2²⁰

-1-08

W9-BFP-579

The Editor

DANIEL JAVITCH is Professor of Comparative Literature at
New York University. He is the author of *Poetry and Courtliness in Renaissance England* and *Proclaiming a Classic:
The Canonization of "Orlando Furioso."* He is an associate
editor of *Renaissance Quarterly.*

W. W. NORTON & COMPANY, INC.
Also Publishes

THE NORTON ANTHOLOGY OF AFRICAN AMERICAN LITERATURE
edited by Henry Louis Gates Jr. and Nellie Y. McKay et al.

THE NORTON ANTHOLOGY OF AMERICAN LITERATURE
edited by Nina Baym et al.

THE NORTON ANTHOLOGY OF CONTEMPORARY FICTION
edited by R. V. Cassill and Joyce Carol Oates

THE NORTON ANTHOLOGY OF ENGLISH LITERATURE
edited by M. H. Abrams and Stephen Greenblatt et al.

THE NORTON ANTHOLOGY OF LITERATURE BY WOMEN
edited by Sandra M. Gilbert and Susan Gubar

THE NORTON ANTHOLOGY OF MODERN POETRY
edited by Richard Ellmann and Robert O'Clair

THE NORTON ANTHOLOGY OF POETRY
edited by Margaret Ferguson, Mary Jo Salter, and Jon Stallworthy

THE NORTON ANTHOLOGY OF SHORT FICTION
edited by R. V. Cassill and Richard Bausch

THE NORTON ANTHOLOGY OF THEORY AND CRITICISM
edited by Vincent B. Leitch et al.

THE NORTON ANTHOLOGY OF WORLD MASTERPIECES
edited by Sarah Lawall et al.

THE NORTON FACSIMILE OF THE FIRST FOLIO OF SHAKESPEARE
prepared by Charlton Hinman

THE NORTON INTRODUCTION TO LITERATURE
edited by Alison Booth, J. Paul Hunter, and Kelly J. Mays

THE NORTON INTRODUCTION TO THE SHORT NOVEL
edited by Jerome Beaty

THE NORTON READER
edited by Linda H. Peterson, John C. Brereton, and Joan E. Hartman

THE NORTON SAMPLER
edited by Thomas Cooley

THE NORTON SHAKESPEARE, BASED ON THE OXFORD EDITION
edited by Stephen Greenblatt et al.

For a complete list of Norton Critical Editions, visit
www.wwnorton.com/college/english/nce/welcome.htm

A NORTON CRITICAL EDITION

Baldesar Castiglione

THE BOOK
OF THE COURTIER

THE SINGLETON TRANSLATION

AN AUTHORITATIVE TEXT
CRITICISM

Edited by

DANIEL JAVITCH

NEW YORK UNIVERSITY

W • W • NORTON & COMPANY • *New York* • *London*

Copyright © 2002 by W. W. Norton & Company, Inc.

THE BOOK OF THE COURTIER by Baldesar Castiglione, translated by
Charles S. Singleton, edited by Edgar Mayhew. Copyright © 1959 by
Charles S. Singleton and Edgar de N. Mayhew. Used by permission of
Doubleday, a division of Random House, Inc.

All rights reserved.
Printed in the United States of America.
First Edition.

The text of this book is composed in Fairfield Medium
with the display set in Bernhard Modern.
Composition by Publishing Synthesis, New York.
Manufacturing by Courier, Westford.
Book design by Antonina Krass.

Library of Congress Cataloging-in-Publication Data

Castiglione, Baldassarre, conte, 1478–1529.
[Libro del cortegiano. English]
The book of the courtier : an authoritative text, criticism /
Baldesar Castiglione ; edited by Daniel Javitch.
p. cm.—(A Norton critical edition)
Includes bibliographical references.

ISBN 0-393-97606-8 (pbk.)

1. Courts and courtiers. 2. Courtesy. 3. Castiglione, Baldassarre, conte,
1478–1529. Libro del cortegiano. I. Javitch, Daniel. II. Title.

BJ1604.C43 2002
170′.44—dc21

2001044867

W. W. Norton & Company, Inc., 500 Fifth Avenue, New York, N.Y. 10110
www.wwnorton.com

W. W. Norton & Company Ltd., Castle House, 75/76 Wells Street,
London W1T 3QT

1 2 3 4 5 6 7 8 9 0

Contents

Preface   vii

The Text of *The Book of the Courtier*   1

  The Book of the Courtier   3

  INDEX OF PERSONS AND ITEMS   261

Criticism   281

  Amedeo Quondam • On the Genesis of the *Book
of the Courtier*   283

  Harry Berger Jr. • Sprezzatura and the Absence of Grace   295

  Virginia Cox • Castiglione's *Cortegiano*: The Dialogue as a
Drama of Doubt   307

  Daniel Javitch • *Il Cortegiano* and the Constraints
of Despotism   319

  Eduardo Saccone • The Portrait of the Courtier in
Castiglione   328

  Joan Kelly-Gadol • Did Women Have a Renaissance?   340

  David Quint • Courtier, Prince, Lady: The Design
of the *Book of the Courtier*   352

  Wayne Rebhorn • Ottaviano's Interruption   366

  James Hankins • Renaissance Philosophy and Book IV
of *Il Cortegiano*   377

  Peter Burke • The Courtier Abroad: Or, the Uses
of Italy   388

Baldassare Castiglione: A Chronology   401

Selected Bibliography   403

Preface

In the 1970s, when I started writing about *The Book of the Courtier*, the views that then prevailed about the work were neither positive nor sympathetic. An interpretive tradition that went back at least to the influential nineteenth-century criticism of Francesco De Sanctis, dismissed Castiglione's court society as superficial and frivolous and objected to the purely aesthetic identity of the model individual fashioned in the book. Less hostile modern accounts of the *Courtier*, particularly evident in surveys of Italian Renaissance literature, tended to perceive the work as an idyllic and nostalgic portrayal of the refined individuals who graced the court of Urbino and to see the model of courtliness projected by the speakers in the book as belonging to an irretrievable past, or else as so idealized as to have little relation to the political realities of its times. It was quite common to find the idealistic features attributed to the *Courtier* unfavorably compared to the hard-nosed assessment of political realities that Machiavelli provided in *The Prince*.[1] Even though Castiglione had lived and worked in the same chaotic Italy as Machiavelli, the *Courtier*, critics complained, seemed quite unrealistic and showed none of Machiavelli's concern about the ways affairs of state were actually conducted.

These views, especially the tendency to dismiss the work as a nostalgic idealization of an aristocratic code, did not correspond to my perception of *The Courtier*. It must be said that I came to the work as a student of English Renaissance literature; and from that perspective it was apparent that, for late sixteenth-century Englishmen, Castiglione's perfect courtier had become an important and appealing model of civilized conduct. The evidence did not suggest that the code set forth in the book was retrograde or out of touch with social and political realities. If anything, Castiglione's book tended to be mistaken by Tudor readers as a practical handbook of manners. While I realized that Castiglione had deliberately refused to write a prescriptive manual, the function that the work subse-

1. For examples, see Giuseppe Prezzolini's preface to Baldassar Castiglione e Giovanni Della Casa, *Opere* (Milano: Rizzoli, 1937) and Attilio Momigliano, *Storia della letteratura italiana* . . . (Milano: G. Principato, 1956), pp. 187–89. The perception of the work as backward looking, nostalgic, and quite out of touch with political realities persists among Italian critics. For its most recent expression see Walter Barberis's introduction to his edition of the *Cortegiano* (Torino: Einaudi, 1998).

quently acquired as a guide to manners and social advancement
made me more sensitive to pragmatic and forward-looking aspects
of the book.

As Castiglione himself acknowledged, his principal model had
been Cicero's *De oratore*. The comparison between the two works
that he thereby invited also served to reveal the degree to which the
norms of public behavior advocated in *The Courtier*—and they were
quite different from those prescribed the ideal Roman orator—were
conditioned by the changed political and social circumstances of a
modern court. Contrasting the two works, I proposed that the transformation one could discern of the forthright, aggressive, even combative behavior of Cicero's orator into the more indirect, cunning,
prudent comportment of the model courtier was due to the exigencies of a courtly establishment and its autocratic ruler.[2] If the suppression of aggressiveness and belligerence that marked the
courtier's comportment and differentiated him so notably from
Cicero's combative orator was a sign of the courtier's greater civility,
it also betokened his relative disempowerment. For what *The
Courtier* marks historically is the transformation of the late feudal
warrior aristocrat into the polite courtier, the "civilizing process" (as
Elias called it) that occurred as first princely courts and then the
absolutist state forced the nobility to give up its belligerence and
other feudal entitlements and assume a new role as model of
politesse and social refinement.[3] The deference, the moderation, the
indirection, the tact that were part of the code of courtesy the
courtier had to observe did not just affirm his superior breeding but
also indicated the much more limited freedom, indeed the subjuga-
tion that aristocrats had to accept when they became dependent on
princes for their status and privilege.

Even though my first study of *The Courtier* began to make evident
that the political pressures of despotism shaped and required an artful behavior in Castiglione's book quite foreign to Cicero's ideal of
the civilized man, it was in a later essay, eventually published in
1983, that I demonstrated more precisely the extent to which Castiglione's norms of conduct were determined by these pressures.
The essay is reprinted in this volume so I will not dwell on it,[4] except
to say that one reason the more pragmatic aspects of Castiglione's
code have remained so unappreciated is because his speakers *cloak*
the fact that the pressures of autocratic rule shape the norms of

---

2. See my *Poetry and Courtliness in Renaissance England* (Princeton, N.J.: Princeton University Press, 1978), pp. 18–49.
3. See Norbert Elias, *Über den Prozess der Zivilisation* (1939), trans. Edmund Jephcott into
two volumes as *The History of Manners* and *Power and Civility* (New York: Pantheon,
1982). On the way women as well as the prince play a role in pacifying and taming noblemen at court, see Quint's essay on p. 352 herein.
4. See p. 319 herein.

conduct that they advocate. When they recommend various stylistic
attributes that the courtier must possess, they rarely, if ever, point
out that these attributes are especially desirable because they are
pleasing to the prince. Yet virtually every beautiful attribute the
Courtier (which is how I will refer, henceforth, to the model individual fashioned in the book) was asked to cultivate could be successfully used to win the good will of a sovereign or to preserve it.

I still believe that prince-pleasing, albeit of a more elevated kind,
is one of the book's central but deliberately inconspicuous considerations, but I now feel that my claims about the pragmatic value of
Castiglione's code may have been overstated. I was being too reac-
tive to prior critical charges that the work was naively idealistic and
out of touch with political realities. Nor was I alone in reacting this
way. Other critics also challenged those charges and argued that
preferment and political survival shaped the artful behavior recommended in *The Courtier*.[5] Concerned as some of us were, in the
1970s and 1980s, to reassert that Castiglione's code took full
account of the exigencies imposed by the autocrats who ruled and
would continue to rule Renaissance courts, we paid too little attention to the book's idealism. It is now more apparent that both the
readings that dismissed the work as unrealistic (in the Machiavellian sense) as well as those that sought to reclaim its pragmatic
aspects were, in their different ways, unsympathetic to the idealistic intention of the work. As any sixteenth-century reader would
have readily understood, the game chosen by the *brigata*, or company, "to form in words a perfect courtier" aimed to provide a model
of behavior more perfect than the comportment of actual courtiers,
even of the ones gathered at Urbino. This image of the ideal
courtier was to inspire emulation, on the part not only of the
courtiers depicted in the book but of any courtier reading it.

The lack of sympathy for the book's idealistic aims that prevailed
since about 1950 stemmed most probably from a failure to appreciate a system of education in which self-improvement was predicated
on the imitation of past or imagined models of perfection. Yet this
doctrine of *imitatio* was absolutely central to Castiglione's culture.
Virtually every process of learning, whether it was writing, speaking,
virtuous living, or governing, entailed the imitation of such models.

5. See, for example, Eduardo Saccone's "The Portrait of the Courtier in Castiglione," *Italica* 64 (1987), 1–18 (reprinted in part on p. 328 herein). Saccone challenges the idea that
the Courtier was shaped into an autotelic work of art, with no other aim than his self-
perfection, by asserting rather that "the Courtier is always fighting on two fronts: that of
the competition with his peers and the other to gain his Prince's favor." In a review of
modern interpretations Virginia Cox points to the tendency on the part of some critics in
the 1970s and 1980s (myself included) to emphasize the functional and pragmatic
dimensions of the Courtier's *ethos*, previously perceived in a purely aesthetic key. See her
"Castiglione and His Critics," appended to her edition of Thomas Hoby's *Courtyer* (London: J.M. Dent, 1994), pp. 409–26.

And there was something inherently idealistic about the doctrine of *imitatio* since the assumption was that the model, whether a past historical exemplar or a conflation of exemplars or a transcendent idea of perfection, represented a height, an acme of excellence that one could only try to approach. Indeed, the challenge was to try to attain the greatest similarity to the model and, even if one could not equal its perfection, to come as close to it as one's capacity allowed.

Our bias against *imitatio* notwithstanding, there is a need to reaffirm the work's idealism, if only to gain a better understanding of the admiration it elicited for over a century after its publication. The diverse and even conflicting talents that the Courtier is asked to possess offer some of the first indications that he is an idealized projection. He must, for example, be skilled at arms as well as trained in humanistic studies. The aristocracy was normally expected to have military abilities, but when Lodovico Canossa (the first main speaker) states that he wants the Courtier "more than passably learned in letters, at least in those studies that we call humanities" (1.44), he reflects some of the idealistic aspirations of fifteenth-century Italian educators to form a ruling elite as well versed in letters as in handling arms. Canossa goes on to make even more demands. While the Courtier has to know how to write and speak well, he also has to be a good athlete and a proficient dancer. In addition, he has to have some knowledge of music and of the visual arts and even practice them. The expectation that the Courtier will be so versatile, able to *combine* so many talents, is certainly part of the work's idealism; but what I want to highlight in particular are the ways the book asks those who would emulate its model to stretch their virtuosity and their virtue.

Take, for example, the attribute of *grazia*, which, according to Ludovico Canossa, must adorn all of the courtier's actions. Yet, if one doesn't possess it naturally, grace is almost beyond the reach of art (the company is reminded that it is "almost proverbial that grace is not learned" 1.25). When Cesare Gonzaga persists in finding out how grace can be acquired by those not blessed with it by the stars, Canossa recommends, in one of the work's most cited passages, that the Courtier avoid affectation at all costs and practice "sprezzatura," that ability to disguise artful effort so that it seems natural, spontaneous, effortless (see 1.26).[6] However, even though one can cultivate this semblance of nonchalance, the difficulty of practicing *sprezzatura* is made clear almost immediately after it is recommended as a source of *grazia*. Bibbiena, one of the participants in the dialogue, presumes that their colleague, Roberto da Bari, displays proper *sprezzatura* while dancing when," to make it quite plain

6. See Harry Berger's discussion of grace and *sprezzatura* on p. 295 herein.

that he is giving no thought to what he is doing, he lets his clothes fall from his back and his slippers from his feet, and goes right on dancing without picking them up." Such exaggerated nonchalance is immediately criticized by Lodovico Canossa as precisely the kind of affection that the courtier should avoid. "Do you not see that what you are calling nonchalance," Canossa points out,

> is really affectation, because we clearly see him making every effort to show that he takes no thought of what he is about, which means taking too much thought; and because it exceeds certain limits of moderation, such nonchalance is affected, is unbecoming, and results in the opposite of the desired effect, which is to conceal the art (1.27).

In objecting to Roberto's performance Canossa not only reveals how hard it is to carry off the appearance of nonchalance and spontaneity but also reminds his interlocutors how difficult it is not to breach the requisite of *mediocrità*, that moderated balance of extremes or opposites also deemed so graceful an aspect of the courtier's style and personality. Whether *mediocrità* consists of balancing self-display with reserve, seriousness with jest, pride with modesty, the epithet that most often accompanies this requisite attribute is *difficile*. When, for example, the court lady is asked, like her male counterpart, to equilibrate opposing traits she must *"tener una certa mediocrità* difficile *e quasi composta di cose contrarie* (observe a certain mean, *difficult* to achieve, and, as it were, composed of contraries; 3.5). The Courtier's comportment is regularly characterized by this paradoxical and hence difficult balance of opposites: rehearsed spontaneity, reticent exhibitionism. It is reiterated that he must avoid being presumptuous, yet he is also asked constantly to impress beholders.

The standards are so high that for many they are unattainable. One must bear in mind, too, that Castiglione's speakers establish criteria of proper style for an aristocracy. Virtually by definition, then, they cannot be met by just anyone. The distance between the Courtier and the many inferior outsiders who would ape him is maintained by the repeated suggestion that there are inimitable nuances in his graceful behavior. For example, when the Courtier's manner of speaking is discussed, he is asked, at one point, to be able to speak with forceful eloquence when the occasion calls for it and "at other times with such simple candor as to make it seem that nature herself is speaking . . . and all this with such ease as to make the one who listens believe that with little effort he too could attain to such excellence—but who, when he tries, discovers that he is very far from it" (1.34). As this passage suggests, the standards of proper *mediocrità* and *sprezzatura* are made so hard to attain in order to put them and the achievement of courtly grace out of reach of the bourgeoisie and the lesser folk who threaten to encroach on the courtier's social space.

Part of the idealism of the book, then, consists of the demanding, to most quite unattainable, criteria of stylistic and performative virtuosity it sets forth. But another, even more admirable aspect of the speakers' idealism stems from their desire to fashion a person who will retain as much moral integrity as the system of service in which he functions will allow. For instance, when, in Book 2, Federico Fregoso discusses the relationship of the courtier to his prince or lord, he recognizes that, if the courtier is to retain his sovereign's favor, he needs to be unpresumptuous, accommodating, and pliant. But he does not expect nor will he permit the Courtier to be a sycophant. Flexible though he has to be, the Courtier should not bend further than the bounds of morality will allow. "Above all," Federico says at one point in the discussion, "let him hold to what is good . . . nor let him ever bring himself to seek grace or favor by resorting to foul means or evil practices" (2.22). By observing that presumptuous and wicked courtiers do very well in contemporary courts, Vincenzo Calmeta, one of Federico's interlocutors, reminds him how hard it is to observe this ethical directive. Moreover, Calmeta goes on to point out how impossible it can become for a courtier, in the service of an immoral prince, to preserve his ethical principles and remain employed. Federico is quite aware that, to retain their employment, that is to say their masters' favor, actual courtiers are often forced to compromise their moral integrity. Yet he insists that the Courtier must obey his lord "in all things profitable and honorable to him, not in those that will bring him [i.e., his lord] harm and shame" (2.23). Even at the risk of being dismissed, he must not let obedience to his prince make him betray his moral self.[7]

By the time we get to Ottaviano's even more high-minded guidelines about the Courtier's relationship to his prince in Book 4 the issue is no longer how the Courtier can preserve his personal integrity. This is taken for granted. Rather his capacity to persuade his sovereign to act for the good of the state and of his subjects is now the central concern. Ottaviano wants to transform the Courtier from a respectful servant to the prince's moral and political adviser. His first requirement is that the Courtier be able to tell his prince the truth without fear of displeasing him. Then he must try to veer

---

7. Federico's demand—that the courtier obey his moral conscience rather than unprincipled directives from his lord—does not remain unchallenged. His interlocutors suggest that it may be impossible to reconcile the dictates of moral conscience with the demands of the ruler. For an interpretation of this discussion which brings out its more pessimistic conclusion, see Cox's analysis on p. 307 herein.

the prince away from immoral action and induce him to be virtuous
(see 4.5). These are the loftiest demands imposed on the Courtier,
and Ottaviano's elevated vision of the courtier as the prince's mentor is the most idealistic aspiration in the work (even more so than
Bembo's hope of transforming the Courtier into an initiated Platonic lover). Yet Ottaviano does not ignore how arrogant and full of
false self-esteem most modern princes are and, therefore, how intolerant they are of others' truthful opinions. Even worse, some of
them "abhor reason and justice" (4.7). In addition, he knows that,
accustomed as they are to the fawning manners of their subordinates, modern princes would react most adversely if they had to
confront *"l'orrida faccia della vera virtù"* (the harsh face of true
virtue). The solution lies in the Courtier's beautiful and graceful
attributes. These make him so attractive that the prince will desire
his company and may heed his advice. To lead the prince along "the
austere path of virtue" the courtier must adorn it,

> with shady fronds and strewing it with pretty flowers to lessen
> the tedium of the toilsome journey for one whose strength is
> slight; and now with music, now with arms and horses, now
> with verses, now with discourse of love, and with all the means
> whereof these gentlemen have spoken, to keep his mind con-
> tinually occupied in worthy pleasures, yet always impressing
> upon him also some virtuous habit along with these entice-
> ments, as I have said, beguiling him with salutary deception;
> like shrewd doctors who often spread the edge of the cup with
> some sweet cordial when they wish to give a bitter tasting med-
> icine to sick and over delicate children (4.10).

Even though he has genuine misgivings about the largely ornamental function ascribed to the Courtier by earlier speakers, Ottaviano
recognizes here the advantages of his aesthetic talents by disclosing
how they can serve as the vehicle of ethical purpose. How effectively he has reconciled beautiful attributes and moral agency is
indicated by the idea of "salutary deception," since it allows the
Courtier to employ one of his characteristic habits of style in edifying his prince—dissimulation. Ottaviano's "solution" is not merely
meant to accommodate the courtier's aesthetic accomplishments in
his ethical scheme. It takes into account that moral instruction will
be induced in rulers, if at all, by guilefully appealing to their more
superficial instincts. The Courtier's likelihood of redirecting his sovereign on to the more austere path of virtue depends on the cunning
and deceit he is previously asked to cultivate.

As difficult as the requisites of perfect courtiership are, as high-
minded as they become, the ideal envisaged by the speakers is not
made to seem totally unattainable. Or at least when the demands do

appear impossible, the speakers are reminded of their excessive idealism. Ottaviano, for example, eventually gets carried away with his vision of the courtier as "educator of the prince," and il Magnifico Giuliano tries to bring him down to earth by reminding him that the has endowed the Courtier with more dignity than the prince he serves, "which is most unseemly." Furthermore il Magnifico objects that, by giving the Courtier a role that would befit an older, sober, and more severe councilor, yet asking him as well as to delight the prince with his physical accomplishments and ludic pastimes more appropriate for a young man, Ottaviano requires a blend of attributes too incompatible to find in a single individual. Last, il Magnifico (the champion of equality between courtier and court lady in Book 3) accuses Ottaviano of transforming the Courtier into a political mentor out of misogyny, to make sure he is given a role of greater dignity than the lady of the palace can ever possess (see 4.44).

The objections raised in this instance illustrate how the dialogue form that Castiglione chose for his work offered various means of tempering his idealized projection of the Courtier in general. First of all, the give and take of dialogue allowed the participants to question the excessive idealism voiced by the main speakers or occasionally to challenge it by bringing up the real predicaments of court service. Also, Castiglione's decision to resort to the Ciceronian model of dialogue—that is, one set in a real place with historically real participants—allowed him to give his representation of model building a verisimilitude it might otherwise have lacked. He was also inspired by Cicero to depict his speakers with some of the very attributes they demanded of the perfect courtier. This eulogistic strategy—showing that the historical company at Urbino approximated in their conduct aspects of their idealized self-representation—was at the same time an effective way to make his ideal seem attainable. As Cox most succinctly puts it, Castiglione's" definition of the perfect courtier, like Cicero's of the perfect orator, gains an incomparable persuasive force from the fact that it is elaborated by speakers who are themselves living exemplars of the *ethos* which the book is defining, and guarantors of the efficacy of its recipe for social success."[8]

Indeed, by actually displaying the grace, the ironic self-depreciation, the wit, the "moderation" they require of the Courtier, the participants in the dialogue affirm the possibility of emulating the model. Moreover, Castiglione's speakers are not only aware of the social and political constraints imposed on courtiers by their autocratic

8. Virginia Cox, *The Renaissance Dialogue. Literary Dialogue in Its Social and Political Contexts. Castiglione to Galileo* (Cambridge, UK: Cambridge University Press, 1992), p. 15.

masters but also display the discretion, the prudence, the artful indirection that they prescribe because of these constraints. Yet what makes these courtiers especially admirable is less their cunning virtuosity than the moral independence and self-respect that they will not give up in their roles as prince-pleasers. There, again, they are shown to practice what they preach for they insist that, in the service of his ruler, the Courtier not forfeit his moral integrity, however difficult it may be to maintain it.

At the very end of his speech in Book 4 Ottaviano claims that neither Aristotle nor Plato would have scorned the name of perfect Courtier since both philosophers had won the favor of princes (Alexander the Great and the rulers of Syracuse, respectively) and had managed to exert some beneficial moral influence on them by means not unlike the ones Ottaviano has prescribed. In the case of Plato, this was true of his effect on Dion of Syracuse but not on the tyrant Dionysius. When Plato eventually discovered that Dionysius was so vicious, his tyranny so ingrained, that changing or correcting him was futile, he "decided not to make use of the methods of Courtiership with him" but to leave him. This is, Ottaviano proposes,

> what our Courtier also ought to do if he chances to find himself in the service of a prince of so evil a nature as to be inveterate in vice, like consumptives in their sickness; for in that case he ought to escape from such bondage in order not to incur blame for his prince's evil deeds and not to feel the affliction which all good men feel when they serve the wicked (4.47).

Ottaviano reiterates, here, more forcefully than Federico had in Book 2, the need for the Courtier to forego serving a vicious and evil ruler. Yet one was also told, in that earlier exchange, how risky it would be for a courtier to abandon his service on moral grounds. In fact, given the unlikelihood of subsequent employment, it was virtually impossible to leave. "We must pray God," Calmeta had maintained,

> to grant us good masters, for once we have them, we have to endure them as they are; because countless considerations force a gentleman not to leave a patron once he has begun to serve him: the misfortune lies in ever beginning; and in that case courtiers are like those unhappy birds that are born in some miserable valley (2.22).

So Plato's deliberate departure from the tyrant Dionysius, the last example Ottaviano asks to be followed, must have seemed quite utopian to real courtiers reading Castiglione's book. Yet we must not assume, living as we do in an age of cynicism, that Ottaviano's directive was dismissed as totally unfeasible. Sixteenth-century readers were fully accustomed to being asked to exceed their capacities, to emulate models that were, by definition, unreachable. Precisely because Ottaviano's final exemplar was so idealistic it was all the more worthy of emulation. And if, in general, there were goals set in Castiglione's book too lofty to be reached by ordinary courtiers that did not mean these goals were not inspiring. One must not underestimate the heroic dimensions that the Courtier acquires by the end of the work and the noble aspirations this model might have incited. The uplifting effects of the book could only increase later in the sixteenth century as courts became more despotic or monarchs, at least, became increasingly dominant and restricted their courtiers' freedom of expression and of action even further.

If, in my earlier criticism, I suggested that the great fortune of *The Courtier* had to do with its value as an art of successful prince-pleasing, I now feel its ongoing appeal stemmed even more from its having raised that art to such a noble level. In the proem to the first draft of his work Castiglione had stated that the end of courtiership was "knowing how and being able to serve perfectly, and with dignity any great Prince in whatever praiseworthy activity so as to obtain favor and praise from him and from all the others."[9] *Dignity* is, I think, the operative word. Castiglione, as well as the speakers in his dialogue knew full well what the aristocratic class had been forced to give up when its members had to becomes servants of princes: the possibility of military aggressiveness, and the greater personal independence it had previously enjoyed. Yet, when "forming" their ideal, these speakers were not prepared to forfeit the Courtier's independence altogether, at least not his moral one. However disempowered he may have become, they realized that "to serve with dignity" the Courtier could not allow the pressures of autocracy make him behave in the abject and vile ways such a political system encouraged. The Courtier had to retain some moral freedom and, in the best of circumstances, to exercise some moral agency. In their idealized projection of themselves they thus sought to give the Courtier as much range in this regard as the system of princely patronage might allow. It is this range of moral freedom, and the self-respect it allowed the Courtier to preserve, that ennobled their art of prince-pleasing and made it endure.

---

9. *"Altro proemio del* Cortegiano *tratto dalla prima bozza dell'Autore,"* in *Lettere del Conte B. Castiglione, a cura dell'abate,* P. Serassi (Padova, 1769), vol. 1, p. 193: *"il sapere e potere perfettamente servire e con dignità ogni gran Principe in ogni cosa laudabile, acquistandone grazia e laude da esso e da tutti gli altri."*

The Text of
THE BOOK
OF THE COURTIER[†]
THE SINGLETON TRANSLATION

† *The Book of the Courtier* by Baldesar Castiglione, translated by Charles Singleton. Copyright © 1959 by Charles S. Singleton and Edgar de N. Mayhew. Used by permission of Doubleday, a division of Random House, Inc.

To the Reverend and Illustrious Signor Don Michel de Silva,[1] Bishop of Viseu

[1] When signor Guidobaldo of Montefeltro, Duke of Urbino, departed this life, I, together with several other gentlemen who had served him, remained in the service of Duke Francesco Maria della Rovere, his heir and successor in the state. And, as the savor of Duke Guido's virtues was fresh in my mind, and the delight that in those years I had felt in the loving company of such excellent persons as then frequented the Court of Urbino, I was moved by the memory thereof to write these books of the Courtier: which I did in but a few days, meaning in time to correct those errors which had resulted from my desire to pay this debt quickly. But Fortune for many years now has kept me ever oppressed by such constant travail that I could never find the leisure to bring these books to a point where my weak judgment was satisfied with them.

Now being in Spain, and being informed from Italy that signora Vittoria della Colonna, Marchioness of Pescara, to whom I had already given a copy of the book, had, contrary to her promise, caused a large part of it to be transcribed, I could not but feel a certain annoyance, fearing the considerable mischief that can arise in such cases. Nevertheless, I trusted that the wisdom and prudence of that lady (whose virtue I have always held in veneration as something divine) would avail to prevent any wrong from befalling me for having obeyed her commands. In the end I learned that that part of the book was in Naples, in the hands of many persons; and, as men are always avid of new things, it appeared that certain of these persons were trying to have it printed. Wherefore, alarmed at this danger, I decided to revise at once such small part of the book as time would permit, with the intention of publishing it, thinking it better to let it be seen even slightly corrected by my own hand than much mutilated by the hands of others.

And so, to carry out this thought, I started to reread it; and immediately, at the very outset, by reason of the dedication, I was seized by no little sadness (which greatly grew as I proceeded), when I remembered that the greater part of those persons who are introduced in the conversations were already dead; for, besides those who are mentioned in the proem of the last Book, even messer Alfonso Ariosto, to whom the book is dedicated, is dead: an affable youth, prudent, abounding in the gentlest manners, and apt in everything befitting a man who lives at court. Likewise Duke Giuliano de' Medici, whose goodness and noble courtesy deserved to be

---

1. Most of the people mentioned in the text are identified in Singleton's "Index of Persons and Items" on pp. 261–79. Except where otherwise identified, the notes to the *Book of the Courtier* are by Singleton [*Editor*].

3

enjoyed longer by the world. Messer Bernardo, Cardinal of Santa Maria in Pòrtico, who for his keen and entertaining readiness of wit was the delight of all who knew him, he too is dead. Dead also is signor Ottaviano Fregoso, a most rare man in our times: magnanimous, devout, full of goodness, talent, prudence, and courtesy, and truly a lover of honor and worth, and so deserving of praise that his very enemies were always obliged to praise him; and those misfortunes which he so firmly endured were indeed enough to prove that fortune, as she ever was, is, even in these days, the enemy of virtue. Dead, too, are many others named in the book, to whom nature seemed to promise very long life.

But what should not be told without tears is that the Duchess, too, is dead. And if my mind is troubled at the loss of so many friends and lords, who have left me in this life as in a desert full of woes, it is understandable that I should feel sorrow far more bitter for the death of the Duchess than for any of the others, because she was worth more than the others, and I was much more bound to her than to all the rest. Therefore, in order not to delay paying what I owe to the memory of so excellent a lady, and to that of the others who are no more, and moved too by the threat to my book, I have had it printed and published in such form as the brevity of time permitted.

And since, while they lived, you did not know the Duchess or the others who are dead (except Duke Giuliano and the Cardinal of Santa Maria in Pòrtico), in order to make you acquainted with them, in so far as I can, after their death, I send you this book as a portrait of the Court of Urbino, not by the hand of Raphael or Michelangelo, but by that of a lowly painter and one who only knows how to draw the main lines, without adorning the truth with pretty colors or making, by perspective art, that which is not seem to be. And, although I have endeavored to show in these conversations the qualities and conditions of those who are named therein, I confess that I have not even suggested, let alone expressed, the virtues of the Duchess, because not only is my style incapable of expressing them, but my mind cannot even conceive them; and if I be censured for this or for any other thing deserving of censure (and well do I know that such things are not wanting in the book), I shall not be gainsaying the truth.

[2] But as men sometimes take so much delight in censuring that they censure even what does not deserve it, to those who blame me because I have not imitated Boccaccio or bound myself to the usage of Tuscan speech in our own day, I shall not refrain from saying that, even though Boccaccio had a fine talent by the standards of his time, and wrote some things with discrimination and

care, still he wrote much better when he let himself be guided
solely by his natural genius and instinct, without care or concern
to polish his writings, than when he attempted with diligence and
labor to be more refined and correct. For this reason his own par-
tisans declare that he erred greatly in judging of his own works,
esteeming those little that have done him honor, and those much
that are without worth. If, then, I had imitated that style of writing for which he is censured by those who otherwise praise him,
I should certainly not have escaped the same blame as is leveled
at him in this regard; and I would have deserved it the more in
that he made his mistake thinking that he did well, whereas I
would now be making mine knowing that I did ill. Moreover, if I
had imitated that manner which many think good, and which he
esteemed least, it would have seemed to me, by such imitation, to
show that my judgment was at variance with that of the author I
was imitating: which thing I thought unseemly. And even if this
concern had not moved me, I could not imitate him in subject
matter, since he never wrote anything at all like these books of the
Courtier; nor did it seem to me that I ought to imitate him in the
matter of language, because the power and true rule of good
speech consists more in usage than in anything else, and it is
always bad to employ words that are not in use. Therefore it was
not fitting that I should use many of those words of Boccaccio,
which were used in his time and are not now used by the Tuscans
themselves. Nor have I wished to bind myself to follow the Tuscan speech of today, because intercourse among different nations
has always had the effect of transporting new words from one
country to another, like articles of merchandise, which words
endure or fall away according as usage accepts or rejects them.
And this, besides being attested by the ancients, is clearly seen in
Boccaccio, in whom there are so many French, Spanish, and
Provençal words, as well as some perhaps not very intelligible to
Tuscans today, that it would much reduce his book if these were
all taken away. And because, to my mind, we should not wholly
despise the idiom of the other noble cities of Italy where men
gather who are wise, talented, and eloquent, and who discourse
on great matters pertaining to the governing of states, as well as
on letters, war, and business, I deem that among the words which
are current in the speech of these places, I have been justified in
using those which have grace in themselves, and elegance when
pronounced, and which are commonly held to be good and expres-
sive, even though they may not be Tuscan, and may even come
from outside Italy. Moreover, in Tuscany they use many words
which are evident corruptions of the Latin; which same words in
Lombardy and in other parts of Italy have remained intact and

without change whatever, and are so universally used by everyone that they are admitted by the nobility to be good, and are understood by the people without difficulty.

Hence, I do not believe to have erred if I have employed certain of these words in writing, and if I have taken from my own country what is intact and genuine, rather than from another's what is corrupted and mutilated. Nor does that seem to me a good maxim which many repeat, that our common speech is the more beautiful the less it resembles Latin; neither do I understand why so much more authority should be granted to one manner of speech than to another, that Tuscan may nobilitate Latin words that are crippled and mutilated and give them so much grace that, maimed as they are, everyone can use them as good (which is not denied); and yet Lombard or any other speech may not be permitted to keep the Latin words themselves, pure, whole, proper, and unchanged in any part, and make them at least acceptable. And truly, just as to endeavor to coin new words or to preserve old words, regardless of usage, may be called rash presumption, so also, besides being difficult it seems almost impious to endeavor, despite this same force of custom, to destroy and, as it were, bury alive those which have already survived many centuries and have defended themselves with the shield of usage against the envy of time, and have kept their dignity and splendor, when, by way of the wars and ruins of Italy, changes have come about in the language, in the buildings, dress, and customs.

Thus, if in writing I have not chosen to use those of Boccaccio's words which are no longer used in Tuscany, or to subject myself to the rule of those persons who hold that it is not permissible to make use of those words which are not used by the Tuscans of today, it seems to me that I merit excuse. I think, therefore, that both in the subject matter of the book, and in respect to language (in so far as one language can help another), I have imitated authors who are as worthy of praise as Boccaccio. Nor do I believe that it should be imputed to me as an error that I have chosen to make myself known rather as a Lombard speaking Lombard than as a non-Tuscan speaking too much Tuscan—in order not to do as Theophrastus who, because he spoke too much Athenian, was recognized by a simple old woman as non-Athenian.[2]

But since this is sufficiently discussed in the first Book, I shall say no more, save that, to forestall all debate, I confess to my critics that I do not know this Tuscan speech of theirs, so difficult and recondite; and I affirm that I have written in my own, just as I speak, and for those who speak as I do. And thus I do believe that I have not

---

2. The anecdote is told by Cicero, *Brutus* XLVI, 172.

wronged anyone: for, in my opinion, no one is forbidden to write and speak in his own language. Nor is anyone bound to read or listen to what does not please him. Therefore, if such persons do not choose to read my Courtier, I shall not consider myself to be offended by them in the least.

[3] Others say that since it is so difficult, and well-nigh impossible, to find a man as perfect as I wish the Courtier to be, it was wasted effort to write of him, because it is useless to try to teach what cannot be learned. To such as these I answer (without wishing to get into any dispute about the Intelligible World or the Ideas) that I am content to have erred with Plato, Xenophon, and Marcus Tullius,[3] and just as, according to these authors, there is the Idea of the perfect Republic, the perfect King, and the perfect Orator, so likewise there is that of the perfect Courtier. And if I have been unable to approach the image of the latter, in my style, then courtiers will find it so much the easier to approach in their deeds the end and goal which my writing sets before them. And if, for all that, they are unable to attain to that perfection, such as it is, that I have tried to express, the one who comes the nearest to it will be the most perfect; as when many archers shoot at a target and none of them hits the bull's eye, the one who comes the closest is surely better than all the rest.

Still others say I have thought to take myself as a model, on the persuasion that the qualities which I attribute to the Courtier are all in me. To these persons I will not deny having tried to set down everything that I could wish the Courtier to know; and I think that anyone who did not have some knowledge of the things that are spoken of in the book, however erudite he might be, could not well have written of them; but I am not so wanting in judgment and self-knowledge as to presume to know all that I could wish to know.

Thus all defense against these charges, and perhaps many others, I leave for the present to the tribunal of public opinion; because more often than not the many, even without perfect knowledge, know by natural instinct the certain savor of good and bad, and, without being able to give any reason for it, enjoy and love one thing and reject and detest another. Hence, if my book pleases in a general way, I shall take it to be good, and I shall think that it is to survive. If, instead, it should not please, I shall take it to be bad and shall at once believe that the memory of it must needs be lost. And if my censors be not yet satisfied with this verdict of public opinion,

---

3. The works referred to are Plato's *Republic*, Xenophon's *Cyropaedia*, Cicero's *De oratore*.

then let them be content at least with that of time, which reveals the hidden defects of all things, and, being the father of truth and a judge without passion, is wont to pronounce always, on all writing, a just sentence of life or death.

BALDESAR CASTIGLIONE

The First Book

[1] I have long wondered, dearest messer Alfonso, which of two things was the more difficult for me: to deny you what you have repeatedly and so insistently asked of me, or to do it. For, on the one hand, it seemed very hard for me to deny a thing—especially when it was something praiseworthy—to one whom I love most dearly and by whom I feel I am most dearly loved; yet, on the other hand, to undertake a thing which I was not sure I could finish seemed unbecoming to one who esteems just censure as much as it ought to be esteemed. Finally, after much thought, I have resolved that I would try in this to see how much aid to diligence might be had from affection and the intense desire that I have to please, which, in things generally, is so wont to increase men's industry.

Now, you have asked me to write my opinion as to what form of Courtiership most befits a gentleman living at the courts of princes, by which he can have both the knowledge and the ability to serve them in every reasonable thing, thereby winning favor from them and praise from others: in short, what manner of man he must be who deserves the name of perfect Courtier, without defect of any kind. Wherefore, considering this request, I say that, had it not seemed to me more blameworthy to be judged by you to be wanting in love than by others to be wanting in prudence, I should have eschewed this labor, out of fear of being thought rash by all who know what a difficult thing it is to choose, from among so great a variety of customs as are followed at the courts of Christendom, the most perfect form and, as it were, the flower of Courtiership. For custom often makes the same things pleasing and displeasing to us; whence it comes about sometimes that the customs, dress, ceremonies, and fashions that were once prized become despised; and, contrariwise, the despised become prized. Hence, it is clearly seen that usage is more powerful than reason in introducing new things among us and in blotting out old things; and anyone who tries to judge of perfection in such matters is often deceived. For which reason, since I am well aware of this and of many another difficulty in the matter whereof it is proposed that I should write, I am forced to excuse myself somewhat and to submit evidence that this is an error (if indeed it can be called error) which I share with you, so that, if I am to be blamed for it, that blame will be shared by you, because your having put upon me a burden beyond my powers must not be deemed a lesser fault than my own acceptance of it.

So let us now make a beginning of our subject, and, if that be possible, let us form such a Courtier that any prince worthy of being served by him, even though he have but small dominion, may still be called a very great lord.

In these books we shall not follow any set order or rule of distinct precepts, as is most often the custom in teaching anything whatever, but, following the manner of many ancient writers, and to revive a pleasant memory, we shall rehearse some discussions which took place among men singularly qualified in such matters. And even though I was not present and did not take part in them, being in England at the time when they occurred, I learned of them shortly thereafter from a person who gave me a faithful report of them; and I shall attempt to recall them accurately, in so far as my memory permits, so that you may know what was judged and thought in this matter by men worthy of the highest praise, and in whose judgment on all things one may have unquestioned faith. Nor will it be beside the purpose to give some account of the occasion of the discussions that took place, so that in due order we may come to the end at which our discourse aims.

[2] On the slopes of the Apennines toward the Adriatic, at almost the center of Italy, is situated, as everyone knows, the little city of Urbino. And although it sits among hills that are perhaps not as pleasant as those we see in many other places, still it has been blessed by Heaven with a most fertile and bountiful countryside, so that, besides the wholesomeness of the air, it abounds in all the necessities of life. But among the greater blessings that can be claimed for it, this I believe to be the chief, that for a long time now it has been ruled by excellent lords (even though, in the universal calamity of the wars of Italy, it was deprived of them for a time). But, to look no further, we can cite good proof thereof in the glorious memory of Duke Federico, who in his day was the light of Italy. Nor are there wanting many true witnesses still living who can testify to his prudence, humanity, justice, generosity, undaunted spirit, to his military prowess, signally attested by his many victories, the capture of impregnable places, the sudden readiness of his expeditions, the many times when with but small forces he routed large and very powerful armies, and the fact that he never lost a single battle; so that not without reason may we compare him to many famous men among the ancients.

Among his other laudable deeds, he built on the rugged site of Urbino a palace thought by many the most beautiful to be found anywhere in all Italy and he furnished it so well with every suitable thing that it seemed not a palace but a city in the form of a palace; and furnished it not only with what is customary, such as silver vases, wall hangings of the richest cloth of gold, silk, and other like things, but for ornament he added countless ancient statues of marble and bronze, rare paintings, and musical instruments of every sort; nor did he wish to have anything there that was not most rare and excellent. Then, at great expense, he collected many very excellent and rare books in Greek, Latin, and Hebrew, all of which he adorned with gold and silver, deeming these to be the supreme excellence of his great palace.

[3] Following then the course of nature and being already sixty-five years old, he died as gloriously as he had lived, leaving as his successor his only son, a child ten years of age and motherless, named Guidobaldo. This boy, even as he was heir to the state, seemed to be heir to all his father's virtues as well, and in his remarkable nature began at once to promise more than it seemed right to expect of a mortal; so that men judged none of the notable deeds of Duke Federico to be greater than his begetting such a son. But Fortune, envious of so great a worth, set herself against this glorious beginning with all her might, so that, before Duke Guido had reached the age of twenty, he fell sick of the gout, which grew upon him with grievous pain, and in a short time so crippled all his members that he could not stand upon his feet or move. Thus, one of the fairest and ablest persons in the world was deformed and marred at a tender age.

And not even content with this, Fortune opposed him so in his every undertaking that he rarely brought to a successful issue anything he tried to do; and, although he was very wise in counsel and undaunted in spirit, it seemed that whatever he undertook always succeeded ill with him whether in arms or in anything, great or small; all of which is attested by his many and diverse calamities, which he always bore with such strength of spirit that his virtue was never overcome by Fortune; nay, despising her storms with stanch heart, he lived in sickness as if in health, and in adversity as if most fortunate, with the greatest dignity and esteemed by all. So that, although he was infirm of body in this way, he campaigned with a most honorable rank in the service of their Serene Highnesses Kings Alfonso and Ferdinand the Younger of Naples; and later with Pope Alexander VI, as well as the signories of Venice and Florence.

Then when Julius II became Pope, the Duke was made Captain of the Church; during which time, and following his usual style, he saw to it that his household was filled with very noble and worthy gentlemen, with whom he lived on the most familiar terms, delighting in their company; in which the pleasure he gave others was not less than that which he had from them, being well versed in both Latin and Greek and combining affability and wit with the knowledge of an infinitude of things. Besides this, so much did the greatness of his spirit spur him on that, even though he could not engage personally in chivalric activities as he had once done, he still took the greatest pleasure in seeing others so engaged; and by his words, now criticizing and now praising each man according to his deserts, he showed clearly how much judgment he had in such matters. Wherefore, in jousts and tournaments, in riding, in the handling of every sort of weapon, as well as in revelries, in games, in musical performances, in short, in all exercises befitting noble cavaliers, everyone strove to show himself such as to deserve to be thought worthy of his noble company.

[4] Thus, all the hours of the day were given over to honorable and pleasant exercises both of the body and of the mind; but because, owing to his infirmity, the Duke always retired to sleep very early after supper, everyone usually repaired to the rooms of the Duchess, Elisabetta Gonzaga, at that hour; where also signora Emilia Pia was always to be found, who being gifted with such a lively wit and judgment, as you know, seemed the mistress of all, and all appeared to take on wisdom and worth from her. Here, then, gentle discussions and innocent pleasantries were heard, and on everyone's face a jocund gaiety could be seen depicted, so much so that this house could be called the very abode of joyfulness. Nor do I believe that the sweetness that is had from a beloved company was ever savored in any other place as it once was there. For, not to speak of the great honor it was for each of us to serve such a lord as I have described above, we all felt a supreme happiness arise within us whenever we came into the presence of the Duchess. And it seemed that this was a chain that bound us all together in love, in such wise that never was there concord of will or cordial love between brothers greater than that which was there among us all.

The same was among the ladies, with whom one had very free and most honorable association, for to each it was permitted to speak, sit, jest, and laugh with whom he pleased; but the reverence that was paid to the wishes of the Duchess was such that this same liberty was a very great check; nor was there anyone who did not esteem it the greatest pleasure in the world to please her and the greatest grief to displease her. For which reason most decorous customs were there joined with the greatest liberty, and games and laughter in her presence were seasoned not only with witty jests but with a gracious and sober dignity; for that modesty and grandeur which ruled over all the acts, words, and gestures of the Duchess, in jest and laughter, caused anyone seeing her for the first time to recognize her as a very great lady. And, in impressing herself thus upon those about her, it seemed that she tempered us all to her own quality and fashion, wherefore each one strove to imitate her style, deriving, as it were, a rule of fine manners from the presence of so great and virtuous a lady; whose high qualities I do not now intend to recount, this being not to my purpose, because they are well known to all the world, and much more than I could express either with tongue or pen; and those which might have remained some-what hidden, Fortune, as if admiring such rare virtues, chose to reveal through many adversities and stings of calamity, in order to prove that in the tender breast of a woman, and accompanied by singular beauty, there may dwell prudence and strength of spirit, and all those virtues which are very rare even in austere men.

[5] But, passing over this, I say that the custom of all the gentlemen of the house was to betake themselves immediately after supper to the Duchess; where, amidst the pleasant pastimes, the music and dancing which were continually enjoyed, fine questions would sometimes be proposed, and sometimes ingenious games, now at the behest of one person and now of another, in which, under vari-ous concealments, those present revealed their thoughts allegori-cally to whomever they chose. Sometimes other discussions would turn on a variety of subjects, or there would be a sharp exchange of quick retorts; often "emblems," as we nowadays call them, were devised; in which discussions a marvelous pleasure was had, the house (as I have said) being full of very noble talents, among whom, as you know, the most famous were signor Ottaviano Fregoso, his brother messer Federico, the Magnifico Giuliano de' Medici, messer Pietro Bembo, messer Cesare Gonzaga, Count Ludovico da Canossa, signor Gaspar Pallavicino, signor Ludovico Pio, signor Morello da Ortona, Pietro da Napoli, messer Roberto da Bari, and countless other very noble gentlemen. And there were many besides who, although they did not usually remain there continuously, yet spent most of their time there: such as messer Bernardo Bibbiena, the Unico Aretino, Giancristoforo Romano, Pietro Monte, Terpan-dro, messer Nicolò Frisio. So that poets, musicians, and all sorts of buffoons, and the most excellent of every kind of talent that could be found in Italy, were always gathered there.

[6] Now Pope Julius II, having, by his presence and with the help of the French, brought Bologna under the rule of the Apostolic See in the year 1506, and being on his way back to Rome, passed through

Urbino, where he was received with all possible honor and with as magnificent and splendid a welcome as could have been offered in any of the noble cities of Italy: so that, besides the Pope, all the cardinals and other courtiers were highly gratified. And there were some who were so captivated by the charm of the company they found here that when the Pope and his court had departed, they stayed on for many days in Urbino; during which time not only was the usual style of festivities and ordinary diversions kept up, but every man endeavored to contribute something more, and especially in the games that were played almost every evening. And the order of these was such that, as soon as anyone came into the presence of the Duchess, he would take a seat in a circle wherever he pleased or where chance would have it; and so seated, all were arranged alternately, a man, then a woman, as long as there were women (for almost always the number of men was much the larger); then, the company was governed as it pleased the Duchess, who most of the time left this charge to signora Emilia.

So, the day following the departure of the Pope, when the company had gathered at the usual hour and place, after many pleasant discussions, it was the Duchess's wish that signora Emilia should begin the games; and she, after having declined the task for a time, spoke thus: "Madam, since it is your pleasure that I should be the one to begin the games this evening, and since I cannot in reason fail to obey you, I will propose a game for which I think I can have little blame and even less labor: and this shall be that each propose some game after his own liking that we have never played; then we shall choose the one which seems the worthiest of being played in this company."

And, so saying, she turned to signor Gaspar Pallavicino, bidding him to tell his choice; and he replied at once: "It is for you, Madam, to tell yours first."

"But I have already told it," said signora Emilia; "now do you, Duchess, bid him obey."

To this the Duchess said, laughing: "So that all shall be bound to obey you, I make you my deputy, and give you all my authority."

[7] "It is indeed a remarkable thing," replied signor Gasparo, "that women are always permitted such exemption from labor, and it is only right to wish to understand why; but, in order not to be the first to disobey, I will leave that for another time, and will speak now as required"; and he began: "It seems to me that in love, as in everything else, our minds judge differently; and so it often happens that what is most pleasing to one is most odious to another; but, for all that, our minds do, however, agree in prizing highly what is loved; so that often the excessive affection of lovers beguiles their judg-

ment, causing them to think that the person whom they love is the only one in the world who is adorned with every excellent quality and is wholly without defect. But, since human nature does not admit of such complete perfection, nor is anyone to be found in whom something is not wanting, it cannot be said that these lovers are not deceived, or that the lover is not blinded suspecting the beloved. I would therefore have our game this evening be so: let each one say which virtue above all others he would wish the one he loves to be adorned with; and, since it is inevitable that everyone have some defect, let him say also which fault he would desire in the beloved: so that we may see who can think of the most praiseworthy and useful virtues and of the faults which are the most execrable and least harmful either to the lover or to the beloved."

When signor Gasparo had spoken thus, signora Emilia made a sign to madam Costanza Fregosa, as she sat next in order, that she should speak; and she was making ready to do so, when suddenly the Duchess said: "Since signora Emilia does not choose to go to the trouble of devising a game, it would be quite right for the other ladies to share in this ease, and thus be exempt from such a burden this evening, especially since there are so many men here that we risk no lack of games."

"So be it," replied signora Emilia; and, imposing silence on madam Costanza, she turned to messer Cesare Gonzaga who sat next, and bade him speak; and he began thus:

[8] "Whoever considers carefully all our actions will always find various defects in them; the reason being that, in this, nature is variable, as in other things, bestowing the light of reason on one man in one respect and on another man in another: wherefore it happens that as one man knows what another does not know, and is ignorant of what the other knows, each easily perceives his neighbor's error and not his own; and we all think that we are very wise and perhaps the more so in that wherein we are most foolish. Thus, we have seen it happen in this house that many who were at first held to be very wise have been known, in the course of time, to be full of folly, and this came about through nothing save the attention we gave to it. For, even as they say that in Apulia many musical instruments are used for those who are bitten by the tarantula, and various tunes are tried until the humor which is causing the malady is (through a certain affinity which it has with some one of those tunes) suddenly stirred by the sound of it and so agitates the sick man that he is restored to health by that agitation: so we, whenever we have detected some hidden trace of folly, have stimulated it so artfully and with such a variety of inducements and in so many different ways that finally we have understood what its tendency was; then,

having recognized the humor, we agitated it so thoroughly that it was always brought to the perfection of an open folly. Thus, one turned out to be foolish in verse, another in music, another in love, another in dancing, another in morrises,[4] another in riding, another in fencing—each one according to the native quality of his metal; wherein, as you know, we have had some wonderful entertainment. I hold this, then, to be certain: that in each of us there is some seed of folly which, once awakened, can grow almost without limitation.

"Hence, I wish that for this evening our game might be a discussion of this matter, and that each would say: 'In case I should openly reveal my folly, what sort mine would be and about what, judging such an eventuality by the sparks of folly which are seen to come forth from me every day'; and let the same be said of all the others, keeping to the order of our games, and let each one seek to base his opinion on some real sign and evidence. Thus, each of us will profit from this game of ours by knowing his faults, the better thereby to guard against them. And if the vein of folly which we discover chances to be so abundant that it seems beyond repair, we will encourage it and, according to the doctrine of fra Mariano, we shall have saved a soul, which will be no small gain."

There was much laughter about this game, nor was there anyone who could keep from talking. One said: "My folly would be in thinking"; another "in looking"; and another said: "I am already a fool in love," and the like.

[9] Then fra Serafino said, laughing as usual: "That would take too long; but if you want a good game, let everyone say why he thinks it is that nearly all women hate rats and love snakes; and you will see that no one will hit upon the reason except myself, for I know this secret by a strange way." And already he was starting his usual stories. But signora Emilia bade him keep quiet, and, passing over the lady who sat next, she made a sign to the Unico Aretino, whose turn it was. And he, without awaiting further bidding, said: "Would that I were a judge with the authority to use any sort of torture to extract the truth from criminals; and this in order to uncover the deceits of a certain ingrate who, with an angel's eyes and a serpent's heart, never speaks as she thinks, and with a deceitful, feigned compassion attends to nothing but dissecting hearts. Nor is there in sandy Libya a snake so venomous, so avid of human blood, as this false one; who not only with the sweetness of her voice and her honeyed words, but also with her eyes, her smiles, her looks, and in all her ways, is a veritable Siren. However, since I am not allowed (as I could wish I

---

4. Old folk dances in which fancy costumes were worn, but the Italian *moresche* refers to elaborate choreographed mimes of Arab origin [*Editor*].

were) to make use of chains, rope, or fire, in order to learn a certain truth, I wish to learn it with a game, which is this: let each one say what he thinks that letter *s* means that the Duchess is wearing on her forehead; because, though this is certainly but another artful veil to make deception possible, perchance some interpretation will be given of it such as she would not have expected; and it will be found that Fortune, compassionate spectator of the sufferings of men, has led her to reveal by this little sign, and in spite of herself, her secret desire to kill and bury alive in calamities anyone who looks upon her or serves her."

The Duchess laughed, and Aretino, seeing that she wished to exonerate herself from this imputation, said: "Nay, Madam, it is not now your turn to speak."

Then signora Emilia turned to him and said: "Signor Unico, there is no one among us here who does not yield to you in all things, but most of all in your knowledge of our Duchess's mind. And just as you know it better than the rest, even so do you love it more than the rest, who are like those weak-sighted birds that fix not their eyes upon the orb of the sun and thus cannot well know how perfect it is. Hence, any attempt to clear up this doubt would be in vain, save by your own judgment. Therefore, let this task be left to you alone, as to the only one who can perform it."

Aretino remained silent for a while; then, being urged to speak, he at last recited a sonnet on the aforesaid subject, declaring what was meant by that letter *s*; which sonnet was thought by many to have been improvised; but because it was more ingenious and polished than the brevity of time would seem to have allowed, some thought that it had been prepared.

[10] Then, when the sonnet had been praised with merry applause, and after some further talk, signor Ottaviano Fregoso, whose turn it was, began laughingly as follows: "Gentlemen, if I should affirm that I have never felt any passion of love, I am sure that the Duchess and signora Emilia, even if they did not believe it, would make a show of believing it, and would say that this is because I have mistrusted my own ability to induce any woman ever to love me: wherein, to speak the truth, up to now I have not made any such persistent effort as to have reason to despair of being able to succeed some day. Nor certainly have I refrained from making that effort because I esteem myself so much, or women so little, as to think that many are not worthy of being loved and served by me. But I have rather been frightened away by the continual laments of certain lovers who, pale, sad, and taciturn, seem always to wear their unhappiness depicted in their eyes; and whenever they speak, they accompany every word with tripled sighs and talk of nothing but

tears, torments, despairs, and longings for death. So that even if at times any spark of love did kindle my heart, I have immediately made every effort to extinguish it, not out of any hate that I feel towards women, as these ladies may think, but for my own good.

"And then I have known other lovers utterly different from such lamenters, who not only take joy and satisfaction in the kind looks and tender words and gentle mien of their ladies, but flavor all woes with sweetness, so that they say that their ladies' quarrels, wrath, and scorn are things most sweet: wherefore such lovers as these strike me as being exceedingly happy. For if they find such sweetness in those amorous fits of temper which the others hold to be more bitter than death, I think that in the manifestations of love they must experience that final beatitude which we seek in vain in this world. I wish therefore that our game this evening might be that each one should say, in case she whom he loves must be angry with him, what he would wish the cause of that anger to be. For if there be some here who have experienced such sweet outbursts of anger, I am sure that out of courtesy they will elect one of those causes that make these so sweet; and perhaps I shall find the courage to venture a little further in love, in the hope that I too may find this sweetness where some find bitterness; and thus these ladies will no longer be able to defame me for not loving."

[11] All liked this game and were already preparing to speak on such a topic; but, as signora Emilia said nothing about it, messer Pietro Bembo, who sat next in order, spoke thus: "Gentlemen, the game proposed by signor Ottaviano has brought no little doubt to my mind, since he has spoken of the angers of love, which, even though they have variety, yet have always been most bitter to me, nor do I think that there could be learned from me any flavoring sufficient to sweeten them; but it may be that they are more or less bitter according to the cause whereby they arise. For I remember having seen the lady whom I was serving angry with me, either out of an idle doubt as to my faithfulness which she herself had conceived, or out of some other false notion awakened in her by what someone had said to my detriment; so that I judged no suffering could be compared to mine, and it seemed to me that the greatest pain that I felt was in having to suffer when I had not deserved it and in having this affliction through no fault of mine but through her lack of love. At other times I saw her angry at some error of mine, and recognized that her wrath was caused by my fault; and at such a point I would judge that my former woe was light indeed compared with what I now felt. And it seemed to me that the fact of having displeased (and through my own fault) the sole person whom I desired and sought so to please was the torment that surpassed all others. I

wish therefore that our game might be that each should tell, if she whom he loves must be angry with him, where he would wish the cause of her anger to lie, in her or in himself, so that we may know which is the greater suffering, to give displeasure to one's beloved, or to receive the same from her."

[12] Everyone was awaiting signora Emilia's reply; but she, saying nothing more to Bembo, turned to messer Federico Fregoso and signified that he should tell his game; and he began at once as follows: "Madam, I wish that, as sometimes happens, I might be allowed to defer to someone else's judgment, since I, for one, would gladly approve any of the games proposed by these gentlemen, because truly it seems to me that they would all be amusing. Still, so as not to upset our order, I will say that if anyone should wish to praise our court—apart from the merits of our Duchess which, together with her divine virtue, would suffice to uplift from earth to heaven the meanest souls of this world—he might well say, without suspicion of flattery, that in all Italy it would perhaps be hard to find an equal number of cavaliers as outstanding and as excellent in different things, quite beyond their principal profession of chivalry, as are found here: wherefore, if there are anywhere men who deserve to be called good courtiers and who can judge of what belongs to the perfection of Courtiership, we must rightfully think that they are here present. So, in order to put down the many fools who in their presumption and ineptitude think to gain the name of good courtiers, I would have our game this evening be this, that one of this company be chosen and given the task of forming in words a perfect Courtier, setting forth all the conditions and particular qualities that are required of anyone who deserves this name; and that everyone be allowed to speak out against those things which seem not right, as in the schools of the philosophers it is permitted to offer objections to anyone maintaining a thesis."

Messer Federico was going on in his discourse when signora Emilia interrupted him, saying: "This, should it please the Duchess, shall be our game for the present."

"It does please me," the Duchess replied.

Whereupon nearly all of those present began to say, both to the Duchess and among themselves, that this was the finest game that could possibly be played. And no one waited for the other's answer, but all urged signora Emilia to decide who should begin. And she, turning to the Duchess, said: "Madam, will you command him who it most pleases you should have this task, for I do not wish, in choosing one rather than another, to appear to decide which I judge to be more capable than the others in this matter, and so offend anyone."

The Duchess replied: "Nay, make the choice yourself, and take care lest you set others an example of not obeying, prompting them to refuse obedience in their turn."

[13] Then signora Emilia laughed and said to Count Ludovico da Canossa: "So, in order not to lose more time, you, Count, shall be the one to undertake this task in the way messer Federico has said; not indeed because we think you so good a Courtier that you know what befits one, but because if you say everything contrariwise, as we hope you will do, the game will be the livelier since everyone will have something to answer you; whereas, if another with more knowledge than you had this task, nothing could be objected to him because he would speak the truth, and so the game would be tedious."

The Count answered at once: "Madam, there could be no danger that anyone who speaks the truth would lack someone to gainsay him, so long as you are present." And when the company had laughed a while at this retort, he went on: "But truly I should be very glad to escape from this labor, since it seems too difficult for me; and I recognize as true in myself what you have affirmed in jest, namely, that I do not know what befits a good Courtier. Nor do I seek to prove this by any other witness than by the fact that since I do not perform the deeds of one such, it can be concluded that I do not have the knowledge. I believe that I may be blamed less in this, for it is surely worse not to wish to perform well than not to know how. Still, since it is your pleasure that I should have this charge, I cannot and will not refuse it, for I would not contravene our rule and your judgment, which I esteem far more than my own."

Then messer Cesare Gonzaga said: "As it is already rather late in the evening and we have many other kinds of entertainment ready at hand, perhaps it may be well to postpone this discussion until tomorrow; and this will give the Count time to think about what he is going to say, for truly it is a difficult thing to improvise on such a subject."

The Count replied: "I do not wish to be like the man who stripped to his doublet and jumped less far than he had done in his great-coat; wherefore it seems to me fortunate that the hour is late, for by the brevity of the time I shall be forced to say very little, and shall be excused by the fact that I have given no thought to this matter and so, free of censure, I shall be permitted to say whatever comes first to my lips. Therefore, in order not to bear this burden of obligation longer upon my shoulders, I will say that in all things it is so difficult to know what true perfection is that it is well-nigh impossible; and this is due to the diversity of our judgments. Thus, there are many who will welcome a man who talks a great deal, and will call him pleasing. Others will prefer a modest man; others, an active and restless man; still others, someone who shows calm and deliberation in all things. And so everyone praises or blames according to his own opinion, always hiding a vice under the name of the corresponding virtue, or a virtue under the name of the corresponding vice: for example, calling a presumptuous man, frank; a modest man, dull; a simpleton, good; a rascal, discreet; and likewise throughout. Still I do think that there is a perfection for everything, even though it be hidden; and that this perfection can be determined by someone reasoning about it who has knowledge of the subject. And because, as I have said, the truth is often hidden, and I do not claim to have this knowledge, I can only praise the manner of Courtier that I most esteem, and can approve of what seems to me to be nearest the right, according to my poor judgment: which you may follow if it seems good to you; or you may hold to your own, should it differ from mine. Certainly I will not protest that mine is better than yours, for not only can you think one thing and I another, but I myself may sometimes think one thing and sometimes another.

[14] "Thus, I would have our Courtier born of a noble and genteel family; because it is far less becoming for one of low birth to fail to do virtuous things than for one of noble birth, who, should he stray from the path of his forebears, stains the family name, and not only fails to achieve anything but loses what has been achieved already. For noble birth is like a bright lamp that makes manifest and visible deeds both good and bad, kindling and spurring on to virtue as much for fear of dishonor as for hope of praise. And since this luster of nobility does not shine forth in the deeds of the lowly born, they lack that spur, as well as that fear of dishonor, nor do they think themselves obliged to go beyond what was done by their forebears; whereas to the wellborn it seems a reproach not to attain at least to the mark set them by their ancestors. Hence, it almost always happens that, in the profession of arms as well as in other worthy pursuits, those who are most distinguished are men of noble birth, because nature has implanted in everything that hidden seed which gives a certain force and quality of its own essence to all that springs from it, making it like itself: as we can see not only in breeds of horses and other animals, but in trees as well, the shoots of which nearly always resemble the trunk; and if they sometimes degenerate, the fault lies with the husbandman. And so it happens with men, who, if they are tended in the right way, are almost always like those from whom they spring, and often are better; but if they lack someone to tend them properly, they grow wild and never attain their full growth.

"It is true that, whether favored by the stars or by nature, some men are born endowed with such graces that they seem not to have been born, but to have been fashioned by the hands of some god, and adorned with every excellence of mind and body; even as there are many others so inept and uncouth that we cannot but think that nature brought them into the world out of spite and mockery. And just as the latter, for the most part, yield little fruit even with constant diligence and good care, so the former with little labor attain to the summit of the highest excellence. And take, as an example, Don Ippolito d'Este, Cardinal of Ferrara, who enjoyed such a happy birth that his person, his appearance, his words, and all his actions are so imbued and ruled by this grace that, although he is young, he evinces among the most aged prelates so grave an authority that he seems more fit to teach than to be taught. Similarly, in conversing with men and women of every station, in play, in laughter, in jest, he shows a special sweetness and such gracious manners that no one who speaks with him or even sees him can do otherwise than feel an enduring affection for him.

"But, to return to our subject, I say that there is a mean to be found between such supreme grace on the one hand and such stupid ineptitude on the other, and that those who are not so perfectly endowed by nature can, with care and effort, polish and in great part correct their natural defects. Therefore, besides his noble birth, I would wish the Courtier favored in this other respect, and endowed by nature not only with talent and with beauty of countenance and person, but with that certain grace which we call an 'air,' which shall make him at first sight pleasing and lovable to all who see him; and let this be an adornment informing and attending all his actions, giving the promise outwardly that such a one is worthy of the company and the favor of every great lord."

[15] At this point, without waiting any longer, signor Gaspar Pallavicino said: "So that our game may have the form prescribed and that we may not appear to esteem little that privilege of opposing which has been allowed us, I say that to me this nobility of birth does not seem so essential. And if I thought I was uttering anything not already known to us all, I would adduce many instances of persons born of the noblest blood who have been ridden by vices; and, on the contrary, many persons of humble birth who, through their virtue, have made their posterity illustrious. And if what you said just now is true, that there is in all things that hidden force of the first seed, then we should all be of the same condition through having the same source, nor would one man be more noble than another. But I believe that there are many other causes of the differences and the various degrees of elevation and lowliness among

us. Among which causes I judge Fortune to be foremost; because we see her hold sway over all the things of this world and, as it seems, amuse herself often in uplifting to the skies whom she pleases and in burying in the depths those most worthy of being exalted.

"I quite agree with what you call the good fortune of those who are endowed at birth with all goodness of mind and body; but this is seen to happen with those of humble as well as with those of noble birth, because nature observes no such subtle distinctions as these. Nay, as I said, the greatest gifts of nature are often to be seen in persons of the humblest origin. Hence, since this nobility of birth is not gained either by talents or by force or skill, and is rather due to the merit of one's ancestors than to one's own, I deem it passing strange to hold that if the parents of our Courtier be of humble birth, all his good qualities are ruined, and that those other qualities which you have named would not suffice to bring him to the height of perfection; that is, talent, beauty of countenance, comeliness of person, and that grace which will make him at first sight lovable to all."

[16] Then Count Ludovico replied: "I do not deny that the same virtues can rule in the lowborn as in the wellborn: but (in order not to repeat what we have said already, along with many further reasons which might be adduced in praise of noble birth, which is always honored by everyone, because it stands to reason that good should beget good), since it is our task to form a Courtier free of any defect whatsoever, and endowed with all that is praiseworthy, I deem it necessary to have him be of noble birth, not only for many other reasons, but also because of that public opinion which immediately sides with nobility. For, in the case of two courtiers who have not yet given any impression of themselves either through good or bad deeds, immediately when the one is known to be of gentle birth and the other not, the one who is lowborn will be held in far less esteem than the one who is of noble birth, and will need much time and effort in order to give to others that good impression of himself which the other will give in an instant and merely by being a gentleman. And everyone knows the importance of these impressions, for, to speak of ourselves, we have seen men come to this house who, though dull-witted and maladroit, had yet the reputation throughout Italy of being very great courtiers; and, even though they were at last discovered and known, still they fooled us for many days and maintained in our minds that opinion of themselves which they found already impressed thereon, even though their conduct was in keeping with their little worth. Others we have seen who at first enjoyed little esteem and who, in the end, achieved a great success.

"And there are various causes of such errors, one being the judgment of princes who, thinking to work miracles, sometimes decide to show favor to one who seems to them to deserve disfavor. And they too are often deceived; but, because they always have countless imitators, their favor engenders a great fame which on the whole our judgments will follow. And if we notice anything which seems contrary to the prevailing opinion, we suspect that we must be mistaken, and we continue to look for something hidden: because we think that such universal opinions must after all be founded on the truth and arise from reasonable causes. And also because our minds are quick to love and hate, as is seen in spectacles of combats and of games and in every sort of contest, where the spectators often side with one of the parties without any evident reason, showing the greatest desire that this one should win and the other should lose. Moreover, as for the general opinion concerning a man's qualities, it is good or ill repute that sways our minds at the outset to one of these two passions. Hence, it happens that, for the most part, we judge from love or hate. Consider, then, how important that first impression is, and how anyone who aspires to have the rank and name of good Courtier must strive from the beginning to make a good impression.

[17] "But to come to some particulars: I hold that the principal and true profession of the Courtier must be that of arms; which I wish him to exercise with vigor; and let him be known among the others as bold, energetic, and faithful to whomever he serves. And the repute of these good qualities will be earned by exercising them in every time and place, inasmuch as one may not ever fail therein without great blame. And, just as among women the name of purity, once stained, is never restored, so the reputation of a gentleman whose profession is arms, if ever in the least way he sullies himself through cowardice or other disgrace, always remains defiled before the world and covered with ignominy. Therefore, the more our Courtier excels in this art, the more will he merit praise; although I do not deem it necessary that he have the perfect knowledge of things and other qualities that befit a commander, for since this would launch us on too great a sea, we shall be satisfied, as we have said, if he have complete loyalty and an undaunted spirit, and be always seen to have them. For oftentimes men are known for their courage in small things rather than in great. And often in important perils and where there are many witnesses, some men are found who, although their hearts sink within them, still, spurred on by fear of shame or by the company of those present, press forward with eyes shut, as it were, and do their duty, God knows how; and in things of little importance and when they think they can avoid the

risk of danger, they are glad to play safe. But those men who, even when they think they will not be observed or seen or recognized by anyone, show courage and are not careless of anything, however slight, for which they could be blamed, such have the quality of spirit we are seeking in our Courtier.

"However, we do not wish him to make a show of being so fierce that he is forever swaggering in his speech, declaring that he has wedded his cuirass,[5] and glowering with such dour looks as we have often seen Berto do; for to such as these one may rightly say what in polite society a worthy lady jestingly said to a certain man (whom I do not now wish to name) whom she sought to honor by inviting him to dance, and who not only declined this but would not listen to music or take any part in the other entertainments offered him, but kept saying that such trifles were not his business. And when finally the lady said to him: 'What then is your business?' he answered with a scowl: 'Fighting.' Whereupon the lady replied at once: 'I should think it a good thing, now that you are not away at war or engaged in fighting, for you to have yourself greased all over and stowed away in a closet along with all your battle harness, so that you won't grow any rustier than you already are'; and so, amid much laughter from those present, she ridiculed him in his stupid presumption. Therefore, let the man we are seeking be exceedingly fierce, harsh, and always among the first, wherever the enemy is; and in every other place, humane, modest, reserved, avoiding ostentation above all things as well as that impudent praise of himself by which a man always arouses hatred and disgust in all who hear him."

[18] Then signor Gasparo replied: "As for me, I have known few men excellent in anything whatsoever who did not praise themselves; and it seems to me that this can well be permitted them, because he who feels himself to be of some worth, and sees that his works are ignored, is indignant that his own worth should lie buried; and he must make it known to someone, in order not to be cheated of the honor that is the true reward of all virtuous toil. Thus, among the ancients, seldom does anyone of any worth refrain from praising himself. To be sure, those persons who are of no merit, and yet praise themselves, are insufferable; but we do not assume that our Courtier will be of that sort."

Then the Count said: "If you took notice, I blamed impudent and indiscriminate praise of one's self: and truly, as you say, one must not conceive a bad opinion of a worthy man who praises himself modestly; nay, one must take that as surer evidence than if it came

---

5. A piece of close-fitting armor for protecting the breast and back [*Editor*].

from another's mouth. I do say that whoever does not fall into error in praising himself and does not cause annoyance or envy in the person who listens to him is indeed a discreet man and, besides the praises he gives himself, deserves praises from others; for that is a very difficult thing."

Then signor Gasparo said: "This you must teach us."

The Count answered: "Among the ancients there is no lack of those who have taught this; but, in my opinion, the whole art consists in saying things in such a way that they do not appear to be spoken to that end, but are so very apropos that one cannot help saying them; and to seem always to avoid praising one's self, yet do so; but not in the manner of those boasters who open their mouths and let their words come out haphazardly. As one of our friends the other day who, when he had had his thigh run through by a spear at Pisa, said that he thought a fly had stung him; and another who said that he did not keep a mirror in his room because when he was angry he became so fearful of countenance that if he were to see himself, he would frighten himself too much."

Everyone laughed at this, but messer Cesare Gonzaga added: "What are you laughing at? Do you not know that Alexander the Great, upon hearing that in the opinion of one philosopher there were countless other worlds, began to weep, and when asked why, replied: 'Because I have not yet conquered one'[6]—as if he felt able to conquer them all? Does that not seem to you a greater boast than that of the fly sting?"

Then said the Count: "And Alexander was a greater man than the one who spoke so. But truly one has to excuse excellent men when they presume much of themselves, because anyone who has great things to accomplish must have the daring to do those things, and confidence in himself. And let him not be abject and base, but modest rather in his words, making it clear that he presumes less of himself than he accomplishes, provided such presumption does not turn to rashness."

[19] When the Count paused here briefly, messer Bernardo Bibbiena said, laughing: "I remember you said before that this Courtier of ours should be naturally endowed with beauty of countenance and person, and with a grace that would make him lovable. Now this grace and beauty of countenance I do believe that I have myself, wherefore it happens that so many ladies, as you know, are ardently in love with me; but, as to the beauty of my person, I am rather doubtful, and especially as to these legs of mine which in truth do not seem to me as well disposed as I could wish; as to my

6. The anecdote is found in Valerius Maximus, *Factorum et dictorum memorabilium* VIII, 14.

chest and the rest, I am quite well enough satisfied. Now do determine a little more in detail what this beauty of body should be, so
that I can extricate myself from doubt and put my mind at ease."

After some laughter at this, the Count added: "Certainly such
grace of countenance you can truly be said to have; nor will I
adduce any other example in order to make clear what that grace is;
because we do see beyond any doubt that your aspect is very agreeable and pleasant to all, although the features of it are not very delicate: it has something manly about it, and yet is full of grace. And
this is a quality found in many different types of faces. I would have
our Courtier's face be such, not so soft and feminine as many
attempt to have who not only curl their hair and pluck their eyebrows, but preen themselves in all those ways that the most wanton
and dissolute women in the world adopt; and in walking, in posture,
and in every act, appear so tender and languid that their limbs seem
to be on the verge of falling apart; and utter their words so limply
that it seems they are about to expire on the spot; and the more they
find themselves in the company of men of rank, the more they make
a show of such manners. These, since nature did not make them
women as they clearly wish to appear and be, should be treated not
as good women, but as public harlots, and driven not only from the
courts of great lords but from the society of all noble men.

[20] "Then, coming to bodily frame, I say it is enough that it be neither extremely small nor big, because either of these conditions
causes a certain contemptuous wonder, and men of either sort are
gazed at in much the same way that we gaze at monstrous things.
And yet, if one must sin in one or the other of these two extremes,
it is less bad to be on the small side than to be excessively big;
because men who are so huge of body are often not only obtuse of
spirit, but are also unfit for every agile exercise, which is something
I very much desire in the Courtier. And hence I would have him well
built and shapely of limb, and would have him show strength and
lightness and suppleness, and know all the bodily exercises that
befit a warrior. And in this I judge it his first duty to know how to
handle every kind of weapon, both on foot and on horse, and know
the advantages of each kind; and be especially acquainted with
those arms that are ordinarily used among gentlemen, because,
apart from using them in war (where perhaps so many fine points
are not necessary), there often arise differences between one gentleman and another, resulting in duels, and quite often those
weapons are used which happen to be at hand. Hence, knowledge
of them is a very safe thing. Nor am I one of those who say that skill
is forgotten in the hour of need; for he who loses his skill at such
times shows that out of fear he has already lost his heart and head.

[21] "I deem it highly important, moreover, to know how to wrestle, because this frequently accompanies the use of weapons on foot. Then, both for his own sake and for his friends', he must understand the quarrels and differences that can arise, and must be alert to seize an advantage, and must show courage and prudence in all things. Nor should he be quick to enter into a fight, except in so far as his honor demands it of him; for, besides the great danger that an uncertain fate can bring, he who rushes into such things precipitately and without urgent cause deserves greatly to be censured, even though he should meet with success. But when he finds that he is so far involved that he cannot withdraw without reproach, he must be very deliberate both in the preliminaries to the duel and in the duel itself, and always show readiness and daring. Nor must he do as some who spend their time in wrangling and arguing over points of honor; and, when they have the choice of weapons, select those which neither cut nor prick, and arm themselves as if they were expecting to stand against cannonades; and, thinking it enough not to be defeated, stand always on the defensive and give ground to such a degree that they show extreme cowardice. And so they make themselves the laughingstock of children, like those two men from Ancona who fought at Perugia recently and made everyone laugh who saw them."

"And who were they?" asked signor Gaspar Pallavicino.

"Two cousins," replied messer Cesare.

Then the Count said: "In their fighting they seemed true brothers." Then he went on: "Weapons are also often used in various exercises in time of peace, and gentlemen are seen in public spectacles before the people and before ladies and great lords. Therefore I wish our Courtier to be a perfect horseman in every kind of saddle; and, in addition to having a knowledge of horses and what pertains to riding, let him put every effort and diligence into outstripping others in everything a little, so that he may be always recognized as better than the rest. And even as we read that Alcibiades[7] surpassed all those peoples among whom he lived, and each in the respect wherein it claimed greatest excellence, so would I have this Courtier of ours excel all others in what is the special profession of each. And as it is the peculiar excellence of the Italians to ride well with the rein, to manage wild horses especially with great skill, to tilt and joust, let him be among the best of the Italians in this. In tourneys, in holding a pass, in attacking a fortified position, let him be among the best of the French. In stick-throwing, bull-fighting, in casting spears and darts, let him be outstanding among the Spaniards. But, above all, let him temper his every action with a cer-

---

7. See Cornelius Nepos, *Vitae: Alcibiades*, ch. xi.

tain good judgment and grace, if he would deserve that universal favor which is so greatly prized.

[22] "There are also other exercises which, although not immediately dependent upon arms, still have much in common therewith and demand much manly vigor; and chief among these is the hunt, it seems to me, because it has a certain resemblance to war. It is a true pastime for great lords, it befits a Courtier, and one understands why it was so much practiced among the ancients. He should also know how to swim, jump, run, throw stones; for, besides their usefulness in war, it is frequently necessary to show one's prowess in such things, whereby a good name is to be won, especially with the crowd (with whom one must reckon after all). Another noble exercise and most suitable for a man at court is the game of tennis which shows off the disposition of body, the quickness and litheness of every member, and all the qualities that are brought out by almost every other exercise. Nor do I deem vaulting on horseback to be less worthy, which, though it is tiring and difficult, serves more than anything else to make a man agile and dextrous; and besides its usefulness, if such agility is accompanied by grace, in my opinion it makes a finer show than any other.

"If, then, our Courtier is more than fairly expert in such exercises, I think he ought to put aside all others, such as vaulting on the ground, rope-walking, and the like, which smack of the juggler's trade and little befit a gentleman.

"But since one cannot always engage in such strenuous activities (moreover, persistence causes satiety, and drives away the admiration we have for rare things), we must always give variety to our lives by changing our activities. Hence, I would have our Courtier descend sometimes to quieter and more peaceful exercises. And, in order to escape envy and to enter agreeably into the company of others, let him do all that others do, yet never depart from comely conduct, but behave himself with that good judgment which will not allow him to engage in any folly; let him laugh, jest, banter, frolic, and dance, yet in such a manner as to show always that he is genial and discreet; and let him be full of grace in all that he does or says."

[23] Then messer Cesare Gonzaga said: "Certainly no one ought to interrupt the course of this discussion; but if I were to remain silent, I should neither be exercising the privilege I have of speaking nor satisfying the desire I have of learning something. And I may be pardoned if I ask a question when I ought to be speaking in opposition; for I think this can be allowed me, after the example set by our messer Bernardo who, in his excessive desire to be thought hand-

some, has violated the laws of our game by asking instead of gainsaying."

Then the Duchess said: "You see how from a single error a host
of others can come. Therefore, he who transgresses and sets a bad
example, as messer Bernardo has done, deserves to be punished not
only for his own transgression but for that of the others as well."

To this messer Cesare replied: "And so, Madam, I shall be exempt
from penalty, since messer Bernardo is to be punished both for his
own error and for mine."

"Nay," said the Duchess, "you both must be doubly punished: he
for his own transgression and for having brought you to yours, you
for your transgression and for having imitated him."

"Madam," answered messer Cesare, "I have not transgressed as
yet; however, in order to leave all this punishment to messer
Bernardo alone, I will keep quiet."

And he was already silent, when signora Emilia laughed and said:
"Say what you will, for, with the permission of the Duchess, I pardon both the one that has transgressed and the one that is about to
do so ever so little."

"So be it," the Duchess went on, "but take care lest you make the
mistake of thinking it more commendable to be clement than to be
just; for the excessive pardon of a transgressor does wrong to those
who do not transgress. Still, at the moment, I would not have my
austerity in reproaching your indulgence cause us not to hear
messer Cesare's question."

And so, at a sign from the Duchess and from signora Emilia, he
began forthwith:

[24] "If I well remember, Count, it seems to me you have repeated
several times this evening that the Courtier must accompany his
actions, his gestures, his habits, in short, his every movement, with
grace. And it strikes me that you require this in everything as that
seasoning without which all the other properties and good qualities
would be of little worth. And truly I believe that everyone would easily let himself be persuaded of this, because, by the very meaning of
the word, it can be said that he who has grace finds grace. But since
you have said that this is often a gift of nature and the heavens, and
that, even if it is not quite perfect, it can be much increased by care
and industry, those men who are born as fortunate and as rich in
such treasure as some we know have little need, it seems to me, of
any teacher in this, because such benign favor from heaven lifts
them, almost in spite of themselves, higher than they themselves
had desired, and makes them not only pleasing but admirable to
everyone. Therefore I do not discuss this, it not being in our power
to acquire it of ourselves. But as for those who are less endowed by

nature and are capable of acquiring grace only if they put forth labor, industry, and care, I would wish to know by what art, by what discipline, by what method, they can gain this grace, both in bodily exercises, in which you deem it to be so necessary, and in every other thing they do or say. Therefore, since by praising this quality so highly you have, as I believe, aroused in all of us an ardent desire, according to the task given you by signora Emilia, you are still bound to satisfy it."

[25] "I am not bound," said the Count, "to teach you how to acquire grace or anything else, but only to show you what a perfect Courtier ought to be. Nor would I undertake to teach you such a perfection; especially when I have just now said that the Courtier must know how to wrestle, vault, and so many other things which, since I never learned them myself, you all know well enough how I should be able to teach them. Let it suffice that just as a good soldier knows how to tell the smith what shape, style, and quality his armor must have, and yet is not able to teach him to make it, nor how to hammer or temper it; just so I, perhaps, shall be able to tell you what a perfect Courtier should be, but not to teach you what you must do to become one. Still, in order to answer your question in so far as I can (although it is almost proverbial that grace is not learned), I say that if anyone is to acquire grace in bodily exercises (granting first of all that he is not by nature incapable), he must begin early and learn the principles from the best of teachers. And how important this seemed to King Philip of Macedon can be seen by the fact that he wished Aristotle, the famous philosopher and perhaps the greatest the world has ever known, to be the one who should teach his son Alexander the first elements of letters. And among men whom we know today, consider how well and gracefully signor Galeazzo Sanseverino, Grand Equerry of France, performs all bodily exercises; and this because, besides the natural aptitude of person that he possesses, he has taken the greatest care to study with good masters and to have about him men who excel, taking from each the best of what they know. For just as in wrestling, vaulting, and in the handling of many kinds of weapons, he took our messer Pietro Monte as his guide, who is (as you know) the only true master of every kind of acquired strength and agility—so in riding, jousting, and the rest he has ever had before his eyes those men who are known to be most perfect in these matters.

[26] "Therefore, whoever would be a good pupil must not only do things well, but must always make every effort to resemble and, if that be possible, to transform himself into his master. And when he feels that he has made some progress, it is very profitable to observe

different men of that profession; and, conducting himself with that good judgment which must always be his guide, go about choosing now this thing from one and that from another. And even as in green meadows the bee flits about among the grasses robbing the flowers, so our Courtier must steal this grace from those who seem to him to have it, taking from each the part that seems most worthy of praise; not doing as a friend of ours whom you all know, who thought he greatly resembled King Ferdinand the Younger of Aragon, but had not tried to imitate him in anything save in the way he had of raising his head and twisting one side of his mouth, which manner the King had contracted through some malady. And there are many such, who think they are doing a great thing if only they can resemble some great man in something; and often they seize upon that which is his only bad point.

"But, having thought many times already about how this grace is acquired (leaving aside those who have it from the stars), I have found quite a universal rule which in this matter seems to me valid above all others, and in all human affairs whether in word or deed: and that is to avoid affectation in every way possible as though it were some very rough and dangerous reef; and (to pronounce a new word perhaps) to practice in all things a certain *sprezzatura* [nonchalance], so as to conceal all art and make whatever is done or said appear to be without effort and almost without any thought about it. And I believe much grace comes of this: because everyone knows the difficulty of things that are rare and well done; wherefore facility in such things causes the greatest wonder; whereas, on the other hand, to labor and, as we say, drag forth by the hair of the head, shows an extreme want of grace, and causes everything, no matter how great it may be, to be held in little account.

"Therefore we may call that art true art which does not seem to be art; nor must one be more careful of anything than of concealing it, because if it is discovered, this robs a man of all credit and causes him to be held in slight esteem. And I remember having read of certain most excellent orators in ancient times who, among the other things they did, tried to make everyone believe that they had no knowledge whatever of letters; and, dissembling their knowledge, they made their orations appear to be composed in the simplest manner and according to the dictates of nature and truth rather than of effort and art; which fact, had it been known, would have inspired in the minds of the people the fear that they could be duped by it.

"So you see how art, or any intent effort, if it is disclosed, deprives everything of grace. Who among you fails to laugh when our messer Pierpaolo dances after his own fashion, with those capers of his, his legs stiff on tiptoe, never moving his head, as if he were a stick of wood, and all this so studied that he really seems to be counting his steps? What eye is so blind as not to see in this the ungainliness of affectation; and not to see the grace of that cool *disinvoltura* [ease] (for when it is a matter of bodily movements many call it that) in many of the men and women here present, who seem in words, in laughter, in posture not to care; or seem to be thinking more of everything than of that, so as to cause all who are watching them to believe that they are almost incapable of making a mistake?"

[27] Here messer Bernardo Bibbiena said, without waiting: "Now you see that our messer Roberto has at last found someone to praise his style of dancing, as it seems that none of the rest of you esteem it at all. For if this excellence consists in nonchalance, in showing no concern, and in seeming to have one's thoughts elsewhere rather than on what one is doing, then in dancing messer Roberto has no peer on earth, because to make it quite plain that he is giving no thought to what he is doing, he lets his clothes fall from his back and his slippers from his feet, and goes right on dancing without picking them up."

Then the Count replied: "Since you are determined that I shall go on talking, I will say something more of our faults. Do you not see that what you are calling nonchalance in messer Roberto is really affectation, because we clearly see him making every effort to show that he takes no thought of what he is about, which means taking too much thought; and because it exceeds certain limits of moderation, such nonchalance is affected, is unbecoming, and results in the opposite of the desired effect, which is to conceal the art. Hence, I do not believe that the vice of affectation is any less present in a nonchalance (in itself a praiseworthy thing) wherein one lets his clothes fall of than in a studied concern for one's personal appearance (also, in itself, a praise-worthy thing), bearing the head so stiff for fear of spoiling one's coiffure, or carrying a mirror in the fold of one's cap and a comb in one's sleeve, and having one's page follow about through the streets with a sponge and brush; because such care for personal appearance and such nonchalance both tend too much to extremes, which is always a fault, and is contrary to that pure and charming simplicity which is so appealing to all. Consider how ungraceful that rider is who tries to sit so very stiff in his saddle (in the Venetian style, as we are wont to say), compared with one who appears to give no thought to the matter and sits his horse as free and easy as if he were on foot. How much more pleasing and how much more praised is a gentleman whose profession is arms, and who is modest, speaking little and boasting little, than another who is forever praising himself, swearing and blustering about as if to defy the whole world—which is simply the affectation of wanting to cut a bold figure. And the same holds true in every practice, indeed in everything that is said or done."

[28] Then the Magnifico Giuliano said: "It holds true as well in music, wherein it is a great mistake to place two perfect consonances one after the other, for our sense of hearing abhors this, whereas it often enjoys a second or a seventh which in itself is a harsh and unbearable discord. And this is due to the fact that to continue in perfect consonances generates satiety and gives evidence of a too affected harmony, which is avoided when imperfect consonances are mixed in, establishing a kind of comparison, by which our ears are held in greater suspense, and more avidly wait upon and enjoy the perfect consonances, delighting in that discord of the second or seventh as in something that shows nonchalance."

"So, you see," replied the Count, "that affectation is detrimental in this as in other things. Moreover, it is said to have been proverbial with certain most excellent painters of antiquity that excessive care is harmful, and Protogenes is said to have been censured by Apelles for not knowing when to take his hands from the board.[8]

Then messer Cesare said: "It seems to me that our fra Serafino has this same fault of not knowing when to take his hands from the board,[9] at least not before all of the food has been taken from it too."

The Count laughed and added: "Apelles meant that Protogenes did not know when to stop in painting, which was nothing if not a kind of reproach for his being affected in his work. Thus, this excellence (which is opposed to affectation, and which, at the moment, we are calling *nonchalance*), besides being the real source from which grace springs, brings with it another adornment which, when it accompanies any human action however small, not only reveals at once how much the person knows who does it, but often causes it to be judged much greater than it actually is, since it impresses upon the minds of the onlookers the opinion that he who performs well with so much facility must possess even greater skill than this, and that, if he were to devote care and effort to what he does, he could do it far better.

"And, to multiply such examples, take a man who is handling weapons and is about to throw a dart or is holding a sword or other weapon in his hand: if immediately he takes a position of readiness, with ease, and without thinking, with such facility that his body and all his members fall into that posture naturally and without any effort, then, even if he does nothing more, he shows himself to be

8. Pliny, *Nat. hist.* XXXV, 80.
9. The play of words is on the word *tavola*, which can mean either the *panel* used by a painter or a *dining table*.

perfectly accomplished in that exercise. Likewise in dancing, a sin-gle step, a single movement of the body that is graceful and not forced, reveals at once the skill of the dancer. A singer who utters a single word ending in a group of four notes with a sweet cadence, and with such facility that he appears to do it quite by chance, shows with that touch alone that he can do much more than he is doing. Often too in painting, a single line which is not labored, a single brush stroke made with ease and in such a manner that the hand seems of itself to complete the line desired by the painter, without being directed by care or skill of any kind, clearly reveals that excellence of craftsmanship, which people will then proceed to judge, each by his own lights. And the same happens in almost every other thing.

"Therefore our Courtier will be judged excellent, and will show grace in all things and particularly in his speech, if he avoids affec-tation: which error is incurred by many and sometimes, more than others, by our Lombards who, if they have been away from home for a year, come back and start right off speaking Roman, or Spanish, or French, and God knows how! All of which stems from an exces-sive desire to appear very accomplished, and so they put effort and diligence into acquiring a most odious fault. Certainly it would require no little effort on my part if in these discussions I attempted to use those antique Tuscan words which the Tuscans of today have already dropped from use; moreover, I believe you would all laugh at me."

[29] Then messer Federico said: "It is true that in discussing among ourselves, as we are now doing, it would be bad perhaps to use those antique Tuscan words, because, as you say, they would be irksome both to the speaker and to the listener, and many would understand them only with difficulty. But if one is writing, then I do believe it would be wrong not to use them, because they give much grace and authority to writing, and result in a diction of more gravity and majesty than is had with modern words."

"I do not know," replied the Count, "what grace or authority can be given to writing by words that ought to be avoided, not only in such talk as we are presently engaged in (which you yourself admit) but also in any circumstance whatever that one can imagine. For if any man of good judgment had to deliver an oration on weighty mat-ters before the very senate of Florence, which is the capital of Tus-cany, or had to speak privately about important business with some person of rank in that city, or yet about amusing things with some close acquaintance, or about love with ladies or gentlemen, or in jokes or jests at feasts, games, or where you will, whatever the time, place, or matter, I am sure he would take care to avoid using those

antique Tuscan words; and if he used them, not only would he bring
ridicule upon himself but he would give no little annoyance to anyone hearing him.

"Therefore it strikes me as very strange to use as good words in
writing those which are eschewed as bad in whatever sort of speech,
and to maintain that what is never proper when spoken should be
the most proper usage possible in writing. For it is my opinion that
writing is simply a form of speaking which endures even after it is
uttered, the image, as it were, or better, the soul of our words.
Hence, in speech, which vanishes as soon as it is uttered, some
things are permissible; but not so in writing, because writing preserves the words and submits them to the judgment of the reader,
giving him time to consider them at length. Wherefore, in the case
of writing it is reasonable that greater care should be taken to make
it more polished and correct; not, however, that the written words
should be different from the spoken, but that in writing those words
should be chosen which are the most beautiful in speech. And if
what is not permitted in speaking should be permitted in writing, in
my opinion a most unhappy thing would result: namely, more
license would be taken in that wherein one should take the most
care; and the effort that goes into writing would be detrimental
rather than good.

"Therefore it is surely true that what is proper in writing is also
proper in speaking; and that manner of speaking is most beautiful
which resembles beautiful writing. Furthermore, I deem it far more
essential to be understood in writing than in speaking, since those
who write are not always present to their readers as those who speak
are present to those with whom they speak. But I would praise any
man who, besides avoiding many antique Tuscan words, would
make certain, whether in speaking or writing, that he uses those
words which are in current usage in Tuscany and in other parts of
Italy and which have a certain grace when pronounced. And it
seems to me that he who imposes upon himself any other rule is not
quite sure of avoiding that affectation which is so much condemned
and about which we were speaking a moment ago."

[30] Then messer Federico said: "I cannot deny you, Count, that
writing is a kind of speech; but I do say that if spoken words have
any obscurity in them, such discourse will not penetrate the mind
of the listener, and, since it passes without being understood, is to
no purpose; which does not happen in writing, because if the words
which a writer uses have in them a little, I will not say difficulty, but
subtlety that is hidden, and thus are not so familiar as the words
that are commonly used in speaking, they do give a certain greater
authority to the writing and cause the reader to proceed with more

restraint and concentration, to reflect more, and to enjoy the talent and the doctrine of the writer; and, by judiciously exerting himself a little, he tastes that pleasure which is had when we achieve difficult things. And if the ignorance of the one who reads is so great that he cannot overcome these difficulties, that is no fault of the writer, nor on this account must such a style be judged to be without beauty.

"Therefore I believe that in writing one should use Tuscan words and those only which have been used by the ancient Tuscans, because that is a great proof, tested by time, that they are good and effective in expressing what they signify. And, besides this, they have the grace and venerableness which great age gives not only to words, but to building, statues, pictures, and to everything that is able to take it on; and often by such splendor and dignity they make the diction beautiful, by the power and elegance whereof every subject, no matter how mean it may be, can be adorned so as to deserve the highest praise. But this matter of current usage, by which you set such store, to me seems very risky; and it can often be bad. And if some fault of speech is found to prevail among many ignorant persons, it seems to me that it ought not on this account to be taken as a rule and be followed by other persons. Moreover, usage varies a great deal, nor is there a noble city in Italy without its own manner of speech different from all the others. But since you have not felt bound to declare which speech among these is the best, a man might adopt Bergamasque[1] as well as Florentine, and, according to you, there would be nothing wrong in this.

"It seems to me, therefore, that anyone who wishes to avoid all doubt and feel quite sure must set himself to imitating someone who by common consent is acknowledged to be good, and hold to him as to a guide and shield against any adverse critic. And such a model (in the vernacular, I mean) should be none other than Petrarch and Boccaccio; and whoever strays from these two is groping, like someone walking through the darkness without a light, and he will often lose his way. But we are today so forward that we do not stoop to do what the good writers of old did, namely, to practice imitation, without which I deem it impossible to write well. And it seems to me that a great witness of this is seen in Virgil who, though by his own genius and divine judgment he deprived all posterity of the hope of being able to imitate him well, still choose to imitate Homer."

---

1. Bergamasque is often ridiculed in the Renaissance theater and considered one of the harshest of Italian dialects.

[31] Then signor Gaspar Pallavicino said: "Certainly, this discussion about writing is well worth listening to; and yet it would be more to our purpose if you would teach us the manner the Courtier should observe in speaking, for I think he has greater need of that, since he has to use speech more often than writing."

The Magnifico replied: "Indeed, there is no doubt that a Courtier so excellent and perfect will need to have knowledge of both the one and the other; and without these two abilities perhaps all the rest would not be deserving of much praise. Therefore, if the Count wishes to perform his duty, he will teach the Courtier not only how to speak well but also how to write well."

Then the Count said: "Signor Magnifico, I would not think of undertaking such a task, for it were great folly on my part to presume to teach others what I do not know myself, and (even if I did know it) to think that I could teach in so few words what very learned men have barely been able to do by so much labor and effort—to whose works I would refer our Courtier if I had to teach him to write and speak."

Messer Cesare said: "The Magnifico means speaking and writing in the vernacular and not in Latin; therefore those works of learned men are not to our purpose. But it is for you to tell us what you know about this, and more than that we shall not expect of you."

"I have already told you that," replied the Count; "but if we are speaking of the Tuscan language, perhaps the Magnifico, more than anyone else, ought to give us his judgment on that."

The Magnifico replied: "I cannot, and in reason should not, gainsay anyone who holds that the Tuscan language is more beautiful than the others. It is true, of course, that one meets with many words in Petrarch and Boccaccio that have now been dropped from usage. And I for one would never use these either in speaking or writing; nor do I think that they themselves would use them any longer if they had lived into our time."

Then messer Federico said: "Nay, but they would! And you Tuscans ought to renew your language and not allow it to die, as you are doing—so that by now we can say that it is less known in Florence than in many other places in Italy."

Then messer Bernardo said: "Those words which are no longer used in Florence have remained with the peasants, and are rejected by the gentry as words that have been corrupted and spoiled by age."

[32] Then the Duchess said: "Let us not stray from our original purpose; but let the Count teach the Courtier how to speak and write well, whether it be Tuscan or whatever."

"Madam," the Count replied, "I have already told you what I know about this; and I maintain that the same rules which serve to teach the one thing serve also to teach the other. But since you command me to do so, I will say what I have to say to messer Federico, who differs from me on this. And it may be that I shall have to speak at somewhat greater length than is suitable, but it will be all that I am able to say.

"First I will say that, in my opinion, this language of ours which we call the vulgar tongue is still tender and new, although it has been in use now for quite a long time. For, since Italy has not only been harried and ravaged, but long inhabited, by the barbarians, the Latin language has been corrupted and spoiled by contact with those peoples, and out of that corruption other languages have arisen: and, like the rivers that divide at the crest of the Apennines and flow into the sea on either side, so these languages also have divided, and some that were tinged with Latinity have flowed in various channels and in different directions; and one that was tinged with barbarism remained in Italy. The latter was for a long time disordered and uneven, having no one to take any care of it or to attempt to give it any splendor or grace. Yet finally it was cultivated somewhat more in Tuscany than in other parts of Italy. And for this reason it seems to have flourished there from those early times, because that people more than others have kept gentle accents in their speech and a proper grammatical order, and have had three noble writers who expressed their thoughts ingeniously and in the words and terms that were current in their time; wherein it fell to Petrarch to do this in amorous subjects with more felicity than the others, in my opinion.

"Then, from time to time, not only in Tuscany but in the rest of Italy, among wellborn men versed in the usages of courts, in arms, and in letters, a concern arose to speak and write more elegantly than in that first rude and uncultivated age when the fires of calamity set by the barbarians were not yet extinguished. Thus, both in the city of Florence itself and in all Tuscany, as well as in the rest of Italy, many words were abandoned, and others were taken up in their stead, thereby bringing about the change which takes place in all things human and has always taken place in other languages as well. For if the earliest writings in ancient Latin had survived until now, we should see that Evander and Turnus and the other Latins of those times spoke differently from the last Kings of Rome or the first consuls. For note that the verses which the Salians[2] sang were hardly understood by later generations; but since they had been so composed by those who first gave them their form, out of a religious reverence they were left unchanged. Thereafter, orators and poets

---

2. The *Carmina Saliaria* were no longer understood by Cicero's time. Cf. Quintilian, *Instit. orat.* I, VI.

gradually abandoned many words that had been used by their predecessors; thus, Antonius, Crassus, Hortensius, and Cicero avoided
many of Cato's words, and Virgil many of Ennius'; and so did many
others. For, although they had reverence for antiquity, they did not
hold it in so great esteem as to feel bound by it as you would have
us be today. On the contrary, wherever they saw fit, they censured
it, as Horace who says that his forebears were foolish in their praise
of Plautus, and insists on his right to acquire new words. And
Cicero in many places reprehends many of his predecessors, and in
censuring Sergius Galba declares that his orations have an antique
cast to them; and he says that Ennius himself spurned his predecessors in certain things: so that, if we attempt to imitate the
ancients, we shall not be imitating them. And Virgil, who (as you
say) imitated Homer, did not imitate him in language.

[33] "Therefore I for my part would always avoid using these
antique words, save only in certain places and rarely even there; and
it strikes me that one who otherwise uses them errs, no less than
one who, in order to imitate the ancients, would choose to feed on
acorns when wheat in quantity was already at hand. And because
you say that by their very splendor of antiquity, antique words so
greatly adorn every subject, however mean, that they can make it
worthy of much praise—I say that I do not set such great store
either by these antique words or even by good words as to think that
in reason they are to be prized if devoid of the pith of fine thoughts;
for to separate thoughts from words is to separate soul from body:
in neither case can it be done without destruction.

"So, as I believe, what is most important and necessary to the
Courtier in order to speak and write well is knowledge: because one
who is ignorant and has nothing in his mind worth listening to can
neither speak nor write well.

"Next, what one has to say or write must be given a good order. It
must then be well expressed in words, which words (if I am not mistaken) must be proper, select, lustrous, and well formed, but above
all be words which are still used by the people. Now it is the words
themselves that make the greatness and magnificence of an oration;
for if a speaker uses good judgment and care, and understands how
to choose those words which best express what he wishes to say; and
if he elevates them, and shapes them to his purpose like so much
wax, he can give them such a disposition and an order such as to
cause them to reveal at a glance their dignity and splendor, like
paintings when placed in a good and natural light. And I say this as
well of writing as of speaking; except that in speaking some things
are required that are not needed in writing: such as a good voice,
not too thin or soft as a woman's, nor yet so stern and rough as to

have a boorish quality, but sonorous, clear, gentle, and well constituted, with distinct enunciation and with fitting manner and gestures. The latter, in my opinion, consist in certain movements of the
entire body, not affected or violent, but tempered by a seemly
expression of the face and a movement of the eyes such as to give
grace and be consonant with the words, together with such gestures
as shall signify as well as possible the intention and the feeling of
the orator. But all this would be empty and of little moment if the
thoughts expressed by the words were not fine, witty, acute, elegant,
and solemn, according to the need."

[34] Then signor Morello said: "If this Courtier of ours speaks with
so much elegance and gravity, I fear there may be those among us
who will not understand him."

"Nay," replied the Count, "all will understand him, because words
that are easy to understand can still be elegant. Nor would I have
him always speak of grave matters, but of amusing things, of games,
jests, and jokes, according to the occasion; but sensibly in everything, with readiness and a lucid fullness; nor must he show vanity
or a childish folly in any way. Then, whenever he speaks of anything
that is obscure or difficult, I would have him explain his meaning
down to a fine point, with precision in both words and thoughts,
making every ambiguity clear and plain in a manner that is careful
but not tiresome. Likewise, when occasion demands, let him know
how to speak with dignity and force, and how to stir up those sentiments which are latent within us, kindling and moving them as the
need may be; and speak at other times with such simple candor as
to make it seem that nature herself is speaking, to soften such sentiments and inebriate them with sweetness, and all this with such
ease as to cause the one who listens to believe that with little effort
he too could attain to such excellence—but who, when he tries, discovers that he is very far from it.

"Such is the manner in which I would have our Courtier speak
and write; and let him not only choose fine and elegant words from
every part of Italy, but I should praise him as well if sometimes he
used some of those French or Spanish terms that are already current with us. Thus, should the need arise, I should not be displeased
if he used *primor* (excellence); or used *accertare* (to succeed); *avven-
turare* (to hazard); or *ripassare una persona con ragionamento*, meaning to observe someone and associate with him in order to get to
know him well; or *un cavaliere senza rimproccio* (a knight without
reproach), *attilato* (elegant), *creato d'un principe* (the dependent of
a prince) and other like terms, provided he has reason to think he
will be understood. I would have him use certain words sometimes
in a sense they do not usually have, transferring them aptly, and, so

to say, grafting them like the scion of a tree on some better trunk, in order to make them more attractive and beautiful and, as it were, put things before our very eyes; and, as we say, make us feel them with our hands, to the delight of the listener or the reader. Nor would I have him be afraid even to coin some new words; and he should use new figures of speech, taking these elegantly from the Latins, even as the Latins themselves once took them from the Greeks.

[35] "Therefore if today, among men of letters of good talent and judgment, some took pains to write in this language (in the manner I have described) things worthy of being read, we should soon see it polished and replete with terms and fine figures, and capable of being used in writing as well as any other; and if this were then not pure old Tuscan, it would be Italian, universal, copious, and varied, and like a delightful garden full of a variety of flowers and fruits. Nor would this be anything new, for out of the four languages[3] of which they were able to avail themselves, Greek writers chose words, expressions, and figures from each as they saw fit, and brought forth another that was called the "common" language; then later all five were called simply Greek. And although Athenian was more elegant, pure, and copious than the others, good writers who were not Athenian by birth did not affect it so much as to be unrecognizable by their style and, as it were, by the savor and essence of their native speech. Yet they were not scorned for this; on the contrary, those who tried to seem too Athenian were blamed for it. Among Latin writers also there were many non-Romans who were much esteemed in their day, even though they were not seen to possess that purity of the Roman tongue which is rarely acquired by men born elsewhere. Certainly Titus Livius was not rejected, although there was one who claimed to find a Paduan flavor in him; nor was Virgil rejected on any charge that he did not speak Roman. Moreover, as you know, many writers of barbarian extraction were read and esteemed at Rome.

"But we, being far more strict than the ancients, impose upon ourselves certain new laws that are inept; and although we have well-traveled roads before our eyes, we try to proceed along byways, for in our own language—the function of which, as of all other languages, is to express well and clearly what the mind conceives—we take pleasure in what is obscure; and, calling it the 'vulgar tongue,' we choose to use words in it which are not only not understood by the vulgar, but not even by noble men of letters, and are no longer in use anywhere, careless of the fact that all good writers among the

3. Attic, Doric, Ionian, and Aeolic dialects.

ancients condemn words that have been rejected by usage. Which usage you do not well understand, in my opinion, because you say that if some fault of speech has become prevalent among the ignorant, it ought not to be called usage for that reason, nor accepted as a rule of speech; and, from what I have heard you state on other occasions, you would have us say *Campidoglio* instead of *Capitolio*; *Girolamo* instead of *Jeronimo*; *aldace* instead of *audace*; *padrone* instead of *patrone*—and other like words which are corrupt and spoiled—because they are so written by some ignorant old Tuscan, and because they are so used by Tuscan peasants today.

"Thus, good usage in speech, as I believe, springs from men who have talent, and who through learning and experience have attained good judgment, and who thereby agree among themselves and consent to adopt those words which to them seem good; which words are recognized by virtue of a certain natural judgment and not by any art or rule. Do you not know that figures of speech, which give so much grace and luster to discourse, are all abuses of grammatical rules, yet are accepted and confirmed by usage, because (it being impossible to give any other reason for this) they please, and seem to offer suavity and sweetness to the ear itself? And this, I believe, is what good usage is, whereof Romans, Neapolitans, Lombards, and the rest can be quite as capable as Tuscans.

[36] "It is indeed true that in all languages some things are always good, such as facility, good order, fullness, fine periods of harmonious clauses; and that, on the contrary, affectation and the other things that are opposed to these are bad. But among words there are some that remain good for a time, then grow old and lose their grace completely, whereas others gain in strength and come into favor; because, just as the seasons of the year divest the earth of her flowers and fruits, and then clothe her again with others, so time causes those first words to fall, and usage brings others to life, giving them grace and dignity, until they are gradually consumed by the envious jaws of time, when they too go to their death; because, in the end, we and all our things are mortal. Consider that we no longer have any knowledge of the Oscan tongue. Provençal, which we might say was but recently celebrated by noble writers, is not now understood by the inhabitants of that region. Hence, I think, even as the Magnifico has well said, that if Petrarch and Boccaccio were living today, they would not use many of the words we find in their writings: hence, it does not seem good to me that we should imitate them in those words. I do indeed praise highly those who can imitate what is to be imitated; nonetheless, I do not think it at all impossible to write well without imitation; and particularly in this language of ours in

which we can be helped by usage—which is something I would not venture to say of Latin."

[37] Then messer Federico said: "Why would you have usage be more esteemed in the vernacular than in Latin?"

"Indeed," replied the Count, "I hold that usage is the guide in both the one and the other. But since those to whom Latin was as natural as the vernacular is to us today are no longer among the living, we are obliged to learn from their writings what they learned from usage. Nor does ancient speech mean anything more than ancient usage in speech. And it would be a silly thing to love ancient speech for no other reason than to wish to speak as men used to speak rather than as they speak now."

"So," replied messer Federico, "the ancients did not imitate?"

"I believe," said the Count, "that many of them did imitate, but not in everything. And if Virgil had imitated Hesiod in everything, he would not have surpassed him; nor Cicero, Crassus; nor Ennius, his predecessors. Consider that Homer is so ancient that many believe him to be the first heroic poet in time as well as in excellence of style: and whom would you say he imitated?"

"Someone," answered messer Federico, "more ancient than he, of whom we have no knowledge owing to his great antiquity."

"Then whom," said the Count, "will you say Petrarch and Boccaccio imitated, who we might say have been in the world but a few days?"

"I do not know," replied messer Federico, "but we can believe that they too were bent on imitating, even though we do not know whom."

The Count replied: "It must be thought that the imitated were better than their imitators; and, if they were good, it would be very strange if their name and fame had completely vanished so soon. But I think that their true master was talent and their own native judgment. And at this no one should wonder, for it is almost always possible to advance toward the summit of all excellence by several paths. Nor is there anything that does not comprise in its own kind a multiplicity of things which are different from one another and yet equally deserving of praise among themselves.

"Consider music, the harmonies of which are now solemn and slow, now very fast and novel in mood and manner. And yet all give pleasure, although for different reasons, as is seen in Bidon's manner of singing which is so skilled, quick, vehement, impassioned, and has such various melodies that the spirits of his listeners are stirred and take fire, and are so entranced that they seem to be uplifted to heaven. Nor does our Marchetto Cara move us less by his singing, but only with a softer harmony. For, in a manner serene and full of plaintive sweetness, he touches and penetrates our souls, gently impressing a delightful sentiment upon them.

"Moreover, different things give equal pleasure to our eyes, so that it is difficult for us to judge which things please them most. Consider that in painting Leonardo da Vinci, Mantegna, Raphael, Michelangelo, and Giorgio da Castelfranco are most excellent; and yet they are all unlike one another in their work: so that in his own manner no one of them appears to lack anything, since we recognize each to be perfect in his own style.

"The same holds true of many Greek and Latin poets who, though different in their writing, are equal in fame. Orators, too, have always shown so much diversity among themselves that nearly every age has produced and prized a certain kind of orator peculiar to its time; and these have been different, not only from their predecessors, but also from one another: as it is written of Isocrates, Lysias, Aeschines, and many others among the Greeks, all excellent, yet each resembling no one but himself. Then, among the Latins, Carbo, Laelius, Scipio Africanus, Galba, Sulpicius, Cotta, Gracchus, Marcus Antonius, Crassus, and so many others that it would take long to name them, all good, yet very different from one another; so that if one were to take thought of all the orators that have ever existed, he would find as many kinds of oratory as orators. I seem to remember too that Cicero somewhere[4] has Marcus Antonius say to Sulpicius that there are many who imitate no one and yet attain to the highest degree of excellence; and he speaks of certain others who had begun a new manner and type of oratory, beautiful, but unusual among orators at that time, in which they imitated no one but themselves. Thus, he affirms also that teachers must consider the nature of their pupils and, taking that as a guide, must direct them and help them in the path toward which their talent and natural disposition inclines them. Hence, my dear messer Federico, I do believe that if someone does not feel congenial to a given author, it is not well to force him to imitate him, because the strength of his talent will be weakened and impeded in being turned from the path which it might profitably have taken, if it had not been denied it.

"Therefore, I do not see how it can be well, in place of enriching our language and giving it spirit, greatness, and luster, to make it poor, thin, humble, and obscure, and to attempt to limit it so narrowly that everyone should be forced to imitate only Petrarch and Boccaccio; and that one may not place trust in Poliziano, Lorenzo de' Medici, Francesco Diacceto, and some others who are also Tuscans and perchance not inferior in learning and judgment to

4. Cicero, *De oratore* II, xxiii, 97.

Petrarch and Boccaccio. And truly it would mean a great poverty to call a halt and not go beyond what some one of the earliest writers may have achieved, and to lose hope that so many men of such noble talents might ever devise more than one beautiful way of expressing themselves in a language which is proper and natural to them. But there are today certain scrupulous souls who, in a kind of cult of the ineffable mysteries of this their Tuscan language, do frighten all so who listen to them as to inspire in many a noble man of learning so much timidity that he dares not open his mouth, and confesses that he does not know how to speak the very language he learned in swaddling clothes from his nurse. But I think we have said more than enough about this. So let us proceed now with our discussion of the Courtier."

[38] Then messer Federico replied: "I should like to say a little more: I certainly do not deny that the opinions and the talents of men differ from one another; nor do I think it well that someone who has a vehement and impassioned nature should undertake to write about calm things, or that another who is severe and grave should write jests, for in this matter it seems right to me that everyone should follow his own bent. And Cicero was speaking of this, I believe, when he said that teachers should have regard for the nature of their pupils, in order not to act like bad husbandmen who sometimes sow grain in ground that is productive only for vineyards. But I cannot comprehend why, in the case of a particular language which does not belong to all men as do speaking and thinking and many other functions, but is an invention bound by certain limitations, it is not more reasonable to imitate those who speak well than it is to speak at random; or why, just as in Latin we must try to conform to Virgil's language and Cicero's rather than to that of Silius or Cornelius Tacitus, it is not better in the case of the vernacular to imitate the language of Petrarch and Boccaccio rather than another's, but express one's own thoughts in it, of course, and by so doing to follow one's own natural instinct, even as Cicero teaches. And in this way it will be found that the difference which you say exists among good orators lies in sense and not in language."

Then the Count replied: "I fear that we shall enter on a wide sea and depart from our first subject of the Courtier. Still I would ask you, in what does the excellence of this language consist?"

Messer Federico replied: "In respecting its proprieties, employing it so, and adopting that style and those harmonies which all who have written well have used."

"I should like to know," said the Count, "whether this style and these harmonies that you speak of arise from the thought or from the words."

"From the words," replied messer Federico.

"Then," said the Count, "do you not think that the words of Silius and of Cornelius Tacitus are the same as those which Virgil and Cicero employ? Are they not used in the same sense?"

"They are indeed the same," replied messer Federico, "but some of them are not preserved well and are used in a different sense."

The Count replied: "And if from a book of Cornelius and from one of Silius all those words were removed that are used in a sense different from that of Virgil or Cicero (which would be very few), then would you not say that Cornelius was the equal of Cicero in language, and Silius the equal of Virgil, and that it were well to imitate their manner of speech?"

[39] Then signora Emilia said: "It seems to me that this debate of yours has now become too long and tiresome; therefore it would be well to postpone it to another time."

Messer Federico was about to reply, even so, but signora Emilia kept interrupting him.

Finally the Count said: "There are many who want to judge of styles and who talk about harmonies and imitation, but they are quite unable to explain to me what style and harmonies are, or in what imitation consists, or why things which are taken from Homer or from someone else are so proper in Virgil as to seem enhanced rather than imitated. Perhaps that is due to my inability to understand such persons. But since it is good evidence that a man knows a thing if he is able to teach it, I fear that they understand it but little and that they praise Virgil and Cicero because they hear many praise them, not because they can recognize the difference between these two and the others; for it is truly not a matter of preserving two or three or ten words in a usage different from that of the others.

"In Sallust, in Caesar, in Varro, and in the other good writers, there are some terms used differently from the way Cicero uses them; and yet both ways are all right, because the excellence and force of a language does not lie in such a trifling matter as that: as Demosthenes well said to Aeschines,[5] who made a thrust at him, asking if certain words which he had used (which were not Attic) were monsters or portents; and Demosthenes laughed and answered that the fortunes of Greece did not depend on that. So I too should care little if some Tuscan reproached me for saying *satisfatto* rather than *sodisfatto*, or *onorevole* rather than *orrevole*, *causa* rather than *cagione*, *populo* rather than *popolo* and the like."

Then messer Federico rose to his feet and said: "Listen to these few words, I beg of you."

5. Cicero, *De oratore* VIII, 26.

"The pain of my displeasure," replied signora Emilia, laughing, "be upon him among you who speaks any more about this matter at this time, for I wish to postpone it to another evening. But do you, Count, continue with this discussion of the Courtier, showing us what a good memory you have; for, if you are able to take it up where you left it, I think you will be doing not a little!"

[40] "Madam," replied the Count, "I think the thread is broken. Still, if I am not mistaken, I believe we were saying that the bane of affectation always produces extreme gracelessness in all things and that, on the other hand, the greatest grace is produced by simplicity and nonchalance: in praise of which, and in blame of affectation, many other things could be said; but I wish to add only one thing more. All women have a great desire to be—and when they cannot be, at least to seem—beautiful. Therefore, wherever nature has failed in this regard, they try to remedy it with artifice: whence that embellishing of the face with so much care and sometimes with pain, that plucking of the eyebrows and the forehead, and the use of all those methods and the enduring of those nuisances which you ladies think are hidden to men, but which are well known."

Here madam Costanza Fregosa laughed and said: "It would be much more courteous of you to go on with your discussion, and tell us what the source of grace is, and speak of Courtiership, instead of trying to uncover the defects of women, which is not to the purpose."

"On the contrary, it is much to the purpose," replied the Count, "for the defects that I am speaking of deprive you ladies of grace, since they are caused by nothing but affectation, through which you openly let everyone know your inordinate desire to be beautiful. Do you not see how much more grace a woman has who paints (if at all) so sparingly and so little that whoever sees her is uncertain whether she is painted or not; than another woman so plastered with it that she seems to have put a mask on her face and dares not laugh so as not to cause it to crack, and never changes color except in the morning when she dresses; and, then, for the rest of the entire day remains motionless like a wooden statue and shows herself only by torchlight, like wily merchants who display their cloth in a dark place. And how much more attractive than all the others is one (not ugly, I mean) who is plainly seen to have nothing on her face, it being neither too white nor too red, but has her own natural color, a bit pale, and tinged at times with an open blush from shame or other cause, with her hair artlessly unadorned and in disarray, with gestures simple and natural, without showing effort or care to be beautiful. Such is that careless purity which is so pleasing to the eyes and minds of men who are ever fearful of being deceived by art.

"Beautiful teeth are very attractive in a woman, for since they do not show as openly as the face, not being visible most of the time, we may believe that less care has been taken to make them beautiful than with the face: and yet whoever laughs without cause and solely to display the teeth would betray his art, and, no matter how beautiful they are, would seem most ungraceful to all, like Catullus' Egnatius.[6] The same is true of the hands which, if they are delicate and beautiful, and are uncovered at the proper time, when there is need to use them and not merely to make a show of their beauty, leave one with a great desire to see them more and especially when they are covered with gloves again; for whoever covers them seems to have little care or concern whether they are seen or not, and to have beautiful hands more by nature than by any effort or design.

"Have you ever noticed when a woman, in passing along the street to church or elsewhere, unwittingly happens (in play or through whatever cause) to raise just enough of her dress to show her foot and often a little of her leg? Does this not strike you as something full of grace, if she is seen in that moment, charmingly feminine, dressed in velvet shoes and dainty stockings. Certainly to me it is a pleasing sight, as I believe it is to all of you, because everyone thinks that such elegance of dress, when it is where it would be hidden and rarely seen, must be natural and instinctive with the lady rather than calculated, and that she has no thought of gaining any praise thereby.

[41] "In such a way one avoids or hides affectation, and you may now see how opposed the latter is to grace, how it deprives of grace every act of the body and the soul: of which so far we have spoken but little, and yet this is not to be neglected; for, as the soul is far more worthy than the body, it deserves to be more cultivated and adorned. And as to what ought to be done in the case of our Courtier, we will lay aside the precepts of the many wise philosophers who have written on this subject to define the virtues of the soul and who discuss their worth with such subtlety; and, holding to our purpose, we will declare in a few words that it suffices if he is, as we say, a man of honor and integrity: for included in this are prudence, goodness, fortitude, and temperance of soul, and all the other qualities proper to such an honored name. And I maintain that he alone is a true moral philosopher who wishes to be good; and for this he has need of few precepts beyond that wish. Socrates was right, therefore, in saying that all his teachings seemed to him

6. Catullus, *Carmen* XXXIX, which begins "Because Egnatius has white teeth, he smiles wherever he goes."

to bear good fruit when anyone was incited by them to wish to know and understand virtue: for those persons who have reached the point of desiring nothing more ardently than to be good manage easily to learn all that is needed for that. Hence, we will discuss this no further.

[42] "But, besides goodness, for everyone the true and principal adornment of the mind is, I think, letters; although the French recognize only the nobility of arms and reckon all the rest as nought; and thus not only do they not esteem, but they abhor letters, and consider all men of letters to be very base; and they think that it is a great insult to call anyone a clerk."

Then the Magnifico Giuliano replied: "What you say is true; this error has prevailed among the French for a long time now. But if kind fate will have it that Monseigneur d'Angoulême succeed to the crown, as is hoped, then I think that just as the glory of arms flourishes and shines in France, so must that of letters flourish there also with the greatest splendor. Because, when I was at that court not so long ago, I saw this prince; and, besides the disposition of his body and the beauty of his countenance, he appeared to me to have in his aspect such greatness (yet joined with a certain gracious humanity) that the realm of France must always seem a petty realm to him. Then later, from many gentlemen, both French and Italian, I heard much about his noble manners, the greatness of his spirit, his valor and liberality; and I was told, among other things, how he loved and esteemed letters and how he held all men of letters in the greatest honor; and how he condemned the French themselves for being so hostile to this profession, especially as they have in their midst a university such as that of Paris, frequented by the whole world."

Then the Count said: "It is a great wonder that, at such a tender age, and solely by natural instinct and against the custom of his country, he should of himself have chosen so worthy a path; and, since subjects always imitate the ways of their superiors, it could be, as you say, that the French will yet come to esteem letters at their true worth: which they can easily be persuaded to do if they will but listen to reason, since nothing is more naturally desired by men or more proper to them than knowledge, and it is great folly to say or believe that knowledge is not always a good thing.

[43] "And if I could speak with them or with others who hold an opinion contrary to mine, I would try to show them how useful and necessary to our life and dignity letters are, being truly bestowed upon men by God as a crowning gift; nor should I lack instances of many excellent commanders in antiquity, who all added the orna-

ment of letters to valor in arms. For, as you know, Alexander vener-
ated Homer so much that he always kept the *Iliad* by his bed.[7] And
he gave the greatest attention not only to these studies but to philosophical speculations as well, under Aristotle's guidance. Alcibiades
increased his own good qualities and made them greater through
letters and the teachings of Socrates.[8] Also the effort that Caesar
devoted to study is witnessed by the surviving works he so divinely
wrote. Scipio Africanus, it is said, always kept in his hand the works
of Xenophon,[9] wherein, under the name of Cyrus, a perfect king is
imagined. I could tell you of Lucullus, Sulla, Pompey, Brutus, and
many other Romans and Greeks; but I will only remind you that
Hannibal, so excellent a military commander, and yet fierce by
nature and a stranger to all humanity, faithless and a despiser of
men and the gods—had nonetheless some knowledge of letters and
was conversant with Greek.[1] And, if I am not mistaken, I think I
once read that he even left a book written by him in Greek.

"But there is no need to tell you this, for I am sure you all know how
mistaken the French are in thinking that letters are detrimental to
arms. You know that the true stimulus to great and daring deeds in
war is glory, and whosoever is moved thereto for gain or any other
motive, apart from the fact that he never does anything good,
deserves to be called not a gentleman, but a base merchant. And it is
true glory that is entrusted to the sacred treasury of letters, as all may
understand except those unhappy ones who have never tasted them.

"What soul is so abject, timid, and humble that when he reads of
the great deeds of Caesar, Alexander, Scipio, Hannibal, and many
others, does not burn with a most ardent desire to resemble them,
and does not reckon this transitory life of a few days' span as less
important, in order to win to an almost eternal life of fame which,
in spite of death, makes him live on in far greater glory than before.
But he who does not taste the sweetness of letters cannot know how
great the glory is that letters so long preserve, and measures it only
by the life of one or two men, because his own memory extends no
further. Hence, he cannot value so brief a glory as he would one that
is almost eternal (if, to his misfortune, he were not denied knowledge of it); and since he does not much esteem it, we may with reason think that he will not risk such danger to win it as one would
who knows of it.

"But I should not want some objector to cite me instances to the
contrary in order to refute my opinion, alleging that for all their
knowledge of letters the Italians have shown little worth in arms for

7. So Plutarch in his *Life of Alexander*.
8. Plutarch, *Life of Alcibiades*.
9. Cicero, *Tusculanae disputationes* II, 26.
1. Cornelius Nepos, *Life of Hannibal*, ch. 13.

some time now—which, alas, is only too true. But it must be said that the fault of a few men has brought not only serious harm but eternal blame upon all the rest, and that they have been the true cause of our ruin and of the prostrate (if not dead) virtue of our spirits. Yet it would be a greater shame if we made this fact public than it is to the French to be ignorant of letters. Hence, it is better to pass over in silence what cannot be remembered without pain: and, leaving this subject, upon which I entered against my will, to return to our Courtier.

[44] "I would have him more than passably learned in letters, at least in those studies which we call the humanities. Let him be conversant not only with the Latin language, but with Greek as well, because of the abundance and variety of things that are so divinely written therein. Let him be versed in the poets, as well as in the orators and historians, and let him be practiced also in writing verse and prose, especially in our own vernacular; for, besides the personal satisfaction he will take in this, in this way he will never want for pleasant entertainment with the ladies, who are usually fond of such things. And if, because of other occupations or lack of study, he does not attain to such a perfection that his writings should merit great praise, let him take care to keep them under cover so that others will not laugh at him, and let him show them only to a friend who can be trusted; because at least they will be of profit to him in that, through such exercise, he will be capable of judging the writing of others. For it very rarely happens that a man who is unpracticed in writing, however learned he may be, can ever wholly understand the toils and industry of writers, or taste the sweetness and excellence of styles, and those intrinsic niceties that are often found in the ancients.

These studies, moreover, will make him fluent, and (as Aristippus said to the tyrant)[2] bold and self-confident in speaking with everyone. However, I would have our Courtier keep one precept firmly in mind, namely, in this as in everything else, to be cautious and reserved rather than forward, and take care not to get the mistaken notion that he knows something he does not know. For we are all by nature more avid of praise than we ought to be and, more than any other sweet song or sound, our ears love the melody of words that praise us; and thus, like Sirens' voices, they are the cause of shipwreck to him who does not stop his ears to such beguiling harmony. This danger was recognized by the ancients, and books were written to show how the true friend is to be distinguished from the flatterer.[3] But to what avail is this, if many, indeed countless persons

---

2. Told by Diogenes Laërtius in his *Lives of the Philosophers.*
3. The reference is to one of Plutarch's *Moralia* entitled "How to Tell Friend from Flatterer."

know full well when they are being flattered, yet love the one who flatters them and hate the one who tells them the truth? And finding him who praises them to be too sparing in his words, they even help him and proceed to say such things of themselves that they make the impudent flatterer himself feel ashamed.

"Let us leave these blind ones to their error, and let us have our Courtier be of such good judgment that he will not let himself be persuaded that black is white, or presume of himself more than he clearly knows to be true; and especially in those points which (if your memory serves you) messer Cesare said we had often used as the means of bringing to light the folly of many persons. Indeed, even if he knows that the praises bestowed upon him are true, let him avoid error by not assenting too openly to them, nor concede them without some protest; but let him rather disclaim them modestly, always showing and really esteeming arms as his chief profession, and the other good accomplishments as ornaments thereto; and do this especially when among soldiers, in order not to act like those who in studies wish to appear as soldiers, and, when in the company of warriors, wish to appear as men of letters. In this way, for the reasons we have stated, he will avoid affectation and even the ordinary things he does will appear to be very great things."

[45] Messer Pietro Bembo replied: "Count, I do not see why you insist that this Courtier, who is lettered and who has so many other worthy qualities, should regard everything as an ornament of arms, and not regard arms and the rest as an ornament of letters; which, without any other accompaniment, are as superior to arms in worth as the soul is to the body, because the practice of them pertains properly to the soul, even as that of arms does to the body."

Then the Count replied: "Nay, the practice of arms pertains to both the soul and the body. But I would not have you be a judge in such a case, messer Pietro, because you would be too much suspected of bias by one of the parties. And as this is a debate that has long been waged by very wise men, there is no need to renew it; but I consider it decided in favor of arms; and since I may form our Courtier as I please, I would have him be of the same opinion. And if you are contrary-minded, wait until you can hear of a contest wherein the one who defends the cause of arms is permitted to use arms, just as those who defend letters make use of letters in defending their own cause; for if everyone avails himself of his own weapons, you will see that the men of letters will lose."

"Ah," said messer Pietro, "a while ago you damned the French for their slight appreciation of letters, and you spoke of what a light of glory letters shed on a man, how they make him immortal; and now it appears that you have changed your mind. Do you not remember that

Giunto Alessandro alla famosa tomba
del fero Achille, sospirando disse:
"O fortunato, che sì chiara tromba
trovasti, e chi di te sì alto scrisse!"[4]

When Alexander had come to the famous tomb of Achilles, sighing, he said: "O fortunate man, to find so clear a trumpet and someone to write of you so loftily!"

And if Alexander envied Achilles, not for his exploits, but for the fortune which had granted him the blessing of having his deeds celebrated by Homer, we see that the esteemed Homer's letters above Achilles' arms. What other judge would you have, or what other sentence on the worthiness of arms and of letters than what has been pronounced by one of the greatest commanders that have ever been?"

[46] Then the Count replied: "I blame the French for thinking that letters are detrimental to the profession of arms, and I hold that to no one is learning more suited than to a warrior; and I would have these two accomplishments conjoined in our Courtier, each an aid to the other, as is most fitting: nor do I think I have changed my opinion in this. But, as I said, I do not wish to argue as to which of the two is more deserving of praise. Let it suffice to say that men of letters almost never choose to praise any save great men and glorious deeds, which in themselves deserve praise because of the essential worthiness from which they derive; besides this, such men and deeds are very noble material for writers, and are in themselves a great ornament and partly the reason why such writing is perpetuated, which perhaps would not be so much read or prized if it lacked a noble subject, but would be empty and of little moment.

"And if Alexander envied Achilles for being praised by Homer, this does not prove that he esteemed letters more than arms; wherein if he had thought himself to be as far beneath Achilles as he deemed all those who were to write of him to be beneath Homer, I am certain that he would have much preferred fine deeds on his own part to fine talk on the part of others. Hence, I believe that what he said was tacit praise of himself, expressing a desire for what he thought he lacked, namely, the supreme excellence of some writer, and not for what he believed he had already attained, namely, prowess in arms, wherein he did not at all take Achilles to be his superior. Wherefore he called him fortunate, as though to suggest that if his own fame had hitherto not been so celebrated in the world as Achilles' had (which was made bright and illustrious by a poem so divine), this was not because his valor and merits were fewer or less

4. The first quatrain of a sonnet by Petrarch (*Canzoniere* 187), based on Cicero, *Pro Archia poeta* X, 24.

deserving of praise, but because Fortune had granted Achilles such a miracle of nature to be the glorious trumpet for his deeds. Perhaps he wished also to incite some noble talent to write about him, thereby showing that his pleasure in this would be as great as his love and veneration for the sacred monuments of letters: about which by now we have said quite enough."

"Nay, too much," replied signor Ludovico Pio, "for I believe it is not possible in all the world to find a vessel large enough to contain all the things you would have be in our Courtier."

Then the Count said: "Wait a little, for there are yet many more to come."

"In that case," replied Pietro da Napoli, "Grasso de' Medici will have much the advantage over Pietro Bembo!"

[47] Here everyone laughed, and the Count began again: "Gentlemen, you must know that I am not satisfied with our Courtier unless he be also a musician, and unless, besides understanding and being able to read music, he can play various instruments. For, if we rightly consider, no rest from toil and no medicine for ailing spirits can be found more decorous or praiseworthy in time of leisure than this; and especially in courts where, besides the release from vexations which music gives to all, many things are done to please the ladies, whose tender and delicate spirits are readily penetrated with harmony and filled with sweetness. Hence, it is no wonder that in both ancient and modern times they have always been particularly fond of musicians, finding music a most welcome food for the spirit."

Then signor Gasparo said: "I think that music, along with many other vanities, is indeed well suited to women, and perhaps also to others who have the appearance of men, but not to real men; for the latter ought not to render their minds effeminate and afraid of death."

"Say not so," replied the Count, "or I shall launch upon a great sea of praise for music, reminding you how greatly music was always celebrated by the ancients and held to be a sacred thing; and how it was the opinion of very wise philosophers that the world is made up of music, that the heavens in their motion make harmony, and that even the human soul was formed on the same principle, and is therefore awakened and has its virtues brought to life, as it were, through music. Wherefore it is recorded that Alexander was sometimes so passionately excited by music that, almost in spite of himself, he was obliged to quit the banquet table and rush off to arms; whereupon the musician would change the kind of music, and he would then grow calm and return from arms to the banquet.[5] And,

5. As related by Plutarch, *Moralia* II, 2.

I tell you, grave Socrates learned to play the cithara when he was very old.[6] I remember also having heard once that both Plato and Aristotle wish a man who is well constituted to be a musician; and with innumerable reasons they show that music's power over us is very great; and (for many reasons which would be too long to tell now) that music must of necessity be learned from childhood, not so much for the sake of that outward melody which is heard, but because of the power it has to induce a good new habit of mind and an inclination to virtue, rendering the soul more capable of happiness, just as corporal exercise makes the body more robust; and that not only is music not harmful to the pursuits of peace and of war, but greatly to their advantage.

"Moreover, Lycurgus approved of music in his harsh laws. And we read that the bellicose Lacedemonians and the Cretans used citharas and other delicate instruments in battle;[7] that many very excellent commanders of antiquity, like Epaminondas, practiced music, and that those who were ignorant of it, like Themistocles, were far less esteemed. Have you not read that music was among the first disciplines that the worthy old Chiron taught the boy Achilles,[8] whom he reared from the age of nurse and cradle; and that such a wise preceptor wished the hands that were to shed so much Trojan blood to busy themselves often at playing the cithara? Where, then, is the soldier who would be ashamed to imitate Achilles, not to speak of many another famous commander that I could cite? Therefore, do not wish to deprive our Courtier of music, which not only makes gentle the soul of man, but often tames wild beasts; and he who does not take pleasure in it can be sure that his spirit lacks harmony among its parts.

"Consider that its power is such that it once caused a fish to let itself be ridden by a man over the stormy sea.[9] You find it used in sacred temples to give praise and thanks to God, and we must believe that it is pleasing to Him, and that He has given it to us as a sweet respite from our toils and vexations. Wherefrom rude laborers in the fields under the burning sun will often beguile their heavy time with crude and rustic song. With it the simple peasant lass, rising before dawn to spin or weave, wards off sleep and makes pleasant her toil. This is the happy pastime of poor sailors after the rains and the winds and the storms. This is the consolation of tired pilgrims in their long and weary journeys, and oftentimes of miserable prisoners in their chains and fetters.

6. Valerius Maximus, *Fact. et dict. mem.* VIII, 7.
7. Plutarch, *On Music*, ch. XXVI.
8. *Iliad* X, 390; XVI, 199; Plutarch, *On Music*, ch. XL.
9. According to legend, Arion, a Greek poet of Lesbos, was saved by a dolphin which he had lured to him by the music of his lyre. Herodotus, *History* I, chs. 23–24.

"Thus, as stronger evidence that even rude melody provides the greatest relief from every human toil and care, nature seems to have taught it to the nurse as the chief remedy for the continual crying of tender babes who by the sound of her voice are lulled to restful and placid sleep, forgetting the tears which are so much their lot and at that age are given us by nature as a presage of our later life."

[48] As the Count now remained silent for a little, the Magnifico Giuliano said: "I am not at all of signor Gasparo's opinion. Indeed I think, for the reasons given by you and for many others, that music is not only an ornament but a necessity to the Courtier. Yet I would have you state how this and the other accomplishments which you assign to him are to be practiced, and at what times and in what manner. For many things which are praiseworthy in themselves often become most unseemly when practiced at the wrong times; and, on the contrary, others which appear to be quite trivial are much prized when done in a proper way."

[49] Then the Count said: "Before we enter upon that subject, I would discuss another matter which I consider to be of great importance and which I think must therefore in no way be neglected by our Courtier: and this is a knowledge of how to draw and an acquaintance with the art of painting itself.

"And do not marvel if I require this accomplishment, which perhaps nowadays may seem mechanical and ill-suited to a gentleman; for I recall reading that the ancients, especially throughout Greece, required boys of gentle birth to learn painting in school, as a decorous and necessary thing, and admitted it to first rank among the liberal arts; then by public edict they prohibited the teaching of it to slaves. Among the Romans, too, it was held in highest honor and from it the very noble house of the Fabii took its name; for the first Fabius was called *Pictor*; and was in fact a most excellent painter, and so devoted to painting that, when he painted the walls of the Temple of Salus, he inscribed his name thereon; for, even though he was born of a family illustrious and honored by so many consular titles, triumphs, and other dignities, and even though he was a man of letters and learned in law, and was numbered among the orators, still it seemed to him that he could add splendor and ornament to his fame by leaving a memorial that he had been a painter. Nor was there any lack of others too who were born of illustrious families and were celebrated in this art; which, besides being most noble and worthy in itself, proves useful in many ways, and especially in warfare, in drawing towns, sites, rivers, bridges, citadels, fortresses, and the like; for, however well they may be stored away in the memory (which is something that is very hard to do), we cannot show them to others so.

"And truly he who does not esteem this art strikes me as being quite lacking in reason; for this universal fabric which we behold, with its vast heaven so resplendent with bright stars, with the earth at the center girdled by the seas, varied with mountains, valleys, rivers, adorned with such a variety of trees, pretty flowers, and grasses—can be said to be a great and noble picture painted by nature's hand and God's; and whoever can imitate it deserves great praise, in my opinion: nor is such imitation achieved without the knowledge of may things, as anyone knows who attempts it. For this reason the ancients held art and artists in the greatest esteem, wherefore art attained to the pinnacle of the highest excellence, very sure proof of which is to be found in the antique statues of marble and bronze that can still be seen. And, although painting differs from sculpture, both spring from the same source, namely, good design. Therefore, since those statues are divine, we can believe that the paintings were divine too; and the more so in being susceptible of greater artistry."

[50] Then signora Emilia turned to Giancristoforo Romano who was sitting there with the others, and said: "What do you think of this opinion? Do you agree that painting is susceptible of greater artistry than sculpture?"

Giancristoforo replied: "I think, Madam, that sculpture requires more labor and more skill and is of greater dignity than painting."

The Count rejoined: "Because statues are more durable, one might perhaps say they have a greater dignity; for, since they are made as memorials, they serve better than painting the purpose for which they are made. But, apart from this service to memory, both painting and sculpture are made to adorn, and in this painting is much superior; for if it is not so diuturnal, so to say, as sculpture, still it lasts a long time: and the while it lasts, it is much more beautiful."

Then Giancristoforo replied: "I truly believe that you are speaking contrary to your own persuasion, and that you do this entirely for your Raphael's sake; and you may also be thinking that the excellence in painting which you find in him is so supreme that sculpture in marble cannot attain to such a mark. But, take care, this is to praise an artist and not an art."

Then he went on: "I do indeed think that both the one and the other are artful imitations of nature; but I do not know how you can say that that which is real and is nature's own work is any less imitated by a marble or bronze figure, in which all the members are round, fashioned and proportioned just as nature makes them, than on a panel where one sees only a surface and colors that deceive the eyes; nor will you tell me, surely, that being is not nearer truth than seeming. Besides, I consider sculpture to be more difficult because, if you happen to make a mistake, you cannot correct it, since marble cannot be patched up again, but you have to execute another figure; which does not happen in painting wherein you can make a thousand changes, adding and taking away, improving it all the while."

[51] The Count said, laughing: "I am not speaking for Raphael's sake, nor must you think me so ignorant as not to know Michelangelo's excellence in sculpture, your own, and that of others. But I am speaking of the art and not of the artists.

"What you say is quite true, that both the one and the other are imitations of nature; but it is not a matter of painting seeming and of sculpture being. For, although statues are in the round as in life and painting is seen only on the surface, statues lack many things which paintings do not lack, and especially light and shade (for the color of flesh is one thing and that of marble another). And this the painter imitates in a natural manner, with light and dark, less or more, according to the need—which the sculptor in marble cannot do. And even though the painter does not fashion his figure in the round, he does make muscles and members rounded in such a manner as to join up with the parts which are not so seen, whereby we see clearly that the painter knows and understands those parts as well. And in this an even greater skill is needed to depict those members that are foreshortened and that diminish in proportion to the distance, on the principle of perspective; which, by means of proportioned lines, colors, light, and shade, gives you foreground and distance on the surface of an upright wall, and as bold or as faint as he chooses. And do you think it a trifle to imitate nature's colors in doing flesh, clothing, and all the other things that have color? This the sculptor cannot do; neither can he render the grace of black eyes or blue eyes, shining with amorous rays. He cannot render the color of blond hair or the gleam of weapons, or the dark of night, or a storm at sea, or lightnings and thunderbolts, or the burning of a city, or the birth of rosy dawn with its rays of gold and red. In short, he cannot do sky, sea, land, mountains, woods, meadows, gardens, rivers, cities, or houses—all of which the painter can do.

[52] "Therefore I deem painting more noble and more susceptible of artistry than sculpture, and I think that among the ancients it must have had that excellence which other things had; and this we can still see from certain slight remains, particularly in the grottoes of Rome; but we can know it much more clearly from the writings of the ancients in which there is such frequent and honored men-

tion both of the works and of the masters, from which we learn how much the latter were always honored by great lords and republics.

"So we read that Alexander loved Apelles of Ephesus dearly[1]—so much so that once, when he had him paint one of his favorite women and heard that the worthy painter had conceived a most passionate love for her because of her great beauty, he made him an outright gift of her: a generosity truly worthy of Alexander, to give away not only treasures and states, but his own affections and desires; and a sign of a very great love for Apelles to care nothing if, in pleasing the artist, he displeased that woman whom he so dearly loved—whereas we may believe that the woman was sorely grieved to exchange so great a king for a painter. Many other instances are cited of Alexander's kindness to Apelles; but he showed his esteem for him most clearly in giving order by public edict that no other painter should be so bold as to paint his portrait.[2]

"Here I could tell of the rivalry of many noble painters who were the praise and wonder of nearly the whole world; I could tell you with what majesty the ancient emperors adorned their triumphs with paintings, dedicated them in public places, bought them as cherished objects; how some painters have been known to make a gift of their works, deeming gold and silver insufficient to pay for them; and how a painting by Protogenes was so highly prized that when Demetrius was laying siege to Rhodes and could have entered the city and set fire to the quarter where he knew the painting was, he refrained from giving battle and so did not take the city;[3] how Metrodorus, a philosopher and very excellent painter, was sent by the Athenians to Lucius Paulus to teach his children and to decorate the triumph which he had to make ready.[4] And many noble authors have also written about this art, which is a great sign of the esteem it enjoyed: but I would not have us discuss it any further.

"So let it be enough simply to say that it is fitting for our Courtier to have knowledge of painting also, since it is decorous and useful and was prized in those times when men were of greater worth than now. And even if no other utility or pleasure were had from it, it helps in judging the excellence of statues both ancient and modern, vases, buildings, medallions, cameos, intaglios, and the like, and it also brings one to know the beauty of living bodies, not only in the delicacy of the face but in the proportions of the other parts, both in man and in all other creatures. And so you see how a knowledge of painting is the source of very great pleasure. And let those consider this who are so enraptured when they contemplate a woman's

1. Pliny, *Natural History* XXXV, ch. 86.
2. Pliny, *Natural History* VII, ch. 125.
3. Pliny, *Natural History* XXXV, ch. 104.
4. Pliny, *History* XXXV, ch. 135.

beauty that they believe themselves to be in paradise, and yet cannot paint; but if they could, they would gain much greater pleasure because they would more perfectly discern the beauty that engenders so much satisfaction in their hearts."

[53] Here messer Cesare Gonzaga laughed and said: "I, of course, am no painter; still I am sure I take much greater pleasure in looking at a certain woman than would that most worthy Apelles whom you mentioned a moment ago, were he to return to life now."

The Count replied: "This pleasure of yours does not derive entirely from her beauty but from the affection that you perchance feel for her; and if you were to tell the truth, the first time you beheld that woman, you did not feel a thousandth part of the pleasure that you later felt, even though her beauty was the same. Thus, you can see how much greater a part affection had in your pleasure than did beauty."

"That I do not deny," said messer Cesare; "but just as my pleasure arises from affection, so my affection arises from beauty; hence, we can still say that beauty is the cause of my pleasure."

The Count replied: "Many other causes besides beauty inflame our souls: such as manners, knowledge, speech, gestures, and a thousand other things (which might, however, in some way be called beauties too); but, above all, the feeling that one is loved. Thus, it is possible to love most ardently even in the absence of that beauty of which you speak; but the love which arises solely from the outward beauty we see in bodies will surely give far greater pleasure to him who discerns that beauty more than to him who discerns it less. Therefore, to return to our subject, I think Apelles must have taken more pleasure in contemplating the beauty of Campaspe than did Alexander, because we can readily believe that both men's love sprang solely from her beauty, and that for this reason, perhaps, Alexander decided to give her to Apelles who appeared to have the ability to discern it more perfectly.

"Have you not read that those five girls of Crotone, whom the painter Zeuxis chose from among the others of that city for the purpose of forming from all five a single figure of surpassing beauty,[5] were celebrated by many poets for having been judged beautiful by one who must have been a consummate judge of beauty?"

[54] Messer Cesare seemed not to be satisfied with this, and would not at all grant that anyone except himself could experience the

5. The Greek painter Zeuxis, commissioned to paint a figure of Helen for a temple to the goddess Hera in Croton, in southern Italy, used as models five beautiful girls of the city, selecting the most beautiful features of each. Pliny, *Natural History* XXXV, ch. 64; also Cicero, *De inventione* 2, 1, 1–3 [*Editor*].

pleasure he felt in contemplating a certain woman's beauty, and was starting to speak again. But in that moment a great tramping of feet was heard and the noise of loud talking; whereupon everyone turned to see a great light from torches appear at the door of the room; and immediately following there arrived, with a numerous and noble company, the Prefect, who was just coming back from accompanying the Pope part of his way. On entering the palace he had at once asked what the Duchess was doing and had learned what kind of game was being played that evening and the charge given to Count Ludovico to speak of Courtiership. Hence, he was hurrying as fast as he could in order to arrive in time to hear something. Thus, when he had at once made his reverence to the Duchess and had urged the others to be seated (all had stood when he came in), he too sat down in the circle along with some of his gentlemen, among whom were the Marquess Febus da Ceva and his brother Ghirardino, messer Ettore Romano, Vincenzo Calmeta, Orazio Florido, and many others; and, as everyone remained silent, the Prefect said: "Gentlemen, my coming here would indeed do great harm if I were thus to put an obstacle in the way of such fine discussions as I believe those are that were taking place among you just now. But do not do me the wrong of depriving yourselves and me of such pleasure."

Then Count Ludovico said: "Nay, Sir, I think we all must find it far more pleasant to keep silent than to talk; for since this labor has fallen more to me this evening than to the others, I am weary now of speaking, as I think all the others must be of listening; for my talk was not worthy of this company nor equal to the great matter I was charged with; in which, having little satisfied myself, I think I have satisfied the others even less. Hence, you, Sir, were fortunate to come in at the end. And it is well now to give the charge of what remains to someone else who can take my place, because whoever he may be, I know he will do much better than I should if I tried to go on, tired as I now am."

[55] "Certainly I," replied the Magnifico Giuliano, "shall in no way allow myself to be cheated of the promise you made me; and I am sure that the Prefect will not be displeased to hear this part of it."

"And what was the promise?" asked the Count.

"To tell us how the Courtier should put into effect those good qualities which you have said befit him," replied the Magnifico.

The Prefect, although a mere boy, was more wise and discreet than it seemed could be in such tender years, and in his every movement showed a greatness of spirit together with a certain vivacity of temper that gave true presage of the high mark of virtue to which he would attain. Wherefore he said quickly: "If all this is still to be told, it seems to me that I have arrived in very good time; for in hearing how the Courtier must put into effect those good qualities, I shall also hear what they are, and in this way I shall come to know all that has been said up to now. Therefore, do not refuse, Count, to pay the debt, a part of which you have already settled."

"I should not have such a heavy debt to pay," replied the Count, "if labors were more equally distributed; but the mistake was in giving the authority of command to a lady who is too partial." And thus, laughing, he turned to signora Emilia, who quickly said: "It is not you who should complain of my partiality; but since you do so without reason, we will give someone else a portion of this honor which you call a labor," and, turning to messer Federico Fregoso, she said: "It was you who proposed this game of the Courtier; therefore it is only right that it should fall to you to carry on with part of it; and that part shall be to satisfy the request of the Magnifico Giuliano, declaring in what way, manner, and time, the Courtier is to put into effect his good qualities and practice those things which the Count said befitted him."

Then messer Federico said: "Madam, you are trying to separate what cannot be separated, for these are the very things that make his qualities good and his practice good. Therefore, since the Count has spoken so long and so well, and has also said something of such matters as these and has prepared in his mind the remainder of what he has to say, it was only right that he should continue up to the end."

"Consider yourself to be the Count," signora Emilia replied, "and say what you think he would say; and in this way all satisfaction will be done."

[56] Then Calmeta said: "Gentlemen, since the hour is late and in order that messer Federico may have no excuse for not telling what he knows, I think it would be well to put off the rest of this discussion until tomorrow, and let the brief time that remains be spent in some other more modest entertainment."

When everyone agreed, the Duchess desired that madonna Margherita and madonna Costanza Fregosa should dance. Whereupon Barletta, a delightful musician and an excellent dancer, who always kept the court amused, began to play upon his instruments; and the two ladies, joining hands, danced first a *bassa*, and then a *roegarze*[6] with extreme grace, much to the delight of those who watched. Then, the night being already far spent, the Duchess rose to her feet, whereupon everyone reverently took leave and retired to sleep.

6. *Bassa danza:* a dance of Spanish origin, much in vogue at the time, often danced by two or three persons; *roegarze:* a dance of French origin (cf. Old French *rouergasse*), sometimes danced by four or eight persons.

The Second Book

To Messer Alfonso Ariosto

[1] I have often considered—and not without wonder—how a certain error arises which, as it is universally present in old people, can be thought to be proper and natural to them. And this is that they nearly all praise bygone times and denounce the present, railing against our doings and our ways and at everything that they, in their youth, did not do; affirming too that every good custom and good way of life, every virtue, all things, in short, are continually going from bad to worse.

And truly it seems quite contrary to reason and a cause for wonder that a ripe age, which in all other respects is wont to make men's judgment more perfect, should so corrupt it in this respect that they do not see that if the world were always growing worse, and if fathers were generally better than their children, we should long since have reached that lowest grade of badness beyond which it is impossible to go. And yet we see that, not only in our own time, but in the past as well, this fault was ever peculiar to old age, which is something we clearly gather from the writings of many ancient authors, and especially the writers of comedy who, more than the others, set forth the image of human life.

Now, for my part, I do believe that the cause of this mistaken opinion among old people is that the passing years take with them many of the good things of life and, among others, deprive the blood of a great part of the vital spirits; wherefore the constitution is changed, and these organs through which the soul exercises its powers become weak. Thus, in old age the sweet flowers of contentment fall from our hearts, as in autumn the leaves fall from their trees, and in place of bright and clear thoughts there comes a cloudy and turbid sadness attended by a thousand ills. So that not only the body but the mind also is enfeebled, and retains of past pleasures merely a lingering memory and the image of that precious time of tender youth in which (while we are enjoying it), wherever we look, heaven and earth and everything appear merry and smiling, and the sweet springtime of happiness seems to flower in our thoughts as in a delightful and lovely garden.

Therefore, when the sun of our life enters the cold season and begins to go down in the west, divesting us of such pleasures, it would perhaps be well if along with them we might lose their memory too; and, as Themistocles said, discover an art that could teach us to forget.[7] For the senses of our body are so deceitful that they often beguile the judgment of our minds as well. Hence, it seems to me that old people in their situation resemble people who, as they sail out of the port, keep their eyes fixed upon the shore and think that their ship is standing still and that the shore is receding, although it is the other way round. For the port, and similarly time and its pleasures, stay the same, while one after the other we in our ship of mortality go scudding across that stormy sea which takes all things to itself and devours them; nor are we ever permitted to touch shore again, but, tossed by conflicting winds, we are finally shipwrecked upon some reef.

Since the senile spirit is thus an unfit vessel for many pleasures, it cannot enjoy them; and even as to those who, when sick with a fever and with a palate spoiled by corrupt vapors, all wines seem bitter, though they be rare and delicate—so to old people in their indisposition (in which, however, there is still the desire) pleasures seem insipid and cold and very different from those which they remember enjoying once, although the pleasures in themselves are still the same. Hence, feeling themselves deprived of them, they complain and denounce present times as bad, not perceiving that the change is in themselves and not in the times; and, contrariwise, they call to mind the past pleasures along with the time in which they had those pleasures; and so they praise that time as good because it seems to carry with it a savor of what they felt when it was present. For our minds, in fact, hate all things that have accompanied our sorrows, and love those things that have accompanied our joys.

This is why sometimes to a lover it is a thing most dear to look upon a window, even if it is shuttered, because there it was that he once knew the bliss of gazing upon his lady love; and similarly, to see a ring, a letter, a garden or other place, or anything whatever that may seem to have been a conscious witness of his joys; and, on the contrary, a room that is most splendid and beautiful will often be distasteful to one who has been a prisoner there or has suffered there some other unhappiness. And I have known persons who would never again drink from a cup like the one from which they had taken medicine when sick. For just as, to the one, the window or ring or letter brings back the sweet memory that is so delightful and seems a part of bygone joy, so, to the other, the room or the cup seems to bring back to the memory the sickness or the imprison-

7. Cicero, *De oratore* II, ch. 74.

ment. For this same reason, I think, old people are brought to praise bygone times and to condemn the present.

[2] Of courts therefore they speak as of all else, declaring those they remember to have been far more excellent and full of outstanding men than those we see nowadays. And when such discussions get under way, they begin at once to extol with boundless praise the courtiers of Duke Filippo or Duke Borso; and they recount the sayings of Niccolò Piccinino, and remind us that in those days there were no murders (or rarely), that there were no fights, no ambushes, no deceits, but only a certain loyal and kindly good will among all men, and a loyal trust; and that in the courts of that time so many good customs prevailed along with such goodness, that the courtiers were all like monks; and woe unto him who spoke a bad word to another or so much as paid some less than honorable attention to a woman. And, on the contrary, they say that everything is the reverse these days, and that not only have courtiers lost that fraternal love and that sober manner of life, but that in the courts nothing prevails save envy, malevolence, corrupt manners, and a most dissolute life given over to every kind of vice—the women lascivious and shameless, the men effeminate. They condemn our dress also as indecent and too womanish.

In short, they censure a multitude of things, among which there are many actually deserving of censure, for it cannot be denied that there are many evil and wicked men among us, or that our times abound much more in vices than the times they praise. But I do believe they ill discern the cause of this difference, and that they are foolish. For they would have the world contain all good things, and nothing evil—which is impossible; because, since evil is the opposite of good, and good the opposite of evil, it is necessary that, by way of opposition and a certain counter-balance, the one sustain and reinforce the other, and that if the one diminishes or increases, so must the other, because there is no contrary without its contrary.

Who does not know that there would be no justice in the world if there were no wrongs? No magnanimity, if none were pusillanimous? No continence, if there were no incontinence? No health if there were no sickness? No truth, if there were no falsehood? No happiness, if there were no misfortunes? Thus, Socrates puts it very well when, as Plato has it,[8] he expresses his wonder that Aesop did not write a fable imagining that, as God had never been able to unify pleasure and pain, He had joined them end to end, so that the beginning of the one should be the end of the other;

8. Plato, *Phaedo*, ch. 3.

for we know that we can never enjoy any pleasure if something unpleasant does not precede it. Who can appreciate rest without first feeling the weight of fatigue? Who relishes food, drink, or sleep, unless he has first endured hunger, thirst, or want of sleep? Therefore I think that sufferings and sickness were given to man by nature, not chiefly to make him subject to them (since it does not seem right that she who is mother of every good should give us so many ills by her own deliberate design), but as nature created health, pleasure, and other goods, so sickness, vexation, and other ills followed as consequents. Thus, when virtues were bestowed upon the world through grace and as a gift of nature, at once the vices necessarily joined company with them by way of that conjoined opposition; so that whenever the one waxes or wanes, so must the other.

[3] Therefore, when our old men praise bygone courts for not having such vicious men in them as some that are in our courts, they overlook the fact that their courts did not contain some men as virtuous as ours—which is no marvel, since no evil is as evil as that which is born of the corrupted seed of good; hence, as nature produces much greater talents now than she did then, so those who aim at the good do far better now than did those of former times, and those who aim at the bad do far worse. Hence, we must not say that those who refrained from doing evil because they did not know how deserve any praise for this; for, though they did little harm, they did the worst they could. And that the talents of those times were, on the whole, far inferior to those of our own time is evident enough in all that we see of theirs, in letters as well as in paintings, statues, buildings, and everything else.

These old men also condemn many things that we do (which things are in themselves neither good nor bad) simply because they did not do them. And they say it is unseemly for young men to ride about the city on horseback, especially in slippers, or to wear fur linings or long garments in winter, or wear a cap before the age of eighteen, at least, and the like: in which they are quite wrong, because these customs, besides being convenient and useful, are established by usage and appeal to all, as once to go about in gala dress with uncovered breeches and dainty slippers and, in order to be dashing, to carry always a sparrow hawk on the wrist (to no purpose), to dance without touching the lady's hand, and to follow many other customs that were as much prized then as they would be outlandish now.

Therefore, let it be permitted us to follow the customs of our time without being slandered by these old men who, in their desire to praise themselves will often say: "I was still sleeping with my mother and sisters when I was twenty, and for a long time after that I didn't know what women were; and now boys are hardly dry behind the ears when they know more mischief than grown men did in those days." Nor do they see that in saying this they are confirming the fact that boys today are more talented than old men were then.

Therefore, let them leave off censuring our times as being full of vices, because to take away these would mean to take away the virtues. And let them remember that among the worthy ancients, in the age when those more than human talents and those spirits lived who were glorious and truly divine in every virtue, many vicious men were also to be found, who, if they were alive today, would surpass our wicked men in evil deeds, even as the good men of that age would in good deeds. And to this all history bears ample witness.

[4] But this I think must suffice as a rejoinder to these old men. Hence, we will end this argument, already too lengthy, no doubt, but surely not beside the purpose; and, since it is enough to have shown that the courts of our time are no less deserving of praise than those which are so much praised by old men, we will attend to the discussion that took place concerning the Courtier, from which we readily understand the rank held by the Court of Urbino among other courts, and what manner of Prince and Lady they were who were served by such noble spirits, and how fortunate all could count themselves to live in such a society.

[5] Now the following day there were many and varied discussions among the gentlemen and the ladies of the court regarding the debate of the evening before, this due in large measure to the fact that the Prefect, eager to know what had been said, kept questioning everybody about it; and, as often happens, he got a variety of answers, because some praised this and some that, and many disagreed also as to what the Count's opinion had really been, since everyone's memory had not fully retained what had been said.

The matter was thus discussed nearly all day; and when night began to fall, the Prefect decided they should eat, and took all the gentlemen to supper with him. And when supper was over, he repaired to the rooms of the Duchess; who, on seeing such a numerous company assembled earlier than was customary, said: "Messer Federico, it seems to me that a great burden has been put upon your shoulders, and great is the expectation you must satisfy."

Whereupon, without waiting for messer Federico to answer, the Unico Aretino said: "But what is this great burden? Who, when he knows how to do something, is so foolish as not to do it in his own good time?"

And so, discoursing of this, all took their seats in their usual place and order, eagerly awaiting the proposed discussion.

[6] Then messer Federico turned to the Unico Aretino and said: "So, signor Unico, you do not think that a laborious part and great burden have been put upon me for this evening, obliged as I am to set forth in what way, manner, and time the Courtier ought to exercise his good qualities, and practice those things that have been declared to befit him?"

"To me it seems no great thing," replied the Unico, "and it would be quite enough in this to say that the Courtier must have good judgment, as the Count quite rightly said; in which case I think he will surely be able to practice what he knows, at the right time and in the proper way. And any attempt to reduce this matter to more precise rules would be too difficult, and perhaps superfluous. For I do not know who would be so stupid as to engage in arms when others are engaging in music; or to go about the streets dancing a morris dance, however clever he might be at it; or to go and comfort a mother whose son had died and begin with pleasantries and with trying to play the wit. I think surely no gentleman who is not a complete fool would do such things."

Then messer Federico said: "It seems to me, signor Unico, that you indulge too much in extremes. For it can sometimes happen that one is silly in ways not readily apparent, nor are our errors always of the same sort. And a man may happen to refrain from some public and all too obvious folly, such as dancing a morris dance around the square, and yet not have sense enough to refrain from praising himself on the wrong occasion, or from indulging in tiresome presumption, or from saying something which he thinks will provoke laughter but which, because said at the wrong time, falls cold and completely flat. And often these errors are covered with a kind of veil that prevents the one who commits them from seeing them unless he keeps in this a diligent watch; and, although there are many reasons why our eyes are wanting in discernment, it is by ambition that they are especially blurred, because everyone is ready to put himself forward in that wherein he thinks himself to be knowledgeable, no matter whether it be true or not.

"Therefore, it seems to me that the right rule of conduct in this regard consists in a certain prudence and wise choice, and in discerning what the relative gain or loss is in things if done opportunely or done out of season. And although the Courtier may be of such good judgment as to perceive these differences, it will surely be easier for him to do what he is striving to do if his mind's eye is made attentive by some precept and if he is shown the ways and, as it were, the foundations on which he must build—than if he were to follow mere generalities.

[7] "The Count spoke last evening so fully and beautifully about Courtiership as to arouse in me no little fear and doubt whether I should be able to satisfy this noble company so well in what it falls to me to say, as he did when it was his turn. Still, in order to share as much as I can in the praise he has won, and be certain not to err at least in this part, I shall not gainsay him in anything.

"So, agreeing with his opinions and, among other points, with those about the Courtier's noble birth, his talent, bodily disposition, and comely aspect—I say that to win praise deservedly, and a good opinion on the part of all, and favor from the princes whom he serves, I deem it necessary for him to know how to order his whole life and how to make the most of his own good qualities generally in associating with all men, without exciting envy thereby. And how difficult this is in itself can be inferred from the rarity of those who are seen to reach such a goal; for, truly, we are all naturally more ready to censure errors than to praise things well done; and many men, from a kind of innate malice, and even when they clearly see the good, strive with all effort and care to discover some fault or at least something that seems a fault.

"Thus, our Courtier must be cautious in his every action and see to it that prudence attends whatever he says or does. And let him take care not only that his separate parts and qualities be excellent, but that the tenor of his life be such that the whole may correspond to these parts, and may be seen to be, always and in everything, such as never to be discordant in itself, but form a single whole of all these good qualities; so that his every act may stem from and be composed of all the virtues (which the Stoics hold to be the duty of the wise man) and, even though in every act one virtue is chief, still all the virtues are so conjoined as to move toward the same end, informing every effect and furthering it. Hence, he must know how to avail himself of them and, by the test and, as it were, the opposition of the one, cause another to be more manifestly known; as good painters who, by their use of shadow, manage to throw the light of objects into relief, and, likewise, by their use of light, to deepen the shadows of planes and bring different colors together so that all are made more apparent through the contrast of one with another; and the placing of figures in opposition one to another helps them achieve their aim. Thus, gentleness is most striking in a man who is valiant and impetuous; and as his boldness seems greater when accompanied with modesty, so his modesty is enhanced and made more evident by his boldness. Hence, to talk little and to do much, and not to praise oneself for deeds that are praiseworthy, but tact-fully to dissimulate them, serves to enhance both the one virtue and the other in anyone who knows how to employ this method dis-creetly; and so it is with all other good qualities.

"Therefore, in all that he does or says, I would have our Courtier follow certain general rules which, in my opinion, briefly comprise all I have to say. And the first and most important of these is that he should avoid affectation above all else, as the Count rightly advised last evening. Next, let him consider well what he does or says, the place where he does it, in whose presence, its timeliness, the reason for doing it, his own age, his profession, the end at which he aims, and the means by which he can reach it; thus, keeping these points in mind, let him act accordingly in whatever he may choose to do or say."

[8] With this messer Federico appeared to pause for a moment. Whereupon signor Morello da Ortona said at once: "These rules of yours teach us little, it seems to me; and, for my part, I know about as much now as I did before you declared them to us—although I do remember having heard them sometimes from friars when I was at confession, and they call them 'the circumstances,' it seems to me."

Then messer Federico laughed and said: "If you well remember, the Count wished the chief business of the Courtier to be arms, and spoke at length of the way in which he should apply himself to that; therefore, we will not repeat this. Yet you may also take it to be implied in our rule that whenever the Courtier chances to be engaged in a skirmish or an action or a battle in the field, or the like, he should discreetly withdraw from the crowd, and do the out-standing and daring things that he has to do in as small a company as possible and in the sight of all the noblest and most respected men in the army, and especially in the presence of and, if possible, before the very eyes of his king or the prince he is serving; for it is well indeed to make all one can of things well done. And I think that even as it is wrong to seek false glory or what is not deserved, so is it wrong also to rob oneself of a deserved honor and not to seek that praise which alone is the true reward of virtuous labors.

"And I recall that in the past I have known men who, though very able, were stupid on this score, and would risk their lives as much to capture a flock of sheep as to be the first to scale the walls of a besieged town—which is something our Courtier will not do, if he will but keep in mind the motive that leads him to war, which is nothing except honor. Whereas, if he happens to engage in arms in some public show—such as jousts, tourneys, stick-throwing, or in any other bodily exercise—mindful of the place where he is and in whose presence, he will strive to be as elegant and handsome in the exercise of arms as he is adroit, and to feed his spectators' eyes with all those things that he thinks may give him added grace; and he will take care to have a horse gaily caparisoned, to wear a becoming attire, to have appropriate mottoes and ingenious devices that will attract the eyes of the spectators even as the loadstone attracts iron. He will never be among the last to show himself, knowing that the crowd, and especially women, give more attention to the first than to the last; for in the beginning our eyes and our minds are eager for this kind of novelty and take notice of the least thing and are impressed thereby, whereas in the continuation they are not only sated but wearied. Thus, there was an excellent actor in ancient times who for this reason wished always to be the first to appear on the stage to speak his part.

"So also, in the matter of arms, our Courtier will have regard for the profession of those with whom he speaks and conduct himself accordingly—speaking with men in one way, and with women in another; and if he wishes to touch on something in praise of himself, he will do it with dissimulation, as if by chance and in passing, and with the discretion and caution that Count Ludovico declared to us yesterday.

[9] "Now do you not think, signor Morello, that our rules are able to teach something? Do you not believe that that friend of ours, of whom I spoke to you the other day, had completely forgotten with whom he was talking and why, when, to entertain a lady he had never seen before, he began right off to tell her that he had slain so many men, how fierce he was, and that he could wield a sword with either hand; and did not leave her until he had come to the point of attempting to teach her how certain blows of the battle-ax should be parried, both when one is armed and when one is unarmed, and to show her certain grips of the sword handle: so that the poor soul was on pins and needles and could hardly wait to be rid of him, as if she feared he might slay her as he had those others. Such are the errors committed by those who have no regard for the 'circumstances,' which you say you heard of from the friars.

"And so, I say that, as for bodily exercises, there are some that are almost never practiced except in public, such as jousts, tourneys, stick-throwing, and all those others that involve arms. Hence, whenever our Courtier has to engage in such, he must first see to it that he is well equipped as to horses, weapons, and dress, and lacks nothing; and if he should feel that all is not in order in every respect, he must in no wise enter in; because, if he should fail to do well, he cannot use the excuse that that is not his profession. Then also he must carefully consider who will see him and who his companions are, because it would not be seemly for a gentleman to honor a country festival with his presence where the spectators and the company were persons of low birth."

[10] Then signor Gaspar Pallavicino said: "In our Lombard country we do not stand so on ceremony. On the contrary, there are many young gentlemen who, on festive occasions, dance all day in the sun with peasants, and play with them at throwing the bar, wrestling, running, and jumping. And I do not think this amiss, because then the contest is not one of nobility, but one of strength and agility, at which villagers are quite as good as nobles; and such familiarity would seem to have about it a certain charming liberality."

"For my part," replied messer Federico, "this dancing of yours in the sun pleases me not at all, nor do I see what can be gained by it. But if anyone is determined to wrestle, run, or jump with peasants, he ought, in my opinion, to do so in the manner of trying his hand at it and out of courtesy, as we say, not as though competing with them. And one must be well-nigh sure of winning, else he ought not to enter in, because it is too unseemly and too ugly a thing, and quite without dignity, to see a gentleman defeated by a peasant, and especially at wrestling. Hence, I believe it would be well to abstain, at least when there are many present, because the gain in winning is very slight and the loss in case of defeat is very great.

"The game of tennis also is almost always played in public, and is one of those spectacles to which the presence of a crowd lends great attraction. Therefore I would have our Courtier engage in it (and in all other exercises except arms) as in something which is not his profession, and in which he will make it evident that he does not seek or expect any praise; not let it appear that he devotes much effort or time to it, even though he may do it ever so well. Neither must he do as some men who delight in music, and who, in speaking with anyone, always start to sing *sotto voce* the moment there is a pause in the conversation; or others who, as they go about through the streets or in church, are forever dancing; or others who, whenever they encounter a friend in the square or wherever, begin suddenly to act as if they were fencing or wrestling, whichever exercise they like best."

Here messer Cesare Gonzaga said: "One of our young cardinals in Rome does even better: for, out of a great pride in his own physical strength, he leads into his garden all persons who come to visit him, even if he never saw them before, and invites them with the greatest insistence to take off their coats and try if they can outjump him."

[11] Messer Federico laughed and went on: "There are certain other exercises that can be practiced in public and in private, such as

dancing. And in this I think the Courtier should take great care; because, when dancing in the presence of many and in a place full of people, I think he should maintain a certain dignity, though tempered with a fine and airy grace of movement; and even though he may feel himself to be most agile and a master of time and measure, let him not attempt those quick movements of foot and those double steps which we find most becoming in our Barletta, but which would perhaps little befit a gentleman. Yet privately, in a chamber, as we are now, I think he could be allowed to try this, and try morris dances and *branles*[9] as well; but not in public, unless he is masquerading, for then it is not unseemly even if he should be recognized by all. Indeed, there is no better way of showing oneself in such things, at public spectacles, either armed or unarmed; because masquerading carries with it a certain freedom and license, which among other things enables one to choose the role in which he feels most able, and to bring diligence and a care for elegance into that principal aim, and to show a certain nonchalance in what does not matter: all of which adds much charm; as for a youth to dress like an old man, yet in a loose attire so as to be able to show his vigor; or for a cavalier to dress as a rustic shepherd, or in some other such costume, but astride a perfect horse and gracefully attired in character: because the bystanders immediately take in what meets the eye at first glance; whereupon, realizing that here there is much more than was promised by the costume, they are delighted and amused.

"However, in such games and shows where there is masquerading, it would not be proper for a prince to elect to play the part of the prince himself, for the pleasure which comes to the spectators from the novelty of the thing would be wanting for the most part, since it is nothing new to anyone that the prince is the prince; and when he is seen to wish to play the prince as well as be the prince, he loses the license of doing all those things that are beneath a prince's dignity. And if there should happen to be any competition in those games, especially in arms, he might even make people think he wished to maintain the identity of the prince so as not to be beaten by others but spared. Moreover, if he were to perform in play what he must really do when the need arises, he would deprive what is real of its due authority and it might appear that the reality were mere play. But if on such occasions the prince puts off his identity as prince, and mingles with his inferiors as an equal (yet so that he can be recognized), then, in rejecting his own, he attains to a higher greatness, which is to seek to surpass others not by authority but by

---

9. *Branles:* a dance of Spanish origin resembling the cotillion, sometimes performed by masked figures and very popular in Castiglione's day.

ability, and to show that his own worth is not the greater merely because he is a prince.

[12] "Therefore I say that in these martial spectacles the Courtier must observe the same discretion according to his rank. Moreover, in horseback vaulting, in wrestling, in running and jumping, I should be very glad to have him shun the vulgar herd or at most put in a rare appearance with them, because there is nothing in the world so excellent that the ignorant will not grow tired of it and esteem it little, from seeing it often.

"About music I am of the same opinion: hence, I would not have our Courtier behave as many do who have no sooner come into any place (and even into the presence of gentlemen of whom they know nothing) when, without waiting for much urging, they set about doing what they know how to do, and often enough what they do not know how to do; so that it seems they have put in an appearance for that alone, and that that is their principal profession. Therefore, let the Courtier turn to music as to a pastime, and as though forced, and not in the presence of persons of low birth or where there is a crowd. And although he may know and understand what he does, in this also I would have him dissimulate the care and effort that is required in doing anything well; and let him appear to esteem but little this accomplishment of his, yet by performing it excellently well, make others esteem it highly."

[13] Then signor Gaspar Pallavicino said: "There are many kinds of music, vocal as well as instrumental: therefore I should be pleased to hear which is the best kind of all and on what occasion the Courtier ought to perform it."

Messer Federico answered: "In my opinion, the most beautiful music is in singing well and in reading at sight and in fine style, but even more in singing to the accompaniment of the viola,[1] because nearly all the sweetness is in the solo and we note and follow the fine style and the melody with greater attention in that our ears are not occupied with more than a single voice, and every little fault is the more clearly noticed—which does not happen when a group is singing, because then one sustains the other. But especially it is singing recitative with the viola that seems to me most delightful, as this gives to the words a wonderful charm and effectiveness.

"All keyboard instruments are harmonious because their consonances are most perfect, and they lend themselves to the performance of many things that fill the soul with musical sweetness. And

---

1. The instrument referred to is the *viola da mano* (Spanish *vihuela*), to be distinguished from the *viola da arco* (see note 2 below).

no less delightful is the music of four viols[2] which is most suave and exquisite. The human voice gives ornament and much grace to all these instruments, wherewith I deem it enough if our Courtier be acquainted (but the more he excels in them the better) without troubling himself about those which Minerva and Alcibiades scorned,[3] because it seems that they have something unpleasant about them.

"Then, as to the time for engaging in these several kinds of music, I think that must be whenever one finds himself in a familiar and cherished company where there are no pressing concerns; but it is especially appropriate where ladies are present, because their aspect touches the souls of the listeners with sweetness, makes them more receptive to the suavity of the music, and arouses the spirits of the musicians as well.

"As I have said, I favor shunning the crowd, especially the ignoble crowd. But the spice of everything must be discretion, because it would really not be possible to imagine all the cases that do occur; and if the Courtier is a good judge of himself, he will adapt himself to the occasion and will know when the minds of his listeners are disposed to listen and when not; and he will know his own age, for it is indeed unbecoming and most unsightly for a man of any station, who is old, gray, toothless, and wrinkled, to be seen viola in hand,[4] playing and singing in a company of ladies, even though he may do this tolerably well. And that is because the words used in singing are for the most part amorous, and in old men love is a ridiculous thing: although, among other miracles, it sometimes seems that Love delights in kindling cold hearts regardless of years."

[14] Then the Magnifico replied: "Do not deprive the poor old men of this pleasure, messer Federico; for I have known aged men who had quite perfect voices, and hands highly gifted with instruments, far more than some young men."

"I do not wish to deprive old men of this pleasure," said messer Federico, "but I do indeed wish to deprive you and these ladies of the chance to laugh at such an absurdity; and if old men wish to sing to the viola, let them do so in secret and simply in order to relieve their spirits of the troubling thoughts and great vexations of which our life is full, and to taste that something divine in music

2. "The string quartet, as we think of it, did not exist as yet. The violin is a more modern instrument. The four viols were a treble, alto, tenor, and bass viol. Here the *viola da arco* is specifically mentioned to distinguish it from the *viola da mano* mentioned above." (I am grateful to Dr. Isabel Pope Conant for these remarks. See on these points her article "Vicente Espinel as a Musician," in *Studies in the Renaissance* V [1958], pp. 135 ff.)

3. The instruments which Minerva and Alcibiades scorned are wind instruments which deform the face of the musician. Cf. Aristotle, *Politics* VIII, ch. 6; Plutarch, *Life of Alcibiades*, ch. 2.

4. Again this must be the *viola da mano* mentioned above.

which I believe Pythagoras and Socrates sensed in it. And even if they do not practice it themselves, they will enjoy it much more when they listen to it, for having habituated their minds to it, than will those who know nothing about it. For just as the arms of a smith, who is otherwise weak, are often stronger through exercise than those of another man who is more robust but not used to working with his arms—so ears that are practiced in harmony will hear it better and more readily, and appreciate it with far greater pleasure than ears which, however good and sharp they may be, are not trained in the varieties of musical consonances; because those modulations do not penetrate ears that are unaccustomed to hearing them, but pass them by without leaving any savor of themselves—although even wild beasts enjoy melody in some degree.

"This then is the pleasure old men may fittingly take in music. And I say the same of dancing, because truly we ought to desist from these exercises before age obliges us to do so against our will."

Here signor Morello replied, as though angry: "And so it is better to rule out all old men, and to say that only young men are to be called courtiers!"

At this messer Federico laughed and said: "Consider, signor Morello, that those who are fond of these things, even if they are not young, try to appear so. Hence, they dye their hair and shave twice a week: and this for the reason that nature is tacitly telling them that such things are becoming only to the young."

All the ladies laughed, for each of them understood that these words were aimed at signor Morello; and he seemed a little disconcerted by them.

[15] "But, of course," messer Federico quickly added, "there are proper ways of passing the time with the ladies that are suitable for old men."

"And what are they," said signor Morello, "telling stories?"

"That too," replied messer Federico. "But, as you know, every age brings with it its own cares, and has its own peculiar virtue and its own peculiar vice. Thus, old men, although they are commonly more prudent, more continent, and wiser than young men, are also more loquacious, miserly, difficult, and timid; are always ranting about the house, are harsh to their children, and insist that everyone should do things their way. And, on the contrary, young men are spirited, generous, frank, yet prone to quarrel, changeable, liking and disliking in the same instant, immersed in their own pleasures, and hostile to anyone who gives them good advice.

"But, of all ages, that of manhood is the most tempered, because it has already left the bad points of youth behind it and has not yet arrived at those of old age. Thus, the young and the old, being placed as it were at the extremes, must learn how to follow reason and correct the faults that nature implants in them. Hence, old men must guard against too much self-praise and those other bad faults which we have said are peculiar to them, and use that prudence and knowledge which they will have acquired out of long experience, and be like oracles to whom everyone will turn for advice, and show grace in speaking appropriately about what they know, and in tempering the gravity of their years with a certain gentle and jocund humor. In this way they will be good courtiers and will take much pleasure in the company of men and women, and, without singing or dancing, will be most welcome in such company at all times. And, when the need arises, they will give proof of their worth in matters of importance.

[16] "Let young men observe the same care and judgment, not indeed in the manner of the old (for what is becoming to the one would scarcely be so to the other, and we are wont to say that too much wisdom is a bad sign in the young) but in correcting their own natural faults. Thus, I very much like to see a young man, especially when he is engaging in arms, be somewhat grave and taciturn and be self-possessed, without those restless ways that are so often seen in that age; because such youths appear to have a certain something which the others lack. Moreover, such a quiet manner has a kind of impressive boldness about it, because it seems to arise not from anger but from deliberation, and to be ruled by reason rather than by appetite. This quality is nearly always found in men of great courage, and we also see it in those brute animals that surpass the rest in nobility and strength, as the lion and the eagle. Nor is this strange, because an impetuous and sudden movement which, without words or other show of anger, bursts forth abruptly, like the explosion of a cannon, with all its force and from that quiet which is its contrary—is far more violent and furious than one that waxes by degrees, growing hotter little by little. Thus, those who do so much talking and jumping about and are unable to stand still when they undertake to do anything would seem to waste their powers in that way; and, as our messer Pietro Monte rightly says, they act like children who go about at night singing through fear, as if to give themselves courage with their song.

"Hence, just as a calm and judicious youthfulness is most praiseworthy in a young man, because the levity that is the peculiar fault of that age seems to be tempered and corrected—so in an old man a green and spirited old age is to be highly esteemed, because the vigor of his spirit seems to be so great that it warms and strengthens an age that is so weak and chill, maintaining it in that middle condition which is the best part of our life.

[17] "But in the end all these qualities in our Courtier will still not suffice to win him universal favor with lords and cavaliers and ladies unless he have also a gentle and pleasing manner in his daily conversation. And, truly, I think it difficult to give any rule in this, because of the infinite variety of things that can come up in conversation, and because, among all men on earth, no two are found that have minds totally alike. Hence, whoever has to engage in conversation with others must let himself be guided by his own judgment and must perceive the differences between one man and another, and change his style and method from day to day, according to the nature of the person with whom he undertakes to converse. Nor could I, for my part, give him other rules in this than those already given, which signor Morello learned at confession as a child."

Here signora Emilia laughed and said: "You do too much shirk your labors, messer Federico. But you shall not succeed, for you shall be required to talk on until it is time to go to bed."

"And what, Madam, if I have nothing to say?" replied messer Federico.

"Thereby we shall see how ingenious you are," said signora Emilia, "and if it is true, as I have heard, that a man has been known to be so clever and eloquent as not to want for material in writing a book in praise of a fly, others in praise of the quartan, another in praise of baldness, then can you not manage to talk about Courtiership for one evening?"

"By now," replied messer Federico, "we have said enough about that to make two books; but since no excuse avails me, I will talk on until you are satisfied that I have done, if not my duty, at least all that lies within my powers.

[18] "I think the conversation which in every way the Courtier must try to make pleasing is that which he has with his prince; and, although this term 'conversation' implies a certain equality which would not seem possible between a lord and a servant, still we will so name it for the present. Therefore, in addition to making it evident at all times and to all persons that he is as worthy as we have said, I would have the Courtier devote all his thought and strength of spirit to loving and almost adoring the prince he serves above all else, devoting his every desire and habit and manner to pleasing him."

Here, without waiting further, Pietro da Napoli said: "Nowadays you will find many such courtiers, for it strikes me that you have, in few words, sketched us a noble flatterer."

"You are quite wrong," replied messer Federico, "for flatterers love neither their prince nor their friends, which I wish our Courtier to do above all else; and it is possible to obey and to further the wishes of the one he serves without adulation, because by wishes I mean such as are reasonable and right, or those which in themselves are neither good nor bad as, for instance, to play or to devote oneself to one kind of exercise rather than to another. And I would have our Courtier bend himself to this, even if by nature he is alien to it, so that his prince cannot see him without feeling that he must have something pleasant to say to him; which will come about if he has the good judgment to perceive what his prince likes, and the wit and prudence to bend himself to this, and the considered resolve to like what by nature he may possibly dislike; and, with these precautions in mind, he will never be ill-humored or melancholy before his prince, nor taciturn as many are who seem to bear a grudge against their masters, which is something truly odious. He will not speak ill, especially not of his lords; which happens often enough, for in courts there seems to blow a tempest that drives those who are most favored by their lord and who are raised from low to high estate, to be always complaining and speaking ill of him: which is not only unseemly in them, but is so even in those who chance to be maltreated.

"Our Courtier will not indulge in foolish presumption; he will not be the bearer of unpleasant news; he will not be careless in speaking words which can offend, instead of trying to please; he will not be obstinate and contentious, as are some who seem to delight only in being troublesome and obnoxious like flies, and who make a profession of contradicting everybody, spitefully and indiscriminately. He will not be an idle or lying babbler nor a boaster or inept flatterer, but will be modest and reserved, observing always (and especially in public) the reverence and respect that befit a servant in relation to his master; and he will not behave like many who, when they meet a great prince (and even if they have spoken to him only once before), go up to him with a certain smiling and friendly countenance, as if they meant to embrace an equal or show favor to an inferior.

"Rarely or almost never will he ask of his lord anything for himself, lest his lord, not wishing to deny it to him directly, should perchance grant it to him with ill grace, which is much worse. And when asking something for others, he will be discreet in choosing the occasion, and will ask things that are proper and reasonable; and he will so frame his request, omitting those parts that he knows can cause displeasure, and will skillfully make easy the difficult points, so that his lord will always grant it, or do this in such wise that, should he deny it, he will not think the person whom he has thus not wished to favor goes off offended; for often when lords refuse some favor to someone who requests it so importunately, they judge that the person who asks for the thing with such insistence must desire it greatly, and that, in failing to obtain it, such a one must bear an ill will toward him who denies it; and with this thought they begin to hate the man and can never again look upon him with favor.

[19] "He will not try to make his way into his master's chamber or private quarters when not invited, even though he be a person of authority; for when princes are in private, they often like to feel free to do and say what they please, and thus do not wish to be seen or heard by anyone who might criticize them; and this is most proper. Hence, I think those men are wrong who blame princes for keeping in their rooms persons of little worth except in their service to them personally, for I do not see why princes should not have the same freedom to relax their spirits as we should wish for ourselves.

"But if a Courtier who is accustomed to handling affairs of importance should happen to be in private with his lord, he must become another person, and lay aside grave matters for another time and place, and engage in conversation that will be amusing and pleasant to his lord, so as not to prevent him from gaining such relaxation.

"But in this, as in all things, above all let him take care not to cause his lord any annoyance and let him wait until favors are offered to him rather than fish for them openly as many do, who are so avid of them that it seems they would die if they did not get them; and if they chance to meet with any disfavor, or if they see others favored, they suffer such agony that they are quite unable to conceal their envy. Thus, they make themselves the laughingstock of everyone and often cause their masters to favor anyone at all, merely in order to spite them. Then again, if they happen to be favored beyond the ordinary, they are so inebriated thereby that they are paralyzed with joy, and seem not to know what to do with their hands and feet, and can hardly keep from calling the whole company to come and see and congratulate them as though for something they were never accustomed to receive before.

"I would not have our Courtier be of this sort. I am quite willing that he should like favors, but not set such store by them as to appear unable to do without them; and when he obtains them, let him not seem unaccustomed or strange to them, or marvel that they should be offered to him; nor let him refuse them as some do who refrain from accepting out of a real ignorance, and in that way show bystanders that they think themselves unworthy.

"Yet a man ought always be a little more humble than his rank would require; not accepting too readily the favors and honors that are offered him, but modestly refusing them while showing that he esteems them highly, yet in such a way as to give the donor cause to press them upon him the more urgently. For the greater the resistance shown in accepting them in this way, the more will the prince who is granting them think himself to be esteemed, and his benefaction will appear the greater the more the recipient of it shows his appreciation and how great he considers the honor done him by it. And these are the true and solid favors that cause a man to be esteemed by outsiders, for, as they are unsought, everyone assumes that they are the reward of true worth and the more so in proportion to the modesty that attends them."

[20] Then messer Cesare Gonzaga said: "It seems to me that you have stolen that passage from the Gospel where it is said: 'When thou art bidden to a wedding, go, and sit down in the lowliest place; that when he that bade thee cometh, he may say: Friend, go up higher: and thus thou shalt have honor in the presence of them that sit at meat with thee.'"[5]

Messer Federico laughed and said: "It would be too great a sacrilege to steal from the Gospel; but you are more learned in Holy Writ than I thought"; then he went on: "You see to what a great danger those men expose themselves who rashly enter into conversation in a prince's presence without being invited; and the prince, to put them to shame, will often not answer and will turn his head another way, or even if he does answer, all will see, when he does, that he is annoyed.

"To receive favors of princes, then, there is no better way than to deserve them. And when one sees another man who is pleasing to a prince for whatever reason, he must not think that, by imitating such a one, he too can attain to that same mark, for not everything is suited to everybody. And there will sometimes be a man who by nature is so clever at jesting that whatever he says brings laughter, and he seems to have been born only for this; and if another man of sober manner (even if he be well endowed) tries to do the same thing, it will fall so cold and flat as to disgust his listeners, and he will be precisely like the ass who tried to imitate the dog in playing with his master.[6] Thus, everyone must know himself and his own powers, and govern himself accordingly, and consider what things he ought to imitate and what things he ought not."

[21] Here Vincenzio Calmeta said: "Before you go any further, if I well understood, I believe you said a while ago that the best way to get favors is to deserve them; and that the Courtier ought to wait until they are offered to him rather than seek them presumptuously.

5. Luke 14:8–10.
6. Cf. the Aesop fable, *Asinus domino blandiens*.

Now I greatly fear that this precept is to little effect, and I believe experience shows us quite the contrary. For nowadays few indeed enjoy the favor of princes, except those who are presumptuous; and I know you can testify to the fact that some who found themselves in small favor with their princes have managed to please them only through presumption; but, as for there being those who have risen through modesty, I for my part do not know of any; and I will even give you time to think on this, but I believe you will discover few. And if you consider the court of France, which is today one of the noblest in Christendom, you will find that all those who there enjoy universal favor tend to be presumptuous, not only toward one another but toward the King himself."

"Do not say so," replied messer Federico; "on the contrary, there are very modest and courteous gentlemen in France. It is true that they behave with a certain freedom and with an unceremonious familiarity which is peculiar and natural to them; and which should therefore not be called presumption because in this very manner of theirs, the while they laugh at the presumptuous and make sport of them, they highly esteem those who appear to them to be worthy and modest."

Calmeta replied: "Look at the Spaniards, who seem to be the masters in Courtiership, and ask yourself how many you find who are not exceedingly presumptuous both with ladies and with gentlemen; and more even than the French, in that they at first make a show of the greatest modesty: and in this they are truly discerning because, as I have said, the princes of our time favor those only who have such manners."

[22] Then messer Federico replied: "But I will not suffer you to cast this slur upon the princes of our time, messer Vincenzio. For there are indeed many who love modesty, which, however, I do not say will in itself suffice to make a man well liked; but I do say that when it is joined to great worth, it honors its possessor greatly. And although it is silent of itself, praiseworthy deeds speak out, and are far more admirable than if they were attended by presumption and rashness. Nor will I deny that there are many presumptuous Spaniards, but I say that those who are highly esteemed are very modest on the whole.

"Then there are certain others who stand so aloof that they shun human society too much, and so far exceed a certain mean that they cause themselves to be regarded either as too timid or too proud; and I have no praise at all for such as these, nor do I wish modesty to be so dry and arid as to amount to boorishness. But let the Courtier be eloquent when it suits his purpose and, when he speaks on political matters, let him be prudent and wise; and let him have the good judgment to adapt himself to the customs of the countries where he happens to be; then, let him be entertaining in lesser matters and well spoken on every subject. But, above all, let him hold to what is good; be neither envious nor evil-tongued; nor let him ever bring himself to seek grace or favor by resorting to foul means or evil practices."

Then Calmeta said: "I assure you that all other means are far more uncertain and take longer than these you are censuring. For, to repeat what I said, princes today love those only who resort to such practices."

"But do not say this," messer Federico then rejoined, "for that would be too plain an argument that the princes of our day are all corrupt and bad—which is not true, because there are some who are good. But if our Courtier happens to find himself in the service of one who is wicked and malign, let him leave him as soon as he discovers this, that he may escape the great anguish that all good men feel in serving the wicked."

"We must pray God," replied Calmeta, "to grant us good masters, for, once we have them, we have to endure them as they are; because countless considerations force a gentleman not to leave a patron once he has begun to serve him: the misfortune lies in ever beginning; and in that case courtiers are like those unhappy birds that are born in some miserable valley."

"In my opinion," said messer Federico, "duty should come before all other considerations. And provided a gentleman does not leave his lord when he is at war or in adversity—for it could be thought that he did so to improve his own fortunes or because he feared that his chances for profit had failed him—in any other time I think he has a right to quit, and ought to quit, a service which in the eyes of all good men is sure to disgrace him; for everyone assumes that whoever serves the good is good, and whoever serves the bad is bad."

[23] Then signor Ludovico Pio said: "There is a doubt in my mind that I wish you would clear up for me: namely, whether a gentleman who serves a prince is bound to obey him in all that he commands, even if it is something dishonorable and disgraceful."

"In dishonorable things we are not bound to obey anyone," replied messer Federico.

"How now?" answered signor Ludovico, "if I am in the service of a prince who treats me well and who has confidence that I will do for him all that can be done, and who orders me to go out and kill a man or do anything whatever, am I to refuse to do it?"

"You ought to obey your lord," replied messer Federico, "in all things profitable and honorable to him, not in those that will bring him harm and shame. Thus, if he should command you to do some deed of treachery, not only are you not bound to do it, but you are bound not to do it—both for your own sake and in order not to minister to the shame of your lord. It is true that many things that are evil appear at first sight to be good, and many appear evil and yet are good. Hence, when serving one's masters it is sometimes permitted to kill not just one man but ten thousand men, and do many other things that might seem evil to a man who did not look upon them as one ought, and yet are not evil."

Then signor Gaspar Pallavicino replied: "I pray you, by your faith, go into this a bit more, and teach us how one can distinguish what is really good from what appears to be good."

"Excuse me," said messer Federico, "I do not wish to go into that, for there would be too much to say; but let the whole question be left to your discretion."

[24] "Clear up another doubt for me at least," replied signor Gasparo.

"And what is that?" said messer Federico.

"It is this," replied signor Gasparo. "If the lord I am serving should tell me exactly what I am to do in a given undertaking or in any affair whatever; and if I, when actually engaged in it, should decide that by doing more, or less, or otherwise, than I was told to do, I could make the affair succeed to the greater advantage and profit of him who had given me the task, I should like to know if I must hold to that original order without exceeding the limits of it, or, on the contrary, do what seems best to me?"

Then messer Federico replied: "I would give the rule in this by citing the example of Manlius Torquatus (who in such a circumstance killed his own son out of too great a sense of duty)[7] if I thought him worthy of much praise, which truly I do not; and yet I do not venture to condemn him either and oppose the judgment of so many centuries. For, no doubt, it is a quite dangerous thing to depart from our superiors' commands, trusting more in our own judgment than in theirs, when in reason we ought to obey; because if our design should happen to fail, and the affair should turn out badly, we incur the error of disobedience, and ruin what we have to do, without having any means of excusing ourselves or any hope of pardon; on the other hand, if the thing turns out according to our wish, we must give the praise to Fortune, and be content with that. Moreover, in this way we begin the practice of making light of our lords' commands; and, following the example of one man who happened to succeed and who perhaps was prudent and had reasoned well, and may also have been helped by Fortune, a thousand other ignorant

7. Plutarch, *Parallel Lives*. See also Aulus Gellius, *Noctes Atticae* I, 13.

triflers will venture to follow their own ideas in matters of great importance and, in order to make a show of being wise and having great authority, will deviate from their lords' commands: which is a very bad thing and frequently the cause of countless errors.

"But in such a case I think that the man involved must consider carefully and, as it were, weigh in the balance the good and the advantages he stands to gain, should he disobey the order and his design turn out as he hopes; and, on the other hand, weigh the evil and the disadvantages that could result if, in disobeying the order, the affair should chance to turn out badly. And if he sees that, in case of failure, the damage would be greater and more serious than the gain would be in case of success, he should refrain and should obey to the letter what he was told to do; and, conversely, if in case of success the gain is likely to be greater than the damage in case of failure, I believe that he may set about doing what his reason and good judgment dictate, and disregard somewhat the letter of his orders—doing as good merchants do who risk little to gain much, but will not risk much to gain little.

"I deem it well above all that he reckon with the character of the prince he serves, and govern himself accordingly; for if the prince's character happens to be severe, as is true of many, I would never advise him, if he were a friend of mine, to change by the least bit the order given: lest there happen to him what is recorded to have happened to a master engineer of the Athenians, to whom Publius Crassus Mucianus, when he was in Asia and planning to besiege a town, sent a request for one of two ship's masts that he had seen at Athens, in order to make a ram with which to batter down a wall, stating that he wished the larger one. The engineer, as an expert in such matters, recognized that the larger mast was ill-suited to such a purpose, and, since the smaller one was easier to transport and was even more suitable for making such a machine, he sent it to Mucianus. The latter, hearing how things had gone, sent for the poor engineer, demanding to know why he had not obeyed him; and, refusing to accept any reason he gave him, he had him stripped naked and flogged and scourged with rods until he died, because it seemed to Mucianus that, in place of obeying, the man had tried to advise him.[8] Hence, with such severe men one must exercise great caution.

[25] "But let us leave this question of how to deal with princes and come to the matter of intercourse with one's equals or with those who are nearly so. For to this we must give some attention also, since it is more universally the case, and a man finds himself more

---

8. The story is told by Aulus Gellius, *Noctes Atticae* I, 13.

often engaged with such company than with princes—although
there are some fools who, even if they are in the company of the
best friend in the world, upon meeting with someone better dressed,
attach themselves at once to him; and then, if they happen on someone even better dressed, they do the same again. And if the prince
should pass through the square, church, or other public place, then
they elbow their way past everyone until they stand beside him; and
even if they have nothing to say to him, they insist on talking,
and hold forth at great length, laughing and clapping their hands,
and slapping their heads to make a show of having important business, so that the crowd may see that they are in favor. But since
such as these deign to speak only with princes, I would not have us
speak of them."

[26] Then the Magnifico Giuliano said: "Now that you mention
those who are so ready to associate with well-dressed men, I wish
you would show us, messer Federico, how the Courtier ought to
dress, and what attire best suits him, and in what way he ought to
govern himself in all that concerns the adornment of his person. For
in this we see an infinite variety: some dressing after the French
manner, some after the Spanish, some wishing to appear German;
nor are those lacking who dress in the style of Turks; some wearing
beards, some not. It would therefore be well to know how to choose
the best out of this confusion."

Messer Federico said: "I do not really know how to give an exact
rule about dress, except that a man ought to follow the custom of
the majority; and since, just as you say, that custom is so varied, and
the Italians are so fond of dressing in the style of other peoples, I
think that everyone should be permitted to dress as he pleases.

"But I do not know by what fate it happens that Italy does not
have, as she used to have, a manner of dress recognized to be Italian: for, although the introduction of these new fashions makes the
former ones seem very crude, still the older were perhaps a sign of
freedom, even as the new ones have proved to be an augury of servitude, which I think is now most evidently fulfilled. And as it is
recorded that when Darius had the Persian sword he wore at his
side made over into the Macedonian style, the year before he fought
with Alexander, this was interpreted by the soothsayers to mean that
the people into whose fashion Darius had transformed his Persian
sword would come to rule over Persia.[9] Just so our having changed
our Italian dress for that of foreigners strikes me as meaning that all
those for whose dress we have exchanged our own are going to con-

9. This anecdote is told by Q. Curtius Rufus, *Historiorum Alexandri Magni* III, 6. This Darius is Darius III who was King of Persia 336–330 B.C.

quer us: which has proved to be all too true, for by now there is no nation that has not made us its prey. So that little more is left to prey upon, and yet they do not leave off preying.

[27] "But I would not have us enter into unpleasant matters. Therefore we shall do well to speak of the clothes that our Courtier shall wear; which, provided they are not unusual or inappropriate to his profession, will be well in all respects if only they satisfy the wearer of them. It is true that, for my part, I should prefer them not to be extreme in any way, as the French are sometimes in being over-ample, and the Germans in being overscanty—but be as the one and the other style can be when corrected and given a better form by the Italians. Moreover, I prefer them always to tend a little more toward the grave and sober rather than the foppish. Hence, I think that black is more pleasing in clothing than any other color; and if not black, then at least some color on the dark side. I mean this of ordinary attire, for there is no doubt that bright and gay colors are more becoming on armor, and it is also more appropriate for gala dress to be trimmed, showy, and dashing; so too on public occasions, such as festivals, games, masquerades, and the like. For such garments, when they are so designed, have about them a certain liveliness and dash that accord very well with arms and sports. As for the rest, I would have our Courtier's dress show that sobriety which the Spanish nation so much observes, since external things often bear witness to inner things."

Then messer Cesare Gonzaga said: "This would trouble me little, for if a gentleman is worthy in other respects, his clothes will never enhance or diminish his reputation."

"What you say is true," replied messer Federico. "Yet who of us, on seeing a gentleman pass by dressed in a habit quartered in varied colors, or with an array of strings and ribbons in bows and crosslacings, does not take him to be a fool or a buffoon?"

"Such a one would be taken neither for a fool," said messer Pietro Bembo, "nor for a buffoon by anyone who had lived for any time in Lombardy, for there they all go about like that."

"Then," said the Duchess, laughing, "if all go dressed like that, it must not be imputed to them as a fault, since such attire is as fitting and proper to them as it is for the Venetians to wear puffed sleeves, or for the Florentines to wear hoods."

"I am not speaking," said messer Federico, "more of Lombardy than of elsewhere, for the foolish and the wise are to be found in every nation. But to say what I think is important in the matter of dress, I wish our Courtier to be neat and dainty in his attire, and observe a certain modest elegance, yet not in a feminine or vain fashion. Nor would I have him more careful of one thing than of another, like many we see, who take such pains with their hair that they forget the rest; others attend to their teeth, others to their beard, others to their boots, others to their bonnets, others to their coifs; and thus it comes about that those slight touches of elegance seem borrowed by them, while all the rest, being entirely devoid of taste, is recognized as their very own. And such a manner I would advise our Courtier to avoid, and I would only add further that he ought to consider what appearance he wishes to have and what manner of man he wishes to be taken for, and dress accordingly; and see to it that his attire aid him to be so regarded even by those who do not hear him speak or see him do anything whatever."

[28] Then signor Gaspar Pallavicino said: "It does not seem fitting to me, or even customary among persons of worth, to judge the character of men by their dress rather than by their words or deeds, for then many would be deceived; nor is it without reason that the proverb says: "The habit does not make the monk."'"

"I do not say," replied messer Federico, "that by dress alone we are to make absolute judgments of the characters of men, or that men are not better known by their words and deeds than by their dress; but I do say that a man's attire is no slight index of the wearer's fancy, although sometimes it can be misleading; and not only that, but ways and manners, as well as deeds and words, are all an indication of the qualities of the man in whom they are seen."

"And what is there, according to you," replied signor Gasparo, "on which to base our judgment, if not on words or deeds?"

Then messer Federico said: "You are too subtle a logician. But to explain what I mean: there are some acts that still endure after they are done, such as building, writing, and the like; and others that do not endure, as those which I now have in mind. In this sense, therefore, I do not call walking, laughing, looking, or the like, acts—and yet all these outward things often make manifest what is within. Tell me, did you not immediately judge that friend of ours about whom we spoke only this morning to be a vain and frivolous man, when you saw him walking with that twist of his head, wriggling about, and with his smiling countenance inviting the company to doff their caps to him? So, too, whenever you see anyone staring too intently, with senseless eyes, like an idiot, or laughing stupidly like those goitered mutes of the mountains of Bergamo—do you not take him to be an utter dolt even though he says or does nothing else? Thus, you see that these ways and manners (which at the moment I do not mean to regard as acts) are in large measure what men are known by.

[29] "But there is another thing which seems to me to create or take away greatly from reputation, and this is our choice of the friends

with whom we are to live in intimate relations; for reason doubtless requires that persons who are joined in close friendship and in indissoluble companionship must be alike in their desires, in their minds, their judgments, and talents. Thus, he who associates with the ignorant or the wicked is held to be ignorant or wicked; and, on the contrary, he who associates with the good, the wise, and the discreet is taken to be such himself. For it seems that everything naturally and readily joins with its like. Hence, I think we should take great care in beginning these friendships, because anyone who knows one of a pair of close friends at once imagines the other to be of the same sort."

Then messer Pietro Bembo replied: "It seems to me that we must indeed take great care in the matter of contracting such close friendships as you say, not only because of the gain or loss of reputation, but because nowadays true friends are very few. For I do not believe that there exist any more in the world a Pylades and Orestes, a Theseus and Pirithous, a Scipio and Laelius. Nay, I know not by what fate it happens every day that two friends who have lived for many years in the most cordial love will end by finally deceiving one another in some way or other, either out of malice or envy or inconstancy or some other evil motive: and each will blame the other for what both deserve.

"Thus, since it has happened to me more than once to be deceived by the one whom I most loved and by whom I was confident of being loved above every other person—I have sometimes thought to myself it would be well for us never to trust anyone in the world, or give ourselves over to any friend (however dear and cherished he may be) so as to tell him all our thoughts without reserve as we would tell ourselves; for there are so many dark turns in our minds and so many recesses that it is not possible for human discernment to know the simulations that are latent there. Therefore, I think it is well to love and serve one person more than another according to merit and worth; and yet never be so trusting of this sweet lure of friendship as to have cause later to regret it."

[30] Then messer Federico said: "Truly, the loss would be far greater than the gain if human intercourse were to be deprived of that supreme degree of friendship which, in my opinion, yields all the good that life holds for us; therefore, I will in no way grant you that what you say is reasonable; nay, I would go so far as to maintain, and with most evident reasons, that without this perfect friendship man would be far more unhappy than all other creatures. And if some do profanely desecrate this sacred name of friendship, we ought not on that account to uproot it from our hearts and, because of the fault of wicked men, deprive good men of so much felicity. And for my

part I believe that here among us there is more than one pair of friends whose love is steadfast and without shadow of deceit, and such as to continue unto death to share in like desires, no less than if they were those ancients whom you mentioned a moment ago; and so it happens whenever one chooses a friend like himself in character, quite apart from the influence which comes from the stars. And I mean all this to apply to the good and the virtuous, for the friendship of the wicked is not friendship.

"I think it well that a tie so close should join or bind no more than two, for otherwise it would perhaps be dangerous; because, as you know, it is more difficult to attune three musical instruments together than two. Therefore, I should wish our Courtier to have one special and cordial friend, of the sort we have described, if possible; and then, that he should love, honor, and respect all others according to their worth and merits, and seek always to associate more with those who enjoy high esteem, are noble, and known to be good men, than with the ignoble and those of little worth; in such a way that he too may be loved and esteemed by such men. And he will succeed in this if he is courteous, humane, generous, affable, and gentle in his association with others, active and diligent in serving and caring for the welfare and honor of his friends, whether they be absent or present, tolerating their natural and bearable defects, without breaking with them for some trivial reason, and correcting in himself such defects as are in kindness pointed out to him; never putting himself before others in seeking the first and most honored places; nor doing as some who appear to hold the world in scorn, and insist on laying down the law to everyone with a certain tiresome severity; and who, besides being contentious in every little thing at the wrong time, blame their friends for what they do not do themselves; and are always seeking a pretext to complain of them— which is a most odious thing."

[31] When messer Federico paused here, signor Gaspar Pallavicino said: "I wish you would speak a little more in detail than you do concerning this matter of converse with our friends; for truly you hold much to generalities and show us the matter in passing, as it were."

"How 'in passing'?" replied messer Federico. "Would you perhaps have me tell you the very words you must use? But does it not strike you that we have talked enough about this?"

"Enough, I think," replied signor Gasparo, "yet I should like to hear a few more particulars concerning this converse with men and women; which is something that seems to me of great importance, considering that most of our time at courts is given over to it; and if such converse were always uniform, it would soon become tiresome."

"In my opinion," replied messer Federico, "we have given the Courtier knowledge of so many things that he can easily vary his conversation and adapt himself to the quality of the persons with whom he has to do, assuming that he has good judgment and acts accordingly, and attends sometimes to grave matters and sometimes to festivals and games, depending on the occasion."

"And which games?" asked signor Gasparo.

Then messer Federico replied, laughing: "Let us ask the advice of fra Serafino, who invents new ones every day!"

"Jesting aside," replied signor Gasparo, "do you think it a vice in the Courtier to play at cards and dice?"

"I do not," said messer Federico, "unless he should do so too constantly and as a result should neglect other more important things, or indeed unless he should play only to win money and to cheat the other player; and, when he lost, should show such grief and vexation as to give proof of being miserly."

"And what," replied signor Gasparo, "do you say of the game of chess?"

"It is certainly a pleasing and ingenious amusement," said messer Federico, "but it seems to me to have one defect, which is that it is possible to have too much knowledge of it, so that whoever would excel in the game must give a great deal of time to it, as I believe, and as much study as if he would learn some noble science or perform well anything of importance; and yet in the end, for all his pains, he only knows how to play a game. Thus, I think a very unusual thing happens in this, namely, that mediocrity is more to be praised than excellence."

Signor Gasparo replied: "Many Spaniards excel in this and in many other games; yet they do not devote much study to them or leave off doing other things."

"You can be sure," replied messer Federico, "that they do put a great deal of study into it, although they hide the fact. The other games you refer to, besides chess, are perhaps like many I have seen played that are of little account and serve only to cause the vulgar to marvel; hence, they seem to me worthy of no other praise or reward than that which Alexander the Great gave the fellow who at a good distance could impale chickpeas on a needle.

[32] "But because it seems that, in this as in many other things, Fortune has great power over men's opinions, we sometimes see that a gentleman, no matter how good his character may be, and though endowed with many graces, will find little favor with the prince, and will, as we say, go against the grain; and this for no understandable reason. So that as soon as he comes into the presence of the prince, and before he has been recognized by the others, although he may

be quick at repartee and may cut a good figure by his gestures, manners, words, and all else that is needful, that prince will show that he esteems him little, nay, will be the readier to offend him in some way. And thus it will come about that the others will immediately follow the prince's bent, and everyone will find the man to be of little worth, nor will there be any who prize or esteem him, or laugh at his witticisms, or hold him in any respect; nay, all will begin to make fun of him and persecute him. Nor will it avail the poor man at all if he makes fair retorts or takes all this as if it were in jest, for the very pages will buzz about him, so that he can be the worthiest man in the world and still be put down and derided.

"On the other hand, if the prince shows a liking for some dullard who knows neither how to speak nor how to act, this man's manners and ways (however silly and uncouth they may be) will often be praised with exclamations and wonderment by everyone, and the whole court will appear to admire and respect him, and everyone will laugh at his clever sayings and at certain rustic and pointless jests that ought to provoke vomit rather than laughter: so are men set and obstinate in the opinions that are engendered by the favor and disfavor of princes.

"Therefore I would have our Courtier bring talent and art to support his own worth; and always, when he has to go where he is a stranger and unknown, let him see to it that a good repute precedes him and that men there know that he is highly esteemed in other places, among other lords, ladies, and gentlemen; for a fame that is thought to result from many judgments generates a certain firm belief in a man's worth, which then, in minds already disposed and prepared in this way, is easily maintained and increased by actual performance: moreover, he escapes the annoyance that I feel when I am asked who I am and what my name is."

[33] "I do not see how this can help," replied messer Bernardo Bibbiena, "for more than once it has happened to me (as, I think, to many others) that because I was told by persons of good judgment that a certain thing was excellent, I made up my mind about it before I had seen it; and then, when I saw it, it fell greatly in my esteem and far short of what I had expected. And this came about only from having relied too much on report, and from having formed in my mind such an exaggerated notion that, even though the real thing was great and excellent, yet later, when measured by the fact, it seemed to me meager indeed compared with what I had imagined. And so it can happen with our Courtier too, I fear. Hence, I do not see the advantage of heightening such expectations and having our fame precede us; for our minds often imagine things that cannot be matched by the reality, and so we lose more than we gain."

Here messer Federico said: "The things which to you and to many others fall far short of their renown are, for the most part, such that the eye can judge of them at a glance—as if you had never been at Naples or Rome and had heard them much talked about, and you were to imagine something far exceeding what they later proved to be when you saw them; but this does not happen when it is a matter of a man's character, because what is outwardly visible is the least part. Thus, if on first hearing some gentleman speak you should not find him to be as worthy as you had previously imagined, you would not so readily change your good opinion of him as you would of those things of which the eye can instantly judge; but you would expect to discover from day to day some other hidden virtue, always holding fast to the good impression that had come to you through the words of so many persons; and then, assuming that such a one is as well endowed as I take our Courtier to be, your faith in his reputation would be constantly confirmed because his performance would give you cause, and you would always be imagining something more than met the eye.

[34] "And certainly it cannot be denied that these first impressions bear great weight, and that we must be most careful of them. And, in order that you may see how important they are, I want to tell you that I have known a gentleman in my time who, though he was most fair of aspect and modest of manner, and worthy in arms as well, was not, however, so outstanding in any of these things as not to have many who were his equals and even his superiors. And yet, as his destiny would have it, a certain lady fell ardently in love with him, and as her love grew daily, because of the signs the young man gave of loving her in return, and as there was no way for them to speak together, she was moved by excess of passion to disclose her desires to another lady, from whom she hoped to get some help. This second lady was in no way inferior to the first in rank or beauty; whence it came about that on hearing the young man (whom she had never seen) spoken of so affectionately, and, perceiving that he was exceedingly loved by her friend (whom she knew to be most prudent and of excellent judgment), she at once imagined him to be the handsomest, the wisest, the most discreet of men, and, in short, the man most worthy of her love in all the world. And thus, without ever having seen him, she conceived such a passionate love for him that she began making every effort to get him for herself instead of for her friend and to cause him to return her love: which with little effort she succeeded in doing, for she was indeed a lady to be wooed and not one obliged to do the wooing.

"And now listen to this: not long afterwards it happened that a letter which this second lady had written to her lover fell into the hands of yet another lady, she also very noble and outstanding for her cultivation and beauty who—being like most women curious and eager to learn secrets, and especially other women's—opened this letter and, as she read it, saw that it was dictated by an extremely passionate love. At first the sweet and ardent words she read moved her to compassion for that lady, for she well knew from whom the letter came and to whom it was addressed; then those words gained so in power that, as she turned them over in her mind and considered what sort of man this must be who could bring this lady to love him so much, straight-way she also fell in love with him; and the letter was perhaps more effective than if it had been sent to her by the young man. And as it can sometimes happen that the poison in a dish intended for some prince kills the first person who tastes it, so this poor lady, in her excessive greed, drank the love poison that had been prepared for another.

"What more need I say? The affair became so well known that many other ladies besides these, partly in order to spite the others and partly to ape them, put every effort and care into gaining this man's love and contended for it with one another as boys for cherries. This all came about from the first impression of that lady who saw that he was so much loved by another."

[35] Here signor Gaspar Pallavicino replied, laughing: "As reasons to support your opinion, you cite me the doings of women, who for the most part are quite beyond the pale of reason. And if you would tell the whole truth, this man who was favored by so many women must have been a simpleton and practically worthless. For it is the way of women always to favor the worst, and like sheep to do what they see the first one do, be that for good or ill. Moreover, they are so jealous among themselves that this man could have been a monster and they would still have tried to steal him away from one another."

Here many began to speak, and nearly everyone wanted to contradict signor Gasparo; but the Duchess imposed silence on all, and then said, laughing: "If the evil you speak of women were not so far from the truth that the uttering of it casts blame and shame on him who speaks it rather than on them, I should allow you to be answered. But I do not wish you to be cured of this bad habit by the many reasons that could be adduced to refute you, so that you may incur the direst punishment for your sin, which punishment shall be the bad opinion in which all will hold you who hear you argue so."

Then messer Federico replied: "Signor Gasparo, do not say that women are so beyond the pale of reason, even if sometimes they are more moved to love by others' judgment than by their own; for gentlemen and many wise men often do the same. And if I may be allowed to speak the truth, you yourself, and all the rest of us here, do often and even now rely more on the opinion of others than on our own. And in proof of this, it is not long ago that certain verses were presented here as being Sannazaro's, and they seemed most excellent to everyone and were praised with exclamations and marvel; then when it was known for certain that the verses were by someone else, they at once sank in reputation and were found to be less than mediocre. And a certain motet that was sung before the Duchess pleased no one and was not thought good until it was known to be by Josquin de Près.

"What clearer proof of the weight of opinion could you wish for? Do you not remember that, when drinking a certain wine, you would at one time pronounce it to be most perfect and at another to be most insipid? And this because you were convinced they were different wines, one from the Riviera of Genoa and the other from this region; and even when the mistake was discovered, you refused to believe it—so firmly was that wrong opinion fixed in your mind, which opinion came however from the report of others.

[36] "Therefore the Courtier must take great care to make a good impression at the start, and consider how damaging and fatal a thing it is to do otherwise. And they of all men run this risk who make a profession of being very amusing and think by these pleasantries of theirs to enjoy a certain freedom by virtue of which it is proper and permissible for them to do and say whatever comes into their heads, without giving it a second thought. Thus, they often begin certain things without knowing how to finish them, and then try to come to their own aid by raising a laugh; yet even this they do so clumsily that it does not succeed, so that they arouse the utmost disgust in anyone who sees or hears them, and they fail miserably.

"Sometimes, thinking to be witty and droll, they say the dirtiest and most indecent things, in the presence of ladies and often to the ladies themselves; and the more they see them blush, the more they think themselves good courtiers, and they go right on laughing and priding themselves on having the fine virtue they think they have. Yet they do these many stupidities for no other reason than that they wish to be thought jolly good fellows: this being the one name that seems to them worthy of praise, and in which they take more pride than in any other; and to acquire it they engage in the crudest and most shameful improprieties in the world. They often push one another downstairs, deal each other blows with sticks and bricks, throw fistfuls of dust in one another's eyes, cause their horses to roll one on the other in ditches or downhill; then at table they throw soups, gravies, jellies, and every kind of thing in one another's face: and then they laugh. And the one who knows how to do the most things of this kind deems himself the better Courtier and the more gallant, and thinks to have won great glory. And if sometimes they invite a gentleman to take part in these antics of theirs and he does not choose to join in such boorish jests, they at once say that he wants to appear too wise, stands too much on dignity, and is not a jolly good fellow. But I can tell you worse: there are some who vie among themselves and lay wager as to who can eat and drink the most vile and nauseating things; and they concoct things so abhorrent to human sense that it is impossible to mention them without the greatest disgust."

[37] "And what can these be?" asked signor Ludovico Pio.

Messer Federico replied: "Get Marquess Febus to tell you, who has often seen them in France; and perhaps they were done to him."

Marquess Febus replied: "I have seen nothing of the kind done in France that is not also done in Italy; but everything that is good among the Italians in the way of dress, sports, banquets, handling arms, and everything else that befits a Courtier—they have gotten it all from the French."

"I do not say," replied messer Federico, "that very fine and modest cavaliers are not also to be found among the French, and I myself have known many that are truly worthy of every praise. Still, there are some who are careless; and, generally speaking, it strikes me that the customs of the Spaniards suit the Italians better than do those of the French, because the calm gravity that is peculiar to the Spaniards is, I think, far more suited to us than the ready vivacity we see in the French in almost all their movements: which is not unbecoming to them, nay, is charming, because it is so natural and proper to them as not to appear an affectation on their part. There are indeed many Italians who devote every effort to imitating that manner; and they do nothing but shake their heads as they speak, bowing clumsily to the side; and when they pass through town they walk so fast that their lackeys cannot keep up with them. By way of such manners they deem themselves to be good Frenchmen and to have the free manner of the French, which actually happens rarely save in those who have been reared in France and have acquired the manner from childhood.

"The same is true of knowing many languages, which is something I very much approve of in the Courtier, especially Spanish and French, because intercourse with both of these nations is very frequent in Italy, and they have more in common with us than any of the others; and their two princes, being very powerful in war and most magnificent in peace, always have their courts full of noble cavaliers, who are then spread abroad in the world; and we do indeed have occasion to hold converse with them."

[38] "Now I would not go on to speak in any more detail of things too well known, such as that our Courtier ought not to profess to be a great eater or drinker, or be dissolute in any bad habit, or be vile or disorderly in his way of life, or have certain peasant ways that bespeak the hoe and the plow a thousand miles away; because a man of this sort not only may not hope to become a good Courtier, but no suitable job can be given him other than tending sheep.

"And, to conclude, I declare that it would be well for the Courtier to know perfectly all we have said befits him, so that everything possible may be easy for him, and that everyone may marvel at him and he at no one. It is understood, however, that in this there is to be no proud and inhuman rigidity, such as some have who refuse to show any wonder at all at what others do, because they think they are able to do much better, and by their silence they scorn those things as unworthy of any mention; and act as if they wished to show that no one is their equal, let alone able to understand the profundity of their knowledge. The Courtier must avoid these odious ways, and praise the good achievements of others with kindness and good will; and, although he may feel that he is admirable and much superior to all others, yet he ought not to appear to think so.

"But because such complete perfection as this is very rarely, and perhaps never, found in human nature, a man who feels himself wanting in some particular ought not to lose confidence in himself or the hope of reaching a high mark, even though he cannot attain to that perfect and highest excellence to which he aspires. For in every art there are many ranks besides the highest that are praise-worthy, and he who aims at the summit will seldom fail to mount more than half the way. Therefore if our Courtier knows himself to be excellent in something besides arms, I would have him with propriety derive profit and honor from it; and let him have the discretion and good judgment to know how to bring people adroitly and opportunely to see and hear what he considers himself to excel in, always seeming to do this without ostentation, casually as it were, and rather when begged by others than because he wishes it. And in everything that he has to do or say, let him, if possible, always come prepared and ready, but give the appearance that all is done on the spur of the moment. But, as for those things in which he feels himself to be mediocre, let him touch on them in passing, without dwelling much upon them, though in such a way as to cause others to think that he knows much more about them than he lays claim to know: like certain poets who have sometimes suggested the most subtle things in philosophy or other sciences, when probably they understood very little about them. Then, in those things wherein he knows himself to be totally ignorant, I would never have him claim ability in any way or seek

to gain fame by them; on the contrary, when need be, let him confess openly that he knows nothing."

[39] "That," said Calmeta, "is not what Nicoletto[1] would have done,
who, being an excellent philosopher, but with no more knowledge of
law than of flying, when a certain mayor of Padua decided to give
him a lectureship in law, was never willing (although many students
so urged him) to undeceive that mayor and confess his ignorance;
saying always that he did not agree with the opinion of Socrates in
this matter, and that it was not for a philosopher ever to declare
himself ignorant in anything."

"I do not say," replied messer Federico, "that the Courtier, unre-
quired by others, should venture of himself to confess his own
ignorance; for I too dislike this folly of accusing and depreciating
oneself. And sometimes therefore I laugh to myself at certain men
who are so ready, without any coercion, to tell of certain things,
which, even though they may have happened through no fault of
theirs, yet imply a certain disgrace; like a cavalier you all know, who,
every time mention was made of the battle fought against King
Charles in the Parmesan,[2] would begin at once to tell how he had
fled, making it clear that on that day he had seen and heard nothing else; or, whenever a certain famous joust was mentioned, would
always tell how he had fallen; and in his conversation he often
appeared to try to create the occasion for telling how one night,
when he was on his way to speak with a certain lady, he had gotten
a sound beating.

"I would not have our Courtier say such silly things; but rather,
should the occasion arise when he might show his ignorance in
something, then I think he ought to avoid it; and if compelled by
necessity, then he ought openly to confess his ignorance rather than
expose himself to that risk. And in this way he will escape the censure that many nowadays deserve who (out of I know not what perverse instinct or imprudent judgment) are always attempting things
of which they are ignorant and avoiding things they know how to do.
And, in proof of this, I know a very excellent musician who has
abandoned music and given himself over entirely to composing
verses, and, thinking himself very great at that, has made himself
the laughingstock of everyone, and by now has lost even his music.
Another, one of the first painters of the world, scorns that art
wherein he is most rare, and has set about studying philosophy; in

---

1. Paolo Nicola Vernia (d. 1499) professor of physics at the University of Padua, called
   Nicoletto because of his shortness of stature.
2. The reference is to the Battle of Fornovo (July 6, 1495), between the Italian forces under
   the Marquess Gianfrancesco Gonzaga of Mantua and the French army of Charles VIII of
   France. Both sides claimed the victory.

which he comes up with such strange notions and new chimeras that, for all his art as a painter, he would never be able to paint them. And countless instances like these are to be found.

"There are of course some who know their own excellence in one thing and yet make a profession of something else, though something in which they are not ignorant; and every time they have an occasion to show their worth in the thing wherein they feel they have talent, they give evidence of their considerable ability. And it sometimes happens that the company, seeing this ability of theirs in something that is not their profession, think they must be able to do far better in what is their profession. Such an art, when accompanied by good judgment, does not displease me in the least."

[40] Then signor Gaspar Pallavicino replied: "This seems to me to be not an art, but an actual deceit; and I do not think it seemly for anyone who wishes to be a man of honor ever to deceive."

"This," said messer Federico, "is an ornament attending the thing done, rather than deceit; and even if it be deceit, it is not to be censured. Will you also say that, in the case of two men who are fencing, the one who wins deceives the other? He wins because he has more art than the other. And if you have a beautiful jewel with no setting, and it passes into the hands of a good goldsmith who with a skillful setting makes it appear far more beautiful, will you say that the goldsmith deceives the eyes of the one who looks at it? Surely he deserves praise for that deceit, because with good judgment and art his masterful hand often adds grace and adornment to ivory or to silver or to a beautiful stone by setting it in fine gold. Therefore let us not say that art—or deceit such as this, if you insist on calling it that—deserves any blame.

"Neither is it unseemly for a man who feels he has talent in a certain thing adroitly to seek the occasion for displaying it and in the same way to conceal what he thinks would deserve little praise—doing this always with circumspect dissimulation. Do you not recall that, without appearing to seek them out, King Ferdinand found occasions aplenty to go about in his doublet, and did this because he felt he had a good physique; and that, as his hands were not too good, he rarely or almost never took off his gloves? And there were very few who took any notice of this precaution on his part. Also it seems to me I have read that Julius Caesar liked to wear the laurel wreath because it hid his baldness.[3] But in all these matters it is necessary to exercise great prudence and good judgment in order not to exceed the bounds; for often a man falls into one error when avoiding another, and, in seeking to win praise, wins blame.

3. Suetonius, *Life of Julius Caesar*, ch. 45.

[41] "Therefore, in our manner of life and in our conversation, the safest thing is to govern ourselves always according to a certain decorous mean, which indeed is a very great and strong shield against envy, which we ought to avoid as much as possible. Also I would have our Courtier take care not to acquire the name of liar or boaster, which can sometimes befall even those who do not merit it. Therefore, in all he says, let him be always careful not to exceed the limits of verisimilitude, and not to tell too often those truths that have the appearance of falsehoods—like many who never speak of anything except miracles and yet expect to be held in such authority that every incredible thing they say should be believed. Others, at the start of a friendship, in order to gain favor with their new friend, swear, on the first day they speak with him, that there is no one in the world whom they love more, and that they would gladly die to do him some service, and such unreasonable things. And when they leave him, they make a show of weeping and of being unable to utter any word for grief. Thus, in their wish to be thought so exceedingly loving, they cause others to judge them to be liars and silly flatterers.

"But it would be too long and wearisome to attempt to speak of all the faults that can occur in the manner of our converse. Hence, as to what I desire in the Courtier, let it suffice to say (beyond what has already been said) that he should be one who is never at a loss for things to say that are good and well suited to those with whom he is speaking, that he should know how to sweeten and refresh the minds of his hearers, and move them discreetly to gaiety and laughter with amusing witticisms and pleasantries, so that, without ever producing tedium or satiety, he may continually give pleasure.

[42] "But by this time I think that signora Emilia will give me leave to be silent. And should she refuse me, by my own words I shall be persuaded that I am not the good Courtier of whom I have spoken, because not only does fine talk (which you have perhaps neither now nor ever heard from me) fail me completely, but even such talk (whatever its worth) as I am capable of."

Then the Prefect said, laughing: "I would not have this false opinion —namely, that you are not an excellent Courtier—stick in the mind of any of us; for your desire to say no more must stem rather from a wish to avoid labor than from lack of anything to say. So, in order that nothing may appear to be neglected in such a worthy company as this and in so excellent a discussion, be pleased to teach us how we are to make use of those pleasantries which you have just mentioned, and show us the art that pertains to all this sort of amusing talk, calculated to excite laughter and gaiety with propriety, for truly this seems most important to me, and very well suited to the Courtier."

"Sir," replied messer Federico, "pleasantries and witticisms are the gift and bounty of nature rather than of art. Certain peoples are quicker than others, like the Tuscans who are truly very sharp. It also appears that such quips come quite naturally to the Spaniards. Yet there are many among these and other peoples who, out of an excessive loquacity, go beyond bounds and become insipid and inept because they pay no attention whatever to the kind of person they are speaking with, or to the place where they are, or to the occasion or the soberness and modesty which they themselves ought to practice."

[43] Then the Prefect replied: "You deny that there is any art in pleasantries, and yet in speaking ill of those persons who do not observe modesty and soberness in making use of them, and who have no regard for the time and the persons with whom they are speaking, you seem to me to bear witness to the fact that this too can be taught and has some method in it."

"These rules, Sir," replied messer Federico, "are so universal that they fit and apply to everything. But I stated that there was no art in pleasantries because I believe that there are only two kinds thereof to be found: one of which is sustained through a long and continuous discourse, as we see in the case of certain men who so gracefully and entertainingly narrate and describe something that has happened to them or that they have seen or heard, that with gestures and words they put it before our eyes and almost bring us to touch it with our hand; and this, for lack of another term, we may call *festivity* or *urbanity*. The other kind of pleasantry is very short and consists in sayings that are quick and sharp, such as are often heard among us, or biting; nor are they well turned unless they sting a little, and these formerly were called *detti*; now some call them *arguzie*.

"So I say that in regard to the first kind, in humorous narrative, that is, there is no call for any art because nature herself creates and fashions men with a gift for amusing stories, and gives them the face, the gestures, the voice, and the words, all suited to imitating what they will. As for the other kind, the *arguzie*, what can art avail? For a pungent saying must come forth and hit the mark before he who utters it appears to have had time to give it a thought; otherwise it is flat and no good. Therefore I deem it to spring wholly from genius and from nature."

Then messer Pietro Bembo spoke up and said: "The Prefect is not denying what you say, that nature and genius play the main part, especially as regards invention. But surely witty thoughts, good and bad and in varying degree, come to anyone's mind, whatever his talent, and then it is judgment and art that polish and correct these, choosing the good and rejecting the bad. Therefore, leave aside what pertains to talent and explain to us what part art plays in this; namely, as among those pleasantries and witticisms that provoke laughter, which befit the Courtier and which do not, and on what occasions and in what ways they are to be used; for this is what the Prefect is asking you."

[44] Then messer Federico said, laughing: "There is no one here to whom I do not yield in all things, and especially in the matter of being facetious; unless perhaps witless things (which often make others laugh more than bright sayings) be counted as wit also." Then, turning to Count Ludovico and to messer Bernardo Bibbiena, he said: "Here are the masters in this matter, from whom, if I am to speak of jocose sayings, I must first learn what to say."

Count Ludovico replied: "It strikes me that you are already ready beginning to practice what you claim to know nothing about, trying, that is, to make this company laugh by ridiculing messer Bernardo and me; for every one of them knows that you yourself are far better endowed than we are with what you would praise us for. Therefore, if you are weary, then you had better beg the Duchess to postpone the rest of our discussion until tomorrow, rather than try to escape from your task by subterfuge."

Messer Federico was beginning to make an answer, but signora Emilia at once interrupted him and said: "It is not our plan that this discussion should be devoted to praise of you: for we know all of you very well. But, as I recall that you accused me last evening, Count, of not apportioning labor equally, it is well for messer Federico to rest a while; and we shall give messer Bernardo Bibbiena the task of discussing pleasantries, for not only do we know him to be most amusing in sustained discourse, but we remember that several times he promised us he would write on this subject, and hence we can believe that he has given it much thought and will therefore fully satisfy us. Then when we have done with pleasantries, messer Federico shall go on with what he has yet to say about the Courtier."

Then messer Federico said: "Madam, I do not know what I can have left to say; but, like the wayfarer at noon, weary from the toil of the long journey, I will find rest in what messer Bernardo says and in the sound of his words, as if under some most pleasant and shady tree alongside the soft murmur of a flowing spring. Then, perhaps refreshed a little, I shall be able to say something more."

Messer Bernardo replied, laughing: "If I showed you my head, you would see what shade could be expected from the leaves of my tree. As for listening to the murmur of that flowing spring, this perhaps you will do: for I was once turned into a spring, not by any of the ancient gods, but by our friend fra Mariano, and never since have I lacked water!"

Then everyone began to laugh, for the pleasantry alluded to by messer Bernardo was well known to all, having occurred at Rome in the presence of Cardinal Galeotto of San Pietro ad Vincula.

[45] When the laughter had ceased, signora Emilia said, "Now stop making us laugh with your pleasantries, and teach us how we are to use them, how they are devised and all that you know about this subject. And begin at once, so as not to lose more time."

"I fear," said messer Bernardo, "that the hour is late; and, in order that my talk about pleasantries may not be unpleasant and wearisome, perhaps it is well to postpone it until tomorrow."

Here many replied at once that the usual hour for ending the discussion was not for some time yet. Then, turning to the Duchess and to signora Emilia, messer Bernardo said: "I am not trying to escape from this task, although, even as I am wont to marvel at the daring of those who venture to sing to the viol in the presence of our friend Giacomo Sansecondo, I should not speak on the subject of pleasantries before an audience that understands what I ought to say far better than I do. Still, in order not to give any of these gentlemen cause for refusing the charge that may be put upon them, I will state as briefly as I can whatever occurs to me in the matter of those things that provoke laughter: which is something so peculiarly ours, that, to define man, we are wont to say that he is a risible animal. For laughter is found only in man, and it is nearly always a sign of a certain hilarity inwardly felt in the mind, which by nature is attracted to pleasure, and desires rest and recreation; wherefore we notice many things devised by men to this end, such as festivals and so many different kinds of shows. And because we like those who provide us with such recreation, it was the custom of ancient rulers (Roman, Athenian, and many others), in order to gain the favor of the people and feed the eyes and the mind of the multitude, to construct great theaters and other public buildings, and therein to offer new sports, horse and chariot races, combats, strange beasts, comedies, tragedies, and mimes. Nor were grave philosophers averse to such shows who, at spectacles of this sort and in banquets, gave repose to their minds, wearied by lofty discourse and divine thoughts; which is something all kinds of men willingly do: for not only laborers in the fields, sailors, and all those who do hard and rough work with their hands, but holy men of religion and prisoners awaiting death from hour to hour, all persist in seeking some remedy and medicine in recreation. Hence, whatever moves to laughter restores the spirit, gives pleasure, and for the moment keeps one from remembering those vexing troubles of which our life is full. So you can see that laughter is most pleasing to everyone and that he who produces it at the right time and in the right way is greatly to be praised.

"But what laughter is, where it abides, and how it sometimes takes possession of our veins, our eyes, our mouth, and our sides, and seems apt to make us burst, so that no matter what we do we are unable to repress it—this I will leave to Democritus to tell, who would be unable to do so, even if he should promise as much.

[46] "Now the place and as it were the source of the laughable consists in a certain deformity, for we laugh only at those things that have incongruity in them and that seem to be amiss and yet are not. I know not how to state it otherwise; but if you will think about it yourselves, you will see that what we laugh at is nearly always something incongruous, and yet is not amiss.

"Now, as to the means the Courtier ought to employ for the purpose of exciting laughter, and within what limits, I shall try to expound these to you, in so far as my own judgment enlightens me; for it is not seemly that the Courtier should always make men laugh, nor yet after the fashion of fools, drunken men, the silly, the inept, or buffoons. And although these kinds of men appear to be in demand at courts, yet they do not deserve to be called courtiers, but each should be called by his own name and judged for what he is.

"Moreover, we must carefully consider the scope and the limits of provoking laughter by derision, and who it is that we deride; for laughter is not produced by poking fun at some poor unfortunate soul, nor at some rascal or open criminal, because these latter seem to deserve a punishment greater than ridicule; and we are not inclined to make sport of poor wretches unless they boast of their misfortune and are proud and presumptuous. One must also take care not to make fun of those who are universally favored and loved by all and who are powerful, because in doing so a man can sometimes call down dangerous enmities upon himself. Yet it is proper to ridicule and laugh at the vices of those who are neither so wretched as to excite compassion, nor so wicked as to seem to deserve capital punishment, nor of so great a station that their wrath could do us much harm.

[47] "Moreover, you must know that the same sources from which laughable witticisms are derived provide us with serious phrases for praising or censuring, sometimes in the same words. Thus, in praising a generous man who shares all he has with his friends, we are accustomed to say that what he has is not his own; the same may be said in censuring a man who has stolen or acquired what he possesses by other evil means. We say too, 'She is a lady of parts,' mean-

ing to praise her for discretion and goodness; the same could be said in disprise of her, implying that she is the lady of many. But it is more a matter of these being the same situations rather than the same words: thus recently, when a lady was attending mass in church with three cavaliers, one of whom served her in love, a poor beggar came up who stood before the lady and began to beg alms of her; and he kept on begging of her with much insistence and pitiful plaint, yet she neither gave him alms withal nor refused him by any sign that told him to go his way in peace, but stood there distracted as if her mind were elsewhere. Then the cavalier who was in love with her said to his two companions: 'You see what I can expect from my lady, who is so cruel that she not only gives no alms to that poor naked wretch who is dying of hunger and is begging of her so eagerly and so repeatedly, but she doesn't even send him away: so much does she enjoy seeing a man languish in misery before her and implore her favor in vain.'

"One of his two friends replied: 'That is not cruelty; it is this lady's tacit way of teaching you that she is never pleased with an importunate suitor.'

"The other answered: 'Nay, it is a warning to signify that, even though she does not give what is asked of her, she still likes to be begged for it.'

"There you see how the fact that the lady did not send the poor man away gave rise to words of severe censure, of modest praise, and of cutting satire.

[48] "To go back now and declare the kinds of pleasantries that pertain to our subject, I say that in my opinion there are three varieties, even though messer Federico mentioned only two: one, the long narrative, urbane and amusing, that tells how something turned out; the other, the sudden and sharp readiness of a single phrase. But we will add a third sort called practical jokes, in which both long narratives and short sayings find their place, and sometimes action as well.

"Now the first is of such extended discourse as to amount almost to storytelling; and to give you an example: at just the time when Pope Alexander the Sixth died and Pius the Third was created Pope, your fellow Mantuan, Duchess, messer Antonio Agnello, being at Rome and in the palace, happened to be speaking of the death of the one Pope and the creation of the other; and in the course of expressing various opinions about this to some of his friends, he said: 'Gentlemen, even in the time of Catullus, doors began to speak without tongues and to hear without ears,[4] and thus to disclose adulteries. Nowadays, although men are not as worthy as in those

4. Catullus, *Carmen* LXVII, a dialogue between the poet and a door.

times, it may be that doors (many of which are made of ancient marble, at least here in Rome) have the same powers they had then; and for my part I believe that the two doors we see here might dispel all our doubts if we cared to learn from them.'

"Then the gentlemen present were very curious, waiting to see what the outcome of this was to be. Whereupon messer Antonio, continuing to walk back and forth, suddenly looked up at one of the doors of the hall in which they were strolling, paused a moment, and pointed out to his companions the inscription over it, which bore the name of Pope Alexander, followed by a V and an I, signifying Sixth, as you know; and he said: 'See what this door says: *Alessandro Papa VI*, which means that he became Pope by means of the violence he resorted to, and that he made use of violence rather than reason.[5] Now let us see if from this other door we can learn anything about the new Pope.' And, turning to that other door quite casually, he showed the inscription *N PP V*, which meant *Nicolaus Papa Quintus*; and at once he said: 'Alas, bad news! This one says, *Nihil Papa Valet*.'[6]

[49] "Now you see how this kind of pleasantry has something elegant and admirable about it, and how becoming to a Courtier it is, whether the thing said be true or not; for in such cases a man can without blame invent as much as he pleases; and if he speaks the truth, he can adorn it with some little falsehood, in varying degree, according to the need. But perfect grace and true ability in this consist in setting forth what one wishes to express, with word and with gesture, so well and with such ease that those who hear will seem to see the things one tells take place before their very eyes. When done thus, it is so effective that it sometimes adorns and makes very amusing something which in itself may be neither very humorous nor very clever.

"And, although this kind of narrative requires gestures and the effectiveness of the spoken word, still even when written it sometimes proves effective. Who does not laugh when, in the Eighth Day of his *Decameron*, Giovanni Boccaccio tells how hard the priest of Varlungo would try to sing a *Kyrie* and a *Sanctus* when he knew that his Belcolore was in the church? His stories of Calandrino and many others are also amusing narratives.[7] Of much the same kind is the provoking of a laugh by mimicry or by imitation, as we say— in which up to now I have seen no one surpass our messer Roberto da Bari."

---

5. The play of words is on *vi* construed as the ablative form of the Latin noun *vis* meaning "force" or "violence," hence "vi" = "by force."

6. *Nihil Papa Valet:* "The Pope is worthless." The judgment on Pius III has reference to his gentle character and above all to the fact that he was Pope for only twenty-six days.

7. The priest of Varlungo is described in Boccaccio, *Decameron* VIII, 2; the stories about tricks played on Calandrino are in VIII, 3 and 6, and IX, 3 [*Editor*].

[50] "This would be no small praise," said messer Roberto, "if it were true, because certainly I would try to imitate the good rather than the bad, and if I could make myself resemble some men I know, I should count myself most fortunate. But I am afraid I know how to imitate only those things which provoke laughter, which things you have already said consist in some fault."

Messer Bernardo replied: "In some fault, yes, but not one that is unbecoming. And one must know that this imitation of which we are speaking requires talent; because, in addition to making our words and gestures fit, and setting before our hearers' eyes the face and manners of the man we are speaking of, we must be prudent and give much attention to the place, the time, and the persons with whom we speak, and not descend to buffoonery or go beyond bounds—which things you observe admirably, and therefore I think that you must know them all. For in truth it would be unseemly for a gentleman to make faces, weep and laugh, mimic voices, wrestle with himself, as Berto does, or put on peasant's clothes in front of everyone, like Strascino—and things of that sort, which suit them very well since that is their profession.

"But it behooves us to make use of this kind of imitation covertly and in passing, maintaining always the dignity of a gentleman, without using dirty words or performing acts wanting in decorum, nor contorting the face or person so beyond measure; but make our movements such that whoever hears or sees us may imagine from our words and gestures far more than what he sees and hears, and be moved thereby to laughter.

"Moreover, in this sort of imitation one must avoid jibes that are too cutting, especially when aimed at deformities of face or person; for just as bodily defects often provide excellent material for laughter to a man who makes discreet use of them, yet to adopt too sharp a manner in this is the act not only of a buffoon but of an enemy. Thus, although it is difficult, we must in this hold to the manner of our messer Roberto, as I have said, who mimics all men, and not without stinging them in their defects and when they themselves are present, yet no one is disturbed or seems to find reason to take it amiss. And I will not cite any instance of this, because we witness endless examples of it in him every day.

[51] "Much laughter is to be had (and this too in the manner of a narrative) from a well-turned account of certain slips on the part of some persons—small ones, however, and not deserving of any greater punishment—such as certain foolish utterances, sometimes simple and sometimes attended by a quick and cutting dash of madness; likewise certain extreme affectations; and sometimes an enormous and well-constructed lie. As when, a few days ago, our Cesare

told of a delightful piece of folly: he happened to be in the presence of the Podestà of this place and saw a peasant come forward to complain that he had been robbed of a donkey; who, on telling of his poverty and the way he had been deceived by that thief, to make his loss seem all the heavier, said: 'Messere, if you had seen my donkey, you would understand even better how much cause I have to complain; for, when he had his pack on, he looked like a very Tully.'[8]

"And one of our friends, meeting up with a herd of goats led by a huge buck, stopped and with a look of wonder said: 'Look at the fine buck: he looks like a St. Paul!'[9]

"Signor Gasparo tells of having known an old servant of Duke Ercole of Ferrara, who had offered his two sons to the Duke as pages; but, before they could begin to serve him, both boys died. When the Duke heard this, he condoled with the father affectionately, saying that he was very sorry, because the only time he had seen them they had seemed to him very pretty and intelligent lads. The father replied: 'My lord, what you saw was nothing; for in their last few days they had grown far more handsome and good than I could ever have believed, and they already sang together like two sparrow hawks.'

"And it was only the other day that one of our doctors was watching a man who had been condemned to be flogged about the public square, and took pity on him because (although his shoulders were bleeding fiercely) the wretch was walking as slowly as if he were out for a stroll to pass the time; whereupon this doctor said to him: 'Hurry along, poor fellow, and get your suffering over quickly.' At which the good man turned and stood a moment without speaking, gazing at the doctor as if amazed, then said: 'When you are flogged, you will hold to the gait that suits you, and now I will hold to the one that suits me.'

"You will not have forgotten the foolishness of that abbot of whom the Duke was telling not so long ago, who was present one day when Duke Federico was discussing what should be done with the great mass of earth which had been excavated for the foundations of this palace, which he was then building, and said: 'My lord, I have an excellent idea where to put it. Give orders that a great pit be dug, and without further trouble it can be put into that.' Duke Federico replied, not without laughter: 'And where shall we put the earth that is excavated in digging this pit of yours?' Said the abbot: 'Make it big enough to hold both.' And so, even though the Duke repeated several times that the larger the pit was made, the more earth would be excavated, the man could never get it into his head that it could not

8. Marcus Tullius Cicero.
9. St. Paul is traditionally depicted wearing a long beard.

be made big enough to hold both, and replied nothing save: 'Make it that much bigger!' Now you see what good judgment this abbot had."

[52] Then messer Pietro Bembo said: "And why do you not tell the one about your friend the Florentine commander, who was besieged in Castellina[1] by the Duke of Calabria? Finding one day certain poisoned crossbow missiles that had been shot from the camp, he wrote to the Duke that if war was to be waged so barbarously, he would have medicine put on his cannon shot, and then woe to the side that had the worst of it!"

Messer Bernardo laughed, and said: "Messer Pietro, if you do not hold your tongue, I will tell all the things (and they are not few) that I have myself seen and heard of your dear Venetians, especially when they try to ride horseback."

"Please don't tell them," replied messer Pietro, "and I will keep quiet about two delightful tales I know of the Florentines."

Messer Bernardo said: "They must have been Sienese rather, who often slip in this way; such as one recently who, on hearing certain letters read in Council, wherein the phrase 'the aforesaid' was used (to avoid repeating so often the name of the man spoken of), said to the one who was reading: 'Stop there a moment and tell me, is this Aforesaid friendly to our city?'"

Messer Pietro laughed and said: "I am speaking of the Florentines, not of the Sienese."

"Then speak on," added signora Emilia, "and do not be so on your guard about it."

Messer Pietro continued: "When the Florentines were waging war against the Pisans, they sometimes found that their funds were exhausted by the many expenses; and one day when in the Council they were discussing the means of finding money for current needs, after many ways had been proposed, one of the eldest citizens said: 'I have thought of two ways in which we could raise a fair sum of money without much trouble. One of these is this: Since we get no revenue greater than what comes from the customs levied at the gates of Florence, and since we have eleven gates, let us at once have eleven more built, and thus we shall double our revenue from that source. The other way is to give orders immediately that the mints in Pistoia and Prato be set running as in Florence, and that they do nothing there day and night but mint money, and let it all be gold ducats: this latter course, to my mind, is the quicker and less costly."

---

1. Castellina, a fortified town in the Chianti region between Florence and Siena. The date alluded to is probably 1478.

[53] There was much laughter at this citizen's subtle scheme; and when the laughter had subsided, signora Emilia said: "Messer Bernardo, will you allow messer Pietro to ridicule the Florentines in this manner without taking your revenge?"

Still laughing, messer Bernardo replied: "I will forgive him this affront, for if he has displeased me in ridiculing the Florentines, he has pleased me in obeying you, which I too would always do."

Then messer Cesare said: "I heard a delightful blunder uttered by a Brescian who went to Venice this year for the Feast of the Ascension, and in my presence was telling some of his companions about the fine things he had seen there: how much merchandise there was, and how much silverware, spices, cloth, and fabrics; then the Signory went forth with great pomp to wed the sea in the *Bucentaur*,[2] with so many handsomely dressed gentlemen on board, so much music and singing, that it seemed a paradise. And when one of his companions asked him which kind of music he liked best of what he had heard, he said: 'It was all good; but I noted especially a man playing on a strange trumpet which with every move he would shove down his throat more than two palms' length, and then suddenly he would draw it out, then shove it down again; you never saw a greater marvel!'"

Then everyone laughed, understanding the silly notion of the man, who imagined that the player was thrusting down his throat the part of the trombone that disappears when it slides in.

[54] Then messer Bernardo went on: "Affectation is tedious when it is mediocre, but it can cause much laughter when it is extravagant: such as that which we hear sometimes from the mouth of some persons on the subject of greatness, courage, or nobility; or sometimes from women on beauty or fastidiousness. As was the case recently with a lady at a certain great festival where she appeared loath and abstracted; and when asked what she was thinking about that could make her so unhappy, she answered: 'I was thinking of something that disturbs me much whenever it comes to my mind, and I cannot drive it from my heart; and this is that on the universal Judgment Day, when all must rise in their bodies and appear naked before the tribunal of Christ, I cannot endure the distress I feel at the thought that my body will have to be seen naked along with the rest.' Such affectations, because they exceed a limit, cause laughter rather than tedium.

"You are all familiar with those splendid lies so well turned that they cause us to laugh. And that friend of ours who never lets us want for them told me an excellent one of the kind the other day."

2. *Bucentaur* (Italian *Bucentoro*), the name of the galley used in the great ceremony of "wedding the sea," held in Venice on Ascension Day.

[55] Then the Magnifico Giuliano said: "Be that as it may, it cannot be better or more subtle than the one a fellow Tuscan of ours, a certain merchant of Lucca, reported the other day as a positive fact."

"Do tell us," said the Duchess.

The Magnifico Giuliano replied, laughing: "This merchant, so the story goes, finding himself in Poland once, decided to buy a lot of sables with the intention of taking them to Italy and making a great profit from them. After many negotiations, being unable to enter Muscovy himself (because of the war between the King of Poland and the Duke of Muscovy), he arranged through some persons of the country that on an appointed day certain Muscovite merchants should come with their sables to the frontier of Poland, where he promised to be to transact the affair. And so, proceeding with his companions toward Muscovy, the man of Lucca reached the Dnieper, which he found frozen over as hard as marble, and saw that the Muscovites were already on the other bank, but approached no nearer than the width of the river (being fearful of the Poles because of suspicions aroused by the war). So, when the parties had recognized one another, the Muscovites, after some signaling, began to shout and declare the price they wanted for their sables; but the cold was so extreme that they were not heard, for before reaching the other bank (where the merchant of Lucca and his interpreters were) the words froze in the air and hung there frozen and caught in such a way that the Poles, who knew how this could be, resorted to the measure of building a great fire in the very middle of the river, because, to their way of thinking, the words reached there still warm before they were frozen and stopped; and the river was quite solid enough to bear the fire easily. Whereupon, this being done, the words (that had remained frozen for all of an hour) began to melt and descend with a murmur like snow melting from the mountains in May; and at once the words were clearly heard, even though the Muscovites had already departed: but, because it seemed to the merchant that the words asked too high a price for the sables, he would not accept the offer and so came back without them."

[56] Thereupon everyone laughed, and messer Bernardo said: "Truly, the story I want to tell you is not so clever; however, it is a good one, and goes so:

"Some days ago a certain friend you have heard me speak of before was telling about the country or world recently discovered by the Portuguese sailors, and of the various animals and other things they bring back to Portugal from there, and he told me he had seen a monkey (of a sort very different from those we are accustomed to see) that played chess most admirably. And, among other occasions, when the gentleman who had brought it was one day before the King of Portugal and engaged in a game of chess with it, the monkey made several moves so skillful as to press him hard, and finally it checkmated him. Whereupon, being annoyed, as losers at that game usually are, the gentleman took up the king piece (which, in the Portuguese fashion, was very big) and struck the monkey a great blow upon the head with it; whereupon the monkey jumped back, complaining loudly and seemed to be demanding justice of the King for the wrong that had been done it. Then the gentleman invited it to play again; and, after refusing for a while by means of signs, it finally began to play again and, as it had done before, once more drove him into a corner. At last, seeing that it was going to be able to checkmate the gentleman, the monkey conceived a clever way to keep from being struck again: without revealing what it was about, it quietly put its right paw under the gentleman's left elbow (which was fastidiously resting on a taffeta cushion) and, in the same moment that with its left hand it checkmated him with a pawn, with its right it quickly snatched the cushion and held it over its head as a protection against the blows. Then it leaped before the King gleefully, as though to celebrate its victory. Now you see how wise, wary, and discreet that monkey was."

Then messer Cesare Gonzaga said: "That monkey must have been a doctor among monkeys, and a great authority; and I think that the Republic of Indian Monkeys must have sent it to Portugal to win fame in a foreign land."

Thereupon everyone laughed, both at the story and at the addition that messer Cesare had given it.

[57] Then, continuing the discussion, messer Bernardo said: "Now you have heard all that I have to set forth regarding those pleasantries that achieve their effect by extended discourse; hence, it is well to speak now of those that consist of a single saying and the ready wit whereof lies in a mere remark or word. And just as in the first kind of humorous talk one ought in his narrative and mimicry to avoid resembling buffoons and parasites and those who make others laugh by their own foolishness, so in these short sayings the Courtier must take care not to appear malicious and spiteful, and not to utter witticisms and *arguzie* solely to annoy and hurt; because such men often suffer deservedly in all their person for the sins of their tongue.

[58] "Now, of the ready pleasantries that consist of a brief saying, those are the keenest which arise from an ambiguity (although they do not always cause laughter because they are oftener praised for being ingenious rather than for being comical); as our messer Anni-

bale Paleotto said some days ago to someone who was recommending
a tutor to teach his sons grammar and who, after praising the tutor as
being very learned, said (coming to the matter of the stipend) that,
besides money, the man desired a room furnished for living and sleeping because he had no *letto* (bed); whereupon messer Annibale at
once replied: 'And how can he be learned if he has not *letto* (read)?'
Here you see how well he played upon the double meaning of the
phrase *non aver letto* ['to have no bed' or 'not to have read']. But since
these punning witticisms are very sharp, in that a man takes words in
a sense different from that in which everyone else takes them, they
seem, as I have said, to cause marvel rather than laughter, except
when they are combined with some other kind of saying.

"Now the kind of witticism that is most used to excite laughter is
made when we are expecting to hear one thing and the speaker
utters another, and this is called 'the unexpected.' And if punning be
combined with this, the witticism becomes most pungent, as when
the other day there was a discussion about making a fine brick floor
(*un bel mattonato*) in the Duchess's room, and after much talk, you,
Giancristoforo, said: 'If we could take the Bishop of Potenza and
have him well flattened out, it would be much to the purpose,
because he is the craziest man born (*il più bel matto nato*).' Everyone laughed much, for by dividing the word *mattonato* you made the
pun; moreover, saying that it would be well to flatten out a bishop
and lay him as the floor of a room was the unexpected thing for the
listener; and so the quip was very sharp and laughable.

[59] "But there are many kinds of punning witticisms; and we must
take care, using our words to twit subtly, and avoiding those that
cause the quip to fall flat or appear forced; and avoid those, as we
have said, that are too cutting. As where several had gathered in the
house of one of their friends who was blind in one eye, and when
the blind man invited the company to stay for dinner, all took their
leave except one who said: 'I will stay with you because I see you
have an empty place for one'; and so saying he pointed with his finger to the empty socket. You see that this is too bitter and rude, for
it wounded the man without any reason, nor had the speaker first
been wounded himself; moreover, he said what could be said to any
and all blind men, and such universal things give no pleasure
because they have the appearance of being thought up beforehand.
And of this sort was the jibe at a man who had lost his nose: 'And
where do you hang your spectacles?' or 'With what do you smell
roses in the summer?'

[60] "But, among other witticisms, those are very well turned that
are made by taking the very words and sense of another man's jibe

and turning them against him, piercing him with his own weapons; as when a litigant, to whom his adversary had said in the judge's presence: 'Why do you bark so?' replied at once: 'Because I see a thief.'

"Another of this sort was when Galeotto da Narni was passing through Siena and stopped in the street to ask where the inn was; and a Sienese, seeing how fat he was, said, laughing: 'Other men carry their valise behind but this man carries his in front.' Galeotto at once replied: 'So one does in a land of thieves.'

[61] "There is yet another kind that we call 'a play on words,' and this consists in changing a word by either adding or omitting a letter or a syllable; as when someone said: 'You are more learned in the Latrin tongue than in Greek.' And you, signora, had a letter addressed to you, 'To Signora Emilia *Impia*.'[3]

"It is also amusing to quote a verse or so, putting it to a use other than that intended by the author, or some other well-known saying, used in the same way or with a word in it changed. As when a gentleman who had an ugly and disagreeable wife, when asked how he was, replied: 'You can imagine when *Furiarum maxima juxta me cubat*.'[4] And messer Geronimo Donato, while visiting the stations[5] at Rome in Lent along with many other gentlemen, met up with a company of beautiful Roman ladies; and when one of the gentlemen said: '*Quot coelum stellas, tot habet tua Roma puellas*,' he replied at once: '*Pascua quotque haedos, tot habet tua Roma cinaedos*,' pointing to a company of young men coming from the other direction.[6]

"And messer Marcantonio della Torre addressed the Bishop of Padua in like manner. There being a nunnery at Padua in charge of a friar believed to be a man of very upright life and learned, it came to pass that, as the friar went familiarly about the convent and often confessed the nuns, five of them (more than half of them) became pregnant; and the thing being discovered, the friar wanted to flee but could not. The bishop had him seized, and he at once confessed that, being tempted of the devil, he had gotten those five nuns with child; so that the bishop was firmly resolved to punish him most severely. But as this man was learned, he had many friends who all made the effort to help him; and, among others, messer Marcanto-

---

3. The name *Pio* means *pious*, and *impio, impia* the opposite.
4. The play is on Virgil's *"Furiarum maxima iuxta accubat"* (*Aeneid* VI, 605–6): "reclining hard by, the greatest of the Furies . . ." here changed to read: "The greatest of the Furies sleeps beside me."
5. The stations of the cross, a series of fourteen images, in a church or along a path leading to a shrine, representing the stages of Jesus' sufferings; they are visited in succession by worshipers [*Editor*].
6. Ovid's verse (*Ars amatoria* I, 59): "Your Rome has as many girls as the heaven has stars" is altered to mean "Your Rome has as many satyrs in it as the meadows have lambs."

nio went to the bishop to implore some pardon for him. The bishop did not wish to hear them at all, but finally, as they kept on pleading and recommending the culprit, urging in his excuse the temptations of his position, the frailty of human nature, and many other things, the bishop said: 'I will do nothing for him, because I shall have to give account to God of this matter.' And when they repeated their pleas, the bishop said: 'What answer shall I give to God on the Judgment Day when He says to me, *Give an account of thy stewardship?*' Then messer Marcantonio at once answered: 'My lord, say what the Evangelist says: *Lord, thou deliveredst unto me five talents: behold I have gained beside them five talents more.*'[7] Whereupon the bishop could not refrain from laughing, and greatly mitigated his anger and the punishment that was in store for the offender.

[62] "It is also amusing to interpret names and pretend some reason why the man who is spoken of has such a name, or why something is done. As a few days ago when Proto da Lucca (who is quite a wit, as you know) asked for the bishopric of Caglio, and the Pope replied: 'Do you not know that in the Spanish tongue *caglio* means *I keep silent*? You are a babbler, and it would not be fitting for a bishop never to be able to utter his title without telling a lie. So be silent now (*caglia*)!' Here Proto made a reply which, although it was not of this kind, yet was no less to the point; for having repeated his request several times, and, seeing that it was to no avail, at last he said: 'Holy Father, if Your Holiness grants me this bishopric, it will not be without some gain, for I shall leave Your Holiness two offices (*ufficii*).' 'And what offices have you to leave?' said the Pope. Proto replied: 'The full office (*ufficio grande*), and the office of the Madonna (*ufficio della Madonna*).'[8] Then the Pope could not help laughing, although he was a very stern man.

"Another man, also at Padua, said that Calfurnio was so named because he used to stoke (*scaldare*) ovens (*forni*).[9] And when one day I asked Fedra why it was that on Good Friday, when the Church prayed not only for Christians but even for pagans and Jews, no mention was made of cardinals along with bishops and other prelates, he answered me that cardinals were intended in the prayer that says: 'Let us pray for heretics and scismatics.'

7. Cf. Luke 16:2: "Give an account of thy stewardship," said by the rich man to his servant. And Matthew 25:20: "And so he that had received five talents came and brought other five talents, saying, Lord, thou deliveredst unto me five talents: behold, I have gained beside them five talents more."
8. The play is on the word *ufficio*: "office," in its meanings (1) post and (2) the breviary. The "office of the Madonna" was much shorter than the other or "full office."
9. A rival of Calfurnio is said to have written to him that he got his name from the fact that he was born in the mountains near Bergamo and was the son of a charcoal burner. The play on words is based on the Latin *calescit furnos*.

"And our Count Ludovico said that the reason why I reproached a lady for using a certain very shiny cosmetic was that I could see myself in her face when it was painted, as in a mirror, and that, being ugly, I did not like to see myself.

"Of this sort was that quip of messer Camillo Paleotto to messer Antonio Porcaro, who, in speaking of a friend of his who told the priest at confession that he fasted willingly and went to mass and the sacred offices and did all the good in the world, said: 'Instead of accusing himself, that man praises himself; to which messer Camillo replied: 'On the contrary, he confesses these things because he thinks it is a great pity (*gran peccato*) to do them.'[1]

"Do you not remember what an excellent reply the Prefect made the other day? Giantommaso Galeotto was surprised that a certain man was asking two hundred ducats for a horse because, as Giantommaso said, it was not worth a cent and, among its other faults, would shy so at weapons that no one could make it go near them—the Prefect (wishing to censure the man for cowardice) said: 'If that horse has the habit of running away from weapons, I wonder that he does not ask a thousand ducats for it!'

[63] "Moreover, the same word is sometimes used, but in a sense different from the usual one. As the Duke, when about to cross a very rapid river, said to a trumpeter: 'Cross over' (*passa*), and the trumpeter turned, hat in hand, and said respectfully: 'After Your Lordship' (*passi la Signoria vostra*).

ᐅ "Another amusing kind of jest is that in which a man appears to take the speaker's words but not his meaning. As happened this year, when a German at Rome, meeting one evening our messer Beroaldo, whose pupil he was, said: '*Domine magister, Deus det vobis bonum sero*'; and Beroaldo at once answered: '*Tibi malum cito.*'[2]

"Again, once when Diego de Chignones was at the Great Captain's table, and another Spaniard, who was dining with them and who, meaning to ask for drink, said: '*Vino*'; Diego replied: '*Y no lo conoscistes,*' with a dig at the fellow for being a heretic.[3]

"Again, messer Giacomo Sadoleto asked Beroaldo, who was insisting on going to Bologna at all costs: 'What brings you to leave Rome at this time where there are so many pleasures, to go to Bologna which is full of turmoil?' Beroaldo replied: 'I am obliged to go to Bologna on three counts,' and had already raised three fingers

---

1. The play is on *gran peccato* which can mean either (1) a great sin or (2) "It's a great pity."
2. The German means to say "May God grant you a good morning," but mistakenly says "May God give you good *late*" (i.e., "be long in giving you good"). Beroaldo's reply is in kind: "May He *quickly* give you evil."
3. The play is on the word *vino* in Spanish meaning (1) "wine" and (2) "He came." "*Vino y no lo conoscistes*" thus echoes John 8:55: "Yet ye have not known him."

of his left hand to enumerate three reasons for his going, when messer Giacomo quickly interrupted him and said: 'The three counts that make you go to Bologna are: first, Count Ludovico da San Bonifacio; second, Count Ercole Rangone; third, the Count of Pepoli.' Whereupon everyone laughed, because these three counts had been pupils of Beroaldo and were handsome youths who were then studying at Bologna.

"Now we laugh much at this kind of witticism, because it brings with it a reply different from what we were expecting to hear and our very error amuses us in such matters; and when we find that we are wrong in expecting what we did, we laugh.

[64] "But the modes of speech and the figures that belong to grave and serious talk are nearly always suited to pleasantries and games as well. Consider that words set in opposition increase the charm, when one contrasting clause is counterbalanced by another. This same manner is often most witty. Thus, a Genoese, who was a great spendthrift, was reproached by a very miserly usurer, who said to him: 'When will you ever stop throwing away your riches?' And he replied: 'When you stop stealing other men's.'

"And since, as we have said, the same topics which are the source of sharp pleasantries can often yield serious words of praise as well, it is a most graceful and apt method in either case for a man to admit or confirm what another speaker says, but take it in a way that was not intended. Thus, some days ago a village priest was saying mass to his flock, and, after he had announced the festivals of the week, he began the general confession in the people's name, saying: 'I have sinned in doing evil, in speaking evil, in thinking evil,' and what follows, naming all the deadly sins; at which a friend and close companion of the priest, to play a joke on him, said to the bystanders: 'Bear witness all of you to what by his own mouth he confesses he has done, for I mean to inform the bishop of this.'

"This same method was used by Sallaza dalla Pedrada to pay a compliment to a lady with whom he was speaking. When he had praised her not only for her virtue but for her beauty, and when she had replied to him that she did not deserve such praise because she was already an old lady, he said to her: 'Madam, your age is nothing but your resemblance to the angels, who are the first and eldest creatures that God ever made.'

[65] "Jocose sayings are very useful as taunts, even as are grave sayings for the purpose of praise; and so are well-turned metaphors, and especially if used in repartee and if the one who replies keeps the same metaphor the other person used. Of such kind was the answer given to messer Palla de' Strozzi, who, being exiled from Flo-

rence, sent back one of his men on a certain business and told him in a threatening tone: 'And tell Cosimo de' Medici for me that the hen is brooding.'[4] The messenger did the errand commanded him, and Cosimo, without pausing to think, replied to him at once: 'And do you tell messer Palla for me that a hen cannot brood well outside the nest.'

"Again, messer Camillo Porcaro gracefully praised signor Marc 'Antonio Colonna with a metaphor. The latter, having heard that in an oration messer Camillo had celebrated certain Italian gentlemen who were famous in war and had spoken very highly of him among the rest, thanked him, saying: 'Messer Camillo, you have dealth with your friends as merchants sometimes do with their money who, finding that they have a false ducat, put it among many good coins and pass it off in this way: so you, to honor me (although I am worth little), have put me among such worthy and excellent gentlemen that I may pass for good through their merit.' Then messer Camillo replied: 'Those who counterfeit ducats are given to gilding them so well that they seem to the eye much finer than the good ones; thus, if there were counterfeiters of men as there are of ducats, we might rightfully suspect that you were false since you are of much finer and brighter metal than any of the rest.'

"Consider that this situation provided the occasion for both kinds of witticism; and so do many others, of which countless instances could be cited, and especially in the case of serious sayings. Like the one uttered by the Great Captain, who, when he was seated at the table and all the places were already taken, saw that there remained standing two Italian gentlemen who had fought very well in the war: he at once stoop up and had all the others rise, to make a place for these two, saying: 'Allow these gentlemen to find a seat and eat, for were it not for them, the rest of us would now not have anything to eat.' Another time he said to Diego Garzia, who was urging him to withdraw from a dangerous position where cannon shot was falling: 'Since God did not put any fear in your heart, do not try to put any in mine.'

"And King Louis, now King of France, on being told soon after his coronation that then was the time to punish his enemies who had so much wronged him while he was Duke of Orléans, replied that it was not up to the King of France to avenge wrongs done to the Duke of Orléans.

[66] "A cutting witticism can often be facetious and have a certain gravity that does not cause laughter. As when Djem Othman,

---

4. In Italian and in this context, the expression "la gallina cova" can mean "to brood revenge."

brother to the Grand Turk, being a captive at Rome, said that jousting, as we practice it in Italy, seemed to him too much if done in
play and too little if done in earnest. And on being told how agile
and active King Ferdinand the Younger was in running, jumping,
vaulting, and the like, he said that in his country slaves engaged in
such exercises but that from boyhood gentlemen learned to be liberal, and were praised for that.

"Of much the same kind too, but somewhat more laughable, was
what the Archbishop of Florence said to Cardinal Alessandrino, that
men have only their goods, their body, and their soul: their goods are
harried by lawyers, their body by physicians, and their soul by theologians."

Then the Magnifico Giuliano replied: "One might add to this
what Nicoletto used to say, that we seldom find a lawyer who goes
to law himself, a physician who takes physic, or a theologian who is
a good Christian."

[67] Messer Bernardo laughed, then went on: "Of this sort there are
countless instances, uttered by great lords and very grave men. But
we also laugh often at comparisons, such as the one our Pistoia
wrote to Serafino: 'Send back the big traveling bag that looks like
you'; for, if you remember, Serafino did look very much like a big
traveling bag.

"There are some, moreover, who take pleasure in comparing
men and women to horses, dogs, birds, and often to chests, chairs,
wagons, chandeliers; which is sometimes to the point and sometimes falls very flat, for in this one has to take into consideration
the time, place, persons, and other things that we have repeatedly
mentioned."

Then signor Gaspar Pallavicino said: "That was an amusing comparison that signor Giovanni Gonzaga made of Alexander the Great
and his own son Alessandro."

"I do not know it," replied messer Bernardo.

Signor Gasparo said: "Signor Giovanni was playing at three dice
and, as was his wont, had lost many ducats and was still losing; and
his son signor Alessandro (who, though a mere boy, yet is quite as
fond of gambling as his father) stood watching him with great attention and seemed very sad. The Count of Pianella, who was present
with many other gentlemen, said: 'Look, Sir, how little pleased
signor Alessandro is at your losing: he can't wait for you to win so
that he can have some of the winnings. Therefore, relieve him of his
suffering and, before you lose what is left, give him at least one
ducat so that he too can go gamble with his companions.' Then
signor Giovanni said: 'You are mistaken, because Alessandro is not
thinking of any such trifle. But just as it is written that Alexander

the Great, while still a boy, on hearing that his father Philip had won a great battle and had taken a certain kingdom, began to weep; and, when asked why he wept, answered that it was because he was afraid his father would conquer so much territory that he would leave nothing for him to conquer; in the same way my son Alessandro is grieved and on the point of weeping, seeing that I, his father, am losing, because he fears I am losing so much that I shall leave nothing for him to lose.'"

[68] Whereupon, after some laughter, messer Bernardo continued: "Moreover, we must avoid impiety in our jests, for then the thing reaches the point of trying to be witty by blaspheming and seeking new ways to do that; wherein a man is seen to look for glory in a thing that deserves not only blame but severe punishment: which is abominable; hence, those persons who try to be amusing by showing little reverence for God deserve to be banished from the society of all gentlemen. And those persons too who are obscene and foul in their speech, and who show no respect for the presence of ladies, and seem to have no other amusement than to make them blush with shame, and who to that end are constantly seeking witticisms and *arguzie*. As in Ferrara this year, at a banquet attended by many ladies, there were a Florentine and a Sienese (who are usually hostile, as you know). To taunt the Florentine the Sienese said: 'We have married Siena to the Emperor, and have given Florence to him as a dowry'—and he said this because it was reported at the time that the Sienese had given the Emperor a certain sum of money and that he had taken the city under his protection. The Florentine quickly replied: 'Siena will first be possessed' ("possessed" in the French sense, but he used the Italian word), 'then in good time the dowry will be discussed.' The retort, as you see, was clever, but, being made in the presence of ladies, became indecent and unseemly."

[69] Then signor Gaspar Pallavicino said: "Women delight in hearing nothing else, and you wish to deprive them of it. For my part, moreover, I have found myself blushing with shame far more often at words uttered by women than by men."

"I was not speaking of such women," said messer Bernardo, "but of virtuous ladies who deserve reverence and honor from every gentleman."

Signor Gasparo said: "One would have to invent a very subtle rule for distinguishing between them, because more often than not those who seem to be the best are in fact quite the contrary."

Then messer Bernardo said, laughing: "If our signor Magnifico were not present here, who is everywhere held to be the protector of women, I should undertake to reply to you; but I do not wish to offend him."

Here signora Emilia, also laughing, said: "Women have no need of any defender against an accuser of so little authority. Therefore, let signor Gasparo hold to this perverse opinion of his, which arises from his never having found a lady who would look at him, rather than from any fault on the part of women—and go on with your discussion of pleasantries."

[70] Then messer Bernardo said: "Indeed, Madam, it seems to me I have spoken of the many topics that are the sources of sharp witticisms and which have the more grace the more they are presented in a fine narrative. There are many others that could still be mentioned. As when, by overstatement or understatement, we say things that exceed verisimilitude in some incredible way; and of this sort was what Mario da Volterra said of a certain prelate, that he held himself to be so great a man that, when he entered St. Peter's, he would stoop in order not to strike his head against the architrave of the portal. Again, our Magnifico here said that his servant Golpino was so lean and thin that one morning, in blowing on the fire to kindle it, the fellow had been carried by the smoke all the way up the chimney to the top; but, happening to catch crosswise against one of the little openings, he had had the good fortune not to drift away with the smoke. Again, messer Agostino Bevazzano said that a miser, who had been unwilling to sell his grain while the price was high, had afterward hanged himself in despair from a rafter of his bedroom when he found that the price had fallen very low; and, on hearing the noise, one of his servants ran in, saw the miser hanging, and quickly cut the rope, thus saving him from death. Whereupon the miser, when he had regained his senses, was determined his servant should pay him for the rope that had been cut. Of this same sort also would seem to be what Lorenzo de' Medici said to a boring buffoon: 'You wouldn't make me laugh if you tickled me.' And similarly he answered another stupid fellow who had found him in bed very late one morning and who rebuked him for sleeping so late, saying: 'Already I have been to the New Market and the Old, and outside the San Gallo gate and around the walls for exercise, and have done a thousand things besides, and you are still asleep!' Then said Lorenzo: 'What I have dreamed in one hour is worth more than what you have done in four.'

[71] "It is also good when by a retort we reprehend something without seeming to mean to do so. As when the Marquess Federico of Mantua, father of our Duchess, was at table with many gentlemen, and one of them, after eating a whole tureen of stew, said: 'Marquess, pardon me' and, so saying, began to guzzle the broth that was

left. To which the Marquess at once replied: 'Ask pardon of the swine, for to me you do no offense at all.' Again, to censure a tyrant who was falsely reputed to be generous, messer Niccolò Leonico said: "Think what generosity there is in this man: he gives away not only his own property, but that of other men as well.'

[72] "Quite a nice sort of pleasantry is that too which consists in a certain dissimulation, when one thing is said and another is tacitly understood. To be sure, I do not mean something wholly contrary, such as calling a dwarf a giant, a Negro white, or a very ugly man most handsome, for these are contraries that are too evident—although these too sometimes bring laughter; but I mean when, in a stern and solemn manner of speech, someone says humorously in jest what he does not really think. As when a gentleman was telling what was plainly a lie to messer Augustino Foglietta and was affirming it stoutly (since he appeared to be having great difficulty in believing it), messer Augustino at last said: 'My good man, if I may ever hope to enjoy a kindness from you, please do me the great favor of allowing me not to believe what you are saying.' But when the other kept on repeating and swearing that it was the truth, he at last said: 'Since you insist, I will believe it for your sake, because the fact is, I would do you an even greater favor than this.' Don Giovanni di Cardona said something much like this about a man who wished to leave Rome: 'In my opinion, the fellow is ill-advised, because he's so wicked that if he stayed on in Rome, he could in time become a cardinal.' Of this sort too is what Alfonso Santa Croce said (who had shortly before suffered certain outrages at the hands of the Cardinal di Pavia) who, as he was strolling with certain gentlemen outside Bologna near the place of public execution and saw a man who had recently been hanged, turned toward the body with a certain pensive air, and said loudly enough that everyone heard him: 'Happy you who do not have to deal with the Cardinal of Pavia.'

[73] "This sort of pleasantry with an ironic twist seems most becoming in great men, since it is grave and pungent and can be used in jocose as well as in grave matters. Hence, many ancients (and these among the most esteemed) have employed it, like Cato and Scipio Africanus the Younger; but the philosopher Socrates is said to have excelled above all men in this; and, in our own time, King Alfonso I of Aragon: who, when about to dine one morning, took off the many precious rings he was wearing on his fingers in order not to get them wet when he washed his hands, and so gave them to the first person who happened to be at hand, as if without looking to see who he was. This servant thought that the King had not noticed who took them, and that because of much weightier cares he might well forget all

about it; and in this he was the more confirmed when he saw that the King did not ask for them again. Then when days and weeks passed and he heard never a word about this, he thought he was surely safe. And thus, nearly a year after this had happened, he came forward again one morning when the King was about to dine, and held out his hand to receive the rings; at which the King, bending close to his ear, said to him: 'Let those be enough for you, because these will do nicely for someone else.' You see how pungent, ingenious, and solemn the saying was, and truly worthy of the lofty spirit of an Alexander.

[74] "Similar to this manner tending to the ironical is another in which an evil thing is called by a polite name. As in what the Great Captain said to one of his gentlemen, who, after the Battle of Cerignola when the day had been won, came up to him in the richest armor imaginable as though ready for battle. Whereupon the Great Captain, turning to Ugo di Cardona, said: 'Fear the storm no more, for St. Elmo has appeared'; and with these polite words he stung the man, for you know that St. Elmo always appears to sailors after the storm, giving the sign of fair weather; and thus the Great Captain meant that this gentleman's appearance was the sign that the danger was entirely over. Another time, signor Ottaviano Ubaldini was at Florence in the company of certain citizens of great authority when the discussion turned on soldiers, and one of them asked him if he knew Antonello da Forlì, who had at that time fled the Florentine State. Signor Ottaviano replied: 'I do not know him except that I have always heard him spoken of as a prompt soldier.' Whereupon another Florentine said: 'You see how prompt he is, when he sallies forth without asking leave.'

[75] "Clever too are those witticisms in which we twist another's words to a meaning not intended. And I take to be of this sort what our Duke replied to the castellan who lost San Leo⁵ when that state was taken by Pope Alexander and given to Duke Valentino. The Duke was in Venice at the time and many of his subjects came continually to give him secret news as to how the affairs of state were going; and among others there came this castellan, who excused himself as best he could, putting the blame on his own bad luck, and saying: 'Never fear, my lord: I am still capable of bringing about the recovery of San Leo.' Then the Duke replied: 'Don't go to any more trouble about this, for the losing of it was already one way of making it possible to recover it.'

"There are certain other sayings, such as when a known wit says something in the manner of a fool: as, the other day, messer Camillo

5. San Leo was a fortress some eighteen miles from Urbino (near San Marino), vital to her system of defenses.

Palleotto said of someone: "The man was such a fool, to die when he was just beginning to get rich.'

"Of like kind is a certain spicy and keen dissimulation wherein a man (a man of wit, as I have said) pretends not to understand what he does understand. As what the Marquess Federico of Mantua said when he was being plagued by a tiresome fellow who complained that certain neighbors of his were snaring the doves in his dovecote, and stood holding one of them hanging dead by one foot in a snare just as he had found it, replied that he would have the matter looked into. But the fellow persisted in complaining of his loss, not once but repeatedly, continuing to hold up the hanged dove and to say: 'And what, my lord, do you think should be done about this?' At last the Marquess said: 'I think the dove ought on no account to be buried in church, for, since it hanged itself, we must regard it as a suicide.'

"Of somewhat the same kind was the retort which Scipio Nasica made to Ennius. Once when Scipio went to Ennius' house to speak with him, and called to him from the street, one of his maids replied that he was not at home. Scipio clearly heard Ennius himself tell the maid to say he was not at home; and so he went away. Not long afterward, Ennius came to Scipio's house and called to him from below; whereupon Scipio himself called out that he was not at home. Then Ennius replied: 'What! Do I not know your voice?' Scipio said: 'You are very discourteous. The other day I believed your maid when he said you were not at home, and now you will not believe the like from me.'[6]

[76] "It is delightful too when a man is given a jibe in the very thing in which he first jibed his fellow. As in the case of messer Alonso Carillo who, being at the Spanish court and having committed some trifling youthful errors, was put in prison by the King's order and left there overnight. The following day he was taken out; whereupon he went to the palace in the morning and came into the hall where there were many cavaliers and ladies. And as they laughed about his imprisonment, signora Boadilla said: 'Signor Alonso, I felt very sorry about this misadventure of yours, because all who know you thought that the King was going to have you hanged.' Then Alonso said quickly: 'Madam, I too was much afraid of that; but then I had hope that you would ask my hand in marriage.' You see how sharp and witty this one was, because in Spain (as in many other places also) it is a custom that when a man is led to the gallows, his life is spared if a public courtesan asks to marry him.

"In like manner the painter Raphael replied to two cardinals with

6. The anecdote is told by Cicero, *De oratore* II, chs. 6–8.

whom he was on familiar terms and who in his presence (in order to make him talk) were finding fault with a picture he had painted—in which St. Peter and St. Paul were shown—saying that the two figures were too red in the face. Then Raphael replied at once: 'Gentlemen, you must not wonder at this, for I have made them so quite on purpose, since we must believe that St. Peter and St. Paul are as red in heaven as you see them here, out of shame that their church should be governed by such men as you.'

[77] "Those witticisms are very acute that contain a certain hidden touch of laughter: as in the case of a husband who was lamenting and weeping for his wife who had hanged herself on a fig tree, when another man came up to him, plucked him by the robe, and said: 'Brother, as a great favor, might I have a little branch of your fig tree to graft upon some tree in my garden?'

"There are certain other witticisms uttered slowly, with an air of patience and with a certain gravity, as when a peasant, who was carrying a box on his shoulders, jostled it against Cato, saying: 'Look out!' Cato replied: 'Have you anything on your shoulders other than that chest?'

"Moreover, we laugh when a man who has committed a blunder tries to mend it by saying something studied that seems silly, and yet aims at the end he intends, and with that attempts to recover himself. As not long ago in the Florentine Council, there were two enemies (as often happens in these republics), and one of them, a member of the Altoviti family, fell asleep. And, although his adversary, who was of the Alamanni family, did not have the floor and had not spoken, yet in order to raise a laugh, the man who sat next to Altoviti aroused him with a nudge of the elbow and said: 'Do you not hear what that man is saying? Make answer, as the Signors are asking for your opinion.' Whereupon Altoviti stood up all drowsy and, without stopping to think, said: 'Gentlemen, I say just the opposite of what Alamanni said.' Alamanni replied: 'Oh, but I have said nothing!' 'Then,' said Altoviti at once, 'the opposite of what you will say.' Of this kind too was what your Urbino physician, master Serafino, said to a peasant who had suffered such a blow in one eye that it was actually driven from his head, and yet had decided to go to master Serafino to be cured. On seeing him, although he knew it was impossible to cure him, yet in order to force money from his hands (even as the blow had forced the eye from his head), the doctor made him great promises to cure him. And thus he went on demanding money of him every day, declaring that within five or six days he would begin to recover his sight. The poor peasant gave him what little he had; then, seeing that the affair was going to be a lengthy one, he began to complain to the doctor and to say that he felt no better at all, and that he could no more see out of that eye than he might have done if he had never had it in his head. Finally master Serafino, seeing that he could no longer get much out of the man, said: 'Brother, you must have patience. You have lost your eye and there is no cure for you; and may God grant that you not lose your other eye as well.' On hearing this, the peasant began to weep and complain mightily, saying: 'Master, you have ruined me and stolen my money. I will complain to the Duke'; and he was shouting loudly. Then master Serafino was angry, and, to clear himself, said: 'Ah, wretched peasant! So you would wish to have two eyes like city folk and respectable people. Away with you, and be dammed!' And he put such fury into these words that the poor peasant was frightened to silence and went his way very quietly, believing himself to be in the wrong.

[78] "It is also delightful to explain or interpret a thing jocosely. As when at the court of Spain there appeared in the palace one morning a cavalier who was very ugly, with a wife who was most beautiful, both dressed in white damask[7] (*damasco*)—the queen said to Alonso Carillo: 'What do you think of these two, Alonso?' 'Madam!' replied Alonso, 'I think she is the *dama* (lady) and he is the *asco*' (which means a repulsive person). Again, Rafaello de' Pazzi saw a letter which the Prior of Messina had written to a lady of his acquaintance, the superscription of which read: 'This missive is to be delivered to the one who is the cause of my woes.' 'I think,' said Rafaello, 'that this letter must be addressed to Paolo Tolosa.' You know how the bystanders laughed, as everyone knew that Paolo Tolosa had lent the Prior ten thousand ducats, and he, being a great spend-thrift, never found any way to repay them.

"Similar to this is the giving of some friendly admonition in the form of advice, yet in a veiled way. As Cosimo de' Medici did to one of his friends who was very rich but had little learning, and who through Cosimo had obtained a mission away from Florence. When the man was setting out and asked Cosimo what method he thought he ought to follow to do well in this office of his, Cosimo replied: "Dress in rose color,[8] and say little.' Of the same sort was what Count Ludovico said to a man who wished to travel incognito through a certain dangerous place and did not know how he should disguise himself; and the Count, being asked about it, replied: 'Dress like a doctor or some other man of learning.' Again, Giannotto de' Pazzi said to someone who wished to make a military cloak

7. Figured woven material, often made of silk. "Cavalier": knight [*Editor*].
8. Rose was the color worn by the Florentine nobility.

of as many different colors as he could find: 'Imitate the Cardinal of Pavia in word and deed.'[9]

[79] "We laugh too at some things involving discrepancy. As when someone said the other day to messer Antonio Rizzo about a certain man from Forlì: 'His name is Bartolommeo, so you see how crazy he is!' And another: 'You are looking for master Stalla[1] and you have no horses!' Also: 'And yet the fellow lacks only money and brains!'

"And we laugh at certain other inconsistent things. Recently, a friend of ours was suspected of having the renunciation of a benefice forged, and, upon another priest's falling sick, Antonio Torello said to him: 'Why are you wasting time and don't send for that notary of yours and see if you can't get your hands on this benefice too?' And we laugh likewise at some things that are not consentaneous: as the other day when the Pope sent for messer Gianluca da Pontremolo and messer Domenico dalla Porta (who are both hunchbacks, as you know) and made them Auditors, saying that he wished to set the Wheel (*Rota*) right—messer Latino Giovenale said: 'His Holiness is mistaken if he thinks he can make the Wheel right with two wrongs (*due torti*).[2]

[80] "We often laugh too when a man concedes what is said to him and more too, yet pretends to take it in a different sense. As when Captain Peralta was conducted to the field to fight a duel with Aldana, and Captain Molart (who was Aldana's second) asked Peralta to take oath if he was wearing any amulets or charms to keep him from being wounded; Peralta swore that he was wearing no amulets or charms or relics or any objects of devotion whatever in which he had faith. Whereupon, to taunt him with being a heretic, Molart said: 'Do not trouble yourself about this, for even without your oath I can believe that you have no faith even in Christ himself.'

"It is also delightful in such cases to use timely metaphors. As when our master Marcantonio said to Botton da Cesena, who was goading him with words: 'Botton, Bottone, you will one day be the button (*bottone*), and your buttonhole will be the noose.' Another time, when master Marcantonio had composed a very long comedy in several acts, this same Bottone said to him: 'All the lumber of

9. The play here is on the Italian idiomatic expression *"farne di tutti i colori"* meaning "to do all kinds of outrageous things." Thus, the Cardinal of Pavia had "done things of all colors."
1. A stable (Italian) [*Editor*]. Apparently the name Bartolommeo is far too illustrious or imposing for the man in question to bear.
2. The "wheel" is the *Ruota della Giustizia*, the highest civil and criminal court of the Vatican. The play is on the word *torto* which can mean "a wrong" or "a twisted man," i.e., such as the hunchbacks in question.

Slavonia will be needed for the stage set of your comedy.' Master
Marcantonio replied: 'And for the stage set of your tragedy, three
planks will be quite enough.'

[81] "Again we often use a word in which there is a hidden meaning quite different from the one we seem to intend. As when our
Prefect here, on hearing a certain captain spoken of, who had for
the most part lost battles in his time, and had just then chanced to
win one; and when the speaker recounted how, as the captain made
his entry into the city, he wore a very beautiful crimson velvet cloak,
which he always wore following his victories, the Prefect said: 'It
must be new.'

"It is no less amusing when we reply to something that our interlocutor has not said or when we pretend to believe he has done
something he has not done but ought to have done. As when Andrea
Coscia, having gone to visit a gentleman who rudely kept his seat
and left his guest standing, said: 'Since Your Lordship commands
me, I will sit down to obey you.' Whereupon he sat down.

[82] "We laugh too when a man blithely accuses himself of some
fault. As when I told the Duke's chaplain the other day that the Cardinal had a chaplain who said mass faster than he, he replied: 'That
is not possible!' And, bending over to my ear, he said: 'I want you to
know that I do not say one-third of the silent prayers.' Or there was
Biagino Crivello who, when a priest died at Milano, begged his
benefice of the Duke, who, however, stood firm in his intention to
give it to another person. Finally Biagino, seeing that his arguments
were of no avail, said: 'What! Now that I have had the priest killed,
why will you not give his benefice to me?'

"Also it is often entertaining to manifest a desire for those things
which cannot be. As the other day one of our friends who, when
he saw all these gentlemen jousting, whereas he was lying
stretched out on his bed, said: 'Ah, how glad I should be if this
too were a fitting exercise for a worthy man and a good soldier.'
Moreover, it is a fine and pungent manner of talk, and especially
for grave and dignified persons, to reply the opposite of what the
person spoken to would wish, but slowly and with a certain air of
doubtful and hesitating deliberation. As once with King Alfonso I
of Aragon, who had given one of his servants weapons, horses, and
clothes, because the fellow said that he had dreamed the night
before that His Highness had given him all these things; and then,
not long afterwards, the same servant said he had dreamed that
night that the King was giving him a goodly sum of gold florins;
whereupon the King replied: 'From now on do not believe in
dreams, for they are not true.' Similar also was the Pope's reply to

the Bishop of Cervia who said to him, in order to sound out his intentions: 'Holy Father, it is being said all over Rome, and throughout the palace too, that Your Holiness intends to make me governor.' Then the Pope replied: 'Let them talk—they are only rascals: have no fear, there is no truth in it.'

[83] "Gentlemen, I could perhaps cite other sources of humorous sayings, such as things uttered with timidity, with admiration, with threats, things beside the point, or said in excessive anger; and, in addition to these, certain other unusual cases which provoke laughter when they occur; sometimes taciturnity joined to a certain wonder; sometimes laughter itself, when out of place. But I think I have now said enough, for I believe pleasantries that consist in words do not go beyond those we have discussed.

"Then, as for those that depend on the outcome of an action, although they take endless forms, they are reduced to a few categories. But in both kinds the main thing is to cheat expectation and reply in a way the listener does not expect; and if a pleasantry is to be nicely turned, it must be flavored with deceit, or dissimulation, or ridicule, or censure, or comparison, or whatever other manner one chooses to adopt. And, although plesantries generally provoke laughter, yet they produce diverse effects in this regard: for some have a certain elegance and a modest capacity to amuse, others have a hidden or an open sting, others have a touch of the lascivious, others move to laughter as soon as they are heard, others the more we think about them; others cause blushes as well as laughter, others stir a little anger. But in all kinds one has to consider the state of mind of the hearers, because jests often bring greater affliction to the afflicted, and there are certain maladies that grow worse the more medicine is employed.

"Therefore, if the Courtier, with his banter and witticisms, has regard for time, person, and his own rank, and takes care not to use them too often (for it proves really tedious to persist in this all day long unseasonably and in every discussion) he may be called a humorous man; and if he takes care also not to be so sharp and biting that he be known as malicious and as one who attacks without cause or with evident rancor either those who are very powerful, which is imprudent; or those who are too weak, which is cruel; or those who are too wicked, which is useless; or says things that offend persons whom he would not wish to offend, which is ignorance. For there are some who feel bound to speak and attack indiscriminately whenever they can and regardless of what may come of it. And among the latter there are some who do not scruple to stain the honor of some noble lady for the sake of pronouncing a witticism; which is a very bad thing, and deserving of the gravest punishment, for in this respect ladies are to be numbered among the weak, and so should not be attacked, as they have no weapons with which to defend themselves. But, besides these points, one who would be witty and entertaining must have a certain natural aptitude for all kinds of pleasantries and must adapt his behavior, gestures, and face accordingly; and the more grave and severe and impassive his face is, the more pungent and keen will he make what he says appear to be.

[84] "But as for you, messer Federico, who thought to find rest under this leafless tree and in my arid discussion, I am sure that you have repented of it and are thinking that you must have found your way to the Montefiore Inn.[3] Hence, it would be well for you, like an experienced courier, to rise somewhat earlier than usual and proceed on your journey in order to avoid stopping at a bad inn."

"On the contrary," replied messer Federico, "I have come to such a good inn that I intend to stay here longer than I had at first meant to do. Hence, I shall go on resting while you complete the proposed discussion, of which you have left out a part which you mentioned in the beginning—that is, practical jokes; and it is not well that you should cheat the company of this. But, as you have taught us many fine things in the matter of pleasantries, and have made us bold in the use of them by the examples of so many singular wits and great men, princes, kings, and popes—so too in the matter of practical jokes I believe you will give us such daring that we shall venture to play some of them even on you."

Then messer Bernardo said, laughing: "You will not be the first: but it may be that you will not succeed, because I have already been the butt of so many of them that I am wary of everything, like dogs that are afraid of cold water once they have been scalded with hot. However, since you would have me speak of this too, I think I can dispatch it in a few words.

[85] "It seems to me that a practical joke is nothing but an amicable deception in matters that do not offend, or only slightly. And just as in pleasantries laughter is aroused by saying something contrary to expectation, so in practical joking it is produced by doing something contrary to expectation. And the more clever and discreet these jokes are, the more they please and the more they are praised; for one who is careless in playing a practical joke often gives offense and provokes quarrels and serious enmities.

"But the sources of material for practical jokes are almost the same as for pleasantries. Therefore, in order not to repeat them, I

3. A notoriously bad inn at Montefiore, a village between Pesaro and Urbino.

will say merely that there are two kinds of practical jokes, each of which may be further divided into several varieties. One kind is that wherein someone is cleverly deceived in a fine and amusing manner; the other is where a net is spread, as it were, and a little bait is put out, so that a man easily tricks himself. Of the first kind was the joke that two great ladies, whom I do not wish to name, had played on them recently by a Spaniard named Castillo."

Then the Duchess said: "And why do you not wish to name them?"

Messer Bernardo replied: "I do not want them to be offended."

The Duchess answered, laughing: "It is not amiss to play jokes sometimes even on great lords. Indeed, I have heard of many played on Duke Federico, on King Alfonso of Aragon, on Queen Isabella of Spain, and on many other great princess; and not only did they take no offense, but they liberally rewarded the pranksters."

Messer Bernardo replied: "Not even in the hope of that will I name them."

"Then speak on as you please," answered the Duchess.

Messer Bernardo continued: "The other day at the court I have in mind, there arrived a peasant of Bergamo on business for a courtier gentleman. This peasant was so well dressed and so elegantly decked out that, although he was accustomed to nothing save tending cattle and knew no other occupation, anyone not hearing him speak would have thought him a gallant cavalier. Now, on being told that a Spanish retainer of Cardinal Borgia had arrived by the name of Castillo and that he was exceedingly clever, was a musician, a dancer, a *ballatore*,[4] and the most accomplished Courtier in all Spain—these two ladies conceived a great desire to speak with him and at once sent for him. After receiving him with much ceremony, they invited him to be seated and began to show him the greatest regard in speaking with him before all the company; and there were few of those present who did not know that the fellow was a Bergamasque cowherd. So when these ladies were seen entertaining him with so much respect and honoring him so, there was great laughter, all the more so as the good man spoke only his native Bergamasque dialect. But the gentlemen who played the trick had previously told these ladies that this man, among other things, was a great joker and spoke all languages admirably and especially rustic Lombard. Hence, they thought all the while that he was pretending, and often turned to each other, marveling, and said: 'What a wonder to hear! how well he mimics the language!' In short, their conversation lasted so long that everyone's sides ached from laughing, and he himself could not help giving such proof of his gentility that

4. A *ballatore* would be called *ballerino* today.

even these ladies were at last persuaded, though with great difficulty, that he was what he was.

[86] "We see this kind of practical joke all the time; but those are
more amusing than others which scare at first and turn out well in
the end; for even the victim laughs at himself when he sees that his
fears were groundless. As when I was lodging at Paglia[5] one night,
and in the same inn where I was there happened to be three other
guests besides myself (two men from Pistoia and another man from
Prato), who sat down after supper to gamble, as men often do. And
they had not been playing long before one of the Pistoians lost all
he had, and was left without a cent, so that he began to lament and
swear and curse loudly, and went off to bed blaspheming. After continuing the game for a while, the other two decided to play a joke
on the one who had gone to bed. Whereupon, making sure that he
was already asleep, they put out all the lights and covered the fire;
then they began to talk loud and make all the noise they could, pretending they were quarreling over the game, and one of them said:
'You took the card from underneath,' and the other denied this, saying: 'You have bet on a flush; the deal is off,' and the like, with such
an uproar that the man who was asleep awoke. And, hearing that his
friends were playing and talking as if they saw the cards, he opened
his eyes a little and seeing no light in the room he said: 'What the
devil, do you intend to shout all night?' Then he lay back again to
sleep. His two friends did not answer him but went on as before, so
that the man began to wonder (now that he was wider awake); and,
seeing for certain that there was neither fire nor light of any kind,
and that the two went right on playing and quarreling, he said: 'And
how can you see the cards without light?' One of the pair replied:
'You must have lost your sight along with your money; can't you see
by the two candles we have here?' The man in bed raised himself on
his elbows and said in anger: 'Either I am drunk or blind, or you are
lying.' The two stood up and groped their way to the bed, laughing
and pretending to believe that he was making fun of them; and he
kept on repeating: 'I say I do not see you.' Finally the two began to
feign great surprise, and one said to the other: 'Alas, I believe he is
serious. Hand me that candle and let's see if it can be that something has gone wrong with his sight.' Then the poor fellow was certain that he had gone blind, and, weeping bitterly, he said: 'Oh, my
friends, I am blind!' and he began at once to pray to Our Lady of
Loreto and to implore her to pardon the blasphemies and curses he
had heaped upon her for having lost his money. His two companions kept on comforting him and saying: 'It is not possible that you

5. Paglia is in the vicinity of Orvieto and near the river Paglia which flows into the Tiber.

do not see us; this is some fantasy that you've taken into your head.' 'Alas,' replied the other, 'this is no fantasy, for I can see no more than if I had never had eyes in my head.' 'But your sight is clear,' the two replied; and one said to the other: 'See how well he opens his eyes! Look how bright they are! Who could believe he can't see?' All the while the poor man wept all the more loudly and prayed for God's mercy. At last the two said to him: 'Make a vow to go in penance to Our Lady of Loreto, barefoot and naked, for this is the best remedy that can be found; and meanwhile we will go to Acqua Pendente and to those other towns nearby to see if we can find some doctor, and we shall not fail to do anything we can for you.' Then the poor fellow straightway knelt by his bed and, with endless tears of bitter penitence for his blasphemy, made a solemn vow to go naked to Our Lady of Loreto and to offer her a pair of silver eyes, to eat no flesh on Wednesday, or eggs on Friday, and to fast on bread and water every Saturday in honor of Our Lady, if she would grant him the mercy of restoring his sight. His two companions went into another room, lighted a candle, and, holding their sides with laughter, came back to the unhappy man who, even though relieved of so great an anguish, as you can imagine, was still so stunned by the fright he had gotten that he was not only unable to laugh, he could not even speak; and his two companions did nothing but tease him, saying that he was bound to fulfill all those vows, because he had obtained the mercy he sought.

[87] "Of the other kind of practical joke, where a man tricks himself, I shall give no example other than the one that was played on me not long ago. During the past carnival, my friend Monsignor of San Pietro ad Vincula (who knows how much I enjoy playing jokes on friars when I am masked, and who had carefully arranged beforehand what he intended to do) came one day with Monsignor of Aragon and other cardinals to certain windows in the *Banchi*[6] as though he meant to remain there to watch the maskers pass by, as is the custom at Rome. I came along in my mask, and, seeing a friar standing off to one side with a hesitant air, I judged that I was in luck, and at once I swooped down on him like a hungry falcon on its prey. And having first asked him who he was and heard his answer, I pretended I knew him and with many words I began to make him believe that the chief of police was out searching for him because of some ill reports that had been lodged against him, and I urged him to go with me to the Chancery,[7] that I would provide him

---

6. *Banchi*, the "Banks," a well-known street, popular for promenading at the time, so-called from the many banks and offices in it.
7. The Chancery (*Cancelleria*), a palace which was then given over to public offices but was also the residence of Cardinal Galeotto della Rovere.

some refuge there. Fearful and trembling all over, the friar seemed not to know what he ought to do, and said he was afraid of being seized if he went far from San Celso.[8] I kept on urging him, and talked with him until I got him to mount behind me; and with that I thought I had finally succeeded in my scheme. So at once I started to spur toward the *Banchi*, with my horse bucking and kicking constantly. Now you can imagine what a fine figure a friar cut mounted up behind a masker, with his cloak flying and his head jerking back and forth, and always seeming to be on the verge of falling.

"Witnessing this fine spectacle, those gentlemen began to throw eggs at us from the windows; as did the people of the quarter and everyone there, so that hail never fell from heaven with greater force than those eggs fell from the windows, and most of them on me. Masked as I was, I passed it off and thought that the laughter was all for the friar, and not for me; and so I went up and down the *Banchi* several times under that hailstorm, although the friar with tears in his eyes begged me to let him dismount and not to desecrate a friar's habit in this way. Then the rascal had eggs passed to him on the sly by some lackeys stationed there on purpose, and, pretending to hold tight to me to keep from falling, he crushed them on my chest, frequently on my head, and sometimes on my very brow until I was completely covered. Finally, when everyone was tired of laughing and throwing eggs, he jumped down from my horse and, throwing back his cowl, showed me his long hair and said: 'Messer Bernardo, I am one of the grooms of San Pietro ad Vincula, and it is I who take care of your little mule!' Then I do not know whether it was grief or anger or shame I felt most. However, as the lesser evil, I made for home and did not have the courage to put in an appearance the next morning; but the laughter over this trick lasted not only through the following day, but almost until now."

[88] When they had again laughed for a while at this story, messer Bernardo continued: "There is another very amusing kind of practical joke that is also a source of pleasantries, when we pretend to think that someone wishes to do something which in fact he does not wish to do. For example, I was once on the bridge at Lyons in the evening after supper, and was going along jesting with Cesare Becadello. We began to seize each other by the arm as if we wished to wrestle, for it happened that no one appeared to be on the bridge at that time. While we were engaged in these antics, two Frenchmen came up who, seeing our dispute, asked what the matter was, and stayed to try to separate us, believing we were quarreling in earnest. Then I said quickly: 'Help me, gentlemen, for at certain

8. San Celso was a street near Banchi.

phases of the moon this poor man goes out of his mind and now, you see, he is even trying to jump off the bridge into the river.' Thereupon the pair ran and joined me in seizing Cesare and holding him very tight. He, telling me the while that I was mad, tried all the harder to free himself from their hands, and they held him all the tighter; so that quite a crowd began to gather to watch this disturbance and everyone ran up. And the more the good Cesare flailed about with hands and feet (for by now he was getting into a rage), the more people gathered; and, because of the great struggle he was making, they firmly believed he was trying to jump into the river, and they held him the tighter for that. So that a great crowd of men carried him bodily to the inn, without his cap and all disheveled, pale with anger and shame, since nothing that he said availed him, partly because the French did not understand him and also partly because, as I led them to the inn, I kept lamenting the poor man's misfortune in being thus stricken in mind.

[89] "Now, as we have said, one could go on at length about practical jokes; but let it suffice that the sources of them are the same as for pleasantries. Moreover, we have an infinity of examples because we see them every day; and, among others, many amusing ones are found in Boccaccio's tales, such as those played by Bruno and Buffalmacco on their friend Calandrino and on Master Simone,[9] and many others played by women that are truly ingenious and fine.

"I recall having formerly known many entertaining men of this sort; and among others a certain Sicilian student at Padua called Ponzio, who once saw a peasant with a pair of fat capons. Pretending that he wanted to buy them, he struck a bargain and told the man to come home with him, that he would give him some lunch in addition to the price agreed on. He led the peasant thus to a place where there was a bell tower standing free of its church so that one could walk all around it; and directly at one of the four sides of the tower a little street ended. Here Ponzio, who had already conceived what he planned to do, said to the peasant: 'I have wagered these capons with a friend of mine who says that this tower is all of forty feet around, while I say it is not. And when I met up with you, I had just bought this twine to measure it. Now, before we go home, I want to see which of us has won.' And, so saying, he took the twine from his sleeve, gave one end of it to the peasant, and said: 'Here, hand them to me,' and took the capons; and, holding the other end of the twine as if he meant to measure, he began to walk around the tower, having first made the peasant stay where he was and hold the twine on the side of the tower opposite the side where the little

---

9. These are characters in Boccaccio's *Decameron* VIII, 3, 6, 9; IX, 5.

street ended. When he came around to this other side, he stuck a nail into the wall, tied the twine to it, and, leaving the man standing there, he quietly went off up the little street with the capons. The peasant stayed there for a good while, waiting for Ponzio to finish measuring; finally, after he had said several times: 'Why are you taking so long?'—he went to look, and found that it was not Ponzio holding the twine, but a nail stuck in the wall—which was all the pay he got for the capons. Ponzio played countless jokes of this sort.

"There have also been many other men who were entertaining in this way, such as Gonnella, Meliolo in his day, and at present our friends fra Mariano and fra Serafino here, and many whom you all know. And this method is truly praiseworthy in men who have no other profession, but it seems that the Courtier's practical jokes ought to be somewhat more removed from scurrility. One must take care too that practical jokes do not amount to fraudulence, as we see in the case of many rascals who go about the world with various money-making wiles, feigning now one thing and now another. The Courtier's tricks, moreover, must not be too rough; and let him show respect and reverence to women above all, in this as in everything, and especially when some damage might be done their honor."

[90] Then signor Gasparo said: "Surely, messer Bernardo, you are too partial to the women. And why would you have men show more respect for women than women for men? Can it be that our honor is not as dear to us as theirs to them? So you think that women ought to sting men with words and practical jokes without any reserve at all, and that men should keep silent and thank them in the bargain?"

Then messer Bernardo replied: "I do not say that in their pleasantries and practical jokes women should not show men the same respect that we have already said; but I do say that they may sting men for their faults more freely than men may sting them. And this is because we ourselves have set a rule that a dissolute life in us is not a vice, or fault, or disgrace, while in women it means such utter opprobrium and shame that any woman of whom ill is once spoken is disgraced forever, whether what is said be calumny or not. Therefore, since even to speak of women's honor runs the risk of doing them grave offense, I say that we ought to refrain from this and sting them in some other way; because to deal too hard a thrust with our pleasantries or practical jokes is to exceed the bounds that we have already held to be proper to a gentleman."

[91] When messer Bernardo paused a little, signor Ottaviano Fregoso said, laughing: "Signor Gasparo could answer you that this rule which you say we ourselves have made is perhaps not as unreason-

able as it seems to you. For since women are very imperfect creatures, and of little or no worth compared with men, and since of themselves they were not able to do any worthy thing, it was necessary, through shame and fear of infamy, to put a curb on them which would give them some good quality. And it was chastity that seemed more needful for them than any other quality, in order for us to be certain of our offspring; hence, it was necessary to use our wits, art, and all possible ways, to make women chaste, and, as it were, allow them in all other things to be of little worth and to do constantly the opposite of what they should. Therefore, since they are permitted without blame to commit all other faults, if we try to sting them for all those defects which, as we have said, are permitted them, and hence are not unseemly in them and to which they pay no attention—we shall never incite laughter; for you have said already that laughter is produced by certain things which are incongruous."

[92] Then the Duchess said: "You speak of women in this way, signor Ottaviano, and then you complain that they do not love you."

"I do not complain of that," said signor Ottaviano, "on the contrary, I thank them, since they do not, by loving me, oblige me to love them. Neither am I speaking my own mind, but only saying that signor Gasparo could use these arguments."

Messer Bernardo said: "Truly women would gain much if they could conciliate two such great enemies of theirs as you and signor Gasparo."

"I am not their enemy," replied signor Gasparo, "but you are certainly an enemy of men; for if you would not have women stung in their honor, you ought also to impose a law on them that they not sting men in what is as shameful to us as unchastity is to women. And why was not Alonso Carillo's retort to signora Boadilla (about hoping to escape with his life through her taking him for her husband) as seemly in him as it was for her to say that all who knew him thought the King was going to have him hanged? And why was it not as permissible for Ricciardo Minutolo to deceive Filippello's wife and cause her to go to that bathhouse as it was for Beatrice to make her husband Egano get out of bed and get a sound beating from Anichino, when she had been lying with the latter long since? And for that other woman to tie a string to her toe and make her husband believe that she was someone else?[1]—since you say that in Giovanni Boccaccio these practical jokes by women are so clever and fine."

---

1. Ricciardo Minutolo is a character in Boccaccio's *Decameron* III, 6; Beatrice and Anichino are in VII, 7; "that other woman" appears in VII, 8 [*Editor*].

[93] Then messer Bernardo said, laughing: "Gentlemen, it was my task merely to discuss pleasantries and I do not propose to go beyond that limit. And I think I have already stated why it does not seem to me a seemly thing to attack women in their honor either by word or deed, and then have a rule put over them that they may not sting men where it hurts. As for the pranks and witticisms cited by you, signor Gasparo, I do grant you that, although what Alonso said to signora Boadilla does touch a little on chastity, it does not displease me, because it is done in an offhand way and is so veiled that it can be understood on the face of it, so that he could have dissimulated and claimed that he did not mean it in that way. He said another which in my opinion is most unseemly. And it was this: once when the Queen was passing signora Boadilla's house, Alonso noticed that the door was covered with charcoal drawings of those lascivious animals that are painted about inns in so many ways; and, turning to the Countess of Castagneto, he said: 'Behold, Madam, the heads of the beasts that signora Boadilla slays every day in the hunt.' You see that while the metaphor is clever and well taken from hunters (who take pride in having many heads of beasts mounted on their doors), still it is scurrilous and shameful. Besides, it is not an answer to anything; for an answer is something much more courteous in that it seems to have been provoked and needs must be on the spur of the moment.

"Returning, however, to the subject of tricks that are played by women, I do not say that they do well to deceive their husbands, but I say that some of those deceptions that Giovanni Boccaccio tells of women are fine and very clever, and especially those which you yourself have mentioned. But, to my mind, the trick played by Ricciardo Minutolo goes too far and is much crueler than the one played by Beatrice; because Ricciardo Minutolo took much more from the wife of Filippello than Beatrice did from her husband, for Ricciardo by his deception violated the woman and made her do of herself a thing she did not wish to do, whereas Beatrice deceived her husband in order that she might do of herself what she liked."

[94] Then signor Gasparo said: "Beatrice can be excused on no other grounds than those of love, which is something that ought to be allowed to men as well as to women."

Then messer Bernardo replied: "It is true that the passion of love brings its own ample excuse for every fault. However, for my part, I hold that a gentleman of worth, who is in love, ought to be sincere and truthful in this as in all other things; and if it is true that to betray an enemy is baseness and a most abominable wrong, think how much more grave the offense ought to be considered when done to one whom we love. And I believe that every gentle lover endures so many toils, so many vigils, exposes himself to so many dangers, sheds so many tears, uses so many ways and means to please his lady love—not chiefly in order to possess her body, but to take the fortress of her mind and to break those hardest diamonds and melt that cold ice, which are often found in the tender breasts of women. And this I believe is the true and sound pleasure and the goal aimed at by every noble heart. Certainly, if I were in love, I should wish rather to be sure that she whom I served returned my love from her heart and had given me her inner self—if I had no other satisfaction from her—than to take all pleasure with her against her will; for in such a case I should consider myself master merely of a lifeless body. Hence, those who pursue their desires by these tricks, which might perhaps rather be called treacheries than tricks, do wrong to others, nor do they gain that satisfaction withal which is sought in love if they possess the body without the will. I say the same of certain others who in their love make use of enchantments, charms, sometimes force, sometimes sleeping potions, and such things. And you must know that gifts do much to lessen the pleasures of love; for a man can suspect that he is not loved but that his lady makes a show of loving him in order to gain something by it. Hence, you see that the love of some great lady is prized because it seems that it cannot arise from any other source save that of real and true affection, nor is it to be thought that so great a lady would ever pretend to love an inferior if she did not really love him."

[95] Then signor Gasparo replied: "I do not deny that the purpose, the labors, and the dangers of lovers should be chiefly directed to the conquest of the beloved's mind rather than the body. But I say that these deceits, which you call treacheries in men and tricks in women, are excellent means of attaining this aim, for whoever possesses a woman's body is always master of her mind also. And if you well recall, Filippello's wife, after complaining so much of the deceit practiced on her by Ricciardo, discovered how much sweeter than her husband's were the kisses of her lover, and changed her coldness to Ricciardo into sweet affection, and from that day on loved him most tenderly. Consider therefore that what his pressing attentions, the gifts, and the many other tokens constantly proffered could not effect was accomplished in no time by lying with her. And now you see this same trick or treachery (as you choose) was a good way to capture the fortress of her mind."

Then messer Bernardo said: "You are setting up a very false premise, for if women always surrendered their mind to the man who possessed their body, no wife would be found who failed to love her husband more than any other person in the world; whereas we see the contrary. But Giovanni Boccaccio was a very great enemy of women, even as you are."

[96] Signor Gasparo replied: "Indeed I am not their enemy; but there are very few men of worth who hold women in any esteem at all, even though for their own purposes they sometimes feign the contrary."

Then messer Bernardo replied: "You do wrong not only to women but also to all men who reverence them. However, as I have said, I do not wish to go beyond my original topic of practical jokes at this time and enter upon so difficult an undertaking as would be the defense of women against you, who are so great a warrior. So I will make an end of this talk of mine, which has perhaps been far more lengthy than was needed and certainly less entertaining than you expected. And since I see the ladies sitting so quietly and suffering your wrongs as patiently as they are doing, I shall henceforth think that a part of what signor Ottaviano said is true, namely, that they care not what other evil is spoken of them, provided they are not charged with any lack of chastity."

Then, at a sign from the Duchess, many of the ladies rose to their feet and all rushed laughing upon signor Gasparo as if to assail him with blows and treat him as the bacchantes treated Orpheus,[2] saying the while: "Now you shall see whether we care if we are slandered."

[97] Thus, partly because of the laughter and partly because all had risen to their feet, the drowsiness which by now was in the eyes and the mind of some seemed to be dispelled; but signor Gasparo began to say: "You see that because they are in the wrong, they wish to resort to force and end the discussion in this way by giving us a Braccesque leave,[3] as the saying goes."

Then signora Emilia replied: "You shall not succeed in this, for when you saw messer Bernardo wearied by his long talk, you began to speak so much evil of women, thinking you had no one to stand against you. But we shall put a fresh champion in the field to fight you, so that your offense may not go long unpunished." Then, turning to the Magnifico Giuliano, who up to then had spoken lit-tle, she said: "You are held to be the defender of women's honor;

---

2. Orpheus, the son of Apollo and husband of Euridice, descended to Hades to bring Euridice back to life, but lost her there and later met his death at the hands of infuriated Thracian maenads or bacchantes because he had scorned women.
3. The expression is thought to derive from the name of a famous *condottiere* Braccio For-tebracci, whose followers were called Bracceschi. Bracci was famous for his violence, hence a Braccesque leave would be one most violent and rude.

therefore, now is the time for you to show that you have not won this title falsely. And if heretofore you have ever enjoyed any remuneration in such a profession, you must now consider that, by putting down this fierce enemy of ours, you will obligate all women to you, so much so that even if every effort is made to repay you, the obligation will always stand and can never be fully repaid."

[98] Then the Magnifico Giuliano replied: "Madam, I think you do your enemy much honor and your defender very little; for certainly signor Gasparo has so far said nothing against women that messer Bernardo has not answered excellently well. And I believe we all know that it is fitting for the Courtier to show women the greatest reverence, and that he who is discreet and courteous must never charge them with lack of chastity, either in jest or in earnest. Thus, to discuss such an evident truth as this is almost to cast doubt upon what is beyond doubt. But I think that signor Ottaviano went a little too far when he said that women are very imperfect creatures, incapable of any virtuous action, and of little or no worth in comparison with men. And, because we often place trust in those who have great authority, even when they do not speak the whole truth and even when they speak in jest, signor Gasparo has let himself be led by the words of signor Ottaviano into saying that men who are wise hold women in no esteem whatever, which is most false. Indeed, I have known very few men of merit who do not love and honor women—whose virtue and consequently whose worth I deem not a jot inferior to men's. Yet if this were to be the subject of dispute, the cause of women would be at a serious disadvantage; because these gentlemen have conceived a Courtier so excellent and of such divine accomplishments that whoever imagines him so must think that women's merits could never attain such a mark. But if things were to be made equal, we should first need someone as witty and as eloquent as Count Ludovico and messer Federico, to imagine a Court Lady with all the perfections proper to woman, just as they have imagined the Courtier with the perfections proper to man. And then, if the champion of their cause were a man of but ordinary wit and eloquence, I think that, having truth as his ally, he would clearly show that women have quite as much virtue as men."

"Nay," replied signora Emilia, "far more; and, to bear this out, you see that virtue (*la virtù*) is feminine, and vice (*il vizio*) is masculine."

[99] Then signor Gasparo laughed, and, turning to messer Niccolò Frisio, said: "What do you think of this, Frisio?"

Frisio replied: "I feel sorry for the Magnifico who, beguiled by signora Emilia's promises and blandishments, has fallen into the error of saying things that I blush for, as one who wishes him well."

Signora Emilia replied, still laughing: "You will rather blush for yourself when you see signor Gasparo converted and confessing his error and your own, and beseeching the pardon that we shall refuse to grant him."

Then the Duchess said: "Since the hour is very late, let us postpone the whole matter until tomorrow; and the more so because it seems to me wise to follow the advice of signor Magnifico, namely, that, before we enter into this dispute, a Court Lady perfect in every way should be imagined, just as these gentlemen have imagined the perfect Courtier."

Then signora Emilia said: "Madam, God forbid that we should chance to entrust this task to any fellow conspirator of signor Gasparo, who should fashion us a Court Lady unable to do anything except cook and spin!"

Frisio said: "But that is her proper business."

Then the Duchess said: "I am willing to put my trust in signor Magnifico who (with the wit and good judgment that I know to be his) will imagine the highest perfection that can be desired in woman, and will express it in beautiful language as well; and then we shall have something to hold up against signor Gasparo's false calumnies."

[100] "Madam," replied the Magnifico, "I am not sure how well advised you are to assign to me an undertaking so important that I truly do not feel equal to it. Nor am I like the Count and messer Federico, who with their eloquence have imagined a Courtier that never existed and perhaps never can exist. Still, if you would have me bear this burden, at least let it be on the same conditions as in the case of these other gentlemen, that is, that anyone may contradict me when he pleases, and I shall take it not as contradiction but as help; and perhaps, with this correcting of my mistakes, we shall discover the perfection of the Court Lady which we are seeking."

"I hope," replied the Duchess, "that your talk will be such as to invite little in the way of contradiction. So set your whole mind to it, and devise us such a woman that these our adversaries will be ashamed to say she is not equal in worth to the Courtier; about whom it will be well for messer Federico to say no more, since he has adorned him all too well and especially as we are now to place him in competition with a woman."

Then messer Federico said: "Madam, there now remains little or nothing for me to say about the Courtier; and what I had thought to say has slipped my mind because of messer Bernardo's pleasantries."

"In that case," said the Duchess, "let us meet together again tomorrow, at an early hour, so that we shall have time to settle both matters."

They all rose to their feet when she had said this; and, having reverently taken leave of the Duchess, everyone went to his own room.

The Third Book

To Messer Alfonso Ariosto

[1] We read that Pythagoras most ingeniously and admirably ascertained the size of Hercules' body, and his method was this: it being known that the space where the Olympic games were celebrated every five years, in front of the temple of Olympic Jove near Elis, in Achaia, had been measured by Hercules, and that the stadium had been made 625 times as long as his own foot; and that the other stadiums which were afterward established throughout Greece by later generations were likewise made 625 feet long, and yet were somewhat shorter than the first one; following this proportion, Pythagoras easily determined how much larger Hercules' foot was than other men's feet; and thus, knowing the measure of the foot, he ascertained by this that Hercules' body was as much larger than other men's as the first stadium was larger than the other stadiums.[4]

Thus, you, my dear messer Alfonso, by the same reasoning may clearly know, from this small part of the whole, how superior the Court of Urbino was to all others in Italy, considering how much these games, which were devised for the relaxation of minds wearied by more arduous endeavors, were superior to those practiced in the other courts of Italy. And if these were such, imagine what the other worthy pursuits were to which our minds were bent and wholly given over; and of this I confidently make bold to speak in the hope of being believed, for I am not praising things so ancient that I am free to invent, and I can prove my claims by the testimony of many men worthy of credence who are still living and who personally saw and knew the life and the customs that once flourished in that court: and I consider myself obliged, as far as I can, to make every effort to preserve this bright memory from mortal oblivion, and make it live in the mind of posterity through my writing.

Wherefore, perhaps, in the future, someone will not be wanting who will envy our century for this as well; because no one reads of the marvelous deeds of the ancients without forming a certain

---

4. The whole anecdote is taken from Aulus Gellius, *Noctes Atticae* I, 1.

higher opinion of those who are written of than the books themselves seem able to express, though they are divinely written. Even
so we hope that all those into whose hands this work of ours shall
come (if indeed it prove so worthy of favor as to deserve to be seen
by noble cavaliers and virtuous ladies) will suppose and firmly
believe that the Court of Urbino was far more excellent and adorned
with singular men than we can set down in writing; and if we had
as much eloquence as they had worth, we should need no other
proof to bring those who did not see it to believe our words.

[2] Now when the company had assembled the next day at the usual
hour and place, and was seated and silent, everyone turned his eyes
to messer Federico and to the Magnifico Giuliano, waiting to see
which of them would start the discussion. Wherefore the Duchess,
after remaining silent a while, said: "Signor Magnifico, all of us
desire to see this Lady of yours well adorned; and if you do not show
her to us in such a way as to display all her beauty, we shall think
that you are jealous of her."

The Magnifico replied: "Madam, if I thought her beautiful, I
should display her unadorned, and in the same fashion wherein
Paris chose to see the three goddesses; but if the ladies here, who
well know how, do not help me to array her, I fear that not only
signor Gasparo and Frisio, but all these other gentlemen, will have
good reason to speak ill of her; hence, while she still has some reputation of beauty, perhaps it will be better to keep her hidden, and
see what messer Federico has still to say about the Courtier, who
without doubt is fairer by far than my Lady can be."

"What I had in mind," replied messer Federico, "is not so pertinent to the Courtier that it cannot be omitted without sacrifice;
indeed, it is rather a different matter from what has so far been
discussed."

"And what is it then?" said the Duchess.

Messer Federico replied: "I had decided to explain, in so far as I
could, the origins of these companies and orders of knighthood
which great princes have founded under various emblems: such as
that of St. Michael in the House of France; that of the Garter which
bears the name of St. George in the House of England; the Golden
Fleece in that of Burgundy; and how these dignities are bestowed
and how persons who have deserved such are deprived of them;
whence they arose, who established them, and to what end: for
these knights are always honored even in great courts.[5]

5. The Order of St. Michael was a knightly order established by Louis XI of France in 1469.
The Order of the Garter was established by King Edward III of England in 1344. The
Golden Fleece was established by Philip the Good, duke of Burgundy, in 1429 [Editor].

"I thought too, had I time enough, to speak not only of the diversity of the customs that prevail at the courts of Christian princes in serving them, in observing festivals, and in appearing at public shows, but also to say something of the Grand Turk's court, and even more particularly something of the court of the Sophi, King of Persia.[6] For I have heard from merchants who have been long in that region that the noblemen there are of great worth and of gracious customs, and that in their intercourse with one another, in serving their ladies, and in all their actions, they observe much courtesy and discretion, and, when it is called for, much magnificence, great liberality, and elegance in arms, games, and festivals; and I have been delighted to learn what fashions they esteem most in these matters, and in what their ceremonies and elegance of dress and arms consist; wherein they differ from us and wherein they resemble us; what manner of amusements their ladies practice and how modestly they show favor to those who pay court to them. But, truly, now is not the proper time for this discussion, especially as something else is to be said, which is far more to our purpose than this."

[3] "Nay," said signor Gasparo, "this and many other things are more to the purpose than imagining this Court Lady, considering that the same rules apply to her as to the Courtier; for she, like the Courtier, ought to have regard for time and place and (in so far as her inability permits) follow all those other ways that have been so much discussed. And therefore, instead of this, it would perhaps not have been amiss to teach some of the particulars that pertain to the service of the prince's person, for the Courtier must indeed know these things and do them well; or to speak of the manner to be followed in bodily exercises, such as riding, handling weapons, and wrestling, and to say wherein lies the difficulty of these practices."

Then the Duchess said, laughing: "Princes ought not to employ such an excellent Courtier as this in the service of their persons; and, as for bodily exercises and physical strength and agility, we will leave our messer Pietro Monte to concern himself with the teaching of these things, whenever he may find the most convenient time; because at present the Magnifico has no other duty than to speak of this Lady, of whom I think you are already beginning to be afraid and so would like to make us stray from our purpose."

Frisio replied: "Surely it is out of place and beside the purpose to speak of women now, particularly when more remains to be said of the Courtier, for we ought not to mix one thing with another."

6. By "Grand Turk" is meant the Sultan of Constantinople and by "the Sophi," Ismail Suphi (1480–1524).

"You are greatly mistaken," replied messer Cesare Gonzaga, "because just as no court, however great, can have adornment or splendor or gaiety in it without ladies, neither can any Courtier be graceful or pleasing or brave, or do any gallant deed of chivalry, unless he is moved by the society and by the love and charm of ladies: even discussion about the Courtier is always imperfect unless ladies take part in it and add their part of that grace by which they make Courtiership perfect and adorned."

Signor Ottaviano laughed, and said: "There you have a little sample of the kind of bait that makes men fools."

[4] Then the Magnifico, turning to the Duchess, said: "Since it is your pleasure, Madam, I will say what I have to say, but with great fear that I shall give no satisfaction. Certainly, it would cause me far less toil to imagine a lady worthy of being the queen of the world than to imagine a perfect Court Lady, because I do not know where to find my model for the latter; whereas, for the Queen, I should not need to go very far, since it would be enough for me to set forth the divine accomplishments of a lady whom I know and, in contemplating those accomplishments, set all my thoughts to expressing clearly in words what many see with their eyes; and if I could do no more, I should have performed my task by merely uttering her name."

Then said the Duchess: "Do not exceed bounds, signor Magnifico, but hold to the order given, and describe the Court Lady so that such a noble lady may have someone capable of serving her worthily."

The Magnifico continued: "Then, Madam, in order to show that your commands can induce me to attempt what I do not even know how to do, I will speak of this excellent Lady as I would wish her to be; and when I have fashioned her to my taste, and since then I may not have another, like Pygmalion I will take her for my own. And, though signor Gasparo has said that the same rules which serve for the Courtier serve also for the Lady, I am of a different opinion; for although some qualities are common to both and are as necessary for a man as for a woman, there are yet others that befit a woman more than a man, and others that befit a man and to which a woman ought to be a complete stranger. I say this of bodily exercises; but above all I think that in her ways, manners, words, gestures, and bearing, a woman ought to be very unlike a man; for just as he must show a certain solid and sturdy manliness, so it is seemly for a woman to have a soft and delicate tenderness, with an air of womanly sweetness in her every movement, which, in her going and staying, and in whatever she says, shall always make her appear the woman without any resemblance to a man.

"Now, if this precept be added to the rules which these gentlemen have taught the Courtier, then I think she ought to be able to follow many such and adorn herself with the best accomplishments, as signor Gasparo says. For I hold that many virtues of the mind are as necessary to a woman as to a man; also, gentle birth; to avoid affectation, to be naturally graceful in all her actions, to be mannerly, clever, prudent, not arrogant, not envious, not slanderous, not vain, not contentious, not inept, to know how to gain and hold the favor of her mistress and of all others, to perform well and gracefully the exercises that are suitable for women. And I do think that beauty is more necessary to her than to the Courtier, for truly that woman lacks much who lacks beauty. Also she must be more circumspect, and more careful not to give occasion for evil being said of her, and conduct herself so that she may not only escape being sullied by guilt but even by the suspicion of it, for a woman has not so many ways of defending herself against false calumnies as a man has. But since Count Ludovico has set forth in great detail the chief profession of the Courtier, and has insisted that this be arms, I think it is also fitting to state what I judge that of the Court Lady to be, and when I have done this I shall think to have discharged the greater part of my assignment.

[5] "Leaving aside, then, those virtues of the mind which she is to have in common with the Courtier (such as prudence, magnanimity, continence, and many others), as well as those qualities that befit all (such as kindness, discretion, ability to manage her husband's property and house and children, if she is married, and all qualities that are requisite in a good mother), I say that, in my opinion, in a Lady who lives at court a certain pleasing affability is becoming above all else, whereby she will be able to entertain graciously every kind of man with agreeable and comely conversation suited to the time and place and to the station of the person with whom she speaks, joining to serene and modest manners, and to that comeliness that ought to inform all her actions, a quick vivacity of spirit whereby she will show herself a stranger to all boorishness; but with such a kind manner as to cause her to be thought no less chaste, prudent, and gentle than she is agreeable, witty, and discreet: thus, she must observe a certain mean (difficult to achieve and, as it were, composed of contraries) and must strictly observe certain limits and not exceed them.

"Now, in her wish to be thought good and pure, this Lady must not be so coy, or appear so to abhor gay company or any talk that is a little loose, as to withdraw as soon as she finds herself involved, for it might easily be thought that she was pretending to be so austere in order to hide something about herself which she feared others might discover; for manners so unbending are always odious. Yet, on the other hand, for the sake of appearing free and amiable she must not utter unseemly words or enter into any immodest and unbridled familiarity or into ways such as might cause others to believe about her what is perhaps not true; but when she finds herself present at such talk, she ought to listen with a light blush of shame.

"Likewise, she must avoid an error into which I have seen many women fall, which is to gossip and eagerly listen to evil spoken of other women. For those women who, when they hear of the unchaste ways of other women, bristle and pretend that the thing is incredible and that a woman so immodest is a monster, in making so much of the fault give cause to think that they might be guilty of it themselves. And those others who continually go about prying into other women's love affairs, relating them in such detail and with such glee, appear envious and desirous that everyone should know of this case in order that the same thing may not through error be imputed to them; and thus they emit certain laughs and assume certain attitudes, making it evident that they relish it all. And the result of this is that men, although they appear to listen to them willingly, usually conceive a bad opinion of such women and have little respect for them, and take these ways of theirs to be an invitation to go further; and they often do go so far with them that it quite justly brings shame upon them, and in the end they esteem them so little as to care nothing for their company, and even come to despise them. On the other hand, there is no man so profligate and so forward as not to have reverence for those women who are esteemed to be good and virtuous, because a certain gravity, tempered with wisdom and goodness, is like a shield against the insolence and brutishness of presumptuous men; wherefore we see that a word, a laugh, or an act of kindness, however small, coming from a virtuous woman is more esteemed by everyone than all the blandishments and caresses of those who so openly show their want of shame—and if they are not unchaste, by their wanton laughter, loquacity, insolence, and scurrilous behavior of this sort, they appear to be so.

[6] "And since words that have no subject matter of importance are vain and puerile, the Court Lady must have not only the good judgment to recognize the kind of person with whom she is speaking, but must have knowledge of many things, in order to entertain that person graciously; and let her know how in her talk to choose those things that are suited to the kind of person with whom she is speaking, and be careful lest, unintentionally, she might sometimes utter words that could offend him. Let her take care not to disgust him

by indiscreet praise of herself or by being too prolix. Let her not proceed to mingle serious matters with playful or humorous discourse, or mix jests and jokes with serious talk. Let her not show ineptitude in pretending to know what she does not know, but let her seek modestly to do herself credit in what she does know—in all things avoiding affectation, as has been said. In this way she will be adorned with good manners; she will perform with surpassing grace the bodily exercises that are proper to women; her discourse will be fluent and most prudent, virtuous, and pleasant; thus, she will be not only loved but revered by everyone, and perhaps worthy of being considered the equal of this great Courtier, both in qualities of mind and of body."

[7] Having spoken thus far, the Magnifico paused and was silent as if he had ended his talk. Then signor Gasparo said: "Truly, signor Magnifico, you have greatly adorned the Lady and given her excellent qualities. Yet it seems to me that you have held much to generalities, and mentioned some things in her so great that I believe you were ashamed to expound them; and, rather than explain them, you have wished they were so, like those persons who sometimes desire things that are impossible and miraculous. Hence, I would have you set forth to us a little better what the bodily exercises proper to a Court Lady are, and in what way she ought to converse, and what those many things are of which you say it is fitting that she should have knowledge; and whether you mean that prudence, magnanimity, continence, and the many other virtues you have named are supposed to help her merely in the management of her house, children, and family (which, however, you do not wish to be her principal profession), or rather in her conversation and graceful practice of these bodily exercises; and, by your faith, take care not to set these poor virtues to such menial tasks that they will be ashamed."

The Magnifico laughed and said: "Signor Gasparo, you cannot help showing your ill will toward women. But, truly, I thought I had said quite enough and especially to such an audience as this; for I think there is none here who does not recognize that, as for bodily exercises, it is not seemly for a woman to handle weapons, ride, play tennis, wrestle, and do many other things that are suited to men."

Then the Unico Aretino said: "With the ancients it was the custom for women to wrestle naked with men,[7] but we have lost that good practice, along with many others."

Messer Cesare Gonzaga added: "And, in my time, I have seen women play tennis, handle weapons, ride, hunt, and engage in nearly all the exercises that a cavalier can."

7. Cf. Plato, *Republic* V, 3.

[8] The Magnifico replied: "Since I may fashion this Lady as I please, not only would I not have her engage in such robust and strenuous manly exercises, but even those that are becoming to a woman I would have her practice in a measured way and with that gentle delicacy that we have said befits her; and so when she dances, I should not wish to see her make movements that are too energetic and violent; nor, when she sings or plays, use those loud and oft-repeated diminutions that show more art than sweetness; likewise the musical instruments that she plays ought in my opinion to be appropriate to this intent. Consider what an ungainly thing it would be to see a woman playing drums, fifes, trumpets, or other like instruments; and this because their harshness hides and removes that suave gentleness which so adorns a woman in her every act. Hence, when she starts to dance or to make music of any kind, she ought to begin by letting herself be begged a little, and with a certain shyness bespeaking a noble shame that is the opposite of brazenness.

"Moreover, she must make her dress conform to this intent, and must clothe herself in such a way as not to appear vain and frivolous. But since women are not only permitted but bound to care more about beauty than men—and there are several sorts of beauty—this Lady must have the good judgment to see which are the garments that enhance her grace and are most appropriate to the exercises in which she intends to engage at a given time, and choose these. And when she knows that hers is a bright and cheerful beauty, she must enhance it with movements, words, and dress that tend toward the cheerful; just as another who senses that her own style is the gentle and grave ought to accompany it with like manners, in order to increase what is a gift of nature. Thus, if she is a little stouter or thinner than normal, or fair or dark, let her help herself in her dress, but in as hidden a way as possible; and all the while she keeps herself dainty and clean, let her appear to have no care or concern for this.

[9] "And since signor Gasparo asks further what these many things are that she should know about, and in what manner she ought to converse, and whether her virtues are to contribute to her conversation—I declare that I would have her know that which these gentlemen wished the Courtier to know. And, as for the exercises that we have said are unbecoming to her, I would have her at least possess such understanding of them as we may have of those things we do not practice; and this in order that she may know how to value and praise cavaliers more or less according to their merits.

"And, to repeat briefly a part of what has already been said, I wish this Lady to have knowledge of letters, of music, of painting, and know how to dance and how to be festive, adding a discreet modesty and the giving of a good impression of herself to those other things that have been required of the Courtier. And so, in her talk, her laughter, her play, her jesting, in short in everything, she will be most graceful and will converse appropriately with every person in whose company she may happen to be, using witticisms and pleasantries that are becoming to her. And although continence, magnanimity, temperance, fortitude of spirit, prudence, and the other virtues might appear to matter little in her association with others (though they can contribute something there too), I would have her adorned with all of these, not so much for the sake of that association as that she may be virtuous, and to the end that these virtues may make her worthy of being honored and that her every act may be informed by them."

[10] Then signor Gasparo said, laughing: "Since you have granted letters and continence and magnanimity and temperance to women, I am quite surprised that you do not wish them to govern cities, make laws, lead armies, and let the men stay at home to cook or spin."

The Magnifico replied, also laughing: "Perhaps that would not be so bad either." Then he added: "Don't you know that Plato, who certainly was no great friend to women, put them in charge of the city and gave all martial duties to the men?[8] Don't you believe that many women could be found who would know how to govern cities and armies as well as men do? But I have not given them these duties, because I am fashioning a Court Lady, not a Queen. I know full well that you would like tacitly to renew the false aspersion which signor Ottaviano cast on women yesterday, representing them as very imperfect creatures, incapable of any virtuous action, and of very little worth and of no dignity compared to men; but, in truth, both you and he would be making a very great mistake in thinking so."

[11] Then signor Gasparo said: "I do not wish to repeat things that have been said already; but you would very much wish to make me say something which would hurt these ladies' feelings and make them my enemies, just as you wish to win their favor by flattering them falsely. But they are so far superior to other women in their discretion that they love the truth (even if the truth is not so much to their credit) more than they love false praise; nor do they resent it if anyone says that men have greater dignity, and they will declare that you have said surprising things in attributing to the Court Lady certain absurd impossibilities and so many virtues that Socrates and

8. Plato, *Republic* V, 15; *Laws* VI, 21.

Cato and all the philosophers in the world are as nothing by comparison; for, to tell the truth, I wonder that you are not ashamed to have gone so far beyond bounds. For it should have been enough for you to make this Court Lady beautiful, discreet, chaste, affable, and able to entertain (without getting a bad name) in dancing, music, games, laughter, witticisms, and the other things that we see going on at court every day; but to wish to give her knowledge of everything in the world, and allow her those virtues that have so rarely been seen in men during the past centuries, is something one cannot endure or listen to at all.

"Now, that women are imperfect creatures, and consequently have less dignity than men, and that they are not capable of the virtues that men are capable of, is something I am not disposed to maintain, because the worthiness of the ladies here present would be enough to prove me wrong: but I do say that very learned men have written that, since nature always intends and plans to make things most perfect, she would constantly bring forth men if she could; and that when a woman is born, it is a defect or mistake of nature, and contrary to what she would wish to do: as is seen too in the case of one who is born blind, or lame, or with some other defect; and, in trees, the many fruits that never ripen. Thus, a woman can be said to be a creature produced by chance and accident. That such is the case, consider a man's actions and a woman's, and conclude from these regarding the perfection of the one and the other. Nevertheless, since these defects in women are the fault of nature that made them so, we ought not on that account to despise them, or fail to show them the respect which is their due. But to esteem them to be more than what they are seems a manifest error to me."

[12] The Magnifico waited for signor Gasparo to continue; then, seeing that he remained silent, he said: "As for the imperfection of women, you have advanced a very feeble argument; to which, although this may not be the time to enter into these subtleties, I answer (on good authority and according to the truth) that the substance of anything whatever cannot be said to be more or less. For just as no stone can be more perfectly a stone than another, as regards the essence stone, nor one piece of wood more perfectly wood than another piece—so one man cannot be more perfectly man than another; and consequently the male will not be more perfect than the female as regards their formal substance, because the one and the other are included under the species man, and that in which the one differs from the other is an accident and is not of the essence. Thus, if you tell me that man is more perfect than woman, if not in essence, at least in accidental qualities, I will answer that these accidental qualities necessarily belong either to the body or to

the mind; if to the body, man being more robust, more quick and agile, and more able to endure toil, I say that this little argues perfection, because among men themselves those who have these qualities more than others are not more esteemed for that; and in wars, where the operations are, for the most part, laborious and call for strength, the sturdiest are not more esteemed; if to the mind, I say that women can understand all the things men can understand and that the intellect of a woman can penetrate wherever a man's can."

[13] After pausing here a moment, the Magnifico Giuliano added, laughing: "Do you not know that the proposition is held in philosophy that those who are weak in body are able in mind? So that there is no doubt that women, being weaker in body, are abler in mind, and are by nature better fitted for speculation than men are." Then he went on: "But, apart from this, since you have told me that I should conclude from their works regarding the perfection of the one and of the other, I say that if you will consider nature's works, you will find that she makes women as they are, not by chance but adapted to the necessary end: for, although she makes them unsturdy of body and gives them a placid spirit and many other qualities opposed to those of men, yet the characters of the one and the other tend to a single end that regards usefulness itself. For just as women are less courageous because of their feebleness, so are they more cautious: thus, a mother nourishes her children, a father instructs them and with his strength earns outside the home what she with sedulous care conserves within it, which is something no less praiseworthy.

"Then, if you examine ancient histories (although men have always been very chary in writing praise of women) and modern histories, you will find that worth has constantly prevailed among women as among men; and that there have always been women who have undertaken wars and won glorious victories, governed kingdoms with the greatest prudence and justice, and done all that men have done. As for the sciences, do you not remember reading of many women who were learned in philosophy? Others who excelled in poetry? Others who prosecuted, accused, and defended before judges with great eloquence? As for manual works, it would be too long to tell of them, nor is there need to adduce any proof as to that.

"Therefore, if man is not more perfect in essential substance than woman, nor in accidentals (and quite apart from any argument, the effects of this can be seen), I do not know wherein lies this perfection of his.

[14] "And since you said that nature's aim is always to produce the most perfect things, and that if she could, she would always produce

man; and that producing woman is rather an error or defect on her part than an aim—this I deny completely; nor do I see how you can say that nature does not aim to produce women, without whom the human species cannot be preserved, which is something that nature herself desires more than anything else. For by means of the union of male and female she produces children, who return the benefits received in childhood by maintaining their parents when they are old; then they in turn beget other children of their own, from whom they expect to receive in old age what they in their youth gave their parents; thus nature, moving as it were in a circle, completes the figure of eternity and in such a way gives immortality to mortals. Therefore, since woman is as necessary in this as man, I do not see why one would be made more by chance than the other.

"It is quite true that nature always aims to produce the most perfect things, and hence means to produce the species man, with no preference of male over female. Nay, if she were always to produce the male she would be working an imperfection; for just as there results from body and soul a composite more noble than its parts, which is man, so from the union of male and female there results a composite which preserves the human species, and without which its parts would perish. And hence male and female are by nature always together, nor can the one be without the other; thus, we must not apply the term male to that which has no female, according to the definition of the one and of the other; nor the term female to that which has no male. And as one sex alone shows imperfection, ancient theologians attribute both sexes to God: hence, Orpheus said that Jove was male and female; and we read in Holy Writ that God created man male and female in His own likeness; and the poets, in speaking of the gods, often confuse the sex."

[15] Then signor Gasparo said: "I would not have us get into such subtleties, for these ladies would not understand us; and, even if I should answer you with the best of arguments, they would believe (or at least pretend to believe) that I am wrong, and would proceed to pronounce judgment according to their own liking. Yet since we have already begun, I will say only that in the opinion of very wise men, as you know, man is as the form and woman as the matter; and therefore, just as the form is more perfect than the matter—nay, gives it its being—so man is far more perfect than woman. And I recall once having heard that a great philosopher says in his *Problems*:[9] 'Why is it that a woman always naturally loves the man to whom she first gave herself? And why, on the contrary, does a man hate the woman he first enjoyed?' And, in giving the reason, he

9. Aristotle, *Problems* IV, 9–10.

affirms that this is because in such an act the woman takes on perfection from the man, and the man imperfection from the woman; and that everyone naturally loves that which makes him perfect, and hates that which makes him imperfect. And, besides this, it greatly argues the perfection of man and the imperfection of woman that all women without exception desire to be men, by a certain natural instinct that teaches them to desire their own perfection."

[16] The Magnifico Giuliano replied immediately: "The poor creatures do not desire to be men in order to become more perfect, but in order to gain freedom and to escape that rule over them which man has arrogated to himself by his own authority. And the analogy you give of matter and form does not apply in every respect; for woman is not made perfect by man as matter by form, because matter receives its being from form, and cannot exist without it; nay, in the degree that forms have matter, they have imperfection, and are most perfect when separated from matter. But woman does not receive her being from man; on the contrary, even as she is perfected by him, she also perfects him; hence, they come together in procreation, which neither of them can effect without the other. Besides, I will attribute the cause of woman's lasting love for the first man to whom she has given herself, and of man's hatred for the first woman he enjoyed, not to what is stated by your philosopher in his *Problems*, but to woman's firmness and constancy and to man's inconstancy, and not without a natural reason: for, since the male is warm, he naturally derives lightness, movement, and inconstancy from that quality, while on the other hand woman derives quietness, a settled gravity, and more fixed impressions from her frigidity."

[17] Then signora Emilia turned to the Magnifico and said: "For Heaven's sake, leave all this matter and form and male and female for once, and speak so as to be understood; for we have heard and understood very well the ill that signor Ottaviano and signor Gasparo spoke of us, but we do not at all see in what way you are now defending us: so it strikes me that you are straying from the subject and leaving in the minds of all the bad impression that these enemies of ours have given of us."

"Do not give such a name to us, Madam," replied signor Gasparo, "for it rather fits signor Magnifico who, in giving false praises to women, shows that no true praises can be found for them."

The Magnifico Giuliano continued: "Do not doubt, Madam, that answers will be made to everything. But I do not wish to utter such gratuitous abuse of men as they have uttered of women; and if anyone here should chance to record these discussions, I should not wish that, hereafter, in some place where these questions of matter and form might be known, that the arguments and reasons which signor Gasparo brings against you should go without reply."

"I do not see, signor Magnifico," signor Gasparo then said, "how on this point you can deny that man is by his natural qualities more perfect than woman, who by temperament is frigid as man is warm. And warmth is far more noble and more perfect than cold, because it is active and productive; and, as you know, the heavens shed only warmth upon us here, and not cold, which does not enter into the works of nature. And hence I believe that the frigidity of women's temperament is the cause of their cowardice and timidity."

[18] "So, you still wish to enter into subtleties," replied the Magnifico Giuliano, "but you shall see that you will always have the worst of it; and, in proof of this, hear me. I grant you that warmth is in itself more perfect than cold; but this is not true of things that are mixed and composite, for if it were, the warmer body would be the more perfect; which is false, because temperate bodies are most perfect. Moreover, I say to you that woman is of frigid temperament in comparison with man, who by excess of warmth is far from temperate; but woman, taken in herself, is temperate, or at least more nearly temperate than man, because the moisture she has in her is proportionate to her natural warmth, which in man more readily evaporates and is consumed because of excessive dryness. Furthermore, woman has a coldness that resists and moderates her natural warmth and renders it more nearly temperate; while in man the excessive warmth soon brings his natural heat to the highest point, and for lack of sustenance it wastes away. And thus, since men dry out more than women in the act of procreation, it frequently happens that they do not keep their vitality as long as women; thus, this further perfection can be ascribed to women, that, living longer than men, they carry out the intention of nature better than men.

"I am not speaking now of the warmth which the heavens shed upon us, because such warmth is of a different sort from that which we are discussing; for since it preserves all things beneath the moon's orb, both warm and cold, it cannot be opposed to cold. But the timidity of women, although it argues a certain imperfection, has yet a laudable source in the subtlety and readiness of their spirits which quickly present images to their minds, hence they are easily disturbed by external things. Many times you will see men who have no fear of death or of anything else and yet cannot be called courageous, because they do not know what the danger is, and heedlessly enter in like fools where they see the way open; and this comes from a certain dull-witted grossness: for which reason a fool cannot be said to be brave. But true courage comes from actual deliberation and a determined resolve to act in a given way, and from setting honor and duty above all the dangers in the world; and from being so stout of heart and mind, even in the face of death, that the senses are neither impeded nor frightened, but function in speech and thought as if they were quite undisturbed. We have seen and heard of great men of this sort; likewise many women, in both ancient and modern times, who have shown greatness of spirit and who no less than men have done things in the world worthy of infinite praise."

[19] Then Frisio said: "Such things had their beginning when the first woman, by her transgression, induced a man to sin against God and left to the human race a heritage of death, travails, and sorrows, and all the miseries and calamities that are suffered in the world today."

The Magnifico Giuliano replied: "Since you wish thus to take refuge in the sacristy, do you not know that this very transgression was repaired by a Woman, who brought us so much greater gain than the other had done us damage that the sin that was atoned by such merits is called most fortunate? But I do not wish now to expound to you how inferior in worth all human creatures are to Our Lady the Virgin (in order not to mingle divine things with these foolish discussions of ours); nor do I wish to tell how many women with infinite steadfastness have suffered themselves to be cruelly slain by tyrants for Christ's name; nor speak of those women who, in learned disputation, have confounded so many idolaters. And if you should tell me that this was a miracle done through the grace of the Holy Spirit, I say that no virtue deserves more praise than that which is approved by the testimony of God. And you can think of many other women also who are less talked about, especially if you will read St. Jerome, who celebrated certain women of his time with such marvelous praise that it would indeed suffice for the holiest man on earth.

[20] "Then think how many other women there have been who are never mentioned at all, because the poor creatures are kept shut in, and do not have the great pride to seek the name of saint with the vulgar herd as many accursed hypocrites among men do today, who—forgetful, or rather scornful, of Christ's teaching, which requires a man to anoint his face when he fasts in order that he may not be known to fast, and commands that prayers, alms, and other good works shall be done, not in the public square nor in synagogues, but in secret, so that the left hand shall not know what the right hand does—affirm that there is no better thing in the world than setting a good example: and so, with head bent to one side and with downcast eyes, letting it be known they do not wish to speak to

women or eat anything save raw herbs—grimy, with their habits all torn, they deceive the simple. They do not refrain from forging wills, fomenting mortal enmities between man and wife, or from resorting sometimes to poison, from using sorceries, incantations, and every sort of villainy. And then out of their own head they cite a certain authority which says, *Si non caste, tamen caute*;[1] and with this they think to cure every great evil, and to persuade with valid reasons those persons who are not very cautious that all sins, however grave, are readily pardoned by God, provided they remain hidden and a bad example is not set. Thus, under a veil of sanctity and in secret they frequently devote all their thoughts to corrupting the pure mind of some woman; sowing hatred between brothers; governing states; raising up one and putting down another; getting men beheaded, imprisoned, and proscribed; serving as instruments of crime and, as it were, repositories of the thefts that many princes commit. Others take shameless pleasure in appearing dainty and fresh, with well-shaven crown and fine dress, and, as they go along, lift their habit to show their neat hose—and bow to show their physique. Others use certain glances and gestures even while saying mass, and in so doing think they are graceful and that they cause others to pay attention to them. Evil and wicked men, utter strangers not only to religion but to all good conduct; and when they are reprehended for their dissolute life, they make a jest of it, laugh at all who speak to them about it, and almost pride themselves on their vices."

Then signora Emilia said: "It gives you so much pleasure to speak ill of friars that you have strayed quite from the purpose in this. But you do a great wrong to murmur against them, and you burden your conscience without gaining anything by it; for, were it not for them, who pray God for the rest of us, we should suffer much greater scourges than we do."

Then the Magnifico Giuliano laughed and said: "How, Madam, have you guessed so well that I was speaking of friars when I did not name them? But, truly, what I am doing should not be called murmuring, for I am speaking quite openly and plainly; nor am I talking about good friars, but only about the bad and guilty ones, about whom, moreover, I am not telling the thousandth part of what I know."

"Now do not speak of friars," replied signora Emilia, "because I, for one, deem it a grave sin to listen to you; therefore, I shall leave the room so as not to hear you."

---

1. "If not chastely, then discreetly."

[21] "I am willing to speak no more of this," said the Magnifico Giuliano, "but, to return to the praises of women, I say that, for every admirable man that signor Gasparo finds me, I will show you a wife or daughter or sister of equal and sometimes greater merit. Moreover, many women have been the cause of countless benefits to their menfolk, and have sometimes set right many an error of theirs. Thus, since women are naturally capable of the same virtues as men (as we have shown) and as we have several times seen the results thereof, I do not see—when I allow them what it is possible for them to have, what they have many times had, and what they still have—why I should be thought to be speaking of miracles, (whereof signor Gasparo has accused me), seeing that there have always been in the world, and still are women quite like the Court Lady I have fashioned, as there are men like the man who has been fashioned by these gentlemen."

Then signor Gasparo said: "Arguments that are contradicted by experience do not seem good to me; and certainly, if I were to ask you who these great women were that have been as worthy of praise as the great men whose wives or sisters or daughters they were, or that have been the cause of some good, and who those were who have set right the errors of men—I think you would be embarrassed."

[22] "Truly," replied the Magnifico Giuliano, "I should be embarrassed only by the number of them; and if I had time enough, I would tell you here the story of Octavia, wife of Mark Antony and sister of Augustus; of Porcia, Cato's daughter and wife of Brutus; of Caia Caecilia, wife of Tarquinius Priscus; of Cornelia, Scipio's daughter, and of countless others who are very famous: and not only of our own but of barbarian nations; as Alexandra, wife of Alexander, King of the Jews, who—after the death of her husband, when she saw the people aflame with rage and already up in arms to slay the two children he had left her, in revenge for the cruel and harsh servitude in which the father had always kept them—was able to appease their just wrath and by her prudence immediately win over to her children those minds which the father, by countless wrongs over the many years, had rendered so hostile to his offspring."

"Tell us at least," replied signora Emilia, "how she did it."

"When she saw her children in so much danger," said the Magnifico, "she at once had Alexander's body thrown into the middle of the public square. Then, calling the citizens to her, she said that she knew they were incensed with a very just hatred of her husband because the cruel injuries he had so iniquitously done them deserved it; and just as she had always wished, while he was alive, that she could bring him to abandon such a wicked life, so now she was ready to give proof of this and, in so far as that was possible, help them punish him for these things, now that he was dead; and that therefore they should take his body and feed it to dogs, and tear it to bits in the cruelest ways they could devise: but she begged them to have mercy on her innocent children, who could have no knowledge of their father's evil deeds, much less any guilt. These words were so effective that the fierce wrath prevailing in the minds of all the people was at once mitigated and converted to such a feeling of pity that with one accord they not only chose those children as their rulers, but they even gave a most honorable burial to the body of the dead man."

Here the Magnifico paused a moment, then added: "Don't you know that the wife and sisters of Mithridates showed much less fear of death than Mithridates did? And Hasdrubal's wife than Hasdrubal?[2] Don't you know that Harmonia, daughter of Hiero the Siracusan, chose to die in the burning of her native city?"[3]

Then Frisio said: "Where it is a matter of obstinacy, it is certain that some women are occasionally found who would never abandon their purpose; like the one who, when she could no longer say 'scissors' to her husband, made the sign of them to him with her hands."[4]

[23] The Magnifico Giuliano laughed, and said: "Obstinacy directed to a worthy end ought to be called constancy; as in the case of the famous Epicharis,[5] a Roman freed-woman, who, being privy to a great conspiracy against Nero, was of such constancy that, although racked by the worst tortures imaginable, she never betrayed any of her accomplices; whereas, many noble knights and senators, in the same peril, timorously accused brothers, friends, and the dearest and nearest they had in the world.

"What will you say of that other woman named Leona in whose honor the Athenians dedicated a tongueless lioness (leona) in bronze before the gate of the citadel, to exhibit the steadfast virtue of silence that had been hers; because, being likewise privy to a conspiracy against the tyrants, she was not dismayed by the death of two great men her friends, and, though torn by countless and most cruel tortures, never betrayed any of the conspirators."[6]

---

2. For the heroic actions of Hasdrubal's wife, see Valerius Maximus, *Factorum et dictorum* III, 2.
3. See Valerius Maximus, *op. cit.*, III, 2.
4. The reference is to the anecdote of the wife who was thrown into a well by her husband when she persisted too long in asking him to get her a pair of scissors, and who, as she came to the surface time and again, choked by the water and unable to utter the word, with her fingers made the sign of scissors to her husband. Cf. C. Speroni, "The Obstinate Wife," *Italica* XXVIII (1951), p. 181.
5. Tacitus (*Annales* XV, 57) tells of the heroic death of this Greek courtesan in A.D. 65.
6. Cf. Pausanias, *Periegesis of Greece* I, 23; Plutarch, "On Garrulity." Leaena was accused of being a party to the conspiracy that led to the slaying of Hipparchus of Athens in 514 B.C.

Then madonna Margherita Gonzaga said: "I think that you tell all too briefly of these virtuous deeds of women; for these enemies of ours, although they have heard and read of them, yet pretend not to know them and would have the memory of them lost: but if you will let us women hear them, at least we shall take pride in them."

[24] Then the Magnifico Giuliano replied: "Very well. Now I want to tell you of a woman who did something which I think signor Gasparo himself will admits is done by very few men." And he began: "In Massilia there was once a custom thought to have been brought from Greece, which was this: they publicly kept a poison concocted of hemlock, and anyone was allowed to take it who proved to the Senate that he ought to depart this life because of some trouble suffered, or for some other just reason, to the end that whoever endured too great a misfortune or enjoyed too prosperous a fortune should not continue in the one or change the other. Now Sextus Pompey, finding himself . . ."

Here Frisio, not waiting for the Magnifico Giuliano to go on, said: "It strikes me that this is the beginning of a long story."

Then the Magnifico Giuliano turned to madonna Margherita, laughing, and said: "You see: Frisio will not let me speak. I was going to tell you about a woman who, when she had demonstrated to the Senate that she ought rightfully to die, cheerfully and fearlessly took the poison in the presence of Sextus Pompey, with such constancy of spirit and with such thoughtful and loving remembrances to her family, that Pompey and all the others who saw such wisdom and steadfastness in a woman in the face of death's dark passage wept and were overcome by wonder."[7]

[25] Then signor Gasparo said, laughing: "I too recall having read an oration in which an unhappy husband asks the permission of the Senate to die, and proves that he has just cause in that he cannot endure the continual annoyance of his wife's chatter, and prefers to swallow the poison (which you say was publicly kept for such a purpose) rather than his wife's words."

The Magnifico Giuliano replied: "How many poor women would have just cause for asking leave to die, because they cannot endure, I will not say the evil words, but the most evil deeds, of their husbands! For I know several such who suffer in this world the pains that are said to be in hell."

"Do you not think," replied signor Gasparo, "that there are also many husbands who have such torment from their wives that they continually yearn for death?"

7. The anecdote is told by Valerius Maximus, *op. cit.*, II, 6.

"And what annoyance," said the Magnifico, "can wives give their husbands that is as incurable as that which husbands give their wives? —who, if not for love, at least for fear, are submissive to their husbands?"

"Certain it is," said signor Gasparo, "that the little good they sometimes do is done out of fear, since there are few women in the world who in their hearts do not hate their husbands."

"Nay, quite the contrary," replied the Magnifico, "and if you well remember what you have read, we see in all the histories that wives nearly always love their husbands more than husbands love their wives. When did you ever see or read of a husband giving his wife such proof of love as the famous Camma gave her husband?"

"I do not know," replied signor Gasparo, "who the woman was, or what proof she gave."

"Nor I," said Frisio.

"Listen then," replied the Magnifico, "and you, madonna Margherita, take care to remember it.

[26] "This Camma[8] was a very beautiful young woman, adorned with such modesty and comely manners that she was admired for this no less than for her beauty; and above all else and with all her heart she loved her husband, whose name was Synattus. Now it chanced that another man, who was of much higher station than Synattus and who was almost tyrant of the city where they lived, fell in love with this young woman; and, having long tried by all ways and means to possess her, and quite in vain, he became convinced that the love she bore her husband was the sole obstacle to his desires; and he had this Synattus murdered. Then he continued to press her, but never managed to gain anything more than before; whereupon, as his love grew daily, he resolved to take her for his wife, although she was far beneath him in station. So when Sinoris (for this was the name of the lover) had asked her of her parents, they began to urge her to make her peace with this, showing her that her consent would be very advantageous, and her refusal dangerous to her and to them all. And she, after withstanding them for a time, replied that she was willing.

"Her parents sent word to Sinoris, who was exceedingly glad, and arranged that the marriage should be performed at once. Then, when the two had entered into the Temple of Diana in the usual rite, Camma had a certain sweet drink brought which she had prepared; and so, before Diana's image and in the presence of Sinoris, she drank half of it; then with her own hand (for such was the custom at marriages) she gave the rest to the groom, who drank it all.

8. The story of Camma is told in Plutarch's tract "On the Virtue of Women."

"When Camma saw that her design had succeeded, rejoicing she knelt at the foot of Diana's image and said: 'O Goddess, thou that knowest the secrets of my heart, be thou good witness how hard it was for me to keep from making an end of my life after the death of my dear husband, and with what weariness I have endured the pain of lingering on in this bitter life, wherein I had no other good or pleasure save the hope of that vengeance which I now know I have attained. Thus, joyous and content, I go to join the sweet company of that soul which in life and in death I have always loved more than myself. And you, wretch, who thought to be my husband, give orders that your tomb be made ready for you in place of the marriage bed, for I am offering you as a sacrifice to the shade of Synattus.'

"Terrified by these words, and feeling already the effect of the poison steal over him, he sought various remedies but none availed; and Camma had the good fortune (or whatever it was) to know, before dying, that Sinoris was dead. Learning this, she lay down most contentedly on her bed, her eyes turned toward heaven, uttering continually the name of Synattus and saying: "Oh, dearest husband, now that I have given both tears and vengeance as last offerings for your death, and cannot see what else is left me to do for you, I quit this world and a life so cruel without you and once dear to me for your sake alone. Come then, my lord, to meet me and receive this soul as willingly as it comes to you.' And so saying, with arms spread wide as if she thought to embrace him already, she died. Now, Frisio, what, pray, do you think of this woman?"

Frisio replied: "I think that you would like to make these ladies weep. But, even supposing the story to be true, I tell you such women are no longer found in the world."

[27] "Indeed they are," said the Magnifico, "and, in proof of this, listen. In my time there was a gentleman in Pisa whose name was messer Tommaso; what his family was I do not recall, although I often heard them spoken of by my father, who was a great friend of his. Now, this messer Tommaso, crossing one day in a small boat to Sicily on business, was overtaken by some Moorish galleys[9] which had come up so suddenly that those in charge of the boat did not see them; and, although the men in her put up a strong defense, yet as they were few and the enemy many, the vessel fell into the hands of the Moors together with all who remained in her, wounded or uninjured according to their lot, and among them messer Tommaso, who had fought bravely and with his own hands had slain a brother of one of the captains of the galleys. Wherefore, enraged at the loss of his brother, as you can imagine, the captain claimed him as his

___

9. Low, flat vessels navigated with sails and oars, common in the Mediterranean [*Editor*].

prisoner; and, beating and torturing him every day, carried him to Barbary, resolving to keep him a prisoner there for life, in great misery and suffering.

"After a time, all the others were liberated, by one means or another, and returned home to report to his wife (whose name was madonna Argentina) and to his children the hard life and the great suffering in which messer Tommaso lived and would continue to live without hope unless God should miraculously help him. After his family was told of this and had tried to free him in one way and another, and when he himself was quite resigned to death, it came to pass that a sedulous piety so spurred the wit and daring of one of his sons, whose name was Paolo, that the youth took no thought of any kind of danger and resolved that he would either die or free his father; and in this he succeeded, and brought him out so secretly that he was in Leghorn before it was known in Barbary that he had escaped. From Leghorn messer Tommaso, now safe, wrote to his wife telling her of his deliverance, where he was, and how he hoped to see her on the morrow. Overwhelmed by this great and unexpected joy at being (through the piety and capability of her son) on the point of seeing her husband again so soon, whom she so dearly loved and whom she had firmly believed she would never see again—the good and gentle lady, when she had read the letter, raised her eyes to heaven and, calling her husband's name, fell dead; nor for all the remedies that were brought to her did her departed soul return again to her body. Cruel spectacle, and enough to temper our wishes and restrain us from excessive longings after too much joy."

[28] Then Frisio said, laughing: "How do you know she did not die of grief on hearing that her husband was coming home?"

The Magnifico replied: "Because up to that time her life was not consonant with this; indeed, I think that her soul, unable to endure waiting to see him with the eyes of her body, forsook it, and, drawn by desire, quickly flew to where her thought had flown on reading the letter."

Signor Gasparo said: "It may be that this lady was too much in love, for women always go to extremes in everything, which is bad; and you see that by being too much in love she harmed herself, her husband, and her children, whose joy over his perilous and longed-for liberation she turned into bitterness. Therefore, you should not cite her as one of those women who have been the cause of great benefits."

The Magnifico replied: "I cite her as one of those who can testify that there are wives who love their husbands; as for those who brought great benefits to the world, I could tell you of an infinite number of such, and could set forth to you those who invented such things that among men they deserved to be esteemed as goddesses, like Pallas and Ceres; and the Sibyls, by whose mouth God spoke so often, revealing to the world the things that were to come; and those who have been the teachers of very great men, like Aspasia; and like Diotima,[1] who by her sacrifices delayed for ten years the coming of a pestilence that was due to strike Athens. I could tell you of Nicostrata, Evander's mother, who taught letters to the Latins; and of yet another woman who was the teacher of the lyric poet Pindar;[2] and of Corinna and Sappho, who so excelled in poetry; but I do not wish to go so far afield. I will say, however (to be brief), that women were perhaps no less the cause of Rome's greatness than men."

"This," said signor Gasparo, "would be fine to hear."

[29] The Magnifico replied: "Listen then.[3] After the fall of Troy, many Trojans who escaped that great ruin fled, some in one direction, some in another; of whom one lot, who were tossed by many storms, came into Italy at that place where the Tiber enters the sea. Landing there in quest of necessaries, they began to search the countryside. The women, who had remained in the ships, took thought of a good plan that would put an end to their dangerous and long wanderings by sea and that would give them a new country in place of the one they had lost; and, after conferring together while the men were away, they burned the ships; and the first to set her hand to such a deed had the name Roma. Yet, fearing the wrath of the men, who were returning, they went out to meet them; and with much affection, embracing and kissing, some their husbands and some their kinsmen, they softened the first impulse of anger; then in quiet they explained to the men the reason for their wise scheme. Whereupon the Trojans, both out of necessity and because they had been kindly received by the natives, were well pleased with what the women had done, and dwelt there with the Latins in the place which was later Rome; and from this arose the ancient custom among the Romans that the women kissed their kinfolk when they met. Now you see how much these women helped in the founding of Rome.

[30] "Nor did the Sabine women[4] contribute less to Rome's increase than the Trojan women did to its beginning. For Romulus, having

1. Pallas Athena was the Greek goddess of wisdom; Ceres or Demeter was the goddess of the earth. The Sybils were priestesses who were consulted for their enigmatic prophecies. Aspasia (5th century B.C.), cultured courtesan and the mistress of Pericles, was praised for her learning and eloquence. Diotima was the priestess from Mantinea to whom Socrates attributes his understanding of love in Plato's *Symposium* [*Editor*].
2. The reference is to the Greek poetess Myrtis of the sixth century B.C.
3. The story that follows is taken from Plutarch, "On the Virtue of Women." Cf. *Aeneid* V, 605 ff.
4. The story of the Sabine women is taken from Livy, *History of Rome* I, ch. 12–13.

aroused general enmity among all his neighbors by carrying off their women, was harassed by wars on every side; which, since he was a man of ability, were soon concluded in victory, except the war with the Sabines, which was very great because Titus Tatius, King of the Sabines, was exceedingly able and wise. Wherefore, when a hard battle had been fought between the Romans and the Sabines, with very heavy casualties on both sides, and as a fresh and cruel conflict was brewing, the Sabine women, dressed in black, with hair loosened and torn, weeping and mourning, with no fear for the weapons that were already drawn to strike, rushed in between the fathers and the husbands, begging them not to stain their hands with the blood of fathers-in-law and sons-in-law. And if the men were displeased with the marriage tie, let the weapons be turned against them, the women, for it were better for them to die than to live widowed or without fathers and brothers, and be forever remembering that their children were begotten of those who had slain their fathers or that they themselves were born of those who had slain their husbands. Thus, weeping and groaning, many of the women carried their little children in their arms, some of whom were already beginning to prattle, and who seemed to try to call to their grandfathers and hold out their arms to them; to whom the women showed these their grandchildren, saying in tears: 'Behold your own blood which you are trying so hotly and furiously to spill with your own hands.'

"The piety and wisdom of these women were so effective in this that not only was an indissoluble friendship and confederation brought about between the two hostile kings, but, what was more wonderful, the Sabines came to live in Rome and the two peoples became one. And thus this peace greatly increased the power of Rome, thanks to those wise and courageous women who were repaid by Romulus, in that, when he divided the people into thirty wards, he gave to these the names of Sabine women."

[31] Here, having paused a little, and seeing that signor Gasparo was not going to speak, the Magnifico Giuliano said: "Does it not seem to you that these women were the cause of good to their menfolk and contributed to the greatness of Rome?"

Signor Gasparo replied: "Truly, they were worthy of much praise: but if you had also been pleased to tell of the errors of women as well as of their good works, you would not have kept silent about the fact that in this war against Titus Tatius it was a woman who betrayed Rome and who showed the enemy the way to seize the Capitol, wherein the Romans barely escaped being entirely destroyed."

The Magnifico Giuliano replied: "You cite me a single bad woman, whereas I tell you of countless good ones; and, in addition to those already mentioned, I could name you a thousand other instances of what I am saying, of benefits done to Rome by women; and could tell you why a temple was dedicated of old to Venus Armata, and another to Venus Calva, and how the Festival of the Handmaidens was instituted in honor of Juno because handmaidens had once delivered Rome from the machinations of the enemy.[5] But, leaving all these things aside, did not that great deed—the discovery of Cataline's conspiracy for which Cicero so praises himself —have its beginning with a lowly woman,[6] who therefore could be said to have been the cause of all the good that Cicero boasts of doing for the Roman Republic? And, if I had the time, I should further show you that women have often corrected many of the errors of men; but I fear that this talk of mine is already too long and tiresome: so, having performed as best I could the assignment given me by these ladies, I would now make way for someone who can say things worthier of being listened to than any I can say."

[32] Then signora Emilia said: "Do not rob women of those true praises which are their due; and keep in mind that if signor Gasparo, and perhaps also signor Ottaviano, listen to you with displeasure, we and all these other gentlemen are pleased to hear you."

The Magnifico still wished to have done, but all the ladies began to entreat him to speak; whereupon he said, laughing: "In order not to make signor Gasparo more of an enemy of mine than he already is, I will be brief about a few women who come to mind, omitting many that I could mention." Then he continued: "When Philip, son of Demetrius, was besieging the city of Chios,[7] he issued an edict promising freedom and their masters' wives to all slaves who could escape from the city and come to him. So great was the wrath of the women over this shameful edict that they came forth to the walls armed, and fought so fiercely that in a short while they drove Philip off, to his shame and loss, which is something their husbands had not been able to do.

"When these same women came to Leuconia with their husbands, fathers, and brothers (who were going into exile), they did something not less glorious than this:[8] the Erythraeans, who were there with their allies, declared war on these Chiotes, who were unable to stand against them, and entered into a pact that they

5. The story of how Rome was saved from the Latins by slave-girls (handmaidens) who took the place of free-born girls demanded as hostages by the enemy is told by Plutarch in the *Life of Romulus* and the *Life of Camillus* [Editor].
6. Cataline was a Roman aristocrat who conspired to overthrow the Republic in 63 B.C. The reference is to a Roman woman named Fulvia whose deeds are recounted by Sallust, *Conspiracy of Cataline*, ch. XXIII [Editor].
7. The story is told in Plutarch's "On the Virtue of Women."
8. Cf. Plutarch, *op. cit.*, for this story.

should leave the city dressed only in their cloacks and tunics. When the women heard of this shameful pact, they complained, and upbraided the men for abandoning their weapons and going out almost naked among the enemy; and when the men answered that they had already bound themselves to this, the women told them to leave their clothes behind and to carry their shields and spears; and to tell the enemy that these were their attire. And so, following their women's advice, they undid in great part the shame from which they could not entirely escape.

"Again, when Cyrus had routed an army of Persians in battle,[9] the latter as they fled to their city, met their women outside the gate, who, as they came toward them, said: 'Why are you fleeing, cowardly men? Is it perhaps that you would hide yourselves in us, out of whom you came?' On hearing these and other such words, and feeling how inferior in courage they were to their women, the men were ashamed of themselves and, turning upon the enemy, stood once more against him and routed him."

[33] Having spoken thus far, the Magnifico paused, and, turning to the Duchess, said: "Now, Madam, you will give me leave to be silent."

Signor Gasparo replied: "You will have to be silent, for you do not know what more to say."

The Magnifico said, laughing: "You urge me on so that you run the risk of having to listen all night to praises of women; and of having to hear of many Spartan women who rejoiced in the glorious death of their sons; and of those who disowned or even slew their sons when they saw them act like cowards; also of how, in the ruin of their country, the Saguntine women took up arms against the forces of Hannibal;[1] and how, when Marius defeated the army of the Germans, their women, being unable to gain permission to live free at Rome in the service of the Vestal Virgins, killed themselves and their little children; and of a thousand others of whom all the ancient histories are full."[2]

Then signor Gasparo said: "Ah, signor Magnifico, God alone knows just how all those things happened; for those centuries are so remote from us that many lies can be told, and there is no one to gainsay them."

[34] The Magnifico said: "If you will compare the worth of women in every age to that of men, you will find that they have never been, and are not now a whit inferior to men in worth; for, leaving aside

9. *Ibid.*
1. Cf. Livy, *op. cit.*, XXI, ch. 7–9; XXXXI, ch. 17.
2. Cf. Valerius Maximus, *op. cit.*, VI, ch. 1.

those many ancients and coming down to the time when the Goths ruled in Italy, you will find that there was a queen among them, Amalasontha, who ruled for a long time with admirable wisdom; then Theodolinda, Queen of the Lombards, of singular ability; Theodora, the Greek empress; and in Italy, among many others, Countess Matilda was a most extraordinary woman, in whose praise I will leave Count Ludovico to speak, since she was of his family."

"Nay," said the Count, "that is up to you, for you well know that it ill becomes a man to praise his own."

The Magnifico continued: "And how many famous women do you find in the history of this most noble house of Montefeltro! How many in the house of Gonzaga, of Este, of Pio! Then, if you would speak of present times, we shall not need to look far afield for examples, because we have them here before us. But I shall not avail myself of these lest you pretend out of courtesy to grant me what you can in no way deny. And, to go outside of Italy, remember that in our day we have seen Queen Anne of France, a very great lady no less in ability than in station; and if you will compare her in justice and clemency, liberality and uprightness of life, with Kings Charles and Louis (to both of whom she was consort), you will not find her to be the least bit inferior to them. Consider madonna Margherita (daughter of the Emperor Maximilian) who until now has governed and still governs her state with the greatest wisdom and justice.

[35] "But, leaving all others aside, tell me, signor Gasparo, what king or prince has there been in Christendom in our day, or even for many years past, who deserves to be compared with Queen Isabella of Spain?"

Signor Gasparo replied: "King Ferdinand, her husband!"

The Magnifico continued: "I will not deny that. For since the Queen judged him worthy of being her husband, and loved and respected him so much, we cannot say that he does not deserve to be compared with her; yet I believe that the fame he had because of her was a dowry not inferior to the kingdom of Castile."

"On the contrary," replied signor Gasparo, "I think that Queen Isabella was given credit for many of King Ferdinand's deeds."

Then the Magnifico said: "Unless the people of Spain—lords and commoners, men and women, poor and rich—have all conspired to lie in praising her, there has not been in our time anywhere on earth a more shining example of true goodness, of greatness of spirit, of prudence, of piety, of chastity, of courtesy, of liberality—in short, of every virtue—than Queen Isabella; and, although the fame of that lady is very great everywhere and among all nations, those who lived in her company and who personally witnessed her actions, all affirm that this fame sprang from her virtue and merits. And whoever con-

siders her deeds will easily see that such is the truth. For, leaving
aside countless things that bear witness to this and that could be
recounted if it were to our purpose, everyone knows that, when she
came to rule, she found the greater part of Castile held by the
grandees;[3] nevertheless, she recovered the whole with such justice
and in such manner that the very men who were deprived of it
remained greatly devoted to her and content to give up what they
possessed. Another notable thing is the courage and wisdom she
always showed in defending her realms against very powerful enemies; and likewise to her alone is the honor of the glorious conquest
of the kingdom of Granada to be attributed; for in such a long and
hard war against obstinate enemies—who were fighting for property, for life, for religion, and (to their way of thinking) for God—
she always showed, both in her counsel and in her very person, such
ability that perhaps few princes in our time have dared, I will not
say to imitate her, but even to envy her.

"Besides this, all who knew her affirm that she had such a divine
manner of ruling that her mere wish seemed enough to make every
man do what he was supposed to do; so that men, in their own
houses and secretly, scarcely dared to do anything they thought
might displease her: and this was due in large part to the admirable
judgment she showed in recognizing and choosing able ministers for
those offices in which she intended to use them; and so well did she
know how to combine the rigor of justice with the gentleness of
mercy and liberality that in her day there was no good man who
complained of being too little rewarded by her nor any bad man of
being too severely punished. There arose thus among the people a
very great veneration for her, comprised of love and fear, and a veneration still so fixed in the minds of all that it almost seems that they
expect her to be watching them from heaven, and think she might
praise or blame them from up there; and so those realms are still
governed by her fame and by the methods instituted by her, so that,
although her life is ended, her authority lives on—like a wheel
which, when spun a long while by force, continues to turn by itself
for a good space, even though no one impels it any more.

"Moreover, consider this, signor Gasparo: in our time almost all
the men of Spain that are great or famous for anything whatever
were made so by Queen Isabella; and Gonzalvo Ferrando, the Great
Captain, was much prouder of this than of all his famous victories
or of those egregious and worthy deeds which have made him so
bright and illustrious in peace and war that, unless fame is thank-
less in the extreme, she will always herald his immortal praises to
the world and bear witness that in our time we have had few kings

---

3. Powerful noblemen of high rank [*Editor*].

or great princes who are not surpassed by him in magnanimity, in wisdom, and in every virtue.

[36] "Coming back to Italy now, I say that here too there is no lack of very admirable ladies; for in Naples we have two remarkable queens;[4] also not long ago there died at Naples the Queen of Hungary,[5] such a remarkable lady, as you know, worthy of the unconquerable and glorious king, Matthias Corvinus, her husband. Likewise the Duchess Isabella of Aragon, worthy sister of King Ferdinand of Naples, who (like gold in the fire) showed her virtue and worth amidst the storms of fortune. If you pass into Lombardy, you will find Isabella, Marchioness of Mantua, of whose most admirable virtues it would be offensive to speak as restrainedly as anyone must do here who would speak of her at all. I regret, too, that all of you did not know her sister, the Duchess Beatrice of Milan, in order that you might never again have occasion to marvel at a woman's abilities. And Eleanora of Aragon, Duchess of Ferrara and mother of both of the ladies whom I have mentioned, was such that her most excellent virtues bore fair witness to the entire world that she was not only the worthy daughter of a king, but deserved to be queen of a much greater realm than all her ancestors had possessed. And, to mention another, how many men in the world do you know who have endured the hard blows of fortune as patiently as Queen Isabella of Naples, who, after the loss of her kingdom, the exile and death of her husband, King Federico, and of two children, and the captivity of her first-born, the Duke of Calabria, still proves herself a queen, and so sustains the calamitous vexations of bitter poverty as to give all men proof that, though her fortune has changed, her character has not.

"I shall forgo mentioning countless other ladies, as well as women of low station: like many Pisan women, who in defense of their city against the Florentines showed that generous courage, without any fear whatever of death, which the most unconquerable spirits that ever lived on earth might have shown; wherefore, some of them have been celebrated by many noble poets. I could tell you of some who excelled greatly in letters, in music, in painting, in sculpture; but I do not wish to go on reviewing these instances so well known to you all. It will suffice if you take thought of the women you yourselves have known, for it will not be difficult for you to see that on the whole they are not inferior in worth and merits to their fathers, brothers, and husbands; and that many of them have been the cause

---

4. The queens referred to are doubtless Joanna III of Aragon (d. 1517), wife of Ferdinand I, King of Naples, and Juana IV (d. 1518), her daughter, widow of Ferdinand II of Naples.
5. This is Beatrice of Aragon (1457–1508) who became the wife of Matthias Corvinus, King of Hungary, in 1476 and died in Naples.

of benefits to men and have often corrected many of their errors; and if there are not now found on earth those great queens who go forth to conquer distant lands and erect great buildings, pyramids, and cities—like that famous Tomyris, Queen of Scythia, Artemisia, Zenobia, Semiramis, or Cleopatra—neither are there still men like Caesar, Alexander, Lucullus, and those other Roman commanders."

[37] "Do not say that," replied Frisio, laughing; "for now more than ever are there women to be found like Cleopatra or Semiramis; and if they do not have such great domains, power, and riches, still they do not lack the will to imitate those queens in taking their pleasures and in satisfying all their appetites in so far as they are able."

The Magnifico Giuliano said: "You are still trying to exceed bounds, Frisio; but if there are Cleopatras to be found, there is no lack of a great many Sardanapaluses, which is much worse."

Then signor Gasparo said: "Do not make these comparisons, or believe that men are more incontinent than women; and, even if they were, it would not be worse, for from women's incontinence countless evils arise, as they do not from men's. Therefore, as was said yesterday, it is wisely established that women are permitted to fail in all other things without incurring blame, to the end that they may devote all their strength to holding to this one virtue of chastity; without which there would be uncertainty about offspring, and the bond would be dissolved that binds the whole world through the blood, and through each man's natural love for what he engenders. Hence, a dissolute life is more forbidden to women than to men, who do not carry their children within them for nine months."

[38] Then the Magnifico replied: "These are indeed fine arguments which you present, and I do not see why you do not put them in writing. But, tell me, why has it not been established that a dissolute life is quite as disgraceful a thing in men as it is in women, considering that if men are by nature more virtuous and of greater worth, they might all the more easily practice this virtue of continence also; and there would be neither more nor less certainty about offspring, for, even if women were unchaste, they could in no way bear children of themselves and without other aid, provided men were continent and did not take part in the unchastity of women. But if you will acknowledge the truth, you surely know that of our own authority we men have arrogated to ourselves a license, whereby we insist that in us the same sins are most trivial and sometimes deserve praise which in women cannot be sufficiently punished, unless by a shameful death, or at least a perpetual infamy. Wherefore, this being the prevailing opinion, I judge it a fitting thing to punish

harshly those too who defame women with lies; and I think that every noble cavalier is bound always to take arms, if need be, in defense of the truth, and especially when he knows that some woman is falsely accused of being unchaste."

[39] "And I," replied signor Gasparo, laughing, "not only declare that what you say is the duty of every noble cavalier, but I think it is an act of great courtesy and goodness to conceal the fault which a woman may happen to have committed, either by mischance or out of excessive love; and thus you can see that I am more on the side of women, when reason allows, it than you are. Indeed, I do not deny that men have arrogated to themselves a certain liberty; and this because they know that, according to universal opinion, a loose life does not defame them as it does women, who, due to the frailty of their sex, give in to their appetites much more than men; and if they sometimes refrain from satisfying their desires, they do so out of shame and not because they lack a ready will in that regard. Therefore men have instilled in women the fear of infamy as a bridle to bind them as by force to this virtue, without which they would truly be little esteemed; for the world finds no usefulness in women except the bearing of children.

"But such is not the case with men, who rule cities and armies, and do so many other important things. Since you will have it so, I do not wish to deny that women can do these things; the fact is that they do not do them. And when it has chanced that men were models of continence, they have surpassed women in this virtue as well as in the others, even though you do not grant this. And, in this regard, I will not recite as many stories or fables as you have done, but will simply remind you of the continence of two very great commanders, who were young and were enjoying the fruits of victory, which is wont to make men insolent even in the lowest ranks. One is that of Alexander the Great toward the very beautiful women of Darius, a vanquished enemy;[6] the other is that of Scipio, who, at the age of twenty-four, had taken a city in Spain by force. There was brought to him a beautiful and noble young woman, captured along with many others; and, on hearing that she was the bride of a gentleman of that country, Scipio not only refrained from any unchaste act toward her, but restored her unsullied to her husband and gave her a rich gift besides.[7]

"I could tell you of Xenocrates, who was so continent that, when a very beautiful woman lay down naked beside him and used all the caresses and arts that she knew (and she was very well versed in

6. Cf. Plutarch's *Life of Alexander.*
7. The anecdote is told by Valerius Maximus, *op. cit.*, IV, 3.

such), she was unable to make him show the slightest sign of pruri-
ence, although she tried throughout the night;[8] and of Pericles, who
on merely hearing someone praise a boy's beauty too emphatically
upbraided him sharply;[9] and of many others who have been very
continent by their own choice, and not out of shame or fear of punishment, which is what moves most women to practice this virtue;
who deserve high praise nonetheless, and he who falsely defames
them for unchasteness deserves the harshest punishment, as you
have said."

[40] Then messer Cesare, who had been silent for a long time, said:
"Think how signor Gasparo must speak when he blames women, if
these are the things he says in their praise. But if the Magnifico will
permit me to say a few things in his stead, in reply to those which
signor Gasparo has (in my opinion) falsely spoken against women,
it will be well for both of us; since he can rest for a while and will
then be able to proceed to describe some further excellence of the
Court Lady, while I shall consider myself much favored in having an
opportunity to join him in performing the office of a good cavalier—
which is to defend the truth."

"Nay, please do," replied the Magnifico, "for I was already thinking I had fulfilled my duty to the extent of my powers, and that by
now this discussion is beside my purpose."

Messer Cesare continued: "I certainly do not wish to speak of the
profit the world has from women other than that of bearing of children, for it has been sufficiently shown how necessary they are, not
only to our being, but also to our well-being; but I say, signor Gasparo, that if they are, as you say, more inclined to yield to their
appetites than men, and if, for all that, they abstain therefrom more
than men do (which you admit), they are the more worthy of praise
in that their sex has less strength to resist natural appetites. And if
you say that they do it out of shame, it strikes me that instead of one
virtue you are allowing them two; for if shame is stronger in them
than appetite and if, for that reason, they abstain from bad actions,
I think that this shame (which is really nothing but fear of infamy)
is a rare virtue indeed, and one possessed by very few men. And if,
without bringing infinite disgrace to men, I might tell how many of
them are sunken in shamelessness (which is the vice opposed to this
virtue), it would pollute these chaste ears that hear me. And, what
is more, these offenders against God and nature are men who are
already old, who make a profession, some of priesthood, some of
philosophy, some of sacred law; who govern states with a Catonian

8. *Ibid.*
9. Cf. Cicero, *De officiis* I, ch. 40.

severity of countenance that makes a show of all the integrity in the world; and who are always alleging that the feminine sex is most incontinent; but they never regret anything more than their want of natural vigor to satisfy the abominable desires that still remain in their minds after nature has denied them to their bodies; and hence they often devise ways wherein such vigor is not required.

[41] "But I do not wish to say more; and it is enough if you grant me that women more than men abstain from an unchaste life; and certainly they are not curbed by any other bridle than that which they themselves put on. And that this is true, consider that the greater part of those who are kept under too close a watch, or are beaten by their husbands or fathers, are less chaste than those who have a certain liberty. But a bridle to women generally is their love of true virtue and their desire for honor, which many whom I have known in my time hold dearer than their own life; and, to tell the truth, every one of us has seen very noble youths, discreet, wise, worthy, and handsome, who devote many years to love, and omit nothing in the way of care, gifts, entreaties, tears, in short, everything imaginable—and all in vain. And were it not that you might tell me that my qualities have never made me worthy of being loved, I should cite myself in witness of this, who have more than once been on the verge of death because of the unyielding and all too stern chastity of a woman."

Signor Gasparo replied: "Do not wonder at that; for women who are begged refuse to yield to the one who begs them; and those who are not begged do the begging themselves."

[42] Messer Cesare said: "I have never known these men who are begged by women; but I have known very many who, on finding that their efforts are in vain and that they have foolishly wasted their time, have recourse to a noble revenge by claiming that they have had an abundance of what they have only imagined, and think it a kind of Courtiership to bear ill report and to invent tales in order that slanderous stories about some noble lady may set the crowd to talking. But such men who make a vile boast (whether true or false) of having possessed some fair lady deserve the severest punishment or torture; and if that is sometimes meted out to them, we cannot praise those enough who perform that office. For if such a one is telling lies, what villainy can be greater than to rob a worthy lady of something she values more than her life? And for no other reason than that which ought to win her endless praise? But, if he is telling the truth, what punishment could be heavy enough for a man so base as to repay with such ingratitude a woman who—conquered by false flatteries, feigned tears, ceaseless entreaties, laments, wiles,

tricks, and perjuries—has let herself be brought to an excessive love, and has then surrendered herself blindly and completely, a prey to an evil spirit of that ilk?

"But to answer you further concerning the extraordinary continence of an Alexander and of a Scipio as cited by you, I will not deny that the one and the other performed an act which deserves great praise: nevertheless, so that you may not say that in recounting ancient things I am telling fables, I will cite you a lowly woman of our own time who showed far greater continence than these two great men.

[43] "I say then that once I knew a pretty and winsome girl, whose name I will not tell you, so as not to furnish matter for slander to the many fools who conceive a bad opinion of a woman as soon as they hear that she is in love. This girl, having long been loved by a noble youth of good character, began to love him with all her mind and heart; and of this not only I (to whom she readily confided everything as if I had been, I will not say her brother, but her dearest sister), but all those who saw her in the company of her beloved young man were well aware of her passion. Thus, loving as ardently as any loving soul can love, for two years she maintained such continence that she never gave this young man the least sign of her love for him except such as she could not conceal; nor would she ever speak to him or receive letters or gifts from him, although not a day passed but she was urged to do both. And how much she desired it I well know, because whenever she was able to come into secret possession of anything that had belonged to the youth, she cherished it so much that it seemed to be her lifespring and her every good; and never in all that time would she grant him other pleasure except to see him and let herself be seen, and to dance with him as with others when sometimes she took part in public festivals.

"And since they were well suited to one another in station, the two desired that so great a love as theirs might end happily, and that they might be man and wife. And the same was desired by all the other men and women of that city, except her cruel father who, out of a perverse and strange humor, decided to marry her to another and richer man; and to this the unhappy girl expressed her opposition in no way except by bitter tears. And when the unhappy marriage had been concluded amidst great compassion on the part of the people and despair on the part of the poor lovers, even this blow of Fortune could not destroy a love that lay so deep in their hearts; and it continued for the space of three years, although she most prudently hid it and sought in every way to drive from herself those desires that were now hopeless. All this while she persisted in her determination to remain continent; and since she could not have him honorably whom alone she adored, she resolved not to wish for him in any way, and to continue in her custom of accepting neither messages nor gifts nor even glances from him; and, steadfast in this firm resolve, and, overcome by the cruelest anguish, and wasted by the long passion, she died within three years, preferring to renounce the satisfaction and the pleasures so fervidly desired, and finally her very life, rather than her honor. Nor was she without ways and means of satisfying herself quite in secret, without risking disgrace or loss of anything; and yet she abstained from what she herself so much desired and to which she was so continually exhorted by the only one in the world whom she wished to please: nor was she moved to this by fear or motive other than true virtue.

"What will you say of another, who for six months lay beside her dear lover nearly every night; nonetheless, in a garden full of sweetest fruits and incited by her own most ardent desires and by the entreaties and tears of one dearer to her than her life, she refrained from tasting them; and, although she was taken up and held close in those beloved arms, she never gave in, but kept the flower of her chastity immaculate?

[44] "Does it not seem to you, signor Gasparo, that these are acts of continence equal to those of Alexander?—who, being most ardently in love, not with Darius' women, but with the fame and greatness that drove him to thirst for glory, to endure hardships and dangers, to make himself immortal, scorned not only other things, but his own life, in order to win renown above all other men. And are we to marvel that, with such thoughts in his heart, he abstained from something he did not much desire? For, since he had never seen those women before, it is not possible that he fell in love with them on the spot, but may perhaps even have loathed them because of Darius, his enemy; and, in such a situation, his every wanton act toward them would have been an outrage and not love. Hence, it is no great matter that Alexander, who conquered the world by magnanimity rather than by arms, abstained from such outrage to those women.

"And truly Scipio's continence also deserves great praise. Nonetheless, if you consider it carefully, it cannot be said to equal that of the two women; for he likewise abstained from something which he did not desire—being in an enemy country, new in his command, and at the start of a very important undertaking; having left great expectations of himself at home, and bound as he was to give account of himself to very strict judges who often punished the slightest mistakes as well as great ones, and among whom he knew he had enemies; knowing also that if he were to act otherwise (the lady being very noble and married to a most noble lord), he would make many enemies, and in such a way that they would retard his victory and perhaps prevent it entirely. Hence, for so many important reasons he abstained from a passing indulgence that would have done him harm, showing continence and a generous integrity; which, as is written, gained him the good will of all those peoples, and was worth another army to him, conquering hearts by benevolence that perhaps would have proved unconquerable by force of arms. So that this could be called rather a military stratagem than pure continence—though the report of this deed is not very trustworthy, because some authoritative writers state that Scipio did enjoy the young woman amorously; but there is no doubt whatever in the case I have reported."

[45] Frisio said: "You must have found it in the Gospels!"

Messer Cesare replied: "I witnessed it myself, and so I have a greater certainty of it than you or others can have that Alcibiades always arose from Socrates' bed not otherwise than children from the bed of their parents; for bed and night were indeed a strange place and time for the contemplation of that pure beauty which Socrates is said to have loved without any impure desires, especially since he loved the soul's beauty rather than the body's—but this beauty in boys, and not in grown men, even though the latter have more wisdom. And surely one could not find a better example wherewith to praise the continence of men than that of Xenocrates, who, given to a life of study, held in check by his profession which was philosophy (which consists in good habits and not in words), when old and no longer in possession of his natural vigor, and completely impotent, denied himself a harlot who would have been abhorrent to him because of that name alone. I should rather deem him continent if he had given any sign of carnal desire, and then had observed continence; or if he had abstained from what old men desire more than the skirmishes of Venus, namely, wine: but, as certain evidence of his continence as an old man, it is recorded that he was much given to wine. And what in an old man shall we say is more a stranger to continence than drunkenness? And if abstaining from the delights of Venus in that sluggish and cold time of life is deserving of so much praise, how much more is that same abstinence to be praised in tender girls such as the two I have told you of: one of whom maintained the strictest rule over all her senses, not only denying her eyes their very light, but driving from her heart those thoughts which alone had long been the sweetest sustenance of her life; the other, ardently enamored and finding herself so many times secretly in the arms of the one whom she loved far more than the whole world, struggling against herself and against one who was dearer to her than herself, repressed that ardent desire which has often conquered and conquers so many wise men.

"Now, signor Gasparo, do you not think that writers ought to be ashamed of celebrating Xenocrates in this, and calling him continent? For if we had any way of knowing, I would wager that he slept like a log throughout the night and up to the dinner hour of the next day, drowned in wine; nor was it of any avail for the woman to rub him in order to make him open his eyes, but he was as one drugged."

[46] At this all the company laughed, and signora Emilia said, still laughing: "Indeed, signor Gasparo, if you will think a little harder, I am sure you will remember some other fine instance of continence similar to that one!"

Messer Cesare replied: "Does it not seem to you, Madam, that the case of Pericles cited by him is a fine example of continence? I am only surprised that he did not speak also of the continence and the fine saying that is recorded of the man of whom a woman asked too high a price for a night, and he answered her that he was not accustomed to buy repentance at such a figure."[1]

The company was still laughing; and messer Cesare, after remaining silent for a moment, said: "Forgive me, signor Gasparo, if I speak the truth, for in short these are the instances of the miraculous continence that men have recorded of themselves, the while they denounce women as incontinent: in whom every day we see infinite proofs of continence; for surely, if you will consider well, there is no fortress so unassailable that, were it attacked with a thousandth part of the weapons and wiles as are used to overcome the constancy of a woman, it would not surrender at the first assault. How many retainers of princes, made rich by them and held in the greatest esteem, who were in command of fortresses and strongholds on which that prince's state and life and every good depended, without shame or any fear of being called traitors, have perfidiously and for gain surrendered those to persons who were not to have them? And would to God there were such a dearth of this kind of men in our day that we might not have a much harder time finding a man who had done his duty in such instances than we do in naming those who have failed in theirs! Do we not see many indeed who go about killing men in the forests, and who sail the seas for no other purpose than to steal money? How many prelates sell the things of God's church! How many lawyers forge wills, how many perjurers bear false witness solely to gain money! How many doctors poison their patients for the same motive! And again how many do the

---

1. From Aulus Gellius, *Noctes Atticae* I, ch. 8.

vilest things from fear of death! And yet a tender and delicate girl often resists all these fierce and strong assaults, for many have been known who chose to die rather than to lose their chastity."

[47] Then signor Gasparo said: "Messer Cesare, I do not believe that such women exist in the world today."

Messer Cesare replied: "I will not now cite you the ancients, but I will say this, that many women could be found, and are found, who in such cases are not afraid to die. And this instance occurs to me now: when Capua was sacked by the French (which was not so long ago that you cannot recall it very well) a beautiful young lady of that city was taken from her house where she had been captured by a company of Gascons, and when she reached the river that flows through Capua, she pretended that she wished to tie her shoe, so that the man who was leading her turned loose of her for a moment; whereupon she threw herself into the river. What will you say of a peasant girl[2] who not many months ago, at Gazuolo in the Mantuan region, went with her sister to reap in the fields, and, being overcome by thirst, entered a house for a drink of water; and the master of the house, who was a young man, seeing that she was very beautiful and alone, embraced her and, first with gentle words and then with threats, sought to bring her to do his pleasure; and when she stubbornly resisted more and more, he at last subdued her with many blows and with force. Thus, disheveled and weeping, she returned to her sister in the field, nor for all her sister's urging would she tell the outrage she had suffered in that house; but, as they walked toward home, she pretended to grow calmer little by little and speak without excitement, and asked her sister to do certain things for her. Then when she came to the edge of the Oglio, which is the river that flows by Gazuolo, she drew somewhat apart from her sister, who did not know or imagine what she intended to do, then suddenly she threw herself in. Her sister ran lamenting and weeping after her, following her as best she could along the bank of the river that bore her downstream very rapidly: and every time the poor creature came to the surface, the sister would throw her a cord which she had brought with her for binding sheaves, and although the cord touched her hands several times (for she was still near the bank), the stanch and determined girl continually refused it and put it from her; and thus, spurning every aid that might have saved her life, she quickly perished: driven neither by nobility of birth, nor by fear of a crueler death or of infamy, but solely by grief for her lost virginity. Now from this you can see how many unknown women perform acts so greatly deserving of praise; for this woman gave

2. The story is told by Bandello, *Novelle* I, 8.

such proof of her virtue only a few days ago, you might say, yet no one speaks of her or even mentions her name. But if the death of the Duchess's uncle, the Bishop of Mantua, had not occurred at that time, the bank of the Oglio, at the place where she threw herself in, would now be graced by a very beautiful monument in memory of that glorious soul, which deserved all the brighter fame in death in that in life it dwelt in a less noble body."

[48] Here messer Cesare paused a moment, then continued: "At Rome too, in my day, another such case occurred: a beautiful and noble Roman girl, being long pursued by one who showed a great love for her, was never willing to reward him in any way, even with a single glance. So with money he corrupted a maid of hers, who, wishing to please him in order to get more money, persuaded her mistress to visit the church of San Sebastiano on a certain not very popular feast day; and, having notified the lover of everything, and shown him what he was to do, she brought the girl to one of those dark caves which nearly all who go to San Sebastiano are wont to visit; and here the young man was already secretly hidden. He, finding himself alone with her whom he loved so much, began to beg her in every way, as gently as he could, to take pity on him and change her past hardness to love. But when he saw that all his entreaties were of no avail, he resorted to threats, and when these also failed, he began to beat her cruelly; then, being firmly determined to obtain his aim, by force if necessary, he enlisted the help of the evil woman who had brought her there, but he was unable to force her to consent. Nay, although she was not at all strong, the poor girl defended herself by word and act as best she could: so that partly from anger at seeing that he could not obtain what he desired, partly from fear that her relatives, should they learn of the thing, might make him pay the penalty for it, this wicked man, aided by the maid (who shared his fear), strangled the unhappy girl and left her there. He fled and managed to escape being taken. The maid, blinded by the very crime itself, was not clever enough to flee; and when she was seized because of certain telltale signs, she confessed everything and got the punishment she deserved. The body of the steadfast and noble girl was brought forth from that cave in the greatest honor and taken into Rome for burial, with a laurel crown upon her head, and accompanied by an unending throng of men and women; among whom there was not one who went home without tears in his eyes; and in this way that rare soul was universally mourned as well as praised by all the people.

[49] "But, to speak of persons known to you, do you not recall having heard how signora Felice della Rovere was journeying to Savona

and, fearing that some sails that were sighted might be ships of Pope Alexander in pursuit of her, made ready with steadfast resolution to throw herself into the sea in case they should approach and there were no means of escape. And you must not think that she did this out of any passing whim, for you know as well as anyone else what intelligence and prudence accompanied this lady's singular beauty. Nor can I keep from mentioning our Duchess who has lived with her husband for fifteen years like a widow, and has not only been steadfast in not manifesting this to anyone in the world, but, when urged by her own people to leave such widowhood, she chose to suffer exile, poverty, and all kinds of hardships rather than accept what seemed to all others the great favor and bounty of Fortune"; and as messer Cesare was going on to say more of this, the Duchess said: "Speak of something else, and do not persist in this subject, for you have much else to say."

Messer Cesare continued: "But I know that you will not deny this, signor Gasparo, nor you, Frisio."

"No, indeed," replied Frisio, "but it takes more than one to make a crowd."

[50] Then messer Cesare said: "It is true that few women are capable of such great actions as these; still, those even who resist the assaults of love are all cause for wonder; and those who are sometimes overcome deserve much compassion: for certainly the importunity of lovers, the arts they use, the snares they spread, are so many and so continual that it is a great marvel if a tender girl manages to escape them. What day, what hour ever passes that the pursued girl is not urged by the lover with money, with presents, and with all things calculated to please her? When can she ever go to her window that she does not see the stubborn lover, speaking no word, but with eyes that speak, with pained and languid face, with hot sighs, often with copious tears? When does she ever go out to church or any other place without having the fellow always before her, meeting her at every street corner, his sad passion depicted in his eyes as if he expected to die at any moment. I do not speak of the fopperies, the inventions, mottoes, devices, festivals, dances, games, masquerades, jousts, tourneys!—all of which she knows are done for her. Then at night she cannot awaken without hearing music, or at least that restless soul moving about the walls of the house with sighs and plaints. If by chance she wishes to speak to one of her maids, the latter (already corrupted by money) soon produces a little gift, a letter, a sonnet, or some such thing that she has to give her from her suitor. And then, choosing the right time, her maid tells her how the poor man is consumed with love, how he values his own life at naught to serve her; how he wishes nothing from

her that is not honorable, and how he desires only to speak with her. Means to cope with all impediments are also found, copied keys, rope ladders, sleeping potions; the thing is pictured as being of little consequence; examples are cited of many other women who do far worse: in this way everything is made so easy for her that she need go to no other trouble than to say, 'I will.' And if the poor girl should hold back for a time, so many inducements are brought forward, so many ways are found that are calculated to break down her restraint by their continual battering. And there are many who, when they see that their blandishments are of no avail, resort to threats, saying they will tell their husbands that they are what they are not. Others bargain boldly with fathers and often with husbands who, for money or for favors, force their own daughters and wives to surrender themselves. Others try by means of incantations and sorceries to take from them the liberty God gave their souls, and in this are seen some remarkable effects. But I could not in a thousand years rehearse all of the artifices employed by men to bring women to do their wishes, for these are endless; and, in addition to those which every man invents for himself, there has been no lack of writers who have composed ingenious books and taken every care to teach methods of deceiving women in these matters.

"Now consider how these simple doves can be safe amidst so many snares, tempted as they are by such sweet bait. And so what wonder if a woman (seeing herself so much loved and adored for many years by a handsome, noble, and well-mannered youth, who risks death a thousand times a day to serve her, giving all his thought to pleasing her), finally yields to him as a result of that continual wearing away (as water wears the hardest marble); and, conquered by this passion, contents him with what you say she, in the weakness of her sex, desires more than does her lover? Does this seem to you an error so grave that the poor creature, who has been snared by so many flatteries, would not deserve at least the pardon that is often granted to murderers, thieves, assassins, and traitors? Will you maintain that this is an offense so enormous that, when you find some woman committing it, womankind must be wholly despised and held up as universally wanting in continence, with no thought taken of the many who are unconquerable, who stand as adamant against the continual urgings of love, and firmer in their infinite constancy than the rocks against the waves of the sea?"

[51] Messer Cesare had ceased speaking and signor Gasparo was about to reply, when signor Ottaviano said, laughing: "In Heaven's name, grant him the victory, for I know that you have little to gain in this; and, as I see it, you will make not only all these ladies your enemies, but the greater part of the men as well."

Signor Gasparo laughed and said: "Nay, the ladies have very good reason to thank me; because, if I had not contradicted signor Magnifico and messer Cesare, we should not have heard all the praises they have given to women."

Then messer Cesare said: "The praises that the Magnifico and I have given to women, and many others besides, are very well known and thus have been superfluous. Who does not know that without women we can take no pleasure or satisfaction in this life of ours, which, but for them, would be uncouth and devoid of all sweetness, and wilder than that of wild beasts? Who does not know that women alone take from our hearts all vile and base thoughts, woes, miseries, and those troubled humors that so often attend such things? And if we will carefully consider the truth, we shall see also that in our understanding of great matters women do not distract but rather awaken our minds, and in war they make men fearless and daring beyond measure. Certainly it is impossible that cowardice should ever again prevail in a man's heart where once the flame of love has entered; for one who loves always desires to make himself as lovable as possible, and always fears that he may incur some disgrace that will cause him to fall low in the estimation of the one by whom he desires to be highly esteemed. Nor does he hesitate to risk his life a thousand times a day to prove himself worthy of her love: hence, if one could assemble an army of lovers that would fight in the presence of the ladies they love, that army would conquer the whole world, unless similarly another army of lovers were to oppose it. And be sure that the ten years' stand of Troy against all Greece came from nothing if not the fact that a few lovers, when they made ready to go forth to battle, armed themselves in the presence of their women; and these women often gave a hand and, as they left, spoke to them some word that inflamed them and made them more than men. Then in battle they knew that their women were watching them from the walls and towers; wherefore it seemed to them that every act of courage, every proof they gave, won them their women's praise, which was the greatest reward they could have in the world.

"There are many who believe that the victory of King Ferdinand and Queen Isabella of Spain against the King of Granada was due in large measure to women; for most of the times when the Spanish army went out to meet the enemy, Queen Isabella also went out with all her maids of honor, and in the army there were many noble cavaliers in love. The latter would go along talking with their ladies until they reached the place where the enemy was seen, then each would take leave of his own lady; and, with the ladies looking on, they would go forth to meet the enemy with the fierce spirit that love gave them, and with the desire to show their ladies that they were served by men of valor; hence, a very small band of Spanish cavaliers was often seen to put a host of Moors to flight and death, thanks to the gentle and beloved ladies. So, signor Gasparo, I do not see what perversity of judgment brings you to censure women.

[52] "Do you not see that the cause of all gracious exercises that give us pleasure is to be assigned to women alone? Who learns to dance gracefully for any reason except to please women? Who devotes himself to the sweetness of music for any other reason? Who attempts to compose verses, at least in the vernacular, unless to express sentiments inspired by women? Think how many noble poems we should be deprived of, both in Greek and in Latin, if women had enjoyed little esteem with the poets. But, leaving all others aside, would it not be a very great loss if messer Francesco Petrarca, who wrote of his loves so divinely in this language of ours, had cared only for Latin, as would have happened if love for madonna Laura had not sometimes distracted him? I will not name you the bright talents that there now are in the world, and here present, that every day produce some noble fruit, and yet find their subject matter entirely in the beauties and virtues of women. Consider that Solomon, wishing to write mystically of very lofty and divine things, in order to cover them with a fair veil, imagined an ardent and tender dialogue between lover and lady, thinking that here below among us he could find no similitude more apt and suited to things divine than love of woman; and in this way he chose to give us a little of the savor of that divinity which, both through knowledge and through grace, he knew better than anyone else. Hence, signor Gasparo, there was no need to dispute about this or at least no need to use so many words: but in contradicting the truth you have prevented us from hearing a thousand other fine and important points regarding the perfrection of the Court Lady."

Signor Gasparo replied: "I believe there is nothing I can answer you; but if you think that the Magnifico has not adorned her with enough good qualities, the fault is not with him but with the one who ordained that there should be no more virtues than this in the world; for the Magnifico gave her all there are."

The Duchess said, laughing: "You will see now that signor Magnifico will find yet others."

The Magnifico replied: "Indeed, Madam, I think that I have said enough, and for my part I am content with this Lady of mine; and if these gentlemen will have none of her when she is fashioned so, then let them leave her to me."

[53] When all were silent at this point, messer Federico said: "Signor Magnifico, to encourage you to say more, I should like to

ask you about what you stated to be the main business of the Court
Lady, that is, I wish to hear how she should conduct herself with
respect to one particular that to me seems most important; for,
although the excellent qualities you have attributed to her include
talent, wisdom, judgment, dexterity, modesty, and so many other
virtues (having which she ought in reason to be able to converse
with anyone and on any subject), still I think that more than anything else she needs to have knowledge of what pertains to discourse of love. For just as every gentle cavalier employs those noble
exercises, the elegance of dress, and the fine manners that we have
mentioned as a means of gaining the favor of women, he also uses
words for this same purpose; and not only when he is constrained
by passion, but often also to honor the lady with whom he speaks,
thinking that to show her that he loves her proves that she is worthy of it, and that her beauty and her merits are so great that they
oblige every man to serve her. Hence, I should like to know how this
Lady ought to converse discreetly in such a case, and how she ought
to reply to one who truly loves her, and how reply to one who puts
up a false show of love, and if she must pretend not to understand,
or must return his love, or must refuse, and how she must conduct
herself."

[54] Then the Magnifico said: "It would be necessary first to teach
her to distinguish those who feign love from those who truly love;
and, as for returning love or not, I think she ought to be governed
by nobody's wish but her own."

Messer Federico said: "Then teach her what the sure and positive signs are by which to distinguish false from true love, and with
what proof she ought to be content in order to be sure of the love
shown her."

The Magnifico replied, laughing: "This I do not know, because
nowadays men are so cunning that they make no end of false
demonstrations, and sometimes weep when they can hardly keep
from laughing; hence, they ought to be sent to Isola Ferma under
the True Lovers' Arch.[3] But, in order that this Lady of mine (for
whom I must have a special concern, since she is my creation) may
not incur the errors which I have seen others incur, I should say she
ought not to be easily persuaded that she is loved, nor do as some
do, who not only do not pretend not to understand when anyone
speaks to them of love, even covertly, but at the first word take in all

---

3. The reference is to an episode in the Spanish romance *Amadis of Gaul*: in the enchanted
island named Isola Ferma there is a garden which is entered through an arch on which
there is the statue of a knight holding a trumpet to his mouth. This trumpet emits a horrible blast when unfaithful lovers enter through the arch and sweet music when true
lovers enter.

the praises that are spoken to them, or deny these with a certain air that is more an invitation to love than a denial to those with whom they are speaking. Therefore, the manner I would have my Court Lady follow in discourse of love is always to refuse to believe that whoever speaks to her about love really loves her: and if the gentleman happens to be as forward as many are, and shows her little respect in his words, let her give him such an answer as to make it clear that he is annoying her. Again, if he happens to be discreet and uses modest phrases and covert words of love, with the gracious manner which I think the Courtier these gentlemen have fashioned will follow, the Lady will pretend not to understand, and will put another construction upon his words, always trying modestly to change the subject, with the wit and discretion that have been said to befit her. Again, if the talk is such that she cannot pretend not to understand, she will take it all as being in jest, pretending to recognize that it is said to her more in order to honor her than because it is true, and will disclaim her own merits and attribute the compliments the gentleman pays her to his courtesy; and in this way she will cause others to deem her discreet and she will be better insured against deceit. Such is the manner in which I think the Court Lady ought to conduct herself in discoursing of love."

[55] Then messer Federico said: "Signor Magnifico, you talk of this matter as if all who speak of love to women spoke lies, and were trying to deceive them: and if this were true, I should say that your doctrine was sound: but if the cavalier who speaks so is truly in love and feels that passion which sometimes so greatly afflicts the human heart, will you take no thought of what calamity and mortal anguish you put him in by insisting that the Lady must never believe anything he says in this matter? Are his supplications, tears, and the many other signs to count for nothing? Take care, signor Magnifico, lest it be thought that, in addition to the cruelty which many of these ladies have in them by nature, you are teaching them yet more."

The Magnifico replied: "I was not talking about a man in love, but about one who engages in amorous talk, wherein the most necessary condition is that there be no lack of words. But just as true lovers have burning hearts, so do they have cold tongues, and a speech that hesitates and then stops abruptly; wherefore perhaps it would not be a false assumption to say: 'He who loves much speaks little.' Yet in this matter I think no sure rule can be laid down, because of the variety of men's customs; nor could I say anything more than that the Lady must be very cautious, and always bear in mind that men can manifest their love with much less risk than women can."

[56] Then signor Gasparo said, laughing: "Signor Magnifico, would you not have this excellent Lady of yours love in return, even when she knows she is loved? Especially since, if the Courtier is not loved in return, we cannot think that he will go on loving her; and thus she may lose much favor and especially that service and reverence with which lovers honor and almost adore the virtue of their beloved."

"In this," replied the Magnifico, "I do not wish to give counsel; but I do say that I think love, as you are now speaking of it, is proper only for unmarried women; for when this love cannot lead to marriage, the lady is ever bound to feel the remorse and sting that is caused by illicit things, and risks staining that reputation for chastity which is so important to her."

Then messer Federico replied, laughing: "This opinion of yours, signor Magnifico, strikes me as being very austere, and I think you must have learned it from some preacher—some one of those who upbraid women for loving laymen, in order that they may keep the better part for themselves. And I think you impose too harsh a law on married women, for many are found whose husbands bear them the greatest hatred without cause, and do them grave offense, sometimes in loving other women, sometimes in giving them all the annoyances they can think of; some against their will are married by their fathers to old men who are infirm, loathsome, and disgusting and who make their life a constant misery. If such women were allowed to get a divorce and to separate from those with whom they are ill-mated, then perhaps they would be without excuse if they loved any man except their husband; but when they are ill-starred or ill-suited by temperament or for some other reason, and it comes to pass that in the marriage bed, which ought to be a nest of concord and of love, the accursed infernal fury plants the seed of its venom, which then produces anger, suspicion, and the sharp thorns of hatred which torment those unhappy souls thus cruelly bound by an indissoluble chain even unto death—then why will you not allow the woman to seek some refuge from such a harsh scourge and give to someone else what is not only scorned but abhorred by her husband? I do think that those who have husbands suited to them, and who are loved by them, must not wrong them; but the others wrong themselves by not loving those who love them."

"Nay," replied the Magnifico, "they wrong themselves by loving any man except their husband. Still, since it is oftentimes not in our power to refuse to love, if this mishap should befall the Court Lady (that her husband's hate or another's love should bring her to love), I would have her give her lover a spiritual love only; nor must she ever give him any sure sign of her love, either by word or gesture or by other means that can make him certain of it."

[57] Then messer Roberto da Bari said, laughing: "I appeal this judgment of yours, signor Magnifico, and I believe that many will join with me; but since you are determined to teach married women this rusticity, so to speak, would you also have the unmarried be so cruel and discourteous?—and not allow them to be complacent to their lovers in anything?"

"If my Court Lady is unmarried," replied the Magnifico, "and is to be in love, then I wish her to love someone whom she can marry; nor will I reckon it a fault if she gives him some sign of love—in which case I wish to teach her a general rule in a few words, so that she may not find it hard to remember: let her show her lover every sign of love except such as may give him hope of obtaining something dishonorable from her. And it is necessary to be very careful about this, for it is an error into which countless women fall, who ordinarily desire above all else to be beautiful: and since having many lovers seems to them a proof of their beauty, they put all their efforts into getting as many of them as they can. Thus, they often indulge in immodest behavior; and, abandoning that tempered modesty which so becomes them, they indulge in certain bold glances, in scurrilous words and impudent behavior, thinking they are well viewed and well heard for this, and that by such ways they cause themselves to be loved: which is not true, because the demonstrations of love that are made to them come from a desire excited by the notion that they are willing, and not by love. Hence, I would not have my Court Lady seem wantonly to offer herself to anyone who desires her, doing her best to captivate the eyes and affections of all who gaze upon her, but I would have her by her merits and virtuous behavior, by her charm and her grace, instill in the minds of all who look upon her the true love that lovable things deserve, and the respect that deprives anyone of hope who would think any dishonorable thing. Therefore, he who is loved by such a woman will be obliged to content himself with the slightest sign from her, and to prize a single affectionate glance from her more than the complete possession of any other woman; and I should not know how to add anything to such a Lady save that she be loved by so excellent a Courtier as these gentlemen have imagined, and that she love him also, so that both may attain their entire perfection."

[58] Having spoken thus far, the Magnifico was silent; whereupon signor Gasparo said, laughing: "You cannot complain now that the Magnifico has not fashioned a most excellent Court Lady; and henceforth, if any such Lady be found, I will indeed grant you that she deserves to be judged the equal of the Courtier."

Signora Emilia replied: "I promise to find her, provided that you will find the Courtier."

Messer Roberto added: "Truly it cannot be denied that the Lady imagined by the Magnifico is most perfect: nevertheless, as to those last traits pertaining to love, it does seem to me that he has made her a little too austere, especially when he would have her deprive her lover of all hope by word, gesture, and behavior, and do all she can to bring him to despair. For, as everyone knows, human desires do not attach themselves to things which do not hold out some hope. And although there have been some few women, proud perhaps of their beauty and worth, whose first words to any man who wooed them were that he must never expect to get any wished-for thing from them, yet afterward they were a little more gracious to him in the way in which they looked upon him and received him, so that by their kindly acts they somewhat tempered their haughty words. But if this Lady drives away all hope by her acts, words, and manner, I think our Courtier, if he is wise, will never love her; and thus she will have the imperfection of being without a lover."

[59] Then the Magnifico said: "I would not have my Court Lady drive away hope of everything, but only of dishonorable things which, if the Courtier be as courteous and discreet as these gentlemen have made him, he will not only not hope for, but will not even desire. Because if the beauty, behavior, talents, goodness, knowledge, modesty, and the many other traits we have given the Lady are the cause of the Courtier's love of her, the end of his love will necessarily be worthy too; and if nobility, excellence in arms and letters and music, if gentleness and gracefulness in speech and conversation, are the means whereby the Courtier is to win the Lady's love, the end of that love will necessarily be of the same quality as the means by which it is attained. Moreover, just as there are various kinds of beauty in the world, so are there various desires in men; and so it happens that when they see a woman of such grave beauty (whether she be going or staying, joking or jesting, or doing what you will) that it always tempers her demeanor in such a way as to instill a certain reverence in anyone who looks upon her—many stand in awe and do not dare to serve her; and, drawn by hope, are inclined rather to love those pretty and enticing women who are so delicate and tender as to show in words and acts and looks a certain languid passion that promises easily to grow and change to love.

"To guard against being deceived, some men love another kind of women, who are so free in their looks and words and movements as to do the first thing that comes to their mind, with a certain naïveté which does not hide their thoughts. Nor are there lacking other generous souls who—believing that virtue is proved in difficulty and that there is sweetest victory in conquering what seems to others unconquerable—in order to prove that they are capable of forcing a stubborn mind and persuading even stubborn wills, recalcitrant and rebellious in love, to love them—promptly give themselves to loving the beauties of those women who in their glances, words, and behavior show a more austere severity than the others. Wherefore these men, who have so much self-confidence and think themselves secure against being deceived, readily love also certain women who seem by cunning and art to hide a thousand wiles beneath their beauty; or else certain others who in their beauty have a somewhat disdainful manner of few words and few smiles, with an air of seeming to care little for any man who looks at them or serves them. Then there are certain other men that deign to love only those women who hold in their countenance and words and every movement all comeliness, all gentle manners, all knowledge, and all the graces brought together—like a single flower composed of all the excellences in the world. Thus, if my Court Lady is denied the kinds of love that are prompted by evil hope, she will not be left without a lover on that account; for she will not lack lovers who are moved both by her merits and by a confidence in their own worth, through which they will know themselves worthy of being loved by her."

[60] Messer Roberto still objected, but the Duchess ruled that he was in the wrong, approving the Magnifico's argument; then she continued: "We have no reason to complain of the Magnifico, for truly I do believe that the Court Lady he has imagined can stand comparison with the Courtier, and even show some advantage; for he has taught her how to love, which is something these gentlemen have not done for their Courtier."

Then the Unico Aretino said: "It is indeed well to teach women how to love, for rarely have I seen any who knew how: since nearly always they join to their beauty a cruelty and ingratitude toward those who serve them most gratefully and who, by their nobility of birth, gentleness, and worth, deserve to be rewarded in their love; and instead they often make themselves a prey to men who are very silly, base, and of little worth, and who not only do not love them, but hate them. So, to avoid such monstrous errors as these, perhaps it would have been well to teach them first how to choose a man worthy of their love, and then how to love him; which is not necessary in the case of men who of themselves know it only too well. And of this I can serve as good witness; for I was never taught to love, save by the divine beauty and divinest manners of a lady whom I had no choice but to adore, and was far from needing any teacher in the art; and I think the same must happen to all who truly love. Hence, it would be more to the point to teach the Courtier how to make himself loved rather than how to love."

[61] Then signora Emilia said: "Now do tell us about that, signor Unico."

The Unico replied: "Reason would require, it seems to me, that the favor of ladies should be gained through serving them and pleasing them; but what for them constitutes serving and pleasing I think must needs be learned from the ladies themselves, who often desire such strange things that there is no man who could imagine them, and sometimes they themselves do not know what it is they want. Hence, it were well for you, Madam, who are a woman and must surely know what women like, to undertake this task and do the world a very great service."

Then signora Emilia said: "The fact that you enjoy such universal favor with women is good evidence that you know all the ways by which that favor is gained; hence, it is more fitting that you should teach those ways."

"Madam," replied the Unico, "I could give the lover no more useful admonition than that he should see to it that you have no influence over the lady whose favor he is seeking; because such good qualities as the world appears once to have thought were mine, together with the sincerest love that ever was, have not had as much power to make me loved as you have had to make me hated."

[62] Then signora Emilia replied: "Signor Unico, God save me even from thinking, much less doing, anything to cause you to be hated; for not only would I be doing what I ought not, but I should be thought to show little judgment in attempting the impossible. But since you urge me thus to speak of what pleases women, I will speak; and if you are displeased, blame yourself for it.

"I think, then, that if anyone is to be loved, he must love and he must be lovable; and that these two things suffice to gain the favor of women. Now, to answer what you accuse me of, I say that everyone knows and sees that you are most lovable; but that you love as sincerely as you say, I very much doubt, as perhaps the others do also. For by being so very lovable you have brought it about that you were loved by many women. Now, great rivers, when they divide into many channels, become small streams; even so love bestowed upon more than one object has little strength. But your own constant lamenting and complaining of ingratitude on the part of women whom you have served (which is not to be believed, in view of your great merits) is a certain kind of concealment designed to hide the favors, the joys, and pleasures that you have gained in love, and to assure the women who love you and have given themselves to you that you will not betray them; and hence they in their turn are content that you should thus openly show feigned love to others in order to hide your real love for them. Wherefore, if the women whom you now pretend to love are not so ready to believe you as you could wish, this happens because your art of love is beginning to be understood, and not because I cause you to be hated."

[63] Then the Unico said: "I do not wish to try further to confute your words, because by now it appears as much my fate not to be believed when I speak the truth, as it is yours to be believed when you speak untruth."

"But, signor Unico, you must admit," replied signora Emilia, "that you do not love as you would have us believe; for if you loved, your every desire would be to please your beloved and to wish what she wishes, because this is the law of love; but it denotes deceit when you complain so much of her, as I have said, or indeed is proof that you wish what she does not wish."

"Nay," said the Unico, "I do in fact wish what she wishes, which is evidence that I love her; but I complain because she does not wish what I wish, which is a sign that she does not love me, according to the very rule you have cited."

Signora Emilia replied: "He who begins to love must also begin to please his beloved and to comply entirely with her wishes, and by hers govern his own; and he must see to it that his own desires serve her, and that his soul is like an obedient handmaid, nor ever think of anything except to transform himself into the soul of his beloved, if that is possible, and to reckon this his highest happiness; for they act so who truly love."

"Precisely," said the Unico, "my highest happiness would be to have a single will govern both our souls."

"Then it is for you to act accordingly," replied signora Emilia.

[64] Then messer Bernardo interrupted and said: "Certainly, he who truly loves aims in all his thoughts to serve and please the lady of his love, without being shown the way by others; but, as these services in love are sometimes not clearly recognized, I believe that, besides loving and serving, it is necessary also for him to make some other demonstration so evident that the lady cannot conceal the fact of knowing that she is loved; and yet do this with so much modesty that he will not appear to show her little respect. And since you, Madam, have begun to tell how the soul of the lover must be the obedient handmaid of the beloved, I beseech you to teach us this secret too, which seems to me very important."

Messer Cesare laughed and said: "If the lover is so modest that he is ashamed to tell her of his love, let him write it to her."

Signora Emilia added: "Nay, if he is as discreet as he ought to be, he should make sure, before he declares himself to her, that he will not offend her."

Then signor Gasparo said: "All women like to be asked for their love, even though they intend to refuse what they are asked for."

The Magnifico Giuliano replied: "You are much mistaken; nor would I advise the Courtier ever to resort to this extreme, unless he is quite certain of not being repulsed."

[65] "Then what must he do?" asked signor Gasparo.

The Magnifico continued: "If he wishes to speak or write, let him do it with such modesty and caution that his first words shall test her mind and probe her wish in a manner so ambiguous as to leave her a way of certain escape by making it possible for her to pretend not to see that his talk is actually of love; so that in case he encounters difficulty he may withdraw and make a show of having spoken or written with some other intent, in order safely to enjoy those intimate endearments and courtesies a woman often grants to a man who she believes takes them in a spirit of friendship—and then withholds as soon as she finds they are being taken as demonstrations of love. Hence, those men who are too precipitate and make advances so presumptuously, with a kind of fury and stubbornness, often lose these favors, and deservedly; for every noble lady deems herself to be little esteemed by one who fails to show her respect, seeking to gain her love before he has served her."

[66] "Hence, in my opinion, the method that the Courtier ought to follow in making his love known to the Lady would be to reveal it to her by actions rather than words, for it is certainly true that more of love's affection is sometimes revealed by a sigh, by a reverence, by timidity, than by a thousand words; next, by making his eyes be faithful messengers in bearing the embassies of his heart, since they often reveal the passion within more effectively than the tongue itself, or letters, or messengers; and they not only reveal thoughts but they often kindle love in the beloved's heart. Because those vital spirits that come forth from the eyes, being generated near the heart, enter in through other eyes (at which they are aimed as an arrow at a target) and penetrate naturally to the heart as if it were their proper abode, and, mingling with those other spirits there and with the very subtle kind of blood which these have in them, they infect the blood near the heart to which they have come, and warm it, and make it like themselves and ready to receive the impression of that image which they have brought with them. Passing thus to and fro along the way from the eyes to the heart, and bringing back the tinder and steel of beauty and grace, little by little these messengers fan with the breath of desire that fire which thus burns and never consumes itself, because they are always bringing the substance of hope for it to feed on. Hence, it can indeed be said that

eyes are the guides in love, especially if they are winsome and soft; black, of a bright and sweet black, or blue; gay and smiling, and in their glance gracious and penetrating like some in whom the channels giving egress to the spirits seem so deep that we can see through them all the way to the heart.

"Thus, the eyes remain hidden, even as in war soldiers lie in ambush; and if the form of the whole body is beautiful and well proportioned, it attracts and draws to itself anyone who looks upon it from afar, bringing him closer; and, as soon as he is near, the eyes dart forth and bewitch, like sorcerers; and especially when they send their rays straight into the eyes of the beloved at the moment these are doing the same to the other's; because the spirits meet, and in that sweet encounter each takes on the other's qualities, as we see in the case of a diseased eye which, by looking fixedly into a sound eye, communicates its own disease to it. Thus, it seems to me that in this way our Courtier can in great part make his love for his Lady known.

"It is true that if the eyes are not carefully controlled, they frequently reveal amorous desires to someone to whom one would least wish to do so; because through the eyes there shines forth almost visibly the ardent passion which the lover (while wishing to reveal it only to his beloved) often reveals also to one from whom he would most hide it. Therefore one who has not lost the bridle of reason will govern himself cautiously and take account of time and place, and, when necessary, abstain from gazing too intently, however sweet that may be; for when a love is made public it is too hard a thing."

[67] Count Ludovico replied: "Yet sometimes openness in love will do no harm, for in that case men often think that such a love is not tending to the end that every lover desires, seeing that little care is taken to hide it, or little concern had whether it be known or not; and so, by not denying it, a man gains a certain freedom enabling him to speak openly with his beloved and to be with her without arousing suspicion; which does not happen with those who try to be secret, because they seem to hope for and be about to attain some great reward that they would not like for others to discover. Moreover, I have also seen a most ardent love spring up in a woman's heart toward a man for whom at first she had not the slightest affection, merely from hearing that many persons thought that the two were in love; and I think that the reason for this was that such a universal opinion as that seemed a proof sufficient to convince her that the man was worthy of her love, and it almost seemed that the report brought from her lover messages much truer and more deserving of belief than he himself could have sent to her by letters

and words, or by another person. Hence, this public report sometimes not only will do no harm, but will help."

The Magnifico replied: "Love affairs that are brought about by
common talk risk causing a man to be pointed at in public; and
hence he who wishes to travel this road warily must make a show of
having much less fire within him than he has, and must be content
with little (as it will seem to him), and must conceal his desires,
jealousies, griefs, and pleasures, and often laugh with his mouth
when his heart weeps, and pretend to be prodigal of that whereof he
is most avaricious; and these are things so difficult to do as to be
almost impossible. Therefore if our Courtier would follow my counsel, I would urge him to keep his loves secret."

[68] Then messer Bernardo said: "Therefore you must teach him
this, and to me it seems a matter of no little importance; for—
besides the signs which men sometimes make so covertly, and
almost without a motion, that the person whom they wish reads in
their face and eyes what they have in their heart—I have sometimes
heard a long and open talk of love between two lovers, but of which
those who were present could not clearly understand any particular
whatever, or even be sure that the talk was of love, and this was due
to the discretion and caution of the speakers; for, without giving any
sign that they were displeased at being listened to, they whispered
the only words that mattered, and spoke aloud those words that
could be variously construed."

Then messer Federico said: "To speak in any detail of such ways
to secrecy would be to pursue the infinite; hence, I would rather
have us discuss a little what the lover ought to do in order to keep
his lady's favor, which seems to me much more necessary."

[69] The Magnifico replied: "The means that serve to win that favor
serve also to hold it, I think; and the whole point consists in pleasing
the lady of our love without ever offending her. Wherefore it would be
hard to give any fixed rule for this; since in countless ways a man who
is not very discreet sometimes makes mistakes that appear trifling
and yet gravely hurt the lady's feelings; and this happens to those who
are driven by passion more than to others: like some who, whenever
they get a chance to speak with the lady of their love, lament and
complain most bitterly, and often desire things that are quite impossible; so that by their importunity they become tiresome. Others,
when they are stung by any jealousy, allow themselves to be transported so by grief that they heedlessly take to speaking ill of the man
whom they suspect (and sometimes when neither he nor the lady is at
fault), and demand that she not speak to him or even turn her eyes in
his direction. And by such conduct they often not only offend the

lady, but are the very cause that prompts her to love the other man: because the fear a lover sometimes shows that his lady may forsake him for another reveals that he is conscious of being inferior to the other man in merits and worth, and by this opinion the lady is moved to love the other man; and, seeing that an ill report is made of him in order to put him out of favor, she does not believe it, even though true, but loves him all the more."

[70] Then messer Cesare said, laughing: "I will confess that I am not so wise as to be able to refrain from speaking ill of any rival of mine, unless you can teach me another better way to ruin him."

The Magnifico replied, laughing: "There is an adage which says that when our enemy is in the water up to his waist, we must offer him our hand and rescue him from peril; but when he is in up to his chin, we must put our foot on his head and drown him forthwith. There are some who do this with their rivals: as long as they have no sure way of ruining them, they go about dissimulating and pretending to be their friend rather; then, when the opportunity presents itself— such as to make them know they can ruin them without fail in saying all manner of evil of them (whether true or false)—they do this mercilessly, employing artifice, deception, and all the means they can devise.

"But since I should never wish our Courtier to practice any deceit, I would have him deprive his rival of the Lady's favor by no other means than by loving and serving her and by being worthy, valiant, discreet, and modest; in short, by deserving her more than his rival does, and by being in all matters cautious and prudent, refraining from all those inept follies into which many ignorant men often fall in various ways. For I have known some who use Poliphilian words[4] in writing and speaking to women, and stand so on the subtleties of rhetoric that the women lose confidence, and think themselves very ignorant, and cannot wait to hear the end of such talk and get rid of the fellow. Others are excessively boastful. Others often say things that redound to their discredit and harm, like some I always laugh at, who profess to be in love and sometimes say, in the presence of women: 'I have never found a woman who would love me'; and they do not see that those who hear them decide then and there that this can be due to no other cause than that they deserve neither love nor the water they drink; and take them to be men of little worth, and would not love them for all the gold in the world, since it seems to them that, if they loved such men, they would stand lower than all the other women who had not loved them.

4. "Poliphilian" words are bizarre and obscure words like those of the *Hypnerotomachia Poliphili* of Francesco Colonna, published by Aldus in 1499.

"Others are so silly that, in order to cause some rival of theirs to be hated, they say, in the presence of women: 'So and so is the most fortunate man on earth; for certainly he is neither handsome nor discreet nor valiant, and cannot do or say more than other men; yet all women love him and pursue him'; and by thus showing themselves envious of the man's happiness, they cause others to believe that, although the man appears not to be lovable either in looks or actions, he has in him some hidden quality by which he deserves the love of so many women; hence, those who hear him thus spoken of are moved the more to love him because they believe it."

[71] Then Count Ludovico laughed, and said: "I assure you, the discreet Courtier will never practice these stupidities in order to gain favor with women."

Messer Cesare Gonzaga replied: "Nor such a stupidity as was practiced in my time by a gentleman of high repute, whose name, for the honor of men, shall not be mentioned."

The Duchess replied: "But do tell us what he did."

Messer Cesare continued: "Being loved by a great lady, he came secretly at her request to the town where she was; and when he had seen her and had stayed to talk with her as long as she and time permitted, he took his leave with many bitter tears and sighs, witnessing the extreme grief he felt at such a parting, and implored her to remember him always; and then he added that she ought to pay for his board and lodging, for since he had come at her invitation, it seemed reasonable to him that he should not be out of pocket for having come."

Then all the ladies began to laugh and say that this man was most unworthy of being called a gentleman; and many of the men were ashamed, with that sense of shame that the man himself ought to have felt if at any time he had ever had the sense to see what a disgraceful fault that was.

Then signor Gasparo turned to messer Cesare and said: "It would have been better for the honor of women to refrain from telling this than to refrain from naming him, for the honor of men; because you can well imagine that great lady's good judgment in loving such a witless animal, and it could well be that from among the many who served her she chose this man as the most discreet, and that she rejected and disfavored others whose lackey he was not worthy to be."

Count Ludovico laughed and said: "Who knows if he was not discreet in other things, and erred only in this matter of board and lodging? But many times men do very foolish things from excessive love; and if you would tell the truth, you yourself may have happened to fall into more than one such error."

[72] Messer Cesare replied, laughing: "By your faith, let us not expose our errors!"

"But it is necessary to expose them," replied signor Gasparo, "in order that we may correct them"; then he added: "Signor Magnifico, now that the Courtier knows how to win his Lady's favor and how to maintain it, and knows how to deprive his rival of it, it is for you to teach him how to keep his love secret."

The Magnifico replied: "It seems to me that I have said quite enough; and so, choose someone else now to speak of this matter of secrecy."

Then messer Bernardo and all the others began once more to urge him; and the Magnifico said, laughing: "You want to tempt me. You are all too well versed in love; still, if you want to know more about it, go and read your Ovid."

"And how," said messer Bernardo, "can I have any hope that Ovid's precepts will be useful in love, when he recommends and declares it to be a very good thing, that a man pretend to be drunk in the presence of the beloved? Consider what a fine method that is for winning favor! And he cites a good way to make your love known to a lady at a banquet: dip a finger in the wine and write it on the table!"

The Magnifico replied, laughing: "There was nothing wrong with that in those days."

"Therefore," said messer Bernardo, "since such a sordid thing as this was not offensive to men of that time, we may believe they did not have so gentle a manner of serving women in love as we. But let us not stray from our first purpose, which is to teach how to keep love secret."

[73] Then the Magnifico said: "In my opinion, to keep love secret it is necessary to avoid the causes that make it public, which are many; but there is one chief cause, namely, the desire to be too secret and not to trust anyone. For every lover wishes to make his passion known to his beloved and, if he is alone, he is forced to make many more and stronger demonstrations than if he were aided by some loving and faithful friend; because the demonstrations which the lover himself makes arouse much more suspicion than do those made through intermediaries. And, since the human mind is naturally curious to discover things, as soon as some stranger begins to suspect something, he sets about with such diligence that he discovers the truth; and, having discovered it, he does not scruple to bruit it about—indeed, sometimes he takes pleasure in this; which does not happen in the case of a friend who, besides helping with favors and counsel, often repairs the mistakes made by the blind lover, and always observes secrecy and attends to many things to which the lover him-

self cannot attend. Moreover, a great comfort is felt in telling one's passions to a cordial friend and in unburdening oneself of them; and similarly it greatly increases our joys to share them."

[74] Then signor Gasparo said: "There is something else that discloses love more than this."

"And what is that?" asked the Magnifico.

Signor Gasparo continued: "Vain ambition in women, coupled with madness and cruelty. Women, as you yourself have said, seek to have as many lovers as they can and would have all of them burn (were that possible) and, once they were in ashes and dead, would have them alive again so that they might die a second time. And even though they are in love, still they relish the torment of their lover, because they think that pain and afflictions and the constant invocation of death is the true sign that they are loved, and that by their beauty they can make men miserable or happy, and bestow life and death upon them as they choose. Hence, they feed only on this food, and are so greedy of it that in order not to be without it they neither content their lovers nor reduce them to utter despair; but, in order to keep them continually in worries and in desire, they resort to a certain domineering austerity in the form of threats mingled with hope, and expect a word of theirs, a look, a nod, to be deemed the highest happiness. And in order to be thought modest and chaste, not only by their lovers but by all others, they see to it that their harsh and rude ways are publicly known so that everyone may think that if they maltreat in this manner those who deserve to be loved, they must treat the unworthy much worse. And in this belief, thinking by such an art to be safe from disrepute, they lie every night with the vilest men, men whom they scarcely know; and in order to enjoy the calamities and continual laments of some noble cavalier whom they love, they deny themselves those pleasures which they might perhaps be excused for enjoying and they bring the poor lover to sheer desperation and to acts that make public what with every care ought to be kept most secret.

"Then there are other women who, if they can trick many men into thinking themselves loved by them, keep alive the jealousies among them by showing affection and favor to one in the presence of the other; and then, when they see that the one they most love is already confident that he is loved because of the demonstrations shown him, they put him in suspense by ambiguous words and feigned anger, and pierce his heart, pretending to care nothing for him, and that they mean to give themselves wholly to another; whence arise hatreds, enmities, countless scandals, and manifest ruin, because in such a case a man is bound to show the strong passion that he feels even though it result in blame and disrepute to the lady. Others, not content with torturing by jealousy, after the lover has given all proofs of love and of faithful service, and when they have accepted these with a show of returning them benevolently, begin for no cause at all to manifest a certain reserve when it is least expected, and pretend to believe that he has grown lukewarm; and feigning new suspicions that they are not loved, they make it clear that they wish to break with him entirely. Wherefore, because of these reverses, the poor fellow is of necessity obliged to begin all over again and to court her as though he were just beginning to serve her; and to walk about her part of town daily and, when the lady leaves her house, follow her to church and wherever she goes, never turning his eyes any other way: whereupon more tears and sighs and ill humors come, and when he manages to speak with her, then there are entreaties, blasphemies, despairings, and all those ragings to which unhappy lovers are brought by these wild animals who have a greater thirst for blood than tigers have.

[75] "Such manifestations of suffering are all too evident and well known, more often to others than to the one who causes them; and thus in the space of a few days they become so public that not a step is taken nor the least sign given that is not noted by a thousand eyes. And so it happens that, long before any pleasures have been enjoyed in their love, everyone believes that they have been enjoyed; for when women see that the lover is near to death, is overcome by the cruelty and the tortures inflicted on him, and is really determined to withdraw, they at once begin to show him that they love him dearly, and show him all manner of favors, and give themselves to him: in order that, when his ardent desire is no more, the fruits of love may be even less sweet, and that he may be the less attached to them—so as to turn everything about. And since their love is thus well known, and at the same time all the effects that result from it are also well known, then the woman is dishonored, and the lover finds that he has lost his time and toil, and has shortened his own life through sorrow without gaining any pleasure whatever; because he attains his desire, not when this would have made him most happy by its sweetness, but when he cares little or nothing for the woman because his heart is already so mortified by his cruel passion that no feeling is left for tasting the pleasure or contentment that is offered him."

[76] Then signor Ottaviano said, laughing: "You were quiet for a time and refrained from speaking ill of women; and now you have hit them so hard that it seems as if you had waited to gain strength, like those who draw back in order to make a more forceful assault; truly you are wrong, and you ought by now to be gentler."

Signora Emilia laughed, and, turning to the Duchess, said: "Behold, Madam, our adversaries are beginning to clash and disagree among themselves."

"Do not call me that," replied signor Ottaviano, "for I am not your adversary. This debate has displeased me much, not because I was sorry to see a victory in favor of women, but because it has brought signor Gasparo to disparage them more than he ought, and signor Magnifico and messer Cesare to praise them perhaps a little more than was their due; besides which, owing to the length of the discussion, we have lost the opportunity of hearing many other fine things that remain to be said about the Courtier."

"You see," said signora Emilia, "you are still our adversary; and hence this discussion displeases you, and you would not have wished such an excellent Court Lady to be imagined; not because there was more to be said about the Courtier (for these gentlemen have already said all they knew, and I think that neither you nor anyone else could add anything whatever to it), but because of the envy that you feel of women's honor."

[77] "To be sure," replied signor Ottaviano, "I should like to hear many other things said about the Courtier. Still, since everyone is satisfied to take him as he is, I too am satisfied; nor would I in any way change him, save to make him a little more friendly to women than signor Gasparo is, yet perhaps not as much as some of these other gentlemen are."

Then the Duchess said: "By all means we must see if your genius can give the Courtier a greater perfection than these gentlemen have done. So be pleased to say what you have in mind: otherwise we shall think that you too are at a loss to add anything to what has been said, and that you have wished to detract from the praises of the Court Lady when it seemed to you that she was the equal of the Courtier, whom you would therefore have us believe could be much more perfect than these gentlemen have imagined him."

Signor Ottaviano laughed and said: "The praise and blame that have been given to women beyond their due have so filled the ears and the mind of all listeners as to leave no room there for anything else; besides this, it strikes me that the hour is very late."

"Then," said the Duchess, "by waiting until tomorrow we shall gain more time. Meanwhile, the praise and blame that you say have been excessively given to women from both sides will depart from the minds of these gentlemen, and they will thus be better able to take in the truth that you will tell them."

So saying, the Duchess rose to her feet, and, courteously dismissing all the company, withdrew to her more private room; and everyone retired to sleep.

The Fourth Book

To Messer Alfonso Ariosto

[1] Thinking to record the discussions held on the fourth evening following those reported in the preceding books, I feel amidst various reflections one bitter thought strike upon me, making me mindful of human miseries and of our vain hopes: how often Fortune in midcourse, and sometimes near the end, dashes our fragile and futile designs and sometimes wrecks them before the port can even be seen from afar. Thus I remember that, not long after these discussions took place, untimely death deprived our court of three of its rarest gentlemen, even while they flourished in robust health and in hope of honor. And of these the first was signor Gaspar Pallavicino who, being afflicted and brought low more than once by a sore disease, was still of such strength of spirit that for a time soul and body held together in the face of death; yet he reached the end of his natural course long before his time: a great loss indeed, not only to our court and to his friends and relatives, but to his native land and to all Lombardy.

Not long thereafter messer Cesare Gonzaga died, leaving to all who knew him a bitter and painful memory of his death; for since nature produces such men as rarely as she does, it seemed only right that she should not so soon have deprived us of this man, because certainly it can be said that messer Cesare was taken from us just when he was beginning to give something more than a promise of himself, and to be esteemed for his excellent qualities as much as they deserved; for by many virtuous deeds he had already given good proof of his worth, which shone forth not only in noble birth, but in the adornment of letters and arms as well, and in every kind of praiseworthy behavior; so that, owing to his goodness, his talents, courage, and knowledge, nothing too great could have been expected of him.

And but a short time passed until the death of messer Roberto da Bari also brought deep sorrow to the whole court; for it seemed right that everyone should be grieved by the death of a young man of good manners, agreeable, of handsome aspect, and of the rarest physical grace, and of as stout and sturdy a character as it is possible to wish.

[2] Thus, had these men lived, I think they would have attained such eminence that they would have been able to give to all who knew them clear proof of how praiseworthy the Court of Urbino was, and how adorned it was with noble cavaliers—as nearly all that were ever reared there have adorned it. For truly there did not come forth from the Trojan horse so many lords and captains as from this court have come men singular in worth and most highly regarded by all. Thus, as you know, messer Federico Fregoso was made Archbishop of Salerno; Count Ludovico, Bishop of Bayeux; signor Ottaviano, Doge of Genoa; messer Bernardo Bibbiena, Cardinal of Santa Maria in Portico; messer Pietro Bembo, secretary to Pope Leo; the Magnifico rose to the dukedom of Nemours and to that greatness in which he now finds himself. Signor Francesco Maria della Rovere also, Prefect of Rome, was made Duke of Urbino: although much greater praise may be given the court where he was nurtured and because in it he became such a rare and worthy lord in all manner of virtue, as we now see, than because he achieved the dukedom of Urbino; nor do I believe that this is in small part due to the noble company which he continually kept there, where he always saw and heard laudable manners.

It seems to me, however, that the cause, whether through chance or favor of the stars, that has for so long given excellent lords to Urbino, continues still to produce the same effects; and hence we may hope that good fortune will so continue to favor these virtuous achievements that the blessings of the court and the state shall not only not decline but rather increase at a more rapid pace from day to day; and of this many bright signs are noted, among which I deem the chief to be Heaven's favoring us with such a lady as Eleanora Gonzaga, the new Duchess; for if ever there were joined in a single person wisdom, grace, beauty, intelligence, discreet manners, humanity, and every other gentle quality—they are so joined in her that they form a chain that comprises and adorns her every movement, uniting all these qualities at once.

Now let us continue with the discussions about our Courtier, in the hope that beyond our time there will be no lack of those who will find bright and honored models of worthiness in the present Court of Urbino, even as we are now finding them in that of the past.

[3] It seemed, then, as signor Gaspar Pallavicino used to relate, that on the day following the discussions contained in the preceding Book, little was seen of signor Ottaviano; wherefore many thought he had withdrawn in order to be free to think carefully of what he had to say. Thus, when the company had returned to the Duchess at the usual hour, a diligent search had to be made for signor Otta-

viano, who for a good while did not appear; so that many cavaliers and ladies of the court began to dance, and engage in other pastimes, thinking that for that evening there would be no more talk about the Courtier. And indeed all were occupied, some with one thing and some with another, when signor Ottaviano arrived after he had almost been given up; and, seeing that messer Cesare Gonzaga and signor Gasparo were dancing, he bowed to the Duchess and said, laughing: "I quite expected to hear signor Gasparo speak ill of women again this evening; but now that I see him dancing with one, I think he must have made his peace with all of them; and I am pleased that the dispute (or rather the discussion) about the Courtier has ended so."

"It has not ended at all," replied the Duchess, "for I am not the enemy of men that you are of women, and therefore I would not have the Courtier deprived of his due honor, and of those adornments that you yourself promised him last evening"; and so saying, she directed that, as soon as the dance was over, all should sit in the usual order, which was done; and when all were seated and attentive, signor Ottaviano said: "Madam, since my wish that there should be many other good qualities in the Courtier is taken as a promise that I must declare them, I am content to speak of them, not certainly with the idea of saying all that could be said, but only enough to remove from your mind the charge that was made against me last evening, namely, that I spoke as I did rather to detract from the praises of the Court Lady (by raising the false belief that other excellences can be attributed to the Courtier and, by such wiles make him superior to her) than because such is the truth. Hence, to adapt myself to the hour, which is later than it is wont to be when we begin our discussions, I shall be brief.

[4] "So, to continue the reasoning of these gentlemen, which I wholly approve and confirm, I say that, among the things which we call good, there are some which, simply and in themselves, are always good, such as temperance, fortitude, health, and all the virtues that bring tranquility of mind; others, which are good in various respects and for the end to which they are directed, such as law, liberality, riches, and other like things. Therefore I think that the perfect Courtier, such as Count Ludovico and messer Federico have described him, may indeed be good and worthy of praise, not, however, simply and in himself, but in regard to the end to which he is directed. For indeed if by being of noble birth, graceful, charming, and expert in so many exercises, the Courtier were to bring forth no other fruit than to be what he is, I should not judge it right for a man to devote so much study and labor to acquiring this perfection of Courtiership as anyone must do who wishes to acquire it. Nay, I

should say that many of those accomplishments that have been attributed to him (such as dancing, merrymaking, singing, and playing) were frivolities and vanities and, in a man of any rank, deserving of blame rather than of praise; for these elegances of dress, devices, mottoes, and other such things as pertain to women and love (although many will think the contrary), often serve merely to make spirits effeminate, to corrupt youth, and to lead it to a dissolute life; whence it comes about that the Italian name is reduced to opprobrium, and there are but few who dare, I will not say to die, but even to risk any danger. And certainly there are countless other things, which, if effort and study were put into them, would prove much more useful, both in peace and in war, than this kind of Courtiership taken in and for itself. But if the activities of the Courtier are directed to the good end to which they ought to be directed, and which I have in mind, I feel certain that they are not only not harmful or vain, but most useful and deserving of infinite praise.

[5] "Therefore, I think that the aim of the perfect Courtier, which we have not spoken of up to now, is so to win for himself, by means of the accomplishments ascribed to him by these gentlemen, the favor and mind of the prince whom he serves that he may be able to tell him, and always will tell him, the truth about everything he needs to know, without fear or risk of displeasing him; and that when he sees the mind of his prince inclined to a wrong action, he may dare to oppose him and in a gentle manner avail himself of the favor acquired by his good accomplishments, so as to dissuade him of every evil intent and bring him to the path of virtue. And thus, having in himself the goodness which these gentlemen attributed to him, together with readiness of wit, charm, prudence, knowledge of letters and of many other things—the Courtier will in every instance be able adroitly to show the prince how much honor and profit will come to him and to his from justice, liberality, magnanimity, gentleness, and the other virtues that befit a good prince; and, on the other hand, how much infamy and harm result from the vices opposed to these virtues. Hence, I think that even as music, festivals, games, and the other pleasant accomplishments are, as it were, the flower; so to bring or help one's prince toward what is right and to frighten him away from what is wrong are the true fruit of Courtiership. And because the real merit of good deeds consists chiefly in two things, one of which is to choose a truly good end to aim at, and the other is to know how to find means timely and fitting to attain that good end—it is certain that a man aims at the best end when he sees to it that his prince is deceived by no one, listens to no flatterers or slanderers or liars, and distinguishes good from evil, loving the one and hating the other.

[6] "I think too that the accomplishments attributed to the Courtier by these gentlemen may be a good means of attaining that end—and this because, among the many faults that we see in many of our princes nowadays, the greatest are ignorance and self-conceit. And the root of these two evils is none other than falsehood: which vice is deservedly odious to God and to men, and more harmful to princes than any other; because they have the greatest lack of what they would most need to have in abundance—I mean, someone to tell them the truth and make them mindful of what is right: because their enemies are not moved by love to perform these offices, but are well pleased to have them live wickedly and never correct themselves; and, on the other hand, their enemies do not dare to speak ill of them in public for fear of being punished. Then among their friends there are few who have free access to them, and those few are wary of reprehending them for their faults as freely as they would private persons, and, in order to win grace and favor, often think of nothing save how to suggest things that can delight and please their fancy, although these things be evil and dishonorable; thus, from friends these men become flatterers, and, to gain profit from their close association, always speak and act in order to please, and for the most part make their way by dint of lies that beget ignorance in the prince's mind, not only of outward things but of himself; and this may be said to be the greatest and most monstrous falsehood of all, for an ignorant mind deceives itself and inwardly lies to itself.

[7] "From this it results that, besides never hearing the truth about anything at all, princes are made drunk by the great license that rule gives; and by a profusion of delights are submerged in pleasures, and deceive themselves so and have their minds so corrupted—seeing themselves always obeyed and almost adored with so much reverence and praise, without ever the least contradiction, let alone censure—that from this ignorance they pass to an extreme self-conceit, so that then they become intolerant of any advice or opinion from others. And since they think that to know how to rule is a very easy thing, and that to succeed therein they need no other art or discipline save sheer force, they give their mind and all their thoughts to maintaining the power they have, deeming true happiness to lie in being able to do what one wishes. Therefore some princes hate reason or justice, thinking it would be a kind of bridle and a way of reducing them to servitude, and of lessening the pleasure and satisfaction they have in ruling if they chose to follow it, and that their rule would be neither perfect nor complete if they were obliged to obey duty and honor, because they think that one who obeys is not a true ruler.

"Therefore, following these principles and allowing themselves to be transported by self-conceit, they become arrogant, and with imperious countenance and stern manner, with pompous dress, gold, and gems, and by letting themselves be seen almost never in public, they think to gain authority among men and to be held almost as gods. And to my mind these princes are like the colossi that were made last year at Rome on the day of the festival in Piazza d'Agone,[5] which outwardly had the appearance of great men and horses in a triumph, and which within were full of tow and rags. But princes of this kind are much worse in that these colossi were held upright by their own great weight, whereas these princes, since they are ill-balanced within and are heedlessly placed on uneven bases, fall to their ruin by reason of their own weight, and pass from one error to a great many: for their ignorance, together with the false belief that they cannot make a mistake and that the power they have comes from their own wisdom, brings them to seize states boldly, by fair means or foul, whenever the possibility presents itself.

[8] "But if they would take it upon themselves to know and do what they ought, they would then strive not to rule as they now strive to rule, because they would see how monstrous and pernicious a thing it is when subjects, who have to be governed, are wiser than the princes who have to govern. Take note that ignorance of music, of dancing, of horsemanship, does no harm to anyone; nevertheless, one who is not a musician is ashamed and dares not sing in the presence of others, or dance if he does not know how, or ride if he does not sit his horse well. But from not knowing how to govern peoples there come so many woes, deaths, destructions, burnings, ruins, that it may be said to be the deadliest plague that exists on earth. And yet some princes who are so very ignorant of government are not ashamed to attempt to govern, I will not say in the presence of four or six men, but before the whole world, for they hold such a high rank that all eyes gaze upon them and hence not only their great but their least defects are always seen. Thus, it is recorded that Cimon was blamed for loving wine, Scipio for loving sleep, Lucullus for loving feasts. But would to God that the princes of our day might accompany their sins with as many virtues as did those ancients; who, even though they erred in some things, yet did not flee from the promptings and teachings of anyone who seemed to them able to correct those errors; nay, they made every effort to order their lives on the model of excellent men: as Epaminondas on that of Lysias the Pythagorean, Agesilaus on that of Xenophon, Scipio on that of Panaetius, and countless others. But if some of our

5. The modern Piazza Navona.

princes should happen upon a strict philosopher, or anyone at all who might try openly and artlessly to reveal to them the harsh face of true virtue, and teach them what good conduct is and what a good prince's life ought to be, I am certain they would abhor him as they would an asp, or indeed would deride him as a thing most vile.

[9] "I say, then, that, since the princes of today are so corrupted by evil customs and by ignorance and a false esteem of themselves, and since it is so difficult to show them the truth and lead them to virtue, and since men seek to gain their favor by means of lies and flatteries and such vicious ways—the Courtier, through those fair qualities that Count Ludovico and messer Federico have given him, can easily, and must, seek to gain the good will and captivate the mind of his prince that he may have free and sure access to speak to him of anything whatever without giving annoyance. And if he is such as he has been said to be, he will have little trouble in succeeding in this, and will thus be able always adroitly to tell him the truth about all things; and also, little by little, to inform his prince's mind with goodness, and teach him continence, fortitude, justice, and temperance, bringing him to taste how much sweetness lies hidden beneath the slight bitterness that is at first tasted by anyone who struggles against his vices; which are always noxious and offensive and attended by infamy and blame, just as the virtues are beneficial, smiling, and full of praise. And he will be able to incite his prince to these by the example of the famous captains and other excellent men to whom the ancients were wont to make statues of bronze, of marble, and sometimes of gold, and to erect these in public places, both to honor these men and to encourage others, so that through worthy emulation they may be led to strive to attain that glory too.

[10] "In this way the Courtier will be able to lead his prince by the austere path of virtue, adorning it with shady fronds and strewing it with pretty flowers to lessen the tedium of the toilsome journey for one whose strength is slight; and now with music, now with arms and horses, now with verses, now with discourse of love, and with all those means whereof these gentlemen have spoken, to keep his mind continually occupied in worthy pleasures, yet always impressing upon him also some virtuous habit along with these enticements, as I have said, beguiling him with salutary deception; like shrewd doctors who often spread the edge of the cup with some sweet cordial when they wish to give a bitter-tasting medicine to sick and over-delicate children.

"Thus, by using the veil of pleasure to such an end, the Courtier will reach his aim in every time and place and activity, and for this will deserve much greater praise and reward than for any other good work that he could do in the world. For there is no good more universally beneficial than a good prince, nor any evil more universally pernicious than a bad prince: likewise, there is no punishment atrocious and cruel enough for those wicked courtiers who direct gentle and charming manners and good qualities of character to an evil end, namely to their own profit, and who thereby seek their prince's favor in order to corrupt him, turn him from the path of virtue, and bring him to vice; for such as these may be said to contaminate with a deadly poison, not a single cup from which one man alone must drink, but the public fountain that is used by all the people."

[11] Signor Ottaviano was silent, as if he did not wish to say more; but signor Gasparo said: "It does not seem to me, signor Ottaviano, that this goodness of mind and this continence and the other virtues which you would have our Courtier teach his prince can be learned; but I think that to those who have them they have been given by nature and by God. And that this is so, you will see that there is not a man in the world so wicked and evil by nature, nor so intemperate and unjust, as to confess himself to be such when he is asked; nay, everyone, no matter how wicked, is pleased to be thought just, continent, and good: which would not happen if these virtues could be learned; for it is no disgrace not to know what one has made no effort to know, but it seems blameworthy indeed not to have that with which we should be adorned by nature. Thus, everyone tries to hide his natural defects, both of mind and of body; which is seen in the blind, the crippled, and the twisted, and in others who are maimed or ugly; for, although these defects can be ascribed to nature, yet everyone is displeased at the thought that he has them, because it seems that nature herself bears witness to that imperfection, as if it were a seal and token of wickedness in him. This opinion of mine is also confirmed by the story that is told of Epimetheus, who knew so badly how to apportion the gifts of nature among men that he left them much more wanting in everything than all other creatures: wherefore Prometheus stole from Minerva and from Vulcan that artful knowledge whereby men gain their livelihood; but they did not yet know how to congregate in cities and live by a moral law, for this knowledge was guarded in Jove's stronghold by most watchful warders who so frightened Prometheus that he dared not approach them; wherefore Jove took pity on the misery of men who were torn by wild beasts because, lacking civic virtues, they could not stand together; and sent Mercury to earth to bring them justice and shame, so that these two things might adorn their cities and unite the citizens. And he ordained that these should not be given to men like the other arts, in which one expert suffices for many who are ignorant (as in the case

of medicine), but that they should be impressed upon every man; and he established a law that all who were without justice and shame should be exterminated and put to death as public menaces. So you see, signor Ottaviano, that these virtues are granted to men by God, and are not learned, but are natural."

[12] Then signor Ottaviano said, laughing: "Would you have it, then, signor Gasparo, that men are so unhappy and perverse in their judgments that they have by industry found an art whereby to tame the natures of wild beasts, bears, wolves, lions, and are thereby able to teach a pretty bird to fly wherever they wish and to return of its own will from the woods and from its natural freedom to cages and to captivity—and that by the same industry they cannot, or will not, devise arts to help themselves and to improve their minds by diligence and study? This, to my way of thinking, would be as if physicians were to put all their efforts into finding the method of healing sore nails and milk scab in children, and were to leave off treating fevers, pleurisy, and other grave maladies; and how out of all reason that would be, everyone may consider.

"Therefore I hold that the moral virtues are not in us entirely by nature, for nothing can ever become accustomed to that which is naturally contrary to it; as we see in a stone, which, even though it were thrown upward ten thousand times, would never become accustomed to move so by itself; and if the virtues were as natural to us as weight is to a stone, we should never become accustomed to vice. Nor, on the other hand, are the vices natural in this sense, else we should never be able to be virtuous; and it would be too wrong and foolish to punish men for those defects that proceed from nature without any fault on our part; and this error would be committed by the laws, which do not inflict punishment on evildoers on account of their past error (since what is done cannot be undone), but have regard to the future, to the end that he who has erred may err no more nor by his bad example be the cause of others erring. And thus the laws do assume that virtues can be learned, which is very true; for we are born capable of receiving them and of receiving the vices too, and hence through practice we acquire the habit of both, so that first we practice virtue or vice and then we are virtuous or vicious. The contrary is noted in things that are given us by nature, which we first have the power to practice and then do practice: as with the senses; for first we are able to see, hear, and touch, then we do see, hear, and touch, although many of these activities are improved by discipline. Wherefore good masters teach children not only letters, but also good and seemly manners in eating, drinking, speaking, and walking, with appropriate gestures.

[13] "Therefore, as in the arts, so likewise in virtue it is necessary to have a master who, by his teaching and good reminders, shall stir and awaken in us those moral virtues of which we have the seed enclosed and planted in our souls; and, like a good husbandman, cultivate them and open the way for them by removing from about us the thorns and tares of our appetites which often so overshadow and choke our minds as not to let them flower or produce those fair fruits which alone we should desire to see born in the human heart.

"In this way, then, justice and shame, which you say Jove sent upon earth to all men, are natural in each one of us. But even as a body without eyes, however robust it may be, often goes astray in moving toward some object, so the root of these virtues which are potentially innate in our minds, often comes to nothing if it is not helped by cultivation. For if it is to pass to action and to a perfect operation, nature alone does not suffice, as has been said, but the practice of art and reason is required to purify and clear the soul by lifting from it the dark veil of ignorance, from which almost all the errors of men proceed—because if good and evil were well recognized and understood, no one would fail to prefer good and eschew evil. Hence, virtue can almost be called a kind of prudence and a knowledge of how to choose the good, and vice a kind of imprudence and ignorance that brings us to judge falsely; for men never choose evil, thinking it to be evil, but are deceived by a certain semblance of the good."

[14] Then signor Gasparo replied: "There are, however, many who know well that they are doing evil and yet do it; and this because they put the present pleasure which they feel before the punishment which they fear will befall them: like thieves, murderers, and other such men."

Signor Ottaviano said: "True pleasure is always good and true suffering always evil; therefore these men deceive themselves in taking false pleasure for true, and true suffering for false; wherefore through false pleasures they often incur true sufferings. Therefore the art that teaches how to distinguish the true from the false can indeed be learned; and the virtue by which we choose what is truly good and not what falsely appears so can be called true knowledge, more profitable to human life than any other, because it removes ignorance, from which, as I have said, all evils spring."

[15] Then messer Pietro Bembo said: "I do not see why signor Gasparo should grant you, signor Ottaviano, that all evils are born of ignorance; and that there are not many who know well that they are sinning when they sin, and do not at all deceive themselves regarding true pleasure or true suffering. For it is certain that men who are

incontinent judge reasonably and rightly, and know that what they are brought to by their lusts in despite of duty is evil, and therefore resist and set reason against appetite, whence arises the struggle of pleasure and pain against the judgment. Finally reason gives up, overcome by too strong an appetite, like a ship that for a while resists the stormy seas but at last, beaten by the too furious violence of the winds, with anchor and rigging broken, lets herself be driven at Fortune's will, without helm or any guidance of compass to save her.

"Therefore the incontinent commit their errors with a certain ambiguous remorse and, as it were, in despite of themselves; which they would not do if they did not know that what they are doing is evil, but they would follow appetite lavishly without any struggle on the part of reason, and would then be not incontinent but intemperate, which is much worse: for incontinence is said to be a lesser vice because it has some part of reason in it; and likewise continence is said to be an imperfect virtue because it has a part of passion in it. Therefore in this I think we cannot say that the errors of the incontinent proceed from ignorance, or that they deceive themselves and do not sin, when they well know that they are sinning."

[16] Signor Ottaviano replied: "Truly, messer Pietro, your argument is fine; nonetheless, it strikes me as being specious rather than true. For even though the incontinent do sin in this ambiguous way, reason struggling with appetite in their minds, and, although what is evil seems evil to them, yet they do not have a perfect recognition of it nor do they know it as thoroughly as they would need to know it. Hence, they have a vague notion rather than any certain knowledge of it, and so allow their reason to be overcome by passion; but if they had true knowledge of it, it is certain that they would not err: since that by which appetite conquers reason is always ignorance, and true knowledge can never be overcome by passion (which pertains to the body and not to the soul); and passion becomes virtue if rightly ruled and governed by reason, otherwise it becomes vice. But reason has such power that it always brings the senses to obey it, and extends its rule by marvelous ways and means, provided ignorance does not seize upon what reason ought to possess. So that, although the spirits, nerves, and bones have no reason in them, yet when a movement of the mind begins in us, it is as if thought were spurring and shaking the bridle on our spirits, and all our members make ready: the feet to run, the hands to grasp or to do what the mind thinks. This, moreover, is plainly seen in many who sometimes, without knowing it, eat some loathsome and disgusting food, which seems most dainty to their taste, and then when they learn what thing it was not only suffer pain and distress of mind, but the body so follows the judgment of the mind that perforce they cannot help vomiting that food."

[17] Signor Ottaviano was proceeding with his discourse, but the Magnifico Giuliano interrupted him, saying: "If I have heard aright, signor Ottaviano, you said that continence is an imperfect virtue because it has a part of passion in it; and when there is a struggle in our minds between reason and appetite, I think that the virtue which fights and gives victory to reason ought to be esteemed more perfect than that which conquers when no lust or passion opposes it; for in the latter instance the mind seems not to abstain from evil out of virtue, but to refrain from doing evil because it has no wish to do the thing."

Then signor Ottaviano said: "Which captain would you judge to be of greater worth, the one who by fighting openly puts himself in danger and yet conquers the enemy, or the one who by his ability and knowledge deprives them of their strength, reducing them to such a point that they cannot fight, and conquering them so, without any battle or any danger whatsoever?"

"The one," said the Magnifico Giuliano, "who conquers more in safety is without doubt more to be praised, provided that this safe victory of his is not due to the cowardice of the enemy."

Signor Ottaviano replied: "You have judged well; and hence I say to you that continence may be compared to a captain who fights manfully, and, although the enemy is strong and powerful, still conquers them even though not without great difficulty and danger; but temperance, free of all perturbation, is like that captain who conquers and rules without opposition; and, having not only put down but quite extinguished the fire of lust in the mind wherein it abides, like a good prince in time of civil war, temperance destroys her seditious enemies within, and gives to reason the scepter and entire dominion.

"Thus, this virtue does no violence to the mind, but very gently infuses it with a vehement persuasion which inclines it to honorable things, renders it calm and full of repose, and in all things even and well tempered, and informed throughout by a certain harmony with itself that adorns it with a tranquility so serene as never to be disturbed; and in all things becomes most obedient to reason and ready to direct its every movement accordingly, and to follow it wherever reason may wish to lead, without the least recalcitrance, like a tender lamb which always runs and stops and walks near its mother and moves only when she moves. This virtue, then, is very perfect, and is especially suited to princes because from it many other virtues spring."

[18] Then messer Cesare Gonzaga said: "I do not know what virtues befitting a prince can spring from this temperance, if temperance is what removes the passions from the mind, as you say. Perhaps this

would be fitting in a monk or hermit; but I am not at all sure that it becomes a prince who is magnanimous, liberal, and valiant in arms, never to feel, regardless of what is done to him, either wrath or hate or good will or scorn or lust or passion of any kind; or that without these he could have authority over citizens or soldiers."

Signor Ottaviano replied: "I did not say that temperance entirely removes and uproots the passions from the human mind. Nor would this be well, because even in the passions there are some good elements; but temperance brings under the sway of reason that which is perverse in our passions and which stands against what is right. Therefore it is not well to extirpate the passions altogether in order to get rid of disturbances; for this would be like issuing an edict that no one must drink wine, in order to suppress drunkenness, or like forbidding everyone to run because in running we sometimes fall. Note that those who tame horses do not prevent them from running and jumping, but have them do so at the right time and in obedience to the rider. Hence, the passions, when moderated by temperance, are an aid to virtue, just as wrath aids fortitude, and as hatred of evildoers aids justice, and likewise the other virtues too are aided by the passions; which, if they were wholly taken away, would leave the reason weak and languid, so that it could effect little, like the master of a vessel abandoned by the winds and in a great calm.

"Therefore, do not marvel, messer Cesare, if I have said that many other virtues are born of temperance, for when a mind is attuned to this harmony, then through the reason it easily receives true fortitude, that makes it intrepid and safe from every danger, and almost puts it above human passions. And this is true no less of justice (pure virgin, friend of modesty and of the good, queen of all the other virtues), because she teaches us to do what we ought to do and to shun what we ought to shun; and therefore she is most perfect, because the other virtues perform their works through her, and because she is helpful to whomsoever possesses her, and to others as well as to himself: and, without her, as it is said, Jove himself could not rule his kingdom well. Magnanimity also follows upon these and makes them all greater; but it cannot stand by itself because whoever has no other virtue cannot be magnanimous. Then the guide of these virtues is prudence, which consists of a certain judgment in choosing well. And linked into this happy chain are also liberality, magnificence, desire for honor, gentleness, pleasantness, affability, and many other virtues that there is not time now to name. But if our Courtier will do what we have said, he will find them all in his prince's mind, and every day will see beautiful flowers and fruits put forth there, such as are not found in all the exquisite gardens of the world; and within him he will feel very great satisfaction, remembering that he gave his prince, not what fools give (which is gold or silver, vases, garments, and the like, whereof he who gives them is in great want of them and he who receives them has them in greatest abundance), but gave him that virtue which perhaps among all human things is the greatest and rarest, that is, the manner and method of right rule: which of itself alone would suffice to make men happy and to bring back once again to earth that Golden Age which is recorded to have existed once upon a time when Saturn ruled."

[19] When signor Ottaviano here made a slight pause as if to rest, signor Gasparo said: "Which do you think, signor Ottaviano, is the happier rule and the more capable of bringing back to earth that golden age you mention: the rule of so good a prince or the government of a good republic?"

Signor Ottaviano replied: "I should always prefer the rule of a good prince because such rule is more according to nature, and (if we may compare small things with things infinitely great) more like that of God who singly and alone governs the universe. But, apart from this, you see that in those things that are made by human skill, such as armies, great fleets, buildings, and the like, the whole is referred to one man who governs as he wishes. So too in our body, where all the members do their work and fulfill their functions at the command of the heart. In addition to this, moreover, it seems right that people should be ruled by a single prince, as is the case also with many animals, to whom nature teaches such obedience as a very salutary thing. Note that deer, cranes, and many other birds, when they migrate, always choose a leader whom they follow and obey; and bees, almost as if they had discourse of reason, obey their king with as much reverence as the most obedient people on earth; and hence all this is very certain proof that the rule of a prince is more in keeping with nature than that of republics."

[20] Then messer Pietro Bembo said: "To me it seems that since liberty has been given us by God as a supreme gift, it is not reasonable that it should be taken from us, or that one man should have a larger portion of it than another: which happens under the rule of princes, who for the most part hold their subjects in the closest bondage. But in well-ordered republics, this liberty is fully preserved: besides which, both in judging and in deliberating, one man's opinion happens more often to be wrong than the opinion of many men; because the disturbance that arises from anger or indignation or lust more easily enters the mind of one man than that of the many, who are like a great body of water, which is less subject to corruption than a small body. I will say too that the example of the animals does not seem appropriate to me; for deer, cranes, and

other animals do not always choose to follow and obey the same one, but they change and vary, giving rule now to one, now to another, and come in this way to a kind of republic rather than to monarchy; and this can be called true and equal liberty, when those who sometimes command obey in their turn. Nor do I think that the example of the bees is pertinent, for their king is not of their own species; and therefore whoever wishes to give men a truly worthy lord would need to find one of another species and of a more excellent nature than the human, if men are to be bound in reason to obey him, like the herds which obey, not an animal of their own kind, but a herdsman who is a man, and is of a higher species than theirs. For these reasons, signor Ottaviano, I hold that the rule of a republic is more desirable than that of a king."

[21] Then signor Ottaviano said: "Against your opinion, messer Pietro, I wish only to cite one argument; namely, that there are only three kinds of right rule: one is monarchy; another, the rule of the good, whom the ancients called optimates; the third, popular government. And the excess and opposing vice, so to speak, into which each of these kinds of rule falls when it comes to ruin and decay is when monarchy becomes tyranny; when the rule of the optimates changes into government by a few who are powerful and not good; and when popular government is seized by the rabble, which brings general confusion and surrenders the rule of the whole to the caprice of the multitude. Of these three kinds of bad government, it is certain that tyranny is the worst of all, as could be proved by many arguments: thus, it follows that monarchy is the best of the three kinds of good government, because it is the opposite of the worst; for, as you know, those things that result from opposite causes are themselves opposites.

"Now as to what you said about liberty, I answer that we ought not to say that true liberty is to live as we like, but to live according to good laws. Nor is obeying less natural or less useful or less necessary than commanding; and some things are born and devised and ordained by nature to command, as others are to obey. It is true that there are two modes of ruling; the one absolute and violent, like that of masters toward their slaves, and in this way the soul commands the body; and the other is more mild and gentle, like that of good princes over the citizens by means of laws, and in this way the reason commands the appetite: and both of these modes are useful, for the body is by nature made apt for obeying the soul, and likewise appetite for obeying the reason. There are many men, moreover, whose actions pertain only to the body; and such men differ as much from virtuous men as the soul differs from the body; and, even though they are rational creatures, they have only such share of reason as to be able to recognize this, but do not possess it or derive profit from it. These, therefore, are naturally slaves, and it is better and more useful for them to obey than to command."

[22] Then signor Gasparo said: "The discreet and virtuous, and those who are not by nature slaves, in what mode are they to be ruled?"

Signor Ottaviano replied: "By the gentle kind of rule, kingly and civic. And to such men it is well sometimes to give the charge of those offices for which they are suited, so that they too may be able to command and govern those who are less wise than themselves, yet in such a way that the chief rule shall depend entirely upon the supreme ruler. And since you said that it is an easier thing for the mind of a single man to be corrupted than that of many, I say that it is also easier to find one good and wise man than many. And we must think that a king of noble race will be good and wise, inclined to the virtues by his natural instinct and by the illustrious memory of his forebears, and practiced in good behavior; and even if he is not of another species higher than the human (as you have said of the king of bees), being aided by the teachings and the training and skill of so prudent and good a Courtier as these gentlemen have devised, he will be very just, continent, temperate, strong, and wise, full of liberality, magnificence, religion, and clemency. In fine, he will be most glorious and dear to men and to God, by Whose grace he will attain the heroic virtue that will bring him to surpass the limits of humanity and be called a demigod rather than a mortal man: for God delights in and protects, not those princes who try to imitate Him by a show of great power and by making themselves adored of men, but those who, besides the power they wield, strive to make themselves like Him in goodness and wisdom, by means of which they may wish and be able to do good and be His ministers, distributing for the welfare of mortals the benefits and gifts they receive from Him. Hence, just as in the heavens the sun and the moon and the other stars exhibit to the world, as in a mirror, a certain likeness of God, so on earth a much liker image of God is seen in those good princes who love and revere Him and show to the people the splendid light of His justice accompanied by a semblance of His divine reason and intellect; and with such as these God shares His righteousness, equity, justice, and goodness, and more happy blessings than I could name, that give to the world a much clearer proof of divinity than the sun's light or the continual turning of the heavens and the various courses of the stars.

[23] "Thus, men have been put by God under princes, who for this reason must take diligent care in order to render Him an account of

them like good stewards to their lord, and love them and look upon every good and evil thing that happens to them as happening to themselves, and procure their happiness above every other thing. Therefore the prince must not only be good but also make others good, like the square used by architects, which not only is straight and true itself, but also makes straight and true all things to which it is applied. And it is a very great proof that the prince is good if his people are good, because the life of the prince is a norm and guide for the citizens, and all behavior must needs depend on his behavior; nor is it fitting for an ignorant man to teach, or for a disorderly man to give orders, or for one who falls to raise others up.

"Hence, if the prince is to perform these duties well, he must put every effort and cure into acquiring knowledge; let him then erect within himself and in every regard follow steadfastly the law of reason (not one inscribed on paper or in metal, but graven upon his very mind) so that it will always be not only familiar to him but ingrained in him and that he will live with it as with a part of himself; so that day and night in every place and time, it may admonish him and speak to him within his heart, removing from him those turbulences that are felt by intemperate minds which—because they are oppressed on the one hand, as it were, by a very deep sleep of ignorance, and on the other, by the turmoil which they undergo from their perverse and blind desires—are shaken by a restless frenzy as a sleeper sometimes is by strange and horrible visions.

[24] "Moreover, when greater power is joined to an evil will, greater harm is also joined; and when the prince can do whatever he desires, then there is great danger that he may not desire what he ought. Hence, Bias well said that the office shows the man: for just as vases that are cracked cannot readily be detected so long as they are empty, yet if liquid be put into them, show at once just where the defect lies—in like manner corrupt and depraved minds rarely disclose their defects save when they are filled with authority; because they are then unable to bear the heavy weight of power, and so give way and pour out on every side greed, pride, wrath, insolence, and those tyrannical practices which they have within them. Thus, they recklessly persecute the good and the wise and exalt the wicked; and they allow no friendships in their cities nor unions nor understandings among the citizens, but encourage spies, informers, and murderers in order to make men afraid and cowardly, sowing discord to keep men disunited and weak. And from these ways come endless harm and ruin to the unhappy people; and often cruel death (or at least continual fear) comes to the tyrants themselves; because good princes do not fear for themselves but for those whom they rule, while tyrants fear those whom they rule; hence, the greater the

number of people they rule and the more powerful they are, the more fear they feel and the more enemies they have. How fearful and of what an uneasy mind was Clearchus, tyrant of Pontus, whenever he went into the market place or theater, or to some banquet or other public place; who, as it is written, was wont to sleep shut up in a chest! Or that other tyrant, Aristodemus the Argive, who made his bed into a kind of prison: for in his palace he had a little room suspended in air, so high that it could only be reached by a ladder; and there he slept with his woman, whose mother would remove the ladder at night and replace it in the morning.[6]

"The life of the good prince must be an entirely different life from this, free and secure, and as dear to his citizens as their own life, and so ordered as to partake of both the active and the contemplative life, in the measure that is suited to the welfare of his people."

[25] Then signor Gasparo said: "And which of these two ways of life, signor Ottaviano, do you think is more fitting for the prince?"

Signor Ottaviano replied, laughing: "Perhaps you think that I imagine myself to be the excellent Courtier who must know so many things and make use of them to the good end I have described; but remember that these gentlemen have fashioned him with many accomplishments that are not in me. Therefore let us first try to find him, and I will abide by his decision in this as in the other things that pertain to a good prince."

Then signor Gasparo said: "I think that if there be wanting in you any of the accomplishments which have been attributed to the Courtier, then they are music and dancing and some others of little importance, rather than those belonging to the education of the prince and to this part of Courtiership."

Signor Ottaviano replied: "None are of little importance that serve to gain the prince's favor, which is necessary (as we have said) before the Courtier may venture to try to teach him virtue; which, as I think I have shown you, can be learned, and is as beneficial as ignorance is harmful, from which all sins stem, and especially that false esteem which men conceive of themselves. But I think I have said enough, and perhaps more than I promised."

Then the Duchess said: "We shall be the more indebted to your courtesy, the more your performance surpasses your promise; hence, be pleased to tell us what you think of signor Gasparo's question; and, by your faith, tell us also everything that you would teach your prince if he had need of instruction—and let us assume that you have won his favor completely, so that you are free to tell him whatever comes to mind."

6. The examples here derive from Plutarch's "On the Ignorant Prince."

[26] Signor Ottaviano laughed and said: "If I had the favor of some of the princes I know, and if I were to tell them freely what I think, I fear I should soon lose that favor; moreover, in order to teach him, I myself should first have to learn. Yet since it is your pleasure that I answer signor Gasparo on this point also, I will say that it seems to me that princes ought to lead both kinds of life, but more especially the contemplative, because this in them is divided into two parts: one consists in seeing rightly and in judging; the other in commanding reasonable things (justly and in the proper manner) in which they have authority, and in requiring the same of those who rightly should obey, at appropriate times and places; and of this Duke Federico was speaking when he said that he who knows how to command is always obeyed. And whereas commanding is always the chief office of princes, often also they must witness with their own eyes and be present at the execution of their commands according to the times and needs, and must sometimes take part themselves; and all this pertains to action; but the contemplative life ought to be the goal of the active as peace is of war and as repose is of toil.

[27] "Therefore it is also the office of the good prince to establish his people in such laws and ordinances that they may live in ease and peace, without danger and with dignity, and may worthily enjoy this end of their actions, namely, tranquility. For there have often been many republics and princes most prosperous and great in war; but then, as soon as they achieved peace, they came to ruin and lost their greatness and splendor, like iron in disuse. And this happened from no cause other than from not having been well trained to live in peace, and not knowing how to enjoy the good of repose. And to be always at war, without seeking to achieve the end which is peace, is not right: although some princes think that their chief aim must be to dominate their neighbors, and therefore they incite their people to a warlike ferocity in despoiling, killing, and the like, and dispense rewards to encourage this, and call it virtue. Thus, it was once a custom among the Scythians that whoever had not slain an enemy might not drink from the bowl that was passed around at solemn feasts. In other places it was the custom to set up about a man's tomb as many obelisks as he who was buried there had slain enemies; and all these and like things were done in order to make men warlike, solely with the aim of dominating others: which was wellnigh impossible, since such an undertaking could never end short of subjugating the entire world; and wanting in reason according to the law of nature which will not let us be pleased with that in others which displeases us in ourselves.

"Hence, princes ought not to make their people warlike out of a desire to dominate, but in order to defend themselves and their people against anyone who might try to bring them into bondage or do them wrong in any way; or in order to drive out tyrants and govern well those people who are badly treated; or in order to subject those who by nature deserve to become slaves, with the aim of giving them good government, ease, repose, and peace. To this end also the laws and all the ordinances of justice ought to be directed, by punishing the wicked, not out of hatred, but in order that they may no longer be wicked and to the end that they may not disturb the peace of the good. For truly it is a monstrous thing and worthy of blame for men to show themselves valiant and wise in war (which is bad in itself), and then in peace and quiet (which is good) show themselves ignorant and of so little worth as not to know how to enjoy the good. Hence, just as in war a people ought to aim at the virtues that are useful and necessary in order to attain the end, which is peace—so in peace, to attain its end also, which is tranquility, they ought to aim at those righteous virtues to which the practical virtues lead. In this way his subjects will be good and the prince will be much more occupied in praising and rewarding than in punishing; and his rule will be a most happy one both for his subjects and for himself—not imperious, like that of master over slave, but sweet and gentle like that of a good father over a good son."

[28] Then signor Gasparo said: "I should be glad to know what these virtues are that are useful and necessary in war, and what are the good virtues in peace."

Signor Ottaviano replied: "All virtues are good and helpful, because they tend to a good end; but in war true fortitude is especially useful, freeing the mind from the passions so that it not only has no fear of dangers, but is even unaware of them; so too, steadfastness and a long-suffering patience, and a mind stanch and unperturbed by the blows of Fortune. It is also well, in war, and always, to have all the virtues that tend to moral excellence, such as justice, continence, and temperance; but much more in time of peace and ease, because when men enjoy prosperity and ease, and a favorable Fortune smiles on them, they often become unjust and intemperate, and allow themselves to be corrupted by pleasures: hence, those who find themselves in such a condition greatly need these virtues, because idleness readily engenders bad habits in men's minds. Wherefore it was an ancient saying that slaves should be given no leisure; and it is thought that the pyramids of Egypt were built in order to keep the people occupied, because it is very good that all should be accustomed to endure toil.

"There are still many other virtues, all helpful; but let it suffice for the present that I have spoken thus far; for if I managed to teach my prince and instruct him in the kind of virtuous education we have sketched, then I should think I had attained sufficiently well the aim of the good Courtier."

[29] Then signor Gasparo said: "Signor Ottaviano, since you have praised good education so highly and have shown that you think it the chief means by which a man is made virtuous and good, I should like to know whether this instruction which the Courtier is to give his prince ought to be begun as it were in daily practice and conduct, which may accustom him to doing right without his noticing it; or whether one should begin by explaining to him the nature of good and evil, and making him understand, before he sets out, which is the good way to follow and which is the bad way to avoid: in short, whether his mind must first be imbued and stamped with the virtues through reason and intelligence, or through practice."

Signor Ottaviano said: "You are involving me in too long a discourse; still, so that you may not think I abstain because I do not wish to answer your questions, I will say that, even as our mind and body are two things, so likewise the soul is divided into two parts, one of which has reason in it and the other has the appetite. Thus, just as in generation the body precedes the soul, so the irrational part of the soul precedes the rational: which is clearly seen in children, in whom anger and desire are noted almost as soon as they are born, but reason appears with the passing of time. Hence, we must care for the body before the soul and for the appetite before the reason; but we must care for the body for the sake of the soul, and care for the appetite for the sake of the reason: for just as intellectual virtue is perfected by teaching, so moral virtue is perfected by practice. First, therefore, we should teach through practice, whereby it is possible to govern the appetites that are not yet capable of reason and direct them toward the good by way of such good exercise; then we ought to establish them through the intelligence, which, although it shows its light only later, yet provides a way of bringing the virtues to an even more perfect fruition in one whose mind has learned good habits—in which, in my opinion, the whole matter consists."

[30] Signor Gasparo said: "Before you go further, I should like to know what care must be taken of the body, since you have said that we must care for the body before the soul."

Signor Ottaviano replied, laughing: "Ask some here present about that, who nourish their bodies so well and are fat and fresh; for mine, as you see, is not so well cared-for. Yet on this point too it would be possible to speak at length, as well as of the proper age for marriage so that the children may not be too near or too far from their parents' age; and to speak of the exercises and education to be followed from birth and throughout their life in order to make them handsome, healthy, and strong."

Signor Gasparo replied: "What women would most like in order to make their children well constituted and handsome, I believe, is that community in which Plato in his Republic would have them held, and after that fashion."

Then signora Emilia said, laughing: "It is not any part of our pact that you should begin again to speak ill of women."

"I thought," replied signor Gasparo, "that I was paying them a great tribute in saying that they desired to introduce a custom approved by so great a man."

Messer Cesare Gonzaga said, laughing: "Suppose we see whether this one can stand among signor Ottaviano's precepts (for I do not know if he has yet mentioned all of them), and whether it would be well for the prince to make it a law."

"The few I have mentioned," replied signor Ottaviano, "would perhaps suffice to make the prince good, as princes go nowadays, although if one wished to examine the matter in more detail, he would find much more to say."

The Duchess added: "Since it costs us only words, tell us, by your faith, all that occurs to you in this matter of instructing your prince."

[31] Signor Ottaviano replied: "Madam, I should teach him many other things if only I knew them; among others, that he should choose from among his subjects a number of the noblest and wisest gentlemen, with whom to consult on everything, and that he should give them authority and free leave to speak their mind to him about all things without hesitation; and that he should act toward them in such a way as to show them all that he wished to know the truth in everything and that he detested all falsehood. And, besides such a council of nobles, I should advise that from among the people other men of lower station be chosen who would constitute a popular council to confer with the council of nobles concerning the affairs of the city, both public and private. And in this way there would be made of the prince (as of the head) and of the nobles and the people (as of the members) a single united body, the government of which would depend chiefly on the prince, and yet would also include the others; and such a state would thus have the form of the three good kinds of government, which are monarchy, optimates, and people.

[32] "Next, I should show him that, of the duties that fall to the prince, the most important is justice; for the maintenance whereof wise and proved men ought to be appointed to office, whose pru-

dence should be true prudence joined to goodness—otherwise it is not prudence but cunning; and when this goodness is wanting, the skill and subtlety of prosecutors lead only to the ruin and destruction of law and justice, and, for all that the errors are theirs, the blame must fall on him who put them in office.

"I should tell how from justice springs that piety toward God which all men must have, and especially princes, who ought to love Him above all else, and direct all their actions to Him as to the true end; and, as Xenophon said,[7] honor and love Him always, but much more when they enjoy prosperity, so that afterward they may with more reason feel confident in asking His mercy when they experience some adversity. For it is not possible to govern rightly either one's self or others without God's help, Who sometimes to the good sends good fortune as His minister to save them from grievous perils; and sometimes adverse fortune to prevent their being so lulled by prosperity as to forget Him or human prudence, which often remedies ill fortune, as a good player remedies bad throws of the dice by placing his board well. Nor would I neglect to urge the prince to be truly religious—not superstitious or given to the folly of incantations and soothsaying; for should he join divine piety and true religion to human prudence, he will have good fortune on his side and a protecting God ever to increase his prosperity in peace and war.

[33] "Next I should tell him how he ought to love his own country and his own people, not holding them too much in bondage, lest he make himself hated by them, from which come seditions, conspiracies, and a thousand other evils; nor yet in too great a liberty, lest he be despised, from which come a licentious and dissolute life among the people, rapine, thievery, murders, without any fear of the law; and often the ruin and total destruction of city and realms. Next, how he ought to love those close to him according to their rank, maintaining with all men a strict equality in certain things, such as justice and liberty; and in certain other things, a reasonable inequality, such as in being generous, in rewarding, in distributing honors and dignities according to the differences in their merits, which ought always to be surpassed by their rewards and not the other way around; and in this way he would be not only loved but almost adored by his subjects. Nor would he need to resort to foreigners for the protection of his life, because his people for their own good would guard his life with their own, and all men would willingly obey the laws, when they saw that he himself obeyed them and was, as it were, their custodian and incorruptible executor; and he

7. In his *Cyropaedia* I, 6.

should establish so strong an impression of himself in this respect that, even if sometimes he found it necessary to break the laws in some particular, everyone would recognize that this was done for a good end, and his will would command the same reverence as the law itself. Thus, the minds of the citizens would be so tempered that the good would not seek to have more than they needed and the bad could not do so; for excessive wealth is often the cause of great ruin, as in poor Italy, which has been and still is exposed as a prey to foreign peoples, both because of bad government and because of the great riches of which it is full. Thus, it would be well to have the greater part of the citizens neither very rich nor very poor, for the overrich often become proud and insolent, and the poor, abject and fraudulent. But men of modest fortune do not lay snares for others and are safe from snares: and, constituting the greater number, these men of modest fortune are also more powerful; and therefore neither the poor nor the rich can conspire against the prince or against others, nor foment seditions; wherefore, in order to avoid this evil, it is salutary to observe a mean in all things.

[34] "Therefore, I should say that the prince ought to employ these and many other opportune measures so that there may not arise among his subjects any desire for new things or for a change of government; which they frequently seek either in hope of gain or of some honor, or because of loss or indeed of some shame which they fear. And they are incited in this way sometimes by a hatred and an anger that bring them to despair, through the wrongs and offenses that are done them out of greed, insolence, and cruelty, or the lust of those who are over them; sometimes by the contempt which the neglect and cowardice and worthlessness of their princes cause them to feel. These two errors should be avoided by winning the people's love and obedience; which is won by favoring and honoring the good, and by prudently and sometimes severely preventing the bad and seditious from becoming powerful; and this is much easier to prevent before it happens than it is to deprive them of power once they have acquired it. I should say that, to keep the citizens from falling into these errors, there is no better way than to keep them from evil practices, and especially from those that become established little by little; for these are the secret plagues that ruin cities before they can be remedied or even detected.

"I would advise the prince to strive by such methods to keep his subjects in a tranquil state, and give them the blessings of mind, body, and fortune; but give them those of the body and of fortune, in order that they may practice those of the mind, which are the more profitable the greater and more copious they are; which is not true of those of the body and of fortune. If, therefore, his subjects are good and worthy and rightly directed toward the goal of happiness, the prince will be a very great lord; for rule is true rule and great rule where the subjects are good, well governed, and well commanded."

[35] Then signor Gasparo said: "I think he would be a petty lord whose subjects were all good, for the good are few everywhere."

Signor Ottaviano replied: "If some Circe were to change all the subjects of the King of France into wild beasts, would he not seem to you a petty lord even though he ruled over so many thousands of animals? And, contrariwise, if the flocks roaming our mountains here for pasture were to become wise men and worthy cavaliers, would you not think that those herdsmen who governed them and were obeyed by them had become great lords instead of herdsmen? So you see, it is not the number but the worth of their subjects that makes princes great."

[36] For some time the Duchess and signora Emilia and all the others had been very attentive to signor Ottaviano's discourse; but when he now made a little pause as if he had finished, messer Cesare Gonzaga said: "Truly, signor Ottaviano, one cannot say that your precepts are not good and useful; nevertheless, I should think that if you were to fashion your prince accordingly, you would rather deserve the name of good schoolmaster than of good Courtier, and your prince would be a good governor rather than a great prince. Of course I do not say that princes should not see to it that their people are well ruled with justice and good customs; nevertheless, it is enough, it seems to me, for princes to choose good officials to administer such things, their real office being a much greater one.

"Hence, if I felt that I was that excellent Courtier which these gentlemen have fashioned, and if I had the favor of my prince, I certainly would not lead him to anything vicious; but, in order that he might pursue that good end which you have stated (and which I agree ought to be the fruit of the Courtier's labors and actions), I should seek to implant a certain greatness in his mind, along with a regal splendor, a readiness of spirit, and an unconquered valor in war, that would make him loved and revered by everyone, so that chiefly for this would he be famous and illustrious in the world. I should say too that he ought to join to his greatness a certain familiar gentleness, a sweet and amiable humanity, and a fine manner of showing his favor discreetly to his subjects and to strangers, and in varying measure according to their deserts—holding always, however, to the majesty that befits his rank, never allowing his authority to diminish in the least by lowering himself too much, nor excite hatred by too stern a severity; that he ought to be very generous and splendid, and give to everyone unstintingly because God, as the saying goes, is the treasurer of generous princes; that he ought to offer magnificent banquets, festivals, games, public shows; and have a great many fine horses for use in war and for pleasure in time of peace, falcons, dogs, and all the other things that pertain to the pleasures of great lords and of the people: as in our day we have seen signor Francesco Gonzaga, Marquess of Mantua, do, who in these matters seems King of Italy rather than lord of a city.

"I should also try to induce him to build great edifices, both to win honor in his lifetime and to leave the memory of himself to posterity: as Duke Federico did in the case of this noble palace, and as Pope Julius is now doing in the case of St. Peter's Church and that street which leads from the Palace to his pleasure pavilion the Belvedere, and many other buildings: as also the ancient Romans did, whereof we see so many remains at Rome and at Naples, at Pozzuoli, at Baia, at Civita Vecchia, at Porto, as well as outside Italy, and in many other places—all of which is great proof of the worthiness of those divine minds. So Alexander the Great did also, for, not content with the fame he had rightly won by conquering the world with arms, he built Alexandria in Egypt, Bucephalia in India, and other cities in other countries; and he thought of giving Mount Athos the form of a man, and of building a very spacious city in the man's left hand and in his right a great basin in which were to be gathered all the rivers that rise there, and these were to overflow thence into the sea: a grand thought indeed and worthy of Alexander the Great.

"These are things, signor Ottaviano, which I think befit a noble and true prince, and make him most glorious in peace and in war, rather than such trivial scruples as to fight only in order to conquer and rule over those who deserve to be ruled, or to seek what is good for his subjects, or to deprive of power those who rule badly: for if the Romans, Alexander, Hannibal, and the others had been concerned with such things as these, they would not have reached the pinnacle of glory they did."

[37] Then signor Ottaviano replied, laughing: "Those who showed no concern for these things would have done better to do so; although if you will take thought, you will find many who did, and particularly those first ancients, like Theseus and Hercules. And do not imagine that Procrustes and Sciron, Cacus, Diomed, Antaeus, Geryon were other than cruel and wicked tyrants, against whom these magnanimous heroes waged perpetual and deadly war. Therefore, for his delivering the world from such insufferable monsters (for tyrants should have no other name), temples were raised and sacrifices were offered to Hercules, and divine honors were paid to

him: the extirpation of tyrants being so great a benefit to the world that he who does it deserves far greater reward than any that is due to mortal man. And, as among those whom you named, do you not think that by his victories Alexander did good to those whom he overcame, having taught so many good customs to those barbarous peoples whom he conquered, from wild beasts making them men? He built so many fine cities in lands that were sparsely populated, introducing there a decent way of life and, as it were, uniting Asia and Europe by the bond of friendship and holy laws, so that those who were conquered by him were happier than the others. For he taught marriage to some, to others agriculture, to others religion, to others not to kill their parents but to support them in their old age, others to abstain from copulating with their mothers, and a thousand other things that one could cite in evidence of the benefits that his victories conferred upon the world.

[38] "But, leaving aside the ancients, what more noble, glorious, and profitable undertaking could there be than for Christians to direct their efforts to subjugating the infidels? Does it not seem to you that such a war, if it should meet with good success and were the means of turning so many thousands of men from the false sect of Mohammed to the light of Christian truth, would be as profitable to the vanquished as to the victors? And truly, as Themistocles once said to his household, when he had been banished from his native land and was received by the King of Persia and favored and honored with innumerable very rich gifts: 'My friends, it would have been a disaster if we had not met with disaster,' the same might then be said by the Turks and Moors, because their loss would be their salvation.

"Therefore I hope we may yet see this happy event, if God should grant that Monseigneur d'Angouleme live to wear the crown of France, who gives such promise of himself, as the Magnifico said some four evenings ago; and that Henry, Prince of Wales, wear that of England, who is now growing up in all virtue under his great father, like a tender shoot in the shade of an excellent and fruit-laden tree, to renew it when the time shall come with much greater beauty and fruitfulness; for, as our Castiglione writes us from there and promises to tell us more fully on his return, it seems that nature chose to show her power in this lord by uniting in a single body excellences enough to adorn a multitude."

Then messer Bernardo Bibbiena said: "Don Carlos, Prince of Spain, is also showing very great promise. Although he has not yet reached the tenth year of his age, he already reveals so great a capacity and such sure signs of goodness, prudence, modesty, magnanimity, and every virtue, that if the rule of Christendom is to be in his hands (as men think), we can believe that he will eclipse the name of many ancient emperors and equal the fame of the most famous men who have ever been on earth."

[39] Signor Ottaviano added: "Thus, I think that such divine princes as these have been sent by God on earth and have been made by Him to resemble one another, in youth, in military power, in state, in bodily beauty, and constitution, to the end that they may be of one accord in this good purpose as well. And if there must ever be any envy or emulation among them, may it be solely in the desire on the part of each to be first and the most fervent and zealous in so glorious an undertaking.

"But let us leave this matter and return to our subject. I say, then, messer Cesare, that the things you would have the prince do are very great and deserve much praise; but you must understand that if he does not know what I have said he ought to know, and if he has not formed his mind on that pattern and directed it to the path of virtue, he will scarcely know how to be magnanimous, generous, spirited, prudent, or how to have any of the other qualities he ought to have. Nor would I wish him to have these for any reason save an ability to exercise them: for just as those who build are not all good architects, so those who give are not all generous men; because virtue never harms anyone, yet there are many who rob in order to give away, and thus are generous with the property of others; some give to those they ought not, and leave in misfortune and distress those to whom they are obligated; others give with a certain bad grace, almost with spite, so that it is plain that they do so on compulsion; others not only are not secret about it, but summon witnesses and almost make a public proclamation of their generosities; others foolishly empty the fountain of their generosity at one draught, so that it cannot be used again thereafter.

[40] "Therefore in this as in other things one must know and govern one's self with that prudence which is the necessary companion to all the virtues; which, being at the midpoint, are equally distant from the two extremes, which are the vices; and thus an undiscerning man easily incurs them. For just as with a circle it is difficult to find the point of the center, which is the mean, so it is difficult to find the point of virtue set midway between the two extremes (the one vicious because of excess, the other because of want); and to these we are inclined, now to the one, now to the other. And we see this in the pleasure or the displeasure we feel within us, for by reason of the one we do what we should not do, and by reason of the other we fail to do what we should; but pleasure is the more dangerous, because our judgment lets itself be easily corrupted by it.

But since it is a difficult thing to know how far one is from the mid-point of virtue, we ought of our own accord to withdraw by degrees in the direction opposite to the extreme to which we see ourselves inclined, as those do who straighten crooked timbers; for in such a way we draw near to virtue which, as I have said, consists in that midpoint of the mean. And so it happens that we err in many ways, and perform our office and duty in but one way; as archers, who hit the mark in one way only, and miss the target by many ways. Thus, often, in his wish to be humane and affable, one prince will do countless unseemly things and will so abase himself that he becomes despised; another, to maintain his grave majesty with fit-ting authority, becomes austere and insufferable; another, in order to be thought eloquent, indulges in a thousand strange manners and in long circumlocutions of affected words, listening to himself so much that others for boredom cannot listen to him.

[41] "Therefore, messer Cesare, do not call anything a trifle that can improve a prince, in any way, however little; nor suppose that I think you are condemning my precepts when you say that they would make a good governor rather than a good prince; for perhaps no greater or more fitting praise can be given to a prince than to call him a good governor. Hence, if it were for me to educate him, I would have him take care to govern not only in the ways mentioned, but in much lesser matters, and understand as far as possible all the particular things that pertain to his people, nor ever believe or trust any one of his ministers to such an extent as to give to him alone the bridle and control of all his rule. For there is no man who is entirely apt in all things, and much greater harm results from the trust of princes than from their distrust, which not only does no harm, but often is to the greatest advantage: and yet in this the prince needs good judgment to discern who deserves to be trusted and who does not. I would have him take care to understand his ministers' actions and be the critic of them; abolish and shorten dis-putes among his subjects; bring about peace among them and bind them together by marriage ties; make his city united and peaceful in friendship like a private family—populous, not poor, quiet, full of good workmen; favor merchants and even aid them with money; be generous and handsome in hospitality toward foreigners and eccle-siastics; moderate all superfluities, for through errors committed in these matters, though they may seem trivial, cities often come to ruin. Wherefore it is right that the prince should set a limit upon the too sumptuous houses of private citizens, upon banquets, upon the excessive dowries of women, upon their luxury and display of jewels and dress, which is but augmentation of folly on their part: for besides often wasting their husbands' goods and substance from

ambition and the envy they bear one another, women sometimes sell their honor to anyone who will buy it for the sake of some little jewel or trinket."

[42] Then messer Bernardo Bibbiena said, laughing: "Signor Otta-viano, you are passing to the side of signor Gasparo and Frisio."

Signor Ottaviano replied, also laughing: "That dispute is over, and I certainly do not wish to renew it; so I shall speak no more about women, but shall return to my prince."

Frisio replied: "You may very well leave him now and feel satisfied that he is such as you have described him. For without a doubt it would be easier to find a Lady with the qualities set forth by the Magnifico than a prince with the qualities set forth by you; hence, I fear that he is like the Republic of Plato, and that we shall never see the like of him, unless in heaven perhaps."

Signor Ottaviano replied: "We can still hope for things to come to pass which are possible, even though they may be difficult. Thus, in our time we shall perhaps yet see him on earth; for, although the heavens are so chary of producing excellent princes that one is scarcely seen in many centuries, such good fortune might befall us."

Then Count Ludovico said: "I am myself quite hopeful of it; for, besides those three great princes whom we have named and of whom we may expect what has been declared to befit the highest type of perfect prince, there are also in Italy today several princes' sons who, although they are not destined to have such great power, will perhaps make up for that in virtue. And the one among them all who shows the best temperament and gives more promise than any of the others would appear to be signor Federico Gonzaga, eldest son of the Marquess of Mantua and nephew to our Duchess here. For, besides the comely behavior and the discretion he shows at such a tender age, those who have charge of him tell wonderful things of his talents, his eagerness for honor, his magnanimity, cour-tesy, generosity, love of justice; so that from so good a start we can expect only the best of ends."

Then Frisio said: "No more of this now: we will pray God that we may see this hope of yours fulfilled."

[43] Then signor Ottaviano, turning to the Duchess with an air of having finished his discourse, said: "There, Madam, you have what it occurs to me to say about the aim of the Courtier; wherein, if I may not have given entire satisfaction, it will at least be enough for me to have shown that some further perfection might be given him in addition to the things mentioned by these gentlemen; who, I think, must have omitted this and whatever else I might say, not because they did not know it better than I, but in order to spare

themselves the trouble; therefore, I will let them proceed, if they have anything more to say."

Then the Duchess said: "Not only is the hour so late that soon it will be time to stop for the evening, but it seems to me that we ought not to mingle any other discourse with this one: into which you have put so many diverse and beautiful things that we may say, respecting the aim of Courtiership, not only that you are the perfect Courtier we are looking for, and qualified to educate your prince rightly, but if Fortune is favorable to you, you ought also to be an excellent prince, which would be of great benefit to your country."

Signor Ottaviano laughed, and said: "Perhaps, Madam, if I should hold such rank, it would be with me as it is wont to be with many others, who know better how to speak than act."

[44] At this, when the matter had been bandied about the company, with some contradiction and also some praise of what had been said, and when it was noted that it was not yet time to retire to sleep, the Magnifico Giuliano said, laughing: "Madam, I am such an enemy of deception that I am obliged to contradict signor Ottaviano who, from having (as I fear) conspired secretly with signor Gasparo against women, has fallen into two errors, both most grave in my opinion. One of which is that, in order to set this Courtier above the Court Lady and make him exceed the bounds that she can attain, signor Ottaviano has also set the Courtier above the prince, which is most unseemly; the other is that he has given him a goal ever difficult and sometimes impossible for him to reach, and such that, if he should reach it, he ought not to be called a Courtier."

"I do not understand," said signora Emilia, "how it should be so difficult or impossible for the Courtier to attain this goal of his, nor how signor Ottaviano has set him above the prince."

"Do not grant him these things," replied signor Ottaviano, "for I have not set the Courtier above the prince, nor do I think that I have fallen into any error respecting the aim of Courtiership."

Then the Magnifico Giuliano replied: "You cannot say, signor Ottaviano, that the cause which gives a certain quality to an effect does not always have more of that quality than its effect has. Thus, the Courtier, through whose instruction the prince is to become so excellent, would have to be more excellent than the prince; and in this way he would also be of greater dignity than the prince himself, which is most unseemly. Then, respecting the aim of Courtiership, what you have said holds good when the prince's age is close to that of the Courtier, and yet not without difficulty, for where there is little difference of age, it is natural that there should be little difference in knowledge as well, whereas if the prince is old and the Courtier young, it stands to reason that the old prince would know more than the young Courtier; and if this does not always happen, it does happen sometimes, and then the goal you have given the Courtier is impossible. But if the prince is young and the Courtier old, it will be difficult for the Courtier to win the prince's mind by means of those accomplishments which you have attributed to him. For, to speak truly, jousting and other bodily exercises are for young men and not for the old, and music and dancing and festivals and games and affairs of love are ridiculous in old age; and it strikes me that they would ill become one who directs the life and manners of the prince, for such a one ought to be a very sober and authoritative person, mature in years and in experience and, if possible, a good philosopher, a good commander, and ought to know almost everything. Hence, I think that whoever instructs the prince should not be called a Courtier but deserves a far greater and more honored name. So that you must pardon me, signor Ottaviano, if I have exposed your fallacy; for it seems to me that I am bound to do so for the honor of my Lady, whom you are determined to have of less dignity than this Courtier of yours, and this I will not tolerate."

[45] Signor Ottaviano laughed, and said: "Signor Magnifico, it would be more in praise of the Court Lady to exalt her until she equaled the Courtier rather than abase the Courtier until he equaled the Court Lady; for surely the Lady would not be forbidden to teach her mistress also, and to tend with her to that aim of Courtiership that I have said befits the Courtier with his prince. But you are trying more to blame the Courtier than to praise the Court Lady; hence, I may be allowed to continue to take the Courtier's part.

"To reply, then, to your objections, I will say that I did not hold that the Courtier's instruction should be the sole cause of making the prince such as we would have him be. For if the prince were not by nature inclined and fitted to be so, every care and every exhortation on the part of the Courtier would be in vain: even as the labor of any good husbandman would also be in vain if he were to set about cultivating and sowing the sterile sand of the sea with excellent seed, because such sterility is natural to it; but when to good seed in fertile soil, and to mildness of atmosphere and seasonable rains, there is added also the diligence of man's cultivation, abundant crops are always seen to grow in plenty there. Not that the husbandman alone is the cause of these, although without him all the other things would avail little or nothing. Thus, there are many princes who would be good if their minds were properly cultivated; and it is of these that I speak, not of those who are like sterile ground, and are by nature so alien to good behavior that no training can avail to lead their minds in the straight path.

[46] "And since, as we have already said, our habits are formed according to our actions, and virtue consists in action, it is neither impossible nor surprising that the Courtier should lead the prince to many virtues, such as justice, generosity, magnanimity, the practice of which the prince can easily realize and so acquire the habit of them; which the Courtier cannot do, because he does not have the means of practicing them; and thus the prince, led to virtue by the Courtier, can become more virtuous than the Courtier. Moreover, you must know that the whetstone, though it cuts nothing, sharpens iron. Hence it seems to me that, although the Courtier instructs the prince, he need not on that account be said to be of greater dignity than the prince.

"That the aim of this Courtiership is difficult and sometimes impossible, and that even when the Courtier attains it, he ought not to be called a Courtier but deserves a greater name—I will say that I do not deny this difficulty, because it is no less difficult to find so excellent a Courtier than it is to attain such an end. Yet it seems clear to me that there is no impossibility, even in the case you cited: for if the Courtier is so young as not to know what we have said he ought to know, then we are not speaking of him, since he is not the Courtier we presuppose, nor is it possible that one who must know so many things can be very young. And if it happens that the prince is wise and good by nature, and has no need of precepts or counsel from others (although everyone knows how rare that is), it will be enough for the Courtier to be such a man as could make the prince virtuous if he had any need of that. Moreover, he will be able to realize that other part of his duty, which is not to allow his prince to be deceived, always to make known the truth about everything, and to set himself against flatterers and slanderers and all those who scheme to corrupt the mind of his prince in unworthy pleasures. And in this way he will in large part attain his end, even though he cannot entirely translate it into practice: which will not be a reason for imputing fault to him, since he refrains from it for so good a cause. For if an excellent physician were to find himself in a place where all enjoyed good health, it would not be right on that account to say that this physician failed in his intention, even if he healed no sick. Thus, just as the physician's aim must be men's health, so the Courtier's ought to be his prince's virtue; and it is enough that both of them have this intrinsic aim in potency, even when the failure to realize it extrinsically in act arises with the subject to whom this aim is directed.

"But if the Courtier should be so old that it is unbecoming for him to engage in music, festivals, games, arms, and bodily exercises generally, even then we cannot say it is impossible for him to win his prince's favor in that way. For if his age keeps him from engaging in those things, it does not keep him from understanding them; and if he has practiced them in his youth, age does not prevent his having and knowing the more perfectly how to teach them to his prince, for years and experience bring increase of knowledge in everything. Thus, even if the old Courtier does not practice the accomplishments we have ascribed to him, he will still attain his aim of instructing his prince rightly.

[47] "And if you do not wish to give him the name of Courtier, that does not trouble me; for nature has not set such limits upon human dignities that a man may not rise from one to another. Thus, common soldiers often become captains; private persons, kings; priests, popes; pupils, masters; and so, along with the dignity, they acquire the name. Thus, we might perhaps say that to become his prince's instructor was the goal of the Courtier. And yet I do not know who would refuse this name of perfect Courtier, which I deem to be worthy of the greatest praise. And it seems to me that just as Homer described two most excellent men as models of human life—the one in deeds (which was Achilles), the other in suffering and enduring (which was Ulysses)—so he also described a perfect Courtier (which was Phoenix),[8] for, after telling of his loves and many other youthful things, he tells how he was sent to Achilles by the latter's father, Peleus, as a companion and in order to teach him how to speak and act: which is nothing but the aim we have given our Courtier.

"Nor do I think that Aristotle and Plato would have scorned the name of perfect Courtier, for we clearly see that they performed the works of Courtiership to this same end—the one with Alexander the Great, the other with the Kings of Sicily. And as the office of a good Courtier is to know the prince's nature and his inclinations, and to enter adroitly into his favor by those ways of access that are sure, as we have said, and then lead him to virtue, Aristotle so well knew Alexander's nature and encouraged it so cleverly and well that Alexander loved and honored him more than a father. Thus, among the many other tokens that Alexander gave him of his benevolence, he ordered the rebuilding of his native city of Stagira, which had been destroyed; and besides directing Alexander to that most glorious aim—which was the desire to make the world into one single universal country, and have all men living as one people in friendship and in mutual concord under one government and one law that might shine equally on all like the light of the sun—Aristotle instructed him in the natural sciences and in the virtues of the mind

8. For Phoenix—appointed by Peleus to oversee the upbringing of his son, Achilles [Editor]— cf. Cicero, De oratore III, ch. 15; Iliad, IX, 561 ff.

so as to make him most wise, brave, continent, and a true moral philosopher, not only in words but in works; for one cannot imagine a more noble philosophy than to bring a civilized way of life to such savage peoples as those who inhabited Bactria and Caucasia, India, and Scythia; and to teach them marriage and agriculture, teach them to honor their fathers, to abstain from rapine, murder, and other evil things; to build so many very noble cities in remote lands; so that by his laws countless men were led from a brutish to a human way of life. And Aristotle was the author of these deeds of Alexander, employing the methods of a good Courtier: which is something that Calisthenes did not know how to do, even though Aristotle showed him; for he wished to be a pure philosopher and an austere minister of naked truth, without blending in Courtiership; and he lost his life and brought infamy instead of help to Alexander.

"By this same method of Courtiership, Plato taught Dion of Syracuse; and later, when he found the tyrant Dionysius like a book full of defects and errors and in need of complete erasure rather than of any change or correction (since it was not possible to remove from him that color of tyranny with which he had been stained for so long), he decided not to make use of the methods of Courtiership with him, judging that they would all be in vain; which is what our Courtier ought also to do if he chances to find himself in the service of a prince of so evil a nature as to be inveterate in vice, like consumptives in their sickness; for in that case he ought to escape from such bondage in order not to incur blame for his prince's evil deeds and not to feel the affliction which all good men feel who serve the wicked."

[48] Signor Ottaviano paused at this point, and signor Gasparo said: "I certainly did not expect our Courtier to be honored so; but since Aristotle and Plato are his companions, I think no one henceforth ought to despite the name. Still, I am not quite sure that I believe that Aristotle and Plato ever danced or made music in their lives, or performed any acts of chivalry."

Signor Ottaviano replied: "We are hardly permitted to think that these two divine spirits did not know everything, and hence we can believe that they practiced what belongs to Courtiership, for they write of it on occasion in such a way that the very masters of the subjects of which they write acknowledge that they understood these to the marrow and deepest roots. Wherefore we may not say that all the accomplishments ascribed to him by these gentlemen are not suited to the Courtier (or preceptor of the prince, as you choose to call him) who aims at the good end we have mentioned, even though he were the sternest philosopher and of a most saintly life, because those things do not clash with goodness, discretion, wisdom, or worth, at whatever age and time or place."

[49] Then signor Gasparo said: "I remember that last evening, in discussing the accomplishments of the Courtier, these gentlemen wished him to be in love; and since, in summarizing what has been said so far, we might conclude that a Courtier who has to lead his prince to virtue by his worth and authority will almost have to be old (because knowledge very rarely comes before a certain age, and especially knowledge in those things that are learned through experience)—I do not know how it can be fitting for him, if he is advanced in age, to be in love. For, as has been said this evening, love is not a good thing in old men, and those things which in young men are the delights, courtesies, and elegances so pleasing to women, in old men amount to madness and ridiculous ineptitude, and whoever indulges in them will cause some women to despise him and others to deride him. So if this Aristotle of yours, as an old Courtier, were in love and did the things that young lovers do (like some whom we have seen in our time), I fear he would forget to instruct his prince, and children would perhaps mock him behind his back, and women would scarcely have any pleasure from him except to poke fun at him."

Then signor Ottaviano said: "As all the other accomplishments assigned to the Courtier suit him, even though he be old, I do not think that we ought at all to deprive him of this happiness of loving."

"Nay," said signor Gasparo, "to deprive him of love is to give him a further perfection and to make him live happily, free of misery and calamity."

[50] Messer Pietro Bembo said: "Do you not remember, signor Gasparo, that signor Ottaviano, although he is untutored in love, yet in his game the other evening seemed to know that there are some lovers who say that the indignations and wraths and wars and torments which they receive from their ladies are sweet; and that he asked to be taught the cause of this sweetness? Therefore if our Courtier, though old, were inflamed with those loves that are sweet without bitterness, he would feel in them no calamity or misery; and, being wise, as we suppose him to be, he would not deceive himself by thinking that all that suits young men suits him; but if he loved, he would perhaps love in a way that would not only not bring him blame, but much praise and the highest happiness, free of all vexation, which rarely or almost never happens in the case of young men; and thus he would not leave off instructing his prince, nor would he do anything deserving the mockery of children."

Then the Duchess said: "I am glad, messer Pietro, that you have had little to do in our discussion this evening, for now we shall the more confidently give you the burden of speaking, and of teaching the Courtier a love so happy that it brings with it neither blame nor displeasure; for it could well be one of the most important and useful conditions that have yet been attributed to him. Therefore, by your faith, tell us all that you know about it."

Messer Pietro laughed and said: "Madam, I should not want any claim of mine that it is permissible for old men to love, to cause these ladies to consider me old; be pleased therefore to give this task to someone else."

The Duchess replied: "You ought not to shy at being reputed old in wisdom even if you are young in years; so speak on, and make no more excuses."

Messer Pietro said: "Truly, Madam, if I am to talk about this matter, I should have to go and ask counsel of my Lavinello's[9] hermit."

Then signora Emilia said, half annoyed: "Messer Pietro, there is no one in the company who disobeys more than you; therefore it will be well if the Duchess penalizes you in some way."

Messer Pietro said, still smiling: "Madam, do not be angry with me, for God's love; for I will tell you what you wish."

"Then do so," replied signora Emilia.

[51] Whereupon messer Pietro, having first remained silent for a while, made ready as if to speak of something important, then said: "Gentlemen, in order to show that old men can love not only without blame but sometimes more happily than young men, I am obliged to enter upon a little discourse to explain what love is, and wherein lies the happiness that lovers can have. So I beg you to follow me attentively, for I hope to bring you to see that there is no man here to whom it is unbecoming to be in love, even though he were fifteen or twenty years older than signor Morello."

Then, after there was some laughter among the company, messer Pietro continued: "I say, then, that, according to the definition of ancient sages, love is nothing but a certain desire to enjoy beauty; and, as our desire is only for things that are known, knowledge must always precede desire, which by its nature turns to the good but in itself is blind and does not know the good. Therefore nature has ordained that to every cognitive power there shall be joined an appetitive power; and as in our soul there are three modes of cognition, namely, by sense, by reason, and by intellect: so, from sense comes appetite, which we have in common with animals; from rea-

---

9. In Book III of Bembo's *Gli Asolani* a hermit explains the doctrine of platonic love to Lavinello.

son comes choice, which is proper to man; from intellect, whereby man can communicate with the angels, comes will. Thus, even as sense knows only those things which the senses perceive, appetite desires these and no other; and even as intellect is turned solely to the contemplation of intelligible things, the will feeds only upon spiritual good. Being by nature rational and placed as in the middle between these two extremes, man can choose (by descending to sense or rising to intellect) to turn his desires now in one direction and now in the other. In these two ways, therefore, men can desire beauty, which name is universally applied to all things, whether natural or artificial, that are made in the good proportion and due measure that befit their nature.

[52] "But to speak of the beauty we have in mind, namely, that only which is seen in the human person and especially in the face, and which prompts the ardent desire we call love, we will say that it is an effluence of the divine goodness, which (although it is shed, like the sun's light, upon all created things), when it finds a face well proportioned and composed of a certain radiant harmony of various colors set off by light and shadow and by measured distance and limited outline, infuses itself therein and shines forth most beautifully and adorns and illumines with grace and a wondrous splendor the object wherein it shines, like a sunbeam striking upon a beautiful vase of polished gold set with precious gems. Thus, it agreeably attracts the eyes of men to itself, and, entering through them, impresses itself upon the soul, and moves and delights it throughout with a new sweetness; and, by kindling it, inspires it with a desire of itself.

"Then, seized with a desire to enjoy this beauty as something good, if the soul allows itself to be guided by the judgment of sense, it falls into very grave errors, and judges that the body in which this beauty is seen is the chief cause thereof; and hence, in order to enjoy that beauty, it deems it necessary to join itself as closely to that body as it can, which is mistaken; hence, whoever thinks to enjoy that beauty by possessing the body deceives himself, and is moved, not by true knowledge through rational choice, but by false opinion through sensual appetite: wherefore the pleasure that is consequent upon this is necessarily false and mistaken.

"Hence, all those lovers who satisfy their unchaste desires with the women they love meet with one of two evils: for as soon as they have what they desired, either they feel satiety and tedium or conceive a hatred for the beloved object, as if appetite repented of its error and recognized the deceit practiced upon it by the false judgment of sense, through which it judged what is bad to be good; or else they remain in the same desire and yearning, like those who have not actually attained the end they were seeking. And although, because of the blind opinion with which they are inebriated, they seem to feel pleasure at the moment, as sick men sometimes dream of a draught from some clear spring, still they are not satisfied or quieted. And since quiet and satisfaction always follow upon the possession of the desired good, if that were the true and good end of their desire, they would remain quiet and satisfied upon possessing it; but they do not. Nay, deceived by that resemblance, they soon return to their unbridled desire, and in the same turmoil they felt before, once more they experience that furious and burning thirst for what in vain they hope to possess perfectly. Such lovers therefore love most unhappily: for either they never attain their desires, which is great unhappiness, or if they do attain them, they find that they have attained their woe, and their miseries become even greater miseries; because, both in the beginning and in the midst of this love of theirs, they never feel anything save anguish, torments, sorrows, sufferings, toils: so that to be pale, dejected, to be in continual tears and sighs, to be always silent or lamenting, to long for death, in short, to be most unhappy, such are the conditions that are said to befit lovers.

[53] "The cause, then, of this ruin in the minds of men is chiefly sense, which is very potent in youth, because the vigor of flesh and blood in that time of life gives it as much strength as it takes away from reason, and thus easily induces the soul to follow appetite. For, finding itself deep in an earthly prison, and deprived of spiritual contemplation in exercising its office of governing the body, the soul of itself cannot clearly perceive the truth; wherefore, in order to have knowledge, it is obliged to turn to the senses as to its source of knowledge; and so it believes them and bows before them and lets itself be guided by them, especially when they have so much vigor that they almost force it; and, being fallacious, they fill it with errors and false opinions.

"Thus, it nearly always happens that young men are wrapped up in this love which is sensual and is an outright rebel to reason; and so they make themselves unworthy of enjoying the graces and benefits which love bestows upon its true subject; nor do they feel any pleasures in love save those which unreasoning animals feel, whereas their distress is far more grievous.

"Therefore on this premise (which is most valid) I affirm that the contrary happens to those who are of a maturer age. For if the latter (when the soul is already less oppressed by the weight of the body, and when the natural heat begins to diminish) are smitten by beauty and direct their desire thereto, guided by rational choice, they are not duped then, but come into perfect possession of beauty.

And thus good always comes to them from that possession; because beauty is good; hence, it follows that true love of beauty is most good and holy, always working a good effect in the minds of those who check the perversity of sense with the bridle of reason; which the old can do far more easily than the young.

[54] "Therefore it is not unreasonable to say also that the old can love without blame, and more happily than the young; taking this word old, however, not in the sense of decrepit or as meaning that the organs of the body have already become so weak that the soul cannot perform its operations through them, but as meaning when knowledge in us is in its true prime. I will not refrain from saying this also: I think that, although sensual love is bad at every age, yet in the young it deserves to be excused, and in some sense is perhaps permitted. For although it brings them afflictions, dangers, toils, and the woes we have said, still there are many, who, to win the good graces of the ladies they love, do worthy acts, which (although not directed to a good end) are in themselves good; and thus from that great bitterness they extract a little sweetness, and through the adversities which they endure they finally recognize their error. Hence, even as I consider those youths divine who master their appetites and love according to reason, I likewise excuse those who allow themselves to be overcome by sensual love, to which they are so much inclined by human weakness: provided that in such love they show gentleness, courtesy, and worth, and the other noble qualities which these gentlemen have mentioned; and provided that when they are no longer youthful, they abandon it altogether, leaving this sensual desire behind as the lowest rung of that ladder by which we ascend to true love. But if, even when they are old, they keep the fire of the appetites in their cold hearts, and subjects strong reason to weak sense, it is not possible to say how much they should be blamed. For like senseless fools they deserve with perpetual infamy to be numbered among the unreasoning animals, because the thoughts and ways of sensual love are most unbecoming to a mature age."

[55] Here Bembo paused a moment, as if to rest; and as everyone remained silent, signor Morello da Ortona said: "And if there were an old man more vigorous and sturdier and better looking than many youths, why would you not allow him to love with that love with which young men love?"

The Duchess laughed and said: "If young men's love is so unhappy, signor Morello, why do you wish to have old men love unhappily too? But if you were old, as these gentlemen say, you would not plot evil against old men."

Signor Morello replied: "It is messer Pietro Bembo who is plotting evil against old men, since he wishes them to love in a certain way which I, for one, do not understand; and it seems to me that to possess this beauty which he so much praises, without the body, is a fantasy."

Then Count Ludovico said: "Do you think, signor Morello, that beauty is always as good as messer Pietro Bembo says?"

"Certainly I do not," replied signor Morello, "Nay, I remember having seen many beautiful women who were very bad, cruel, and spiteful, and this seems to be almost always the case, for beauty makes them proud, and pride makes them cruel."

Count Ludovico said, laughing: "Perhaps they seem cruel to you because they do not grant you what you want; but be instructed by messer Pietro Bembo as to how old men ought to desire beauty, and what they ought to seek in women, and with what they ought to be satisfied; and if you do not go beyond those limits, you shall see that they will be neither proud nor cruel, and will grant you what you wish."

Then signor Morello seemed a little annoyed, and said: "I have no wish to know what does not concern me; but be instructed yourself as to how this beauty ought to be desired by young men who are less vigorous and sturdy than their elders."

[56] Here messer Federico, in order to calm signor Morello and to change the subject, did not let Count Ludovico reply, but interrupted him and said: "Perhaps signor Morello is not entirely wrong in saying that beauty is not always good; for women's beauty is often the cause of countless evils, hatreds, wars, deaths, and destructions in the world; to which the fall of Troy bears sure witness. And, for the most part, beautiful women are either proud or cruel, or brazen (as has been said); but this last signor Morello would not consider to be a fault. There are also many wicked men who are graced with fair looks, and it seems that nature made them so to the end that they might be better able to deceive, and that this fair appearance is like the bait on the hook."

Then messer Pietro Bembo said: "You must not believe that beauty is not always good."

Here Count Ludovico, in order to return to the original subject, interrupted and said: "Since signor Morello is not concerned to know that which so deeply touches him, teach it to me and show me how old men acquire this happiness of love, for it will not trouble me if I am thought old, provided only that I profit by it."

[57] Messer Pietro laughed and said: "I wish first to drive error from the minds of these gentlemen, then I will satisfy you too." And so,

beginning again, he said: "Gentlemen, I would not have any of us, like profane and sacrilegious men, incur the wrath of God in speaking ill of beauty, which is a sacred thing. Therefore, in order that signor Morello and messer Federico may be warned and not lose their sight like Stesichorus (which is a most fitting punishment for anyone who despises beauty), I say that beauty springs from God and is like a circle, the center of which is goodness. And hence, as there can be no circle without a center, there can be no beauty without goodness. Thus, a wicked soul rarely inhabits a beautiful body, and for that reason outward beauty is a true sign of inner goodness. And this grace is impressed upon the body in varying degree as an index of the soul, by which it is outwardly known, as with trees in which the beauty of the blossoms is a token of the excellence of the fruit. The same is true of the human body, as we see from the physiognomists, who often discover in the face the character and sometimes the thoughts of men; and what is more, in animals too we discern by the outward aspect the inner qualities which impress themselves upon the body in the degree that is possible. Think how clearly we read anger, ferocity, and pride in the face of the lion, the horse, and the eagle; and a pure and simple innocence in lambs and doves; a cunning guile in foxes and wolves, and so with nearly all other animals.

[58] "Hence, the ugly are also wicked, for the most part, and the beautiful are good: and we may say that beauty is the pleasant, cheerful, charming, and desirable face of the good, and that ugliness is the dark, disagreeable, unpleasant, and sorry face of evil. And if you will consider all things, you will find that those which are good and useful always have the grace of beauty in them as well. Behold the constitution of this great fabric of the world, which was made by God for the health and conservation of every created thing, the round heaven, adorned with so many divine lamps, and the earth in the center, surrounded by the elements and sustained by its own weight; the sun, which in its revolving illumines the whole, and in winter approaches the lowest sign, then by degrees climbs in the other direction; and the moon, which derives her light from it, according as it approaches her or draws away from her; and the five other stars[1] which separately travel the same course. These things have an influence upon one another through the coherence of an order so precisely constituted that, if they were in the least changed, they could not exist together, and the world would fall into ruin; and they also have such beauty and grace that the mind of man cannot imagine anything more beautiful.

1. These five "stars" are of course the planets Mercury, Venus, Mars, Jupiter, and Saturn.

"Think now how man is constituted, who may be called a little world: in whom we see every part of his body precisely framed, necessarily by skill, and not by chance; and then the form taken as a whole is so beautiful that it would be difficult to decide whether it is utility or grace that is given more to human features and the rest of the body by all the parts, such as the eyes, nose, mouth, ears, arms, breast, and the other members. The same can be said of all the animals: look at the feathers of birds, the leaves and branches of trees, which nature gives them to preserve their being, yet they also have the greatest loveliness.

"Leave nature, and come to art: what is so necessary in ships as the prow, the sides, the yards, the mast, the sails, the helm, the oars, the anchors, and the rigging? Yet all these things are so comely that to one who looks upon them they appear to be devised as much to please as to be useful. Columns and architraves support lofty galleries and palaces, yet they are not therefore less pleasing to the eyes of one who looks upon them than they are useful to the buildings. When men first began to build, they put that middle ridge in their temples and houses, not in order that the buildings might have more grace, but in order that the water might flow off nicely on either side; yet comeliness was soon added to usefulness, so that if a temple were built under a sky where no hail or rain ever fell, it would not seem to have any dignity or beauty if it did not have the ridge of a roof.

[59] "Thus, to call them beautiful is to bestow much praise, not only on things but on the world itself. We are praising when we say beautiful sky, beautiful earth, beautiful sea, beautiful rivers, beautiful lands, beautiful woods, trees, gardens; beautiful cities, beautiful churches, houses, armies. In fine, this gracious and sacred beauty is the supreme adornment of all things; and we may say that the good and the beautiful are somehow one and the same thing, and especially in the human body; whose beauty I think is immediately caused by the beauty of the soul, which (as partaker of true divine beauty) graces and beautifies whatever it touches, and especially if the body which it inhabits is not of such base material that the soul cannot impress its character thereon. Therefore beauty is the true trophy of the soul's victory, when with divine power she holds sway over material nature, and by her light conquers the darkness of the body. Hence, we should not say that beauty makes women proud or cruel, even though it may seem so to signor Morello; nor should we impute to beautiful women those enmities, deaths, and destructions of which the unbridled appetites of men are the cause. I will not deny, of course, that it is possible to find beautiful women in the world who are also immodest, but this is not at all because their

beauty inclines them to immodesty; nay, it turns them from it and leads them to the path of virtuous conduct, through the tie that beauty has with goodness. But sometimes a bad upbringing, the continual urgings of their lovers, gifts, poverty, hope, deceits, fear, and a thousand other causes can overcome even the steadfastness of beautiful and good women; and by way of these or similar causes beautiful men can also become wicked."

[60] Then messer Cesare said: "If what signor Gasparo alleged yesterday is true, there is no doubt that beautiful women are more chaste than ugly women."

"And what did I allege?" said signor Gasparo.

Messer Cesare replied: "If I well remember, you said that women who are wooed always refuse to satisfy the man who woos them, and that those women woo who are not wooed. Now it is certain that the beautiful are always more wooed and entreated in love than the ugly; therefore the beautiful always refuse, and hence are more chaste than the ugly, who woo but are not wooed."

Bembo laughed, and said: "There is no answer to this argument." Then he added: "It often happens, too, that like our other senses our sight is deceived and judges a face to be beautiful which in reality is not beautiful; and since in the eyes and entire appearance of some women a certain wantonness is seen depicted, along with immodest blandishments, many (who find such a manner pleasing because it promises them ease in gaining what they desire) call this beauty. But in truth it is impudence in disguise, unworthy of so honored and so sacred a name."

Messer Pietro Bembo was silent, and those gentlemen kept urging him to speak on about this love and about the mode of enjoying beauty truly; and he said at last: "I think I have shown clearly enough that old men can love more happily than young, which was my premise; therefore it is not for me to carry this any further."

Count Ludovico replied: "You have shown the unhappiness of youth rather than the happiness of old men, whom as yet you have not taught what path to follow in their love, but have only told them to be guided by reason; and many deem it impossible for love to follow reason."

[61] Bembo was still trying to make an end of his discourse, but the Duchess begged him to speak; and he began again thus: "Human nature would be too unhappy, if our soul (in which such ardent desire can easily arise) were forced wholly to feed that desire on what the soul has in common with animals, and could not direct it to that other nobler part which is proper to it. Therefore, since it is your wish, I will not refrain from speaking on this noble subject.

And since I feel that I am unworthy to speak of Love's most sacred mysteries, I pray him so to move my thought and tongue that I may be able to show this excellent Courtier how to love beyond the manner of the vulgar herd; and, since from boyhood I have dedicated my whole life to him, so may he cause my words now to accord with this intent and with his praise.

"I say, then, that since human nature in youth is so greatly given over to the senses, the Courtier may be permitted to love sensually while he is young. But if later, in more mature years, he chances to conceive such an amorous desire, he must be very wary and take care not to deceive himself by letting himself be led into those calamities which in the young deserve more compassion than blame, and, on the contrary, in the old deserve more blame than compassion.

[62] "Therefore when the fair aspect of some beautiful woman meets his eye, joined to such comely behavior and gentle manners that he (as one well versed in love) feels that his spirit accords with hers; and as soon as he notices that his eyes seize upon her image and carry it to his heart; and when his soul begins to take pleasure in contemplating her and to feel an influence within that stirs and warms it little by little; and when those lively spirits which shine forth from her eyes continue to add fresh fuel to the fire—then, at the start, he ought to administer a quick remedy and arouse his reason, and therewith arm the fortress of his heart, and so shut out sense and appetite that they cannot enter there by force or deception. Thus, if the flame is extinguished, the danger is also extinguished; but if it continues to live and grow, then the Courtier, feeling himself caught, must firmly resolve to avoid all ugliness of vulgar love, and must enter into the divine path of love, with reason as his guide. And first he must consider that the body wherein this beauty shines is not the source from which it springs, but, rather, that beauty (being an incorporeal thing and, as we have said, a heavenly ray) loses much of its dignity when it chances to be conjoined with base and corruptible matter; for the more perfect it is, the less it partakes of matter, and is most perfect when entirely separated therefrom. And he must consider that, just as one cannot hear with his palate or smell with his ears, so also beauty can in no way be enjoyed, nor can the desire it excites in our minds be satisfied through the sense of touch, but only by way of that sense whereof this beauty is the true object, namely, the faculty of sight.

"Therefore let him keep aloof from the blind judgment of sense, and with his eyes enjoy the radiance of his Lady, her grace, her amorous sparkle, the smiles, the manners and all the other pleasant ornaments of her beauty. Likewise with his hearing let him enjoy the sweetness of her voice, the modulation of her words, the harmony of her music (if his lady love be a musician). Thus, he will feed his soul on the sweetest food by means of these two senses—which partake little of the corporeal, and are reason's ministers—without passing to any unchaste appetite through desire for the body.

"Then let him obey, please, and honor his Lady with all reverence, and hold her dearer than himself, and put her convenience and pleasure before his own, and love in her the beauty of her mind no less than that of her body. Let him take care therefore not to allow her to fall into any error, but through admonishment and good precepts let him always seek to lead her to modesty, temperance, and true chastity, and see to it that no thoughts arise in her except those that are pure and free of all blemish of vice; and thus, by sowing virtue in the garden of her fair mind, he will gather fruits of the most beautiful behavior, and will taste them with wondrous delight. And this will be the true engendering and expression of beauty in beauty, which some say is the end of love.

"In such a way our Courtier will be most acceptable to his Lady, and she will always show herself obedient, sweet, and affable to him, and as desirous of pleasing him as of being loved by him; and the wishes of both will be most virtuous and harmonious, and so they will both be very happy."

[63] Here signor Morello said: "The begetting of a beautiful child in a beautiful woman would be an engendering of beauty in beauty effectively; and pleasing him in this would appear to me a much clearer sign that she loved her lover than treating him with the affability of which you speak."

Bembo laughed and said: "You must not exceed limits, signor Morello; nor does the woman give small sign of her love when she gives her lover her beauty, which is so precious a thing, and by the paths that are the access to her soul (that is, sight and hearing) sends the glances of her eyes, the image of her face, her voice, her words, which penetrate the lover's heart and give him proof of her love."

Signor Morello said: "Glances and words can be, and often are, false witnesses; therefore he who has no better vouchsafe of love is, in my judgment, most uncertain. And truly I was expecting you to make this Lady of yours a little more courteous and generous to the Courtier than the Magnifico made his. But it strikes me that both of you resemble those judges who pronounce sentence against their friends in order to appear wise."

[64] Bembo said: "I am quite willing that this Lady should be much more courteous to my Courtier who is no longer young, than the

Magnifico's is to the young Courtier; and this is reasonable, for my Courtier will desire only seemly things, and therefore the Lady can without blame grant him all of them; but the Magnifico's Lady, who is not so sure of the young Courtier's modesty, ought to grant him only seemly things, and refuse him the unseemly: hence, my Courtier, who is granted what he asks, is happier than the other, to whom part is granted and part refused.

"And in order that you may understand even better that rational love is happier than sensual love, I say that sometimes the same things ought to be refused in sensual love and granted in rational love, because they are unseemly in the one and seemly in the other. Thus, to please her good lover, besides granting him pleasant smiles, intimate and secret conversations, and leave to joke and jest with her and touch her hand, the Lady may in reason and without blame go even so far as to kiss, which in sensual love is not permitted, according to the Magnifico's rules. For since a kiss is the union of body and soul, there is danger that the sensual lover may incline more in the direction of the body than in that of the soul; whereas the rational lover sees that, although the mouth is part of the body, nevertheless it emits words, which are the interpreters of the soul, and that inward breath which itself is even called soul. Hence, a man delights in joining his mouth to that of his beloved in a kiss, not in order to bring himself to any unseemly desire, but because he feels that that bond is the opening of mutual access to their souls, which, being each drawn by desire for the other, pour themselves each into the other's body by turn, and mingle so together that each of them has two souls; and a single soul, composed thus of these two, rules as it were over two bodies. Hence, a kiss may be said to be a joining of souls rather than of bodies, because it has such power over the soul that it withdraws it to itself and separates it from the body. For this reason all chaste lovers desire the kiss as a union of souls; and thus the divinely enamored Plato says that, in kissing, the soul came to his lips in order to escape from his body. And since the separation of soul from sensible things and its complete union with intelligible things can be signified by the kiss, Solomon, in his divine book of the Song, says: 'Let him kiss me with the kiss of his mouth,' to signify the wish that his soul be transported through divine love to the contemplation of heavenly beauty in such manner that, in uniting itself closely therewith, it might forsake the body."

[65] All were most attentive to Bembo's discourse; and he, pausing a moment, and seeing that no one else spoke, said: "Since you have had me begin to teach happy love to our Courtier who is not young, I wish to lead him even a little further; for it is very dangerous to

stop at this point, seeing that the soul is most inclined in the direction of the senses, as we have said several times; and, although reason may choose wisely in its operation and be aware that beauty does not originate in the body, and although it may put a bridle upon unseemly desires, still the continual contemplation of beauty in the body often perverts sound judgment. And even if no other evil resulted therefrom, absence from the beloved brings much suffering with it, because the influence of that beauty gives the lover a wondrous delight when it is present and, by warming his heart, arouses and melts certain dormant and congealed powers in his soul, which, being nourished by the warmth of love, well up around his heart, and send forth through the eyes the spirits that are most subtle vapors made of the purest and brightest part of the blood, that receive the image of her beauty and shape it with a thousand various ornaments. Hence, the soul delights and, as in a stupor, feels, together with the pleasure, the fear and reverence that we are wont to have for sacred things, and judges that it has found its paradise.

[66] "Therefore the lover who considers beauty only in the body loses this good and this happiness as soon as his beloved lady, by her absence, leaves his eyes deprived of their splendor, and consequently leaves his soul widowed of its good. For when her beauty is thus far away, that amorous influence does not warm his heart as when she was present; wherefore his pores become dry, yet the memory of her beauty still stirs those powers of his soul a little, so that they seek to scatter the spirits abroad; and these, finding the ways shut, have no exit, and yet seek to go forth; and shut in thus, they prick the soul with these goads and cause it to suffer painfully, as children do when the teeth begin to come through the tender gums. And from this come the tears, the sighs, the anguish, and the torments of lovers, because the soul is always in travail and affliction, and well-nigh enters into a furor until such time as the cherished beauty appears to it again; and then suddenly it is quieted and breathes easily, and, being wholly intent upon that beauty, it feeds on sweetest food, nor would it ever depart from so delightful a spectacle.

"Hence, to escape the torment of this absence and to enjoy beauty without suffering, the Courtier, aided by reason, must turn his desire entirely away from the body and to beauty alone, contemplate it in its simple and pure self, in so far as he is able, and in his imagination give it a shape distinct from all matter; and thus make it loving and dear to his soul, and there enjoy it; and let him keep it with him day and night, in every time and place, without fear of ever losing it, remembering always that the body is something very different from beauty, and not only does not increase beauty but lessens its perfection.

"In this way our Courtier who is no longer young will be spared the bitterness and calamities that the young almost always experience: such as jealousies, suspicions, disdain, anger, despairs, and certain wrathful furors by which they are often led so into error that some of them not only beat the women whom they love, but take their own lives. He will do no injury to the husband, father, brothers, or kinsfolk of his beloved Lady; he will in no way defame her; he will never be forced to do the hard thing of curbing his eyes and tongue in order not to disclose his desires to others, or to endure suffering at partings or during absences; for he will always carry his precious treasure with him, shut up in his heart, and will also, by the force of his own imagination, make her beauty much more beautiful than in reality it is.

[67] "But among such blessings the lover will find another much greater still, if he will make use of this love as a step by which to mount to a love far more sublime; which he will succeed in doing if he continually considers within himself how narrow a bond it is to be limited always to contemplating the beauty of one body only; and therefore, in order to go beyond such a close limit, he will bring into his thought so many adornments that, by putting together all beauties, he will form a universal concept and will reduce the multitude of these to the unity of that single beauty which sheds itself on human nature generally. And thus he will no longer contemplate the particular beauty of one woman, but that universal beauty which adorns all bodies; and so, dazzled by this greater light, he will not concern himself with the lesser, and, burning with a better flame, he will feel little esteem for what at first he so greatly prized.

"This degree of love, although it is very noble and such that few attain thereto, can still not be called perfect; for, since the imagination is a corporeal faculty, and has no knowledge if not through those principles that are furnished it by the senses, it is not wholly purged of material darkness; and hence, although it may consider this universal beauty in the abstract and in itself alone, yet it does not discern that beauty clearly or without a certain ambiguity, because of the likeness which the shapes in the fantasy have to the body. Wherefore, those who attain this love are like little birds beginning to put on feathers, that, although with their weak wings they can lift themselves a little in flight, yet dare not go far from their nest or trust themselves to the winds and open sky.

[68] "Therefore, when our Courtier shall have reached this goal, although he may be called a very happy lover by comparison with

those who are submerged in the misery of sensual love, still I would not have him be satisfied, but rather go forward boldly along the lofty path, following the guide that leads him to the goal of true happiness. And thus, instead of going outside himself in thought (as all must who choose to contemplate bodily beauty alone), let him turn within himself, in order to contemplate that beauty which is seen by the eyes of the mind, which begin to be sharp and clear-sighted when those of the body lose the flower of their delight. Then the soul, which has departed from vice and is purged by the study of true philosophy and is given to a spiritual life and is practiced in the things of the intellect, facing toward the contemplation of its own substance, as if wakened from deepest sleep, opens those eyes which all have and few use, and sees in itself a ray of that light which is the true image of the angelic beauty communicated to it, and of which it then communicates a faint image to the body. Thus, when it has grown blind to earthly things, the soul acquires a very keen perception of heavenly things; and sometimes when the motive forces of the body are rendered inoperative by assiduous contemplation, or are bound by sleep, then, being no longer fettered by them, the soul senses a certain hidden savor of true angelic beauty, and, ravished by the splendor of that light, begins to kindle and to pursue it so eagerly that it is almost drunk and beside itself in its desire to unite itself to that beauty, thinking to have found the footprint of God, in the contemplation of which it seeks to rest in its blessed end. And thus, burning with this most happy flame, it rises to its noblest part, which is the intellect; and there, no longer darkened by the obscure night of earthly things, it beholds divine beauty; but still it does not yet quite enjoy that beauty perfectly, because it contemplates it in its own particular intellect merely, which is unable to comprehend vast universal beauty. Wherefore, not content with bestowing this blessing, love gives the soul a greater happiness; for, just as from the particular beauty of one body it guides the soul to the universal beauty of all bodies, so in the highest stage of perfection beauty guides it from the particular intellect to the universal intellect. Hence, the soul, aflame with the most holy fire of true divine love, flies to unite itself with the angelic nature; and not only completely abandons the senses, but has no longer any need of reason's discourse; for, transformed into an angel, it understands all things intelligible, and without any veil or cloud views the wide sea of pure divine beauty, and receives it into itself, enjoying that supreme happiness of which the senses are incapable.

[69] "If, then, the beauties which every day with these clouded eyes of ours we see in corruptible bodies (but which are nothing but

dreams and the thinnest shadows of beauty) seem to us so fair and full of grace that they often kindle in us a most ardent fire and one of such delight that we judge no felicity able to equal what we sometimes feel when a single glance from a woman's beloved eyes reaches us—what happy marvel, what blessed awe, must we think is that which fills the souls that attain to the vision of divine beauty! What sweet flame, what delightful burning, must we think that to be which springs from the fountain of supreme and true beauty—which is the source of every other beauty, which never increases or diminishes: always beautiful, and in itself most simple and equal in every part; like only to itself, and partaking of none other; but so beautiful that all other beautiful things are beautiful because they participate in its beauty.

"This is that beauty which is indistinguishable from the highest good, which by its light calls and draws all things unto itself, and not only gives intellect to intellectual things, reason to rational things, sense and desire to sensual things, but to plants also and to stones it communicates motion and the natural instinct proper to them, as an imprint of itself. Therefore this love is as much greater and happier than the others as the cause that moves it is more excellent; and hence, just as material fire refines gold, so this most sacred fire in our souls destroys and consumes what is mortal therein, and quickens and beautifies that celestial part which, in the senses, was at first dead and buried. This is the Pyre whereon the poets record that Hercules was burned atop Mount Oeta, and by such burning became divine and immortal after death. This the Burning Bush of Moses, the Cloven Tongues of Fire, the Fiery Chariot of Elias, which doubles grace and happiness in the souls of those who are worthy to behold it, when they leave this earthly baseness and fly toward heaven.

"Therefore let us direct all the thoughts and powers of our souls to this most holy light, that shows us the path leading to heaven; and, following after it and divesting ourselves of those passions wherewith we were clothed when we fell, by the ladder that bears the image of sensual beauty at its lowest rung, let us ascend to the lofty mansion where heavenly, lovely, and true beauty dwells, which lies hidden in the inmost secret recesses of God, so that profane eyes cannot behold it. Here we shall find a most happy end to our desires, true rest from our labors, the sure remedy for our miseries, most wholesome medicine for our illnesses, safest refuge from the dark storms of this life's tempestuous sea.

[70] "What mortal tongue, then, O most holy Love, can praise thee worthily? Most beautiful, most good, most wise, thou dost flow from the union of beauty and goodness and divine wisdom, and dost

abide in that union, and by that union dost return thereunto as in a circle. Sweetest bond of the universe, midway between celestial and terrestrial things, with benign control thou dost incline the supernal powers to rule the lower powers, and, turning the minds of mortals to their source, joinest them thereto. Thou unitest the elements in concord, movest nature to produce, and movest all that is born to the perpetuation of life. Thou gatherest together things that are separate, givest perfection to the imperfect, likeness to the unlike, friendship to the unfriendly, fruit to the earth, calm to the sea, vital light to the heavens. Thou art father of true pleasures, of all grace, of peace, of gentleness, and good will, enemy of boorish savagery and baseness—in short, thou art beginning and end of all good. And since thou delightest to dwell in the flower of beautiful bodies and beautiful souls, and thence sometimes to reveal thyself a little to the eyes and mind of those who are worthy to behold thee, I think that now thy abode is here among us.

"Deign, then, O Lord, to hear our prayers, shed thyself upon our hearts, and with the splendor of thy most holy fire illumine our darkness and, like a trusted guide, in this blind maze show us the true path. Correct the falseness of our senses, and, after our long raving, give us the true and substantial good; cause us to savor those spiritual odors that quicken the powers of the intellect, and to hear celestial harmony with such accord that there may no longer be room in us for any conflict of passion; inebriate us at that inexhaustible fountain of contentment that ever delights and never satiates, that gives a taste of true blessedness to all who drink of its living and limpid waters; with the beams of thy light purge our eyes of misty ignorance, to the end that they may no longer set store by mortal beauty, and may know that the things which first they seemed to see are not, and that those which they saw not really are. Accept our souls which are offered to thee in sacrifice; burn them in that living flame which consumes all mortal ugliness, so that, being wholly separated from the body, they may unite with divine beauty in a perpetual and most sweet bond, and that we, being outside ourselves, may, like true lovers, be able to become one with the beloved, and, rising above the earth, be admitted to the banquet of angels, where, fed on ambrosia and immortal nectar, we may at last die a most happy death in life, as of old those ancient fathers did whose souls thou, by the most ardent power of contemplation, didst ravish from the body and unite with God."

[71] Having spoken thus far with such vehemence that he seemed almost transported and beside himself, Bembo remained silent and still, keeping his eyes turned toward heaven, as if in a daze; when signora Emilia, who with the others had been listening to his dis-

course most attentively, plucked him by the hem of his robe and, shaking him a little, said: "Take care, messer Pietro, that with these thoughts your soul, too, does not forsake your body."

"Madam," replied messer Pietro, "that would not be the first miracle Love has wrought in me."

Then the Duchess and all the others began urging Bembo once more to go on with his discourse: and everyone seemed almost to feel in his mind a certain spark of the divine love that had inspired the speaker, and all wished to hear more; but Bembo added: "Gentlemen, I have uttered what the holy frenzy of love dictated to me at the moment. But now that it seems to inspire me no longer, I should not know what to say: and I think Love is not willing that its secrets be revealed any further, or that the Courtier should pass beyond that rung of the ladder to which he has been willing to have me show him; therefore it is perhaps not permitted to speak further of this matter."

[72] "Truly," said the Duchess, "if the Courtier who is not young is able to follow the path you have shown him, he will quite rightly content himself with such great happiness, and will feel no envy of the youthful Courtier."

Then messer Cesare Gonzaga said: "The path that leads to this happiness seems to me so steep that I think one can hardly travel it."

Signor Gasparo added: "I think that for men it will be hard to travel, but for women impossible."

Signora Emilia laughed, and said: "Signor Gasparo, if you come back to insulting us so often, I promise that you will not be pardoned again."

Signor Gasparo said: "No wrong is done you by saying that women's souls are not as purged of the passions as those of men, or as versed in contemplation as messer Pietro said those who would taste divine love must be. Thus, we do not read that any woman has had this grace, but that many men have had it, like Plato, Socrates, Plotinus, and many others; and likewise many of our holy Fathers, like St. Francis, upon whom an ardent spirit of love impressed the most holy seal of the five wounds: nor could anything except the power of love lift St. Paul to the vision of those secret things whereof no man is allowed to speak; nor show St. Stephen the opened heavens."

Here the Magnifico Giuliano replied: "Women will by no means be surpassed by men in this; for Socrates himself confesses that all the mysteries of love he knew were disclosed to him by a woman, the famous Diotima; and the angel that wounded St. Francis with the fire of love has also made several women of our time worthy of the same seal. You must remember also that St. Mary Magdalen was forgiven many sins because she loved much, and that she, perhaps in no less grace than St. Paul, was many times rapt to the third heaven by angelic love; and many others, who (as I told at great length yesterday) cared nothing for their own life in their love of Christ's name; nor were they afraid of torments or of any manner of death however horrible and cruel; and they were not old, as messer Pietro would have our Courtier be, but tender and delicate girls, and of that age at which he says sensual love must be permitted in men."

[73] Signor Gasparo was on the point of replying, but the Duchess said: "Let messer Pietro Bembo be the judge of that, and let us abide by his decision whether or not women are as capable of divine love as men. But, as the dispute between you might be too long, it will be well to postpone it until tomorrow."

"Nay, until this evening," said messer Cesare Gonzaga.

"How, this evening?" said the Duchess.

Messer Cesare replied: "Because it is already day"; and he showed her the light that was beginning to come in through the cracks at the windows.

Then everyone rose to his feet in great surprise because it did not seem that the discussion had lasted longer than usual; but because it was begun much later, and, because of its delightfulness, it had so beguiled the company that they had taken no notice of the passing of the hours; nor was there anyone who felt the heaviness of sleep upon his eyes, which happens almost always when we stay up beyond the accustomed bedtime hour. Then the windows were opened on the side of the palace that looks toward the lofty peak of Mount Catria, where they saw that a beautiful rosy dawn had already come into the east, and that all the stars had disappeared except the sweet mistress of the heaven of Venus that holds the border between night and day; from which a soft breeze seemed to come that filled the air with a brisk coolness and began to awaken sweet concerts of joyous birds in the murmuring forests of the nearby hills.

So, having reverently taken leave of the Duchess, they all went off toward their chambers, without torchlight, the light of day being now enough; and as they were about to leave the room, the Prefect turned to the Duchess and said: "To put an end to the dispute between signor Gasparo and the Magnifico, we will come with the judge earlier this evening than yesterday."

Signora Emilia replied: "On condition that if signor Gasparo wishes to accuse and slander women further, as is his wont, let him give bond to stand trial, for I cite him as a suspect and fugitive."

Index of Persons and Items

Accolti, Bernardo (1458–1535), known as the Unico Aretino, because born in Arezzo and "unique" as an improviser of verse, wandered from one Renaissance court to another and was much acclaimed, 13

Achilles, 54, 56, 240

Aeschines (389–314 B.C.), Athenian orator and opponent of Demosthenes, 45, 47

Aesop, 67

Agesilaus (d. ca. 360 B.C.), king of Sparta and noted general, 212

Agnello, Antonio (d. after 1527), Mantuan poet and friend of Castiglione and Bembo, 107

Alamanni, 127

Alcibiades (ca. 450–404 B.C.), Athenian politician and general, pupil and friend of Socrates, 28, 51, 77, 182

Aldana, probably a Spanish captain in command of mercenary troops in Italy, 129

Alessandrino, Cardinal. *See* Sangiorgio

Alexander, known as Alexander the Great (356–323 B.C.), succeeded his father Philip I of Macedon (336 B.C.), 26, 31, 51, 54, 55, 60, 61, 88, 93, 121, 176, 177, 232; continence of, 177ff., 180, 181

Alexander VI (1431–1503), Rodrigo Borgia, elected pope (1492), 11, 107, 108, 125

Alexandra (d. 70 B.C.), queen of the Jews, succeeded her husband Alexander in 79 B.C. (cf. Josephus, *Antiquities of the Jews*, XIII, ch. xv–xvi), 163

Alfonso I of Aragon (1385–1458), king of Naples from 1443, celebrated as a patron of humanists and artists, 124, 130, 133

Alfonso II of Aragon (1448–1495), became king of Naples in 1494; formerly duke of Calabria, 11

Alidosi, Francesco (d. 1511), Bishop of Pavia, served Pope Julius II and was made a cardinal by him in 1505; later became archbishop of Bologna and was killed by Francesco Maria della Rovere, duke of Urbino, 124

Altoviti, 127

Amalasontha (A.D. 498–535), daughter of Theodoric and regent of the East Gothic kingdom, 173

Angoulême, Monseigneur d', afterwards Francis I (1494–1547), succeeding his cousin Louis XII to the throne in 1515; much celebrated as a patron of art and letters, 50, 233

Anne (1476–1514), Anne of Brittany, who married Charles VIII of France in 1491 and his successor Louis XII in 1499, 173

Antaeus, a Libyan giant, son of Earth, slain by Hercules, 232

Antonius, Marcus (143–87 B.C.), famous orator of Republican Rome, 40, 45

Apelles (4th century B.C.), commonly considered the greatest painter of antiquity, 34, 60, 61

Aragon, Eleanora of (1450–1493), daughter of Ferdinand I of Naples, married Ercole I of Ferrara in 1473, mother of Isabella and Beatrice, 175

Aragon, Isabella of (1470–1524), daughter of Alfonso II of Naples, wife of Gian Galeazzo Sforza, Duke of Milan, 175

Aragon, Cardinal Ludovico of (1474–1519), natural son of Ferdinand of Aragon, friend of Castiglione, 135

Aretino (Unico). See Accolti, Bernardo

Ariosto, Alfonso (1475–1525), distant cousin of the poet Ludovico Ariosto. Alfonso appears to have been the one who first urged Castiglione to write the *Courtier* on the suggestion of Francis I of France, and was himself a kind of "perfect courtier." The *Courtier* was first dedicated to him, which dedication, in the *editio princeps* by Aldus, was replaced by that to De Silva (1528, Alfonso no longer living), 9

Aristippus (435?–356 B.C.), Greek philosopher, pupil of Socrates, 52

Aristodemus, 224

Aristotle, 31, 51, 56, 240, 241

Artemisia (d. 350 B.C.), queen of Caria, wife of King Mausolus, built the famous "mausoleum" at Halicarnassus in his memory, 176

Artifice vs. nature, 48

Aspasia (d. 410 B.C.), consort of Pericles, noted for her beauty and learning, 169

Barletta, musician and dancer at the court of Urbino, 63, 75

Bassat, a dance, 63

Bayeux, Bishop of. See Canossa, Ludovico da

Beatrice (character in Boccaccio), 140

Beatrice, Duchess of Milan. See Este, Beatrice d'

Beauty, 244ff.; of body, 27; and goodness, 248; and love, general discussion, 244ff.; universal, 257; in women, 48

Beccadello, Cesare, 136

Bembo, Pietro (1470–1547), of a noble Venetian family. One of the most famous men of letters of the Italian Renaissance and considered a great authority on language and style and on "platonic" love. He resided at the court of Urbino from 1506 to 1512, and later became papal secretary to Leo X, and a cardinal in 1539. Bembo corrected the proofs of the *Courtier* as Castiglione was in Spain, 13

Beroaldo, Filippo (1472–1518), professor of literature in Rome and Librarian of the Vatican, 118

Berto, probably a buffoon at the papal court in the time of Julius II or Leo X, 25, 109

Bevazzano, Augustino (fl. ca. 1525), man of letters, born at Treviso, near Venice. Lived at the Roman court and was Bembo's secretary for a time, 123

Bias of Pirene (6th century B.C.), Greek sage, counted as one of the Seven Sages, 223

Bibbiena, Messer Bernardo Dovizi da (1470–1520), friend of the Medici, created cardinal of Santa Maria in Partico by Pope Leo X. The town of Bibbiena lies near Florence. Messer Bernardo thus figures in the dialogues as a Tuscan as does his patron and friend the Magnifico Giuliano. He is known as the author of *La Calandria*, one of the earliest of the new comedies imitative of Plautus that was first given at the court of Urbino in the carnival of 1513 with a prologue written by Castiglione himself. Messer Bernardo was famous for his wit and love of practical jokes, 13

Bidon, of Asti, Italy, a singer in the chapel of Leo X, 44

Bishop of Cervia. *See* Cattanei

Boadilla, signora, has been identified as Beatriz Fernandez de Boadilla, Marchioness of Moya and a close friend of Queen Isabella, 126, 140

Boccaccio, Giovanni (1313–1375), author of the *Decameron*, whose prose style became a model for 16th-century Italian prose, 37, 38, 43, 44, 46, 108, 137, 140, 142

Borgia, Cardinal Francesco (1441–1511), made bishop and cardinal by his cousin Pope Alexander VI, 133

Borgia, Cesare (Duke Valentino), 125

Borso, Duke. *See* Este, Borso d'

Bottone da Cesena, 129

Brutus, Marcus Junius (85?–42 B.C.), Roman general, politician, headed conspiracy against Caesar, 51

Cacus, in Roman myth the son of Vulcan who stole cattle from Hercules and was slain by him, 232

Caesar, Caius Julius (100–44 B.C.), famous Roman general and statesman, renowned also as orator and writer (*De bello Gallico, De bello civili*), 47, 51, 101, 176

Caia Caecilia, wife of King Tarquinius Priscus, famous for her virtue and wisdom (cf. Livy I, ch. 34–41), 163

Calabria, Duke Alfonso of, after Alfonso II of Naples, 111

Calfurnio, Giovanni (1443–1503), humanist and professor of rhetoric at Padua, 117

Calisthenes (4th century B.C.), Greek philosopher, possibly a cousin of Aristotle, put to death by Alexander the Great, 241

Calmeta, Vincenzio Colli, surnamed il Calmeta (d. 1508) of Castelnuova, poet, improviser of verses, and prose writer, onetime secretary of Beatrice d'Este, 62, 83

Camma, 166

Cammelli, Antonio (1440–1502), called il Pistoia from his native town, a writer of humorous and satirical verse who lived much of his life at the court of the Este at Ferrara, 121

Campaspe, a beautiful slave of Alexander the Great, given (as Pliny relates) by him to Apelles, 61

Canossa, Count Ludovico da (1476–1532), of a noble Veronese family, close friend and relative of Castiglione, bishop of Tricarico (1511), served as ambassador of Leo X to England and France, was bishop of Bayeux (1520) and emissary of Francis I to Venice. He resided at the Court of Urbino as early as 1496, and later at Rome, 13

Captain, the Great Captain. See Fernandez

Cara, Marchetto, celebrated composer of profane music in the service of the Gonzagas of Mantua, ca. 1495–1520, 44

Carbo, Caius Papirius, was consul in 120 B.C. and is praised as an orator by Cicero, 45

Cardinal of Pavia. See Alidosi, Francesco

Cardona, Giovanni di (d. 1512?), a Spanish condottiere, 124

Cardona, Ugo di (d. 1525), Spanish soldier, brother of Giovanni, 125

Carillo, Alonso, a Spanish wit of whose life little is known, 126, 128

Carlos, Prince of Spain, later the Emperor Charles V (1500–58), 233

Castagneto, Countess Brazaida de Almada, a lady-in-waiting to Queen Isabella, 140

Castiglione, Baldesar (1478–1529), 8, 233. In the spring of 1507 Castiglione was in England on a mission from the duke of Urbino to Henry VII, specifically to receive the Order of the Garter for Duke Guidobaldo. As this is precisely the fictional time of the dialogues of the Courtier, the author has introduced his own name into the conversations "as our Castiglione writes from there [England]," (Book IV, ch. 38).

Castillo, 133

Cato, Marcus Porcius (234–149 B.C.), Roman soldier and writer, praised by Cicero for his eloquence, 40, 124, 127

Catullus, Gaius Valerius (84?–54 B.C.), famous Roman lyric poet, born in Verona, 107

Cervia, Bishop of. Tommaso Cattanei, bishop from 1486 to 1515, 131

da Ceva, Marquess Febus, 62

da Ceva, Ghirardino, 62

Charles VIII (1470–1498), succeeded his father to the throne of France in 1483 and invaded Italy in 1494, 100, 173

Chignones, Diego de (d. 1512), a Spanish cavalier and lieutenant of Don Gonsalvo Fernandez de Cordova, called "the Great Captain," 118

Cicero, Marcus Tullius (106–43 B.C.), Roman orator and statesman. Quotations from his work *De oratore* are frequent in the *Courtier*, 40, 44, 45, 46, 47, 110

Cimon (d. 449 B.C.), naval commander responsible for Athens's victories over the Persians in 477–467 B.C., 212

Circe, 231

Clearchus (d. 353 B.C.), governor of Byzantium in 408 B.C., 224

Cleopatra (69–30 B.C.), famous queen of the Egyptians, 176

Colonna, Marcantonio (d. 1522), Roman nobleman who served under "the Great Captain" and other commanders of the day, 120

Colonna, Vittoria (1492–1547), the renowned poetess of the Renaissance was the wife of the Marquess of Pescara, 3

Corinna (fl. 5th century B.C.), Greek lyric poetess, who competed with Pindar, 169

Cornelia (2nd century B.C.), daughter of Scipio Africanus the elder and mother of the Gracchi, 163

Corvinus, Matthias (1443–1490), proclaimed king of Hungary in 1458, 175

Coscia, Andrea, 130

Cotta, Caius Aurelius, Roman Consul in 75 B.C., praised as an orator by Cicero, 45

Court Lady: ability to discourse on love, 190; affability, 151; attack on, 156; defense of, 156ff.; dress, 154; exercises (fitting ones), 153; musical training, 154; true love (how to distinguish from false), 190ff.

Court Lady, qualities: gentle birth, graceful, prudent, mannerly, clever, 150ff.; knowledge, ability to entertain, discretion, fluent discourse, equal to Courtier in qualities of mind and body, 152ff.; temperance, courage, 160

Courtier, moral conduct: allegiance to Prince, 213; attitude toward favors, 82; attitude toward flattery, 80; attitude toward love, 243ff., 251; attitude toward peasants, 74; avoidance of affectation, 32ff., 48, 72, 101; candor in self-evaluation, 99; choice of friends, 90ff.; confession of ignorance, 100; discretion and judgment, 99; duties to princes discriminated, 81, 84ff., 94, 210, 213, 237ff.; judgment, 70; knowledge, 40; lack of presumption, 83ff.; praise of self, 25ff.; prudence, 71; relation to his beloved, 251, 254; relations with his equals, 87ff.; his reputation at large, 94

Courtier, qualities: air, 22; beauty of body, 27; grace, 29, 31ff.; honor and integrity, 49; nobility of birth, 22; nobility of birth opposed, 22ff.; truth and sincerity, 102

Courtier, skills: arms, 24, 53, 72; bullfighting, 28; casting spears and darts, 28; dueling, 27ff.; handling of weapons, 27ff.; horsemanship, 28, 33; hunting, 29; jumping, 29; learning and arms conjoined, 53ff.; running, 29; stick-throwing, 28; stone-throwing, 29; swimming, 29; tennis, 29, 74; tilt and joust, 28, 72; vaulting on horseback, 29; wrestling, 28

Courtier, social graces: conversation, 80ff.; dancing ability, 75; decorum in speech, 35ff.; deportment, 29; dress, 88ff.; how to make himself loved by women, 196; how to make love and approach women, 198ff.; humor, 102ff.; knowledge of drawing and painting, 57ff.; literary and linguistic skill, 52; knowledge of languages, 98; as man of letters, 50, 53ff.; musical ability, 55, 76ff.; nonchalance, 32ff., 48; pleasing voice, 40ff.; problems as a lover, 254; training by good teachers, 31; use of antique words, 40; use of foreign words, 45

Courtiers, classic examples: Phoenix, Aristotle, Plato, 240ff.

Courtiership: beginning of the discussion, 19; proper aims of, 209ff.

Crassus, Lucius Licinius (140–91 B.C.), famous orator of Republican Rome, 40, 44, 45

Crassus Mucianus, Publius Licenius, Roman jurisconsult and military leader, Consul in 131 B.C., 87

Crivello, Biagino, one of Ludovico Sforza's captains, 130

Cuña, Don Pedro de, referred to as Prior of Messina, a Spanish commander who was killed in the battle of Ravenna (1512), 128

Cyrus, 172

Darius III (336–330 B.C.), king of Persia, defeated by Alexander the Great in the battle of Arbela, 331 B.C., 88

Deceit: in love, 140; problem of, 101

Decameron, 108

Demetrius I, of Macedon, surnamed Poliorcetes, (337?–282 B.C.), one of Alexander's most famous generals, 60

Democritus (late 5th–early 4th century B.C.), Greek philosopher, known as "the Laughing Philosopher," 106

Demosthenes (385?–322 B.C.), Athenian orator and statesman, 47

Diacceto, Francesco Cattani da (1466–1522), a Florentine and disciple of Marsilio Ficino, much admired for his literary works and his learning, 45

Diction, 35, 37; excellence of style, 46ff.; use of foreign words, 41

Dion of Syracuse (?408–ca. 354 B.C.), philosopher, friend, and disciple of Plato, was brother-in-law of Dionyisus the Elder, tyrant of Syracuse, and a Sicilian Greek political leader, 241

Diomed, cruel Thrasian king, son of Ares, slain by Hercules, 232

Dionysius, the Younger (fl. 368–344 B.C.), tyrant of Syracuse; when he came to power in 367 Plato was recalled to advise him, but he proved ill-disposed to the teachings of the philosopher, 241

Diotima, priestess of Mantinea, reputed teacher of Socrates, mentioned in Plato's *Symposium*, 169, 259

Djem Othman (1459–1495), younger son of Mohammed II, who was a prisoner of Popes Innocent VIII and Alexander VI in Italy for many years, 120

Dress, Spanish attire, 116

Duchess. *See* Gonzaga, Elisabetta

Duels, 28

Ennius, Quintus (239–109 B.C.), Roman epic poet, 40, 44, 126

Epaminondas (418?–362 B.C.), Theban general, 56, 212

Epicharis, 164

Epimetheus, in Greek mythology the brother of Prometheus and husband of Pandora (cf. Plato, *Protagoras*, XI–XII), 214

Ercole, Duke of Ferrara. *See* Este

Este, Beatrice d' (1475–1497), sister of Isabella, married Ludovico Sforza, duke of Milano in 1491, 175

Este, Borso d' (1413–1471), duke of Ferrara (1450–1471), 67

Este, Duke Ercole d' (1471–1505), 110

Este, Ippolito d' (1479–1520), third son of Duke Ercole of Ferrara and Eleanora of Aragon, made a cardinal by Pope Alexander VI in 1493, friend of Leonardo da Vinci, patron of Ludovico Ariosto, 22

Este, Isabella d' (1474–1539), daughter of Ercole I of Ferrara, became the wife of the Marquess Francesco Gonzaga in 1490, hence was the sister-in-law of the Duchess Elisabetta of the dialogue. Isabella was one of the most celebrated ladies of the Renaissance, 175

Ettore Romano, probably Ettore Giovenale, surnamed Romano as well as Pieraccio, who served Francesco Maria della Rovere and the duke of Ferrara and was one of the thirteen Italian champions in the famous "disfida di Barletta," 62

Evander, king of Pallanteum who welcomed Aeneas (*Aen.* VIII, 52 ff.), 39

Fabius, Caius F. Pictor (late 4th century B.C.), first Roman patrician to practice the art of painting (cf. Pliny, *Natural History*, XXXV, ch. 77), 57
Febus da Ceva, Marquess and his brother Ghirardino, They belonged to an illustrious Piedmontese family, contemporaries of Castiglione, 98
Federico, Duke. *See* Montefeltro, Federico da
Federico, Marquess. *See* Gonzaga, Federico
Fedra. *See* Inghirami
Ferdinand, the Catholic, of Aragon, (1452–1516), king of Spain, married to Isabella of Castile in 1469, 126, 173, 188
Ferdinand II of Aragon (1469–1496), king of Naples, 11, 32, 101, 121, 175
Fernandez, Don Gonsalvo Hernand y Aguilar (1443–1515), known as Gonsalvo de Cordova or more commonly as "the Great Captain." Famous for his military victories in Italy where he fought for Ferdinand II of Naples against the French, 118, 120, 125, 174
Filippo, Duke. *See* Visconti, Filippo Maria
Florence, Archbishop of (Roberto Folco), 121
Filippo, Duke. *See* Visconti
Flattery, 52ff.
Florido, Orazio, native of Fano, near Urbino, secretary and faithful retainer of Francesco Maria della Rovere, 62
Foglietta, Augustino (d. 1527), of a noble Genoese family, served Popes Leo X and Clement VII, 124
Folly, 15ff.
Forlì, Antonello da (d. 1488), a soldier of fortune, 125
Fortune, 86, 93, 207; admiring, 13; cause of elevation and lowliness, 23; compassionate, 17; envious, 11
France, court of, 84; bad manners of, 98
Francis I of France. *See* Angoulême, Monseigneur d'
Fregosa, Costanza, sister of Ottaviano and Federico, and faithful companion of the duchess, wife of Count Marcantonio Landi of Piacenza, 15, 63
Fregoso, Federico (1480–1541), younger brother of Ottaviano, nephew of Duke Guidobaldo, made archbishop of Salerno by Julius II in 1507, 13, 208
Fregoso, Ottaviano (d. 1524), Genoese nobleman, nephew of Duke Guidobaldo. Elected doge of Genoa in 1513 and later appointed governor of the city by Francis I, 13
French, The, Italian imitation of, 98

Friars, attack on, 161ff.

Friendship, 91

Frisio, Niccolò (also spelled Frigio), a friend of Castiglione and one time emissary of Pope Julius II. He became a monk in 1510, retiring to the Certosa of Naples, 13

Galba, Sergius (fl. 144 B.C.), Roman orator, 40, 45

Galeotto, Cardinal. See Rovere, Galeotto della

Galeotto, Giantommaso, 118

Games, 14; cards and dice, 93; chess, 93

Garter, The Order of, 148

Garzia, Diego, perhaps the famous Diego Garcia de Paredes (1466–1530), who fought with "the Great Captain" in Spain and Italy, 120

Geryon, a three-headed king of Spain, slain by Hercules for the sake of his oxen, 232

Giancristoforo Romano (1465–1512), renowned sculptor, goldsmith, medalist, architect, is known to have been at the Court of Urbino around the time of the dialogue of the Courtier, 13

Gianluca da Pontremolo, 129

Giorgio da Castelfranco (ca. 1478–1510), born at Castelfranco northwest of Venice, the famous painter better known as Giorgione, 45

Giorgione. See Giorgio da Castelfranco

Giovenale, Latino (1486–1533), Roman aristocrat, poet, and ambassador, 129

Giuliano, Duke. See Medici, Giuliano de'

Golden Fleece, Order of (Burgundy), 148

Gonnella, jester already famous in the 14th century and protagonist of many tales of practical jokes, 138

Gonzaga, Alessandro (1497–1527), son of Giovanni Gonzaga, 121

Gonzaga, Cesare (1475–1512), of a younger branch of the Gonzaga family of Mantua; a cousin and close friend of Castiglione, reputed a man of great military valor, 13, 83

Gonzaga, Eleanora (d. 1543), eldest daughter of Marquess Francesco Gonzaga of Mantua and Isabella d'Este, married to Francesco Maria della Rovere in 1509, thus becoming the "new Duchess" of Urbino, 208

Gonzaga, Elisabetta (1471–1526), the "Duchess" of the Courtier, second daughter of the Marquess Federico Gonzaga of Mantua and sister of the Marquess Francesco, married Duke Guidobaldo in 1489. She was a close friend of the famous Isabella d'Este, her brother's wife. Due to the frequent illness and retired life of her husband, the Duchess was the central and presiding figure in the life of the court, 12, 13

Gonzaga, Federico (1440–1484), succeeded his father as marquess of Mantua (1478), 123, 126

Gonzaga, Federico (1500–1540), succeeded his father Francesco in the rule of Mantua in 1519, 236

Gonzaga, Francesco (1466–1519), eldest son of Federico of Mantua, succeeding him in 1484; brother of Elisabetta (the Duchess of the dialogue) and husband of Isabella d'Este, 231

Gonzaga, Giovanni (1474–1523), third son of the Marquess Federico of Mantua, a friend of Bembo and of Bibbiena, 121

Gonzaga, Ludovico, bishop of Mantua, 185

Gonzaga, Margherita, illegitimate daughter of Francesco Gonzaga, niece of the Duchess Elisabetta and lady of the court, 63

Good and evil, problem of, 67, 86, 215

Gracchus, Caius Sempronius (d. 121 B.C.), praised by Cicero as one of the greatest Roman orators, 45

Grace, how acquired, 31

Grasso de'Medici, nickname of a very fat (*grasso*) man in the service of the Medici, 55

Hannibal (247–183 B.C.), Carthaginian general, son of Hamilcar, who marched on Rome and was defeated by Scipio Africanus at Zama in North Africa (202), 51, 232

Harmonia (3rd century B.C.), granddaughter of Hiero of Syracuse, 164

Hasdrubal (2nd century B.C.), Carthaginian general who surrendered to Scipio Aemilianus in 146 B.C., 164

Henry, prince of Wales, later Henry VIII (1491–1547), 233

Hercules, 147, 232, 257

Hesiod, 44

Hiero, of Syracuse, 164

Homer, 37, 44, 47, 51, 54, 240

Horace (Quintus Horatius Flaccus) (65–8 B.C.), famous Roman lyric poet and satirist, 40

Hortensius, Quintus H. Hortalus (114–50 B.C.), famous Roman orator praised by Cicero, 40

Humor: arguzie (short jokes and puns), 104, 114–31; decorum in, 109; festivity (narrative humor), 103, 109–14; pleasantry, art of, 105; pleasantries and wit, 104; practical jokes, 107, 132–38

Hungary, Queen of, 175

Ideal government, 228

Ideal Prince, actions of, 235ff.

Imitation: athletic training and arms, 31; diction, 36; of French and Spanish manners, 98; literary style, 46; oratory, 45; painting and sculpture, 58

Incontinence, dangers of, 217

Infidels, war on, 233

Inghirami, Tommaso (ca. 1470–1516), of Volterra, a diplomat of the papal court, actor and poet who got the nickname Fedra from playing that role in Seneca's *Hippolytus*, 117

Isabella. *See* Este, Isabella d'

Isabella of Naples (d. 1533), became the wife of Federico I of Aragon in 1486. She lived at the court of Ferrara in her last years, 175

Isabella (1451–1504), queen of Castile, married Ferdinand of Aragon in 1469 and ruled jointly with him until her death, 128, 133, 173, 174, 175

Isocrates (436–338 B.C.), Athenian orator, 45

Jove, 214

Julius II (1443–1513), was Giuliano della Rovere, first a cardinal, elected Pope in 1503, famous as a patron of art and letters, 11, 13, 232

Justice, 228ff.

Laelius, Caius L. Sapiens, Roman orator and famous friend of Scipio (Cicero, *De amicitia*), 45, 91

Language: developments, 39; manner of speaking, 40ff.; problem of imitation, 44ff.; spoken, 35ff.; use of Tuscan words, 36; written, 35, 36

Latino Giovenale de' Manetti (1486–1553), Roman nobleman, writer of verse in Latin and Italian, acquaintance of Castiglione, 129

Laughter, 105ff.

Laura, 189

Law, 221, 230, 240

Leona, Athenian courtesan tortured to death for her part in assassination of Hipparchus, brother of the tyrant Hippias, in 514 B.C., 164

Leo X, Giovanni de' Medici, second son of Lorenzo the Magnifico, became Pope Leo X in 1513, 130

Leonardo da Vinci (1452–1519), 45

Leonico, Niccolò (1456–1531) of Venice, professor at the University of Padua, 124

Letters, 50ff.; French attitude toward, 50, 51

Liberty, 220ff.

Livius, Titus (Livy) (59 B.C.–A.D. 17), born at Padua, famous historian of Rome, 42

Livy. *See* Livius, Titus

Louis XII (1462–1514), succeeded Charles VIII as king of France (1499), 120, 173

Love, 14, 243ff.; angers of, 18; Courtier and, 242; ideal, 255; secret vs. open, 204ff.; sources of, 61

Lovers, 17

Lucullus (106–57 B.C.), Roman general, 51, 176, 212

Lycurgus, 56

Lysias (445–380 B.C.), Athenian orator, 45, 212

Magnanimity, 219

Magnifico. See Medici, Giuliano de'

Manlius Torquatus, Titus, favorite hero of Roman history, consul in 340 B.C., He killed his own son for disobeying express orders not to engage in single combat with the enemy, 86

Mantegna, Andrea (1431–1506), one of the most celebrated artists of northern Italy, painted his most important works at the Court of Mantua, 45

Marcantonio, Messer, probably a physician of Urbino, 129

Margherita of Austria (1480–1530), daughter of Maximilian I, in 1507 entrusted with the government of the Low Countries, 173

Mariano, Fra (1460–1531), of the Fetti family, a Dominican friar and renowned buffoon who lived first under the protection of Lorenzo, then at the papal court in the time of Julius II, Leo X, and Clement VII, 16, 104, 138

Mario de' Maffei da Volterra (1464–1537), bishop of Aquino and later of Cavaillon in France, friend of Sadoleto, 123

Mark Antony, 163

Masquerading, 75

Matilda of Canossa (1046–1115), ruler of Tuscany and supporter of Gregory VII in his struggle with Henry IV, 173

Maximilian I, emperor of Germany, 122, 173

Medici, Cosimo de' (1389–1464), called Pater Patriae, grandfather of Lorenzo the Magnificent, 120, 128

Medici, Giuliano de' (1479–1516), youngest son of Lorenzo de' Medici, Il Magnifico, and brother of Lorenzo's second son Giovanni who became Pope Leo X. During the exile of the Medici from Florence (1494–1512) Giuliano lived much of the time at the Court of Urbino where he was known as the "Magnifico Giuliano." He was made duke of Nemours by Francis I of France, 13

Medici, Lorenzo de' (1448–1492), the Magnificent, grandson of Cosimo, father of Giovanni who became Pope Leo X and of Giuliano who in the Courtier is called the Magnifico Giuliano, 45, 123

Meliolo, Ludovico, buffoon and steward at the Mantuan court (ca. 1500), 138

Men, continence in: Alexander, Scipio, Alcibiades, Socrates, Xenocrates, Pericles, 181ff.

Men, excellent models: Epaminondas based on Lysias, Agesilaus based on Xenophon, Scipio based on Panaetius, 213

Men, virtue of: Alexander, Scipio, Xenocrates, Pericles, 177

Mercury, 214

Metrodorus, 60

Michelangelo Buonarroti (1476–1564), 45, 59

Minerva, 77, 214

Minutolo, Ricciardo, character in Boccaccio, 139

Mithridates VI (120–63 B.C.), king of Pontus, 164

Mohammed, 233

Molart, Captain, French captain (Molard) in command of mercenary troops in Italy, 129

Monte, Pietro. Little is known about him, except that he excelled as a master of military exercises at the Court of Urbino and may have served in the Venetian army for a time, 13, 31, 79

Montefeltro, Federico of (1422–1482), succeeded his half-brother to the rule of Urbino in 1444 and was made duke of Urbino and captain general of the Church by Pope Sixtus IV in 1474. He married Battista Sforza, niece of Duke Francesco Sforza of Milan, who bore him several daughters and one son, Guidobaldo. The great palace of Urbino, where the scene of the *Courtier* is laid, was built by him and he is one of the outstanding figures of the Renaissance for his wisdom as ruler of a city-state and for his love of art and letters, 10

Montefeltro, Guidobaldo of (1472–1508), son of Federico II of Montefeltro and Battista Sforza, succeeded his father as duke of Urbino in 1482, married Elisabetta Gonzaga, the sister of the Marquess of Mantua. They had no children. In 1504 he adopted as his heir his nephew Francesco Maria della Rovere, who succeeded him (1508), 11

Moral Virtues, not inherent, 215

Morello, Sigismondo da Ortona. Little is known of the life of this "nestor" and misogynist of the group. Ortona is in the Abruzzi region, in the province of Chieti, 13

Moresca, mime, morris dance, 16, 70, 75

Music, 44, 55; as pastime, 76; power of, 55ff.; theory of, 34; value of (in general), 56

Narni, Galeotto da (ca. 1427–90), humanist-adventurer known for his learning and wit, 116

Nature, 68

Nero (A.D. 37–68), became Roman emperor in 54. He was made guardian of Britannicus, the son of Emperor Claudius, but in 55 he murdered the boy. Among his other notorious acts: He murdered his mother, Agrippina, in 59, and his wife, Octavia, in 62. In 64 Rome was half burned in a fire intended (said rumor) to serve as background for a recitation by Nero on the fall of Troy, 164

Nicolas V, Pope (1398–1455), 108

Nicoletto (Paolo Niccolo Vernia), 100

Nicoletto da Orvieto, courtier at the court of Pope Leo X, 121

Nicostrata, also called Carmenta, a legendary figure in the earliest history of Rome, mother of Evander (cf. Livy, I, 7), 169

Octavia (70–11 B.C.), celebrated second wife of Mark Antony (cf. Plutarch, *Life of Antony*), 163

Old age, 65ff.; difficulties of, 78; pleasure in music, 77, 78

Orestes, 91

Orpheus, 142, 158

Ovid, 203

Painting: Apelles, 34; Protogenes, 34

Painting and sculpture: appraisal of, 59ff.; place of, 58, 59

Paleotto, Annibale (d. 1516), of Bologna, made a Senator by Leo X (1514), 114–15

Paleotto Camillo, brother of Annibale, professor of rhetoric at Bologna, friend of Castiglione, 118, 125, 126

Pallavicino, Gasparo (1486–1511), descendant of the marquesses of Cortemaggiore, near Piacenza, hence a Lombard; close friend of Castiglione, 13

Panaetius (2nd century B.C.), Greek Stoic philosopher, 212

Past, the, attitude toward, 68

Paulus, Lucius Aemilius, surnamed Macedonicus, (d. 160 B.C.), Roman general who was given a triumph in Rome (167 B.C.) after his victory over King Perseus of Macedon, 60

Pazzi, Gianotto de', 128

Pazzi, Rafaello de' (1471–1512), Florentine nobleman who served Cesare Borgia and Julius II, 128

Pedrada, Sallaza dalla, Salazar de la Pedrada, a Spanish officer, 119

Pepoli, Count of, 119

Peralta, Captain, Spanish *condottiere*, 129

Pericles, 178, 183

Petrarch, (Francesco Petrarca) (1304–1374). The great lyric poet and humanist who was considered one of the three crowning glories of Italian literature, Dante and Boccaccio being the other two, 37, 38, 43, 44, 45, 46, 189

Philip V (237–179 B.C.), king of Macedonia, son of Demetrius II; joined Hannibal against Rome, 31, 122

Phoenix, 240

Pia, Emilia (d. 1528), daughter of Marco Pio, lord of Carpi, a widow from 1500, living at Urbino as the faithful and constant companion of the Duchess Elisabetta, 12

Pianella, Conte di (Giacomo d'Atri), whom the king of Naples made count of Pianella (in the Abruzzi in 1496), 121

Piccinino, Niccolò (1380–1444), of Perugia, renowned *condottiere*, 67

Pierpaolo. Nothing is known of this man of the court, cited for his comic dancing, 32

Pietro da Napoli. Nothing is known of him, 13

Pindar (518?–ca. 438 B.C.), Greek poet, generally regarded as the greatest Greek lyric poet, 169

Pio, Ludovico (d. 1512), son of Leonello of the noble family of Carpi, a brave military captain and distant cousin of Emilia Pia, 13

Pirithous, 91

Pistoia. *See* Cammelli, Antonio

Pius III, Francesco Todeschini (1439–1503), pope for only twenty-six days (elected Sept. 22, 1503), succeeding Alexander VI, 107

Plato, 56, 67, 155, 228, 240, 241, 253, 259

Plautus (254?–184 B.C.), famous Roman playwright, 40

Plotinus (ca. 204?–270), Greek philosopher and main exponent of neo-platonism, author of the *Enneads*, teacher of philosophy in Rome, 259

Poliziano, Angelo Ambrogini (1454–1494), famous poet and humanist, professor of Latin and Greek and tutor in the Medici household, 45

Pompey, Gnaeus P. Magnus (106–148 B.C.), Roman general and statesman and member of First Triumvirate, 51

Ponzio, Caio Caloria, 138

Porcaro, Antonio, Roman nobleman, brother of Camillo, of whom little is known, 118

Porcaro, Camillo, 120

Porcia (d. 42 B.C.), daughter of Cato the younger, wife of Brutus, who assassinated Caesar; celebrated for her virtue by Plutarch, *Life of Cato the Younger*, 163

Porta, Domenico della, 129

Portugal, Emanuel I of, 114

Potenza, Bishop of (Giacopo di Nino di Ameria), 115

Prefect. *See* Rovere, Francesco Maria della

Près, Josquin de (ca. 1450–1521), celebrated Belgian musician of the Renaissance, in the service of several of the Italian courts of the day, 97

Prince, theory of the: active and contemplative life, 224; as related to the republic, 220; bad prince exemplified (tyrant), 223; danger of arrogance, 212; danger of ignorance, 212; good prince exemplified, 222ff., 225; his office as builder, 232; princely virtues, 226; reciprocity in devotion, 229, 230; religious character, 229; selection of wise counsellors, 228

Prior of Messina. *See* Cuña

Procrustes, in Greek legend a cruel robber who tortured his prisoners on a bed and was killed by Theseus, 232

Prometheus, in Greek mythology the son of Iapetus, brother of Epimetheus and benefactor of mankind, stealing fire from heaven and bringing it to earth, 214

Proto da Lucca (early 16th century), famous buffoon at the papal court, 117

Protogenes (late 4th century B.C.), Greek painter, rival of Apelles, 34, 60

Provençal, 43

Pygmalion, legendary king of Cyprus and sculptor who fell in love with a statue which he had made and to which Aphrodite gave life (cf. Ovid, *Metamorphoses* X, 243 ff.), 150

Pylades, 91

Pythagoras (6th century B.C.), Greek philosopher, 78, 147

Rangone, Count Ercole, 119

Raphael (Rafaello Sanzio) (1483–1520), famous painter, a native of Urbino, and close friend of Castiglione, 45, 58, 126

Rizzo, Antonio, 129

Roberto da Bari (d. ca. 1512), young gentleman of the court of Urbino and close friend of Castiglione, 13

Roegarze, a dance, 63

Rovere, Felice della (d. after 1536), natural daughter of Julius II and wife of Gian Giordano Orsini, lord of Bracciano, 185

Rovere, Francesco Maria della (1490–1538), nephew of Duke Guidobaldo was made Prefect of Rome by Pope Sixtus IV and again by Pope Julius II in 1502 and in 1504 was adopted by his uncle as his heir, succeeding him in the state four years later, and in that year married Eleanora, daughter of the Marquess of Mantua, 62

Rovere, Galeotto della (d. 1508), cardinal of San Pietro ad Vincula, nephew of Pope Julius II, 105, 135

Sadoleto, Giacomo (1477–1547), renowned humanist, secretary to Popes Leo X and Clement VII and later a Cardinal, a friend of Castiglione, 118

St. Elmo, 125

St. Francis, 259

St. George, Order of (The Garter), 148

St. Jerome (340–ca. 420), Church father and translator of the Bible into Latin, 161

St. Mary Magdalen, 259

St. Michael, Order of (France), 148

St. Paul, 260

St. Stephen, 259

Sallust (Gaius Sallustius Crispus) (86–34 B.C.), Roman historian and politician, 47

San Bonifacio, Count Ludovico da, 119

San Pietro ad Vincula. *See* Rovere, Cardinal Galeotto della

Sangiorgio, Giovanni Antonio di (1439–1509), of Piacenza, professor of canon law at Pavia, later bishop of Alexandria, 121

Sannazaro, Jacopo (1458–1530), Italian poet and prose writer of Naples, best known for his work *L'Arcadia*, 97

Sansecondo, Giacomo (fl. 1493–1522), celebrated musician who lived at several of the Italian courts and was a friend of Castiglione, 105

Sanseverino, Galleazzo (d. 1525), a military captain for a time in the service of Ludovico il Moro, whose natural daughter Bianca he married. Louis XII of France appointed him "grand ecuyer" in 1506, 31

Santa Croce, Alfonso. Nothing is known of this Spaniard, 124

Sappho (fl. ca. 600 B.C.), famous Greek lyric poetess, native of Lesbos, 169

Sardanapalus, last king of the Assyrian empire of Nisus (r. 668–26 B.C.), notorious for his luxury and licentiousness, 176

Scipio, continence of, 177, 180, 181

Scipio Africanus (237–183 B.C.), known as Scipio the Elder, the Roman general who defeated Hannibal at Zama (202 B.C.), 177

Scipio Africanus, the Younger (d. 129 B.C.), the conqueror of Carthage in 146 B.C. His literary work was praised by Cicero, 45, 51, 91, 124, 212

Scipio Nasica, Roman politician, jurist, and military commander, who was consul in 191 B.C., 126

Sciron, legendary Attic robber, killed by Theseus, 232

Semiramis (9th century B.C.), legendary queen of Assyria, wife of Ninus and builder of Babylon, 176

Serafino, Ciminelli dall'Aquila (1466–1500), enjoyed great popularity as court poet at Naples, Rome, Mantua, and Urbino, 121, 128

Serafino, Fra, probably a Mantuan, at one time in the service of the Gonzagas, specialist in the organization of festivals; resided at Urbino for some time, 16

Sextus Pompey (d. 35 B.C.), general and son of the famous Pompey, 165

Silius, Caius S. Italicus (A.D. 25–100), Roman epic poet, imitator of Virgil, 46, 47

Silva, Dom Miguel de (d. 1556), Portuguese nobleman, bishop of Viseu in the province of Beira, and ambassador to Pope Leo X, Adrian VI, and Clement VII, where his friendship with Castiglione was established, and where he enjoyed a considerable fame for his prose and verse in Latin. The dedicatory letter to him is not found in the Laurentian ms. of the *Courtier* but only in the editio princeps by Aldus, 1528. Cian thinks it must have been written in 1527, 3

Sinoris, 166

Socrates (470?–399 B.C.), 51, 56, 67, 78, 100, 124, 155, 182, 259

Solomon, 189, 253

Spain, court of, 84

Spaniards: ability at chess, 93; humor, 103; influence of their taste, 98

Sprezzatura (nonchalance), 32

Stesichorus (630–550 B.C.), Greek lyric poet said to have been stricken blind for writing against Helen of Troy, 248

Strascino, nickname of Nicolò Campani (1478–1523), writer of popular comedies and farces and a celebrated actor, 109

Strozzi, Palla di (1372–1462), Florentine nobleman and patron of learning, banished by Cosimo de' Medici (1434), 116

Style, excellence of, 47ff.

Sulla, Lucius Cornelius (138–78 B.C.), Roman general and politician, 51

Sulpicius, Publius S. Rufus (124–88 B.C.), tribune of the Roman plebs, praised by Cicero as an orator, 45

Synattus, 166

Tacitus, Cornelius (55?–after A.D. 117), Roman orator and historian, 46, 47

Tarantula (dance), in Apulia, 15

Temperance, 218ff.

Terpando, Antonio Maria, friend of Bembo and Bibbiena, probably a Roman, 13

Themistocles (527?–460? B.C.), Athenian general and statesman, 56, 233

Theodolinda (d. 625), queen of the Lombards, 173

Theodora (d. 867), virtuous wife of Theophilus, emperor of Constantinople, 173

Theophrastus (d. ca. 287 B.C.), Greek philosopher, a pupil of Aristotle and his successor as head of Peripatetic school, 6

Theseus, legendary hero of Attica, 91, 232

Titus Tatius, legendary king of the Sabines, 170

Tolosa, Paolo, 128

Tommaso, Messer, of Pisa, 167

Tomyris (6th century B.C.), queen of the Massagetae, who resisted the invasion of Cyrus the Great of Persia, 176

Torello, Antonio (d. 1536), a priest from Foligno, was private chamberlain to Julius II and Leo X, 129

Torre, Marcantonio della, famous physician and professor of medicine at Padua, friend of Leonardo da Vinci, 116

Turnus, king of the Rutulians, who fought against Aeneas (*Aen.* VI, 00), 39

Tyrants, extirpation of, Procrustes, Sciron, Cacus, Diomed, Antaeus, Geryon, 233

Ubaldini, Ottaviano (d. 1498), son of a famous *condottiere*, nephew of Duke Federico da Montefeltro and the tutor of the duke's son Guidobaldo, 125

Unico. *See* Accolti, Bernardo

Ulysses, 240

Universal beauty, 256

Urbino: description, 10; palace, 11

Valentino, Duke. *See* Borgia

Varro, Marcus Terentius (116–27 B.C.), Roman writer and scholar renowned for his learning and the variety of his literary works, 47

Vestal Virgins, at first four then six priestesses at the temple of Vesta in Rome. They were daughters of the best families, dedicated to the goddess in childhood and trained in obedience and chastity, 172

Virgil, 37, 40, 42, 44, 46, 47

Virtue, as mean, 234

Virtues, natural or learned, 214

Visconti, Filippo Maria (1391–1447), duke of Milan, 67

Vulcan, 214

Wit: decorum in, 122; decorum of, 115, 131ff.; examples of, 109ff.

Womanly virtue, instances of: classical, 163ff.; medieval and modern, 172ff.

Women, 96, 122, 138ff.; Greek, 171; Roman, 170ff.; Sabine, 169; sources of excellence in men, 188ff.; Trojan, 169

Women, as famous queens: Tomyris, Artemisia, Zenobia, Semiramis, Cleopatra, 176

Women, as famous teachers: Aspasia, Diotima, Nicostrata, Corinna, Sappho, 169

Xenocrates (396–314 B.C.), Greek platonic philosopher and one-time head of the Academy, 177, 182, 183

Xenophon (434?–355 B.C.), Greek historian, author of the *Cyropae-dia* based on the life of Cyrus, the Younger; *Anabasis, Sympo-sium, Hellenica,* 51, 212, 229

Youth: appraisal of, 79; vs. maturity, 250ff.

Zenobia (fl. ca. A.D. 1260), queen of Palmyra, 176
Zeuxis, Greek painter (fl. late 5th century B.C.), 61

CRITICISM

AMEDEO QUONDAM

On the Genesis of the *Book of the Courtier*[†]

The *Book of the Courtier* is important in early modern culture because of its reception: over 150 editions from its initial publication in 1528 until the end of the eighteenth century (not only in Italian but also in Spanish, French, English, German, Dutch, and Latin), all of which provide clear proof of its stable and rooted presence within the literary, social, and intellectual spheres of European culture. The *Book of the Courtier* is equally important in terms of the story of its composition: Castiglione worked on it for nearly twenty years, leaving numerous documents and other traces that allow us to reconstruct the deep and complex nature of its genesis.

Above all, the exceptional nature of the *Book of the Courtier* is to be found in the richness of the documentation that surrounds its long and tormented composition: five manuscripts distributed over a course of at least fifteen years that detail the project's development right up to its final definitive shape. Yet it is also important to recognize that the genesis of the *Book of the Courtier* was followed by numerous intellectuals within the literary circles of early sixteenth-century Italy. For a long time it was known that Castiglione was writing a very innovative work, and many sought to read it before publication in early versions and manuscripts. The author was often well disposed to show his work-in-progress, always ready as he was to receive judgments and advice from influential and discreet readers.

There was nothing exceptional about this, as such interpersonal relations had always defined the camaraderie of Renaissance humanists, even in Castiglione's generation, which had experienced the impact of the printing press and its continual encroachment upon earlier methods of textual production.

The list of these privileged readers of Castiglione's manuscripts and of those involved in the textual history of *The Courtier* is truly remarkable both in terms of their quality and number: Jacopo Sadoleto, Pietro Bembo, Ippolito d'Este, Alfonso Ariosto, Marco Antonio Flaminio, Mario Ecquicola, Matteo Bandello, Vittoria Colonna, Giovanni Battista Ramusio, Ludovico Canossa. United by similarities in age and therefore by shared educational backgrounds, they played leading roles in the cultural, institutional, and political scene of the first decades of the sixteenth century. If Bembo and

---

[†] Translated by Paul Bucklin. For this volume, Amedeo Quondam has kindly excerpted and abridged some segments of his much more extensive argument in "*Questo povero Cortegiano*," *Castiglione, il Libro, la Storia* (Roma: Bulzoni, 2000). Page numbers to *The Book of the Courtier* refer to this Norton Critical Edition.

Ecquicola (born in 1470) are a few years older than Castiglione (born in 1478), then Alfonso Ariosto and Ludovico Canossa (1475), Sadoletto (1477), and Ippolito d'Este (1479) are basically the same age; while the younger protagonists are Bandello and Ramusio (born in 1485), Vittoria Colonna (1490), and Flaminio (1498). With the exception of the two aristocrats Ippolito d'Este and Vittoria Colonna, and the "republican" Ramusio, their lives were marked by more or less extensive stints of courtly service that in many cases ended in ecclesiastical careers: Canossa becomes a bishop beginning in 1511, Sadoleto is made cardinal in 1536, Bembo in 1537, and Bandello auxiliary bishop in 1550.

In 1508, when Castiglione begins to make notes, in Latin, regarding themes to discuss in his future work, he has already been in Urbino since the summer of 1504. The notebook dates back to the years directly preceding 1508 and includes (albeit with cancellations, variants, and integrations) disparate notes and borrowed material, such as a summary outline of *exempla* of women famous for their *virtù*, a collection of moral sayings, even the initial outline of a dialogue in which numerous individuals dispute matters pertaining to love. When taken as a whole it is not much more than a set of initial notes; yet it is certainly surprising to discover that all, or almost all, of its segments correspond to certain parts of the *Book of the Courtier,* at least in the places that are dedicated to the subject of women and of love.

Even if this period was continually interrupted by military campaigns throughout Italy and diplomatic voyages to Europe, Castiglione's sojourn in Urbino is a stable one in terms of his rapport with the house and family of the Montefeltros and continues uninterrupted even after the death of Guidobaldo di Montefeltro (April 11, 1508). When Guidobaldo died, as he writes at the outset of his book: "I together with several other gentlemen who had served him, remained in the service of Duke Francesco Maria della Rovere, his heir and successor to the state."[1] This continues until at least March of 1513 when, upon the death of Pope Giulio II (March 11), Castiglione is sent to Rome as the resident ambassador of the Duke of Urbino.

Between 1509 and 1512 Castiglione takes an active part, as a gentleman in arms in the service of Duke Francesco Maria della Rovere in diverse military campaigns instigated by the warrior pope Giulio II: from May to July of 1509, from June of 1510 to May of 1511, from June to November of 1512. These are the years of the

---

1. Page 3. The Italian reads: *"io insieme con alcun 'altri cavalieri che l'avevano servito restai alli servizi del duca Francesco Maria dell Rovere, erede e successore di quello nel stato."*

terrible battles of Agnadello (May 14, 1509) and of Ravenna (April 11, 1512); times of war that certainly limit or render impractical his ability to concentrate upon the writing of his work, even though he has thought about it but not completely conceived it as early as 1508. In fact, Castiglione is only in Urbino during the intervals between one military campaign and another (between September of 1509 and May of 1510, and between June of 1511 and April of 1512). Certainly, he could have worked on the project during his two long winters passed at Urbino, yet at this moment there exists no documentary evidence that would support such a claim.

In these years, so marked by the wars of Italy, there arise two events that are decisive for the future of the *Book of the Courtier*: first, Castiglione's voyage to England between September of 1506 and March of 1507, which is at the basis of the fictive chronotope of the book, in which the author is absent; and second, the death of Guidobaldo da Montefeltro, Duke of Urbino, in 1508. There is no reason to doubt Castiglione's sincerity when, twenty years later, he writes to Michel de Silva:

> As the savor of Duke Guido's virtues was fresh in my mind, and the delight that in those years I had felt in the loving company of such excellent persons as then frequented the Court of Urbino, I was moved by the memory thereof to write these books of the Courtier: which I did in but a few days, meaning in time to correct those errors which had resulted from my desire to pay this debt quickly. But Fortune for many years now has kept me ever oppressed by such constant travail that I could never find the liesure to bring these books to a point where my weak judgment was satisfied with them.[2]

If this very first draft of the "books of the Courtier" was written, or, as Castiglione himself says, jotted down "in a few days" (after all, Castiglione's memory may have failed him at a distance of twenty years, or he could have intentionally changed the date of its writing in order to bring it closer to the time frame during which the actual dialogues took place in Urbino), it has not survived. The complicity of historical fortune and the author's own dissatisfactions with his labors not only hindered the work's immediate completion but also prevented its earliest traces from surviving.

The first testimony of a textual enlargement of *The Courtier* is a

---

2. Page 3. The Italian reads: "*Et come nell' animo mio era recente l'odor delle virtù del Duca Guido et la satisfattione che io quegli anni haveva sentito della amoravole compagnia di così eccelenti persone, come allhora si ritrovarono nella Corte d'Urbino, fui stimulato da quella memoria a scrivere questi libri del Cortegiano; il che feci in pochi giorni, con intentione di castigar col tempo quegli errori, che dal desiderio di pagar tosto questo debito erano nati. Ma la fortuna già molt' anni m'ha sempre tenuto oppresso in così continui travagli, che io non ho mai potuto pigliar spatio di ridurgli al termine, che il mio debil giudicio ne restasse contento.*"

manuscript notebook labeled A, conserved at Mantova, and documents the very first draft of the *Book of the Courtier*. This document indicates, albeit in broad and fragmentary outlines, the main thematic arguments of the work that will later be divided into four separate books. Moreover, it also includes a prologue which calls upon "the most Christian king," Francis I of France, to instigate a new crusade. Written sometime between 1513 and 1514, its composition occurs between the conclusion of the military campaigns (1509–1512) and Castiglione's Roman sojourn as emissary of the Duke of Urbino that began after the death of Pope Giulio II on March 11, 1513. It is not difficult to hypothesize that something of the original nucleus of ideas quickly written down in 1508 (once again giving credence to the information contained in the dedication to Michel de Silva), as well as that which is contained within the notebook, or whatever else was written in Latin or Italian, may have followed the author to Rome and served as a an initial set of ideas for the first draft written entirely in Castiglione's own hand.

I would like to point out two factors that shed further light upon Castiglione's initial phase of writing *The Courtier* following his prolonged stint of military campaigns: first, their conclusion coincides with Castiglione's intense cultural activity at the court of Urbino, the epicenter of which was surely the Carnival of 1513 and in particular the staging of Bibbiena's *Calandria* and other plays; and second, the death of his very dear friend, Cesare Gonzaga (in September of 1512), whom he had known since childhood—as well as that of Gasparo Pallavicino (in 1511), Roberto da Bari (at the end of 1512), and Giovan Cristoforo Romano (in May of 1512)—all of which surely gave immediate rise to the *"grata memoria"* that solicits writing so as to make amends with death, as set forth in the proem of the fourth book and then in the dedication to Michel de Silva.

From the spring of 1514 Castiglione carries out the functions of ducal orator in Rome. This position not only increases his cultural rapport with the respected group of friends from Urbino (Bembo, Bibbiena, Federico Fregoso) but expands his associations with literati of great repute such as Sadoletto, Beroaldo, and Tebaldeo. He also partakes in the intense artistic experience of this period in Rome (marked by the contemporaneous presence of Michelangelo and Raphael).

It is precisely during these Roman years, between 1514 and January of 1516, that Castiglione has two copyists prepare two manuscripts labeled B and C. With B the first version of *The Courtier* is datable to 1514–1515 and prepared by a scribe under the direct supervision of Castiglione (proven by numerous autograph markings on it). Yet it too is incomplete: it contains entire parts that correspond to the first two books of the authoritative version, as well as the prologue to the third book. Instead, the text of C (datable to 1515–1516) is complete. It was copied by two scribes and subjected to numerous radical interventions by the author (most importantly the insertion of new sections) and other intellectuals (for example, the handwriting of Bembo has been identified).

These years are extremely intense, also because of Castiglione's political and diplomatic responsibilities. From the front lines he follows the unfolding drama of Urbino as it loses its Duke—due to the determination of Pope Leo X to repossess Urbino. In vain he travels to Bologna in December of 1515, pleading his case before King Francis I (no doubt these are the same days in which Castiglione is writing, or had just finished writing, the dedication for the first book to Alfonso Ariosto in which he gives ample praise to Francis "the most Christian king" and exhorts him to start a new crusade against the Turks). Then, and again without success, he accompanies Elizabeth, the Duchess of Urbino, before the pope for the same purpose. In June of 1516 the situation worsens when Francesco Maria della Rovere is relieved of his post and excommunicated. Castiglione follows him into excile (in Mantova) as Lorenzo di Piero de'Medici is nominated the new Duke of Urbino.

When he leaves Rome, Castiglione carries with him the early notes and the two manuscripts (B and C) of the first version of *The Courtier*. He feverishly continued to work on them during the long break in Mantova (in October of 1516 he finds time to marry Ippolita Torelli: and in February of 1517 he accompanies Federico Gonzaga to Venice) that lasted nearly three years and that was rarely interrupted by diplomatic responsibilities. In fact, he is so satisfied with the way his book is shaping up that he sends a copy to Bembo and Sadoletto in September of 1518, as well as to Alfonso Ariosto and the Cardinal Ippolito d'Este before the summer of 1520. The news of his work quickly spreads, especially throughout Lombardy.

Unfortunately, throughout this entire phase of Castiglione's biography, from his first transfer to Rome in 1514 to his return there in 1519, there remain very few documents and letters, even fewer dating from his return to Mantova between June of 1516 and May of 1519. In reality there is nothing strange in this if one considers that of the 271 extant letters, written between 1497 and 1513, nearly all of them (90 percent) were written to his mother, Aloisa. This being the case, it becomes clear that such letters have no reason to be written while Castiglione is at home in Mantova. Yet given Castiglione's propensity for writing home, if nothing else the letters he sent to his mother during his first sojourn in Rome (between 1514 and 1516) were certainly lost. Not that they would have been useful in offering new information regarding his work in composition; for as Castiglione himself states in a missive written on February 13, 1505, the letters sent to his mother shall not discuss anything that "does not pertain to us."

In reality, the documentary discontinuity of the letters marks a change in Castiglione's life that takes place in Mantova between 1516 and 1519 (the period between his two extended stays in Rome). When he re-enters the Roman political and diplomatic arena in May of 1519 he displays determination, knowledge, and lucidity, a professional competence of the highest order; and in the course of a few years Castiglione's public career becomes increasingly important to him: a fact borne out by a remarkable series of new letters, no longer, for the most part, written to family. Also, in 1519 the political and institutional scene changes both in Italy and in Europe: the Emperor Maximilian dies (January 12), as does Francesco Gonzaga, the Marquis of Mantova (March 29), and Lorenzo di Piero de'Medici (May 4); Charles V is the new emperor (June 28). In May of this year Castiglione returns to Rome in order to take care of the interests of the new Marquis of Mantova, Federico Gonzaga, as well as to work towards Francesco Maria della Rovere's repossession of the dukedom of Urbino. After a brief return home in November of 1519, he returns to Rome in July of 1520 where in the course of a few months, two grievous events affect him deeply: the death of Raphael on April 7, 1520; and that of his wife on August 25 of the same year.

It is during these years of great political and diplomatic responsibility that Castiglione also works upon the second version of the *Book of the Courtier*, making significant and ample changes to that which was written by the copyists in C. This document follows him, most probably along with B and A, throughout his travels and reveals the numerous series of tormented interventions with which he reworks its argumentative structure. The manuscript C, full as it is of additions and cancellations, some of which were made by individuals other than Castiglione, with its precise record of the quotidian labor and punctilious revision undertaken by its author offers the fullest testimony of the difficult and laborious process of the work's evolution during its twenty-year voyage toward publication.

While at Rome between July of 1520 and November of 1522, as his political and diplomatic reputation continues to grow, as Francesco Maria della Rovere finally recuperates his Dukedom at Urbino (on December 1, 1521, after the death of Pope Leo X), Castiglione employs four copyists to prepare the new manuscript of his *Book of the Courtier* (between 1520 and 1521) in order to clean up the now chaotic character of C that he and others had laboriously reworked. The new manuscript, labeled D, was completed somewhere between 1520 and 1521 and copied by four different scribes. It provides us with the second version of the *Book of the Courtier* and registers the intense process of revision by Castiglione as well as taking into consideration the observations of Alfonso Ariosto, Bembo, and Sadoleto (all of whom had read and commented upon a copy of C between 1518 and 1520). Yet upon its completion, he quickly begins to make new corrections, cancellations, and integrations. The result is the second version of the *Book of the Courtier*.

When Castiglione leaves Rome to return home on November 15, 1522, he is probably planning the radical restructuring of the work, which he surely carries with him (at least manuscript D), concentrating specifically upon reorganizing the third book with which he is least satisfied. Exactly one year later (November 15, 1523) he is returning to Rome in order to assume the responsibility of resident ambassador for the Marquis of Mantova. At this time he brings with him a heavily reworked manuscript, completely different from that which he had brought with him to Mantova, which contains the third book now rearticulated into the new third and fourth books. There are no direct documents testifying to Castiglione's having produced a clean and intermediate manuscript from the numerous interventions he made to D; but it is clear that immediately upon his re-entry to Rome he entrusts a capable copyist with the production of a new, ordered, clean, and complete copy. It is the fifth and last testimony, a manuscript that has subsequently been labeled L and currently conserved in Florence at the Laurenziana Library (Laurenziano Ashburnhamiano 409). Because of a copyist who followed scribal custom and wrote down when and where he finished his transcription, L is the only testimony with a precise date and place of composition (May 23, 1524, in Rome). The very existence of L is exceptional as there are very few manuscripts that actually survived the process of printing (in the following year, 1525, Castiglione carries this manuscript with him to Spain and sends it on to Venice for its typographical setting and subsequent publication). As a result, L not only bears the visible traces of the typesetter but, more important, that of the editor (who has been identified as the Venetian Giovan Francesco Valier) whose interventions reflect efforts to normalize its vocabulary. L also contains more notable variants when compared to D and records the numerous interventions typical of the author as well as those of other hands. It is with this manuscript that the lengthy period of composition—twenty years of planning, writing, and revision that reflect Castiglione's efforts to perfect his text—finally comes to an end. The result is the version that, with a few ulterior modifications by its ever unsatisfied author, will finally go to the printer.

Yet the calm and quiet earned by Castiglione's completion of his literary labors lasts little more than two months when, on July 19, Pope Clement VII nominates him as his nuncio in Madrid. During this period, one that includes the completion (or nearly so) of transcriptions, there occurs a meeting of particular importance: Castiglione and Canossa, his old friend from Urbino, meet at some point between August and September of 1524 in order to discuss the more important and pressing problems looming on the international political horizon. Castiglione speaks on behalf of Charles V, and Canossa for Francis I. Whatever time they spent discussing issues of absolute public importance, we can also be certain that they found free time and more private occasions during which, one can conjecture, Castiglione may have had Canossa, the great protagonist of *The Courtier*, take a look at his new manuscript.

On October 5, 1524, Castiglione leaves Rome for Mantova with his manuscript. Then, after a long voyage he arrives in Madrid on April 11, 1525. Having made numerous solicitations, he is still unable to recuperate the copy of his manuscript sent to Vittoria Colonna in Naples and becomes worried about its status, concerned that its disappearance might result in the premature publication of his work. Meanwhile, he works feverishly in order to make a few more changes to the third and final version, thus revising the L manuscript he carried with him to Spain. Finally, however, he decides to free his book and give it a life of its own. In April of 1527 he sends the L manuscript as it is, full of interventions by numerous hands, on to Venice where it shall undergo one final change, a linguistic revision to be carried out by someone else.

Yet Castiglione finds no peace. Instead of having the gratification of completing his work, Castiglione's life is once again in turmoil; 1527 proves to be a terrible year for him. The sack of Rome on May 6, 1527 (only a few days after he mailed his manuscript to Venice with minute instructions for the publication of his work), upends his public and private life, radically challenging his beliefs and values. Caught between the Emperor and the Pope, Castiglione is placed in an extremely difficult political position. It is in this context that he writes the new dedication to the Portugese Michel de Silva, Bishop of Viseu.

After these terrible months, in April of 1528, Castiglione's *Book of the Courtier* is finally published, bringing with it a long-awaited conclusion to its twenty-year gestation. Unfortunately, however, its author was unable to enjoy the fruits of his labors. Only a few months after the publication of his work, Castiglione dies in Toledo, Spain (February 8, 1529). Thus the first book of a fifty-

year-old man, his late entrance upon the literary stage, is also his
last.

This impressive set of documents confirms that the genesis of the
Book of the Courtier, a text that in its definitive form was read and
loved for centuries throughout Europe, was far from rectilineal but
rather the result of a complicated process of revision (influenced by
the humanistic preference for a classically inspired aesthetic in
which a variety of elements are ultimately controlled by their organization into a unified and harmonious whole). In fact, much of the
concern in the aforementioned revisions focuses upon the architecture of the *Book of the Courtier,* demonstrating that Castiglione was
first and foremost searching for an orderly, coherent, and organic
form throughout the long process of composing his text. For this
reason his effort is dedicated to shaping the overall structure of his
work and to divide it into the books that will distribute its material
into an appropriate series of proportionate and individually complete sections.

As we have witnessed, the three manuscripts located in the Vatican
Library—respectively titled B (ms. Vat. Lat. 8204), C (ms. Vat. Lat.
8205), and D (ms. Vat. Lat. 8206)—are decisive for documenting the
fundamental phases of development of Castiglione's work. As modern philological analysis has demonstrated, these manuscripts reveal
a tormented and dynamic series of authorial interventions, divisible
into two different and virtually complete stages of composition. The
manuscript C, or the first version of the *Book of the Courtier,* is represented by the manuscript before its later subjection to numerous
additions and variations by Castiglione and concludes the long and
intense process of elaboration that had begun with A (1513–1514),
moved to B (1514–1515), and ended with C (1515–1516). When
compared with the text first published in 1528, C presents a very different structure, in particular its third book which corresponds to
both the third and fourth books in the first published edition.

The most visible element of the textual enlargement is represented by the changes in the architecture of the book during the
major textual "upheaval" that takes place in the passage from D to
L and concerns the radical rewriting of the original third book in its
undefined and chaotinc format into what are now the third and
fourth books.

If the major textual upheaval concerns the old version of the third
book exclusively, the common view of a "fracture" between the third
and fourth books in the final version, a view that has characterized
so much recent critical discourse about the work, not only lacks
documentary evidence but proves to be a reduction and a simplifi-
cation of the much more fully articulated and acute philological

insights that Ghino Ghinassi provided.[3] This notion of a "fracture" between the third and fourth books is nothing, in short, but a phantasm that has come to be passively accepted and reiterated, in the way commonplaces reproduce themselves. If one wants to speak of a "fracture," then one has to recognize that there was a very conspicuous break between the first two books and the excessive (in terms of its dimensions) and chaotic (in terms of its arguments) third book in the first and second versions. Above all, it is necessary to recognize that this fracture produced a resounding defect in the architectural design of the work as a whole, which, as a result, lacked equilibrium and proportion, thus making it terribly flawed according to the aesthetic norms and rules of humanist classicism.

This structural disproportion, retained in version after version, is only resolved positively by Castiglione with the "upheaval" of the final revision from D to L, which is to say with the division of the old third book and its subsequent transformation into the new third and fourth books. In this manner, the four books are distinct and proportionate entities, homogeneous both in their argumentative structure and in individual dimensions when compared to the others. When taken as a whole, they reveal the outline of a coherent architectural structure set forth in a homogeneous and linear rhetorical progression that respects the classical demand for a unified whole, the preference for Horace's *unum et simplex*.

Even from these unelaborated observations, it is not hard to understand why in the dedication of the first printed edition to Don Michel de Silva he reacts with such singular animosity when speaking of the "peril" stemming from Vittoria Colonna's conduct. As will be recalled, Castiglione had sent her a copy of the unauthorized manuscript (certainly modeled upon the second revision as testified by D), the subsequent disappearance of which might have resulted in the premature publication of the *Book of the Courtier* in a format that no longer existed in the mind of its author and far different from the one he had finally completed. It would have been an irreparably outdated book.

Yet one needs to bear in mind another issue, if only because it was the basis of the invention of a "fracture" between the third and fourth books: namely the existence, or lack thereof, of the treatment of the relationship between the courtier and the prince before the second version of *The Courtier* (D). The fact of the matter is that even in A (that is to say, the autograph manuscript of the original draft of *The Courtier*) the education of the prince is already present as a theme. This early treatment of the topic in A does not reveal

3. Ghino Ghinassi, *"Fasi dell'elaborazione del 'Cortegiano'"* in *Studi di filologia italiana*, XXV (1967), pp. 155–196.

any major discrepancies with what will later be presented in the first and second versions (C and D, respectively). Rather, because the evidence demonstrates that the education of the prince is already present in the earliest drafts, its perennial presence throughout *The Courtier*'s twenty-year process of revision reveals that it is undoubtedly the most important *topos* in the entire book.

The reasons behind the major upheaval of the text (from D to L) are not solely aesthetic. They stem, too, from the impracticability, in the 1520s, of a cultural model too tightly linked to the courtly system of regional Italian states and its adherence to a late-feudal courtly code. Above all, they call into play the new cultural and institutional vision of Castiglione. A keen observer of the transformations taking place within the social body of the nobility, he grasps the dynamics of a new patrician order in the process of re-articulating itself in the face of the ancient feudal one, and he knows how to situate them within a larger European context. In this double yet integrated scenario, Castiglione creates a modern model of the noble gentleman founded upon the cultural ideals elaborated by the humanistic classicism of the Italian Renaissance.

Yet Castiglione was also in search of an overall thematic order that would allow him to cover, with brilliant competence, both traditional and new cultural issues of his time, giving particular attention to the great themes of his day like the education of the prince, of women, the philosophy of love, and the question of language, in addition to the parts already dedicated to the formation of the courtier and to the treatment of jokes.

Further observations regarding the textual "upheaval" that accompanied the reorganization of the old third book into the new third and fourth book arise from reflecting upon the courtly features of the third book in the first and second versions, beginning with its formal organization articulated as debates and quarrels, protracted encomiums to princes and princesses, and traditional courtly arguments (the maliciousness of women, the archetypal Ovidian tactics of love, the question of Love, etcetera). This organization, one rooted in the courtly culture and history of northern Italy at the close of the fifteenth century, remains until the revisions made on D (circa 1521). Clearly, it becomes inadequate in providing answers that can measure up to the new cultural dynamics that Castiglione sees emerging.

In the very years that Castiglione returns to the service of the Gonzaga family (from November 15, 1523, when he is at Rome as the ambassador of the Marquis Federico), he begins to reconsider his past literary and courtly experiences in the light of the contemporary political and institutional landscape and recognizes the need to alter his parameters and to modify his point of view, taking into account the changes he perceives. His previous set of registers, formed and nourished within the system of numerous small duchies and their courts that dominated northern Italy, changes as Castiglione begins to look at the great courts of Europe, starting with the curial court in Rome. More than the changing cultural, social, and political references that begin to leave their mark upon the new, evolving *Book of the Courtier*, what is really at stake is its form. In seeking to structure all of the text's parts in a manner ultimately coherent with the first two books and articulated toward an ascending climax, Castiglione also makes changes that have a decisive effect upon the work's overall argumentative strategy and structure that conforms to the rules of a mature classicism by seeking a coherent and homogenous communicative structure.

For this reason the new third book is dedicated to the formation of the lady of the palace (which in the old third book was little more than a marginal consideration, confined, more or less, to the end of the dialogue) and presented in terms that correspond to the ones set forth for the male courtier in the dialogues of the first and second books. It finds its argumentative structure, in terms of its relationship to the whole, in the celebration of the dignity and excellence of women (whereas in the old third book it was carried forth as a quarrel or battle in the terms or topics typical of the late medieval courtly tradition).

It is for this reason that the new fourth book opens with the *institutio principis* (which, in the old third book, had been framed within and then ultimately confused with and dispersed throughout the quarrel over women) as the end of courtliness. And for the same reason the work closes with an apotheosis to spiritual love (also previously linked in the third book, to quarrels over women), in terms quite homologous to the conclusion of Bembo's *Asolani*.

From this, however, there also arises an immediate and extremely clear consequence: this radical reorganization according to order, proportion, symmetry and perspective, eliminates the only conspicuous fracture that the *Book of the Courtier* retained in its old form (in the progression from A to D): the break which marked the distance between the first two books (dedicated to the formation of the courtier) and the third (without a real center, except possibly the outdated quarrel over women).

Given these considerations it becomes easier to see that Castiglione knew he needed to make a radical break from older courtly traditions of northern Italy. As a result, the new *Book of the Courtier* founded a model for the modern courtier that no longer looked to northern Italy and its numerous small courts but sought out, instead, a different point of reference that turned to Europe and its larger courts for inspiration.

The exceptional nature of the *Book of the Courtier* is to be found above all in the richness of the documentation that surrounds its long and tormented composition: five manuscripts distributed over a course of at least fifteen years that detail the project's development right up to its final definitive shape. These textual testimonies and the story they tell about the evolution of *The Book of the Courtier* make Castiglione's case quite exceptional. In the European literary tradition there exists nothing even remotely similar to the ample and continuous firsthand evidence Castiglione provides about the many labors, the indecisions, rethinking, cancellations, changes, and corrections required for a writer to produce a final and "polished" literary work of art. Five authograph manuscripts (or having the value thereof) that extend across the course of fifteen years and allow one to monitor, practically day by day, page by page, all that preceded Castiglione's achievement of the "*leggierezza* and "*discioltura*" in the finished published work. Five manuscripts recording an intense period of authorial engagement and toil, labor concealed beneath the polished, facile style of the published text so that it could conform to its own "universal rule" of *sprezzatura*.[4]

HARRY BERGER JR.

Sprezzatura and the Absence of Grace[†]

The interlocutors in *The Book of the Courtier* spend much of their time elaborating a technology of behavioral performance founded on what Castiglione calls *sprezzatura*. "Sprezzatura" is introduced in Book I, Chapter 26, as "una nova parola," "a new word," by the speaker assigned to supervise the "game" of constructing the ideal courtier, Count Ludovico da Canossa.[1] What he describes under that term is an art that hides art, the cultivated ability to display art-

---

4. "Nor must one be more careful of anything than of concealing art, because if it is discovered, this robs a man of all credit and causes him to be held in slight esteem" (1.26). The Italian reads: "*Né più in altro si ha da poner studio, che nel nasconderla: perché, se è scoperta, leva in tutto il credito et fa l'homo poco estimato.*"
† From *The Absence of Grace: Sprezzatura and Suspicion in Two Renaissance Courtesy Books* (Stanford, Calif.: Stanford University Press, 2000). Reprinted by permission of the publisher. © Copyright 2000 by the Board of Trustees of the Leland Stanford Junior University.
1. B. Castiglione, *Il libro del Cortegiano,* ed. Giulio Carnazzi (Milan: Rizzoli, 1987), p. 81 (abbreviated as C followed by page number in future references); *Book of the Courtier,* trans. C. Singleton (New York: Doubleday, 1959) (abbreviated as S followed by page number to this Norton Critical Edition in future references). Frequently when citing passages or phrases in which the particular context or translation is not at issue, I give only book and chapter numbers (in this case 1.26). At times, where it seems helpful, these may be accompanied by references to C or S.

ful artlessness, to perform any act or gesture with an insouciant or careless mastery that delivers either or both of two messages: "Look how artfully I appear to be natural"; "Look how naturally I appear to be artful." Killjoys might be inclined to dismiss this art as a culturally legitimated practice of hypocrisy or bad faith, but others would appreciate the suppleness of the high-wire act of definitional balance performed by the count and his interlocutors. For the sake of simplicity, I shall call this the sprezzatura of nonchalance even though that name is misleading, since what is involved is not merely nonchalance, *disinvoltura*, insouciance, the ability to conceal effort. Rather it is the ability to show that one is not showing all the effort one obviously put into learning how to show that one is not showing effort.

This, however, touches only on the instrumental or purely aesthetic aspect of sprezzatura. What is it for? A second definitional aspect is beamed up by the count in 1.28, and I give it in Wayne Rebhorn's paraphrase: sprezzatura is "an art of suggestion, in which the courtier's audience will be induced by the images it confronts to imagine a greater reality existing behind them," and this enables the courtier "to make himself into a much more enticing and compelling figure than he might otherwise be."[2] Since, as Frank Whigham concisely renders it, "modesty arouses inference in excess of the facts,"[3] we may think of it as a sprezzatura of conspicuously false modesty. Furthermore, the term's relation to the verb *sprezzare* (to scorn, despise, disdain) and the adjective *sprezzata*, which appears several times in Books 1 and 2, suggests to Rebhorn that sprezzatura designates "an attitude of slightly superior disdain" by which the performer indicates his easy mastery of whatever he is doing, his "scorn for the potential difficulty or restriction involved" and "for normal, human limitations" (34–35). Eduardo Saccone and Daniel Javitch associate the "disdain, misprision, or depreciation" implied by the etymology with a strategy for maintaining class boundaries; they argue for a sprezzatura of elite enclosure founded on the complicity of a coded performance in which the actor and his peers reaffirm their superiority to those incapable of deciphering the code.[4]

Javitch gives sprezzatura a different look by moving it into the political arena and treating it as a strategic response to "the con-

---

2. Wayne Rebhorn, *Courtly Performances. Masking and Festivity in Castiglione's "Book of the Courtier"* (Detroit: Wayne State University Press, 1978), 38. See C, 83–84; S, 34–35.
3. Frank Whigham, *Ambition and Privilege. The Social Tropes of Elizabethan Courtesy Theory* (Berkeley: University of California Press, 1984), 99.
4. Eduardo Saccone, "*Grazia, Sprezzatura, Affetazione* in the *Courtier*," in *Castiglione: The Ideal and the Real in Renaissance Culture*, ed. Robert W. Hanning and David Rosand (New Haven, Conn.: Yale University Press, 1983), 59–64; Daniel Javitch, "*Il Cortegiano* and the Constraints of Despotism," in *idem*, 24–25.

straints of despotism" in the courtly context of "fierce competition for favors":

> The ruler's desire to keep his subordinates in check, as well as the court's standards of polite refinement, compel its members to subdue or at least mask their aggressive and competitive drives. That is why such qualities as reticence, detachment, and understatement are so valued at court. . . . *The courtier* . . . inhabits a world where graceful deceit is valued not only for its intrinsic delight but because the despot who governs that world makes it imperative. (23, 26)

This indeed suggests a fourth definitional aspect of sprezzatura as a form of defensive irony: the ability to disguise what one really desires, feels, thinks, and means or intends behind a mask of "apparent reticence and nonchalance" (Javitch, *"Cortegiano,"* 24). I hesitate to call this the sprezzatura of deceit because, as I'm about to suggest, it involves not deceit *tout court* but rather the menace of deceit, the display of the ability to deceive. I shall therefore, in the interests of vapid generalization and alliteration, refer to it as the sprezzatura of suspicion.[5]

These formulations don't quite catch a reflexive nuance that hovers cloudily about them. Most of them focus on a skill of performative negation, the ability continuously to display that something is being conspicuously withheld; the ability, for example, to present oneself as someone who may have and can keep secrets, who has power in reserve, who does indeed possess the "aggressive and competitive drives" he is masking, who knows how to conceal unpleasant truths under "salutary deception" ("inganno salutifero," 4.10). Deceit is among the "tropes of personal promotion" Whigham discusses in his fine chapter on that topic. He cites George Puttenham's assertion that the "profession of a very Courtier . . . is . . . cunningly to be able to dissemble," and he offers the following comment on the statement by Federico in 2.40 that this "is rather an ornament . . . than deceit": "Deceit is both denied and admitted, redefined and excused; . . . it becomes . . . a sauce or manner" (S, 101).

The push in all these observations is toward more than the ability to deceive; it is toward the ability to represent the ability to deceive, toward the courtier's ability *to show that* he has the art and, if called upon, is capable of deceiving. Disinvoltura is both the behavioral sign

---

5. Different facets of sprezzatura are nicely turned and ambiguated by George Puttenham in discussions that fuse social with rhetorical tropes, courtliness with allegory: (1) "*allegoria*, which . . . not impertinently we call the Courtier or figure of faire semblant," and (2) "the courtly figure Allegoria, which is when we speake one thing and thinke another," and "which for his duplicitie we call the figure of [*false semblant* or dissimulation]": George Puttenham, *The Arte of English Poesie*, ed. Gladys Dodge Willcock and Alice Walker (Cambridge, UK: Cambridge University Press, 1970), 299, 186.

of this capability and the medium through which it will if necessary be actualized. It is also both a competitive act in itself and a sign that its possessor is willing to compete for favors in court; a guarantee that the ambition and aggressiveness the courtier pretends to mask is really there, and available for his prince's use (see 2.18–25, 32).[6] To modify Puttenham's "profession of a very Courtier" in a manner that brings out the pun in "profession" and "very," the true courtier professes himself capable of falsehood; among the accomplishments by which he prefers himself to princes is his ability to show that he is cunningly able to dissemble. Strictly speaking, then, the "trope of personal promotion" is not "deceit"—the ability to dissemble—per se. The courtier promotes himself and tries to win the prince's confidence by displaying his mastery of the behavioral rhetoric, the choreography, that signifies the ability and willingness to deceive.

The performance of sprezzatura is thus a figuration of power. But it is also a figuration of anxiety. The *Cortegiano*'s interlocutors show themselves sensitive to their precarious status in the Italian court culture of their time, a culture dominated by princes who were likely to be despotic and who more often than not were themselves perilously besieged as clients of the militarily superior nation-states. The threat or actuality of disempowerment is a concern not only noted by the book's critics but also expressed by its speakers, and it is against the background of this anxiety that the effortless if not lazy elegance of sprezzatura is depicted as a source and sign of manly inner strength rather than of effeminacy. In other words, sprezzatura is to be worn as a velvet glove that exhibits the contours of the handiness it conceals. But of course the glove could be filled with wet clay. Perhaps this signifier of virile manhood only "camouflages vulnerability," as Whigham phrases it in describing the trope he calls "cosmesis," "the use of cosmetic aids to conceal or repair defects."[7]

The idea of cosmetic sprezzatura puts a mordant and defensive spin on the second of the definitional aspects mentioned above, the "art of suggestion" or conspicuously false modesty picked out by Rebhorn as enabling the courtier "to make himself into a much more enticing and compelling figure than he might otherwise be."[8] Pre-

6. See the wonderfully apt allusion in 2.19–20 to the passage of Scripture (Luke 14:8–11) in which Christ explains to the wedding guest the advantages of strategic self-abasement: those who sneakily try to exalt themselves risk being humbled, but those who make a big show of humbling themselves stand a good chance of getting their host to raise them to a higher place. The interchange at this point between Federico and Cesare dramatizes a wry version of the moral, one that brings out the competitive motive that drives even Christian sprezzatura. Federico lets Cesare identify the allusion and accuse him of theft, and then confesses in effect that he committed a terrible crime but didn't think Cesare was up to catching him out: "It would be too great a sacrilege to steal from the Gospel; but you are more learned in Holy Writ than I thought" (S, 83).
7. Whigham, *Ambition and Privilege*, 116.
8. Rebhorn, *Courtly Performances*, 38. Though I find Whigham's articulation and elaboration of social tropes enormously helpful, I choose here to depart from his scheme, in

sumably this is an art the courtier would cherish and practice with pride, and presumably also, since the discussions about the perfect courtier and his female counterpart are prescriptive, those figures are ideals or models to be distinguished from both their inventors and their imitators. It may therefore be going beyond the purview of a study of sprezzatura in the *Cortegiano* to rewrite Rebhorn's phrase in a manner that highlights cognitive states—"more . . . than he might think himself to be, or fear himself to be"—and to ask what it might mean for a performer to think or fear that he is worse than he appears. Worse not merely as a matter of security or vulnerability (Whigham's chief concern) but as a matter of conscience; an anxiety that is not merely practical but ethical. The *Cortegiano* is a book about self-representation. But self-representation has two dimensions, objective—representing oneself to others—and reflexive—representing oneself to oneself. The explicit theme of the book is learning how to represent oneself to others. Is it then gratuitous to ask how this project may affect and be affected by the questions of trust and self-esteem that come into play when one takes reflexive as well as objective self-representation into account? Do all those who are urged to represent themselves as better than they think they are form a community in which it becomes as difficult to authenticate one's own performances as it is to accredit those of others? Doesn't such a community cast about itself a permanent shadow of representation anxiety? Can it avoid being haunted by its construction and representation of the unrepresented?—by the specter of an unrepresented community of hidden and less worthy selves that its commitment to the culture of sprezzatura conjures up?

In its multifold character, then, sprezzatura creates within and around its performers a self-fulfilling culture of suspicion. An art of behaving as if always under surveillance, an art that aims to ward off danger by appearing dangerous and thus to elicit cautious respect no less than admiration, it motivates increased surveillance and anxiety on the part of the performer as well as the observer. It is within the framework of this hypothesis that I now turn to those passages in Books 1 and 2 that focus on the acquisition of sprezzatura, and that represent this acquisition as a compensatory response to pressures affecting the status of noble families. In part these pressures were caused by the increasing vigor of court-centered seigneurial (as opposed to republican) regimes backed by French or Spanish force. In part they were caused by emergent frictions within the merchant class between new money and old, the

which sprezzatura is merely one in a set of eight "tropes of personal promotion" all on the same level. My narrower focus on Castiglione leads me to treat sprezzatura as a master trope of which deceit and cosmesis are variant inflections responding to different motives and pressures.

nuovi ricchi and the older patrician families. In the *Cortegiano*, as we'll see, these changes are mythologized as a fall from grace, a fall from the *grazia* of divinely bestowed (that is, inborn, inherited) superiority.

Under the nominal topic of what the ideal courtier needs to know and to be able to perform, the interlocutors spend much time in Book 1 going through the standard arguments about the value of mastering techniques of literary, musical, and visual production. But the objective emphasis on the acquisition of learning and art is to some extent a misdirection. From the closing paragraphs of Book 1 through the first twelve paragraphs of Book 2 it gradually becomes clear that the artistic production of objects models the artistic production of subjects. The ultimate aim of the acquisition is to convert painting and writing to living self-portraiture and self-textualization: *ut pictura habitus.*[9] The clichés about learning the arts are continually displaced from the production and evaluation of artifacts to the production and evaluation of courtly behavior as a performance of "nature," "una artificiosa imitazion di natura" (1.50). Does art imitate nature or does nature imitate art? Or is the formula "art imitates nature" itself no more than an artful gesture toward naturalizing the art that creates in its own image the nature it claims only to imitate? In this expressly duplicitous conception, the naturalness art pretends to imitate is an artifact. The passage that immediately precedes the introduction of the term "sprezzatura" glances at another duplicity. In the process of imitating models of comportment, the ideal courtier is urged to combine the selectivity of Zeuxis with the sweet predations of Plato's apian poets, and to do so in the manner of a thief: "even as in green meadows the bee flits about among grasses robbing [carpendo] the flowers, so our Courtier must steal [rubare] this grace from those who seem to him to have it, taking from each the part that seems most worthy of praise" (1.26; S, 32).[1]

At the beginning of Book 2, the emphasis is shifted from the sprezzatura of nonchalance to that of suspicion when Federico's reprise of the previous evening's discussion centers on the importance of constant self-surveillance: "our Courtier must be cautious

9. See the excellent discussion of this and other features in the *Cortegiano* by Jonas Barish in *The Antitheatrical Prejudice* (Berkeley: University of California Press, 1981), 167–83.
1. Why must it be stolen? Is it because the notion of explicit pedagogical transactions between teacher and student contradicts the basic premise of sprezzatura? Robert Hanning associates this advice with the model of Zeuxis and Alberti's use of it to emphasize "the painter's duty to create an idealized yet mimetic art by imitating only the most nearly perfect models. . . . The courtier is both Zeuxis and Zeuxis's portrait, forming one ideal from many fine parts": "Castiglione's Verbal Portrait," in *Castiglione*, ed. Hanning and Rosand, 134–35. Yet behind the blandness of the Zeuxis anecdote is a fantasy of imaginary dismemberment. This aspect of the Zeuxis anecdote is discussed further in Chapter 3.

in his every action and see to it that prudence attends whatever he says or does," and this "diligent watch" is necessary because "we are all naturally more ready to censure errors than to praise things well done" (2.6–7; S, 71). He directs his strictures against the folly of affectation because it betrays the actor's ambition to excel—betrays it and thereby frustrates it, which is to say that this ambition is a precious resource and that it must be concealed in order to be preserved and fulfilled. But not, as I suggested above, simply concealed; it must be represented as concealed. Federico's is a recipe for sustaining the competition of every courtier with every courtier for the prince's favors, and the succeeding conversation (through 2.41) makes it clear that service to princes may both corrupt and disempower the servant.

The discussion of sprezzatura in Book 2 thus opens onto a prospect of apprehensiveness, distrust of hidden motives, fear of exposure, and a general sense of the weakness of the courtier's position. Both as observer and as observed, the courtier focuses his anxiety on the hidden "reality" of the unrepresented self produced by—and haunting—the culture of sprezzatura, with its emphasis on self-misrepresentation. The problems that beset this culture are concentrated in the interpretive combat between performer and spectators/auditors, a field of play charged with the tension between aesthetic *jouissance* and suspicion. Since in order to represent themselves to others performers represent themselves to themselves, since they watch themselves being watched, the force of persuasion and the production of meaning are reversible, alienable, circular: they can originate either in the observer or in the performer. This makes courtly negotiation a struggle for control over the power to determine the self-representation the performer conveys not only to others but also to himself or herself (a disjunction that reminds us the determination may include gender). Courtly practice is fetishistic but ambiguously toned: the subordination of the conspicuously artless performance to the conspicuously artful achievement of it keeps the product, the self-representation, from transcending the etymological limits implied by the term "fetish," which derives from *facticere*—that is, the product remains factlike but factitious and fictitious because made by art. This achievement and the dialectic that enables it may be culture-specific but they are not culture-wide. They are still the privilege of social and political elites trying to protect the continuously changing boundaries of new aristocracies.

Eduardo Saccone has shown how the *Cortegiano*'s conception of courtly performance recognizes the need of boundary maintenance and contributes to it by requiring and producing a double audience: it divides the insiders who appreciate the art of sprezzatura from the outsiders who take it at face value.[2] Saccone cites Canossa's analogy of courtly sprezzatura to the art of ancient orators who concealed their knowledge of letters in order to make "their orations appear to be composed in the simplest manner and according to the dictates of nature and truth rather than of effort and art; which fact, had it been known, would have inspired in the minds of the people the fear that they could be duped by it" (1.26; S, 32). The analogy, as Saccone points out, is misleading because Canossa doesn't distinguish from the "populo" the orator's "fellow advocates," who will admire his art of deception "and in him recognize an excellent compeer" (61).

Saccone emphasizes the exclusivity and bonding of the mutual admiration society. But apart from the fact that compeers are also competitors, courtiers are not orators, princely courts are not popular assemblies, and duchies are not republics. Since courtly audiences are composed mainly of courtiers and princes, aren't the expectation and awareness of duplicity sources of apprehension as well as admiration? The danger, the risk, the *frisson* are part of the game, but so also is the institutionalized distrust that characterizes an apprehensive society—a society based on the desire to take and the fear of being taken. For the insiders in such a society, the value of the face as index of the mind, or of the body as index of the soul, must be imagined to have been problematized. Saccone's benign emphasis responds to the conspicuously reductive focus on the aesthetics of sprezzatura that dominates Book 1. The reductiveness is conspicuous because allusions to violence, duplicity, and the *lex talionis* of court life are scattered throughout the text.

To the extent that the representational techniques associated with sprezzatura rely on study, performance, and dissimulation, they subject physiognomic norms of authenticity and truth to the pressure of continuous mimicry. Such norms are initially associated by Count Ludovico with the gifts of nature when, in 1.14, he defends the proposition that the ideal courtier should be nobly born and introduces the term "grazia" into this discussion. "For noble birth is like a bright lamp that makes manifest and visible deeds both good and bad. . . . And . . . this lust of nobility does not shine forth in the deeds of the lowly born," rather "it almost always happens that, in the profession of arms as well as in other worthy pursuits, those who are most distinguished are men of noble birth, because nature has implanted in everything that hidden seed which gives a certain force and quality of its own essence to all that springs from it, making it like itself" (1.14; S, 21).

2. Saccone, *"Grazia, Sprezzatura, Affettazione,"* 59–64.

Proust's Swann

"Grazia" first appears in 1.14 about halfway through the chapter, and in the passages that follow I leave it untranslated. The count concedes that if aristocrats lack proper tendance they can go bad, and he also concedes that not every aristocrat is "born endowed with such grazie" as the illustrious don Ippolito da Este, cardinal of Ferrara. This appearance of "grazia" is followed shortly after by another: the cardinal "enjoyed such a happy birth that his person, his appearance, his words, and all his actions are . . . ruled by this grazia." But, he adds, "those who are not so perfectly endowed by nature" with "this excellent grazia . . . can, with care and effort, polish and in great part correct their natural defects. Therefore, besides his noble birth, I would wish the Courtier fortunate in this respect"—fortunate, that is, in having been corrected and polished so that he is "endowed by nature not only with talent and with beauty of countenance and person, but also with a certain grazia and, so to speak, an 'air' [sangue], which shall make him at first sight pleasing and lovable to all who see him; and let this be an adornment informing and attending all his actions, giving the promise outwardly that such a one is worthy of the company [commerzio] and the grazia of every great lord" (1.14; S, 22, slightly altered. See C, 69–70).

"Una certa grazia e, come si dice, un sangue" (C, 70). The formula the count uses three times in 1.14, "una certa forza (dolcezza, grazia)," conveys the sense of the *je ne sais quoi*, the mysterious force or sweetness or grace beyond the reach of art. "Sangue" is a physiognomic term connected with the sanguine complexion in humoral psychology, and it therefore suggests the organic and natural—or, to use the more disenchanted anthropological term, ascribed—basis of grazia. It's obvious that the count wishes to embed grazia securely among the qualities guaranteed by noble birth. Even when common sense forces him to concede that noble birth may require help from art, the prerequisite of noble birth remains standing until the very last clause in the chapter, where it is shaken by a small (but eventually serious) jolt: "tale esser degno del commerzio e grazia d'ogni gran signore" (C, 70). Here, as Charles Singleton's translation makes clear, grazia becomes "favor," and the gift together with the power of giving have been alienated from nature to princes. In addition, although Singleton tames "commerzio" by translating it as "company," the term's other—and etymologically salient—senses (commerce, intercourse, trade, negotiation) inject connotations that threaten the autonomy of the aristocrat's possession of grazia.

With the utterance of this phrase, the count betrays the pressure of contemporary reality on a deeply conservative fantasy in which noble birth as a gift of the fathers is conflated with grazia as (in its Christian context) a gift of the Father. Saccone, who notes that the very first occurrence of "grazia" in 1.1 refers to princely favor, demonstrates how the vertical father/son relation-ship is displaced in the *Cortegiano* to the prince and his courtier, where it is not merely a gratuitous gift but a reward for the lat-ter's "good accomplishments."[3] When Gasparo Pallavicino protests that noble birth isn't essential to noble behavior (1.15), the count is forced into a further concession and another defensive maneu-ver: he grants Gasparo's point and argues that since, therefore, upward mobility is possible, the strategic importance of noble birth increases. First impressions are important, and in the competition between the lowborn and the nobly born the aristocrat gets a head start because public opinion sides with the one who "is known to be of gentle birth" (1.16; S, 23). Whether or not he *is* of noble birth, the point is that he exploits that "knowledge" (= rumor) to reinforce his performance of noble behavior.

Saccone notes the significance of a distinction made at 1.19 by Bernardo Bibbiena "between the 'beauty of [his] person', which he doubts, and 'the grace of countenance' . . . , which, as Canossa declares, 'you can truly be said to have.'"[4] This drives a wedge between the physiognomic signs of inherited quality and the (loosely speaking) pathognomic signs of its manifestation in grazia. At 1.24, however, Cesare Gonzaga reminds the count that since he has often described grazia as "a gift of nature and the heav-ens," it cannot be "in our power to acquire it [acquistarlo] of our-selves," though what we are given we can, if it isn't perfect, improve by *studio e fatica*. This is a crucial intervention: grazia is once again assimilated to noble birth as a gift of the fathers and the Father, not something that can be acquired. Cesare then pops the money question that will elicit from the count his recipe for sprezzatura: "for those who are less endowed by nature and are capable of acquiring grace [poter esser aggraziati] only if they put forth labor, industry, and care, I would wish to know by what art, by what discipline, by what method, they can gain [possono acqis-tar] this grace" (S, 30–31; C, 79).[5]

In Saccone's reading, Cesare's move places the emphasis of the remainder of the discussion on the "Aristotelian middle ground between two exceptional conditions," the "absolute perfection" of those who are "perfectly endowed by nature" and the imperfection

3. Saccone, *"Grazia, Sprezzatura, Affettazione,"* 49.
4. Ibid., 52.
5. To translate "aggraziati" as "acquiring grace" is to make Gonzaga's request more arch and perhaps aggressive than it actually is, and to miss the slight but interesting fluctuation in his request. The passive construction "esser aggraziati" places the emphasis on reception (as of a gift) rather than acquisition, and the crescive implication of "ag-graziati" also works to soften the acquisitive force. Sandwiched between two instances of "acquistare," it helps mark a subtle difference between the implication of the first statement, which is that we can't acquire heavenly gifts by our own power, and that of the second, which is that we can.

of "the absolutely ungifted."[6] But I think it does something more complex and interesting. It relegates the ascriptive ideal of natural perfection to the background as a reality possessed by a lucky few, and leaves it standing *as* a real ideal to be imitated by the less fortunate majority, which may include not only klutzy patricians but also clever arrivistes. To reiterate that grazia is a grace beyond the reach of art just before the account of sprezzatura is to make deficiency in grazia the enabling condition of ideal courtiership. The ideal courtier is not the absolute courtier. The latter is a *rara avis*, though a real one; his *grazia* is fully embodied, "organic," and inalienable, the transcendent state of self-possession to which others may aspire but can never attain. The ideal courtier is being imagined by the interlocutors as a simulacrum necessitated by the failure of the ascriptive ideal, which is also a physiognomic and logocentric ideal. They portray a typified abstraction (a schema, an Idea) that may be copied and copiously replicated in rule-governed acts of reincorporation through which the actors transform faces and bodies into signs of the perfect mental and psychic grace denied them by nature. Sprezzatura is envisaged as the false lookalike that threatens to displace grazia.

It is possible to view the construction of this relation—the relation of the real presence of perfect grace in the absolute courtier to its representation by the ideal courtier—as a symptom of nostalgia. Carol Houlihan Flynn claims that conduct manuals "document nostalgic belief in a 'natural' self that 'ought' to be in harmony with its needs and desires," and they seek "a lost unity of body and soul . . . that could exist only in an Edenic imagination."[7] If she is right about the run of conduct books, the *Cortegiano* is an exception on two counts.

First, as a literary performance it dramatizes and criticizes the impulse to nostalgia: on the one hand it represents itself as the memoir of a better time, a lost golden moment (prefatory epistle and I.2); on the other hand it knowingly criticizes such nostalgic evocations as manifestations of the bitterness of the aged who mourn their lost youth (2.l).

Second, the unattainability of the real presence of grazia provides what, in the contemporary parlance of the image industry, would be called a performance opportunity. But at the same time it guarantees performance anxiety. Not only because the courtier is always per-

---

6. Saccone, *"Grazia, Sprezzatura, Affettazione,"* 50. Saccone somewhat tortuously rationalizes grazia as "a modality, an ability," "a virtue . . . become in itself a habit" (51–52). The point is that what the courtier performs is not grazia in its defined character as a gift of nature or the heavens but its dissimulated specter or eidolon. The ability is at the same time the manifestation of the absence of grace.

7. Carol Flynn, "Defoe's Idea of Conduct: Ideological Fictions and Fictional Reality," in *The Ideology of Conduct*, ed. Nancy Armstrong and Leonard Tennenhouse (New York: Methuen, 1987), p. 73.

forming before an audience composed of performers like himself, and not only because he knows they are performing, and knows they know he is performing. There is also anxiety about the performer's own practice of dissimulation—about his need to keep the performance of naturalness from being spoiled by unwanted leakages of the less ideal nature he is expected to suppress/transcend. The by-product of the courtier's performance is that the achievement of sprezzatura may require him to deny or disparage his nature. In order to internalize the model and enhance himself by art, he may have to evacuate—repress or disown—whatever he finds within himself that doesn't fit the model. This complex set of relations places the new ideal in a revisionary rather than nostalgic relation to the genealogical norm introduced by the count at 1.14 as the traditional wisdom.

Freud

The count's is the opening gambit in a series of dialogical moves that conspicuously exclude the norm from consideration in order to open up the space for the performance that dissimulates it. The conspicuousness of the exclusion is important, as I noted, to keep the unattainable norm in play as a prediscursive reality—a real presence—that validates the discourse of courtiership dedicated to its representation. But equally conspicuous is the emphasis on the difference between the absolute and ideal courtiers, the original and the image. This is registered in 1.24 by Cesare's redundant triplets: "as for those who are less endowed by nature and are capable of being aggraziati only if they put forth labor, industry, and care [fatica, industria e studio], I would wish to know by what art, by what disciplines, by what method [con quale arte, con qual disciplina e con qual modo], they can gain this grace" (S, 30–31; C, 79). The first triplet marks the fall from grace by its focus on uncourtly labor and sweat, but the shift to terms of art in the second triplet marks the beginning of the fantasy of renovatio that will be completed by the disclosure that Cesare's art/discipline/method not only conceals labor/industry/care but also theatrically conceals—displays itself as concealing—itself. Part of the signifying activity of sprezzatura is thus to index a mode of behavioral production that selectively abstracts from, doesn't fully correspond with, what may actually have taken place. Its objective is to edge its performances with some form of indexical refrence to the art and difficulty the conspicuous mastery and transcendence of which gives the ideal its value.

It is, finally, the revelation of this double art, this graceful duplicity, that enables "a gentleman living at the court of princes [in corte de' principi] . . . to serve them in every reasonable thing, thereby winning favor from them [acquistandone da essi grazia] and praise from others" (1.1; S, 9; C, 55). In this, the thesis sentence of the *Cortegiano*, Castiglione draws attention to the challenge, the contingency, the jeopardy to which the art responds by juxtaposing the singular "gentleman" ("gentiluomo") to the plural "princes" ("principi"); "the court of princes" possibly denotes a particular court with a series of princes but more probably it denotes the court as an institution, the instability of which forces the courtier to move from one principality to another. Thus to the traditional validation supplied by the real presence of the absolute courtier's unattainable grace is added the validation of the ideal courtier's political art as a response to the real presence of princes.

*　*　*

VIRGINIA COX

Castiglione's *Cortegiano*: The Dialogue as a Drama of Doubt[†]

*　*　*

More typical of Castiglione's art of dialogue are those long passages in the first two books and the first half, at least, of the fourth, in which a principal speaker who carries the burden of exposition— and whom we might be tempted, lazily, to equate with the author— is harried by a questioner, or a number of questioners and forced to defend his views. It is here, where Castiglione's orchestration of the dialogue is at its most 'cautious', that the potential of the form for dramatizing an 'unfinished' thought is most clearly revealed. And it is here—to be precise, in the first half of the second book of the dialogue—when Federico Fregoso rashly broaches the delicate subject of the courtier's relations with his prince.

The discussion starts with the seemingly uncontroversial statement from Fregoso that the courtier should devote himself, heart and soul, to the duty of pleasing his prince. This may appear innocent enough—after all, the courtier's profession is service—but it is immediately met with an accusation, from a minor speaker, Pietro da Napoli, that the courtier, in that case, will be little more than 'un

---

† From *The Renaissance Dialogue: Literary Dialogue in Its Social and Political Contexts, Castiglione to Galileo* (Cambridge University Press, 1992), pp. 51–58. Reprinted by permission of the publisher.
1. *Il Lilbro del Cortegiano*, ed. Bruno Maier (Torino: UTET, 1964), II xviii (p. 216): [Fregoso] 'Voglio adunque che 'l cortegiano . . . si volti con tutti i pensieri e forze dell'animo suo ad amare e quasi adorare il principe a chi serve sopra ogni altra cosa: e le voglie sue e costumi e modi tutti indrizzi a compiacerlo.' [Pietro da Napoli] 'Di questi

nobile adulatore'.[1] Pietro's objection is swiftly dealt with, and his voice carries little authority, but the mention of flattery leaves an awkward resonance in the discussion. Fregoso's reply shows an awareness of having stumbled onto difficult terrain, when he specifies that, even if it is the courtier's duty to sway in the winds of his master's desires, he should never bend further than the bounds of morality permit.[2] However glancingly, the question of the courtier's moral autonomy from the prince has been raised, and, once raised, the issue proves notably reluctant to lie down.

Not long afterwards, indeed, Vincenzo Calmeta interrupts Fregoso with a point which, if conceded, would call into question the premises on which his whole argument, and the whole dialogue is founded. Fregoso, cautioning the courtier against the appearance of grasping for favours, has just stated that 'per aver . . . favor dai signori, non è miglior via che meritargli'.[3] Calmeta counters that this is simply not the case; that 'l'esperienza ci [fa] molto ben chiari del contrario' and that 'oggidi pochissimi sono favoriti da signori eccetto i prosontuosi.'[4] Taken to its logical conclusion, Calmeta's argument would imply that the courtier should measure his actions not by principle, but by expedience: not by what he knows to be right in the comfortable world of absolutes, but by what he suspects will function best in the imperfect courts of the day.

The implications of Calmeta's line of argument are immediately apparent to Fregoso, even if he attempts to steer the conversation onto less dangerous ground. After a brief comparative detour into the manners of the French and Spanish courts he firmly restates his essential point, that the courtier should always '[tendere] al bene . . . né mai s induca a cercar grazia o favor per via viciosa, né per mezzo di mala sorte.'[5] But Calmeta will not relinquish his point, and, perhaps mindful of his own time in the service of

cortegiani oggidi troverannosi assai, perché mi pare che in poche parole ci abbiate dipinto un nobile adulatore.' [F] 'I would have the courtier dedicate his every thought and his every energy to loving and almost worshipping the prince he serves, above all other things; and that he should calculate all his desires and habits and manners to please the prince.' [P] 'There should be no problem in finding such a courtier in the present times, because it seems to me that you have just sketched us a portrait of a prize flatterer.') Almost nothing is known of Pietro da Napoli, a courtier of Julius II: his only other intervention in the dialogue is a *motto*, in I xlvi. p. 168.

2. *Cortegiano*, II xviii, p. 217: ' . . . 'l compiacere e secondar le voglie di quello a chi si serve si po far senza adulare, perché io intendo delle voglie che siano ragionevoli ed oneste, ovvero di quelle che in sé non sono né bone né male, come saria il giocare, darsi più ad uno esercizio che ad un altro.' ('It is possible to indulge the desires of one's master without being a flatterer, because I am only talking about those desires which are reasonable and decent, or those which are morally indifferent, like a preference for one kind of game or activity over another.')

3. ('There is no surer way to gain princes' favour than to deserve it.') *Cortegiano*, II xx. p. 221.

4. ('Experience shows us very clearly that the contrary is true . . . these days, hardly anyone is favoured by princes, except the most grasping.') *Cortegiano*, II xxi. p. 222.

5. ('The courtier must always be guided by what is right and he must never seek grace or favour by vicious or dishonest means.') *Cortegiano*, II xxi. p. 224.

Cesare Borgia, he insists that a man of such high moral scrupulousness would cut little ice with the princes of the day.[6]

Fregoso responds with a concession, acknowledging, for the first time that unprincipled princes *do* exist, and that the exigencies of service may not always be easily squared with the dictates of conscience. He continues to insist, however, that a prince's vice does not exculpate his henchmen. If a courtier discovers his prince to be 'vicioso e maligno', he should instantly leave his service, rather than compromising an inch.[7] Fregoso's attempt at compromise does not release him from the hook, as Calmeta immediately reminds him of something which Castiglione himself had good reason to know from experience, that leaving one's lord is a risky and difficult business. In Calmeta's grim vision, the courtiers of a prince who turns out to be evil 'sono alla condizion di que' malavventurati uccelli, che nascono in trista valle'.[8]

6. *Cortegiano*, II xxii, p. 224. [Calmeta] 'Io v'assicuro che tutte l'altre vie son molto più dubbiose e più lunghe, che non è questa che voi biasimate; perché oggidì, per replicarlo un'altra vólta, i signori non amano se non que' che son volti a tal camino.' ('I assure you that all other routes [to the prince's favour] are far longer and less direct than the one which you are criticizing [i.e. the 'via viciosa' of Fregoso's speech, cited in my previous note]; because, to repeat it once more, these days, princes have no time for anyone who is not prepared to tread that path.') On Calmeta's somewhat turbulent career, see, besides M. Pieri's entry in the *Dizionario biografico degli italiani*, vol. XXVII, pp. 49–52, Cecil Grayson's introduction to his edition of Calmeta's *Prose e lettere edite e inedite* (Bologna, 1959), esp, pp. xvi–xxii, on his service with Borgia; also pp. xxiv–v and xxviii–ix, on his notorious outspokenness—another biographical detail of obvious relevance to his portrayal in the *Cortegiano*. I find no evidence in the text or outside it to justify Piero Floriani's dismissal of Calmeta's role in the dialogue as that of a 'dispettoso portavoce di qualunquistiche lagnanze cortigiane' (*I gentiluomini letterati*, p. 66); his role is a minor, but by no means an unimportant one, and—very differently from the other figures with whom Floriani groups him, like Morello da Ortona and the Unico Aretino, on whom see below, n. 8—he is taken seriously by the other speakers, and there is no attempt to undermine his authority by deconstructing his motives.

7. *Cortegiano*, II xxii, p. 224. [Fregoso] 'Non dite così . . . perché questo sarebbe troppo chiaro argumento che i signori de' nostri tempi fossero tutti viciosi e mali; il che non è, perché pur se ne trovano alcuni di boni. Ma se 'l nostro cortegiano per sorte sua si troverà essere a servicio d'un che sia vicioso e maligno, sùbito che lo conosca, se ne levi, per non provar quello estremo affanno che senton tutti i boni che serveno ai mali.' ('Do not say that, for to say that would be a clear admission that the princes of our time are all vicious and evil; which is not true, since there are some who are good. But if our courtier should find himself by chance in the service of a vicious and ill-intentioned prince, as soon as he realizes it, he should leave, in order not to suffer that anguish which afflicts any good man who finds himself in the service of the wicked.') The flustered obliqueness of the first sentence of Fregoso's reply is a fine dramatic touch: compare his earlier attempt at the same task of defending modern princes, at the beginning of the chapter (p. 223): 'Non voglio già comportar, messer Vincenzio, che voi questa nota diate ai signori de' nostri tempi; perché pur ancor molti sono che amano la modestia.' ('Messer Vincenzio, I would not have you attach this slur to the princes of our day; for there are many who appreciate modesty in their courtiers.')

8. *Cortegiano*, II xxii, p. 224: [Calmeta] 'Bisogna pregar Dio che ce gli dia boni [signori], perché quando s'hanno è forza patirgli tali, quali sono; perché infiniti rispetti astringono che è gentilomo, poi che ha cominciato a servire ad un patrone, a non lasciarlo; ma la disgrazia consiste nel principio: e sono i cortegiani in questo caso alla condizione di que' malavventurati uccelli, che nascono in trista valle.' ('We must pray God to give us good masters, because once we have them it is necessary to put up with them as they are; because there are countless factors which prevent a gentleman, once he has begun to serve a prince not to leave his service. The mistake is to enter a bad prince's service in the

Fregoso replies doggedly that a man's moral duty should outweigh all other considerations.[9] But he is quickly under attack again, this time from Lodovico Pio, who steps up the tempo of the assault and confronts him with his most difficult question so far. Is the courtier obliged to obey his prince 'in tutte le cose che gli comanda, ancor che fossero disoneste e vituperose'? And if not—if, as the flagging Fregoso claims, 'in cose disoneste non siamo obligati ad ubedire a persona alcuna'—then is the alternative simply to refuse, to his master's face?[1] Is a courtier, realistically, in a position to refuse *anything* to his prince? If the prince whose trust and affection he has laboriously gained should ask him, say, to commit murder, can he be expected to sacrifice the labour of a lifetime by questioning his orders?[2]

Hard-pressed, and with the discussion drifting into dangerously concrete and particularized territory. Fregoso is forced into a position of moral equivocation which skews the *Cortegiano* disconcertingly close to the mood of Machiavelli's *Prince*:

> Voi dovete . . . ubidire al signor vostro in tutte le cose che a lui sono utili ed onorevoli, non in quelle che gli sono di danno e di vergogna . . . *Vero é che molte cose paiono al primo aspetto bone, che sono male, e molte paiono male e pur son bone.* Però è licito talor per servizio de' suoi signori ammazzare non un omo ma dieci milia, e far molte altre cose, le quali, a chi non le considerasse come si dee, pareriano male, e pur non sono.[3]

---

first place; and courtiers in this position are like those unfortunate birds, who are born in an evil vale.') Vittorio Cian, in his commentary on *Il Cortegiano*, 2nd edition (Florence, 1916), p. 170, relates Calmeta's last phrase to a Tuscan proverb, 'trist'a quell'uccellino che nasce in cattiva valle'. For Castiglione's extremely problematic relationship with Francesco Gonzaga, after leaving his service in 1504 for that of Guidobaldo da Montefeltro, see J. R. Woodhouse, *Baldesar Castiglione. A Reassessment of 'The Courtier'* (Edinburgh, 1978), pp. 14–15 and p. 17; also Stephen Kolsky, 'Before the Nunciature: Castiglione in Fact and Fiction,' *Rinascimento*, vol. 29 (1989), pp. 339–40.

9. *Cortegiano*, II xxii, pp. 224–5: [Fregoso] 'A me pare, che 'l debito debba valer più che tutti i rispetti; e purché un gentilomo non lassi il patrone quando fosse in su la guerra o in qualche avversità . . . credo che possa con ragion e debba levarsi da quella servitù, che tra i boni sia per dargli vergogna.' ('It seems to me that duty should outweigh all other considerations; and, as long as a gentleman does not leave his master during a war, or some other calamity . . . I believe that he can legitimately leave a post which would bring him shame in the eyes of right-thinking men, and, indeed, that he should leave it.')

1. *Cortegiano*, II xxiii, p. 225: [Pio] 'Should a courtier obey every command his prince gives him, even if he is ordered to do immoral and reprehensible things?' [Fregoso] 'We are not obliged to obey anyone, where it involves immoral action.'

2. *Cortegiano*, II xxiii, p. 225: [Pio] 'E come, s'io starò al servizio d'um principe il qual mi tratti bene, e si confidi ch'io debba far per lui ciò che far si po, commandandomi ch'io vada ad ammazzare un omo, o far qualsivoglia altra cosa, debbo io rifiutar di farla?'

3. ('You should obey your lord in all those things which will bring him profit and honour, and not in those which will bring him only disadvantage and shame . . . But it is true that there are many things which appear right, at first sight, which are in fact wrong, and many things seem wrong and yet are right. And so it can sometimes be justifiable to kill not one man but ten thousand in the service of one's masters, and to do many other things which, to someone who was not looking at them in the right light, would appear wrong, and yet which are not wrong.') *Cortegiano*, II xxiii, pp. 225–6. For examples, from Castiglione's own career, of the kind of moral problems he may have been thinking of here, see Kolsky, 'Before the Nunciature', pp. 346–7.

The distance Fregoso has travelled from conventional discussions of morality may be gauged by comparing a treatment of the same problem by Castiglione's most significant predecessor in the field of court ethics, the Quattrocento Neapolitan statesman, Diomede Carafa, author of the treatise *Dello optimo cortesano* (1479). Carafa is quite clear that, where there is a conflict of duty and conscience a courtier's first duty is not to the prince, but rather to himself and to God. There is no grey area between good and evil; the best of ends can never justify foul means, since God will never allow good to come from morally dubious actions. Carafa's intransigence on this issue is backed by an optimism about the limits of human evil, which calls to mind Castiglione's comments, in the preface to Book II, on the innocence of fifteenth-century court culture: the prelapsarian naïveté of an era less 'copious in vice' than his own.[4] Carafa concludes that, if the courtier is requested to do something which he finds morally repugnant, he should simply refuse, safe in the knowledge that, even if his prince is momentarily offended by his refusal, he will come round, in the long run, to recognizing and respecting his virtue.[5]

4. See *Cortegiano*, II i–iii, pp. 187–95, esp. p. 191, for the admission that the present age is more 'copiosa di vicii' than that immediate past. Of course, Castiglione's main point in this supremely subtle meditation is that the old are misled by nostalgia in their assessment of the present; and he finishes up by defending his own age as more copious in virtue as well as vice (pp. 191–4). It is important for our interpretation of what follows, in Book II, though, to note that Castiglione does explicitly acknowledge that many of the more serious criticisms leveled at his generation by older men are justified.

5. Diomede Carafa, *Dello optimo cortesano* (1479), ed. G. Paparelli (Salerno, 1971), p. 96: 'Per tueti li modi et vie conosce uno servitore possa fare et dire ben de suo signore lo deve fare; dico siano de natura non sia despregio de Idio lo quale ei primo signore di tucti: et non solamente cosa che se ne offende a Dio non la deve cercare di fare uno servidore per compiacerne nè ad signore nè ad altro, ma quando ce fosse comandata, non la facia; che Idio non permette may bene per fare male . . . Et quando ben a tuo signore li dispiacesse quando non lo facessi, non te ne curare; che repusato lo animo, te tenerà per bono homo et li verrà voglia più farte bene et acomandarte soy cose; che per tristo per sia uno signore li piace soy cose li siano fidelmente tenute.' ('A courtier should employ all the means at his disposal to further his lord's interests; all the means, that is, which do not offend God, who is the supreme Lord of all men. And not only should the courtier never do anything offensive to God of his own accord, in order to please his lord or anyone else, but even if he is commanded to do such a thing, he should not do it; for God never permits good to result from evil-doing. And even if your lord is displeased when you do not obey, you should not be concerned about it, for, when he has calmed down, he will recognize you as an upright man, and will be all the more inclined to favour you and to entrust his affairs to you; for, however wicked a prince may be, he likes his goods to be faithfully administered.') Another interesting point of comparison with Castiglione is Giambattista Giraldi Cinzio's much later *Discorso intorno a quello che si conviene a giovane nobile e ben creato nel servire un gran principe* (1569), recently edited by Walter Moretti as *L'uomo di corte*; see pp. 12–15, esp. p. 13: 'E posto che sia comune opinione che in alcune corti si ritrovino più mali uomini che buoni, e in alquante sia forse cosi in fatto, e si vegga spessissime volte che a questi si diano le dignità e gli onori di maggiore importanza . . . dee nondimeno per ogni modo il Giovane di non essere annoverato fra quelli che malvagi sono tenuti; ma dee egli sempre servare una bontà ferma, salda, costante . . . Perchè, quando il Signore usa del giudicio sano, se per qualche rispetto tolera gli uomini di che abbiam detto, al fine esalta quelli che da ben sono . . . E quando pure delle due cose devesse esser l'una, egli è meglio per la virtù e per la bontà sua ricever qualche dispiacere, che per essere malvagio giungere a qualche grado; perché . . . il vizioso non può esser felice.' ('It is commonly reputed that in some courts there are more evil men than good ones, and it is perhaps true that this is so in certain courts, and that

In contrast with Carafa's calm moral certainties—and his own, earlier intransigence—Fregoso's lapse into relativism has the character of a *volte-face*. But his unexpected concession does not win him the truce that he must have been counting on. He is immediately in trouble once more, this time from Gaspare Pallavicino, the *enfant terrible* of the dialogue, who asks whether he would care to explain how one can tell what is right from what merely appears so. Pallavicino's deceptively ingenuous question points up the depth of the water in which Fregoso is floundering. With no room left for manoeuvre, he is compelled to retreat, and blankly refuses to continue, claiming—quite accurately—that, on this subject, 'troppo saria che dire'.[6]

Fregoso's admission of defeat crowns a long and brilliantly orchestrated sequence of dialogue which has brought theory into awkward juxtaposition with practice, and the comfortably ideal with what Machiavelli would call 'la verità effettuale della cosa'.[7] The sequence concludes when, unable to draw him on the definition of virtue, Pallavicino asks Fregoso the less awkward question of the degree to which the courtier charged with performing some commission on behalf of his prince should feel himself free to disobey the letter, if not the spirit of his master's instructions, if circumstances demand such a change.[8] Fregoso replies that it is best to be cautious, and concludes with a chilling example of what disobedience to one's prince can result in: an anecdote about the Roman consul Publius Crassus Mucianus punishing a subordinate's trivial

---

the highest dignities and honours do go to unprincipled men . . . However, the aspiring courtier should on no account allow himself to be counted with the wicked; rather, he should always maintain a firm, steadfast and constant goodness . . . For, when the Prince is judging soundly, even if, for some reason of the moment, he tolerates the evil men we have been talking about, in the long run, he will favour those who are good . . . And, if it comes down to hard choices, it is better to suffer a setback because of one's virtue and goodness, than to achieve success through evil-doing; because the vicious man can never be truly happy.')

6. *Cortegiano*, II xxiii, p. 226: [Pallavicino] 'Deh, per vostra fé, ragionate un poco sopra questo, ed insegnateci come si possan discerner le cose veramente bone dalle apparenti.' [Fregoso] 'Perdonatemi. . . . io non voglio entrar qua, ché troppo ci saria che dire, ma il tutto si rimetta alla discrezion vostra.'

7. I refer, of course, to Machiavelli's famous statement of intent, at the beginning of his treatment of political ethics, in chapter XV of *The Prince*: see *Il Principe*, in *Opere*, ed. Mario Bonfantini (Milan and Naples, 1954), p. 34. For a deliberately overstated, but thought-provoking 'Machiavellian' reading of Castiglione, see Sydney Anglo, *The Courtier's Art, Systematic Immortality in the Renaissance* (Swansea, 1983).

8. *Cortegiano*, II xxiv, p. 226: [Pallavicino] 'Vorrei sapere, essendomi imposto da un mio signor terminatamente quello ch' io abbia a fare in una impresa o negocio di qualsivoglia sorte, s'io, ritrovandomi in fatto, e parendomi con l'operare più o meno o altrimenti di quello che m'è stato imposto, poter fare succedere la cosa più prosperamente o con più utilità di chi m'ha dato tal carico, debbo io governarmi secondo quella prima norma senza passar i termini del comandamento, o pur far quello che a me pare esser meglio?' ('I should like to know what to do if my lord has given me precise orders about how to perform some kind of enterprise or task, and, when I am on the spot, it strikes me that, by doing something less or something more or something other than what I was told to do, I could bring about a better and more profitable result for the prince who commissioned me. Should I follow instructions, without exceeding my original brief? Or should I do what seems best to me?').

and fully justified modification of his orders by having him savagely beaten to death.[9]

On this note of sour warning, with a relief which transpires from the page, Fregoso is finally free to 'lassar da canto . . . questa pratica de signori.[1] The conclusion of his argument is deliberately ambiguous. If Mucianus' behaviour is typical of the arrogance and brutality of princes, as Fregoso suggests it is,[2] then where does that leave his earlier, optimistic assertion that the courtier will be able to reconcile the imperatives of morality and obedience to his lord? Are we to conclude that Calmeta's jaded vision of courtiership was, after all, the correct one: that the only way to survive in the courts is by relinquishing one's own moral standards?

The text, at this point, can offer no answers, only painful and difficult questions. While we are in no way encouraged to question that Fregoso's initial, 'Carafan' position is the correct one, we are forced to recognize that, in the less than ideal world in which the courtier must operate, to attempt to adhere to such high moral standards may bring about his downfall. The kind of morality which can be conveyed in neat sound-bites of 'precept' will be of little use, it is suggested, in a world in which practice corresponds so woefully little to theory.[3] Where there are no easy answers, an honest moralist should not aim to feed readers with comforting or even Machiavellianly chilling 'precetti distinti', but simply to unfold before them a dialogue between conflicting perspectives, to sharpen their sense of the issues involved and open a space for the exercise of this own moral judgment.

The localized tensions which dog Fregoso during his brief dominance of the discussion in Book II call attention to the structurally similar, but far larger-scale tension between his arguments and those expounded by Count Lodovico da Canossa on the previous day. It is a point worth stressing, as it has been insufficiently recognized by critics, that the perspective of the second book of the treatise is subtly but significantly different from that of the first. Canossa's formation of the courtier, in Book I, rests on the reassuring premise that the means to success in the courts is through virtue: that 'grace' is the surest path into the graces of the prince. The effect of Fregoso's contribution, on the other hand, is to insinuate that all is not as it should be in the courts: that rewards are

9. *Cortegiano*, II xxiv, pp. 226–7.
1. ('leave to one side this problem of how to deal with princes') *Cortegiano*, II xxiii, p. 229.
2. The Mucianus episode is introduced by Fregoso as evidence of the need to adjust one's behaviour to the character of one's prince. If the prince is 'di natura austera', like '*molti che se ne trovano*' (*Cortegiano*, p. 228, my italics), then the courtier would do well to resist any temptation to take an initiative.
3. My allusion here is to the *incipit* of one of Francesco Guicciardini's most-quoted *Ricordi*, number 35: 'Quanto è diversa la practica dalla teorica!' (*Ricordi*, ed. Raffaele Spongano [Florence, 1951], p. 42).

allocated less according to merit than to luck or the whim of the prince, and that the surest means to success may not be so much through 'virtù' as 'ingegno' and 'arte'. If Fregoso finds it so hard to contain the cynical Calmeta, in the passage discussed above, this may be, in part, because his antagonist is doing little more than drawing out to the full the implications of certain tendencies present in his own, far more decorous argument.

Fregoso's brief, in the second book, is to discuss how the courtier should put into action all the numerous qualities and talents Canossa has endowed him with in the first.[4] There is no obvious reason why Fregoso's contribution should do anything but smoothly complement his predecessor's and, indeed, he does all he can, at the start of his speech, to represent what he has to say as no more than an appendix to Canossa's dissertation of the previous night.[5] We should not be fooled by this modesty, however, especially when Fregoso's own analysis of courtly behaviour offers a clue for its deconstruction. When disguising himself at Carnival, Fregoso advises, the courtier should not aim at a strictly accurate imitation, but should leave enough clue to enable his audience to guess at his true identity and to revel in the flatteringly paradoxical relationship between the reality and the mask. Thus, a young man may disguise himself as an old man, a noble as a shepherd in rags. But they should be careful to include some detail calculated to give the game away—the latter, perhaps, by riding a horse which would cost a shepherd his life-savings, the former by letting his youthful physique and bearing give the lie to his grey beard.[6]

Fregoso's 'masking' of his speech as a footnote to Canossa's is similarly disingenuous and it does not take long for the muscle of this thesis to emerge.[7] The point around which his arguments

---

4. Fregoso's precise task, as formulated by Emilia Pio when she gives him the commission, in *Cortegiano*, I lv (pp. 183–4), is to '[dechiarare] in qual modo e maniera e tempo il cortegiano debba usar le sue bone condizioni, ed operar quelle cose che 'l Conte ha detto che se gli convien sapere' ('to explain how and in what manner and when the courtier should put into action all those good qualities of his and all those skills which the Count has said he must acquire').

5. See *Cortegiano*, I lv, p. 184, where Fregoso replies to Emilia Pio's command (cited in the previous note) by claiming that 'volendo voi separare il modo e 'l tempo e la maniera dalle bone condizioni e ben operare del cortegiano, volete separar quello che separar non si po' ('if you propose to separate the question of how and when and in what manner the courtier should use his good qualities from those qualities themselves, then you are trying to separate the inseparable'). Pure and applied courtiership are aspects of the same subject and, by rights, it is Canossa who should continue the discussion. See also II vii (p. 198) for Fregoso's assurance, at the outset of his speech, that 'per farmi participe più ch'io posso della sua laude [di Canossa] . . . non gli contradirò in cosa alcuna' ('in order to assure myself some of the Count's reflected glory . . . I shall not dispute anything he has said').

6. *Cortegiano*, II xi, p. 206.

7. It should be noted that the 'framing' of Fregoso's speech is more complex than I have suggested here. A full analysis would have to take into account other pointers, introduced to counterbalance Fregoso's calculatedly self-deprecating presentation of his contribution: like the preface to his speech by the Duchess—the most authoritative speaker of the

revolve is the need for the courtier to respect the norm of decorum: to calculate his behaviour to accord with the time and the place. This may seem incontestable, even banal, when applied to social accomplishments: as one of Fregoso's listeners contemptuously points out, no one needs to be told not to tell jokes at funerals, or go around dancing the *moresca* in the middle of the street.[8] But the far-reaching, perhaps subversive implications of Fregoso's point becomes clear when—in a splendidly sly exposure of the distance between his perspective and Canossa's—he extends this principle from social skills to the virtues of the soul.

Canossa had identified warfare as the 'principal profession' of the courtier and courage in battle as the virtue most crucial for him to possess.[9] Fregoso concurs with this verdict, referring back explicitly to Canossa's statements, and agrees that, on one level, there is nothing more to be said.[1] However, he adds, in a telling postscript, attention to the rule of decorum could teach the courtier that it would be wise for him to calculate the time and place appropriate to his displays of courage, in order to ensure the maximum return from his investment of virtue.

> Pur sotto la nostra regula si potra ancor intendere, che ritrovandosi il cortegiano nella scaramuzza o fatto d'arme o battaglia di terra o in altre cose tali, dee discretamente procurar di appartarsi dalla moltitudine, e quelle cose segnalate ed ardite che ha da fare, farle con minor compagnia che po, ed al cospetto di tutti i piu nobili ed estimati omini che siano nell'e- sercito, e massimamente alla presenzia e, se possibil è, inanzi agli occhi proprii del suo re o di quel signore a cui serve: per-

---

group, whose interventions are all the more crucial because they are so rare—calling attention to the importance of his task (*Cortegiano*, II v, p. 196). For a methodologically interesting example of how to analyse the 'frames' of the discussion, see Rebhorn, *Courtly Performances*, esp. pp. 177–80 on Ottaviano Fregoso's careful stage-management of his appearance in Book IV.

8. *Cortegiano*, II vi, p. 197. The speaker is the poet and extemporizer Bernardo Accolti, known as the Unico Aretino: a speaker whose dignity has already been subtly undermined in I ix and whose only subsequent appearance of any importance in the dialogue will be in III lx–lxiv, where he came off the worse in a bout of love casuistry with Emilia Pio. The function of Accolti's intervention here—like that of the similarly 'unreliable' Morello da Ortona at II viii (p. 200)—is simply to underline the importance of Fregoso's contribution by offering the latter a pretext for explaining at some length the utility of the rules he is setting out to teach.

9. *Cortegiano*, I xvii, p. 109: [Canossa] 'Estimo che la principale e vera profession del Cortegiano debba esser quella dell'arme: la qual sopra tutto voglio che egli faccia vivamente e sia conosciuto tra gli altri per ardito e sforzato e fidele a chi serve.' ('I consider the courtier's principal and true profession to be that of warfare: and I desire him to cultivate this art above all others and to make a name for himself as daring and bold and faithful to his prince.')

1. *Cortegiano*, II viii, p. 200: [Fregoso] 'Se ben vi ricorda, volse ierisera il Conte che la prima profession del cortegiano fosse quella dell'arme e largamente parlò di che modo far la doveva: però questo non replicaremo più.' ('If you remember, the Count stated last night that the courtier's principal profession was warfare and he spoke at length on how this profession should be practised: so I shall not go over the same ground again.')

ché in vero è ben conveniente valersi delle cose ben fatte. Ed io estimo, che si come è male cercar gloria falsa e di quello che non si merita, cosi sia ancor male defraudar se stesso del debito onore, e non cercarne quella laude, che sola è vero premio delle virtuose fatiche.[2]

The discrepancy between this and Canossa's opinion, in Book I, is so marked that it cannot be anything other than intentional. Fregoso's predecessor had insisted on the need for the courtier to manifest his courage regardless of circumstance: indeed, he had specified that the only men who show the quality of spirit required of the perfect courtier are those who perform acts of courage 'ancor quando pensano di *non esser d'alcuno nè veduti, nè mirati, nè conosciuti*'.[3] What Fregoso is presenting as a gloss on Canossa's teaching on virtue is in fact a full-scale revision. Discretion—in Canossa's sterner judgment, a token of pusillanimity—has become, for Fregoso, something dangerously close to the better part of valour.

The implications of this shift of values is, unsurprisingly, not spelled out in the *Cortegiano*. Fregoso's treatment of the need for flexibility in ethics is as sinuous as the subject demands, and he is quick to backtrack when an interlocutor like Calmeta, in the passage above, incautiously stretches his arguments to their logical conclusions. But, by the end of his contribution, the tendency of his arguments is clear. What, for Canossa, had been intrinsic qualities,

---

2. *Cortegiano*, II viii, pp. 200–1 ('Yet my rule [i.e. the rule of paying attention to time and place] can teach us something new: that, when the courtier finds himself in a skirmish, or a clash or a pitched battle, or something of the sort, he should attempt to withdraw discreetly from the main body of troops and to accomplish those bold and striking deeds he proposes to perform with as little company as possible and within sight of the most noble and respected men in the army and, above all, in the presence of and, if possible, under the very eyes of his king, or the lord he is serving; for it is entirely justified to capitalize on one's good actions. And I consider that, just as it is wrong to seek out false and undeserved glory, it is also wrong to cheat oneself of the honour which is one's due and not to seek out that acclaim which is the only true prize of virtuous deeds.')

3. ('even when they think they are not being watched, or observed, or noticed') *Cortegiano*, I xvii, p. 110: my italics. The point is insisted on throughout the chapter: see, for example, p. 109, where Canossa insists that 'l nome di queste bone condicioni [i.e., courage, daring and loyalty] si acquisterà facendone l'opere in ogni tempo e loco, imperò che non è licito in questo mancar mai, senza biasimo estremo' ('and to gain this reputation, he will need to exercise these qualities in every place and on every occasion, for, where these virtues are concerned, it is impossible to lapse without bringing on oneself the most severe opprobrium'). The distance between Fregoso and Canossa's perspectives is also apparent in their differing views on the wisdom of exercising one's valour in minor skirmishes. Canossa (p. 110) insists that 'molte volte più nelle cose piccole che nelle grandi si conoscono i coraggiosi' ('it is often in minor episodes, rather than major ones, that men's bravery is best judged') and he is disparaging about those who screw their courage to the sticking-point for major actions, but 'nelle cose che poco premono e dove par che possano senza esser notati restar di mettersi a pericolo, volentier si lasciano acconciare al sicuro' ('in unimportant matters, when they feel they can avoid exposing themselves to danger without it being noticed, thankfully remain in safety'). Fregoso, on the other hand, is almost equally disparaging about soldiers he has known who 'metteano la vita a pericolo per andar a pigliar una mandra di pecore, come per esser i primi che montassero le mura d'una terra' ('put their lives at risk as willingly to capture a herd of sheep as to be among the first to scale the walls of a besieged town') (p. 201).

rooted in the soul of the courtier, Fregoso, in the course of Book II, gradually but inexorably uproots.

   The premise of Canossa's argument, in Book I, had been that virtue brings its due reward, that—as he asserts with a neat etymological legerdemain Fregoso later takes pleasure in exposing—'chi ha grazia quello è grato'. Fregoso is less optimistic. Social success depends crucially on the perceptions of those around us and human perceptions are notoriously fickle and subject to distortion. It by no means follows that, just because a courtier possesses the qualities Canossa has allotted to him, he will necessarily win the applause and promotion he deserves. Indeed, the contrary may occur:

> Ma perché par che la fortuna, come in molte altre cose, così ancor abbia grandissima forza nelle opinioni degli omini, vedesi talor che un gentilomo, per ben condizionato che egli sia e *dotato di molte grazie, sarà poco grato* ad un signore e, come si dice, non gli arà sangue, e questo senza causa alcuna che si possa comprendere [. . .] e da questo nascerà che gli altri subito s'accommodaranno alla volontà del signore [. . .] di sorta che, se fosse il più valoroso uomo del mondo, sarà forza che resti impedito e burlato. E per contrario se 'l principe si mostrarà inclinato ad un ignorantissimo, che non sappia né dir né far, saranno spesso i costumi e modi di quello, per sciocchi ed inetti che siano, laudati con le esclamazioni e stupore da ognuno, e parerà che tutta la corte lo ammiri ed osservi . . . [4]

The implications of this admission are far-reaching. Once it is accepted that there is no automatic link between virtue and its reward, then it becomes possible—and perhaps necessary—to construct an alternative, parallel art of behaviour, addressed specifically to the problem of how to please an audience. 'Oltre al valore', as Fregoso concludes the passage cited above 'voglio che 'l nostro cortegiano . . . s'aiuti ancora con ingegno ed arte'.[5] The way to achieve social success becomes not to improve the intrinsic quality of the product—the self—but rather to learn to package and market it more effectively.

Perhaps the best way of defining what takes place in Book II of the *Cortegiano* is as a *rhetoricization* of ethics. An essential element in

---

4. ('But because fortune holds sway over men's judgment, as over so many other things, it sometimes happens that a gentleman, for all his fine accomplishments and pleasing graces, may not please his prince; that, for no discernible reason, they will simply not, as people say, "hit it off". And, since all the other courtiers will go along with the prince's judgment, this means that he will get nowhere and become a figure of fun, even if he is the worthiest man in the world. And, on the contrary, if the prince happens to take to some clumsy and inarticulate imbecile, his manners, however stupid and awkward, will often start attracting extravagant praise from all around him, and the entire court will admire and respect him.') *Cortegiano*, II xxxii, pp. 240–1.
5. ('Besides his actual worth, I would have the courtier draw on his wits and his skill.')

classical rhetoric—one increasingly stressed in the Renaissance—
was the skill of 'accommodating' one's language and *ethos* to appeal to
a particular audience. What Fregoso does, in Book II of the *Cortegiano*, is to apply this rhetorical paradigm beyond speech to realms of
human behaviour traditionally governed by ethics. When the courtier
is advised to accommodate his discourse to the different audiences
he may find himself speaking to, we are still safely within the bounds
of classical rhetorical theory. But when he is told to adjust his *behaviour* to his audience—say, to hold back in battle when no-one is
watching—this introduces a kind of slippage, a destabilization of
ethics which, as is plain from the dispute discussed above, between
Fregoso and Calmeta, could have dangerous results.

An accusation frequently levelled at rhetoric, from Plato onwards,
has been that of providing equally powerful support for the false and
the true. If rhetoric—at least in its sophistic and Aristotelian
guise—is a morally neutral art of discourse,[6] so Fregoso's 'rhetori-
cized ethics' comes dangerously close to providing a morally neutral
science of human behaviour, in which virtue is effectively replaced
by the ability to simulate virtue. It never quite comes to this, of
course: Fregoso continues to insist, like his predecessor, that the
courtier should actually *be* virtuous, as well as appearing so. But his
emphasis on techniques of manipulating appearances is such that,
without compromising himself, he provides all the necessary hints
for one less scrupulous than himself—a Machiavelli, or a Iago—to
develop into a fully-fledged art of simulation.[7]

It would be impossible, in the present context, to follow Fregoso's
argument in Book II through all its intricately dramatized sequence
of feelers and feints and retractions. The point it is essential to
stress here is that Fregoso's contribution, replying at a discreet distance to Canossa's, fulfils precisely the same function within the
macrostructure of the *Cortegiano*, as the more telling and least
manageable interjections of the minor speakers have in the
microstructure of individual discussions. Fregoso's implicit critique
of Canossa casts a veil of doubt over his predecessor's arguments,
without definitively invalidating or superseding them. The two perspectives on behaviour embodied by Canossa and Fregoso are jux-

6. On the debate on the moral status of rhetoric in classical and Renaissance culture, see
   my 'Rhetoric and Politics in Tasso's "Nifo"', *Studi secenteschi* 30 (1989), pp. 81–3, and
   the bibliography cited there.
7. The moral dangers involved in Fregoso's recommendation that the courtier should cultivate appearances are dramatized in the discussion: see, for example, *Cortegiano*, II
   xxvii–xxviii, pp. 232–4, where Fregoso's contention that 'le cose estrinseche spesso fan
   testimonio delle intrinseche' ('outward things are often a testimony to what is inside') is
   contested by Gaspare Pallavicino and Cesare Gonzaga; also II xl, p. 252, where
   Pallavicino responds to Fregoso's teachings on the art of cultivating an image that 'questa
   a me non par arte ma vero inganno: né credo io che si convenga, a chi vuol esser omo da
   bene, mai lo ingannare' ('this sounds to me less like art than outright deception; and I do
   not believe that a decent and upright man should ever stoop to deceit').

taposed, unreconciled: in dialogue. It is only outside the text, in the mind of the reader, that a possible synthesis can be found.

* * *

DANIEL JAVITCH

Il Cortegiano and the Constraints of Despotism[†]

> *When I was young, I used to scoff at knowing how to play, dance, and sing, and other such frivolities. I even made light of good penmanship, knowing how to ride, to dress well, and all those things that seem more decorative than substantial in a man. But later, I wished I had not done so. For although it is not wise to spend too much time cultivating the young toward the perfection of these arts, I have nevertheless seen from experience that these ornaments and accomplishments lend dignity and reputation even to men of good rank. It may even be said that whoever lacks them lacks something important. Moreover, skill in this sort of entertainment opens the way to the favor of princes, and sometimes becomes the beginning or the reason for great profit and high honors. For the world and princes are no longer made as they should be, but as they are.*
>
> —Francesco Guicciardini, *Ricordi* (1530)

One of the chief novelties of the *Cortegiano*, and a basic reason for its tremendous fortune in the sixteenth century, is that it set forth an art of conduct tailored to the social and political exigencies of Renaissance despotism. This pragmatic and forward-looking aspect of Castiglione's code has been obscured by modern commentators who have tended to dwell on the book's idealistic, escapist, and nostalgic features.[1] To be sure, the game of fashion-

---

[†] From *Castiglione: The Ideal and the Real in Renaissance Culture*, ed. Robert W. Hanning and David Rosand (New Haven and London: Yale University Press, 1983), pp. 17–28. Copyright © 1983 by Yale University. Reprinted by permission of the publisher.

1. For an exaggerated and polemical account of Castiglione's escapist idealism, see Giuseppe Prezzolini's introduction to his edition of B. Castiglione—G. Della Casa, *Opere* (Milan and Rome, 1937). Similar, if less extreme, claims that Castiglione's ideal is divorced from reality recur in modern discussions of the *Cortegiano*, especially whenever it is compared with Machiavelli's *Principe*. Among interpretations that emphasize the work's elegiac or nostalgic character, see Giuseppe Toffanin, *Il "Cortegiano" nella trattatistica del Rinascimento* (Naples, 1960?), pp. 37–39, and, more recently, Wayne Rebhorn, *Courtly Performances: Masking and Festivity in Castiglione's Book of the Courtier* (Detroit, 1978), especially pp. 91–115.

In my *Poetry and Courtliness in Renaissance England* (Princeton, 1978) I have already proposed that the pressures of Renaissance despotism shaped the behavior of Castiglione's ideal courtier, but after reconsidering my discussion of the *Cortegiano* in that earlier study (see pp. 18–49) I felt that it needed this supplementary essay to demonstrate more precisely and more emphatically the extent to which Castiglione's norms of conduct are determined by these political pressures.

ing a perfect courtier that constitutes the book allows Castiglione's speakers to fabricate a composite ideal that, at best, can only be partly approximated in actual society. But even though this game permits its participants to ignore many claims of daily existence, Castiglione's speakers rarely disregard the real constraints of the autocratic political order to which the courtier belongs. As I want to show in the following observations, the proper conduct they recommend reveals their full awareness that the model individual they fashion has to depend on his ruler's favor for his existence and that his prime objective, therefore, is to secure or preserve such favor.

The pragmatism of the *Cortegiano* can be more fully appreciated once it is recognized that Castiglione's speakers *cloak* the fact that the pressures of autocratic rule shape the norms of conduct they advocate. Until Federico Fregoso mentions it on the second evening of discussion, it is left to be assumed that the courtier has to "devote all his thought and strength of spirit to loving and almost adoring the prince he serves above all else, devoting his every desire and habit and manner to pleasing him" (2.18). And except for Federico's brief treatment of the matter (2.18–20), the speakers give no explicit consideration to the courtier's subservient duties as prince pleaser—despite their paramount importance. Ludovico da Canossa points out near the beginning of his talk that *grazia* must be "an adornment informing and attending all his actions" in order for the courtier to show himself "worthy of the company and the favor of every great lord" (1.14). But it is virtually the only time he indicates that the courtier's graceful self-display is primarily intended to win the prince's approbation. In general, when Castiglione's speakers recommend various stylistic attributes that the courtier must possess, they rarely, if ever, point out that these attributes are especially desirable because they are pleasing to the prince. One might think that they, not their sovereign, are the principal arbiters of graceful conduct at court. This deceptive impression is further reinforced, of course, by the absence of Urbino's ruler, Duke Guidobaldo, from the parlor game taking place in his palace. Appearances to the contrary, however, the ruler is not excluded from the conversations at Urbino: Castiglione's speakers obfuscate but never ignore the prince's decisive influence while they fashion their model individual. For if we consider some of the courtier's principal stylistic attributes and try to establish why they are valued, it gradually becomes apparent that these attributes are not simply advocated because they appeal to the social and esthetic tastes of a courtly elite but, more importantly, because they are necessary and effective means of maintaining a favorable relationship with the prince.

Consider an attribute such as *mediocrità*, the difficult moderation deemed so graceful an aspect of the courtier's style and personality. Basically, *mediocrità* consists of balancing with their opposites predominant traits determined by habit, inclination, office, age, or state of mind. For instance, older men display it when they temper their gravity with lighthearted wit, younger ones when they balance their boisterousness with sober calm. So, *mediocrità* can be achieved by moderating seriousness with jest, pride or presumption with modesty, fervor with detachment, or exhibitionism with reticence. Because this requires the individual to behave in ways contrary to his natural inclinations, or to disguise innate tendencies with their opposites, *mediocrità* calls for enormous flexibility. Castiglione's speakers stipulate that the courtier display this flexibility in his opinions and attitudes as well as in his external behavior. Exemplified by Ludovico da Canossa in the course of the debates he provokes in book 1, the tempered style demands that the courtier be ready not only to concede the validity of views contrary to his own but also to moderate his beliefs so that they will accommodate contrary views.

As Castiglione portrays them, the courtiers at Urbino show little tolerance for earnest partisanship or single-mindedness of any kind, but prize, instead, flexibility and even paradox in demeanor and points of view. It is consistent, therefore, that they should advocate and value *mediocrità*. Moreover, the claims of politeness and deference that are shown to prevail in courtly company—and made all the more pronounced by the presence and participation of women—demand the balanced restraint and flexible accommodation that define mediocrità. But the main reason for possessing such moderation and flexibility—namely, that the courtier has to master *mediocrità* to win or retain the favor of his ruler—remains virtually unstated by the discussants. Unyielding tenacity on the part of a courtier may provoke criticism and mockery from his equals, but what inhibits such obstinate behavior even more is that the prince will simply not tolerate it in his subordinates. Conversely, the courtier's elasticity may win admiration among his peers but he has to possess it primarily because, as companion and servant of his ruler, he must always be ready to accommodate himself to the latter's changing and unpredictable whims. I maintained earlier that the company at Urbino devotes little specific discussion to the courtier's ingratiating conduct in the company and service of his sovereign. However, when Federico Fregoso does offer some brief advice on the subject (2.18–20), pliability is the first quality he recommends for maintaining a good relationship with the ruler. Federico proposes that the courtier must always be ready to accommodate his ruler's wishes for playful diversions. "Ed a questo voglio," he explains, che il cortegiano *si accomodi, se ben da natura sua vi fosse alieno*, di modo che, sempre che 'l signore lo vegga, pensi che a parlar gli abbia di cosa che gli sia grata; il che interverrà, se in costui sarà il bon giudicio per conoscere ciò che piace al principe, e lo ingegno e la prudenzia *per sapersegli accommodare, e la deliberata voluntà per farsi piacer quello che forse da natura gli despiacesse*. [2.18, italics mine]

[And I would have our Courtier *bend himself to this, even if by nature he is alien to it*, so that his prince cannot see him without feeling that he must have something pleasant to say to him; which will come about if he has the good judgment to perceive what his prince likes, and the wit and prudence *to bend himself to this, and the considered resolve to like what by nature he may possibly dislike*. . . .]

Mediocrità, as I said, calls upon the individual to perform in ways contrary to his natural inclinations. But until Federico offers the above advice, one might forget how indispensable this quality becomes in the company of the rulers and, hence, a main reason for valuing it as a courtly attribute. So, when Federico goes on to warn against presumption and obstinacy in conversations with the prince, one more fully realizes that unyielding single-mindedness is deemed undesirable not only because it violates the *mediocrità* required in polite company but because it is bound to alienate the prince.

Federico's discussion of the courtier's proper relationship with the ruler does not last very long. Still, it suffices to help the modern reader recognize that political motives underlie most of the courtier's beautiful stratagems. For instance, Federico goes on to stipulate that

se 'l cortegiano, consueto di trattar cose importanti, si ritrova poi secretamente in camera, dee vestirsi un'altra persona, e differir le cose severe ad altro loco e tempo ed attendere a ragionamenti piacevoli e grati al signor suo, per non impedirgli quel riposo d'animo. [2.19]

[if a Courtier who is accustomed to handling affairs of importance should happen to be in private with his lord, he must become another person, and lay aside grave matters for another time and place, and engage in conversation that will be amusing and pleasant to his lord, so as not to prevent him from gaining such relaxation.]

One is led to suppose, before this brief directive, that the ability to shift from gravity to facetiousness, or to embody them simultaneously, is an aspect of *mediocrità* desired by the courtiers as a group rather than by the ruler dominating the group. Certainly Urbino's courtiers display a marked intolerance of unrelieved seriousness. Given their admiration of the individual's capacity to embody opposites, they consider it much more graceful to blend seriousness with levity. From their point of view this blend does not jeopardize serious intention but rather makes it more attractive. In fact, the very activity engaging them as a group—fashioning an ideal of civilized man while playing a parlor game—serves to exemplify the *serio ludere* they consider so attractive an aspect of the courtier's tempered style. Yet, again, as Federico's above directive indicates, it is primarily in order to relieve and delight his prince that the courtier must know how to offset gravity with play. Norms of elegance at court may well call for an ability to treat serious matters playfully, but more essential for the courtier's social and political survival is the fact that this ability can serve to enhance his relationship with this ruler. Similarly, because the courtier wins admiration among his equals by balancing seriousness with jest, one can understand why so much discussion is devoted to the means and range of joking at the end of book 2. But if one keeps in mind the courtier's duty to engage in "ragionamenti piacevoli e grati al signor suo," it becomes even clearer why the capacity to raise laughter has to be one of his necessary talents. In general, it is because the ruler's favor or assent can be won more easily by appealing to his pleasurable instincts that the courtier must possess and develop artistic and recreative skills.

Federico devotes most of his brief account of the courtier's relationship with his prince to proper ways of suing for favors. The courtier, he warns, must particularly avoid aggressive or importunate solicitation. He must wait

> che i favori gli siano offerti, più presto che uccellargli così scopertamente come fan molti, che tanto avidi ne sono, che pare che, non conseguendogli, abbiano da perder la vita. (2.19)

> [until favors are offered to him rather than fish for them openly as many do, who are so avid of them that it seems they would die if they did not get them.]

Modest but studied reticence, on the other hand, will prove much more effective in obtaining princely rewards:

> Dee ben l'omo star sempre un poco più rimesso che non comporta il grado suo; e non accettar così facilmente i favori ed onori che gli sono offerti, e rifutargli modestamente, mostrando estimargli assai, con tal modo però, che dia occasione a chi gli offerisce d'offerirgli con molto maggior instanzia; perché quanto più resistenzia con tal modo s'usa nello accettargli, tanto più pare a quel principe che gli concede d'esser estimato. . . . (2.19)

[A man ought always to be a little more humble than his rank
would require; not accepting too readily the favors and honors
that are offered him, but modestly refusing them while showing that he esteems them highly, yet in such a way as to give the
donor cause to press them upon him the more urgently. For
the greater the resistance shown in accepting them in this
way, the more will the prince who is granting them think himself to be esteemed.]

Prescriptive comments made earlier in the book already establish
the comeliness of ironic reticence and studied indirection. But it
takes Federico's directives to remind us when and how the courtier's
sprezzatura and *disinvoltura* can be put to most effective use. His
recommendations serve to remind us, moreover, that fierce competition for favors is a pressing and an ever present condition of
courtly existence. Again, this constant rivalry for preferment is left
to be inferred in previous conversations. For example, when
Ludovico da Canossa initially recommends that the courtier "put
every effort and diligence into outstripping others in everything a little, so that he may be always recognized as better than the rest"
(1.21), he neglects to mention that such competitiveness is
prompted by the need to impress the ruler and thereby win his
preferment. To be sure, the ruler's desire to keep his subordinates
in check, as well as the court's standards of polite refinement, com-
pel its members to subdue or at least mask their aggressive and
competitive drives. That is why such qualities as reticence, detachment, and understatement are so valued at court. Castiglione's
speakers repeatedly suggest that the more sprezzatura and disinvoltura the courtier displays when disguising his efforts at outperforming others, the more admiration he will win from his peers. For
instance, on an earlier occasion, when Federico speaks of the
courtier's musical skills, he says,

> Venga adunque il cortegiano a far musica come a cosa per pas-
> sar tempo e quasi sforzato; . . . e benché sappia ed intenda
> ciò che fa, in questo ancor voglio che dissimuli il studio e la fat-
> ica che è necessaria in tutte le cose che si hanno a far bene, e
> mostri estimar poco in se stesso questa condizione, ma, col
> farla eccellentemente, la faccia estimar assai dagli altri. (2.12)

> [Let the Courtier turn to music as to a pastime, and as though
> forced. . . . And although he may know and understand
> what he does, in this also I would have him dissimulate the
> care and effort that is required in doing anything well; and let
> him appear to esteem but little this accomplishment of his,
> yet by performing it excellently well, make others esteem it
> highly.]

Such displays of *sprezzatura*, however, are not simply recommended to the courtier because they will delight his peers. It must be kept in mind that the courtier exhibits his various skills in order to impress his sovereign and win his good graces. His displays of virtuosity are, in effect, bids for preferment and, just like his actual requests for favor, they are likelier to be effective when disguised by apparent reticence and nonchalance. As Federico subsequently makes clear, the prince's intolerance of presumptuous self-promotion on the part of his suitors makes it particularly important to master *sprezzatura* and *disinvoltura*. The deference, moreover, that the courtier must show in the presence of his ruler demands that he veil and underplay his various talents in order not to outshine his superior. Too open a display of his skills or virtues might expose by contrast his sovereign's lack of such qualities, thereby calling into question a supremacy that the courtier cannot afford to challenge. Furthermore, when one keeps in mind how unpredictable and whimsical the sovereign's bestowal of grace can be, the need for *sprezzatura* and *disinvoltura* becomes all the more apparent. Despite his real merits, however appealing his prince-pleasing stratagems, the courtier can never be sure to obtain his patron's grace and favor. He always faces the risk that, for reasons beyond his control, the efforts he exerts to gain such favor will be ignored or discounted. His ability therefore to disguise and minimize such efforts when outperforming others becomes indispensable if he is to avoid losing face and status whenever these efforts fail or are simply unacknowledged by his ruler.

Indirection is so prized in the courtier's world, and obviousness so unseemly, that dissimulation has to characterize most aspects of his conduct. *Sprezzatura*, considered one of the chief sources of *grazia*, always requires deliberate subterfuge because in entails making artifice seem natural, studied effort seem easy and casual. Even *mediocrità* is deceptive because it often demands that the courtier consciously disguise a particular disposition by cultivating an appearance of its contrary. In general, the courtier's conduct is deemed most graceful when it is most ironic, when his actions or stances subtly imply their opposites. Why do the courtiers at Urbino prize such discrepancy between being and seeming? Or conversely, why do they show such distaste for plain and perspicuous conduct? Sheer esthetic preference aside, it seems very consistent that an aristocratic elite, seeking to exclude all but a privileged few, should cherish and promote all ornamental behavior or discourse that refines, obscures, and even defies common usage. Castiglione's speakers repeatedly indicate that the pleasure derived from the covert and ironic guises they recommend will escape individuals of plainer and therefore baser taste. To some extent, then, the courtier's tactics of indirection and deception are ploys by which he asserts his social superiority and refinement. But to an equal, if not greater extent, these ploys are conditioned by the prudential relation he must maintain with his sovereign and even his peers. Transactions with a despotic ruler require ingratiating deceit. Again, lest we might forget, Federico's directives on currying favors from the prince remind us how ineffective and risky undisguised truth can be at court. Federico tells the courtier:

> Rarissime volte o quasi mai non domanderà al signore cosa alcuna per se stesso, acciò che quel signor, avendo rispetto di negarla così a lui stesso, talor non la conceda con fastidio, che è molto peggio. Domandando ancor per altri, osserverà discretamente i tempi; . . . ed assetterà talmente la petizion sua, levandone quelle parti che esso conoscerà poter dispiacere e facilitando con destrezza le difficultà, che 'l signor la concederà sempre, o se pur la negarà, non crederà aver offeso colui a chi non ha voluto compiacere. (2.18)

> [Rarely or almost never will he ask of his lord anything for himself, lest his lord, not wishing to deny it to him directly, should perchance grant it to him with ill grace, which is much worse. And when asking something for others, he will be discreet in choosing the occasion; . . . and he will so frame his request, omitting those parts that he knows can cause displeasure, and will skillfully make easy the difficult points, so that his lord will always grant it, or do this in such wise that, should he deny it, he will not think the person whom he has thus not wished to favor goes off offended.]

Obviously, a relation that calls for this kind of obfuscation would only be jeopardized if the courtier chose to be plain and direct with his master. As Ottaviano remarks on a later occasion, "If I had the favor of some of the princes I know, and if I were to tell them freely what I think, I fear I should soon lose that favor" (4.26). The courtier, such observations make apparent, inhabits a world where graceful deceit is not only valued for its intrinsic delight but because the despot who governs that world makes it imperative.

The ties between the courtier's ingratiating deceits and the exigencies of despotic rule are finally made explicit on the last evening of discussion, when Ottaviano Fregoso takes his turn as main speaker. Ottaviano attempts, it will be recalled, to transform the model courtier from the beautiful parasite he thinks his colleagues have fashioned into a moral counselor of the prince. However, he is sagacious enough to recognize that modern princes, accustomed to the fawning ways of their servants, would react most adversely if they had to countenance the "orrida faccia della vera virtù." So even though he considers insufficient the graceful style and accomplishments the other speakers have prescribed, he realizes that without them the courtier would be quite unable to exert any moral influence on his prince. As he laments,

> Poiche oggidì i principi son tanto corrotti dalle male consuetudini e dalla ignoranzia e falsa persuasione di se stessi, e che tanto è difficile il dar loro notizia della verità ed indurgli alla virtù, e che gli omini con le bugie ed adulazioni e con così viciosi modi cercano d'entrar loro in grazia, il cortegiano, per mezzo di quelle gentil qualità che date gli hanno il conte Ludovico e messer Federico, po facilmente e deve procurar d'acquistarsi la benivolenzia ed adescar tanto l'animo del suo principe. (4.9)

> [Since the princes of today are so corrupted by evil customs and by ignorance and a false esteem of themselves, and since it is so difficult to show them the truth and lead them to virtue, and since men seek to gain their favor by means of lies and flatteries and such vicious ways—the Courtier, through those fair qualities that Count Ludovico and messer Federico have given him, can easily, and must, seek to gain the good will and captivate the mind of his prince.]

And he goes on to stipulate that the courtier use his beautiful and ingratiating talents as a "salutary deception" by means of which he can edify his sovereign (4.10). However idealistic the courtier may be, Ottaviano recognizes that dissimulation must remain his most characteristic habit of style. Eventually Ottaviano's attempt to transform the courtier into a didactic agent becomes too unrealistic, but even when he is carried away by his own moral fervor he remains aware that, given the fallibility of princes, didactic persuasion demands even more guileful subterfuge than the courtier's other rhetorical intents.

Ottaviano displays exemplary *mediocrità* when he tempers his idealism and acknowledges that the courtier's likelihood of edifying his sovereign depends on the cunning and deceit he is previously asked to cultivate. Although he is more idealistic than the previous speakers, he reveals the pragmatism that he shares with them by acknowledging more openly than they do that the political pressures of an autocratic order make necessary the artful behavior advocated in the book. On the other hand, his more open recognition of such political exigencies entails, as we can see, a criticism of modern princes that such despots would find intolerable to hear. This undisguised criticism makes us aware, in retrospect, of why speakers such as Ludovico and Federico are relatively silent about the political constraints that shape their stylistic prescriptions—for the very same reasons that they stipulate indirection and subterfuge. To point out the unpleasant realities of despotic rule that determine their norms of conduct would contradict the prudential cunning they recommend. In other words, by so often leaving us to construe that their primary objective is to fashion a cunning prince pleaser, they exemplify the covertness that must perforce be practiced under princely rule. This deliberate resemblance between the speakers' conduct and the graceful manners they advocate was, of course, Castiglione's own subtle way of commemorating the civilized refinement that he had seen achieved at Urbino. For it showed that the behavior of its courtiers in reality could approximate an ideal of courtiership imagined in a game.

As I have tried to show, however implicit they remain for most of the book, the constraints of an autocratic order shape the art of conduct set forth in Castiglione's book. The *Cortegiano* is, in effect, an art of prince pleasing since virtually every beautiful attribute the courtier is asked to cultivate can be successfully used to win the good will of a sovereign or to preserve it. This pragmatic aspect of the book needs to be emphasized, if only to explain the tremendous success of the *Cortegiano* in Renaissance Europe. We, as modern readers, may feel dismayed by the growing sense that most of the beautiful manners advocated in the book are made necessary by the loss of sincerity and free expression, by the sycophancy and servitude that individuals are made to bear in a despotic political system. Yet in the sixteenth century, when autocratic rule gained such ascendance in Europe, when despotic courts became the centers of power and fashion, was it not precisely because Castiglione provided an ideal of artful behavior tailored to suit the dictates of such institutions that readers found his book so pertinent and instructive?

EDUARDO SACCONE

The Portrait of the Courtier in Castiglione†

The title of this paper reflects, as it happens, only in a general and rather undetermined (but perhaps also overdetermined) way my actual concern with Baldesar Castiglione's text. The important word is, of course, "portrait." But how is it to be taken? First of all, I hasten to say, as a quotation: from the preface to the book, the dedica-

† From *Italica* 64 (1987): 1–10. Reprinted by permission of the American Association of Teachers of Italian.

tory letter to Don Michel de Silva, "the Reverend and Illustrious Signor Don Michel de Silva, Bishop of Viseu." It is there that the author, after briefly narrating the circumstances of the composition of his work and those that have led him to publish it, tells the bishop how in rereading it he was "seized by no little sadness (which greatly grew as I proceeded), when I remembered that the greater part of those persons who are introduced in the conversations were already dead."[1] And here a long list follows: "messer Alfonso Ariosto, to whom the book is dedicated, is dead"; "likewise Duke Giuliano de' Medici, whose goodness and noble courtesy deserved to be enjoyed longer by the world. Messer Bernardo [Bibbiena], Cardinal of Santa Maria in Pòrtico, who for his keen and entertaining readiness of wit was the delight of all who knew him, he too is dead." And dead also is Ottaviano Fregoso; "dead, too, are many others named in the book, to whom nature seemed to promise very long life. But what should not be told without tears is that the Duchess, too, is dead" (4). It is, Castiglione adds, with the mind "troubled at the loss of so many friends and lords, who have left me in this life as in a desert full of woes," that he has decided not to delay any longer paying what he owes (*a pagar quello, che io debbo*) to the memory of the Duchess, and earlier to the memory of Duke Guidobaldo, and, of course, to that of the others who are no more; and to publish the book, which he is now sending to the bishop of Viseu:

> And since, while they lived, you did not know the Duchess or the others who are dead (except Duke Giuliano and the Cardinal of Santa Maria in Pòrtico), in order to make you acquainted with them, in so far as I can, after their death, I send you this book as a portrait of the Court of Urbino, not by the hand of Raphael or Michelangelo, but by that of a lowly painter and one who only knows how to draw the main lines, without adorning the truth with pretty colors or making, by perspective art, that which is not seem to be (4).

"As a portrait," *come un ritratto di pittura.* Much, indeed, too much, has been made, particularly in recent years, of this characterization. I have specifically in mind a book by Wayne A. Rebhorn, *Courtly Performances: Masking and Festivity in Castiglione's "Book of the Courtier"* (Detroit: Wayne State UP, 1978), and some of the essays gathered by Robert W. Hanning and David Rosand in their *Castiglione. The Ideal and the Real in Renaissance Culture* (New Haven: Yale UP, 1983), and, for example, the ones written by the editors themselves: Rosand's "The Portrait, the Courtier, and

1. Baldesar Castiglione, *The Book of the Courtier*, trans. Charles S. Singleton (Garden City, N.Y.: Anchor Books, 1959) 3. All quotations will be from this edition; page numbers to the Norton Critical Edition will be given in the text.

Death," and Hanning's "Castiglione's Verbal Portrait: Structures and Strategies." But their ideas are shared, and have been shared in the past, by a good number of readers, and they substantially amount to stressing on the one hand the literality of the portrait, "representing the image of a society described in all its complexity, with all its ambiguities and contradictions," to repeat Rosand's words.[2] An idealized image, to be sure, "the ideal, timeless portrait of themselves that the courtiers of Urbino collectively fabricate," as Hanning writes[3]—a portrait that is "analogous to and rivaling that of a certain type of narrative painting (*istoria*) practiced by his contemporaries" (and this is Rebhorn summarized by Hanning).[4] On the other hand, the elegiac and nostalgic element of this 'portrait' is emphasized and its "major . . . function" described as "commemorative" the *Book of the Courtier* is finally presented as "the preservation of a social memory,"[5] "the record of a vanished world";[6] its art as "a commemorative art that claims to evoke the dead, to substitute itself for life."[7] A good and obvious, even too obvious instance of humanistic art: an art, that is, that "tries to reconcile in creative tension what is held to be unreconcilable." These last words are from Louise George Clubb's essay, "Castiglione's Humanistic Art and Renaissance Drama," included in the same collection published by Yale UP and quoted approvingly by Hanning.[8]

It is not that I do not believe in some of what is said by these critics; what I object to, however, is the absence of certain important distinctions, which, if not made, risk making the whole picture of the text not only messy but false. Let me move immediately to another moment of the text, in Book I, when the decision is taken by Emilia Pia, approved by the Duchess, to accept the game proposed by messer Federico Fregoso, i.e., that "one of this company be chosen and given the task of forming in words a perfect Courtier [*formar con parole un perfetto cortegiano*], setting forth all the conditions and particular qualities that are required of anyone who deserves this name" (I, 12, p. 19). *Formar con parole*, a "verbal portrait," as it were, and as the concept is aptly translated by Robert Hanning. But let me quote the entire passage, since it is necessary, in order to appreciate it, to hold before us the portrait and its frame:

2. David Rosand, "The Portrait, the Courtier, and Death," *Castiglione: The Ideal and the Real in Renaissance Culture,* eds. Robert W. Hanning and David Rosand (New Haven: Yale UP, 1983) 91.
3. Robert W. Hanning, "Castiglione's Verbal Portrait: Structures and Strategies," *Castiglione: The Ideal and the Real* 135.
4. Hanning 134.
5. Hanning 132.
6. Rosand 92.
7. Rosand 92.
8. Hanning 193.

I will say that if anyone should wish to praise our court . . .
he might well say, without suspicion of flattery, that in all Italy
it would perhaps be hard to find an equal number of cavaliers
as outstanding and as excellent in different things, quite
beyond their principal profession of chivalry, as are found here:
wherefore, if there are anywhere men who deserve to be called
good courtiers [*bon cortegiani*] and who can judge of what
belongs to the perfection of Courtiership [*quello che alla perfezion della cortegiania s'appartiene*], we must rightfully think
that they are here present. So, in order to put down the many
fools who in their presumption and ineptitude think to gain the
name of good courtiers, I would have our game this evening be
this, that one of this company be chosen and given the task of
forming in words a perfect Courtier (I, 12, p. 19).

What the text says here is that there is a difference between the
court of Urbino, between even the "good courtiers" of Urbino, the
equal of whom it would be hard to find in such number in any other
place in Italy, and the ideal, that *perfezion della cortegiania* that is
their task to find with the game of that evening: to find, that is to
say, to conceive, to imagine, to fashion with words. That is to say
(and I wish to stress the point), the exercise, the serious game the
court of Urbino is called upon to perform during four evenings, is
not so much a self-reflexive act—particularly if it is claimed, as
Thomas M. Greene does, that "a chrysalis of a culture," existing "in
its own static, circumscribed self-sufficiency . . . proposes to mirror its contentment by a game of autocontemplation"[9]—not so
much a self-reflexive act, as it is a projective one: turned not inward
["a community . . . turned inward, flawless in the perfection of its
withdrawal, protected momentarily by its mountains, its palace, its
style, its harmony, from the violence and vulgarity beyond it",[1] but
outward and upward. I will consider later what the nature of this
project is; suffice it to note now, in anticipation, that the game to be
played is not at all innocent, static, or aesthetic. It is, instead, a dangerous or, if you will, a subversive one: an exercise that eventually
will have to be taken more as a manifesto than as a beautiful and
harmonious picture; more as a poster to advertise or to publicize
something than as a painting.

  This in part is also the reason why in the preface, the letter to
Don Michel de Silva, which was written in the spring of 1527 and
is clearly already responding to reactions (*accusationi*, or charges),
criticism and interpretations of a text that had been circulating in
its present form since 1524, and in a previous version at least since

9. Thomas M. Greene, "*Il Cortegiano* and the Choice of a Game," *Castiglione: The Ideal and the Real* 7.
1. Greene 7.

1518, Castiglione feels obliged to refuse the dubious compliment, actually a misreading that what he had done was nothing less than a self-portrait:

> Still others[2] say I have thought to take myself as a model [*ho creduto formar me stesso*], on the persuasion that the qualities which I attribute to the Courtier are all in me. To these persons I will not deny having tried to set down everything that I could wish the Courtier to know; and I think that anyone who did not have some knowledge of the things that are spoken of in the book, however erudite he might be, could not well have written of them; but I am not so wanting in judgment and self-knowledge as to presume to know all that I could wish to know (7).

The author is therefore—and rightly, I believe—denying that this is a self-portrait; but it is then the text itself that refuses the understated characterization of a portrait modestly offered by the author in 1527, post factum that is, if only because the text is obviously and chiefly a treatise. A treatise in the form of a reported dialogue, of course.

I have dealt elsewhere at length with this issue.[3] But I should note here, however, in the briefest possible manner, what for me are the reasons for the adoption of this form. They are essentially two, strictly interrelated, and thematically and structurally inextricable from the core of the book: first, the dispersion, or rather the diffusion of the statement's authority, and second, the artful, the artistic deployment of the same statement, amounting to an exercise in *sprezzatura*. Let me try to be more specific and phrase it differently. What Castiglione needs is to present not *his* statement, but rather that of the court *as a collective body*. He manages to succeed in this task by deferring the fashioning by words, by means of words, of the courtier to a series of speakers, so that the final portrait, and the final treatise, is the result of a cumulative effort. Indeed, one can speak, as one Italian critic has recently done, of a *prosopopea della corte*.[4] The court speaks, but not in the first person: "Moi la vérité, je parle," as Truth did once in a text by Jacques Lacan;[5] rather, it speaks as a *noi*, as a "we"; as an indirect "we." Indirect in two senses: because ours, of course, are fictional characters—not the real Ludovico da Canossa, Federico Fregoso, Giuliano de' Medici,

---

2. Vittoria Colonna, for one, who wrote to him on September 20, 1524: "Che abbia ben formato un perfetto cortegiano non me ne maraviglio, ché con solo tenere uno specchio denanzi, et considerare le interne et externe parti sue, posseva descriverlo qual lo ha descritto" [quoted by Vittorio Cian, *Il Cortegiano del conte Baldesar Castiglione* annotato e illustrato da Vittorio Cian, seconda edizione accresciuta e corretta (Firenze: Sansoni, 1910) 9, n. 16].
3. See my "Trattato e ritratto: l'Introduzione del *Cortegiano*," *MLN* 93 (1978) 1–21.
4. Giancarlo Mazzacurati, *Il Rinascimento dei moderni* (Bologna: Il Mulino, 1985).
5. Jacques Lacan, "La chose freudienne," in his *Écrits* (Paris: Seuil, 1966) 409.

etc.; and because the "we" is, as I noted above, the result of an accumulation: Ludovico plus Federico plus Giuliano plus Bibbiena plus Ottaviano Fregoso plus Bembo, etc., equal the Court. I shall clarify further the reasons for applying here the criterion, recommended everywhere in the text, of *sprezzatura*, when I address the question of the audience at which this performance, the statement of the book is directed.

Now all this has little or nothing to do with the portrait of Urbino as the platonic idea of the court, the myth of Urbino, as so many continue to repeat. Castiglione's chief intentions are *not* representative, concerned with representation, that is, as much as with something else. Rather, the representation, the graceful, "aesthetic" representative element in the text could be compared to the bait or the sugar coating recommended—as we shall see—to the courtier-advisor of the prince so that he may obtain the required or wished-for result. This also shows, as will soon become clear, the marvelously tight consistency of Castiglione's text at all levels. But why did I say that this has little to do with the portrait of the court at Urbino? Because if one only pays a little attention to the text, looking concretely, as an anthropologist-historian recently did, at the 'portrait' for information about the court of Urbino, one must honestly concur with him that "nothing or almost nothing . . . is said in the whole work about the court" [*nulla o quasi . . . viene detto riguardo alla corte in tutta l'opera*].[6] All we know about it, all we are told, is what takes place in the evening—and what is more, on very special evenings—when the daily business of the court (of which nothing is said, which is never described) is suspended, and *otium*, leisure intervenes. Consequently, we know something and only something about *otium* at Urbino, and nothing about *negotium*.

So much for the portrait, the *ritratto di pittura* of the court of Urbino. Now what about the elegiac, rather than the nostalgic element in Castiglione's treatment of his subject? Again I will have to refer to my detailed discussion in another essay.[7] Here I will only repeat that if that element is certainly there—and I will not deny it—, it is mainly in the preface of 1527, which has wrongly projected over the entire text a mood that even there can only color the whole picture up to a point. Undoubtedly more representative of the historical situation to which the book is reacting is the extremely symptomatic rejection of the *laudatio temporis acti* typical of old age, and the celebration of the present time, as they are elaborated upon at the beginning of Book II. It was Giancarlo Mazzacurati who

---

6. Giuseppe Papagno, "Corti e cortegiani," *La corte e "Il Cortegiano", II. Un modello europeo*, a cura di A. Prosperi. Centro Studi "Europa delle Corti" (Roma: Bulzoni, 1980) 195.
7. "Trattato e ritratto," particularly 7–17.

spoke some twenty years ago of Castiglione's book as an *apologia del presente*.[8] And, indeed, the entire project of the *Book of the Courtier* cannot be properly understood outside the new historical coordinates into which it wishes to insert itself, providing an answer to certain new needs arising in those years: an answer which was proved to be relevant and important by the very success enjoyed by the book not only in Italy but in the rest of Europe. I am, of course, referring to the claim, made by the author in an earlier proem to his work, that the profession of the courtier is a new one. Let me quote the exact words of the text:

> Although Princes and great Lords have always had many people serving them . . . perhaps never in the past, but only very recently [*da non molto tempo in qua*] some men have made a profession of this Courtiership, so to say, and transformed it almost into an art and a discipline [*e riduttasi quasi in arte e disciplina*], as we can observe it nowadays. So that, as for any other science, for this too some precepts can be offered, and the ways leading to its end [*le vie per conseguirne il fine*] shown. An end which we affirm to be knowing how and being able to serve perfectly, and with dignity any great Prince in whatever is praiseworthy so as to obtain favor and praise from him and from all the others [*il sapere e potere perfettamente servire e con dignità ogni gran Principe in ogni cosa laudabile, acquistandone grazia e laude da esso e da tutti gli altri*].[9]

And here is how this last part of the passage is worded in the present proem to Book I:

> You have asked me to write my opinion as to what form of Courtiership most befits a gentleman living at the courts of princes, by which he can have both the knowledge and the ability to serve them in every reasonable thing [*in ogni cosa ragionevole*], thereby winning favor from them and praise from others [*da essi grazia e dagli altri laude*]: in short, what manner of man he must be who deserves the name of perfect Courtier, without defect of any kind (I, 1, p. 9).

The profession—this is Castiglione's claim—is new, involving a particular social group, if not a class, in search of promotion, or more precisely, a group that wants to be identified, or to identify itself, and be recognized: a recognition implying, no doubt, a political role and, consequently, a claim to power.

Let us now return to the other portrait, the verbal one, the one of the ideal courtier, or, to quote the exact words of the text, the "per-

---

8. Giancarlo Mazzacurati, *Misure del classicismo rinascimentale* (Napoli: Liguori, 1967).
9. "Altro proemio del *Cortegiano* tratto dalla prima bozza dell'Autore," *Lettere del conte B. Castiglione,* a cura dell'abate P. Serassi, Vol. I (Padova, 1769) 193.

fect Courtier," the *perfetto cortegiano*. We should pay more attention than has usually been paid in the past to what this word, "perfect" or "perfection," means in the text. But let us first review briefly
the requirements put forth in the first three books of the *Courtier*
by both Ludovico Canossa and Federico Fregoso, the ones that still
do not seem to satisfy entirely Ottaviano Fregoso, who, in fact, complains, at the end of Book III, about the lost opportunity "of hearing many other fine things that remain to be said about the
Courtier" (206), thus causing the Duchess to challenge him for the
following evening to "give the Courtier a greater perfection [*maggior
perfezione*] than these gentlemen have done" (206). What particularly in the first and in the second evening has been described is a
composite character endowed with many excellent qualities and
abilities, important and less important, in fields as distant or different as arms, letters, arts, music, conversation, sports, dancing, and
telling jokes—qualities and abilities sufficient to make an amiable
and excellent *amateur*, never a specialist—, one, however—and the
prescription is essential—whose "actions, . . . gestures, . . .
habits, in short, . . . every movement" should be accompanied
"with grace" (30). The point is, of course, a most important one, and
on its clarification depends an understanding not only of much that
is at stake in the book but also of the controlling principle of its
form. Again, I will not repeat here the demonstration I have
attempted in another essay,[1] but will let brief mention of a few
points suffice. First, of course, that *grazia* consists of, or rather is
obtained through, *sprezzatura*, the master trope of the courtier, one
whose application is the most general: a *regula universalissima*,
quite a universal rule, "which in this matter seems to me valid above
all others, and in all human affairs whether in word or deed":

> And that is to avoid affectation in every way possible as though
> it were some very rough and dangerous reef; and (to pronounce
> a new word perhaps) to practice in all things a certain *sprez-
> zatura* [nonchalance], so as to conceal all art and make what-
> ever is done or said appear to be without effort and almost
> without any thought about it. . . . [An] art which does not
> seem to be art; nor must one be more careful of anything than
> of concealing it, because if it is discovered, this robs a man of
> all credit and causes him to be held in slight esteem (I, 26,
> p. 32).

The result must be one of effortlessness; but why *sprezzatura*, a
word that suggests disdain, misprision, depreciation, despise? Of
course, these negative terms "at the most immediate and evident

---

1. "*Grazia, sprezzatura, affettazione* in the *Courtier*," *Castiglione: The Ideal and the Real*
45–67, and previously, in a slightly different form, in *Glyph* 5 (1979) 34–54.

semantic level . . . apply to (and qualify) *diligentia*, the very art that is put into operation by the practitioner,"[2] whose effort—it is constantly emphasized—must be concealed. But the real target, against which disdain, despise, or depreciation are levelled, is affectation. This is the well or pit into which the bad courtier, the would-be courtier who is not able to play the difficult game, is bound to fall, in that he oversteps the "certain limits of moderation" [*certi termini di mediocrità*], wherein resides the excellence of *sprezzatura*. On the other hand, as we have seen, concealment—as in irony—is essential: an honest dissimulation, *dissimulazione onesta*, as a later theorist, Torquato Accetto, will call it. And still a dissimulation, a deception or, at any rate, a discrepancy between being and seeming. And dissimulation, if not necessarily intended for the disadvantage of someone, is always intended for someone's advantage. The advantage for the courtier is obvious: what he wants to obtain is *grazia*, acceptance, recognition, praise, and favor from his peers and from the prince. We will have to consider later the other side of the question: the disadvantage for someone. Let us stress for the moment only the one element of indirection that is proper to the good courtier's behavior: indirection as opposed to being direct; irony and understatement as opposed to straightforwardness or ἀλήθεια, as Aristotle would have called it (and of course to ἀλαζονεία, boastfulness, affectation). Everything has to be subtle and clever, implicit rather than explicit, if the boat of the courtier wants to avoid the shipwreck against the "very rough and dangerous reef," the *asperissimo e pericoloso scoglio* that was evoked in a deceivingly casual manner in a passage I have already quoted.

We may pause for a moment and consider the relevance of the concept of *sprezzatura*, of the particular theory of *grazia* advocated by Castiglione, to the very project of his book, to its dialogic structure that manages to avoid the ungracefulness of the traditional treatise: direct, didactic—authoritatively direct and didactic, I should add. But the disappearance from the scene of both the real and the fictional "I"—Castiglione fictively being away from Urbino when the fictive dialogues are supposed to have taken place—finds a correspondence in another disappearance, in the fact that another character is missing from the text: or, to be more precise, is missing from the scene where one would have expected to find him. So, the author is missing; and who else? The Prince, of course: Guidobaldo, who "owing to his infirmity—we are told— . . . always retired to sleep very early after supper" (I, 4, p. 12). Consequently, his place is taken by a substitute, the Duchess Elisabetta Gonzaga, in whose rooms we know that the evening gatherings take place. And we

<hr>

2. Saccone, *"Grazia, sprezzatura, affettazione* in the *Courtier"* 57.

shoùld add, perhaps, without elaborating, that even in these rooms the presiding, the exercise of authority is further relayed, deferred to Emilia Pia, the lady-in-waiting.

The importance of this structuring of the book, of the situation in the book—of the frame, that is, wherein the Court makes an indirect statement of intents, outlines its portrait, makes its plea for recognition and for power, writes, as it were, its manifesto—, the importance of this second structural element cannot be underestimated. For the statement to remain indirect, it was necessary that the Prince be absent. But that the statement is addressed to the Prince, there can be no doubt. No doubt, to be more precise, that the Prince is one of the two addressees of the *Book of the Courtier*, the other being, of course, the courtier himself, or rather, the worthy would-be courtier. This is what in particular the last book of the treatise, the fourth, makes clear. This is, in fact, the book in which the question of the perfection of the courtier is specifically addressed. And this will also be for us the place and the moment to pay, as I promised, more attention than has possibly been paid in the past to the word *perfezione* itself.

It is the fourth evening of the dialogues. Ottaviano Fregoso, who had been invited by the Duchess to say what he had in mind, and who on the day following the discussions contained in the third book had not been seen, having probably "withdrawn in order to be free to think carefully of what he had to say," arrives late, when "many cavaliers and ladies of the court" had already "[begun] to dance, and engage in other pastimes, thinking that for that evening there would be no more talk about the Courtier" (IV, 3, p. 209). Clearly, all this preparation, this staging of Ottaviano's speech is meant to call attention to its importance. What Ottaviano will have to say will not amount to finding *altre bone condicioni al Cortegiano* ("more good qualities for the Courtier"), as the Duchess' words at the end of Book III read in an earlier version,[3] but, as in the final one, *a dare maggior perfectione al Cortegiano che non han dato questi signori*, to "[giving] the Courtier a greater perfection than these gentlemen have done" (III, 77, p. 206). Or even better, to giving the Courtier—as we could say—*his* perfection. In fact, as Ottaviano's speech will make clear, the question is not that of adding more or new qualities, or even more perfections to the Courtier, as much as it is to finalize them, to establish a *buon fine* (IV, 4), a "good end" for them.

Strangely enough, greatly expanding some of Burckhardt's observations about the *Book of the Courtier*, and extending to the entire

---

3. Recorded in the Ashburnham manuscript (MS. Ashb. 409 f. 06r) of the Biblioteca Laurenziana, Florence, as noted by Lawrence V. Ryan, "Book Four of Castiglione's *Courtier*: Climax or Afterthought?," *Studies in the Renaissance* 19 (1977) 168.

fourth book what the great historian had to say about the relationship between the rest of the work and "the magnificent, almost lyri-
cal praise of ideal love, which occurs at the end of the . . . book,"
that for him "has no connection whatever with the special object of
the work" [*vollends nichts mehr zu tun mit der speziellen Aufgabe des
Werkes*],[4] much of recent scholarship has insisted on what has been
variously described as a "structural break," a "structural crisis,"[5] a
"sudden break in atmosphere and argument,"[6] that supposedly takes
place in this fourth book, which—according to at least one of these
critics, Woodhouse, amounts to the "virtual destruction . . . by
Fregoso of the previous 'ideal' of courtly behaviour."[7] And according
to another critic, Rebhorn, Castiglione's changes in the last book
"open a vast gulf between the ideas and ideals of the fourth book
and those of the first three." "Ottaviano's and Bembo's visions of the
ideal courtier—we are told—are essentially incompatible in some
basic respects with the vision of the first three books."[8] An even
more skeptical critic, actually one of the few who has done much to
offer a balanced solution to the question raised by Book IV,
Lawrence Ryan, summarizes part of the problem—the part relative
to Ottaviano's speech—with the following words: "The discussion
suddenly seems to shift from concern with the ideal courtier, possessing a self-contained excellence too lofty for any function in the
real world, into an attempt to establish a meaningful role for him in
an actual society."[9]

I am afraid that what has created the problem is not so much Castiglione's text, as Burckhardt's interpretation of it, an "aesthetisch-
idealisierende" interpretation—to use Erich Loos' words—[1]which
insisted precisely on the "purely general and almost abstract idea of
individual perfection" which characterized and motivated the
Courtier, and on the "self-contained excellence too lofty for any function in the real world," of which Ryan speaks. In fact, let me quote a
characteristic passage from Burckhardt. Castiglione's Courtier was
actually:

4. Jakob Burckhardt, *The Civilization of the Renaissance in Italy,* trans. S. G. C. Middlemore (New York, 1954) 287; *Die Kultur der Renaissance in Italien,* herausgegeben von Werner Kaegi (Berlin und Leipzig: Deutsche Verlags-Anstalt Stuttgart, 1930) 278.
5. See, among others, Amedeo Quondam, who speaks of "una frattura tra i primi libri e l'ul-timo" in his Introduction to *Il libro del Cortegiano,* I grandi libri Garzanti (Milano: Garzanti, 1981) IX, and Piero Floriani, who talks of a "crisi strutturale" in *Bembo e Castiglione. Studi sul classicismo del Cinquecento* (Roma: Bulzoni, 1976) 153.
6. J. R. Woodhouse, "Book Four of Castiglione's *Cortegiano.* A Pragmatic Approach," *The Modern Language Review* 73 (1978) 62.
7. Woodhouse 62.
8. Wayne A. Rebhorn, "Ottaviano's Interruption: Book IV and the Problem of Unity in *Il libro del Cortegiano,*" *MLN* 87 (1972) 37–59.
9. Ryan, "Book Four of Castiglione's *Courtier*" 156–157.
1. Erich Loos, *B. Castigliones "Libro del Cortegiano". Studien zur Tugendauffassung des Cinquecento* (Frankfurt a. M., 1955) 25.

of. Janitch

the ideal man of society, and was regarded by the civilization of that age as its choicest flower [*der gesellschaftliche Idealmensch, wie ihn die Bildung jener Zeit als notwendige, höchste Blüte postuliert*]; and the court existed for him rather than he for the court [*und der Hof ist mehr für ihn als er für den Hof bestimmt*]. Indeed such a man would have been out of place at any court, since he himself possessed all the gifts and the bearing of an accomplished ruler and because his calm, unaffected virtuosity in all things both outward and spiritual [*seine ruhige, unaffektierte Virtuosität in allen äussern und geistigen Dingen*] implied a too self-sufficient nature [*ein zu selbständiges Wesen*]. The inner impulse which inspired him was directed, though our author does not acknowledge the fact, not to the service of the prince, but to his own perfection [*nicht auf den Fürstendienst, sondern auf die eigene Vollendung*].[2]

In other words, the Courtier as a work of art, the Courtier as a typical example of Renaissance self-fashioning. The reality, however, is, and from the beginning, a different and a very dramatic one. From the start, the fashioning of the Courtier depends very much on the public, the audience, the others. Far from self-contained excellence and autonomous personality being his goals, the Courtier is always fighting on two fronts: that of the competition with his peers and the other to gain his Prince's favor. From the beginning—and it is, of course, a truism—the Courtier cannot exist without the court, that is, without the favor of the Prince who holds court. And the relationship, the dependence is, of course, both economic and political. The service of the Prince is from the start—and Burckhardt himself could not ignore it—the stated "Triebkraft, die ihn bewegt," the proclaimed "impulse that moves him."[3] There can never be any doubt about this. The problem is rather a different one, and can be formulated as follows: is there a real opposition—gap, gulf, contradiction, to use the words of other critics—between the service generally postulated in the preceding three books and the specific one outlined by Ottaviano in Book IV?

* * *

2. Burckhardt, *The Civilization of the Renaissance in Italy* 287; *Die Kultur der Renaissance* 277.
3. Burckhardt, *The Civilization of the Renaissance in Italy* 287; *Die Kultur der Renaissance* 277.

JOAN KELLY-GADOL

Did Women Have a Renaissance?[†]

The kind of economic and political power that supported the cultural activity of feudal noblewomen in the eleventh and twelfth centuries had no counterpart in Renaissance Italy. By the fourteenth century, the political units of Italy were mostly sovereign states, that, regardless of legal claims, recognized no overlords and supported no feudatories. Their nobility held property but not seigniorial power, estates but not jurisdiction. Indeed, in northern and central Italy, a nobility in the European sense hardly existed at all. Down to the coronation of Charles V as Holy Roman Emperor in 1530, there was no Italian king to safeguard the interests of (and thereby limit and control) a "legitimate" nobility that maintained by inheritance traditional prerogatives. Hence, where the urban bourgeoisie did not overthrow the claims of nobility, a despot did, usually in the name of nobility but always for himself. These *signorie*, unlike the bourgeois republics, continued to maintain a landed, military "class" with noble pretensions, but its members increasingly became merely the warriors and ornaments of a court. Hence, the Renaissance aristocrat, who enjoyed neither the independent political powers of feudal jurisdiction nor legally guaranteed status in the ruling estate, either served a despot or became one.

In this sociopolitical context, the exercise of political power by women was far more rare than under feudalism or even under the traditional kind of monarchical state that developed out of feudalism. The two Giovannas of Naples, both queens in their own right, exemplify this latter type of rule. The first, who began her reign in 1343 over Naples and Provence, became in 1356 queen of Sicily as well. Her grandfather, King Robert of Naples—of the same house of Anjou and Provence that hearkens back to Eleanor and to Henry Plantagenet—could and did designate Giovanna as his heir. Similarly, in 1414, Giovanna II became queen of Naples upon the death of her brother. In Naples, in short, women of the ruling house could assume power, not because of their abilities alone, but because the principle of legitimacy continued in force along with the feudal tradition of inheritance by women.

In northern Italy, by contrast, Caterina Sforza ruled her petty principality in typical Renaissance fashion, supported only by the Machiavellian principles of *fortuna* and *virtù* (historical situation

† From *Becoming Visible: Women in European History*, ed. Renate Bridenthal and Claudia Koonz (Boston: Houghton Mifflin Company, 1977), pp. 148–52, 154–61. Copyright © 1977 by Houghton Mifflin Company. Used by permission.

and will). Her career, like that of her family, follows the Renaissance pattern of personal and political illegitimacy. Born in 1462, she was an illegitimate daughter of Galeazzo Maria Sforza, heir to the Duchy of Milan. The ducal power of the Sforzas was very recent, dating only from 1450, when Francesco Sforza, illegitimate son of a condottiere and a great condottiere himself, assumed control of the duchy. When his son and heir, Caterina's father, was assassinated after ten years of tyrannous rule, another son, Lodovico, took control of the duchy, first as regent for his nephew (Caterina's half brother), then as outright usurper. Lodovico promoted Caterina's interests for the sake of his own. He married her off at fifteen to a nephew of Pope Sixtus IV, thereby strengthening the alliance between the Sforzas and the Riario family, who now controlled the papacy. The pope carved a state out of papal domains for Caterina's husband, making him Count of Forlì as well as the Lord of Imola, which Caterina brought to the marriage. But the pope died in 1484, her husband died by assassination four years later—and Caterina made the choice to defy the peculiar obstacles posed by Renaissance Italy to a woman's assumption of power.

Once before, with her husband seriously ill at Imola, she had ridden hard to Forlì to quell an incipient coup a day before giving birth. Now at twenty-six, after the assassination of her husband, she and a loyal castelan held the citadel at Forlì against her enemies until Lodovico sent her aid from Milan. Caterina won; she faced down her opponents, who held her six children hostage, then took command as regent for her young son. But her title to rule as regent was inconsequential. Caterina ruled because she mustered superior force and exercised it personally, and to the end she had to exert repeatedly the skill, forcefulness, and ruthless ambition that brought her to power. However, even her martial spirit did not suffice. In the despotisms of Renaissance Italy, where assassinations, coups, and invasions were the order of the day, power stayed closely bound to military force. In 1500, deprived of Milan's support by her uncle Lodovico's deposition, Caterina succumbed to the overwhelming forces of Cesare Borgia and was divested of power after a heroic defense of Forlì.

Because of this political situation, at once statist and unstable, the daughters of the Este, Gonzaga, and Montefeltro families represent women of their class much more than Caterina Sforza did. Their access to power was indirect and provisional, and was expected to be so. In his handbook for the nobility, Baldassare Castiglione's description of the lady of the court makes this difference in sex roles quite clear. On the one hand, the Renaissance lady appears as the equivalent of the courtier. She has the same virtues of mind as he and her education is symmetrical with his. She learns everything—well, almost everything—he does: "knowledge of letters, of music, of painting, and . . . how to dance and how to be festive."[1] Culture is an accomplishment for noblewoman and man alike, used to charm others as much as to develop the self. But for the woman, charm had become the primary occupation and aim. Whereas the courtier's chief task is defined as the profession of arms, "in a Lady who lives at court a certain pleasing affability is becoming above all else, whereby she will be able to entertain graciously every kind of man" (p. 151).

One notable consequence of the Renaissance lady's need to charm is that Castiglione called upon her to give up certain "unbecoming" physical activities such as riding and handling weapons. Granted, he concerned himself with the court lady, as he says, not a queen who may be called upon to rule. But his aestheticizing of the lady's role, his conception of her femaleness as centered in charm, meant that activities such as riding and skill in weaponry would seem unbecoming to women of the ruling families, too. Elisabetta Gonzaga, the idealized duchess of Castiglione's *Courtier*, came close in real life to his normative portrayal of her type. Riding and skill in weaponry had, in fact, no significance for her. The heir to her Duchy of Urbino was decided upon during the lifetime of her husband, and it was this adoptive heir—not the widow of thirty-seven with no children to compete for her care and attention—who assumed power in 1508. Removed from any direct exercise of power, Elisabetta also disregarded the pursuits and pleasures associated with it. Her letters express none of the sense of freedom and daring Caterina Sforza and Beatrice d'Este experienced in riding and the hunt. Altogether, she lacks spirit. Her correspondence shows her to be as docile in adulthood as her early teachers trained her to be. She met adversity, marital and political, with fortitude but never opposed it. She placated father, brother, and husband, and even in Castiglione's depiction of her court, she complied with rather than shaped its conventions.

The differences between Elisabetta Gonzaga and Caterina Sforza are great, yet both personalities were responding to the Renaissance situation of emerging statehood and social mobility. Elisabetta, neither personally illegitimate nor springing from a freebooting condottiere family, was schooled, as Castiglione would have it, away from the martial attitudes and skills requisite for despotic rule. She would not be a prince, she would marry one. Hence, her education,

---

1. From *The Book of the Courtier*, by Baldesar Castiglione, a new translation by Charles S. Singleton (New York: Doubleday, 1959), p. 20. Copyright © 1959 by Charles S. Singleton and Edgar de N. Mayhew. This and other quotations throughout the chapter are reprinted by permission of Doubleday & Co., Inc. Page numbers to *The Book of the Courtier* refer to this Norton Critical Edition.

like that of most of the daughters of the ruling families, directed her toward the cultural and social functions of the court. The lady who married a Renaissance prince became a patron. She commissioned works of art and gave gifts for literary works dedicated to her; she drew to her artists and literati. But the court they came to ornament was her husband's, and the culture they represented magnified his princely being, especially when his origins could not. Thus, the Renaissance lady may play an aesthetically significant role in Castiglione's idealized Court of Urbino of 1508, but even he clearly removed her from that equal, to say nothing of superior, position in social discourse that medieval courtly literature had granted her. To the fifteen or so male members of the court whose names he carefully listed, Castiglione admitted only four women to the evening conversations that were the second major occupation at court (the profession of arms, from which he completely excluded women, being the first). Of the four, he distinguished only two women as participants. The Duchess Elisabetta and her companion, Emilia Pia, at least speak, whereas the other two only do a dance. Yet they speak in order to moderate and "direct" discussion by proposing questions and games. They do not themselves contribute to the discussions, and at one point Castiglione relieves them even of their negligible role:

> When signor Gasparo had spoken thus, signora Emilia made a sign to madam Costanza Fregosa, as she sat next in order, that she should speak; and she was making ready to do so, when suddenly the Duchess said: "Since signora Emilia does not choose to go to the trouble of devising a game, it would be quite right for the other ladies to share in this ease, and thus be exempt from such a burden this evening, especially since there are so many men here that we risk no lack of games." (p. 15)

The men, in short, do all the talking; and the ensuing dialogue on manners and love, as we might expect, is not only developed by men but directed toward their interests.

The contradiction between the professed parity of noblewomen and men in *The Courtier* and the merely decorative role Castiglione unwittingly assigned the lady proclaims an important educational and cultural change as well as a political one. Not only did a male ruler preside over the courts of Renaissance Italy, but the court no longer served as the exclusive school of the nobility, and the lady no longer served as arbiter of the cultural functions it did retain. Although restricted to a cultural and social role, she lost dominance in that role as secular education came to require special skills which were claimed as the prerogative of a class of professional teachers. The sons of the Renaissance nobility still pursued their military and diplomatic training in the service of some great lord, but as youths, they transferred their nonmilitary training from the lady to the humanistic tutor or boarding school. In a sense, humanism represented an advance for women as well as for the culture at large. It brought Latin literacy and classical learning to daughters as well as sons of the nobility. But this very development, usually taken as an index of the equality of Renaissance (noble) women with men,[2] spelled a further decline in the lady's influence over courtly society. It placed her as well as her brothers under male cultural authority. The girl of the medieval aristocracy, although unschooled, was brought up at the court of some great lady. Now her brothers' tutors shaped her outlook, male educators who, as humanists, suppressed romance and chivalry to further classical culture, with all its patriarchal and misogynous bias.

The humanistic education of the Renaissance noblewoman helps explain why she cannot compare with her medieval predecessors in shaping a culture responsive to her own interests. In accordance with the new cultural values, the patronage of the Este, Sforza, Gonzaga, and Montefeltro women extended far beyond the literature and art of love and manners, but the works they commissioned, bought, or had dedicated to them do not show any consistent correspondence to their concerns as women. They did not even give noticeable support to women's education, with the single important exception of Battista da Montefeltro, to whom one of the few treatises advocating a humanistic education for women was dedicated. Adopting the universalistic outlook of their humanist teachers, the noble-women of Renaissance Italy seem to have lost all consciousness of their particular interests as women, while male authors such as Castiglione, who articulated the mores of the Renaissance aristocracy, wrote their works for men. Cultural and political dependency thus combined in Italy to reverse the roles of women and men in developing the new noble code. Medieval courtesy, as set forth in the earliest etiquette books, romances, and rules of love, shaped the man primarily to please the lady. In the thirteenth and fourteenth centuries, rules for women, and strongly patriarchal ones at that, entered French and Italian etiquette books, but not until the Renaissance reformulation of courtly manners and love is it evident how the ways of the lady came to be determined by men in the context of the early modern state. The relation of the sexes here assumed its modern form, and nowhere is this made more visible than in the love relation.

---

2. An interesting exception is W. Ong's "Latin Language Study as a Renaissance Puberty Rite," *Studies in Philology*, 56 (1959), 103–124; also Margaret Leah King's "The Religious Retreat of Isotta Nogarola (1418–1466)," *Signs*, Winter 1977.

*   *   *

Overtly, as we saw, Castiglione and his class supported a comple-mentary conception of sex roles, in part because a nobility that did no work at all gave little thought to a sexual division of labor. He could thus take up the late medieval *querelle des femmes* set off by the *Romance of the Rose* and debate the question of women's dig-nity much to their favor. Castiglione places Aristotle's (and Aquinas's) notion of woman as a defective man in the mouth of an aggrieved misogynist, Gasparo; he criticizes Plato's low regard for women, even though he did permit them to govern in *The Republic*; he rejects Ovid's theory of love as not "gentle" enough. Most signif-icantly, he opposes Gasparo's bourgeois notion of women's exclu-sively domestic role. Yet for all this, Castiglione established in *The Courtier* a fateful bond between love and marriage. One index of a heightened patriarchal outlook among the Renaissance nobility is that love in the usual emotional and sexual sense must lead to mar-riage and be confined to it—for women, that is.

The issue gets couched, like all others in the book, in the form of a debate. There are pros and cons; but the prevailing view is unmis-takable. If the ideal court lady loves, she should love someone whom she can marry. If married, and the mishap befalls her "that her hus-band's hate or another's love should bring her to love, I would have her give her lover a spiritual love only; nor must she ever give him any sure sign of her love, either by word or gesture or by other means that can make him certain of it" (p. 192). *The Courtier* thus takes a strange, transitional position on the relations among love, sex, and marriage, which bourgeois Europe would later fuse into one familial whole. Responding to a situation of general female dependency among the nobility, and to the restoration of patriarchal family values, at once classical and bourgeois, Castiglione, like Renaissance love theorists in general, connected love and marriage. But facing the same realities of political marriage and clerical celibacy that beset the medieval aristocracy, he still focused upon the love that takes place outside it. On this point, too, however, he broke with the courtly love tradition. He proposed on the one hand a Neo-Platonic notion of spiritual love, and on the other, the dou-ble standard.[3]

Castiglione's image of the lover is interesting in this regard. Did he think his suppression of female sexual love would be more justi-fiable if he had a churchman, Pietro Bembo (elevated to cardinal in

3. For historical context, Keith Thomas, "The Double Standard," *Journal of the History of Ideas*, 20 (1959), 195–216; N. J. Perella, *The Kiss Sacred and Profane: An Interpretive History of Kiss Symbolism*, University of California Press, Berkeley, 1969; Morton Hunt, *The Natural History of Love*, Funk & Wagnalls, New York, 1967.

1539), enunciate the new theory and had him discourse upon the love of an aging courtier rather than that of a young knight? In any case, adopting the Platonic definition of love as desire to enjoy beauty, Bembo located this lover in a metaphysical and physical hierarchy between sense ("below") and intellect ("above"). As reason mediates between the physical and the spiritual, so man, aroused by the visible beauty of his beloved, may direct his desire beyond her to the true, intelligible source of her beauty. He may, however, also turn toward sense. Young men fall into this error, and we should expect it of them, Bembo explains in the Neo-Platonic language of the Florentine philosopher Marsilio Ficino. "For finding itself deep in an earthly prison, and deprived of spiritual contemplation in exercising its office of governing the body, the soul of itself cannot clearly perceive the truth; wherefore, in order to have knowledge, it is obliged to turn to the senses . . . and so it believes them . . . and lets itself be guided by them, especially when they have so much vigor that they almost force it" (p. 245). A misdirection of the soul leads to sexual union (though obviously not with the court lady). The preferred kind of union, achieved by way of ascent, uses love of the lady as a step toward love of universal beauty. The lover here ascends from awareness of his own human spirit, which responds to beauty, to awareness of that universal intellect that comprehends universal beauty. Then, "transformed into an angel," his soul finds supreme happiness in divine love. Love may hereby soar to an ontologically noble end, and the beauty of the woman who inspires such ascent may acquire metaphysical status and dignity. But Love, Beauty, Woman, aestheticized as Botticelli's Venus and given cosmic import, were in effect denatured, robbed of body, sex, and passion by this elevation. The simple kiss of love-service became a rarefied kiss of the soul: "A man delights in joining his mouth to that of his beloved in a kiss, not in order to bring himself to any unseemly desire, but because he feels that that bond is the opening of mutual access to their souls" (p. 253). And instead of initiating love, the kiss now terminated physical contact, at least for the churchman and/or aging courtier who sought an ennobling experience—and for the woman obliged to play her role as lady.

Responsive as he still was to medieval views of love, Castiglione at least debated the issue of the double standard. His spokesmen point out that men make the rules permitting themselves and not women sexual freedom, and that concern for legitimacy does not justify this inequality. Since these same men claim to be more virtuous than women, they could more easily restrain themselves. In that case, "there would be neither more nor less certainty about offspring, for even if women were unchaste, they could in no way bear children of themselves . . . provided men were continent and did not take part in the unchastity of women" (p. 176). But for all this, the book supplies an excess of hortatory tales about female chastity, and in the section of the dialogue granting young men indulgence in sensual love, no one speaks for young women, who ought to be doubly "prone," as youths and as women, according to the views of the time.

This is theory, of course. But one thinks of the examples: Eleanor of Aquitaine changing bedmates in the midst of a crusade; Elisabetta Gonzaga, so constrained by the conventions of her own court that she would not take a lover even though her husband was impotent. She, needless to say, figures as Castiglione's prime exemplar: "Our Duchess who has lived with her husband for fifteen years like a widow" (p. 186). Bembo, on the other hand, in the years before he became cardinal, lived with and had three children by Donna Morosina. But however they actually lived, in the new ideology a spiritualized noble love *supplemented* the experience of men while it *defined* extramarital experience for the lady. For women, chastity had become the convention of the Renaissance courts, signaling the twofold fact that the dominant institutions of sixteenth-century Italian society would not support the adulterous sexuality of courtly love, and that women, suffering a relative loss of power within these institutions, could not at first make them responsive to their needs. Legitimacy is a significant factor here. Even courtly love had paid some deference to it (and to the desire of women to avoid conception) by restraining intercourse while promoting romantic and sexual play. But now, with cultural and political power held almost entirely by men, the norm of female chastity came to express the concerns of Renaissance noblemen as they moved into a new situation as a hereditary, dependent class.

This changed situation of the aristocracy accounts both for Castiglione's widespread appeal and for his telling transformation of the love relation. Because *The Courtier* created a mannered way of life that could give to a dependent nobility a sense of self-sufficiency, of inner power and control, which they had lost in a real economic and political sense, the book's popularity spread from Italy through Europe at large in the sixteenth and seventeenth centuries. Although set in the Urbino court of 1508, it was actually begun some ten years after that and published in 1528—after the sack of Rome, and at a time when the princely states of Italy and Europe were coming to resemble each other more closely than they had in the fourteenth and fifteenth centuries. The monarchs of Europe, consolidating and centralizing their states, were at once protecting the privileges of their nobility and suppressing feudal power.[4] Likewise in Italy, as the entire

4. Fernand Braudel, *The Mediterranean World*, Routledge & Kegan Paul, London, 1973; A. Ventura, *Nobiltà e popolo nella società Veneta*, Laterza, Bari, 1964; Lawrence Stone, *The Crisis of the Aristocracy, 1558–1641*, Clarendon Press, Oxford, 1965.

country fell under the hegemony of Charles V, the nobility began to be stabilized. Throughout sixteenth-century Italy, new laws began to limit and regulate membership in a hereditary aristocratic class, prompting a new concern with legitimacy and purity of the blood. Castiglione's demand for female chastity in part responds to this particular concern. His theory of love as a whole responds to the general situation of the Renaissance nobility. In the discourse on love for which he made Bembo the spokesman, he brought to the love relation the same psychic attitudes with which he confronted the political situation. Indeed, he used the love relation as a symbol to convey his sense of political relations.

The changed times to which Castiglione refers in his introduction he experienced as a condition of servitude. The dominant problem of the sixteenth-century Italian nobility, like that of the English nobility under the Tudors, had become one of obedience. As one of Castiglione's courtiers expressed it, God had better grant them "good masters, for, once we have them, we have to endure them as they are" (p. 85). It is this transformation of aristocratic service to statism, which gave rise to Castiglione's leading idea of nobility as courtiers, that shaped his theory of love as well. Bembo's aging courtier, passionless in his rational love, sums up the theme of the entire book: how to maintain by detachment the sense of self now threatened by the loss of independent power. The soul in its earthly prison, the courtier in his social one, renounce the power of self-determination that has in fact been denied them. They renounce *wanting* such power; "If the flame is extinguished, the danger is also extinguished" (p. 251). In love, as in service, the courtier preserves independence by avoiding desire for real love, real power. He does not touch or allow himself to be touched by either. "To enjoy beauty without suffering, the Courtier, aided by reason, must turn his desire entirely away from the body and to beauty alone, [to] contemplate it in its simple and pure self" (p. 254). He may gaze at the object of his love-service, he may listen, but there he reaches the limits of the actual physical relation and transforms her beauty, or the prince's power, into a pure idea. "Spared the bitterness and calamities" of thwarted passion thereby, he loves and serves an image only. The courtier gives obeisance, but only to a reality of his own making: "for he will always carry his precious treasure with him, shut up in his heart, and will also, by the force of his own imagination, make her beauty [or the prince's power] much more beautiful than in reality it is" (p. 255).

Thus, the courtier can serve and not serve, love and not love. He can even attain the relief of surrender by making use of this inner love-service "as a step" to mount to a more sublime sense of service. Contemplation of the Idea the courtier has discovered within his own soul excites a purified desire to love, to serve, to unite with intellectual beauty (or power). Just as love guided his soul from the particular beauty of his beloved to the universal concept, love of that intelligible beauty (or power) glimpsed within transports the soul from the self, the particular intellect, to the universal intellect. Aflame with an utterly spiritual love (or a spiritualized sense of service), the soul then "understands all things intelligible, and without any veil or cloud views the wide sea of pure divine beauty, and receives it into itself, enjoying that supreme happiness of which the senses are incapable" (p. 256). What does this semimystical discourse teach but that by "true" service, the courtier may break out of his citadel of independence, his inner aloofness, to rise and surrender to the pure idea of Power? What does his service become but a freely chosen Obedience, which he can construe as the supreme virtue? In both its sublimated acceptance or resignation and its inner detachment from the actual, Bembo's discourse on love exemplifies the relation between subject and state, obedience and power, that runs through the entire book. Indeed, Castiglione regarded the monarch's power exactly as he had Bembo present the lady's beauty, as symbolic of God: "As in the heavens the sun and the moon and the other stars exhibit to the world a certain likeness of God, so on earth a much liker image of God is seen in . . . princes." Clearly, if "men have been put by God under princes" (p. 222), if they have been placed under princes as under His image, what end can be higher than service in virtue, than the purified experience of Service?

The likeness of the lady to the prince in this theory, her elevation to the pedestal of Neo-Platonic love, both masks and expresses the new dependency of the Renaissance noblewoman. In a structured hierarchy of superior and inferior, she seems to be served by the courtier. But this love theory really made her serve—and stand as a symbol of how the relation of domination may be reversed, so that the prince could be made to serve the interests of the courtier. The Renaissance lady is not desired, not loved for herself. Rendered passive and chaste, she merely mediates the courtier's safe transcendence of an otherwise demeaning necessity. On the plane of symbolism, Castiglione thus had the courtier dominate both her and the prince; and on the plane of reality, he indirectly acknowledged the courtier's actual domination of the lady by having him adopt "woman's ways" in his relations to the prince. Castiglione had to defend against effeminacy in the courtier, both the charge of it (p. 67) and the actuality of faces "soft and feminine as many attempt to have who not only curl their hair and pluck their eyebrows, but preen themselves . . . and appear so tender and languid . . . and utter their words so limply" (p. 27). Yet the close-fitting costume of the Renaissance nobleman displayed the courtier exactly as Castiglione would have him, "well built and shapely of limb" (p. 27). His clothes set off his grace, as did his nonchalant ease, the new manner of those "who seem in words, laughter, in posture not to care" (p. 33). To be attractive, accomplished, and seem not to care; to charm and do so coolly—how concerned with impression, how masked the true self. And how manipulative: petitioning his lord, the courtier knows to be "discreet in choosing the occasion, and will ask things that are proper and reasonable; and he will so frame his request, omitting those parts that he knows can cause displeasure, and will skillfully make easy the difficult points so that his lord will always grant it" (p. 81). In short, how like a woman—or a dependent, for that is the root of the simile.

The accommodation of the sixteenth- and seventeenth-century courtier to the ways and dress of women in no way bespeaks a greater parity between them. It reflects, rather, that general restructuring of social relations that entailed for the Renaissance noblewoman a greater dependency upon men as feudal independence and reciprocity yielded to the state. In this new situation, the entire nobility suffered a loss. Hence, the courtier's posture of dependency, his concern with the pleasing impression, his resolve "to perceive what his prince likes, and . . . to bend himself to this" (p. 81). But as the state overrode aristocratic power, the lady suffered a double loss. Deprived of the possibility of independent power that the combined interests of kinship and feudalism guaranteed some women in the Middle Ages, and that the states of early modern Europe would preserve in part, the Italian noblewoman in particular entered a relation of almost universal dependence upon her family and her husband. And she experienced this dependency at the same time as she lost her commanding position with respect to the secular culture of her society.

Hence, the love theory of the Italian courts developed in ways as indifferent to the interests of women as the courtier, in his self-sufficiency, was indifferent as a lover. It accepted, as medieval courtly love did not, the double standard. It bound the lady to chastity, to the merely procreative sex of political marriage, just as her weighty and costly costume came to conceal and constrain her body while it displayed her husband's noble rank. Indeed, the person of the woman became so inconsequential to this love relation that one doubted whether she could love at all. The question that emerges at the end of *The Courtier* as to "whether or not women are as capable of divine love as men" (p. 259) belongs to a love theory structured by mediation rather than mutuality. Woman's beauty inspired love but the lover, the agent, was man. And the question stands unresolved at the end of *The Courtier*—because at heart the spokesmen for Renaissance love were not really concerned about women or love at all.

Where courtly love had used the social relation of vassalage to work out a genuine concern with sexual love, Castiglione's thought moved in exactly the opposite direction. He allegorized love as fully as Dante did, using the relation of the sexes to symbolize the new political order. In this, his love theory reflects the social realities of the Renaissance. The denial of the right and power of women to love, the transformation of women into passive "others" who serve, fits the self-image of the courtier, the one Castiglione sought to remedy. The symbolic relation of the sexes thus mirrors the new social relations of the state, much as courtly love displayed the feudal relations of reciprocal personal dependence. But Renaissance love reflects, as well, the actual condition of dependency suffered by noblewomen as the state arose. If the courtier who charms the prince bears the same relation to him as the lady bears to the courtier, it is because Castiglione understood the relation of the sexes in the same terms that he used to describe the political relation: i.e., as a relation between servant and lord. The nobleman suffered this relation in the public domain only. The lady, denied access to a freely chosen, mutually satisfying love relation, suffered it in the personal domain as well. Moreover, Castiglione's theory, unlike the courtly love it superseded, subordinated love itself to the public concerns of the Renaissance nobleman. He set forth the relation of the sexes as one of dependency and domination, but he did so in order to express and deal with the political relation and its problems. The personal values of love, which the entire feudality once prized, were henceforth increasingly left to the lady. The courtier formed his primary bond with the modern prince.

In sum, a new division between personal and public life made itself felt as the state came to organize Renaissance society, and with that division the modern relation of the sexes made its appearance,[5] even among the Renaissance nobility. Noblewomen, too, were increasingly removed from public concerns—economic, political, and cultural—and although they did not disappear into a private realm of family and domestic concerns as fully as their sisters in the patrician bourgeoisie, their loss of public power made itself felt in new constraints placed upon their personal as well as their social lives. Renaissance ideas on love and manners, more classical than medieval, and almost exclusively a male product, expressed this new subordination of women to the interests of husbands and male-dominated kin groups and served to justify the removal of women from an "unlady-like" position of power and erotic indepen-

5. The status of women as related to the distinction of public and private spheres of activity in various societies is a key idea in most of the anthropological studies in *Women, Culture, and Society,* eds. Michelle Zimbalist Rosaldo and Louise Lamphere, Stanford University Press, Stanford, 1974.

dence. All the advances of Renaissance Italy, its protocapitalist
economy, its states, and its humanistic culture, worked to mold the
noblewoman into an aesthetic object: decorous, chaste, and doubly
dependent—on her husband as well as the prince.

DAVID QUINT

Courtier, Prince, Lady: The Design of the *Book of the Courtier*†

A consensus has emerged in feminist criticism of the *Book of the
Courtier*, particularly concerning the discussions in Book 3 of the
court lady—the *donna di palazzo*—that end with the violent misogynist outburst of Gasparo Pallavicino, a tirade which for its length
and vehemence can barely be contained within the decorum of the
court society and of Castiglione's book. The general lines of this
reading go as follows. a) The ladies present at Urbino have little to
say about their identity and role in the court, for these are defined
for them by the male courtiers; and their lack of a voice of their own
reflects the more general subordination of women in the patriarchal
culture in Renaissance Italy. b) Insofar as the defenders of women
(Cesare Gonzaga, the Magnifico Giuliano de' Medici) are able to
counter their detractors (Gasparo, Niccolò Frisio, Ottaviano
Fregoso) and to assign positive virtues to the court lady beyond
patriarchy's absolute requirement of chastity, these virtues are for
the most part passive and decorative: the lady is ascribed cultural
accomplishments in order that she be able to receive and appreciate those of the courtier; the lady should be beautiful. c) In her subordination to men, in her transformation into an aesthetic object,
the court lady holds up a disturbing mirror to the male courtier himself, subordinated as he is politically to the prince whom he serves,
his own role reduced to being a cultural ornament to the court. As
Ottaviano Fregoso ruefully concedes in Book 4, the courtier has
himself become effeminate (4.4).[1]

---

† From *Italian Quarterly* 37.143–46 (Winter–Fall 2000): 185–95. Reprinted by permission
of the publisher and the author.
1. "If the courtier who charms the prince bears the same relation to him as the lady bears
to the courtier, it is because Castiglione understood the relation of the sexes in the same
terms that he used to describe the political relation: i.e., as a relation between servant and
lord." This is the formula of Joan Kelly in her polemical article, "Did Women Have a
Renaissance," in *Women, History, & Theory: The Essays of Joan Kelly* (Chicago and
London: The University of Chicago Press, 1984), p. 46; it is cited by Carla Freccero in
her essay, "Politics and Aesthetics in Castiglione's *Il Cortegiano*: Book III and the
Discourse on Women," in *Creative Imitation: New Essay on Renaissance Literature in
Honor of Thomas M. Greene*, ed. David Quint et al. (Binghamton, N.Y.: Medieval and

This reading has the merit of asking us to think about how the discussions of Book 3, too easily written off by earlier criticism as a mere rehearsal of the tropes of the *querelle des femmes*, fit into the larger argument of the *Book of the Courtier*. It counters Jacob Burckhardt's assertion, to be sure a vast overstatement of the case, that in the Renaissance women achieved equality with men—though, in doing so, it may underestimate the innovation of Castiglione's assigning value to female learning and female beauty.[2] It acknowledges, furthermore, the political dimension of the *Courtier*, which describes the role of the princely court in the efforts of the early modern state to tame and control a feudal warrior nobility: that transformation of soldier-aristocrat into polite courtier that Norbert Elias called the "civilizing process."[3] But its political alignment of the court lady with

Renaissance Texts and Studies, 1992), pp. 259–279. Valeria Finucci in *The Lady Vanishes: Subjectivity and Representation in Castiglione and Ariosto* (Stanford: Stanford University Press, 1992) evokes Kelly's argument in her own discussion of how Castiglione's courtiers have to "cancel . . . the possibilities that they themselves have been feminized in their daily lives" (p. 43). Finucci criticizes Kelly for having, like Burckhardt, used "rhetorical, literary images of women to draw conclusions about real women." I would add the differences that Kelly finds between the medieval courts of love and Castiglione's court at Urbino masks far greater literary continuities between the two.

Kelly may have known that she was arguing against the grain of the *Courtier*: she acknowledges, only to deny, the "likeness of the lady to the prince" in Bembo's exposition of Neoplatonic love (p. 44). In *Renaissance Feminism* (Ithaca and London: Cornell University Press, 1990), Constance Jordan provides a more subtle account of the power relations of the *Courtier*, she seems to echo Kelly when she writes that the courtier's "status vis-a-vis his lord is similar to that of a wife in relation to her husband" (77–78), but goes on to explore how Castiglione's courtier is subject to the women of the court of Urbino.

2. See Burckhardt's chapter on "The Position of Women" (V.6) in *The Civilization of the Renaissance in Italy*, trans. Ludwig Geiger and Walther Götz (New York: Harper and Brothers, 1958), 2:389–395. The question of whether and to what extent the role that Castiglione assigns to the court lady was emancipatory for real noblewomen at court is a vexed one. In a distinguished essay, "Osservazioni sul terzo libro del *Cortegiano*," *Aevum* 66 (1992): 519–537, Claudio Scarpati argues that Castiglione's book does, indeed, affirm the equality of the court lady and the courtier. Marina Zancan sees the court lady as complementary to the courtier and the possessor of equal social value, though his and her roles are gendered; see Zancan, "La donna e il cerchio nel *Cortegiano* di B. Castiglione. Le funzioni del femminile nell'imagine di corte," in *Nel cerchio della luna: Figure di donna in alcuni testi del XVI secolo*, ed. Marina Zancan (Venice: Marsilio, 1983), pp. 13–56.

Taking an opposing position, Adriana Chemello contrasts to the court lady defined by the *Courtier* both the professional, culturally accomplished courtesan and the protests against the oppression of "real" women voiced by a Renaissance woman author, Moderata Fonte, in "Donna di palazzo, moglie, cortigiana: ruoli e funzioni sociali della donna in alcuni trattati del Cinquecento," in *La corte e il "cortegiano": II. Un modello europeo*, ed. Adriano Prosperi (Rome: Bulzoni, 1980), pp. 113–132. Francesco Sberlati, in "Dalla donna di palazzo alla donna di famiglia, *I Tatti Studies* 7 (1997): 119–174, underscores the importance for later sixteenth century "feminist" writings of Castiglione's insistence on the lady's learning and her literary and artistic education; however Renaissance women's lives may have been enriched by these new cultural possibilities, he nonetheless acknowledges that their lives remained regimented in the three traditional stages of virgin, wife and mother, and widow. José Guidi draws somewhat similar conclusions in "De l'amour courtois a l'amour sacré: la condition de la femme dans l'oeuvre de B. Castiglione," in Guidi, Marie-Françoise Piejus, and Adelin-Charles Fiorato, *Images de la femme dans la littérature italienne de la Renaissance: Préjugés misogynes et aspirations nouvelles* (Paris: Université de la Sorbonne Nouvelle, 1980), pp. 9–80.

3. See Elias, *The Civilizing Process* (1939), translated from the German by Edmund Jephcott into two volumes, *The History of Manners* (New York: Pantheon Books, 1982)

the courtier seriously distorts the way that Castiglione shows women at court participating in this process of "civilizing" the nobleman—pacifying him and rendering him dependent on princely favor. If the ladies at the court contribute little to the conversation that spells out what their ideal role should be, it is ladies who nonetheless have the last say, who control the discussions of the *Courtier* itself: the Duchess who attends the evening games at Urbino and who appoints her lady-in-waiting, Emilia Pia, to oversee them.[4] It is for women that the male courtiers of the *Courtier*—and, by implication, its author, too—perform, an audience that both makes possible and perhaps limits the book's achievement. The political homology that structures and unifies the book aligns the court lady not with the disempowered courtier, but with the prince who has power over him—they have become one and the same in the person of the Duchess.

It should come as no surprise that this is so. The discourse of courtly love in the Middle Ages described the relationship of the male lover to his lady in the terms of service and reward that also characterized the relationship of the feudal vassal to his overlord: the lady is the lover's lord or "domina." So Pietro Bembo speaks of "serving"—"io servava" (1.11)—his lady as he and the courtiers at Urbino propose different games for the evening's entertainment at the beginning of the book.[5] The ensuing discussion of the courtier, in fact, take the place of the games about the questions of love that we gather are the usual fare at the palace and that continue to encode the language of courtly love.[6] This language, moreover, is commutable in the *Book of the Courtier*: not only does the lover serve the lady he loves, but the courtier is to love the prince he serves. Federico Fregoso describes the relationship—the "conversazione"—that should obtain between lord and servant: "I would have *the Courtier* devote all his thought and strength of spirit to loving and almost adoring the prince he serves above all else, devoting his every desire and habit and manner to pleasing him." ("si volti con tutti i pensieri e forze dell'animo suo ad amare e quasi adorare

and *Power and Civility* (New York: Pantheon Books, 1982). See also Elias, *The Court Society* (1969; English trans. Edmund Jephcott, New York: Pantheon Books, 1983). For the case of England, see Lawrence Stone, *The Crisis of the Aristocracy 1558–1641* (1965; abr. ed. Oxford: Oxford University Press, 1967).

4. Jordan, in *Renaissance Feminism*, pp. 76–85, acknowledges this subordination of the courtiers to the ladies of the court, but understands the discussions of Book III as Castiglione's demonstration of "the power of men to control even the duchess and Emilia Pia, women who have greater social and political status than they do" (84).

5. Citations of the Italian text of the *Courtier* are taken from the edition of Bruno Maier, *Il libro del Cortegiano con una scelta delle Opere minori* (Turin: UTET, 1964). The English translation is that of Charles Singleton, *The Book of the Courtier* (Garden City, N.Y.: Anchor Books, 1959). Numbers in parentheses indicate book and section.

6. On these courtly games, see Thomas M. Greene, "*Il Cortegiano* and the Choice of a Game," *Renaissance Quarterly* 32 (1979): 173–86; reprinted in *Castiglione. The Ideal and the Real in Renaissance Culture*, ed. Robert W. Hanning and David Rosand (New Haven: Yale University Press, 1983), pp. 1–15.

il principe a chi serve sopra ogni altra cosa; e le voglie sue e costumi e modi tutti indrizzi a compiacerlo") (2.18). In return for their devotion, the courtier and lover expect from their prince and lady the reward that the *Courtier* from its very beginning (1.1) calls "grazia." The term covers both the more general favor—"quella universal grazia"—of the prince and of other nobles and ladies (2.17; 4.5)), and the specific mercenary favors which the prince may grant the courtier but for which the astute courtier will rarely, almost never ask (2.18; 2.19). It covers as well the favor—up to and including sexual favors—that the beloved lady will show her servant (3.4): see, for example, the discussion between the Unico Aretino and Emilia Pia on how to gain the favor of women—"acquistar la grazia delle donne"—in 3.61–62. This "grazia" is, furthermore, the recompense awarded to the "grazia" or grace of the courtier, itself, that winning quality of gracefulness and apparent effortlessness that accompanies his actions and that Ludovico Canossa in Book 1 derives from the calculated pose of *sprezzatura* (1.14; 1.25–28).[7]

In fact, the court lady and women in general emerge in Book 3 as a rival audience for whom, as well as for the Prince, the courtier puts on display the exquisite accomplishments that are outlined for him in Book 1. In Books 2 and 4, Frederico Fregoso and then Ottaviano Fregoso speak of how the courtier acquires the favor ("grazia") of the Prince through his good qualities—"per acquistar . . . grazia da quie signori ai quali serve, parmi necessario che e' sappia componere tutta la vita sua e valersi delle sue bone qualita" (2.7); "con gentil modo valersi della grazia acquistata con le sue bone qualità" (4.5). The same Federico Fregoso acknowledges in Book 3 that these qualities and abilities are aimed as well—or instead—at women: "every gallant cavalier employs those noble exercises, the elegance of dress, and the fine manners that we have mentioned as a means of gaining the favor ("grazia") of women"—"ogni gentil cavalliero usa per instrumento d'acquistar grazia di donne quie nobili esercizi, attillature e bei costumi che avemo nominati" (3.53). The courtiership which seeks to have an influence on the Prince, either for the courtier's benefit and self-promotion in Book 2 or, in Ottaviano's more idealistic vision in Book 4, for the goal of good government, can also become an entertainment for the ladies, an instrument of erotic courtship. It may, at one of the darkest moments of Castiglione's book in 3.50, be little more than a means to break down female chastity: Cesare Gonzaga speaks of the difficulty the lady experiences in defending her honor under the assault that her lover makes on her through "the fopperies, the inventions, mottoes, devices, festivals, dances, games,

---

7. On the grace of the courtier, see Eduardo Saccone, "Grazia, Sprezzatura, Affettazione in the *Courtier*," *Glyph* 5 (1979): 34–54, reprinted in *Castiglione*, pp. 45–67.

masquerades, jousts, tourneys—all of which she knows are done for
her"—"attilature, invenzioni, motti, imprese, feste, balli, giochi,
maschere, giostre, torniamenti, le quia cose essa conosce tutte esser
fatte per sé." The festive life of the court takes on a sinister hue, and
the courtier with all his art is reduced in this passage to a cynical
seducer. Does he behave any better, we are left to wonder, in his relationship to the Prince that mirrors his relationship to women?

This symmetry between the Prince and the Lady, each the recipient of the courtier's devoted attention, each the bestower or with-
holder of "grazia," continues in and shapes the discussions of Book
4, which Castiglione added to the final rendition of the *Courtier*. He
filled out further and moved from the earlier three-book version of
his book Ottaviano Fregoso's portrait of the courtier as the educator
of his prince in virtue and justice—Cesare Gonzaga complains that
he has made the courtier into a schoolmaster (4.36). The second
part of the book is taken up with Pietro Bembo's Neoplatonic discourse on love, where the courtier is no less of an educator, this
time of his lady. Ottaviano and Bembo use the same horticultural
metaphor to describe bringing the Prince and the Lady to the fruits
of virtue. Ottaviano speaks of the need of a master—Cesare's
schoolmaster—who can "awaken in us those moral virtues of which
we have the seed enclosed and planted in our souls"—"risvegli in
noi quelle virtú morali, delle quali avemo il seme incluso e sepulto
nell'anima"—in order to let them "flower or produce those fair fruits
which alone we should desire to see born in the human heart"—
"produr quie felici frutti, che soli si dovriano desiderar che
nascessero nei cori umani" (4.13). Bembo's lover will so improve his
Lady that, "by sowing virtue in the garden of her fair mind, he will
gather fruits of the most beautiful behavior, and will taste them with
wondrous delight"—"cosí seminando virtú nel giardin di quel bell
'animo, raccorrà ancora frutti di bellissimi costumi e gustaragli con
mirabil diletto" (4.62). The parallel suggests a common logic of sublimation and an underlying similarity between the apparently contrasting roles that Ottaviano and Bembo assign the courtier in the
active, political life and in the life of contemplation. Ottaviano tries
to teach the Prince to temper his desire for power—his "libido dom-
inandi"—just as Bembo's lover teaches his lady and himself a love
that transcends the desires of the flesh.[8]

8. On Ottaviano's role and the shape of the new fourth book of the *Courtier*, see Wayne
Rebhorn, "Ottaviano's interruption: Book IV and the problem of unity in *Il libro del
Cortegiano*," *Modern Language Notes* 87 (1972): 37–69; the essay is incorporated into
Rebhorn, *Courtly Performances: Masking and Festivity in Castiglione's "Book of the
Courtier"* (Detroit: Wayne State University Press, 1978), pp. 177–204. See also Laurence
V. Ryan, "Book IV of Castiglione's *Courtier*—Climax or Afterthought," *Studies in the
Renaissance* 19 (1972): 156–79; J. R. Woodhouse, *Castiglione* (Edinburgh: University of
Edinburgh Press, 1978), pp. 137–166; Daniel Javitch, *Poetry and Courtliness in
Renaissance England* (Princeton: Princeton University Press, 1978), pp. 40–49.

What both Ottaviano and Bembo would teach, however, is a lesson that the presence of women at court has already taught the courtier, the lesson of civilization itself: the restraint of aggression and the cultivation of good manners—that beautiful behavior which Bembo seeks to inculcate. The role of the court and particularly of its women in reshaping the behavior and identity of the Renaissance nobleman is nicely epitomized in a comic anecdote that Ludovico da Canossa tells early in Castiglione's book. Count Ludovico has just begun to outline the qualities that the ideal courtier should possess and he asserts that "the principal and true profession of the Courtier must be that of arms"—the Courtier is first and foremost a soldier. However, Ludovico immediately concedes that there is a situation where it is not appropriate to show off one's martial qualities, and that is precisely at court:

> We do not wish him to make a show of being so fierce that he is forever swaggering in his speech, declaring that he has wedded his cuirass, and glowering with such dour looks as we have often seen Berto [the court jester] do; for to such as these one may rightly say what in polite society a worthy lady [una valorosa donna in una nobile compagnia] jestingly said to a certain man (whom I do not now wish to name) whom she sought to honor by inviting him to dance, and who not only declined this but would not listen to music or take any part in the other entertainments offered him, but kept saying that such trifles were not his business. And when finally the lady said to him: 'What then is your business?' he answered with a scowl: 'Fighting.' Whereupon the lady replied at once: 'I should think it a good thing, now that you are not away at war or engaged in fighting, for you to have yourself greased all over and stowed away in a closet along with your battle harness, so that you won't grow any rustier than you already are'; and so, amid much laughter from those present, she ridiculed him in his stupid presumption. (1.17)

> Il quale non volemo però che si mostri tanto fiero, che sempre stia in su le brave parole e dica aver tolto la corazza per moglie, e minacci con quelle fiere guardature che spesso avemo vedute fare a Berto, ché a questi tali meritamente si po dir quello, che una valorosa donna in una nobile compagnia piacevolmente disse ad uno, ch'io per ora nominar non voglio; il quale essendo da lei, per onorarlo, invitato a danzare, e rifiutando esso e questo e lo udir musica e molti altri intertenimenti offertigli, sempre con dir cosí fatte novelluzze non esser suo mestiero, in ultimo, dicendo la donna, "Qual è dunque il mestier vostro," rispose con un mal viso: "Il combattere"; allora la donna sùbito: "Crederei," disse "che or che non siete alla guerra, né in termine de combattere, fosse bona cosa che vi faceste molto ben

untare ed insieme con tutti i vostri arnesi da battaglia riporre in
un armario finché bisognasse, per non ruginire piú di quello
che siate," e cosí, con molte risa de' circunstanti, scornato las-
ciollo nella sua sciocca prosunzione.

If the conversations of the *Courtier* are a game, the game is
already up here, even as it is first getting under way. The anecdote
announces the structure and tone of Book 1, which now moves
increasingly away from fighting to the arts of peace that are the
other accomplishments of the courtier, more precisely the accomplishments that define him as courtier. The ensuing definition of
sprezzatura turns discussion from the martial athleticism of the
knight on horseback to the grace of the dancer (compare 1.21–25
with 1.26–27), and subsequently to issues of writing, music, and
painting, and this movement from soldiering to high culture is further thematized in the debate between arms and letters in sections
45–46.[9] But, in effect, the entire *Book of the Courtier* moves the
courtier away from the battlefield and military life that is supposedly
his first profession and into a polite realm where he had better hang
up his armor and fighting ways at the door or risk the ridicule that
befalls the boorish soldier in Ludovico's anecdote. The court and its
etiquette become an instrument by which the prince can pacify,
keep an eye on, and control his warlike noble subjects: Castiglione
outlines a scenario that, as Elias and others have documented,
would be repeated over and over in early modern statebuilding.

In Castiglione's scenario, in the story of the scowling soldier who
has no time for dancing, it is the lady who represents the court and
stands in for the prince: a lady in whose presence another kind of
behavior is demanded of the nobleman, just as he is required to defer
before his prince. The lady offers to dance in order to *honor* him; that
is, she and the court, and behind them both, the prince, become an
alternate, rival source or dispenser of that honor—a sense of noble
selfhood and place in the larger social world—which the soldier
would claim to authenticate for himself from his own lineage and
from his fighting, an honor about which, Gasparo Pallavicino goes on
to object in the next section, he should be permitted himself to boast
(1.18).[1] The adjective, "valorosa," that describes the worthiness of

---

9. On dancing at court, see Stephen Kolsky, "Graceful Performances: The Social and
   Political Context of Music and Dance in the *Cortegiano,*" *Italian Studies* 53 (1998): 1–19.
1. On boasting and honor in the *Courtier*, see David Quint, "Bragging Rights: Honor and
   Courtesy in Shakespeare and Spenser," in *Creative Imitation*, pp. 391–430. See also the
   remarks of Scarpati in "Osservazioni": "La società feudale e cavalleresca, in cui l'onore
   era l'unica forma di possesso che i cadetti potevano esibire, trovava nell'autoelogio una
   via obbligata di affermazione dell'individuo. La nuova aristocrazia può invece recuperare
   il valore stoico dell'attenuazione coniugandolo con quello cristiano della non presunzione
   . . ." (524). Scarpati argues that the avoidance of presumption—the ostentation or praise
   of oneself—is the key virtue that Castiglione prescribes for both the courtier and the
   court lady and that lies behind all the modes of behavior his book recommends for them.

the lady is highly charged, for it suggests an equivalent to the military valor of the soldier. His refusal to dance is a refusal of court culture and of a whole political as well as social arrangement that would make him dependent on the prince for his noble identity. Yet the ease with which the lady rebukes him suggests that this warrior-aristocrat is behind the times, that such identity has already been transformed —that he had better learn how to give up his aggression and to dance and please ladies or be laughed out of the court and noble society ("nobile compagnia") itself. Arms may still be the first profession of the noble courtier, but he is now a courtier first, soldier second.

The design and logic of the *Book of the Courtier* as a whole is thus circular. The princely court and its ladies tame the aggression of a military aristocracy, turn them into the prince's servants, and diminish their potential threat to his rule. Taught restraint and polite manners by the court, Castiglione's courtier (Ottaviano Fregoso, Pietro Bembo) seeks, in turn, in Book 4 to teach temperate rule to the prince and a sublimated, Neoplatonic love to the lady. Lady and Prince are consistently paralleled, and the lady—as the object for whom the courtier learns the skills of civilization and arts of peace—does the prince's work for him, creating a more docile and tractable nobility. If the nobleman comes to court to serve and be near his prince, his main activity there is to associate and converse with ladies: "most of our time at court is given over to it," comments Gasparo Pallavicino (2.31).

Hence the resentment against women that percolates through the *Courtier*, women who set the tone of the court society and its culture. In no small part, the misogyny of some of the courtiers who participate in its conversation can be understood as a response to their situation at court itself, to their being both the dependent creatures of the prince and the pleasing servants of ladies. Ottaviano Fregoso, one of the enemies of women in the book, suggests in his opening remarks in Book 4 that the pacification of the nobility at court has been only too successful. The art of pleasing women practiced at the courts, he comments, makes the courtier womanish: "these elegances of dress, devices, mottoes, and other such things as pertain to women and love (although many will think the contrary), often serve merely to make spirits effeminate"—"queste attilature, imprese, motti ed altre tai cose che appartengono ad intertenimenti di donne e d'amori, ancora che forse a molti altri paia il contrario, spesso non fanno altro che effeminar gli animi" (4.4)—and he sees in this effeminized court culture a cause of Italy's military decline. Turned into women-serving courtiers, the Italian nobility, Ottaviano suggests, have become womanish and all but abandoned their principal profession of arms, leaving the peninsula defenseless before its foreign invaders: "there are but few who dare, I will not say, to die, but even to risk any danger."[2] No wonder, then, that the fighting man of Count Ludovico's anecdote bridles at dancing before the ladies. Ottaviano, however, mystifies the story of disempowerment he tells, ascribing to the women at court the transformation of Italy's martial nobility into peaceable courtiers—rather than to the prince who brings the noble-man to the women-dominated court in the first place.

We may feel, in fact, that the attacks on women in the *Book of the Courtier* are partly a displacement of the resentment that the male courtier feels, but cannot allow himself fully to express, toward the prince and toward the position of subordination in which he finds himself at court. Women, already criticized by a long Western tradi-tion of misogny, are an easier, safer target than the prince; they become a safety-valve that allows the courtier to vent anger that may not be exclusively directed toward them. They are so, however, because the terms of Castiglione's book repeatedly align the court lady with the prince, both holding power at court over the courtier, both the recipients of his love and services. These terms lend Gasparo Pallavicino's outburst against women at the end of Book 3 (74–75) its particular power and, despite its comic excess, its poignancy. Castiglione moved the passage to the very end of Book 3 and made it the climax of the discussion of the court lady. Gasparo speaks the language of unrequited love, of service gone unrewarded.

> they neither content their lovers, nor reduce them to utter despair, but in order to keep them continually in worries and in desire, they resort to a certain domineering austerity in the form of threats mingled with hope, and expect a word of theirs, a look, a nod, to be deemed the highest happiness. . . . They lie every night with the vilest men, men whom they scarcely know; and in order to enjoy the calamities and continual laments of the noble cavaliers whom they love, they deny them-selves those pleasures which they might perhaps be excused for enjoying. . . . There are other women who, if they trick many men into thinking themselves loved by them, keep alive the jealousies among them by showing affection and favor to one in the presence of the other; and then, when they see that the one they most love is already confident that he is loved because of the demonstrations shown him, they put him in suspense by ambiguous words and feigned anger, and pierce his heart, pre-tending to care nothing for him, and that they mean to give themselves wholly to another. . . .

2. In the penultimate, second redaction of the *Courtier* in three books, these words of Ottaviano are spoken by Gasparo Pallavicino and placed in the middle of the discussions about the court lady and women more generally. Gasparo's conclusion is unequivocal: "And women are the cause of all this situation"—"E di tutto questo sono causa le donne." See *La seconda redazione del "Cortegiano" di Baldassarre Castiglione*, ed. Ghino Ghinassi (Florence: Sansoni, 1968), p. 280. See also Scarpati, "Osservazioni," p. 535.

non contentano né disperano mai gli amanti del tutto; ma per mantenergli continuamente negli affanni e nel desiderio usano una certa imperiosa austerità di minacce mescolate con speranza, e vogliono che una loro parola, uno sguardo, un cenno sia da essi riputato per somma felicità. . . . Si giaceno tutte le notti con omini vilissimi e da esse a pena conosciuti, di modo che per godere delle calamità e continui lamenti di qualche nobil cavaliero e da esse amato, negano a se stesse que' piaceri che forse con qualche escusazione potrebbono conseguire. . . . Alcun'altre sono le quali, se con inganni possono indurre molti a credere d'essere da loro amati, nutriscono tra essi le gelosie col far carezze e favore all'uno in presenza dell'altro; e quando veggon che quello ancor che esse più amano già si confida d'esser amato per le demostrazioni fattegli, spesso con parole ambigue e sdegni simulati lo suspendeno e gli traffiggono il core, mostrando non curarlo e volersi in tutto donare all'altro. . . . (3.74)

What happens if, given the symmetry the *Courtier* establishes between the two, we read this courtier's complaint about his ungrateful lady as a description as well of his relationship to his prince, if we substitute "prince" for "women" in the charges Gasparo makes against womankind? The frustration toward the lady he serves parallels the experience of the courtier frustrated by a prince 1) who keeps his servants in perpetual uncertainty by alternately promising and withholding his favor, 2) who raises up unworthy men to positions of favor instead of his faithful gentlemen, 3) who plays his courtiers off one against the other, raising one to favor and causing jealousy and envy among the rest, only to discard him and raise another. Early on the *Courtier* has criticized "the judgment of princes who, thinking to work miracles, sometimes decide to show favor to one who seems to them to deserve disfavor"—"la ostinazion dei signori, i quali, per voler far miracoli, talor si mettono a dar favore a chi par loro che meriti disfavore" (1.16)—that is, who deliberately raise "omini vilissimi" to places of favor and influence in order to demonstrate their own godlike, miracle-working power over the court and the other courtiers whom he thereby snubs. In Book 2, the god in question whom the Prince imitates is Fortune; in his capriciousness, he can refuse favor to the man of good character ("ben condizionato") and show his liking for a dullard ("un

3. For a discussion of Castiglione's prince as the godlike creator of the courtier and dispenser of grace upon him—in analogy with the *potentia absoluta* that nominalist thought ascribed to the Christian God—see Ullrich Langer, *Divine and Poetic Freedom in the Renaissance* (Princeton: Princeton University Press, 1990), 51–83; for the analogy with Fortune, see p. 62. Kenneth Burke examines some implications of the relationship between sovereign and deity in the *Courtier* in *A Rhetoric of Motives* (1950; rpt. Berkeley, Los Angeles and London: University of California Press, 1969), pp. 221–233.

ignorantissimo") (2.32).[3] The courtier, meanwhile, is cautioned not
to behave as some do: "if they chance to meet with disfavor, or if
they see others favored, they suffer such agony that they are quite
unable to conceal their envy"—"e se per sorte hanno qualche disfavore, o vero veggono alri esser favoriti, restano con tanta angonia,
che dissimular per modo alcuno non possono quella invidia" (2.19).
Such envy was perceived to be the particular vice of the
Renaissance court, caused precisely, in the words of one near contemporary writer, Matteo Bandello, by the changing favor of the
Prince that "in one moment lifts him who was low and lowers him
who found himself on high."[4] The *Courtier* at its beginning declares
that it will teach the gentleman how to win favor from the prince
"and praise from others"—"e dagli altri laude" (1.1)—the others in
question being his fellow courtiers, and the book repeatedly seeks to
find "a very great and strong shield against envy, which we ought to
avoid as much as possible"—"grandissimo e fermissimo scudo contra la invidia, la qual si dee fuggir quanto piú si po" (2.41). The envy
the prince's capricious favor arouses among his courtiers matches
the jealousy that Gasparo's lady kindles among her lovers.

To observe that Gasparo's complaints about the courtship he pays
to his lady have their counterpart in the courtiership he practices
before his prince is not to explain away Gasparo's misogyny, but to
explain its place in Castiglione's larger book. To be a Renaissance
courtier, the *Courtier* makes clear, means both to serve a prince and
to enter into a court society where women enjoy an unusual position of prominence and have to be pleased and served as well. The
first kind of service may be bad enough for an aristocrat forced to
civilize himself and to give up the traditional aggressiveness and personal independence of his class; on top of it, the second, Gasparo
suggests, is intolerable. The parallel between the two kinds of service, moreover discloses the element of instinctual repression that
is involved in the courtier's accommodation to the codes of civility.[5]
He needs to sublimate the pleasures of open aggression, both political and erotic, in the polite confines of the court culture and in the
worshipful stance it takes towards both prince and beloved lady;
Bembo's discourse on love in the following book shows how such

4. "È ben vero che ne le cose de le corti si può trovare qualche fondamento di ragione di
queste mutazioni, e questo è il pungente e venenoso stimolo de la pestifera invidia, il quale
di continuo tien i favori del prencipe su la bilancia, *ed in un momento alza chi era basso
e abassa chi in alto si trovava*, di maniera che ne le corti non ci è peste piú nociva né piú
dannosa del morbo de l'invidia." (Novella, I.2) Bandello, *Tutte le Opere di Matteo
Bandello*, ed. Francesco Flora (Verona: Mondadori, 1934–1935), 1:40.

5. Northrop Frye comments in an essay on the *Courtier*: "An extraordinary amount of sexual hostility is expressed in this book, and again the reason is the same: sexuality is normally aggressive and domineering, and education is largely a matter of channelling its
energy into something more in keeping with civilized life." Frye, "Il *Cortegiano*," *Quaderni
d'italianistica* 1 (1980); 1–14, p. 10.

sublimation might become complete. Gasparo's outburst is comic—even his fellow misogynist Ottaviano laughs at him (3.76)—both in its violation of decorum and in the sexual frustration it manifests. He says what the courtier-suitor may think about the lady but is not supposed to say, and he thus risks looking as ridiculous and out of place at court as the soldier in Count Ludovico's anecdote. The violence of his attack on women responds in kind to the episode at the end of Book 2 that provides the cue for the discussion of the ideal court lady in Book 3: there, the real court ladies at Urbino, on signal from the Duchess herself, "rushed laughing upon signor Gasparo as if to assail him with blows and treat him as the bacchantes treated Orpheus, saying the while: 'Now you shall see whether we care if we are slandered'"—"ridendo tutte corsero verso il signor Gasparo, come per dargli delle busse, e farne come le Baccanti d'Orfeo, tutavia dicendo:—Ora vedrete, se ci curiamo che di noi si dica male" (2.96). It is mock-violence, of course, but the allusion to the silencing and death of Orpheus, dismembered at the hands of the maenads, suggests the extent to which the courtiers at this women-dominated court are subject to an emasculating censorship. We sense in Gasparo, the constant, needling figure of dissent in Castiglione's book, a voice that refuses to censor itself and that, in the very intensity of his outburst at the end of Book 3, attests to how heavy are the restraints and discontents that the process of civilization have imposed on it. At the end of the *Courtier* Gasparo is still atacking women (4.72)—and, by doing so, attacking the institution and culture of the court itself—while in the final words of the book, Emilia Pia tries once again to bring him into line.[6]

In the *Book of the Courtier*, the court lady is not, then, represented in the conventional terms of patriarchal culture that subordinate women to men and that would make the lady subservient to

6. This Gasparo is very much the product of Castiglione's final revision of the *Courtier*. In the second redaction, the great enemy of women is Ottaviano Fregoso; it is he whom the court ladies attack like bacchantes at the end of Book 2 (Seconda redazione, p. 179) and whom Emilia Pia cites as a suspect and a fugitive at the end of the book (p. 324). Furthermore, Gasparo's outburst was placed in the mouth of Niccolò Frisio (pp. 316–318); the historical Frisio would confirm his antagonism to women by becoming a monk in 1510. Gasparo thus inherits the speeches and attitudes of these other protagonists and achieves a much greater prominence and consistency of character in Castiglione's final version. (By the same token, Ottaviano's misogyny is now somewhat downplayed, and can be more easily dissociated from his political idealism in Book 4). Gasparo's outburst at the end of Book 3, moreover, is followed almost immediately by the announcement of his premature death in the great elegiac opening of Book 4: Gasparo was the first of the company celebrated in the *Courtier* to die. The effect of the announcement of his death is at least twofold. It reminds us that Gasparo was young, and that we are to understand his refractory, iconoclastic energy, and perhaps his misogyny as well, as the attitudes of youth and immaturity (see Frye, "Il *Cortegiano*," p. 10). It also suggests a final silencing of Gasparo's dissenting voice: what the court society could not completely contain is put to rest by death. The further implication may be that, with the death of this voice, court culture twenty years later is less ready to question its civilized assumptions.

the male courtier as he is, in turn, subservient to the prince. These are the terms, to be sure, with which the misogynists of Book 3 would seek to put women back in their traditional social place. But Castiglione's larger book portrays rather the unusual role the court gives the lady in civilizing the courtier and which makes him her servant much as he is the servant of the prince. The lady is a princely servant as well, but she is seen to act in concert with the prince in carrying out the court's cultural and political project, and she thus acquires a measure of social power. And it is for this reason that the discussions of the status of women in Book 3 take on such importance in the *Book of the Courtier*. For the question of the dignity of women, a question still left open at the end of the book, directly concerns the dignity of court life itself, where the courtier devotes so much time and energy to pursuits that will please ladies. For would such civilized and polite activities be worthwhile, if women were the inferior creatures their detractors Gasparo and Ottaviano make them out to be?[7]

As a product of this court culture, the *Book of the Courtier* is itself implicated and has a stake in this question. In Book 3, Cesare Gonzaga praises women as the recipients and hence the cause of the courtier's cultural refinements.

> Do you not see that the cause of all gracious exercises that give us pleasure is to be assigned to women alone? Who learns to dance gracefully for any reason except to please women? Who devotes himself to the sweetness of music for any other reason? Who attempts to compose verses, at least in the vernacular, unless to express sentiments inspired by women . . . would it not be a very great loss if messer Francesco Petrarca, who wrote of his loves so divinely in this language of ours, had cared only for Latin, as would have happened if love for madonna Laura had not sometimes distracted him? (52)

> Non vedete voi che in tutti gli esercizi graziosi e che piaceno al mondo a niun altro s'ha da attribuire la causa, se alle donne no? Chi studia di danzare e ballar leggiadramente per altro, che per compiacere a donne? Chi intende nella dolcezza della musica per altra causa, che per questa? Chi a compor versi,

---

7. The same question is asked about the prince, but in a more muted way, in Book 2, where in sections 21 and 22, Vincenzio Calmeta suggests that the princes of the present day love only presumption on the part of their courtiers. Federico Fregoso tells him he must not say so, "for that would be too plain an argument that the princess of our day are all corrupt and bad—which is not true, because there are some who are good" (22). This answer suggests that most princes are, indeed, bad, and in the next sentence Fregoso advises the courtier to leave the service of such princes. To serve an unworthy prince would be the same as serving unworthy ladies: it would make court life itself unworthy. Calmeta responds however that the courtier can only pray to God to grant him a good master, "for, once we have them, we have to endure them as they are." Castiglione, the servant of the murderer Francesco Maria della Rovere, knew this only too well.

almen nella lingua vulgare, se no per esprimere quegli affetti
che dalle donne sono causati? . . . non saria grandissima
perdita se messer Francesco Petrarca, il qual cosí divinamente
scrisse in questa nostra lingua gli amor suoi, avesse volto l'animo solamente alle cose latine, come aria fatto se l'amor di
madonna Laura da ció non l'avesse talor desviato?

The references to writing in the Italian vernacular and to
Petrarch are especially pointed. The civilization of the court,
directed to a public that includes, and may even be centrally constituted by, cultured ladies, makes possible a high-culture literature in Italian, rather than in the learned language of Latin. Such
writing cannot become too learned or the ladies—and men similarly unversed in philosophy and Latinity—will not understand it:
so Emilia Pia complains at 3.17 when the debate between Gasparo and the Magnifico Giuliano becomes too technical, a
moment that is as much about the cultural level of the *Book of
the Courtier* as about the conversation at Urbino it purports to
recount. The implied female audience of the court is both a limit
upon the writing it fosters and what enables this writing to carve
out a cultural domain for itself: to declare itself to be what we call
"literature" or "polite letters," as opposed to philosophy, theology,
and other learned disciplines. The *Courtier* would, in fact, join
Petrarch's poetry to become a new classic of this literature; here
Castiglione concedes that it, too, like the other cultural endeavors
of the court, depends upon the ladies who preside over the court
society and set its tone.[8] Like his character Cesare Gonzaga, Castiglione acknowledges that to defend women is to defend the
Courtier who aims to please them, in this case the book as well
as the man.

8. The passage in the second redaction was much longer and included a list of Castiglione's
   contemporary writers, among them Sannazaro, Bembo, Ariosto, and Ecquicola, all of
   whom are said to have written for and about women (Seconda redazione, pp. 277–278).
   Gasparo counters with a list of his own—Sadoleto, Vida, Navagero—sixteenth century
   writers who composed largely in Latin and on religious and historical subjects (p. 281).
   The passage neatly distinguished a vernacular courtly literature from a learned humanist
   one—perhaps too neatly, Castiglione may have subsequently felt when he deleted it; see
   Scarpati, "Osservazioni," pp. 534–535. The prominence of the *Courtier* in the emerging
   sixteenth century Italian literary canon that, in its refined courtly forms of expression, distinguished itself both from the erudite Latin of scholars and from the localized Italian
   literature (Florentine, Neapolitan, Ferrarese) of the fifteenth century is the subject of
   studies by Giancarlo Mazzacurati; see his *Il rinascimento dei moderni* (Bologna: Il
   Mulino, 1985), especially pp. 149–207, and *Conflitti di culture nel cinquecento* (Naples:
   Liguori, 1977).

WAYNE REBHORN

Ottaviano's Interruption[†]

Castiglione emphasizes the patterned, stylized character of social life at his ideal court by dividing *Il Cortegiano* into four separate evenings of discussion and having each evening open in approximately the same fashion: the group has assembled at the usual time in the usual place; the duchess or Emilia Pia entreats the principal speaker to expound his views; and after the latter has played some variation on the elaborate deference ritual performed by every principal speaker before beginning his exposition, he does in fact accept his assignment, and the discussions finally get under way. For this highly formalized opening Castiglione could have found no precedent in dialogue writers like Plato or Cicero; even Bembo, who has *Gli Asolani* take place on three successive afternoons, presents his characters' discussions as exceptional occurrences, not as parts of a regularly recurring, elaborately patterned, social routine. Moreover, comparison between the final, published text of *Il Cortegiano* and Castiglione's earlier versions of the work reveals him consciously revising his manuscript in order to underscore the ceremonial character of life at Urbino. For instance, not only does the *Seconda redazione* of *Il Cortegiano*, which Castiglione completed sometime before 1520 or 1521, have one less book than his final version and thus one less opportunity to display the routines of his characters' social life. but its first book opens by describing a full day's activities at the court rather than focusing immediately and exclusively, as the final text does, on the elaborate ceremonies that initiate the after-dinner discussions.[1] The *Seconda redazione* also contains fewer direct references to the patterned, game-like nature of life at Urbino, and at one point it actually stresses the great variety of disparate activities in which the courtiers engage themselves: "E benché questa vita non fosse sempre di una medema [*sic*] stampa.

---

† From *Courtly Performances: Masking and Festivity in Castiglione's Book of the Courtier* (Detroit: Wayne State University Press, 1978), 177–89, 220–22. Reprinted by permission of the publisher.

1. For the date of the second version of *Il Cortegiano*, see Ghino Ghinassi, "Fasi dell'elaborazione del 'Cortegiano,'" *Studi di filologia italiana* 25 (1967): 177–84. In the *Seconda redazione*, Castiglione explains how Duke Guidobaldo spends his time after lunch taking care of official business and describes the varied activities of the courtiers (I, 2–3, 5–8). Only then does he describe how they ate dinner together and afterwards retired to the duchess's chambers. In the final version of this passage. Castiglione reduces his description of the afternoon activities to a most summary statement in order to move directly to the evening ceremonies: "Erano adunque tutte l'ore del giorno divise in onorevoli e piacevoli esercizi così del corpo come dell'animo; ma perché il signor Duca continuamente, per la infirmitá, dopo cena assai per tempo se n'andava a dormire, ognuno per ordinario dove era la signora duchessa Elisabetta Gonzaga a quell'ora si riduceva . . ." (I, 4, 85). References to the *Cortegiano* are to the edition of Bruno Maier (Torino, UTET, 1964).

pur mai d'altro che di vertuose operazioni non era variata" (I, 3, 8: "And although this life was not always of the same character, it was really never varied by other than virtuous activities"). Castiglione carefully excised this sentence from his final text lest it impair the impression he wished to create of stylization and ritualization at his ideal court.

Consequently, because *Il Cortegiano* establishes so firmly the repeated patterns distinguishing Urbino's social life, when Ottaviano Fregoso interrupts its standard opening procedures at the start of Book IV, his delicate, subtly calculated action acquires great force by frustrating the well-entrenched expectations of courtiers and readers alike. Castiglione describes how, at the beginning of that fourth evening, the lords and ladies of Urbino have come together "all'ora consueta" (IV, 3, 448) in the usual place, and are waiting with anticipation for the arrival of Ottaviano, who has strangely been in retirement all day. No Ottaviano appears, however, and after searching for him in vain, the courtiers and ladies turn to dancing. By the time Ottaviano finally does walk in unexpectedly sometime later, his small alteration of the normal routine must appear a brilliantly calculated, dramatic gesture which proves him a true embodiment of the courtly ideal. For while it does not threaten the others, because it puts Ottaviano in the slightly indecorous position of arriving late, it interrupts the routine just enough to surprise everyone and to gain the fixed attention of the entire company for the speech he is about to give (IV, 3, 449: "stando ognuno con molta attenzione").

Castiglione's revisions of his book reveal that he paid particular attention to this passage describing Ottaviano's late entry and that he altered it in several significant ways. In the first place, although both the *Seconda redazione* and the final text begin by describing how Ottaviano spent the day in retirement, the earlier version suggests facetiously that he was hiding because of the odious nature of his task (i.e., defending his misogynism), while the final text simply stresses his need for solitude in which to think carefully about what he would say and thus implies a greater respect for the seriousness of his ideas and his concern. Secondly, although both passages then describe how all the inhabitants of Urbino arrived in the duchess's chambers at the usual hour and had to search out the missing Ottaviano, both passages continue and conclude in strikingly different fashions:

> . . . bisognò con diligenzia fa[r] cercare il signor Ottaviano; il quale in ultimo venne, e vedendo messer Camillo in mezo delle donne, che ciascuna come suo diffensore lo accarezzava, disse: "Fategli vezzi, ché lo merita, volendo dire così gran bugie per amor vostro come si apparecchia di far questa sera!"
> (*Sec. red.*, III, 3, 186–87

. . . they had to have signor Ottaviano searched out with diligence; finally he came, and seeing messer Camillo in the midst of the women each of whom caressed him as her defender, he said: "Give him those endearments, since he merits them in wanting to tell such grand lies for your love as he is preparing to do this evening!"

. . . bisognò con diligenzia far cercar il signor Ottaviano, il quale non comparse per bon spacio; di modo che molti cavalieri e damigelle della corte cominciarono a danzare ed attendere ad altri piaceri, con opinion che per quella sera più non s'avesse a ragionar del cortegiano. E già tutti erano occupati chi in una cosa chi in un'altra, quando il signor Ottaviano giunse quasi più non aspettato; e vedendo che messer Cesare Gonzaga e 'l signor Gaspar danzavano, avendo fatto riverenzia verso la signora Duchessa, disse ridendo:—Io aspettava pur d'udir ancor questa sera il signor Gaspar dir qualche mal delle donne; ma vedendolo danzar con una, penso ch'egli abbia fatto la pace con tutte; e piacemi che la lite o, per dir meglio, il ragionamento del cortegiano sia terminato così.

(IV, 3, 448)

. . . a diligent search had to be made for signor Ottaviano, who for a good while did not appear; so that many cavaliers and ladies of the court began to dance, and engage in other pastimes, thinking that for that evening there would be no more talk about the Courtier. And indeed all were occupied, some with one thing and some with another, when signor Ottaviano arrived after he had almost been given up; and, seeing that messer Cesare Gonzaga and signor Gasparo were dancing, he bowed to the Duchess and said, laughing: "I quite expected to hear signor Gasparo speak ill of women again this evening; but now that I see him dancing with one, I think he must have made his peace with all of them; and I am pleased that the dispute (or rather the discussion) about the Courtier has ended so."

(208–9)

Note the differences: the later text increases and underscores the length of time Ottaviano is absent; it establishes that the others feel he will not come at all, thus implicitly acknowledging the total inter-
͞otion of their previous routines which they themselves have reaf-
͞d in deciding to dance instead of talk; finally, the later text dra-
Ottaviano's last minute entry and stresses its complete
͞lness ("quasi più non aspettato"). Clearly, as Castiglione
͞ book for publication, not only did he increasingly
͞ted patterns of Urbino's social life, but he also

placed far greater emphasis on the small but dramatic interruption Ottaviano creates by means of his strategically delayed entrance.

Castiglione emphasizes Ottaviano's interruption precisely because it serves as a symbolic cue introducing the greater seriousness and weightiness of the fourth book in comparison with the first three. Such emphasis would not have suited earlier versions of *Il Cortegiano* nearly so well as it does the final text. In the *Seconda redazione*, as in the final version, Castiglione begins his last book with an elegiac passage based on the opening of the last book in Cicero's *De Oratore*,[2] and in both versions, Ottaviano then expounds his elevated conception of the courtier's social and political functions.[3] The final book of the *Seconda redazione* was, however, essentially still in a transitional state; a rambling debate about women and love, it did not end on the high note of Bembo's Neoplatonic idealism but on the low note of Gasparo's misogynistic denunciation of women.[4] As Castiglione reworked this earlier version of his *Cortegiano*, he not only added Bembo's speech, but, more importantly, he also divided and re-arranged all of his material, separating the less lofty debates about women and love, which became his new Book III, from the speeches of Ottaviano and Bembo, which Castiglione's own characters consider more serious and which constitute the present Book IV. As Castiglione moved beyond his earlier conceptions, leaving behind him those popular treatises on women's place in court society that once may have served as a significant motivation for his work, he conceived the speeches of his new fourth book as the most elevated definition of the meaning and purpose of courtly life that he could imagine, and thus as the most fitting conclusion for his masterpiece.[5]

In order to underscore the more elevated, serious character of this last book and its new conceptions, he must have decided that he also had to rewrite the passage describing Ottaviano's interruption. Perhaps his decision was influenced by what Alberti and Bembo had done in the final books of their dialogues, where the former introduced a change of locale and the latter added a crowd and an elaborate ceremony in order to signal the slightly more elevated status of the conceptions about to be offered. In any case, in the final version of the passage, Castiglione stresses the way that

2. Cf. *Sec. red.*, III, 1, 183, and IV, 1, 445–46, with *De Oratore*, III, i–iii.
3. Cf. *Sec. red.*, III, 5–42 with IV, 4–42. The two passages are by no means identical in every regard.
4. Although the germs of Bembo's oration are present in the *Seconda redazione* (III, 112–16), they are completely overwhelmed by the debate between the misogynists and their opponents that dominates this earlier version of Castiglione's final book from the point where Ottaviano finishes his exposition of the courtier's social and political functions to the very end of the work.
5. Ghinassi, op. cit., 173–75; and Lawrence V. Ryan, "Book Four of Castiglione's *Courtier*: Climax or Afterthought?" *SRen* 19 (1972): 159.

Ottaviano's interruption has created an inversion of the normal order of events established on previous evenings: before, the dancing had followed, not preceded conversation, while now, on this fourth evening, conversation takes place only after the implicitly less serious business of dancing is done with. Secondly, Castiglione describes how Ottaviano spent the entire day and, by implication, part of the evening as well, meditating upon his assignment, and nowhere does he suggest that his speaker's absence results from embarrassment over charges of misogynism. Finally, by stressing the considerable amount of time the group spends dancing before Ottaviano finally appears, Castiglione not only makes it seem more reasonable that their conversations should last until morning, but he places their discussions clearly in the middle of the night, perhaps a time of deception and unreality but also traditionally a time of greater truths and more profound exploration of mysterious realms.[6] Ottaviano's interruption is hardly a simple gesture, and it should alert the reader, as it does the lords and ladies of Urbino, to expect the unexpected, to anticipate discussions that probe more deeply and more seriously than before. Thus though Ottaviano reestablishes the ritual forms by his first jesting remarks to the company and by his expected refusal to speak until ordered to do so by the duchess, he has used the social forms available to him in order to prepare auditors—and readers—for the discussions that follow.

  Ottaviano's interruption preludes the far-reaching changes the speakers of the fourth book wreak upon the ideal courtier. Ottaviano and Bembo adopt a far more serious tone in presenting their ideals, replacing the witty, informal presentations of the first three nights with more technical analyses in which explanations and clarifications, formerly less essential, now become prominent. Each implicitly rejects some essential feature of the earlier ideal, Ottaviano criticizing the courtier's uselessness and lack of social productivity, while Bembo rejects the sensual and earthly, though legitimate, love of Book III in favor of the world-denying ecstasy of his Neoplatonic vision.[7] Each speaker redefines the ideal in terms of his own values and attitudes, transforming someone conceived primarily as an actor and an artist, whose prime purposes were to serve his lady and achieve personal honor and dignity, into a mystic

6. Note that Castiglione omits an earlier reference to the coming of dawn at the end of Book II, a reference which would have implied that Bibbiena's speech went on through the depths of the night and which would thus have deprived Bembo's performance of some of its uniqueness. See *Sec. red.*, p. 181 n.
7. A number of critics have stressed the break between the first three books and the fourth in terms of changes of both content and tone. See, for example, Erich Loos, *Baldassare Castigliones "Libro del Cortegiano," Analecta Romanica*, 2 (Frankfurt am Main: Vittorio Klostermann, 1955), pp. 120–30; Giuseppe Toffanin, *Il "Cortegiano" nella trattatistica del Rinascimento* (Naples: Libreria scientifica editrice, n. d.), p. 160; and Ghinassi, op. cit., 175.

lover seeking self-transformation into pure spirit, and a humanist whose sole justification is the service he performs for his prince as educator and advisor.

Castiglione, however, does more than merely emphasize the superiority of this new ideal to the conceptions of previous books; he stresses its absolute differences from them as well. Just as he utilizes Ottaviano's interruption to signal the new and different ideals of Book IV, he has his characters themselves indicate forcefully that Ottaviano's and Bembo's visions of the ideal courtier are essentially incompatible in some basic respects with the vision of the first three books. Ottaviano's conception is rejected because he has turned the ideal courtier into a humanist *maestro di scuola* (IV, 36, 491), and when he later argues that Plato and Aristotle exemplify his ideal, even his fellow misogynist, Gasparo Pallavicino, feels moved to mock his assertion with an ironic comment:

> Io non aspettava già che 'l nostro cortegiano avesse tanto d'onore; ma poiché Aristotile e Platone son suoi compagni, penso che niun più debba sdegnarsi di questo nome. Non so già però s'io mi creda che Aristotile e Platone mai danzassero o fossero musici in sua vita, o facessero altre opere di cavalleria.
>
> (IV. 48, 510)

> I certainly did not expect our Courtier to be honored so; but since Aristotle and Plato are his companions, I think no one henceforth ought to despise the name. Still, I am not quite sure that I believe that Aristotle and Plato ever danced or made music in their lives, or performed any acts of chivalry.
>
> (241)

Similarly, although Bembo claims he accepts earlier notions of sensual love when framing his own ideal, the self-absorbed, spiritual passion he approves for the courtier is possible only after earthly and bodily concerns like sensual love have been transcended. Consequently, his notion of Neoplatonic love really appears the antithesis of the courtly love celebrated by the group in Book III.[8] Clearly, although Castiglione wants the reader to regard Book IV as an essential part of his work, the changes he effects in basic conceptions and which he so forcefully and self-consciously calls attention to open a vast gulf between the ideas and ideals of the fourth book and those of the first three.

At least two fundamentally different approaches to the problem

---

8. I fundamentally disagree with those critics who feel that there is no contradiction between the courtly love of Book III and the Neoplatonic love of Book IV. See, for instance, Joseph A. Mazzeo, *Renaissance and Revolution* (New York: Random House, 1965), p. 143; anod Kenneth Burke, *A Rhetoric of Motives* (Berkeley: University of California Press, 1962), pp. 221–33.

of explaining why Castiglione chose to create a new conception of
the courtier in his last book are possible. The first of these, the biographical approach, looks to the details of Castiglione's life in order
to explain the changes in his book: it generally argues that the
author originally intended a work in three books which he finished
in 1515 or 1516, that he subsequently experienced significant
changes in his life—the dissolution of the court at Urbino, his rise
to prominence in papal service, the death of his wife, and his
assumption of holy orders—and that these experiences led him to
add the material that eventually became the supplemental fourth
book. The last night of discussions is thus considered a revision of
earlier material, an attempt to remold the ideal in the light of a
greater political and religious seriousness.[9] Yet these biographical
explanations accounting for the relationship between the fourth
book and the first three by pointing to the genesis of Castiglione's
work simply do not satisfy. Either they turn *Il Cortegiano* into disguised autobiography, following the lead of Vittorio Cian,[1] or they
simply content themselves by substituting consideration of external,
biographical details for analysis of internal structure. In either case,
they look beyond the book itself rather than within it; they do violence to *Il Cortegiano* as a carefully wrought work of art and frag-
ment its unity into a series of biographical moments. Consequently
a second and better way of approaching the changes in the fourth
book would be to examine the themes and structure of the work
itself, seeking primarily within it explicit reasons for Castiglione's
alteration of his ideal. Looked at in this way, *Il Cortegiano* would
reveal its meaning from within: the new seriousness of the fourth
book could be read as a direct response to certain inadequacies in
the first three; its double reworking of the ideal courtier could be
considered an attempt to solve or at least avoid the two major problems that dogged Castiglione's heels throughout the earlier books—
the problems of deception and triviality.

Considering the first of these problems, it is remarkable how
often the first three books encounter the issue of deception while
failing or refusing to solve the problems it raises. Some issues, like
the question of language and the relative merits of painting and

9. Erich Loos sees the fourth book as Castiglione's response to his disillusionment after the
dissolution of the court at Urbino in 1516; see op. cit., pp. 202–7. Piero Floriani, relying
on the definitive manuscript investigations of Ghino Ghinassi, has argued for composition in three states which reflect Castiglione's concerns with personal problems. The first
three books, completed in early 1516, show Castiglione concerned with the courtier's
success, something he still had not obtained himself. Ottaviano's speech, completed in
1520 or 1521, sees Castiglione, then a political figure in Rome, meditating on his responsibilities. Finally, Bembo's Neoplatonic vision was probably composed between 1521 and
1524, after Castiglione's wife had died and he had taken holy orders. See Piero Floriani,
"La Genesi del 'Cortegiano': Prospettive per una ricerca," *Belfagor* 24 (1969): 373–85.
1. *Un illustre nunzio pontificio del Rinascimento, Baldassar Castiglione, Studi e testi*, 156
(Vatican City: Biblioteca Apostolica Vaticana, 1951), pp. 227–57 and passim.

sculpture, remain unresolved because they are peripheral to the ideal. Other issues, like the questions of nobility and the relative superiority of arms and letters, require compromises, and the courtiers leave them behind almost as soon as they have achieved a satisfactory compromise formulation. Only in the case of the debate on women, which is generated by the structural imbalance between men and women in Urbino's society and is essentially unresolvable, and in the matter of deception, do the courtiers return to the same issues repeatedly. Deception poses an especially complex and troubling problem for them, because they live in a world where appearance reigns supreme and where their chief task is learning how to recognize, understand, and manipulate it. But they worry most about deception because the courtly actor they fashion is the master of masking, the brilliant creator of his social personality who could, on that account, be considered a subtle deceiver, and consequently something less than morally ideal.

Leading the attack on the courtier's masking as deception, Gasparo Pallavicino expresses his reservations on three separate occasions, moving from oblique criticism to head-on assault. A rambunctious spirit of contradiction, Gasparo first attacks Ludovico da Canossa in Book I on the issue of inherited nobility, forcing him to abandon his original position, which simply assumed nobility was something valuable in itself for the ideal courtier, and to argue for it instead on the pragmatic grounds that it disposes others to receive the courtier favorably and thus facilitates his success. Recognizing "no ancestor but Adam,"[2] the egalitarian Gasparo wants a courtier who will win praise and honor through his real qualities and achievements, not through the gifts granted him by fortune or the credulity of men. In other words, by attacking inherited nobility, Gasparo really attacks obliquely a kind of deception where appearances, rather than real qualities, claim the rewards of praise and honor.[3]

Later, in the second book, Gasparo's attack on the courtier's masking as deception becomes much more explicit when he rejects Federico Gonzaga's concern over the ideal's dress and appearance. Criticizing such a concern as a reprehensible affectation for the trivial, Gasparo declares:

> A me non pare, . . . che si convenga, né ancor che s'usi tra abiti, e non alle parole ed alle opere, perché molti s'ingannariano; né senza causa dicesi quel proverbio che l'abito non fa 'l monaco.

> (II, 28, 233)

---

2. Ralph Roeder, *The Man of the Renaissance* (Cleveland, 1933), p. 347.
3. Compare Gasparo's defense of Lombard noblemen for freely engaging themselves in contests of strength with peasants; see II, 10, 204.

> It does not seem fitting to me, or even customary among persons of worth, to judge the character of men by their dress rather than by their words or deeds, for then many would be deceived; nor is it without reason that the proverb says: "The habit does not make the monk."
>
> (90)

Gasparo's challenge forces Federico to abandon his far too simple assertion that in this world "le cose estrinseche spesso fan testimonio delle intrinseche" (II, 27, 232: "external things often bear witness to inner things"), and to agree that he does not think men should be judged by their dress. But he refuses to yield an inch on the importance of external appearances, for in a world of facades where men are usually forced to judge by what they see long before they can judge by what they know, Federico surely argues sensibly that the courtier should try to manipulate his appearance so that it expresses his best qualities. Of course men should be judged by their words and deeds, but in this world, says Federico,

> ancor l'abito non è piccolo argomento della fantasia di chi lo porta, avvenga che talor possa esser falso; e non solamente questo, ma tutti i modi e costumi, oltre all'opere e parole, sono giudicio delle qualità di colui in cui si veggono.
>
> (II, 28, 234)
>
> . . . a man's attire is no slight index of the wearer's fancy, although sometimes it can be misleading; and not only that, but ways and manners, as well as deeds and words, are all an indication of the qualities of the man in whom they are seen.
>
> (90)

In this statement Federico hastens over the problem of deception that has troubled his fellow courtier, admitting only parenthetically ("avvenga che talor possa esser falso") that his ideal courtier could really be a master of deceit. Like Ludovico da Canossa in Book I, Federico refuses to think of the ideal in that way, but prefers to see him as a brilliant actor, the artisan of his apperance and personality. Although Ludovico and Federico would prefer to avoid the unpleasant fact of the courtier's deception, Gasparo's challenges make them face it again and again, for if the courtier deceives, what moral authority can he have?

A few pages after the interchange over the courtier's dress, the issue finally comes into the open. Federico has been describing an ideal strategy for the courtier: he should claim excellence only in his profession, even though he may possess it in other areas, so that when people see him perform well in what is not his profession, they will think him even better at what is. "Quest'arte," concludes

Federico, "s'ella è compagnata da bon giudicio, non mi dispiace punto" (II, 39, 252): "Such an art, when accompanied by good judgment, does not displease me in the least". It does, however, displease Signor Gasparo:

> Questa a me non par arte, ma vero inganno; né credo che si convenga, a chi vol esser omo da bene, mai lo ingannare.
>
> (II, 40, 252)

> This seems to me to be not an art, but an actual deceit; and I do not think it seemly for anyone who wishes to be a man of honor ever to deceive.
>
> (101)

In responding to Gasparo's straightforward, moral indictment, Federico performs a series of intellectual somersaults, first claiming that such deception is really an adornment for the courtier, then admitting it is deception, but not to be blamed, then finally arguing for the identity of deception and art.

> Questo . . . è più presto un ornamento, il quale accompagna quella cosa che colui fa, che inganno; e se pur è inganno, non è da biasimare. Non direte voi ancora, che di dui che maneggian l'arme quel che batte il compagno lo inganna! e questo è perché ha più arte che l'altro. E se voi avete una gioia, la qual dislegata mostri esser bella, venendo poi alle mani d'un bon orefice, che col legarla bene la faccia parer molto più bella, non direte voi che quello orefice inganna gli occhi di chi la vede! E pur di quello inganno merita laude, perché col bon giudicio e con l'arte le maestrevoli mani spesso aggiungon grazia ed ornamento allo avorio o vero allo argento, o vero ad una bella pietra circondandola di fin oro. Non diciamo adunque che l'arte o tal inganno, se pur voi lo volete così chiamare, meriti biasimo alcuno.
>
> (II, 40, 252–53)

> This . . . is an ornament attending the thing done, rather than deceit; and even if it be deceit, it is not to be censured. Will you also say that, in the case of two men who are fencing, the one who wins deceives the other? He wins because he has more art than the other. And if you have a beautiful jewel with no setting, and it passes into the hands of a good goldsmith who with a skillful setting makes it appear far more beautiful, will you say that the goldsmith deceives the eyes of the one who looks at it? Surely he deserves praise for that deceit, because with good judgment and art his masterful hand often adds grace and adornment to ivory or to silver or to a beautiful stone by setting it in fine gold. Therefore let us not say that art—or deceit such as this, if you insist on calling it that—deserves any blame.
>
> (101)

In reply to Gasparo's blunt moral attack, Federico slips out of the line of fire under the cover of a semantic smokescreen where once again aesthetics replace morals and deception metamorphoses into art. Although Gasparo allows the issue to rest without further ado, Federico's slippery redefinition of terms has by no means solved the problem.

*   *   *

Federico's evasive responses do not succeed in laying the question of deception to rest, and whether it continued to bother Castiglione or not in the years after he finished his first three books, he nevertheless revives it in Book IV. This time, however, he offers solutions to the two general problems involved. In the first place, while Ottaviano's new courtier is still a deceiver, he justifies this deception by giving it a moral function. The courtier becomes a humanist educator who will not alienate his prince with the corrections and rebukes of a *severo filosofo* (IV, 8, 456) but will use his talents to make himself and his moral lessons pleasing and ingratiating to his master in order to educate and advise him.[4] In other words, he will deceive the prince into a love of learning and morality by making the unpleasant seem pleasurable, leading his unwitting master up the steep hill of virtue, "ingannandolo con inganno salutifero" (IV, 10, 457: "beguiling him with salutary deception"). In such an educator, the artful manipulation of his personality is not merely excusable; the courtier's good acting is absolutely essential for the ultimate good of the state. No wonder, then, that none of Castiglione's courtiers should think to attack the ideal courtier's deception now.

*   *   *

4. Both More and Erasmus similarly reject the "Stoic philosopher" who would present truth unvarnished, and both insist that the educator and statesman has to be a tactful manipulator of men and even a deceiver if necessary. See Thomas More, *Utopia*, ed. Edward Surtz, S. J. and J. H. Hexter, vol. 4 of *The Complete Works of Saint Thomas More* (New Haven: Yale University Press, 1965), pp. 96–100; and Desiderius Erasmus, *Institutio Principis Christiani*, in *Opera Omnia*, ed. J. Clericus (Leiden, 1703), vol. 4, 594A; and his *Encomium Moriae*, op. cit., vol. 4, 401–504, passim.

JAMES HANKINS

Renaissance Philosophy and Book IV of *Il Cortegiano*†

Baldassare Castiglione was not a philosopher and had not had the benefit of such formal education in philosophy as contemporary universities could provide—that is to say, a thorough immersion in the less readable works of Aristotle. His education was literary and humanistic. At Milan in his youth he had studied with famous humanist masters: Latin literature with Giorgio Merula and Filippo Beroaldo the Elder, Greek with Demetrius Chalcondyles.[1] He was trained to be an orator both in the Renaissance sense of the word—i.e., an ambassador—as well as in the Ciceronian sense. As a Ciceronian orator he would aim to be a statesman, "a good man skilled in speaking," *vir bonus dicendi peritus*, but also a man of broad general culture. Castiglione was thus, in an amateur way, well acquainted with ancient and contemporary philosophy, particularly Aristotelian moral philosophy and Florentine Platonism. As Cicero had urged, he used his philosophical knowledge for the rhetorical purpose of *inventio*: finding and elaborating arguments and topics of discourse. This is not to say that Castiglione was a man without philosophical convictions, but it would clearly be wrong to think of him as a partisan of any one school or doctrine. It is often asserted that humanistic thinkers like Castiglione were as a class given to skepticism or eclecticism. Yet this should not be understood as though humanists adhered to some particular epistemological doctrine. It is simply that the use literary men make of philosophical ideas differs from the use made of them by professional philosophers. Castiglione is above all a literary artist. It is not his purpose to argue for some position, but to paint an ideal. Philosophy in *Il Cortegiano* is a means to that end; it provides a conceptual language in which Castiglione can elaborate and defend his ideas concerning the ideal Courtier.

The fourth book of Castiglione's famous work is particularly philosophical in its subject matter. Indeed, in Aristotelian terms, it has been said to treat primarily of the "final cause," or the reason for being, of the ideal Courtier.[2] In classical and Renaissance moral theory, human beings may find their purpose either in the active or the contemplative life, and the book is accordingly divided into two

---

† This essay was written for this Norton Critical Edition.
1. For Castiglione's biography, see *Dizionario biografico degli italiani*, vol. 22 (Rome, 1979), pp. 53–68.
2. Lawrence V. Ryan, "Book IV of Castiglione's *Courtier*: Climax or Afterthought?" *Studies in the Renaissance* 19 (1972), 156–79, at 160.

parts.[3] The first deals with subjects long associated in humanist literature with the active life: whether virtue is teachable,[4] whether the republican or the princely form of government is preferable, how the prince should be educated, whether the active life is superior to the contemplative life. This part is presided over by the interlocutor Ottaviano Fregoso (1470–1524)—fittingly enough, as he was a famous general and diplomat who became (in 1513) doge of Genoa, then governor of Genoa (1515–22) under Francis I. Pietro Bembo (1470–1547) makes an equally suitable speaker for the latter part of the book, dealing with the contemplative life, as he had given up politics for a literary and ecclesiastical career; he was also, famously, susceptible to the tender passion and an advocate of the dignity of women and Platonic love.[5]

It is sometimes said that the first half of Book IV is Aristotelian, the second, Platonic. This is accurate enough provided it is understood that the two halves are not meant to oppose but to complement each other. That the philosophies of Plato and Aristotle were in fundamental harmony with each other was a pious belief of right-thinking humanist circles in Castiglione's time. Renaissance Platonists, in particular, inclined to concordism, believing that Aristotelianism had a proper role to play in education so long as it was integrated into and subaltern to a Platonic understanding of metaphysics and the soul's destiny. Aristotle's *Ethics* was appropriate as a guide to the active life. But the active life should be subordinate to the contemplative life, and in a double sense. The active life should be lived *for the sake of* the contemplative life, because only contemplation could fulfill the highest potentialities of the human soul; the most godlike happiness possible for human beings was that of contemplatives. This was the argument of Aristotle in Book X of the *Nicomachean Ethics*. But the contemplative life was also primary *causativè* (as the scholastics would say) in that the principles acquired through contemplative experience were meant to guide the life of the person or persons who ideally should rule the

---

3. On the problem of unity between the two parts, see Ryan, "Book IV of Castiglione's *Courtier*," and Wayne A. Rebhorn, "Ottaviano's Interruption: Book IV and the Problem of Unity in *Il Libro del Cortegiano*," *Modern Language Notes* 87 (1972), 37–59. In my view, the problem of unity is largely a false one created by the confusion of genetic with structural issues.

4. This is also the subtitle of Plato's *Meno* in the Thrasyllan catalog of his works (as well as the name of one of the pseudo-Platonic *Spuria*). However, the question as developed in Castiglione owes little to Plato but is instead intended to bring out aspects of the Aristotelian doctrine of virtue.

5. On Fregoso and Bembo see, respectively, *Dizionario biografico degli italiani*, vol. 50 (1998), pp. 423–27, and vol. 8 (1966), pp. 133–51. Bembo is also, of course, the author of *Gli asolani*, a dialogue on love, which ends with a similar description of Platonic love. On the relationship between Bembo's dialogue and *The Courtier*, see Christine Raffini, *Marsilio Ficino, Pietro Bembo, Baldassare Castiglione: Philosophical, Aesthetic, and Political Approaches in Renaissance Platonism* (New York, 1998).

polity. This was the doctrine of Plato's *Republic*. Both teachings are present in Castiglione, who shows here as elsewhere his sympathy with the concordist tendencies of Renaissance Platonism and his hostility to the exclusive Aristotelianism of the schools.[6]

Though the ethical and political teaching of Ottaviano is mostly drawn from Aristotle's *Ethics* and *Politics*, the problem that launches Ottaviano's speech is Platonic: how are wisdom and power to be joined? This was a special preoccupation of Renaissance Platonists, and Plato's solution—that philosophers should rule or rulers should become philosophers—was probably the most widely quoted Platonic *sententia* of the Renaissance. In the *Republic*, which is clearly on Castiglione's mind at the beginning of Book IV,[7] Plato's problem is how one might convince a tyrant that justice is not just a mug's game, that happiness is not just a matter of getting what you want. Real justice in the soul is in fact a precondition of individual happiness; and the man whose soul has been made just and harmonious by intellectual vision, the philosopher, is the only one who can make states happy. This, *mutatis mutandis*, is the problem of Ottaviano's speech. In the Renaissance context it becomes the "problem of counsel" (as it is called in Book I of More's *Utopia*). How can the Courtier encourage the Prince to the practice of virtue when the Prince believes, and is surrounded by people who encourage him to believe, that he can govern a people without governing himself? The Courtier must somehow become an instrument for turning the Prince into a Philosopher-King, but how? If the Prince is already corrupt he will reject his Courtier's advice, even if the Courtier has the courage to speak truth to power (as that other corrupt ruler, Dionysius of Sicily, rejected the advice of that other outspoken courtier, Plato, long ago).[8] This is where the arts of Courtiership come in. The ideal Courtier will have made himself so attractive through his various charms and talents that any Prince who is not wholly corrupt will desire his company and will want to imitate his example. This is why the Courtier must also be virtuous. The Courtier's role is thus boldly transformed from that of parasiti-

6. See esp. IV.24–26. A different view is given by J. R. Woodhouse, *Baldesar Castiglione: A Reassessment of the Courtier* (Edinburgh, 1978), passim, esp. chapter 6.
7. For instance the division of goods at IV.4 recalls the beginning of *Rep.* II, 357b and following; the 'noble lie' at IV.6 recalls *Rep.* III, 414c. The need to unify wisdom and power (alluded to at IV.8) is a major theme in Ficino's *argumenta* to his translation of the *Republic*.
8. IV.47. "By this same method of Courtiership, Plato taught Dion of Syracuse, and later, when he found the tyrant Dionysius like a book full of defects and errors and in need of complete erasure rather than of any change or correction, since it was not possible to remove from him that color of tyranny with which he had been stained for so long, he decided not to make use of the methods of Courtiership with him, judging that they would all be in vain; which is what our Courtier ought also to do if he chances to find himself in the service of a prince of so evil a nature." The passage alludes to the pseudo-Platonic *Letter VII*, 330e.

cal fop (as popular prejudice saw him) into the more dignified role
of *institutor del principe*, the Educator of the Prince.

Castiglione describes the Courtier's technique of captivating the
unsuspecting Prince as a form of trickery, a "salutory deception"
(*inganno salutifero*), a "veil of pleasure" (*velo di piacere*), or a
"snare" (*illecebra*). Like honey smeared on a child's medicine cup,
this benign trickery induces the Prince to drink in the Courtier's virtuous precepts and example along with the pleasure of the
Courtier's companionship.[9] Such duplicity might seem to smack
more of sixteenth-century courts or humanist rhetoricians than of
Plato. But in fact there is good Platonic authority for the use of
deception by the wise for the purpose of leading the blind and the
sensual into virtue. Plato himself in the *Republic* and *Letter VII*
allows that the philosopher must often deceive the unilluminated in
order to compass higher ends,[1] and this rather condescending attitude can often be found in the Platonic tradition. Eusebius for
example describes how Origen used Platonism itself as a "bait" or
"lure" to draw skeptical youths to true religion, an idea that was
taken up by Ficino in many places in his writings.[2] The notion that
pleasure and personal charm can exploited to effect the moral education of political leaders is stated explicitly at the end of the *De
amore* (which, as we shall see, is an important source for *Il
Cortegiano*'s fourth book):

> Since youth is inclined to pleasure, it is held by pleasure alone;
> it flees strict teachers. Hence our protector of youth [Socrates],
> for the good of his country, neglecting the administration of his
> own affairs, undertakes the care of the young, and first cap-
> tures them by the attractiveness of his pleasant company.
> When they are thus snared (*illaqueatos*), he admonishes them
> lightly, then more severely, and finally he chastises them with
> stricter censure. . . . Thus it happened that the companion-
> ship of Socrates was still more useful than it was enjoyable.[3]

It is a commonplace of Renaissance Platonists that truth can not be
imbibed neat by those unused to it, but must be mixed with play-
fulness; the sublime can only be introduced to neophytes through a
mysterious veil or through puzzles that will captivate by degrees the
mind of the young:

---

9. IV.10.
1. See, for example, *Rep.* II, 382c, III, 414c; *Ep.* VII, 332d, 344c.
2. Eusebius, *Hist. Eccles.* VI.8. On Ficino's idea that Platonism was a "bait" for skeptical
   youth, see my *Plato in the Italian Renaissance*, vol. 1 (Leiden, 1990), pp. 286–87.
3. Ficino, *De amore* VII, 16 ed. R. Marcel (Paris 1956), pp. 261–62; Jayne's translation, p.
   173 (n. 8, p. 384 herein). I have modified slightly Jayne's translation. The whole chapter
   ("Quam utilis verus amator") bears study as the problem it addresses—how to bring corrupted youths to virtue using charm, love (*caritas*), wit, and good company—is closely
   analogous to the problem of Book IV of the *Courtier*.

Ficino:

It was the custom of Pythagoras, of Socrates and of Plato to conceal the divine mysteries everywhere under figures and veils (*figuris involucrisque*), modestly hiding their wisdom in contrast to the boasting of the sophists, joking seriously and playing in earnest.[4]

But Plato's games are much more serious than the seriousness of the Stoics. He does not disdain to wander sometimes through more humble subjects so long as he can insensibly captivate his hearers, leading the humbler among them the more readily to higher things. Often, with the gravest purpose in view, he will mix the useful with the sweet, so that by restrained wit and smooth speech he can attract minds naturally prone to pleasure to their [true] food, using pleasure itself as bait.[5]

This strategy, and indeed the whole social and political function of the Courtier, will become moot if it turns out that virtue is not in fact teachable, but rather a gift of nature or divine grace. So Ottaviano continues his speech by countering the view of Gasparo that justice and shame, the building blocks of virtue, are inborn, not acquired qualities.[6] Ottaviano's reply is in effect an exposition of the doctrine of Aristotle's *Ethics,* and particularly of Aristotle's belief that natural moral dispositions have to be shaped by training and repetition into stable ethical habits. Ottaviano here defends a conventional rationalistic ethics inherited from the main schools of ancient philosophy: he accepts that rational control of the appetites and passions is the criterion of good acts and that self-knowledge is the source of virtue. Under questioning from Bembo, he explains the orthodox Aristotelian qualification that the incontinent (those who have not yet formed fixed habits of virtue) have only incomplete knowledge; and he allows to Cesare Gonzaga that some degree of passion is good, so long as it is controlled by reason. The latter point is directed against a well-known Stoic criticism of Aristotelian ethics.[7]

4. Ficino, *Commentaria in Platonem* (Florence, 1496), f. 2v. On this theme see especially M. J. B. Allen, "The Second Ficino-Pico Controversy" in his *Plato's Third Eye: Studies in Marsilio Ficino's Metaphysics and Its Sources* (Aldershot, 1995), essay X, pp. 437–39; and Edgar Wind, *Pagan Mysteries in the Renaissance* (New York, 1968, rev. ed.), p. 236.
5. Ficino, *Opera omnia*, vol. 2 (Basel, 1576; repr. Turin, 1959), p. 1129.
6. The myth of Epimetheus (taken from Plato's *Protagoras*) allows Castiglione to maintain the ambiguity as to whether such gifts are innate or the work of divine providence. Gasparo's position about the sources of virtue here could be interpreted as a broadly Pauline or Lutheran one.
7. These two clarifications are precisely the same points expanded upon by Leonardo Bruni in his very popular summary of Aristotelian ethics, the *Isagogicon moralis disciplinae* (1424), and it is likely that this is Castiglione's source for this passage. Bruni's text can be found in P. Viti, ed., *Leonardo Bruni: Opere letterarie e politiche* (Turin, 1996), pp. 197–241; for its popularity, see my *Repertorium Brunianum: A Guide to the Writings of Leonardo Bruni* (Rome, 1997), and indices. The Stoic view of anger as an undesireable passion is laid out (for example) in Seneca's *De ira.*

Ottaviano can thus conclude that *the Courtier* has the potential, after all, to communicate virtues to the Prince, including "that virtue which perhaps among all human things is the greatest and rarest, that is, the manner and method of right rule."[8] This opens up the question of the best form of government, the *comparatio rei publicae et regni*, a theme much debated in humanist political thought of the fifteenth century.[9] Ottaviano begins by saying that he prefers the rule of a Prince as it is more natural, resembling as it does God's government of the universe, but also the ordering of human activities such as building and warfare. Pietro Bembo, presumably in his character as a Venetian, defends republican rule with four arguments: (1) that princely rule infringes the God-given gift of liberty; (2) that deliberation is better conducted by many than by one; (3) that corruption is less likely in many than in one; and (4) that the principle of power sharing (to rule and be ruled in turn) is not unnatural but can be exemplified in the life cycles of certain animals, like deer and cranes. Three of these arguments are found in Aristotle's *Politics* (III, 15–16, 1286a–1287a)—significantly, in the passage where Aristotle reviews favorably the arguments for kingship. Ottaviano responds to Bembo with the equally Aristotelian arguments that true freedom is not self-will, but to live according to good laws (thereby perfecting one's nature); that to obey as well as to command is human; and that not all forms of princely rule imply slavish obedience on the part of the ruled. In fact, one must distinguish between the rule of masters over slaves and that of good princes over citizens. The latter "kingly and civic" kind of rule (*regio e civile*) is appropriate to governing citizens who are *discreti e virtuosi*.[1] Ottaviano accepts the Aristotelian principle (which is also Platonic) that justice is relative to persons, and that persons superior in virtue have a natural right to rule. It is the superhuman ("heroic") virtue of a king or a royal family which in the end justifies monarchical rule; a good monarch is therefore rightly considered a kind of demigod whose excellence mirrors the divine nature.[2]

8. IV.18.
9. See Quentin Skinner, *The Foundations of Modern Political Theory*, I: *The Renaissance* (Cambridge, 1978); Nicolai Rubinstein, "Monarchies and Republics" in *The Cambridge History of Political Thought, 1450–1700*, ed. J. H. Burns and M. Goldie (Cambridge, 1991), pp. 30–41, and James Hankins, "Humanism and the Origins of Modern Political Thought," in *The Cambridge Companion to Renaissance Humanism*, ed. Jill Kraye (Cambridge, 1996), pp. 118–41.
1. Castiglione is following closely *Pol.* I.5, 1254b. Significantly (and in contrast with later absolutist theory), Castiglione does not follow Aristotle in assimilating royal rule to the rule of a father over children; rather, he sees it as a combination of master/slave rule (over those lacking reason and virtue) and political (*civile*) rule (for the prudent and virtuous). Castiglione's argument is incoherent in Aristotelian terms (political rule being a rule among equals) and may reflect the relatively weaker ideological position of rulers in Italian courts as opposed to northern European absolutist states.
2. Cf. *Pol.* III.17, 1288a.

Ottaviano (and, we may presume, Castiglione himself) thus applies Aristotelian political principles in such a way as to yield conclusions favorable to absolute monarchy. As was not uncommon in the medieval and early modern period, he reads the famously ambiguous passage in Book III of the *Politics* (chapters 14–18, the so-called Treatise on Kingship) as an argument for kingship.[3] His sympathy with absolutism can be seen in the rest of his political advice as well. He urges the Prince to establish himself as the "custodian and incorruptible executor" of the laws, but allows that he can also freely break the laws when necessary. If he is seen, generally speaking, as an upholder of the law, he can be sure "his will [shall] command the same reverence as the law itself." This is hardly different from the advice on the conduct of absolute monarchy given by Cardinal Mazarin to Louis XIV. Nor do the two consultative councils that Ottaviano recommends in any way limit the Prince's power.[4] Both councils are appointed by the Prince and have no legislative functions. If they permit other social ranks a degree of participation, it is nevertheless "passive participation" (as defined by John Najemy).[5] The judiciary is similarly appointed by the Prince. Despite Castiglione's suggestion to the contrary,[6] this is no true mixed constitution in the Aristotelian sense: the optimates and the people do not share power with the King or balance out his authority by exercising political power in their own right. All real power is concentrated in the hands of a quasi-divine monarch.

Having shown how human life in its collective aspect can be perfected through the active life, Castiglione now turns, in the second half of Book IV, to the contemplative life, the life through which the

---

3. For a different view, see Woodhouse, esp. 155–59. In contrast with Woodhouse, I see no evidence that Castiglione favored a republican constitution over princely rule. For the interpretation of the Aristotelian "Treatise on Kingship" (which some have read as a sycophantic compliment to Alexander the Great), see Hans Kelsen, "The Philosophy of Aristotle and the Hellenic-Macedonian Policy," *International Journal of Ethics* 48 (1937), 1–64, reprinted in J. Dunn and I. Harris, eds., *Aristotle*, vol. 1 (Cheltenham, 1997), pp. 103–66. For the use of Aristotle as an authority for medieval monarchy and early modern absolutism theory, see, respectively, Thomas J. Renna, "Aristotle and the French Monarchy, 1260–1303," *Viator* 9 (1978), 309, and James Daly, *Sir Robert Filmer and English Political Thought* (Toronto, 1979).
4. Contrary to what Woodhouse maintains (pp. 158–59), these constitutional arrangements are not "safeguards" against the power of the Prince. In support of his position, Woodhouse misreads "fossero eletti tra'l popolo altri di minor grado, dei quali si facesse un consiglio populare" to refer to "a popular council elected by citizens of lower social rank"; it in fact means that "other men of lower social station should be chosen from among the people to form a popular council."
5. See John Najemy, "Civic Humanism and Florentine Politics," in James Hankins, ed., *Renaissance Civic Humanism: Reappraisals and Reflections* (Cambridge, 2000), pp. 87–92. Najemy defines passive participation as participation without the exercise of political power, office-holding for the sake of honor or money rather than for the sake of self-rule.
6. IV.31: "il governo del quale nascesse principalmente dal principe, nientedimeno participasse ancora degli altri, e cosí aría questo stato forma di tre governi boni, che è il Regno, gli Ottimati e 'l Populo."

individual can attain a godlike perfection or fulfillment. This, perhaps the most famous part of *Il Cortegiano*, is dominated by Pietro Bembo, the well-known literary man and Platonic lover. Bembo's speech is introduced by a dilemma. The ideal Courtier for the purpose of educating a Prince will be old and wise, but the best lover, according to the general view, is young. Since the ideal Courtier by definition must be both the best educator and the best lover, the question arises how the ideal Courtier can be both old and young. The dilemma is a more serious threat to Castiglione's design than the lightness of tone used here might suggest. If valid, the dilemma would demonstrate formally that the perfect Courtier can never exist, even as a pure ideal, and the whole project of *Il Cortegiano* collapses.

Bembo's response is to deny the minor premise, to deny that young men in fact make better lovers, and to show on the contrary that "old men can love not only without blame, but sometimes more happily than young men."[7] This necessitates an inquiry into the nature of love itself: what it is, and in what ways it can make us happy. Here Bembo's analysis is heavily indebted to Marsilio Ficino's *Commentary on Plato's Symposium*, known as the *De amore* (1469), the most influential of Renaissance love-treatises.[8] Following Ficino (and Plato), Bembo defines love as the Desire for Beauty, and specifies that such a Desire for Beauty (ontologically convertible with Good) must be informed by knowledge.[9] All appetitive powers have their actual operations structured by a cognitive power; a good can only be desired as known, as a *bonum intellectum*. Sense appetite operates through the power of sense, while the rational appetite (or will) operates through intellect (or the power of intuiting the intelligible order of reality). Human beings *qua* human have a power of choosing between the sense appetite and the rational appetite; therefore humans can desire beauty in two ways. Either they desire it by descending to the senses, or they desire it by ascending to intellect; they can desire an earthly or a heavenly Venus. Beauty exists both in sense objects and in intelligible objects,

---

7. IV.51. He refutes the dilemma by example as well as precept, insofar as he is himself, as the Duchess says, "old in wisdom even if . . . young in years" (IV.50). Bembo is also for this reason well placed rhetorically to defend his position, since he is arguing against his private interest as a young lover of women.

8. The Latin text is edited by Raymond Marcel, *Marsile Ficin: Commentaire sur le Banquet de Platon* (Paris, 1956); there is an English translation with a useful study of the work's influence by Sears Jayne, *Marsilio Ficino: Commentary on Plato's Symposium on Love* (Dallas, 1985); see also John Charles Nelson, *Renaissance Theory of Love: The Context of Giordano Bruno's Eroici furori* (New York, 1958). An up-to-date and fully documented treatment of Renaissance love theory may be found in Sabrina Ebbersmeyer, *Sinnlichkeit und Vernunft: Studien sur Rezeption und Transformation der Liebestheorie Platons in der Renaissance* (Munich: Fink-Verlag, in press).

9. Cf. *De amore* I.4. Castiglione defines "beauty" as a kind of radiation from the Good, following *De amore* II.3.

though more purely in the latter.[1] What is important for Bembo's argument (as for Ficino's) is to exclude the possibility of a precognitive, self-subsisting, purely material beauty (such as the Stoics, for example, found in natural harmonies and symmetries). If such a beauty is possible, then the whole idea of a material beauty that necessarily points beyond itself to spiritual beauty—and therefore to Platonic love—breaks down.

Since we are born as souls immersed in sense, beauty is more commonly available to us through sensible particulars, but it is cognized more purely and more intensely through intellect. This is because transcendental beauty shines like a ray from God, the source of Being, down the hierarchy of Nature through the angelic nature (identified with Mind or Intellect) to Soul (the source of life and motion), and thence to Body and prime matter, the lowest rungs of Nature. Beauty is more fully cognizable, hence more fully enjoyed, the higher one rises in love, in the contemplative return to God. This means that to seek beauty in bodies, the way young men are inclined to do, is simply an error. The ray of divine beauty shines into bodies,[2] but to try to enjoy bodily beauty by possessing a body sexually is a delusion. It leads only to temporary satisfactions, which turn inevitably to tedium and disgust. That is because beauty's true source is higher, immutable, out of the reach of the senses, unable to be contained by the corporeal; one can no more possess beauty in a body than one can in a sunset. It lies in the realm of intellect, accessible most easily to older men who are less troubled by powerful bodily sensations and passions, whose souls are quiet and free to climb the ladder of love in contemplation of true, intelligible beauty.

The end of Bembo's speech (IV. 61–70) gives us an example of precisely this sort of ascent. To indicate that his inspired utterance comes not from himself but from divine sources, he invokes, like Socrates in the *Symposium*, the god of love, and is rewarded with an exalted state of mental alienation and a speech "dictated by the holy frenzy of love."[3] As always in contemplative experience, Bembo and his audience lose their awareness of the passage of time (IV. 73), an effect of the separation of their consciousness from the world of

---

1. This is mostly taken from Ficino, who is in turn borrowing from Aquinas (e.g., *Summa Contra Gentiles* 3.26). For Ficino's discussion of this issue, with references to his sources, see my commentary on the *De summo bono* of Lorenzo de'Medici, in B. Toscani and J. Hankins, eds., *Lorenzo de'Medici: "De summo bono," testo critico e commentario* (Florence: Istituto Nazionale di Studi sul Rinascimento, in press).
2. For beauty as a "ray" (*raggio*) from the divine nature, see the *De amore* II.5, VI.10, VII.1. The idea that beauty is a simple attribute like gold or a beautiful color or the gleam of a star, which causes harmonies and symmetries in composite things, comes from Plotinus' famous essay *On Beauty* (*Enn.* I.6); see also *De amore* V.3.
3. For Ficino's conception of the four forms of divine furor, see Michael J. B. Allen, *The Platonism of Marsilio Ficino: A Study of His Phaedrus Commentary, Its Sources and Genesis* (Berkeley and Los Angeles, 1984).

change and time. Climbing the ladder of love begins with the contemplation of feminine beauty, which is done using the two higher
senses, sight and hearing, not the lower senses of taste, touch and
smell.[4] This means leaving behind "all the ugliness of vulgar love."
Sight and hearing, "reason's ministers," count as higher senses
because they are less mired in the particular, more oriented toward
the universal (like the intellect). Through the higher senses the
Court Lady can give the Courtier her beauty without actual physical intercourse. The one exception is that she is permitted to give
him a kiss, interpreted spiritually as "the union of body and soul"
(IV. 64); this prefigures the death of the kiss at the height of contemplation (IV. 70), where the soul separates from the body. In
return, the Courtier, inspired by the beauty of his Lady, should also
try to "sow virtue in the garden of her fair mind", just as earlier he
is obliged to lead his Prince into paths of virtue. So it would be
wrong to say that the contemplative ideal is purely selfish, in contrast to the social function of the active life.

Prolonged contemplation of bodily beauty, however, ultimately
has undesireable physiological side effects (IV. 66), which to common sight appear as lover's torments.[5] The Courtier-Lover must
therefore turn away from the bodily instantiation of beauty, turn
away from the particular beauty of one woman and toward universal beauty, "feeling little esteem for what at first he so greatly
prized." This may seem rather ungallant behavior from the Lady's
perspective, but we are now in the realm of Plotinian askesis, where
the soul, purged of all earthly attachments, "turns within," away
from the senses to the intelligible realm within us, regarding with
the "mind's eye"[6] pure transcendant beauty as it is in itself, that
angelic beauty which retains traces and footprints of the Divine
Nature. In a final nisus, "aflame with the most holy flame of true
divine love," the soul leaves behind its particularity and dissolves
into the angelic nature, achieving the highest happiness and enjoying the highest good of which the soul is capable, the ambrosia of
divine vision and the nectar of divine love.[7] Like Lorenzo de'Medici

---

4. Compare *De amore* I.4, II.9, V.2, VI.10.
5. Compare *De amore* VII.11.
6. *De amore* VI.6. The "eye of the soul" is the *mens* or νοῦς, the part of the human soul that
   has access to intelligible reality.
7. For the significance of ambrosia and nectar in Ficino, see Plato's *Phdr.* 247e and Ficino's
   Commentarium in Phaedrum, ad loc.; *De amore* IV, 6; *Lettere* I, 6, lines 42–43, ed. S.
   Gentile, p. 21, and the *De Christiana religione*, in *Opera omnia* I, p. 31; *Commentary on
   the Philebus*, ed. Allen, p. 484. Ambrosia and nectar signify, respectively, the satisfactions
   experienced by the intellect and the will in the enjoyment of God. In Ficino's *De volup-
   tate* (*Opera omnia*, p. 987) ambrosia and nectar are identified with the *contemplatio
   divinitatis* and *gaudium* (the latter being, in the Franciscan/Augustinian tradition, the satisfaction the will enjoys from divine love). In Landino's *Disputationes Camaldulenses*, ed.
   Lohe, p. 17, ambrosia and nectar are identified with the *cognitio Dei* and *voluptas quae
   inde percipitur*. Castiglione, like Ficino, seems purposely to avoid siding with either the

in *L'Altercazione*, Bembo concludes his vision of the *summum bonum* with a prayer to the Highest Good, Highest Beauty, and Most Holy Love, the bond of the universe (*vinculo del mondo*),[8] begging God for a deeper contemplative union with Him (IV.70).

Bembo—and Castiglione—thus ends on a noted of inspired theological vision and prayer, but one should not be misled by this into believing that *The Courtier*'s final speech represents a simple reassertion of Christian mystical piety in its traditional form. To evaluate this courtly strain of Platonic love, one must attend not only to what is being said, but who is saying it and to what purpose. Since the thirteenth century, Italian poets had sought to elevate and refine courtly love by redescribing it in a language drawn from Christian Platonism. The most powerful and self-authenticating of human emotions, which threatened in the twelfth century to challenge clerical moral standards,[9] romantic love was in the end safely domesticated within a Christian system of values by poets like Dante and Petrarch. As Petrarch's *Secret*, especially, reveals, Platonic conceptions of love provided a way to resolve the cognitive dissonance set up by the competing demands of earthly love and the Christian calling.

The Platonic love of the High Renaissance resembles the spiritualized courtly love of the Italian Trecento in many respects and uses some of the same texts and language. Augustine, Boethius, Thomas Aquinas, and Franciscan spiritual writings are important intellectual resources for both traditions. But there are key differences as well, especially with regard to function. Ficino's doctrine of Platonic love is not much interested in adjusting the rival claims of love and faith. It represents, rather, a challenge to traditional Christianity in that it provides an alternative model of social order and an alternative source of transcendence and religious experience that do not depend on institutional Christianity. By invoking the Renaissance language of Platonic love, Castiglione is effectively aligning himself with the broad, anti-dogmatic, anti-institutional spirituality of the sixteenth century, for which Florentine Platonism is an important source and antecedent. This is not to say that Platonism and Platonic love directly threaten the ecclesiastical order. Rather, they marginalize it by transcending it. Bembo's speech is full of deep religious feeling but none of it is specifically Christian or Catholic. The same may be said of Ottaviano's speech earlier in the book. The

---

Thomistic/Dominican view that the highest good is the intellectual vision of God or the Augustinian/Franciscan view that the highest good is the enjoyment in love of the divine nature. On this issue see my remarks in *Lorenzo de'Medici: "De summo bono,"* Introduction, part 4.

8. For love as the bond of the universe, see *De amore* III.4, but the theme is a frequent one in Ficino's work: see my *Plato*, I, p. 289f.

9. Georges Duby, *The Knight, the Lady, and the Priest: The Making of Modern Marriage in Medieval France* (Chicago, 1993).

highest good both of states and of individuals is achieved without reference to the graces or doctrines of the Church.

Hence in Castiglione, as in Ficino, the contemplative ideal is radically transformed. Traditionally associated with saints and religious orders, it has now been appropriated wholesale for the use of courts and princes and removed from the sphere of the Church. It thus provides yet another example of the general sixteenth-century tendency to bracket organized, public religion and to replace it with private forms of spirituality and more secular ways of dealing with human needs and desires, both individual and collective.

PETER BURKE

The Courtier Abroad: Or, the Uses of Italy†

Introduction

Students of the Renaissance have long been discontented with the traditional account of its 'reception' outside Italy, with the unfortunate implication that Italians alone were active and creative, while other Europeans were passive, mere recipients of 'influence'. In order to drive out the simplistic diffusionism embodied in this traditional account, it may be advisable to draw on its opposite or antibody, in other words functionalism, or at least to ask what the 'uses' of Italy were for writers scholars and artists in other parts of Europe, and how far Italian forms or ideas were assimilated into indigenous traditions. To escape the limitations of functionalism, however, it is important to study the ways in which these foreigners interpreted what they saw, heard or read, their perceptual schemata, their horizons of expectation.[1] An ordinary working historian would be ill advised to take sides in current controversies in the field of literary theory, to pronounce on the ultimately metaphysical question whether real meanings are found in texts or projected onto them. All the same, there can be little doubt of the relevance of reception theory (concerned as it is with a temporal process), to the work of cultural historians in general and in particular to historians of the Renaissance (long concerned with

---

† From *Die Renaissance im Blick der Nationen Europas*, Herausgegeben von Georg Kauffmann (Wiesbaden: Otto Harrassowitz, 1991), pp. 1–14. Reprinted by permission of Herzog August Bibliothek Wolfenbuttel.

1. On schemata, A. Warburg, *Gesammelte Schriften* (Leipzig und Berlin, 1932), and E. H. Gombrich, *Art and Illusion* (London, 1960). On 'horizon of expectations', H. Gadamer, *Wahrheit und Methode* (1960: English trans., London 1975), and H. R. Jauss, *Literaturgeschichte als Provokation* (1974; English trans.).

reception in a narrower sense).[2] They need to assimilate the still somewhat alien notion of *Rezeption* (or *Wirkung*) into their own craft traditions.[3]

A few years ago, two enterprising scholars put together a collection of articles on 'The Enlightenment in National Context', stressing regional variation and local needs rather than the French model.[4] It would be extremely useful to have a study of the European Renaissance on similar lines.

To make a small contribution to such a collective volume is the purpose of this paper, an essay in every sense, since it is a provisional report on work in progress presented in order to test reactions to both method and interpretation.[5] It is concerned with "the historical process of acceptance, appropriation, transformation, rejection and substitution" in the case of a work which might be described as unofficially authoritative in some social circles in quite a number of countries. It deals with the reception, or as Italian scholars would say, the "fortune" of one famous Renaissance text, Castiglione's *Courtier*. The area surveyed in this study is essentially Europe minus Italy, though there are odd references to the *Courtier* in Japan and to the New World.[6] Italy is omitted not because reactions to Castiglione were uniform—they were in fact rather diverse—but because the process of adaptation is revealed more clearly by the history of his reception in other countries, other cultures.[7]

The period with which this essay is concerned runs from 1528, when the *Courtier* was first published, in an elegant folio edition (ironically enough, in republican Venice), to the early seventeenth

---

2. D. Hay, *The Italian Renaissance in Its Historical Background* (Cambridge, 1961), entitles two chapters "The Reception of the Renaissance in Italy" and "The Reception of the Renaissance in the North".

3. A somewhat mechanical view of the 'diffusion' or 'spread' of humanism can be found in scholars of the calibre of P. O. Kristeller, "The European Diffusion of Italian Humanism", *Italica* 39 (1962), 1–14, and R. Weiss, *The Spread of Italian Humanism* (London, 1964). On the other hand, F. Simone, *Il rinascimento francese* (Turin, 1961), S. Dresden, "The Profile of the Reception of the Italian Renaissance in France", in *Iter Italicum*, ed. H. Oberman and T. Brady (Leiden, 1975, 119–189), and Q. Skinner, *Foundations of Modern Political Thought* (2 vols, Cambridge, 1978, esp. vol. 1, part 3), are aware, as Dresden puts it, that "whatever is transmitted changes".

4. R. Porter and M. Teich, eds, *The Enlightenment in National Context* (Cambridge, 1981).

5. The footnotes to this essay are intended to reveal both the extent of the secondary literature on Castiglione and the need (given the contradictions and gaps in this literature) for more work on a number of problems.

6. J. Cartwright, *Baldassare Castiglione* (2 vols, London 1908), 2, 440, tells the story of two Japanese ambassadors who visited Mantua in 1585 taking the book home with them. J. M. Corominas, *Castiglione y la Araucana* (Madrid, 1980) claims to be 'estudio de una influencia' but lacks precision. Alonso Ercilla (s. 1533–94), author of the epic *Araucana*, spent much of his life in Chile.

7. The fortunes of the *Courtier* in Italy have not yet been the object of systematic study. Parts of the story are told by V. Cian, *Archivio storico lombardo* 14 (1888), 661–727, G. Mazzacurati, "Percorsi dell'ideologia cortegiana", in *La corte e il cortegiano*, ed. C. Ossola (Rome, 1980), 149–72, and G. Patrizi, "Il *Libro del Cortegiano* e la trattatistica sul comportamento", in *Letteratura italiana*, ed. A. Asor Rosa, 3, part 2 (Turin, 1984).

century, when frequent reprints finally come to an end.[8] In the
ninety years 1528–1619 there were at least 110 editions of *the
Courtier*, 60 in Italian and 50 or more in other languages.[9]

I cannot, however, begin in 1528 and discuss the *Courtier* after
the *Courtier* without more ado. Historians of the reception of texts
face different types of problem according to the kind of book with
which they are concerned. The practical relevance of the *Courtier*
to daily life in some social circles encouraged contemporary comment, favourable and unfavourable, providing a thick dossier for
future historians of its reception.

On the other hand, its combination of ambiguity with a lack of
original ideas makes Castiglione's book particularly difficult to handle. With respect to its ambiguity, I am inclined to agree with those
modern readers who find *The Courtier* what is sometimes called an
"open" work, despite the fact that (as this essay will try to show), the
author's contemporaries generally seem to have seen a clear and distinct message in the book.[1] The dialogue form is exploited in such a
way as to anticipate the objections of most of its later critics.[2] The
ambiguities of the *Courtier* may not all be intentional; they owe
something to the fact that the process of writing and revision was
spread over some twelve years at a time when the situation of the
author, not to mention Italy as a whole, was changing rapidly.[3]

As for the book's lack of originality, it obviously complicates (not
to say undermines) any attempt to study its "influence". We cannot
safely approach this text without bearing in mind the history of the
Courtier before the *Courtier*. The book was far from the first treatise in its genre.[4] It was self-consciously modelled on classical treatises by Cicero and others, and the borrowings from antiquity
include certain central concepts, notably that of "grace".[5] However,
Cicero wrote in a society without a court. Courtesy, like the court
itself, has been described as a medieval "invention".[6] Castiglione

8. However, the book was translated into Dutch in 1662, under the title *De volmaeckte hov-
   elinck*, and translated for the second time into German in 1685, as *Galante
   Nachgespräche*. In 1773 Dr. Johnson was still praising it as "the best book that ever was
   written upon good breeding".
9. L. Opdycke, ed., *The Courtier* (New York, 1901), 419 f: cf. note 8 below.
1. On the idea of the 'open' work, U. Eco, *The Role of the Reader* (London, 1981).
2. Cf. W. A. Rebhorn, *Courtly Performances* (Detroit, 1978), 186.
3. J. Guidi, "Les différentes rédactions et la fortune du 'Courtisan'", in *Réécritures*, ed.
   Guidi (Paris, 1983).
4. On earlier Italian examples, see E. Mayer, *Un opuscolo dedicato a Beatrice d'Aragona*
   (Rome, 1937) and D. Rhodes, "Whose New Courtier?" in *Cultural Aspects of the Italian
   Renaissance*, ed. C. H. Clough (Manchester, 1976), dealing respectively with Diomede
   Caraffa and (probably) Mario Equicola.
5. On the history of 'grace', S. H. Monk, "A Grace Beyond the Reach of Art", *Journal of the
   History of Ideas* 5 (1944), 131–50; on the ancient Roman concern with manners and self-
   presentation, E. S. Ramage, *Urbanitas* (Norman, 1973).
6. D. Brewer, "Courtesy and the Gawain Poet", in *Patterns of Love and Courtesy*, ed. J.
   Lawlor (London, 1966), 54.

has his place in a tradition (going back to the tenth century) of writers who adapt the ancient Roman vocabulary of good manners to the court milieu. He owes an unacknowledged and perhaps indirect debt to medieval discussions of courtly behaviour in France and elsewhere.[7]

Bearing all these problems in mind, we may embark on a study of the reception process, discussing in turn the physical diffusion of the book, its translations, imitations, and other reactions, friendly or hostile.

The Diffusion

The outlines of the story of the diffusion of Castiglione's book abroad are well known, but details can be added almost *ad infinitum*. By 1534 it was possible to read the *Courtier* in Spanish, by 1537 in French, by 1561 in English, by 1566 in German and Polish. In fact two German versions were produced in the sixteenth sentury, two and a quarter Latin renderings (the third being a translation of book 1 alone), and three French translations. Between 1534 and 1619 there were over fifty editions of the *Courtier* in languages other than Italian, including 21 in French, 10 in Spanish and 13 in Latin.[8]

In any case, some foreigners read Castiglione in the original. At least three Italian editions of the text were printed at Lyons (by Rovillio, in 1550, 1553, and 1562). In 1530, only two years after the first edition appeared, Edmund Bonner was writing to Thomas Cromwell asking for the loan of "the book called Cortegiano in Ytalian".[9] There are more than 20 copies of Italian editions of the *Courtier* in Cambridge alone.[1] A few of them have been acquired recently, but most were bought at the time and in some cases the names of former pri-

---

7. S. Anglo, '*The Courtier*' in *The Court of Europe*, ed. A. G. Dickens (London, 1977), with special reference to medieval France. The German contribution to discussions of courtliness is emphasised by C. S. Jaeger, *The Origins of Courtliness* (Philadelphia, 1985); Cf. G. Weise, "Vom Menschenideal und von den Modewörtern der Gotik und der Renaissance" (1936) on medieval terms such as *gracieux, courtoys, hövesch*.

8. The only attempt at a complete list seems to be Opdycke (1901), 419–21, who reached a total of 49. His 17 Spanish editions may include a few ghosts. At any rate his list contrasts with A. Palau y Dulcet, *Manuel del librero Hispano-Americano* (Oxford and Barcelona, 1948–), who mentions only ten, which he has seen personally, and M. Morreale, *Castiglione y Boscán* (Madrid, 1959), who mentions twelve; but R. Klesczewski, *Die französischen übersetzungen des Cortegiano* (Heidelberg, 1966), adds eight French editions which Opdycke missed. He also missed the Polish translation. The number of English editions is also controversial. The D.N.B. claims there were five in Elisabeth's reign, but W. Raleigh, ed., *The Courtier* (London, 1900), lx, could only find four.

9. P. Hogrefe, "Elyot and 'the boke called Cortegiano in Ytalian'", *Modern Philology* 27 (1929–30), 303–9.

1. H. M. Adams, *Catalogue of the Books Printed on the Continent of Europe 1501–1600 in Cambridge Libraries* (2 vols, Cambridge, 1967), lists 20 Italian, one Latin and two Spanish editions; Trinity have acquired three more Italian copies since. These and other modern acquisitions need to be subtracted but on the other side, there are 17th-century editions and English editions to add. Emmanuel College alone, for example, has three copies of the London 1612 edition of the Latin translation.

vate owners are known. One of the copies of the *Courtier* in Italian now in the library of Trinity College Cambridge has a name written in it a sixteenth-century hand, 'Thomas Wryght', presumably the man who was sizar, scholar and chaplain at the college between 1563 and 1572.[2] Of the nine references to Castiglione in Cambridge inventories in the reign of Elizabeth (almost enough to confirm Gabriel Harvey's famous observation on the Cambridge fashion for modern Italian writers), only one is to the Hoby translation. One reference is to the Italian text, owned by Abraham Tillman of Corpus; and seven, in that academic culture, to a Latin translation (three specifically to the Latin translation made by Bartholomew Clerke of King's). Tillman owned both a Latin and an Italian version, perhaps to improve his languages.[3] Similarly, at Oxford, E. Higgins of Brasenose owned copies of the *Courtier* in Italian, Latin, French and English.[4] Sir Thomas Tresham, a compulsive book collector, owned more than one *Courtier* in Italian and in Latin.[5]

Details of this kind, if collected from all over Europe, could offer a basis for a social history of Castiglione's reception. It is, for example, not without interest to note that Castiglione's readers included the emperor Charles V, Francis I, Zygmunt August King of Poland, and James VI and I.[6] It is also intriguing to learn (given Professor Jonathan Brown's recent observations on the painter's calculated spontaneity), that Velazquez owned an Italian edition of the *Courtier* (by his time, the Spanish translation had been banned).[7] A study of the books mentioned in 219 inventories from 16th-century Paris has turned up references to no fewer than 18 copies of the *Courtier*, five in Italian and 13 in French. The owners were generally men of the law (*procureur*, *lieutenant criminel* etc), though there was also one *marchand hostelain*.[8] In provincial Amiens, on the other hand, a similar study of 887 inventories 1503–76 turned up only one reference, to a French edition owned by a *procureur général*.[9] However, researches of this kind on the presence of the *Courtier* in the libraries of individuals from different social groups, and in different parts of Europe has barely begun.

2. I should like to thank the Librarian of Trinity for permission to examine the eleven Italian editions of the *Courtier* now in their possession.
3. E. Leedham-Green, *Books in Cambridge Inventories* (2 vols. Cambridge, 1986).
4. M. H. Curtis, *Oxford and Cambridge in Transition* (Oxford, 1958).
5. British Library, Add. Mss. 39, 830 [a scrap-book with lists of purchases], ff. 178ᵛ, 187ᵛ.
6. D. H. Willson, *James I* (London, 1956), 22.
7. J. Brown, *Velazquez: Painter and Courtier* (New Haven, 1986). Brown does not mention this item in the painter's library, recorded in the 1661 inventory as "Cortesano de Castellon en italiano"; F. Rodríguez Marín, *Francisco Pacheco maestro de Velazquez* (Madrid, 1923), 55. The book had been placed on the Spanish Index of 1612: Palau y Dulcet (1948–), 3, 276. On the other hand, J. Cartwright, *Baldassare Castiglione* (2 vols, London 1908), 2, 443, claims that it was already on the Spanish Index by 1576.
8. A. H. Schutz, *Vernacular Books in Parisian Private Libraries of the Sixteenth Century* (Chapel Hill, 1955), 43.
9. A. Labarre, *Le livre dans la vie amiénois du 16e siècle* (Paris and Louvain, 1971), 385.

The Translations

The translations of the *Courtier*, on the other hand, or at least some of them (English, French and Spanish rather than Latin, German and Polish), have been studied in considerable detail, mainly from a linguistic and literary point of view. It may be worth noting the European languages into which the *Courtier* was not translated in the period, difficult as it is to say whether this is to be explained by the state of society, the state of language (or indeed by accident). There was no translation into Flemish or Dutch until the later seventeenth century (although at least three of the Spanish editions were published in Antwerp); no translation into the Scandinavian languages; or into Slav languages other than Polish; or into Portuguese (unless one includes the adaptation by Rodrigues Löbo, to be discussed in its place); or into Hungarian (despite the receptivity of Hungary to the Renaissance)—but then the book was published two years after the disaster of Mohács, when Hungarians had other things to think about.

In this brief discussion from the point of view of a socio-cultural historian, it seems advisable, however, to focus on the social identity of the translators and on the way in which they rendered certain key passages in the text. The translators included the following: Juan Boscán (c. 1487–1542), a Catalan patrician and poet who probably knew Castiglione in his last years as nuncio in Spain;[1] J. Colin, possibly Jacques Colin (d. 1547), abbé, Latin poet, courtier, and diplomat, who was posted to Italy in 1528 and presumably discovered the *Courtier* there;[2] Gabriel Chappuys (c. 1546–c. 1613), poet, historian, interpreter, theologian, and the translator of Ariosto and Boccaccio as well as Castiglione;[3] Sir Thomas Hoby, a Herefordshire gentleman, a Cambridge man, and a Marian exile (though he spent more of his exile in Catholic Italy than in Protestant Germany), who made his translation at the request of the marquis of Northampton;[4] Bartholomew Clerke (1537–90), Professor of Rhetoric at Cambridge, Fellow of King's and MP for Bramber, a man whose social circle included John Caius and Lord Buckhurst;[5] Lukasz Górnicki (1527–1603), a Polish courtier, encouraged to make his translation by King Zygmunt August;[6] Laurentz Kratzer, customs officer (*Mautzahler*) of Burghausen in Bavaria, who dedicated the book to

---

1. Morreale (1959); D. H. Darst, *Juan Boscán* (Boston, 1978).
2. *Dictionnaire de Biographie Française*; Klesczewski (1966), 24 f, who notes that the authorship of this translation is problematic [the candidates including a Jean Colin as well as Jacques], and that the work may have been shared.
3. *Dictionnaire de Biographie Française*.
4. *Dictionary of National Biography*.
5. *D.N.B.*
6. *Polski Słownik Biografyczny*.

his Duke;[7] and Johann Engelbert Noyse, another Bavarian apparently, who dedicated his version to one of the Fuggers.[8]

It is impossible to discuss the reception of a text in translation without going into philological detail. In a brief account such as this, such detail can only be presented at the price of extreme selectivity. I shall concentrate on the rederings of certain of Castiglione's key terms, notably *cortegianía* and *sprezzatura*, placing the Hoby translation in the foreground but looking at it from a comparative perspective.

Hoby wanted, so he tells us, "to follow the very meaning and wordes of the Authour, without . . . leaving out anye parcell one or other" or "being misledde by fantasie".[9] Like the other translators, however, he encountered serious problems because the language into which he was translating lacked precise equivalents for some of the book's most important concepts.[1] Hoby's difficulties began with the very subject of the book, *cortegianía*. In English the term "courtesy", like "courtier", was in use by the thirteenth century at the latest, but courtesy in the medieval sense is not quite what Castiglione is discussing. Hoby has to coin a new word, "courtiership" or to paraphrase it as "the trade and manner of courtiers". By the end of the sixteenth century, new terms had come into existence, including 'courtliness' or even 'courtship' in a non-amorous sense, thanks perhaps to the vogue for Hoby's translation. However, the terms were not available to him. The French translators had similar problems. Colin coined a word, *courtisannie*, while the anonymous translator tried out alternative paraphrases such as *profession courtisane*, *l'art du courtisan*, or *façon de bon courtisan*.[2]

A still greater challenge was posed, as one might have guessed, by what has become the most famous concept in the whole of Castiglione's book, *sprezzatura*. It is presented as a new coinage. Count Lodovico Canossa, explaining the need to avoid affectation, declares that the courtier must, "per dir forse una nova parola, usar in ogni cosa una certa sprezzatura, che nasconda l'arte, e dimostri ciò che si fa e dice venir fatto senza fatica e quasi senza pensarvi"

7. R. Stöttner, "Die erste deutsche übersetzung von B. Castigliones *Cortegiano*", *Jahrbuch für Münchener Geschichte* 2 (1888), 494–9, who confesses his failure to discover further biographical details.
8. Stöttner (1888), J. Ricius (c. 1520–87), who translated book 1 of *The Courtier* into Latin, was born in Hannover, and educated at Wittenberg before becoming Professor of Poetry at Marburg. He is known to have visited Italy. J. Turler, who also translated *The Courtier* into Latin, may be the same person as the Hieronymus Turler (c. 1550–1602) who published a famous essay *De peregrinatione* and translated Machiavelli's *Istorie fiorentine* into Latin.
9. Prefatory epistle to Lord Henry Hastings; London, 1948 ed., 6.
1. A brief general discussion in C. Gabrieli, "La fortuna de "Il Cortegiano" in Inghilterra", *La Cultura* 16 (1978), 218–52. On his problems with the aesthetic terms in the text, L. Gent, *Picture and Poetry 1560–1620* (Leamington Spa, 1981), 15.
2. Klesczewski (1966).

(Book 1, ch. 26). *Sprezzatura* was not, literally speaking, a new word but rather a new sense given to an old word, the basic meaning of which was 'setting no price on', or as Florio suggested at the end of the century in his *Worlde of Wordes*, "a despising or contemning".

This passage seems to have given some initial trouble to Boscán, who first translated *sprezzatura* literally, as *desprecio* ("contempt"), and then more in accordance with the context as *descuido* ("carelessness"), the term he uses when the word crops up again later. Colin opts for *nonchalance*, which has become a close analogy to the Italian term (whether or not it already was in his day). The anonymous French translator and Chappuys are both more cautious and double words up, *nonchalance et mesprison* in the first case, *mespris et nonchalance* in the second.[3]

As for Hoby, he made more than one attempt at finding the right word. In his rendering of the Italian passage quoted above, he writes that the courtier must "(to speak a new word) . . . use in everye thing a certaine disgracing to cover arte withall, and seeme whatsoever he doth and saith, to doe it without paine, and (as it were) not minding it." Castiglione himself twice used the word *disgrazia* in a similar sense a few lines later on, when Hoby translates it "disgrace". The next time *sprezzatura* occurs, it is again rendered "disgracing", but on the third occasion Hoby chooses "Recklessnesse".[4]

Hoby's choice of terms is precious evidence of his own reaction to Castiglione, if only we can interpret it (which is no easy task, given all the changes which have taken place in the English language in the four hundred odd years which separate us from him). We can begin by asking what alternatives were open to him. He did not opt for "nonchalance" like the French translators.[5] He also avoided the terms "carelessness" and, perhaps more surprisingly, 'negligence', employed in English as early as Chaucer, a word which corresponds to the *non ingrata neglegentia* advocated in Castiglione's own model, Cicero, and adopted by Clerke in his Latin version, referring to the need to behave "negligenter et (ut vulgo dicitur) dissolutè", the latter term being his attempt to render Castiglione's neologism. Clerke also uses the term *incuria*.[6]

What were the associations of the terms which Hoby did use?

3. Discussion in Klesczewski (1966), 168 f.
4. Castiglione Book 1, chs. 26, 27, 28; Hoby, 46, 47, 48.
5. The *Oxford English Dictionary*'s first reference to "nonchalance" is as late as 1678. However, Hoby probably knew one of the French translations of the *Courtier*. He was working on his translation in Paris and his epistle to Hastings refers to the book's high reputation in France.
6. Cicero, *De oratore*, 23.78; B. Clerke, *De curiali sive aulico* (1571: London, 1593 ed.), 45. However, according to the *Middle English Dictionary*, ed. S. E. Kuhn and J. Reidy, Ann Arbor 1954–, in progress, *Necgligence* [sic] is not used (before 1500) except in moral and spiritual contexts, to mean something like 'omission of duty' or "sloth". My thanks to Professor John Stevens for drawing my attention to this point.

Unlike *sprezzatura*, "disgracing" was not newly-coined. It seems to have been strongly pejorative. "Rude and unlearned speech defaceth and disgraceth a very good matter" wrote Robinson in his 1551 translation of More's *Utopia*. "Filthy disgracements" wrote Norton in his 1561 translation of Calvin.[7] We must therefore at least entertain the possibility that the translator was, consciously or unconsciously, subverting his text.[8] Hoby was, after all, a Protestant, indeed a Marian exile, and some other renderings of his have been interpreted as signs of a 'protestant bias', notably 'trifling tales' for Castiglione's *novelle*.[9] There was deliberate paradox and desire to surprise in Castiglione's invention of the term *sprezzatura*, which etymology and context between them rendered highly ambivalent, but Hoby perhaps stressed the negative side at the expense of the positive. It is unfortunate that his journal gives us no clue to his feelings about Italy at the time he was studying there.[1]

If the exact choice of words by Hoby tells us something about the *Courtier's* reception in England, a great deal can be learned from the much freer version by Lukasz Górnicki, the *Dworzanin polski* (1566), a translation which is not a translation.[2] What Górnicki did with Castiglione's text was to transpose it. He transferred the setting from Urbino to a villa near Kraków belonging to his patron, bishop Samuel Maciejowski, chancellor of Poland. It was not only the setting which was naturalised. The *questione della lingua*, which is so important and so topical a theme in the *Cortegiano*, is transformed into a discussion of the advantages and disadvantages of the different Slav languages. There are also significant omissions. Górnicki explains at the start that he has left out Castiglione's discussion of painting and sculpture because, he remarks disarmingly, "we don't know about them here" (*u nas nie znaja*). Still more significant is the omission of the ladies, who have a significant if unobtrusive role to play in the original text. They disappear because in Poland, Górnicki explains, ladies are not learned enough to take part in such a discussion. Their disappearance necessitates other changes. The organisation of the third book, in which the characteristics of the *gentildonna da corte*

---

7. Oxford English Dictionary s.v. "disgrace". The usage closest to Hoby's is Sidney's in his *Defence of Poetry*, [in his *Miscellaneous Prose*, ed. K. Duncan-Jones and J. van Dorsten, Oxford, 1973, 111] where "disgracefulness" seems to mean "inelegance", but this is c. 1580, and so carries on from Hoby and may even allude to him.
8. I should like to thank Professor Stephen Orgel for drawing this possibility to my attention.
9. Raleigh (1900), lix.
1. T. Hoby, *A Booke of the Travaile and Life of me Thomas Hoby*, ed. E. Powell (London, 1902: Camden Miscellany, 10).
2. The edition I have used is that edited by R. Pollak (Kraków, 1954). On the man and the book, R. Löwenfeld, *L. Górnicki* (Breslau, 1884), and D. J. Welsh, "Il Cortegiano Polacco", *Italica* 40 (1963), 22–26. Löwenfeld's book was in Lord Acton's library, now in Cambridge; its pages remained uncut till 1983.

are debated, is of course disrupted by the change, while the misogyny of Castiglione's Gasparo Pallavicino becomes superfluous, and is very neatly replaced by the anti-Italian attitudes of Podlodowski. Given what the original author himself preached and practised on the subject of imitation, we may be allowed to conclude that Górnicki was more faithful to his original than the mere translators like Hoby and Clerke precisely because he was less faithful. All the same, the contrast between the two texts does reveal a good deal about the cultural differences between Poland and Italy and about the problems of reception and assimilation.

This effectively original work which claims to be a translation may be usefully juxtaposed to an example of the reverse. Nicolas Faret's *Honnête homme* first appeared in 1630.[3] It is a treatise, not a dialogue, on "the art of pleasing at court". It makes no reference to Castiglione. However, it soon launches into a discussion of behaviour marked by "une certaine grace naturelle . . . au dessus des préceptes de l'art". The author criticises *la négligence affectée* but recommends *nonchalance*. It is not hard to find Faret's source. What is difficult is to reach a balanced verdict on this book. If you read it as an original work, it looks like pure plagiarism. On the other hand, if you regard is as a translation, its freedom becomes apparent. Faret suppresses the "dialogic" element, thus flattening the text. He draws on later writers on good behaviour, such as Della Casa, Guazzo, and Montaigne (on the education of children). He shortens some sections, such as that dealing with physical exercise, while he amplifies others, on poetry, for example, on boasters, on princes, and, above all, on religion. Once again, the contrast between the two texts reveals something of wider differences— between Italy and France, and between the 1520s and the 1630s.

Adaptations

The freedom of these adaptations has taken us more than half-way to the many works which were inspired by the *Courtier* or imitate it in a more or less precise sense. Too many to discuss here. An American scholar once listed no fewer than 945 treatises on the gentleman published in Europe before 1625, and later discovered 472 more.[4] In a brief essay concerned with general problems of reception, it seems best to discuss a small number of examples in relative detail. There have been many discussions of the importance of the Courtier in the culture of Renaissance England (from Sir

3. I have used the modern reprint of the 1636 edition (ed. M. Magendie, Paris 1925). There is a useful introduction. Cf. M. Magendie, *La politesse mondaine en France de 1600 à 1660* (Paris, 1925).
4. R. Kelso, *The Doctrine of the English Gentleman in the 16th Century* (Urbana, 1929); id., *Doctrine for the Lady of the Renaissance* (Urbana, 1956). She found 891 items on the lady.

Thomas Elyot on), and some of Renaissance France, so it may be more useful to take three examples from the Iberian peninsula, which should indicate in their variety something of the range of possible responses to Castiglione's book.[5]

Luis de Milán is probably best known today for his music for the *vihuela de mano*, but he also deserves to be remembered for a charming dialogue, *El Cortesano*, set in Valencia at the court of the royal duke of Calabria.[6] This dialogue includes a brief discussion of the quality of the perfect courtier by the duke and Don Luis himself, but it is so brief as to be little more than a kind of homage to Castiglione.[7] The rest of the book is taken up with songs and poems, with jests (the court fool takes part, speaking Catalan while the nobles reply in Castillian), and with descriptions of clothes, *impresas* and festivals. The book is a kind of anthology of anecdotes and verses without the central story or argument which gives at least an appearance of unity to Castiglione's work. *El Cortesano* has virtually nothing to do with classical antiquity. It draws on and celebrates late medieval traditions; knights errant, courtly love, tournaments, and so on. What it takes from Castiglione is generally what is most traditional in his book. It exemplifies a 16th-century way of reading his text.

Much closer to the spirit of Castiglione is the "Court in the Village and Winter Nights" [*Côrte na Aldeia e Noites de Inverno*] published in 1618 by a nobleman in the circle of the Duke of Bragança Francisco Rodrigues Lôbo (c. 1573–1621).[8] In sixteen short nights the five main characters discuss a variety of socio-literary subjects, starting with the value and the dangers of romances of chivalry, and going on to the etiquette of visiting, correct forms of speech, the art of love, writing letters, composing impresas, responding wittily when the situation requires it, and even the art of dialogue itself. The conception and some of the themes seem to have been inspired by the *Courtier*, but Rodrigues Lôbo is well aware of Castiglione's own classical models and his dis-

5. On England, W. Schrinner, *Castiglione und die englische Renaissance* (Berlin, 1939); E. R. Vincent, "Il cortegiano in Inghilterra", in *Rinascimento europeo e rinascimento veneziano*, ed. V. Branca (Florence, 1964), 97–107; D. Javitch, *Poetry and Courtliness in Renaissance England* (Princeton, 1978). On France, E. Bourciez, *Les moeurs polies* (Paris, 1886), C. A. Mayer, "L'honnête homme", *Modern Language Review* 46 (1951), 196–217, and P. M. Smith, *The Anti-Courtier Trend in French Renaissance Literature* (Geneva, 1966).
6. L. de Milán, *El Cortesano* (1561: repr. Madrid, 1874). For a good brief account of the author, c. 1500–c. 1561, see the new (1980) edition of Grove's *Dictionary of Music and Musicians*.
7. 79 f, "Reglas del cortesano". Mastre Zapater's description of the universe on the last day of the dialogue, pp. 362 f, is an echo or at least an equivalent of Bembo's famous speech at the end of the *Courtier*.
8. I used the Lisbon, 1972 edition. On the author, W. J. Schnerr, "Two Courtiers: Castiglione and Rodrigues Lôbo", *Comparative Literature* (1961) 138–53.

cussion of grace and urbanity [*graça, urbanidade*] is closer to Cicero and Quintilian and their rhetorical context than it is to Castiglione himself. What he has followed in the *Courtier*, and indeed caught very well, is not so much specific details as the general lightness of touch and in particular the art of presenting a case in the form of an argument between contrasted characters who do impress the reader as individuals; the Doctor of law, the Fidalgo, the Student, the old man, and so on. The characters are all men: in this and other respects the book is reminiscent of the *Dworzanin polski*. Like Górnicki's book, *Côrte na Aldeia* is still very much admired in its country of origin and only the contingent fact that it is written in a language not very well known in Europe has prevented the author from acquiring the literary reputation he deserves. Castiglione would surely have appreciated it as a creative and a graceful imitation in the manner of his own dealings with Cicero.

To imitate Castiglione creatively was easier if one left the court and wrote about another ideal. The obvious example to take is the school or university. It is not so far from the original, in the Fourth Book of which the objection is made to Ottaviano that he is describing a schoolmaster rather than a courtier. One English humanist, who is known to have admired Castiglione's book seems to have been tempted in this direction. Roger Ascham's *Schoolmaster* does in fact begin as a dialogue in a circle of friends who include William Cecil and Walter Mildmay. It is a pity that the book does not continue in the same manner. One wonders whether the author rejected the dialogue form as too playful.

All the same, something similar had already been attempted, as Ascham could hardly have known, in Spain. It was probably in the 1550s that the humanist Cristóbal de Villalón wrote a dialogue on education which remained unpublished until relatively recently.[9] *El Scholástico*, as it is called, is concerned with the ideal student and the ideal teacher at the university, so we may all have something to learn from it. It is set at the University of Salamanca (or nearby, in a garden belonging to the duke of Alba) and it takes the form of a discussion between the rector and a group of nine dons. As in the case of the *Courtier*, the discussion is placed, somewhat nostalgically, a generation earlier (and the choice of the date 1528 is perhaps a kind of homage to Castiglione).

The main subject of this dialogue is the university curriculum, including the place of magic and the role of the pagan classics, but towards the end of the speakers widen their concerns and move closer to the *Courtier* in their discussions of the virtues and failings

9. C. de Villalón, *El Scholastico*, ed. R. J. A. Kerr (Madrid, 1967). On the author (c. 1500–58). J. J. Kincaid, *Cristóbal de Villalón* (New York, 1973).

of women; the importance of music, painting, and other arts; and the behaviour appropriate in a university, a gravity [*gravedad*] which you will be pleased to hear does not exclude grace or wit or the propensity to fall in love (honourable love, of course). The book ends with the speakers swapping funny stories. *El Scholástico* is not a great work of literature, but, like *El Cortesano*, it does have considerable charm and it was a loss to sixteenth-century readers that it was not published in their day, probably because of the criticism of the people who are 'so delicate in their faith' [*tan delicados en la fe*] that they attack Greek and Latin literature as pagan. As the fate of the *Decameron* during the Counter-Reformation demonstrates, the Inquisition was always peculiarly sensitive to reflections on itself.

Baldassare Castiglione:
A Chronology

1478	Baldassare born in Casatico, near Mantua.
1490	Sent to Milan to stay with relatives.
1494	Pursues humanistic studies in Milan with Giorgio Merula and other teachers; attends court of Ludovico Sforza.
1499	Death of father; leaves Milan and life of study, and enters service of Francesco Gonzaga, Marquis of Mantua.
1501	First diplomatic mission on behalf of Marquis of Mantua.
1503	First military campaign, with Marquis of Mantua, against the Spanish in Naples; first visit to Rome.
1504	Transfers to service of Guidobaldo da Montefeltro, duke of Urbino.
1505	Diplomatic mission to Rome on behalf of Duke Guidobaldo.
1506–07	Sent to England to receive Order of the Garter on behalf of Duke Guidobaldo.
1508	Death of Guidobaldo. Stays in Urbino in the service of Duchess Elisabetta, and Guidobaldo's successor, Francesco Maria della Rovere.
1509–12	Under Duke Francesco Maria partakes in campaigns against Romagna and Emilia instigated by Pope Julius II.
1513	Sent to Rome by Duke Francesco Maria as resident ambassador of Urbino. Invested as Count of Novillara.
1513–14	First draft of *The Courtier*. Manuscript A.
1514–16	Completes first version of *The Courtier*. Manuscripts B and C.
1516	Follows Duke Francesco Maria in exile to Mantua after the duke is excommunicated by Leo X, and dispossessed of Duchy of Urbino. Marries Ippolita Torelli.
1517	Birth of first child, Camillo.
1518	Birth of second child, Anna. Drafts second version of *The Courtier* which he sends to Sadoleto and Bembo.
1519	Sent to Rome by new Marquis, Federico Gonzaga, as resident ambassador of Mantua, and also to obtain

restoration of Duchy of Urbino for Francesco Maria della Rovere.

1520   Death of wife after birth of third child, Ippolita. Obtains for Federico Gonzaga nomination of Captain General of papal forces.

1520–21   Completes second version of *The Courtier*. Manuscript D.

1521   Gives up service to Duke Francesco Maria.

1522   Following election of Pope Clement VII sent again to Rome as ambassador of Mantua.

1524   Works on final version of *The Courtier*. Manuscript L. Accepts from Clement VII nomination of papal nuncio to Spain.

1525   Arrives in Madrid as papal nuncio.

1527   Sends final version of *The Courtier* to Venice for publication.

1528   *The Courtier* is published by Aldine press.

1529   Dies in Toledo, having not returned to Italy since 1525.

Selected Bibliography

• indicates works included or excerpted in this Norton Critical Edition.

EDITIONS

Il libro del Cortegiano. Ed. Vittorio Cian. Firenze: Sansoni, 1947. [Originally printed in 1897.]
Il libro del Cortegiano. Ed. Bruno Maier. Torino: UTET, 1955.
La seconda redazione del "Cortegiano." Ed. Ghino Ghinassi. Firenze: Sansoni, 1968.
Il libro del Cortegiano. Ed. Walter Barberis. Torino: Einaudi, 1998.
The Book of the Courtier. Trans. Sir Thomas Hoby. Ed. Virginia Cox. London: J. M. Dent, 1994.

BIOGRAPHY

Ady, Julia Mary Cartwright. *Baldassare Castiglione, The Perfect Courtier.* 2 vols. New York: E. P. Dutton, 1908.

GENERAL STUDIES

Burke, Kenneth. *A Rhetoric of Motives.* Berkeley and Los Angeles: University of California Press, 1969. [Originally published in 1950.]
• Cox, Virginia. *The Renaissance Dialogue. Literary Dialogue in Its Social and Political Contexts. Castiglione to Galileo.* Cambridge, UK: Cambridge University Press, 1992.
Elias, Norbert. *Uber den Prozess der Zivilisation.* Trans. Edmund Jephcott in 2 vols. as *The History of Manners and Power and Civility.* New York: Pantheon, 1982. [Originally published in 1939.]
Javitch, Daniel. *Poetry and Courtliness in Renaissance England.* Princeton, N.J.: Princeton University Press, 1978.
Jordan, Constance. *Renaissance Feminism.* Ithaca, N.Y., and London: Cornell University Press, 1990.
Langer, Ullrich. *Divine and Poetic Freedom in the Renaissance.* Princeton, N.J.: Princeton University Press, 1990.
Lanham, Richard. *The Motives of Eloquence: Literary Rhetoric in the Renaissance.* New Haven, Conn.: Yale University Press, 1976.
Mazzacurati, Giancarlo. *Misure del classicismo rinascimentale.* Napoli: Liguori, 1967.
Posner, David. *The Performance of Nobility in Early Modern European Literature.* Cambridge, UK: Cambridge University Press, 1999.
Saccone, Eduardo. *Le buone e le cattive maniere. Letteratura e galateo nel Cinquecento.* Bologna: il Mulino, 1992.
Scaglione, Aldo. *Knights at Court. Courtliness, Chivalry, and Courtesy from Ottonian Germany to the Italian Renaissance.* Berkeley and Los Angeles: University of California Press, 1991.
Whigham, Frank. *Ambition and Privilege. The Social Tropes of Elizabethan Courtesy Theory.* Berkeley: University of California Press, 1984.

SPECIFIC STUDIES

• Berger, Harry, Jr. *The Absence of Grace: Sprezzatura and Suspicion in Two Renaissance Courtesy Books.* Stanford, Calif.: Stanford University Press, 2000.
Burke, Peter. *The Fortunes of the Courtier: The European Reception of Castiglione's Cortegiano.* Cambridge, UK: Polity Press, 1995.

Cox, Virginia. "Tasso's *Malpiglio overo de la corte: The Courtier* Revisited." *Modern Language Review* 90 (1995): 897–918.

Falvo, Joseph. *The Economy of Human Relations: Castiglione's Libro del Cortegiano*. New York: Lang, 1992.

Finucci, Valeria. *The Lady Vanishes: Subjectivity and Representation in Castiglione and Ariosto*. Stanford, Calif.: Stanford University Press, 1992.

Floriani, Piero. *Bembo e Castiglione: studi sul classicismo del Cinquecento*. Rome: Bulzoni, 1976.

Freccero, Carla. "Politics and Aesthetics in Castiglione's *Il Cortegiano*: Book III and the Discourse on Women," in *Creative Imitation: New Essays on Renaissance Literature in Honor of Thomas M. Greene*, ed. David Quint et al. Binghamton, N.Y.: Medieval and Renaissance Texts and Studies, 1992.

Ghinassi, Ghino. "Fasi dell'elaborazione del *Cortegiano*." *Studi di Filologia Italiana* 25 (1976): 155–96.

Hanning, Robert, and David Rosand, eds. *Castiglione: The Ideal and the Real in Renaissance Culture*. New Haven, Conn.: Yale University Press, 1983.

• Kelly, Joan. "Did Women Have a Renaissance?" in *Women, History, and Theory: The Essays of Joan Kelly*. Chicago and London: University of Chicago Press, 1984.

Kolsky, Stephen. "Graceful Performances: The Social and Political Context of Music and Dance in the *Cortegiano*." *Italian Studies* 53 (1998): 1–19.

Loos, Erich. *Baldassare Castigliones Libro del cortegiano. Studien zur Tugendauffassung des Cinquecento*. Frankfurt: V. Klostermann, 1955.

Ossola, Carlo. *Dal "Cortegiano" all' "Uomo di mondo": storia di un libro e di un modello sociale*. Torino: Einaudi, 1987.

———, ed. *La corte e Il Cortegiano: I: La scena del testo*. Rome: Bulzoni, 1980.

Prosperi, Adriano, ed. *La corte e Il Cortegiano: II. Un modello europeo*. Rome: Bulzoni, 1980.

• Quint, David. "Courtier, Prince, Lady: The Design of the *Book of the Courtier*." *Italian Quarterly* 37 (2000): 185–95.

• Quondam, Amedeo. *"Questo povero Cortegiano," Castiglione, il Libro, la Storia*. Rome: Bulzoni, 2000.

• Rebhorn, Wayne A. *Courtly Performances: Masking and Festivity in Castiglione's Book of the Courtier*. Detroit, Mich.: Wayne State University Press, 1978.

Ryan, Laurence V. "Book IV of Castiglione's *Courtier*,—Climax or Afterthought." *Studies in the Renaissance* 19 (1972): 156–79.

• Saccone, Eduardo. "The Portrait of the Courtier in Castiglione." *Italica* 64 (1987): 1–18.

Woodhouse, John R. *Baldesar Castiglione: A Reassessment of The Courtier*. Edinburgh, UK: Edinburgh University Press, 1978.